THE MAM

MONSTERS

Edited by
Stephen Jones

ROBINSON
London

Constable & Robinson Ltd
3 The Lanchesters
162 Fulham Palace Road
London W6 9ER
www.constablerobinson.com

First published in the UK by Robinson,
an imprint of Constable & Robinson Ltd 2007

A copy of the British Library Cataloguing in Publication Data is available from the British Library.

ISBN: 978 1 84529 594 3

Printed and bound in the EU

1 3 5 7 9 10 8 6 4 2

This monsterrific book is for AMANDA
"—'Twas beauty killed the beast."

CONTENTS

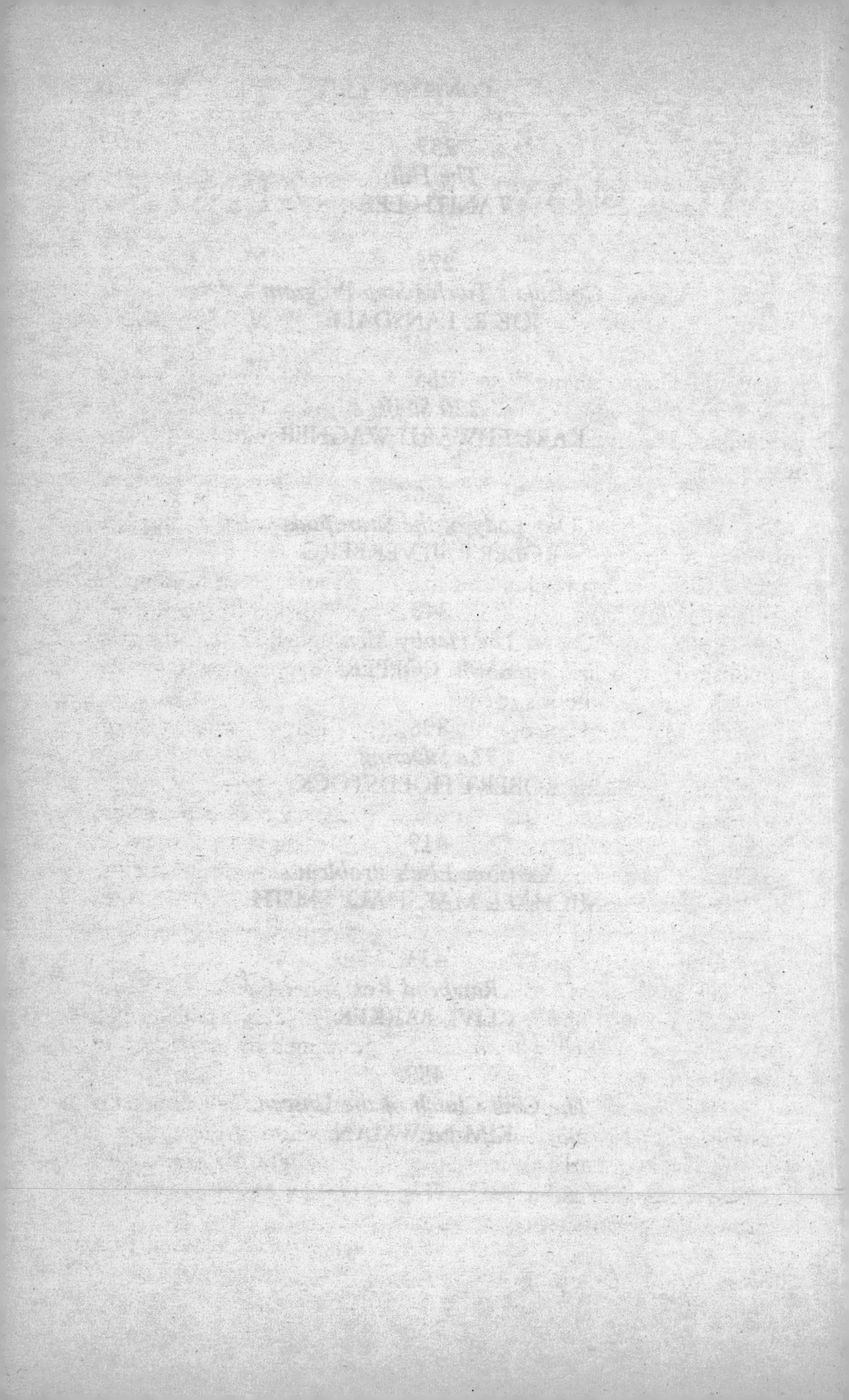

ACKNOWLEDGMENTS

I would like to thank Pete Duncan, Dorothy Lumley, Randy Broecker, Val and Les Edwards, Pam Brooks, Hugh Lamb, Jo Fletcher, Mandy Slater and Michael Marshall Smith for all their help and support.

"Introduction: How to Make a Monster" copyright © Stephen Jones 2007.

"Visitation" copyright © David J. Schow 1981. Originally published in *Seeing Red*. Reprinted by permission of the author.

"Down There" copyright © Ramsey Campbell 1981. Originally published in *Weird Tales* #1. Reprinted by permission of the author and the author's agent.

"The Man He Had Been Before" copyright © Scott Edelman 2007.

"Calling All Monsters" copyright © Mercury Press, Inc. 1973. Originally published in *The Magazine of Fantasy & Science Fiction*, June 1973. Copyright assigned to the author. This version copyright © Dennis Etchison 1982. Reprinted by permission of the author.

"The Shadmock" copyright © R. Chetwynd-Hayes 1975. Originally published in *The Monster Club*. Reprinted by permission of the author's estate and the author's agent.

"The Spider Kiss" copyright © Christopher Fowler 2007.

"Café Endless: Spring Rain" copyright © Nancy Holder 1994. Originally published in *Love in Vein*. Reprinted by permission of the author.

"The Medusa" copyright © Thomas Ligotti 1994. Originally published in *Noctuary*. Reprinted by permission of the author.

"In The Poor Girl Taken by Surprise" copyright © Gemma Files 2003. Originally published in *The Worm in Every Heart*. Reprinted by permission of the author.

"Downmarket" copyright © the estate of Sydney J. Bounds 2007.

"The Horror from the Mound" by Robert E. Howard. Originally published in *Weird Tales*, May 1932.

"Fat Man" copyright © Joseph E. Lake, Jr. 2007.

"The Thin People" copyright Brian Lumley 1987. Originally published in *The Third Book of After Midnight Stories: A Kimber Ghost Book*. Reprinted by permission of the author.

"The Hill" copyright © Tanith Lee 2007.

"Godzilla's Twelve Step Program" copyright © Joe R. Lansdale 1994. First published in *Writer of the Purple Rage*. Reprinted by permission of the author.

".220 Swift" copyright © Karl Edward Wagner 1980. Originally published in *New Terrors 1*. Reprinted by permission of The Karl Edward Wagner Literary Group.

"Our Lady of the Sauropods" copyright © Agberg, Ltd. 1980. Originally published in *Omni*, September 1980. Reprinted by permission of the author.

"The Flabby Men" copyright © Basil Copper 1977. Originally published in *And Afterward, the Dark*. Reprinted by permission of the author.

"The Silvering" copyright © Robert Holdstock 1992. Originally published in *Narrow Houses*. Reprinted by permission of the author.

"Someone Else's Problem" copyright © Michael Marshall Smith 1996, 2007. Originally published in a different version in *Chills*, Issue 10, 1996. Reprinted by permission of the author.

"Rawhead Rex" copyright © Clive Barker 1984. Originally published in *Books of Blood Volume III*. Reprinted by permission of the author.

"The Chill Clutch of the Unseen" copyright © Kim Newman 2004. Originally published in *Quietly Now: An Anthology in Tribute to Charles L. Grant*. Reprinted by permission of the author.

INTRODUCTION:

How to Make a Monster

SO WHAT, EXACTLY, constitutes a "monster"? That's the question I had to ask myself before I started compiling this latest "Mammoth" anthology.

Having previously edited such titles as *The Mammoth Book of Vampires*, *The Mammoth Book of Zombies*, *The Mammoth Book of Werewolves*, *The Mammoth Book of Frankenstein* and *The Mammoth Book of Dracula*, to name just a few, my publishers initially suggested that I put together an omnibus volume containing some of the best stories in those books.

That's something that may happen in the future. However, I felt that because those books had already appeared in various editions and numerous printings around the world, it would be more fun to assemble an entirely new selection of tales, while at the same time introducing readers to some unique and unusual monstrosities.

After careful consideration, I decided not to include stories dealing with demons, ghosts or human monsters (such as psychopaths), as these may – and in some cases, already – have "Mammoth" titles of their own. After that decision was made, any type of creature was up for grabs – the more obscure or original the better.

That is not to say that we don't have all the classic monsters represented in this volume. You would expect nothing less than a vampire story from *Buffy the Vampire Slayer* best-seller Nancy Holder, but it is the unfamiliar location of "Café Endless: Spring Rain" that makes it stand out in my mind. While the resurrected vampire of Robert E. Howard's classic weird tale, "The Horror from the Mound," also originates from a different milieu than that usually associated with the undead.

Scott Edelman's "The Man He Had Been Before" is a contemporary view of a post-apocalyptic world overrun by zombies that has something else to say about growing up, Gemma Files gives the werewolf myth a fairytale twist in "In The Poor Girl Taken by Surprise", and Tanith Lee's "The Hill" is set in and around the creepy home of a missing scientist.

An academic goes in search of the eponymous mythological creature in Thomas Ligotti's "The Medusa", a stone gargoyle is brought to life in "Downmarket" by Sydney J. Bounds, a Big Foot-like creature attacks a town's children in Jay Lake's "Fat Man", and a reclusive islander shares his world with shape-chaging selkies in Robert Holdstock's haunting tale "The Silvering".

The ancient cave-dwellers of Karl Edward Wagner's novella ".220 Swift" have more than a common heritage in the stories of Arthur Machen and Manly Wade Wellman, which can't be said for the nasty little critters found on an InterCity railway train in "Someone Else's Problem" by Michael Marshall Smith.

The King of the Monsters himself turns up in "Godzilla's Twelve Step Program" which, being by hisownself Joe R. Lansdale, is about much more than its humorous title would at first suggest, and the dinosaurs are bio-engineered on the prehistoric planet of Robert Silverberg's "Our Lady of the Sauropods". Reincarnated insects are the problem in "The Spider Kiss" by Christopher Fowler.

Late-night office workers are menaced by hungry horrors from the basement in Ramsey Campbell's claustrophobic "Down There", while the monsters of both Brian Lumley's "The Thin

People" and Basil Copper's "The Flabby Men" share only a semblance with humanity.

R. Chetwynd-Hayes' "The Shadmock" and Clive Barker's "Rawhead Rex" are genuinely new monsters who have both benefited from movie adaptations, and there are multiple monstrosities on display in David J. Schow's exuberant "Visitation" and Dennis Etchison's hallucinatory "Calling All Monsters".

Which brings us, finally, to Kim Newman's melancholy coda, "The Chill Clutch of the Unseen", in which the last monster-fighter and the last classic monster confront each other with surprising results. It is a story that brings this collection full circle while speaking to all of us who grew up on monsters – especially those iconic cinematic characters from Universal Studios.

So there you are: twenty-two stories about all kinds of different monsters. Not all are horrific, but that is only to be expected given the scope of this book and the collective talent of the authors represented.

And if your favourite creature isn't featured this time, then don't worry – as we all know, when it comes to monsters there's usually a sequel . . .

—Stephen Jones
London, England
February, 2007

DAVID J. SCHOW

Visitation

DAVID J. SCHOW IS A SHORT STORY WRITER, novelist, screenwriter (teleplays and features), columnist, essayist, editor, photographer and winner of the World Fantasy and International Horror Guild Awards (for short fiction and non-fiction, respectively).

His association with New Line Cinema began with horror icons Freddy Krueger (*A Nightmare on Elm Street: Freddy's Nightmares*), Leatherface (*Leatherface: Texas Chainsaw Massacre III*) and the eponymous Critters (*Critters 3* and *Critters 4*). In 1994 he wrote the screenplay for *The Crow* and has since worked with such directors as Alex Proyas, James Cameron, E. Elias Merhige, Rupert Wainwright, Mick Garris and William Malone.

For the premiere season of Showtime's *Masters of Horror* TV series he adapted his own short story "Pick Me Up" for director Larry Cohen, and for Season Two he scripted "We All Scream for Ice Cream" (based on a John Farris story) for director Tom Holland.

Among his many books are his fourth novel, *Bullets of Rain*, and seventh short story collection, *Havoc Swims Jaded*. The author's popular "Raving & Drooling" columns for *Fangoria* magazine were collected in *Wild Hairs*.

"*Arēs* was a gaming magazine put out roughly 1980–84 by an outfit called Simulations Publications, Inc.," explains Schow, "then famous for producing *Strategy & Tactics*. The 'simulations' hook was the inclusion of an actual board game into each issue, whole and entire, including die-cut cardboard tokens and pieces.

"They solicited a 'media' column from me, and after a year or so of fending off my story submissions, editor Michael Moore (no relation to the guy who did *Roger & Me*) finally caved and bought a story – the first in the magazine's history having absolutely nothing to do with that issue's game or theme. Michael's replacement, Roger Moore (no relation to Michael or the guy who once played James Bond) gave me the concept for a future issue – 'Nightmare Hotel' – and I gave him 'Visitation' in addition to so much peripheral material that he dubbed the result the 'Dave Schow Memorial Issue' of *Arēs*. (They even incorporated some of the story's characters and settings into the game.)

"Thus the story could be considered as a written-to-order piece, yet done with an extremely free hand. It was most recently adapted to graphic story form for *Doomed* #3 (September, 2006)."

ANGUS BOND CHECKED INTO THE HERMITAGE ALONE, under an assumed name. He had been recognised in consort with too many fanatics to risk a traveling companion, though having Nicholas along would have been comforting. Nicholas was dead.

"Room 713," said the deskman, handing over a bronze key. "One of our suites, mister . . . ah, Orion, yes. Heh." The man's smile looked like a mortician's joke on a corpse, and Angus restrained himself from looking to see if the natty, three-piece clerk's suit was split up the back. The deskman was no zombie.

Close, Angus thought as he hefted his bags. *But no.*

The Hermitage was as Gothically overstated as Angus had expected it to be. Nothing he saw really surprised him – the ornamental iron gargoyles guarding the lobby doors, the unsettling, Bosch-like grotesques hanging in gilt frames beneath low-wattage display lamps, the Marie Antoinette chandeliers, their hexagonal prisms suggesting the imprisonment of lost souls like dragonflies stuck in amber. None of it moved Angus one way or the other. It was all rather standard haunted house crap; occult chintz to get a rise out of the *turistas*.

The wine-red carpeting absorbed his footfalls (greedily, he thought). The Hermitage seemed to be the place. At the door to 713, Angus held his key to the feeble light. He knew how to tilt it so the embossed metal threw down the shadow impression of a death's-head.

Satisfied, he unlocked the door and moved his baggage inside, in order that he might unpack and await the coming of the monsters.

The knock on the door jolted him to instant wariness. Angus took a bite out of a hard roll and left it behind on the leather-topped table with the sausage and cheese he had brought.

It was the zombie clerk, carrying a tarnished salver bearing a brilliantly white calling card, face down. Angus noted that the clerk seemed to smell like the sachets tucked into wardrobes by grandmothers to fend off mildew. The stark whiteness of the card cast deathly shadows on the man's pale features. It seemed to light up the hallway much more efficiently than the guttering yellow bulbs in the brass sconces.

"A gentleman to see you, sir," he said, with all the verve of a ventriloquist's dummy.

Angus picked up the card. It bore two words:

IMPERATIVE.
BRAY.

The clerk stood fast. When Angus realised why, he decided to test the water a little.

"Just a minute." He hurried off to fumble briefly through the depths of his greatcoat. There was the telltale clink of change, and he returned to the door with a silver dollar. Instead of placing it on the salver, he contrived to drop it, apparently accidentally, so that the clerk caught it, smoothly interrupting its fall with his free hand.

He wore dusty butler's gloves that were going threadbare at the fingertips. He weighed the coin in the palm of his hand.

The air in the draftless hallway seemed to darken and roil thickly, like cream in hot coffee, for just a second. The clerk's features darkened, too, making his eyes appear to glow, the way a lightbulb flares just before it burns out. He sucked a quick gulp of air, as though dizzied by an abrupt stab of nausea. His features fought to remain whole, shifting like lard in a skillet, and Angus heard a distant, mad wail. It all took less than a second.

The clerk let the tip slide from the palm of his hand to rattle in the bowl of the metal dish. The queasy, death-rictus smile split across his face again, and he said "Thank you. Sir."

He left. Angus closed his door and nodded to himself in affirmation.

The stranger was swaddled in fog-dampened tweeds, and crowned with a road-weary homburg that had seen better days a few decades earlier. The initial impression left by the bearing of the man was that he was very old – not withered, or incapacitated in the way of those who wore years gracelessly, but old in the sense of worldly experience. An *old* man. Angus felt a stab of kinship here, deep in the midst of hazardous and alien territory.

"You are Angus Bond?" said the old man, arching a snow-white eyebrow. "I am Turquine Bray."

"Nicholas Bray's father?" said Angus, ignoring that no one at the Hermitage knew his real name. The stranger had obviously just arrived.

"Grandfather. Paternal. His father was a null spiritual quantity, neither evil, nor good, like most in the world. He lived out his merchant's life and desired nothing but material things. He led a life of tawdriness and despair; but for seeding Nicholas, no residue of his passage, save the grief he caused others, endures. His fate was a well-deserved insignificance. Nicholas superseded him. Blotted him out. Nicholas once told me you were his closest friend."

The words bit Angus lightly, and the way Bray pulled off his glove advised that the late Nicholas had not dispensed his friendship or loyalty frivolously. The two men shook hands in the dank lobby of the Hermitage, the understanding already shared by them in no need of further words concerning Nicholas.

"I cannot say I am pleased to meet you at last, sir, under such circumstances," said Bray. "But I am relieved. Shall we walk outside? The atmosphere in here could make a vulture's eyes water . . . as it is no doubt intended to do."

The basilisk gaze of the clerk tracked them until they passed through the cataracted glass of the lobby's imposing double doors. Outside, the slate grey bulk of the Hermitage's castellated architecture monitored them dispassionately. It diminished behind them as they walked into the dense southern Kentucky woodland that made up the grounds.

"Gloomy," said Bray. "All this place needs is a tarn."

"Notice how the foliage grows together in tangles?" said Angus. "It meshes, with no nutritional support from the earth. The soil is nearly pure alkaline; I checked it. The stuff grows, and yet is dead. It laces together to keep out the sunlight – see? It's always overcast here."

"The appointments of that hotel are certainly Grand Guignolish. Like a Hollywood set for a horror film."

"Rather like the supposed 'ambience' one gains by patronizing a more expensive restaurant," said Angus. "I suspect you hit it on the head when you mentioned 'atmosphere.' That seems to be the purpose of all this theatrical embroidery – supernatural furniture. Atmosphere."

"Hm." Bray stepped laboriously over a rotting tree trunk. "Sinister chic."

The iron-colored mud stole dark footprints from them as they walked, their breath condensing whitely in the late January chill. Frost still rimed the dead vegetation, even in late afternoon. Angus was glad he had trotted out his muffler. If Poe could have seen this place, he mused, he would have been scared into a writing diet of musical comedy.

"Have you a room?" said Angus, after both men had stood in contemplative silence for a moment.

"I wanted to assure myself of your presence here, first."

"You followed me, then?" said Angus. "For whatever purpose? You certainly know of Nicholas' death already."

"I need you, Mr Bond, to tell me the manner in which he died."

Angus sighed with resignation. "Mr Bray," he said in a tone often rehearsed, "do you know just who I am?"

Bray's steely, chrome-colored eyes shot up to meet with Angus' watery blue ones, and he smiled a cursory smile. "You are Angus Gwyllm Orion Bond. Until roughly two years ago your profession was that of occult debunker – exposer of supernatural hoaxes. Absolute bane of fraudulent mediums, scamming astrologers, warlocks who were more con-men than sorcerers, and all the pop salesmen of lizard's tooth and owlet's wing. Until two years ago."

Bray's breath plumed out as he spoke. His speech was almost a recitation; Angus was impressed with the research.

"Two years ago, you vanished from the considerable media time and space you commanded. You evaporated from the airwaves, the talk shows. Rumor had you seeking the counsel of spiritualists and dabbling in magic yourself. Though you wound up debunking yourself, your books and other franchised items sold better than ever. I presume you've been supporting your now-private life with royalties?"

"Something like that."

"It was at precisely that time that you met up with my grandson. Nicholas was the antithesis of his father – a fantastic intellect and capacity for change. You know how he died."

"It ties together. The change in my life. Nick's death. I'm not sure you'd—"

"I am prepared for the outrageous, Mr Bond. But I'm only interested in the truth. If the truth is merely outrageous, fire away."

"Nicholas came to my estate one night. He was frantic, pounding on the door, sweating, panicked. He couldn't tell me why. He had just moved into his new home at the time – do you recall it?"

"It was next to your estate. The Spilsbury mansion. Where all those actors were slaughtered by the religious cultists in the mid-1960s."

"Yes," said Angus. "Of course, by the time Nick moved in, that was ancient history. That place's allotted fifteen minutes of pop fame had been used up years before."

Bray smiled again.

"He was unnerved. When a horse 'smells' a tornado, it gets

skittish; the closest Nicholas could speculate was that the house 'felt wrong,' and skittish was the word to describe him. I returned with him, to sit and drink by the fireplace. About forty-five minutes later . . ." Angus regretted his dramatic tone. But what occurred had been bloody dramatic.

"It was the first time I ever witnessed an interface," he said simply. "Mr Bray, are you aware how supernatural agencies function physically? What enables the paranormal to coexist with the normal universe – yours and mine?"

"Assuming its reality," said Bray, "I'd speculate that it would be like an alternate dimension."

"Good. But not a physical dimension, not like a parallel world just staggered out of sync with our own. The supernatural is a matter of power potentials. It accumulates, in degrees, like a nuclear pile approaching critical mass. When there's too much, it blows off steam, venting into the real world, *our* world, becoming a temporary reality, sometimes only for a second or two."

"Accumulates? Like dust?" Bray said incredulously. "How?"

"It happens every time someone knocks on wood. Or crosses their fingers for luck, or says *gesundheit*. Every time one avoids walking under a ladder or lighting three on a match. Every time someone makes a joke about ghosts and doesn't disbelieve what he's saying one hundred percent; every time somebody uses a superstitious expression as a reflex cliché – *let the sandman come and take you away; don't let the boogeyman get you*. Every time some idiot in a church mentions the Devil. *Anytime* anyone seriously considers any of millions of minor-league bad-luck totems. It compounds itself *exactly* like dust, Mr Bray – each of those things is a conscious, willful act that requires a minute portion of physical energy in some way. The paranormal energy simultaneously prompted by such action remains unperceived, but it is there, and it stacks up, one imperceptible degree at a time. Just like dust. And when you get an extra infusion of high potency metaphysical force –"

"Like that Jim Jones thing?" said Bray. "Or the Spilsbury murders?"

"Precisely. You boost the backlog of power that much more. Whenever it reaches its own critical mass, it discharges into our reality. The house that Nicholas had moved into was a metaphysical stress point; it was still weak, thanks to the Spilsbury thing. A break point that had not completely healed."

"And during this – this interface, all that accumulated power blew through into my grandson's living room?" Bray shook his head. "I find that difficult to believe."

"Too outrageous?" said Angus, stopping suddenly.

Bray's expression dissolved to neutral. "Go on."

"That night, the 'weakness' was not only at the juncture point of that house, but elsewhere. Temporally, it was a 'weak' time period. Nick was in an agitated fear state – a 'weak', receptive mental condition. But this phenomenon has no regular characteristic save that of overload – you can't count on it venting itself at any regular time, or place, or under any regular conditions. It vented somewhere else that night, and because of the weakened conditions we caught a squirt of it – *bam*! Two or three seconds; a drop of water from a flood. The flood went somewhere else."

Now Bray was frankly interested. "What was it like?"

"I got an impression of tremendous motive force," said Angus. "Blinding black light; a contradictory thing, I know, but there. The air felt pushed out of my lungs by a giant hand. Everything loose in the living room was blown like summer chaff in a hurricane. Overpowering nausea. Vertigo. Disorientation. I was afraid, but it was a vague unfocused kind of terror. It was much worse for Nicholas.

"You see, he – like most people – held latent beliefs in supernatural things. I did not. Too many years debunking special effects led to an utter skepticism for things that go bump in the night – for me. I saw raw, turbulent energy. Nicholas saw whatever he did not totally disbelieve. You might see demons, ghouls, vampire lycanthropes, the Old Ones all hungering for your flesh and soul, dragons gobbling you up and farting brimstone, Satan browsing through your body with a hot fondue fork. Or the Christian God, for that matter."

Bray was taken aback, obviously considering what such an experience would mean for him, given his life's collection of myth and superstition, of fairytale monsters and real-life guilts. All of it would manifest to his eyes. *All* of it, at once. He said "You mean that every superstitious fear I've ever had is waiting to eat me, on the other side of a paranormal power overload?"

"Not as such," said Angus. "Your belief is what makes it real. True disbelief renders it unreal, back into energy – which is what I saw. But that energy, filtered through Nick's mind, made a monster. He said he was trying to hold the doorway to Hell shut, and something horrifying was pulling from the other side. It gave a good yank and the doorway cracked open for a split instant before the briefness of the squirt closed it for good – but Nick, in that instant, saw what was trying to get him. It scared him white."

Bray was quiet for a long moment. Then: "He moved in with you shortly afterward?"

"Yes."

"You could not debunk the supernatural after that?"

"Not and do it with anything like conviction. Investigating the nature of the phenomenon became paramount."

"Nicholas helped you?"

"He was just the ally I needed. He had a propensity for pure research and a keen mind for deduction. We collected data and he indexed it. Using a computer, we were able to produce flowcharts. One of the first things we discovered was the presence of 'pressure points' in the time flow – specific dates that were receptive to the power burst, as the Spilsbury house had been. Lammas, Beltane, Candlemas, Hallowe'en. Almost all holidays. There are short bursts, long bursts, multidirectional bursts, weak and strong ones. Sometimes the proximity of a weak date will magnetize the power, attracting it to a particular time. But most of it concentrates at one physical place. Of course, there might be a dozen such outbursts in a day. Consider Jack the Ripper's reign over Spitalfields, or World War II – the phenomenon would damn near become cyclical, feeding on itself."

"I see," said Bray. "But what about—"

"Nicholas?" Angus interrupted his meandering walk, hands in pockets. "I think the road is just above us, there. Shall we climb up out of this muck and make our way back? I have a flask of arrack in my room, to help cut the chill."

"Thank you," Bray said as Angus helped him through a web of creepers.

"Nicholas was very good at charts," said Angus. "He cross-matched all the power bursts – he was the one who called them 'squirts,' by the way – to ebb and flow grids, and to longitudes and latitudes. He calculated in 'weak spots' and compensated for them. He synthesized a means whereby he could predict, with reasonable accuracy, the location and date of a future 'squirt'. Sometimes he was wrong."

"But he was right for at least one," said Bray.

"In Manhattan," said Angus, "in a dilapidated, condemned office complex called the Dixon Building, he and I faced a full-power blast, alone."

"Oh my god—"

"*God* is right. Nicholas was eaten alive by the demon on the other side of the door. He still believed."

The two old men scrambled up onto the road facing the Hermitage, in the distance. It loomed darkly against the overcast sky, in silhouette, like a dinosaur waiting for dinner.

"In that hotel, tonight, at precisely 1:30 am, there will be an interface such as I've described. On paper, at least, it's one of the biggest I've ever seen. There are a lot of superstitious people out there in the world. I can show you the graphs, in my room."

Together, Angus and Bray entered the maw of the Hermitage.

"Have you taken stock of the clientele here yet?" said Bray as Angus shucked his heavy coat. Since Angus had not been able to coax the room's antediluvian steam coil into boosted output and since the fireplace still held cold tinder, both men kept their sweaters on. The arrack was forestalled when Bray produced a travel decanter of cognac from the depths of his overcoat.

"There is a word for this supernatural power," Angus said. "Some call it mana. It's like electricity – neither good nor evil in itself, but available to those who know how to harness it. Devoid of context, there is no 'good' or 'evil'. I am not the only one who has discovered that the interfaces can be charted. Others will be swift to use such power potentials for selfish or harmful ends. They would embrace the iconography of what the unenlightened blanket with the term *evil*. That desk clerk, for example. I never saw anyone who wanted to be a vampire more, yet to exist as a true vampire would be a pitiable state indeed. I slipped him a silver dollar earlier, one I had charged in accordance with legend as a protective talisman." He dragged a ponderous Victorian chair over to the table where Bray sat nursing his cognac and staring abstractedly through the parted drapes, into the courtyard below them.

Bray saw three men in black awkwardly bearing an enormous foot-locker into the lobby. "You mean like a witchcraft amulet?"

Sipping, Angus said "Amulets are no good if they're not in your possession. This was a *talisman* – charged by the book, in this case, the original text of a grimoire called the *Liber Daemonorum*, published in 1328 by a fellow named Protassus. I have a first edition."

"And the clerk?"

"Since he was behaving by such rigid rules, it was almost boringly simple to anticipate him. He reacted as though he was about to burst at the seams. If not for the gloves he wore, I think that talisman might've burned right through his hand to drop on the floor. But the predictability of a phenomenon or movement does not necessarily decrease its potential threat or danger. Don't kid yourself about the uses some intend for such power. It's backed up like sewage on the other side of the veil, waiting to be tapped, ever-increasing. A lot of *bad* could be created. Power corrupts." He killed his glass and Bray moved to refill it.

"Why expose yourself to something like that?" said Bray, now concerned. "Surely you've had a bellyful of baring your psyche to the tempest – or can you build some kind of tolerance?"

"To a degree, yes. It's still an ordeal, a mental and physical drain. But I can stand, where others would bend." Angus leaned closer; spoke confidentially: "You've missed a more obvious reason for doing so."

"Nicholas?" Bray said finally, "Vengeance?"

Angus swallowed another firebolt of liquor. "Not as an eye-for-an-eye thing. Nicholas' death convinced me that the phenomenon itself must be interrupted. Each outburst is more powerful. Each comes closer on the heels of the last. It is as though it is creating a bigger and bigger space in our reality in which to exist. The 'valve' must be closed before the continuous escalation makes preventive action impossible."

"By god!" said Bray, his eyes lighting up. "The talisman!"

"I hope that wasn't too ostentatious – announcing my presence in the Hermitage with that stunt. As far as the rest of the congregation here is concerned, I'm just another acolyte."

"I haven't seen too many people since I arrived."

"Well, they'd shun the daylight by nature, anyway," said Angus. "Or what passes for daylight around here." He let his eyes drift into infinity focus, regarding the courtyard below. "You know, the Hermitage is quite an achievement, for what it is. But it isn't 'evil'. The power I spoke of, the mana, is what keeps the sunlight from this place and makes dead trees root in dead ground. Channeled and controlled, the mana could be used to build a perfect womb for something that would be evil by anybody's definition. Something designed by people of ill intent to fit every preconcception. Tonight's surge is a big one. Maybe it's going to fuel a birth."

"I don't even want to think about that possibility," said Bray.

"I *must*." Angus dumped one of his satchels onto the bed "During that 1:30 juncture tonight, I must try to put a bogey in the paranormal plumbing."

"How?" said Bray, now visibly unnerved and looking about fruitlessly for a clock. "How does one stop that much power, barreling right at you?"

"One doesn't. You turn it against itself, like holding a mirror up to a gorgon's face. It takes, in this special case, not only protective talismans against the sheer forces themselves, but also my anti-belief in the various physical manifestations – the monsters. The power will exhaust itself through an infinite, echo effect, crashing back and forth like a violently bouncing ball inside a tiny box." He drained his glass again. "In theory, that is."

"Plausible," Bray said. "But then, you're the expert on this sort of thing. I suppose we'll see the truth early this morning . . ."

"No!" Angus, face flushed with sudden panic. "You must leave this place, before—"

"Leave you here alone, to fight such a fight alone? I admit that two old men may not present much of a threat to the powers you describe, but where in hell am I going to go, knowing that such things transpire?" Bray's hand grew white-knuckled around his glass.

"Your own dormant fears might destroy you," Angus said. "Another death on my conscience."

"What am I to do, then?" Bray stiffened. "You may not believe in revenge, but I do. I insist! I side with you or I am less than a man . . . and that is my final word on the matter, sir." As punctuation, he finished his cognac.

The expression on Angus' face was neutrally sober, but within, he was smiling.

Midnight should have been anticlimactic. It was not.

In the funeral quiet of the lobby, an ebony clock boomed out twelve brass tones that resounded through like strikes on a huge dinner gong. A straggler, dressed in tatters, fell to the wine red carpeting in convulsions, thrashing madly about. The stalwart desk clerk had watched the man inscribe three sixes on his forehead earlier, using hot ashes from the lobby fireplace. The ornamental andirons hissed their pleasure, hotly.

An almost sub-aural dirge, like a deep, constant synthesizer note, emanated from the ground floor and gradually possessed the entire structure. A chilling undercurrent of voices seemed to seep through the building's pipework and the hidden, dead spaces between walls.

In the Grand Ballroom the chandeliers began to move by themselves. Below their ghostly tinkling, a quartet of figures in hooded tabards raised their arms in supplication. Candles of sheep tallow were ignited. Mass was enjoined.

Somewhere near the top of the hotel, someone screamed for nearly a whole minute. Unearthly, lowering noises issued from the grounds, now heavily misted in nightfog. There were the sounds of strange beasts in pain, and vague echoes of something large and massy, moving sluggishly as though trapped in a tar pit. It was starlessly dark outside.

"Are you positive you wish to stay?" said Angus, opening the flask of arrack. Bray's private stock was long gone.

"Yes. Just pour me another glass, please." Each new, alien sound made Bray wince a little, inside the folds of his coat, but he maintained bravely.

From within his shirt, Angus fished out a key on a thin chain of silver links. He twiddled it in each of his satchel's two locks. The first thing he produced from the case was a book lashed together with stained violet ribbons.

"Good God, "Bray choked. "Is *that* the—"

"The *Liber Daemonorum*. Pity this must be destroyed tonight. By burning. Damn shame. This is a collector's item." He heaved the volume onto the bed and the rank smell of foxed and mildewed age-old paper washed toward Bray. Brittle pieces of the ragged hide binding flaked to the floor.

Nearby, probably in the hall outside 713, someone howled like a dog until his voice gave out with an adenoidal squeak.

Bray's attention was drawn from the ancient witchcraft tome to the disk of burnished gold Angus removed from the satchel. It was an unbroken ring, big as a salad plate, with free-cast template characters clinging to its inner borders. It caught the feeble light in the room and threw it around in sharp flashes.

"Gold?" said Bray, awestruck.

"Solid, refined twenty-four karat, pure to the fifth decimal point," said Angus, tossing it to the bed. The heavy chain necklace attached to it jingled; the disk bounced a hard crescent of light off the ceiling directly above. "The purity of the metal used in the talisman has protective value. I won't put it on until a few seconds before deadline – keep it as potent as possible, you understand."

From the satchel came more protective fetishes, mojo bags of donkey teeth, copper thread and travertine, hex stones with glyptic symbols, inked spells on parchment bound with hide thongs, tiny corked vials of opaque liquids. Angus tucked these into his clothing.

Something thumped heavily and repeatedly on the floor above them. Drum chants could be faintly heard.

"Any doubts now about there not being a full house here tonight?" Angus said. Bray's hand quivered in betrayal as he drank. Angus regretted that the academic portion of his mind regarded Bray simply as a handicap; his sense of honor could not refuse the older man. He hoped he would survive what was to follow, but would allow no compromising of his own task. Silence hung between them awhile longer.

"Does it matter where we are when it hits?"

"No. This hotel is the place. The psychos surrounding us are like the creepy trappings – more supernatural furniture. Pay them no heed. What we're dealing with has no form. You can be tricked by illusions; if you even consider for a second that something monstrous before your eyes might possibly be real, you're lost – you *must* remember that. The demon Nicholas saw was not real, until he thought it might be, making him afraid. Then it ate him up."

"Angus!" Bray stood from his chair. "I can – I can *feel* something strange . . . palpable, a swelling . . . like a balloon about to burst . . ." He looked around, agitated now.

Angus hauled out his railroad watch. "1:27 am. I set this by the time service in Willoughby late yesterday. Hmm – I suppose no time service is strictly accurate." He slipped quickly into the talisman.

"Exactly like the atmospheric buildup Nicholas sensed, before the squirt at his house," Angus said. "I have no extra power objects, friend Bray. You'll have to stick close behind me. That's about the only aid I can offer you. And something else—" He hurriedly dug a dented tin of Ronson lighter fluid out of the satchel and doused the *Liber Daemonorum*. The pungent liquid soaked slowly into the comforter on the bed and saturated the book of sorcery. Angus then came up with several disposable plastic cigarette lighters, each gimmicked with electrical tape. "Take one of these, and listen to me. During the confrontation, I may become momentarily transfixed. If that happens, I want you to light the book. It must be burned during the interface if my other, lesser shielding spells are to function. The lighter is modified to produce a long jet of flame when you thumb the wheel. Understand that the book is rare, and dangerous, and the supplicants booked into this place would gladly murder us to get it. If I hesitate, destroy it!"

Bray clutched the lighter tightly, like a crucifix against a vampire.

As though in the grip of an earthquake tremor, the Hermitage shuddered. A chunk of the whorled plaster ceiling disengaged and smashed into chalky crumbles at Angus' feet.

"Remember, Bray!" he shouted. "It's not real—"

The rest of his words were obliterated by a thunderclap concussion of moving air as the oak door to 713 blew off its hinges and slapped the floor like a huge, wooden playing card. The French windows past Bray splintered outward in a shrieking hail of needlelike glass bits. The bottles and rickrack on the table scattered toward the window. The cognac flask pegged Bray's temple and brought blood. The vacuum force of the moving air seemed to suck the breath from him. He screamed Angus' name, soundlessly.

Angus labored toward the door, walking ponderously, like a trapper in a snowbank, one hand holding the outthrust talisman, the other readying the lighter for the *Liber Daemonorum* crooked against his chest. Outside, the corridor was awash in stunning yellow light. A high-frequency keen knifed into his ears and numbed his brain. He heard his name being called over and over, coupled with a maniacal laugh that kept shifting speeds, accelerating and slowing, a warped record in the hands of a lunatic disc jockey. Through the shimmer and glare Angus thought he could see stunted, writhing shapes – various monsters struggling to be born of his mind. He stared them down and one by one they were absorbed back into the light that produced them, dissolving as though beaten progressively thinner with a mallet until the light shone through and distintegrated them. The talisman began to radiate heat against his chest. The first echo had been achieved.

The maniac sounds were definitely caused by something in terrific pain, fighting him. In the hallway mirror, Angus saw himself vaporise – hair popping aflame, shearing away, skin peeling back as though sandblasted off, skull rushing backward as sugary powder, blood and brains vanishing in a quick cloud of color and stink.

It was an illusion, and he ignored it.

He tried to ignore the dim, background sound of Bray's screaming.

A grey lizard demon, scales caked in glistening slime, breached the outside window to 713 and pounced on Bray's back, ripping and tearing. More rushed in like a floodtide, their alligator snouts rending his clothing, their flying spittle frying through his skin like brown acid. Curved black talons laid open his chest and they began to devour him organ by organ. His lighter went spinning uselessly across the floor.

Angus caught a glimpse of the carnage taking place behind him. Bray was lost.

Angus stopped his advance. Bray was dead.

Bray was dead, and the typhoon of yellow force petered to nothingness in a second. Standing ridiculously alone in the quiet of the cathedral-like hallway, Angus realised, with a plummeting kind of bright, orange horror in his stomach, that he had lost.

He looked up and down the hallway. Nothing.

Then, distant, indecipherable sounds. Hungry sounds.

The book! The book! his mind screamed. His thumb automatically worked the lighter, and a jet of blue propane fire at least half a foot long spurted up, caressing the *Liber Daemonorum*. It billowed into flame along with his soaked coatsleeve.

But the two iron gargoyles from the lobby were already winging toward Angus with metal-muscled strokes. He heard the grating of their black, iron flesh pumping and looked up to see their diamond eyes fix on him. They peeled to either side of him as the book touched off; one swooped past in a blur, hooking the book away to smother it against its bellows chest, the other jackknifing upward in midair to strafe Angus. He felt cold, sharp pain. His feet left the floor and he crashed onto his back, rolling clumsily, blood daubing into one eye from the gashes the gargoyle's iron, butcher-cleaver claws had carved in his forehead.

His name was still being called, fast and slow and fast and—

"Angus." The tone was first disapproving, then pitying. "Angus, you poor old sod."

Turquine Bray stood over him holding the still-smoking *Liber Daemonorum*. The violet ribbons were charred.

The iron gargoyles circled high in the corridor, lighting behind Bray. They cringed and fidgeted, like greyhounds, grinding their javelin teeth and snorting mist through cast iron nostrils with impatience.

"Since you've delivered this book to us," Bray said "I think you're owed a few words." His hands slithered proudly around the tome and his chromium eyes glittered at Angus.

"The gargoyles—" Angus gasped from the floor.

"Oh, yes, they're real enough. They're a bit piqued because I haven't given you to them yet." Angus could see that Bray spoke around a mouthful of needled fangs like the dental work of a rattlesnake. "Your disbelief in monsters posed an intriguing problem. How to chink such metal armor? How to trick *you*, the expert on all the tricks? You wouldn't believe in the patently unreal, so we made you believe in something else you'd accept with less question. The gargoyles are now real, thanks to your mind. Turquine Bray, however, died in 1974. On Valentine's Day." The Bray thing, its hair gone jet black, eyes sunken to mad ball bearings in seductive, dark pits, grinned wolfishly.

"Impossible!" Breathing was becoming difficult for Angus, as though his lungs were filling with hot candle wax. "Impossible . . . the power burst . . . you existed before the interface took place . . ."

"My dear Angus," the creature rasped in a phlegmatic voice, "you're not paying attention. This power burst was the biggest of all so far. People are more superstitious than ever. They go right on stacking it up. This surge was preceded by what young Nicholas characterised as a 'squirt,' a considerable leakage that primed the paranormal pump, you might say." It pretended to inspect its elongated, spiked nails. "How do you think something as melodramatic as the Hermitage got here in the first place? It came out of your mind. It was what *you* expected; know-nothing cultists and pop Satanists and horror-movie props – supernatural furniture. It was all an illusion, as was I. But it's real now. The *Liber Daemonorum* will help to keep our family corporeal."

Two shuffling corpses battered down the stairway door leading into the hallway. Their sightless, maggoty eyesockets sought Angus' prone form. They made for him with inexorable slowness, rotting flesh dropping off their frames in clots. They hungered.

"Your H.P. Lovecraft might be pleased to know that his Old Ones are finally coming home," the monster growled. It stretched cavernously, bursting from its human clothes, revealing a wide body of insectile armor plating with double-jointed, birdlike legs whose hooked toes gathered the carpet up in bunches. "It's all quite real now, friend Angus." The steely, silver eyes transfixed Angus from a nine-foot height. "As are my other friends. Here. Now."

The gargoyles jumped into the air and hovered like carrion birds. From 713 the reptilian scavengers continued to swarm, champing their oversized jaws, streamers of drool webbing the carpeting. Beyond the steaming, toothy thing that had been Bray, Angus saw a translucent horde of ghostly, humanoid leeches. The scuttling things advanced, worrying their bloodless, watchmaker's claws together in anticipation of a dark, burgundy-hued snack.

He recognised them now, all of the monsters, all of his lifetime's research into the occult, echoing back upon him. If he could be made to believe Bray had been real, then anything could follow . . . Zaebos, a demon with a human head and the body of a crocodile, entreated him from the end of the corridor. Near the ceiling floated the Keres, the Greek vampire entities who appear before death. Windigos – cannibalistic Indian ghosts – crowded past the living-dead corpses to get to Angus's position. They licked their lips. Now Angus knew the name of the monster before him, the spirit who had assumed Bray's form to trick him. It was the Master of Ceremonies to the Infernal Court.

"*Verdelet*!" he croaked, holding the talisman forward. "Swallow this!"

"Now, now," the demon said. "Too late for that hocus-pocus, Angus. You *believe* now." It waved an ebony claw carelessly, and the talisman melted, sizzling through Angus' clothing, scalding and eating into his chest with a geyser of golden steam.

He managed a howling scream.

"I have nought but gratitude for you, friend Angus," Verdelet said. "Thanks to you, as of this night, the Hermitage is open for business."

The last thing Angus heard was the wet sounds of jaws, opening.

RAMSEY CAMPBELL

Down There

RAMSEY CAMPBELL'S LATEST NOVEL, *The Grin of the Dark*, recently appeared in the UK from PS Publishing. He has also completed a new supernatural novel, *Thieving Fear*, which is to be followed by *The Buried City*.

Along with his regular columns in *Video Watchdog* and *All Hallows* magazines, Campbell also now writes a column for *Dead Reckonings* magazine as well.

" 'Down There' was suggested by the failure of the light in a lift at Radio Merseyside's old premises in Sir Thomas Street one day in 1978," recalls the author. "Later I was to develop an entire novel from a different lift, the one that appears in *The Overnight*.

"I generally forget the difficulties the first drafts of most stories give me, but the swine 'Down There' was remains in my memory. Nearly all my stories are substantially rewritten, sometimes reducing their length by as much as a quarter – an uneconomical method, perhaps, but it works for me. In particular I tend to stuff too much into the early pages.

"This has never been truer than in this tale, so that for the first three days of work it seemed that its inert bulk would never achieve the slightest flicker of life. At the moment when Elaine opens the window on the night, however, my imagination finally took hold."

"HURRY ALONG THERE," Steve called as the girls trooped down the office. "Last one tonight. Mind the doors."

The girls smiled at Elaine as they passed her desk, but their smiles meant different things: just like you to make things more difficult for the rest of us, looks like you've been kept in after school, suppose you've nothing better to do, fancy having to put up with him by yourself. She didn't give a damn what they thought of her. No doubt they earned enough without working overtime, since all they did with their money was squander it on makeup and new clothes.

She only wished Steve wouldn't make a joke of everything: even the lifts, one of which had broken down entirely after sinking uncontrollably to the bottom of the shaft all day. She was glad that hadn't happened to her, even though she gathered the subbasement was no longer so disgusting. Still, the surviving lift had rid her of everyone now, including Mr Williams the union representative, who'd tried the longest to persuade her not to stay. He still hadn't forgiven the union for accepting a temporary move to this building; perhaps he was taking it out on her. Well, he'd gone now, into the November night and rain.

It had been raining all day. The warehouses outside the windows looked like melting chocolate; the river and the canals were opaque with tangled ripples. Cottages and terraces, some of them derelict, crowded up the steep hills towards the disused mines. Through the skeins of water on the glass their infrequent lights looked shaky as candle-flames.

She was safe from all that, in the long office above five untenanted floors and two basements. Ranks of filing cabinets stuffed with blue Inland Revenue files divided the office down the middle;

smells of dust and old paper hung in the air. Beneath a fluttering fluorescent tube protruding files drowsed, jerked awake. Through the steamy window above an unquenchable radiator, she could just make out the frame where the top section of the fire-escape should be.

"Are you feeling exploited?" Steve said.

He'd heard Mr Williams's parting shot, calling her the employers' weapon against solidarity. "No, certainly not." She wished he would let her be quiet for a while. "I'm feeling hot," she said.

"Yes, it is a bit much." He stood up, mopping his forehead theatrically. "I'll go and sort out Mr Tuttle."

She doubted that he would find the caretaker, who was no doubt hidden somewhere with a bottle of cheap rum. At least he tried to hide his drinking, which was more than one could say for the obese half-chewed sandwiches he left on windowsills, in the room where tea was brewed, even once on someone's desk.

She turned idly to the window behind her chair and watched the indicator in the lobby counting down. Steve had reached the basement now. The letter *B* flickered, then brightened: he'd gone down to the subbasement, which had been meant to be kept secret from the indicator and from everyone except the holder of the key. Perhaps the finding of the cache down there had encouraged Mr Tuttle to be careless with food.

She couldn't help growing angry. If the man who had built these offices had had so much money, why hadn't he put it to better use? The offices had been merely a disguise for the subbasement, which was to have been his refuge. What had he feared? War, revolution, a nuclear disaster? All anyone knew was that he'd spent the months before he had been certified insane in smuggling food down there. He'd wasted all that food, left it there to rot, and he'd had no thought for the people who would have to work in the offices: no staircases, a fire-escape that fell apart when someone tried to paint it – but she was beginning to sound like Mr Williams, and there was no point in brooding.

The numbers were counting upwards, slow as a child's first sum. Eventually Steve appeared, the solution. "No sign of him," he said. "He's somewhere communing with alcohol, I expect. Most of the lights are off, which doesn't help."

That sounded like one of Mr Tuttle's ruses. "Did you go right down?" she said. "What's it like down there?"

"Huge. They say it's much bigger than any of the floors. You could play two football games at once in there." Was he exaggerating? His face was bland as a silent comedian's except for raised eyebrows. "They left the big doors open when they cleaned it up. If there were any lights I reckon you could see for miles. I'm only surprised it didn't cut into one of the sewers."

"I shouldn't think it could be any more smelly."

"It still reeks a bit, that's true. Do you want a look? Shall I take you down?" When he dodged towards her, as though to carry her away, she sat forward rigidly and held the arms of her chair against the desk. "No thank you," she said, though she'd felt a start of delicious apprehension.

"Did you ever hear what was supposed to have happened while they were cleaning up all the food? Tuttle told me, if you can believe him." She didn't want to hear; Mr Tuttle had annoyed her enough for one day. She leafed determinedly through a file, until Steve went up the office to his desk.

For a while she was able to concentrate. The sounds of the office merged into a background discreet as muzak: the rustle of papers, the rushes of the wind, the buzz of the defective fluorescent like an insect trying to bumble its way out of the tube. She manoeuvred files across her desk. This man was going to be happy, since they owed him money. This fellow wasn't, since he owed them some.

But the thought of the food had settled on her like the heat. Only this morning, in the room where the tea-urn stood, she'd found an ancient packet of Mr Tuttle's sandwiches in the waste-bin. No doubt the packet was still there, since the cleaners were refusing to work until the building was made safe. She seemed unable to rid herself of the memory.

No, it wasn't a memory she was smelling. As she glanced up, wrinkling her nostrils, she saw that Steve was doing so too. "Tuttle," he said, grimacing.

As though he'd given a cue, they heard movement on the floor below. Someone was dragging a wet cloth across linoleum. Was the caretaker doing the cleaners' job? More likely he'd spilled a bottle and was trying to wipe away the evidence. "I'll get him this time," Steve said, and ran towards the lobby.

Was he making too much noise? The soft moist dragging on the floor below had ceased. The air seemed thick with heat and dust and the stench of food; when she lit a cigarette, the smoke loomed reprovingly above her. She opened the thin louvres at the top of the nearest window, but that brought no relief. There was nothing else for it; she opened the window that gave onto the space where the fire-escape should be.

It was almost too much for her. A gust of rain dashed in, drenching her face while she clung to the handle. The window felt capable of smashing wide, of snatching her out into the storm. She managed to anchor the bar to the sill, and leaned out into the night to let the rain wash away the smell.

Nine feet below her she could see the fifth-floor platform of the fire-escape, its iron mesh slippery and streaming. The iron stairs that hung from it, poised to swing down to the next platform, seemed to dangle into a deep pit of rain whose sides were incessantly collapsing. The thought of having to jump to the platform made her flinch back; she could imagine herself losing her footing, slithering off into space.

She was about to close the window, for the flock of papers on her desk had begun to flap, when she glimpsed movement in the unlit warehouse opposite and just below her. She was reminded of a maggot, writhing in food. Of course, that was because she was glimpsing it through the warehouse windows, small dark holes. It was reflected from her building, which was why it looked so large and puffily vague. It must be Mr Tuttle, for as it moved, she heard a scuffling below her, retreating from the lifts.

She'd closed the window by the time Steve returned. "You didn't find him, did you? Never mind," she said, for he was frowning.

Did he feel she was spying on him? At once his face grew blank. Perhaps he resented her knowing, first that he'd gone down to the subbasement, now that he'd been outwitted. When he sat at his desk at the far end of the office, the emptiness between them felt like a rebuff. "Do you fancy some tea?" she said, to placate him.

"I'll make it. A special treat." He jumped up at once and strode to the lobby.

Why was he so eager? Five minutes later, as she leafed through someone's private life, she wondered if he meant to creep up on her, if that was the joke he had been planning behind his mask. Her father had used to pounce on her to make her shriek when she was little – when he had still been able to. She turned sharply, but Steve had pulled open the doors of the out-of-work lift-shaft and was peering down, apparently listening. Perhaps it was Mr Tuttle he meant to surprise, not her.

The tea was hot and fawn, but little else. Why did it seem to taste of the lingering stench? Of course, Steve hadn't closed the door of the room off the lobby, where Mr Tuttle's sandwiches must still be festering. She hurried out and slammed the door with the hand that wasn't covering her mouth.

On impulse she went to the doors of the lift-shaft where Steve had been listening. They opened easily as curtains; for a moment she was teetering on the edge. The shock blurred her vision, but she knew it wasn't Mr Tuttle who was climbing the lift-cord like a fat pale monkey on a stick. When she screwed up her eyes and peered into the dim well, of course there was nothing.

Steve was watching her when she returned to her desk. His face was absolutely noncommittal. Was he keeping something from her – a special joke, perhaps? Here it came; he was about to speak. "How's your father?" he said.

It sounded momentarily like a comedian's catch-phrase. "Oh, he's happier now," she blurted. "They've got a new stock of large-print books in the library."

"Is there someone who can sit with him?"

"Sometimes." The community spirit had faded once the mine owners had moved on, leaving the area honeycombed with mines, burdened with unemployment. People seemed locked into themselves, afraid of being robbed of the little they had left.

"I was wondering if he's all right on his own."

"He'll have to be, won't he." She was growing angry; he was as bad as Mr Williams, reminding her of things it was no use remembering.

"I was just thinking that if you want to slope off home, I won't tell anyone. You've already done more work than some of the rest of them would do in an evening."

She clenched her fists beneath the desk to hold on to her temper. He must want to leave early himself and so was trying to persuade her. No doubt he had problems of his own – perhaps they were the secret behind his face – but he mustn't try to make her act dishonestly. Or was he testing her? She knew so little about him. "He'll be perfectly safe," she said. "He can always knock on the wall if he needs anyone."

Though his face stayed blank his eyes, frustrated now, gave him away. Five minutes later he was craning out of the window over the fire-escape, while Elaine pinned flapping files down with both hands. Did he really expect his date, if that was his problem, to come out on a night like this? It would be just like a man to expect her to wait outside.

The worst of it was that Elaine felt disappointed, which was absurd and infuriating. She knew perfectly well that the only reason he was working tonight was that one of the seniors had to do so. Good God, what had she expected to come of an evening alone with him? They were both in their forties – they knew what they wanted by now, which in his case was bound to be someone younger than Elaine. She hoped he and his girlfriend would be very happy. Her hands on the files were tight fists.

When he slammed the window she saw that his face was glistening. Of course it wasn't sweat, only rain. He hurried away without looking at her, and vanished into the lift. Perhaps the girl was waiting in the doorway, unable to rouse Mr Tuttle to let her in. Elaine hoped Steve wouldn't bring her upstairs. She would be a distraction, that was why. Elaine was here to work.

And she wasn't about to be distracted by Steve and his attempts at jokes. She refused to turn when she heard the soft sounds by the lifts. No doubt he was peering through the lobby window at her, waiting for her to turn and jump. Or was it his girlfriend? As Elaine reached across her desk for a file she thought that the face was pale and very fat. Elaine was damned if she would give her the satisfaction of being noticed – but when she tried to work she couldn't concentrate. She turned angrily. The lobby was deserted.

In a minute she would lose her temper. She could see where he was hiding, or they were: the door of the room off the lobby was ajar. She turned away, determined to work, but the deserted office wouldn't let her; each alley between the filing cabinets was a hiding-place, the buzz of the defective light and the fusillade of rain could hide the sound of soft footsteps. It was no longer at all funny. He was going too far.

At last he came in from the lobby, with no attempt at stealth. Perhaps he had tired of the joke. He must have been to the street door: his forehead was wet, though it didn't look like rain. Would he go back to work now, and pretend that the urn's room was empty? No, he must have thought of a new ruse, for he began pacing from cabinet to cabinet, glancing at files, stuffing them back into place. Was he trying to make her as impatient as he appeared to be? His quick sharp footsteps seemed to grow louder and more nerve-racking, like the ticking of the clock when she was lying awake, afraid to doze off in case her father needed her. "Steve, for heaven's sake, what's wrong?"

He stopped in the act of pulling a file from its cabinet. He looked abashed, at a loss for words, like a schoolboy caught stealing. She couldn't help taking pity on him; her resentment had been presumptuous. "You didn't go down to find Mr Tuttle just now, did you?" she said, to make it easier for him.

But he looked even less at ease. "No, I didn't. I don't think he's here at all. I think he left hours ago."

Why must he lie? They had both heard the caretaker on the floor below. Steve seemed determined to go on. "As a matter of fact," he said "I'm beginning to suspect that he sneaks off home as soon as he can once the building's empty."

He was speaking low, which annoyed her: didn't he want his girlfriend to hear? "But there's someone else in the building," he said.

"Oh yes," she retorted. "I'm sure there is." Why did he have to dawdle instead of coming out with the truth? He was worse than her father when he groped among his memories.

He frowned, obviously not sure how much she knew. "Whoever it is, they're up to no good. I'll tell you the rest once we're out of the building. We mustn't waste any more time."

His struggles to avoid the truth amused and irritated her. The moisture on his forehead wasn't rain at all. "If they're up to no good," she said innocently, "we ought to wait until the police arrive."

"No, we'll call the police once we're out." He seemed to be saying anything that came into his head. How much longer could he keep his face blank? "Listen," he said, his fist crumpling the file, "I'll tell you why Tuttle doesn't stay here at night. The cleaners too, I think he told them. When the men were cleaning out the sub-basement, some of the food disappeared overnight. You understand what that means? Someone stole a hundredweight of rotten food. The men couldn't have cared less, they treated it as a joke, and there was no sign how anyone could have got in. But as he says, that could mean that whatever it was was clever enough to conceal the way in. Of course I thought he was drunk or joking, but now. . . ."

His words hung like dust in the air. She didn't trust herself to speak. How dare he expect her to swallow such rubbish, as if she were too stupid to know what was going on? Her reaction must have shown on her face; she had never heard him speak coldly before. "We must go immediately," he said.

Her face was blazing. "Is that an order?"

"Yes, it is. I'll make sure you don't lose by it." His voice grew authoritative. "I'll call the lift while you fetch your coat."

Blind with anger, she marched to the cloakroom at the far end of the office from the lobby. As she grabbed her coat the hangers clashed together, a shrill violent sound which went some way towards expressing her feelings. Since Steve had no coat, he would be soaked. Though that gave her no pleasure, she couldn't help smiling.

The windows were shaking with rain. In the deserted office her footsteps sounded high-pitched, nervous. No, she wasn't on edge, only furious. She didn't mind passing the alleys between the cabinets, she wouldn't deign to look, not even at the alley where a vague shadow was lurching forward; it was only the shadow of a cabinet, jerked by the defective light. She didn't falter until she came in sight of the lobby, where there was no sign of Steve.

Had he gone without her? Was he smuggling out his girlfriend? They weren't in the room off the lobby, which was open and empty; the over-turned waste-bin seemed to demonstrate their haste. The doors of the disused lift-shaft were open too. They must have opened when Steve had called the other lift. Everything could be explained; there was no reason for her to feel that something was wrong.

But something was. Between the two lift-shafts, the call-button was glowing. That could mean only one thing: the working lift hadn't yet answered the call. There was no other exit from the lobby – but there was no sign of Steve.

When she made herself go to the disused lift-shaft, it was only in order to confirm that her thought was absurd. Clinging to the edges of the doorway, she leaned out. The lift was stranded in the subbasement, where it was very dim. At first all she could distinguish was that the trapdoor in its roof was open, though the opening was largely covered by a sack. Could anything except a sack be draped so limply? Yes, for it was Steve, his eyes like glass that was forcing their lids wide, his mouth gagged with what appeared to be a torn-off wad of dough – except that the dough had fingers and a thumb.

She was reeling, perhaps over the edge of the shaft. No, she was stumbling back into the foyer, and already less sure what she'd glimpsed. Steve was dead, and she must get out of the building; she could think of nothing else. Thank God, she need not think, for the working lift had arrived. Was there soft movement in the disused shaft, a chorus of sucking like the mouthing of a crowd of babies? Nothing could have made her look. She staggered away, between the opening doors – into total darkness.

For a moment she thought she'd stepped out into an empty well. But there was a floor underfoot; the lift's bulb must have blown. As the door clamped shut behind her, the utter darkness closed in.

She was scrabbling at the metal wall in a frantic bid to locate the buttons – to open the doors, to let in some light – before she controlled herself. Which was worse: a quick descent in the darkness, or to be trapped alone on the sixth floor? In any case, she needn't suffer the dark. Hurriedly she groped in her handbag for her lighter.

She flicked the lighter uselessly once, twice, as the lift reached the fifth floor. The sudden plunge in her guts wasn't only shock; the lift had juddered to a halt. She flicked the lighter desperately. It had just lit when the doors hobbled open.

The fifth floor was unlit. Beyond the lobby she could see the windows of the untenanted office, swarming with rain and specks of light. The bare floor looked like a carpet of dim fog, interrupted by angular patches of greater dimness, blurred rugs of shadow. There was no sign of Mr Tuttle or whomever she'd heard from above. The doors were closing, but she wasn't reassured: if the lift had begun to misbehave, the least it could do would be to stop at every floor.

The doors closed her in with her tiny light. Vague reflections of the flame hung on the walls and tinged the greyish metal yellow; the roof was a hovering blotch. All the lighter had achieved was to remind her how cramped the lift was. She stared at the doors, which were trembling. Was there a movement beyond them other than the outbursts of rain?

When the doors parted, she retreated a step. The fourth floor was a replica of the fifth – bare floors colourless with dimness, windows that looked shattered by rain – but the shuffling was closer. Was the floor of the lobby glistening in patches, as though from moist footsteps? The doors were hesitating, she was brandishing her tiny flame as though it might defend her – then the doors closed reluctantly, the lift faltered downwards.

She'd had no time to sigh with relief, if indeed she had meant to, when she heard the lobby doors open above her. A moment later the lift shook. Something had plumped down on its roof.

At once, with a shock that felt as though it would tear out her guts, she knew what perhaps she had known, deep down, for a while: Steve hadn't been trying to frighten her – he had been trying not to. She hadn't heard Mr Tuttle on the fifth floor, nor any imaginary girlfriend of Steve's. Whatever she had heard was above her now, fumbling softly at the trapdoor.

It couldn't get in. She could hear that it couldn't, not before the lift reached the third – oh God, make the lift be quick! Then she could run for the fire-escape, which wasn't damaged except on the sixth. She was thinking quickly now, almost in a trance that carried her above her fear, aware of nothing except the clarity of her plan – and it was no use.

The doors were only beginning to open as they reached the third when the lift continued downwards without stopping. Either the weight on its roof, or the tampering, was sending it down. As the doors gaped to display the brick wall of the shaft, then closed again, the trapdoor clanged back and something like a hand came reaching down towards her.

It was very large. If it found her, it would engulf her face. It was the colour of ancient dough, and looked puffed up as if by decay; patches of the flesh were torn and ragged, but there seemed to be no blood, only greyness. She clamped her left hand over her mouth, which was twitching uncontrollably, and thrust the lighter at the swollen groping fingers.

They hissed in the flame and recoiled, squirming. Whitish beads had broken out on them. In a way the worst thing was the absence of a cry. The hand retreated through the opening, scraping the edge, and a huge vague face peered down with eyes like blobs of dough. She felt a surge of hysterical mirth at the way the hand had fled – but she choked it back, for she had no reason to feel triumphant. Her skirmish had distracted her from the progress of the lift, which had reached the bottom of the shaft.

Ought she to struggle with the doors, try to prevent them from opening? It was too late. They were creeping back, they were open now, and she could see the subbasement.

At least, she could see darkness which her light couldn't even reach. She had an impression of an enormous doorway, beyond which the darkness, if it was in proportion, might extend for hundreds of yards; she thought of the mouth of a sewer or a mine. The stench of putrid food was overwhelming, parts of the dark looked restless and puffy. But when she heard scuttling, and a dim shape came darting towards her, it proved to be a large rat.

Though that was bad enough, it mustn't distract her from the thing above her, on the lift. It had no chance to do so. The rat was yards away from her, and darting aside from her light, when she heard a spongy rush and the rat was overwhelmed by a whitish flood like a gushing of effluent. She backed away until the wall of the lift arrested her. She could still see too much – but how could she make herself put out the flame, trap herself in the dark?

For the flood was composed of obese bodies which clambered over one another, clutching for the trapped rat. The rat was tearing at the pudgy hands, ripping pieces from the doughy flesh, but that seemed not to affect them at all. Huge toothless mouths gaped in the puffy faces, collapsed inwards like senile lips, sucking loudly, hungrily. Three of the bloated heads fell on the rat, and she heard its squeals above their sucking.

Then the others that were clambering over them, out of the dark, turned towards her. Great moist nostrils were dilating and vanishing in their noseless faces. Could they see her light with their blobs of eyes, or were they smelling her terror? Perhaps they'd had only soft rotten things to eat down here, but they were learning fast. Hunger was their only motive, ruthless, all-consuming.

They came jostling towards the lift. Once, delirious, she'd heard all the sounds around her grow stealthily padded, but this softness was far worse. She was trying both to stand back and to jab the lift-button, quite uselessly; the doors refused to budge. The doughy shapes would pile in like tripe, suffocating her, putting out the flame, gorging themselves on her in the dark. The one that had ridden the lift was slithering down the outside to join them.

Perhaps its movement unburdened the lift, or jarred a connection into place, for all at once the doors were closing. Swollen hands were thumping them, soft fingers like grubs were trying to squeeze between them, but already the lift was sailing upwards. Oh God, suppose it went straight up to the sixth floor! But she'd found the ground-floor button, though it twitched away from her, shaken by the flame, and the lift was slowing. Through the slit between the doors, beyond the glass doors to the street, a streetlamp blazed like the sun.

The lift's doors opened, and the doughy face lurched in, its fat white blind eyes bulging, its avid mouth huge as a fist. It took her a moment prolonged as a nightmare to realise that it had been crushed between lift and shaft – for as the doors struggled open, the face began to tear. Screaming, she dragged the doors open, tearing the body in half. As she ran through it she heard it plump at the foot of the shaft, to be met by a soft eager rush – but she was fleeing blindly into the torrent of rain, towards the steep maze of unlit streets, her father at the fireside, his quiet vulnerable demand to know all that she'd done today.

SCOTT EDELMAN

The Man He Had Been Before

AS A WRITER, Scott Edelman has published more than fifty-five short stories in magazines such as *The Twilight Zone*, *Absolute Magnitude*, *The Journal of Pulse-Pounding Narratives*, *Science Fiction Review*, *Fantasy Book* and *PostScripts*, along with the anthologies *Crossroads: Southern Tales of the Fantastic*, *Men Writing SF as Women*, *MetaHorror*, *Once Upon a Galaxy*, *Moon Shots*, *Mars Probes*, *Forbidden Planets* and *Summer Chills*. He has twice been a HWA Bram Stoker Award finalist in the category of Short Story.

As an editor, Edelman is currently responsible for both *Science Fiction Weekly*, the internet magazine of news, reviews and interviews, and *Sci Fi*, the official print magazine of the Sci Fi Channel. He was the founding editor of *Science Fiction Age*, which he edited during its entire eight-year run from 1992–2000. He also edited *Sci-Fi Entertainment* for almost four years, as well as two other SF media magazines, *Sci-Fi Universe* and *Sci-Fi Flix*. He has been a four-time Hugo Award finalist for Best Editor.

"I've always found the end of the world appealing," Edelman admits. "(Well, the *idea* of the end of the world. I could do without the real thing, which unfortunately seems closer each day.) There's something attractive about wiping the slate clean and getting back to basics. It's almost as if the Apocalypse represents a beginning rather than an ending to me.

"Add monsters into that mix and you've *really* got my attention.

"The monsters in the story you're about to read represent my favourite supernatural creatures. (Again, in idea only. Though they have often been the stuff of my actual nightmares, I have no desire to run into them in real life.) As is usual with my stories of monsters, it can be a little unclear who the real monsters are – us or them. But luckily, at the end of the world, we might have a shot at that question being answered."

MOM AND DAD HAD STARTED ARGUING as soon as we'd left the cabin. By the time we topped the ridge in the morning light and peered down into the sleeping subdivision, they'd already moved beyond their usual accusations and recriminations and fallen into the grim silence that always followed.

Had we left early enough to do what we set out to do and still return to the safety of the cabin in time? Had we left late enough to avoid any leftover dangers of the night that might lurk behind each tree? Did we remember to bring enough ammunition? (That was dad, that was always dad.) Was it wise to bring a child along? (That was Mom, always Mom.) The questions had been tossed out insistently and then only debated half-heartedly, because no answers were ever really being sought. Their questions were just sharp sticks with which they liked to poke each other. That's all they ever were.

Dad had led us through the woods, with Mom taking up the rear. Their hostility washed through me as I walked between them. Still, I preferred their quiet fuming to the sounds of their bickering. At least it meant I didn't have to listen to either of them refer to me as a child. I was fourteen years old, a man, with a 12-gauge shotgun slung over my shoulders, finally ready to help them in what was now the most important job in the world and would remain so for some time to come – killing those who wanted to kill us.

No one spoke again until we paused there on the lip of the ridge. I looked at the houses laid out in neat lines in the subdivision in which I could barely remember having lived. There were almost a hundred of them, sitting in a bowl surrounded by hills. I counted out the rows and columns until I found the one I thought had been ours eight long years before.

Dad tossed an arm across my shoulders, hugging both me and the gun.

"Remember," dad said. "Place the barrel in their mouths. Or what's left of their mouths anyway. Point toward the top of the head, then fire. And you can turn away when you pull the trigger . . . if you need to."

He said that last phrase in a way that let me know he would be disappointed in me if I did.

Mom came up beside us, but didn't reach out to touch me. She never did, not if he had his hand on me first.

"Don't worry," Mom said. "As long as the sun shines, you'll be safe from them. So you don't have any reason to be afraid."

Her saying that only told me that *she* was afraid. But whether it was of what waited for us below or what waited slumbering between the two of them to flare back up after I left, I couldn't say for sure. Probably a little bit of both.

I nodded and started down.

"One more thing," dad called out, before I'd gotten more than a dozen feet away.

"I'm ready," I said, curtly, not even turning to look back. "Chill out, dad."

I don't know that I'd ever have dared talk to him like that had I not had a gun in my hands. I knew I'd probably pay for it later, but it seemed worth it. Then it occurred to me that because I'd spoken that way, Mom was likely going to pay for it now, and I regretted my words.

I danced down the slope along the path that deer had been making since before our development had been carved out of the countryside. People might not be long for this world, but deer, well, deer would be forever. I shifted the shotgun tight across my chest and thought of the deer dad and I had brought down in the past. I'd always had trouble making a clean kill, because they were moving targets, and even if I hit one, dad would usually have to step in over a wounded doe to finish the job. Luckily, the targets I was being trusted with today would remain still.

Down in the hollow, I paused before stepping onto the over-grown lawn of the first house, and peered back at my parents silhouetted up on the ridge. I waved at them with one hand while holding up my gun with the other, but I don't think they even noticed. By then, their own hands were moving wildly, and they were taking turns stomping away from each other and then marching back for more finger pointing. With me no longer there to shame them, the real fireworks began.

I walked toward the first door, looking carefully through the tall grass for bodies. I didn't see any lying there out in the open, and a part of me had always known it wouldn't be that easy. I would have to go in.

I jiggled the knob, but the door was locked. I stepped back and lunged at it, putting my whole body behind the blow, the first time a kick, the next a shoulder, but it didn't move. I may have already been fourteen, but there were still some things that only dad could do . . . a thought that made me frown.

I moved to the big picture window to the right of the door and broke the glass with the butt of my gun. The tinkling as the shards rained down made me feel a little better. I cleared away the glass that remained on the windowsill and climbed through.

I could vaguely remember living in a house among houses like this one, instead of the small hunting cabin in the isolated woods we now occupied. As I stood in the centre of the living room and scanned the walls, it all seemed eerily familiar, but perhaps I wasn't remembering reality. Maybe I was only remembering a dream. There was bright wallpaper in a dizzying geometric pattern. A clock in the shape of a cat hung by the door that I hadn't been able to open. It should have blinked at me as each second passed, but its batteries were long dead, just like the original occupants them-selves probably were. Off in the kitchen, I could see a wall calendar with a picture of a toucan, an incorrect month, and a year I hadn't known since I was six.

I was alone in the living room, but I wasn't alone in the house. I found a body in the den, the first I'd ever found without dad by my side, and I immediately knew that my heart was not quite as ready as my head had said it was. The shotgun was slippery in my sweaty hands. He (I know I was only supposed to think of him as "it", Mom had said it would be easier that way, but still, I couldn't stop seeing them as people) was lying facedown on the floor even though there was a comfortable couch nearby. Mom said they just drop wherever they happen to be standing when the sun comes up. Which meant he'd been hunting for one of the living right there when dawn cut him down for the day. I knew that. And yet, he looked strange to me all twisted in the carpeting, his arms and legs bent at angles they shouldn't be. One arm had been flung over his face, so I couldn't even really tell for sure that he had once been human. He could just as easily have been a mannequin.

I poked him with the barrel of my shotgun, and it was like stabbing a sack of flour. I trusted Mom that I was safe until darkness fell, so I relaxed and looked around the room. The television caught my attention the most. What I would have given to see someone move across that screen, someone other than my own reflection. I posed with the gun, but that only reminded me of my favourite show, and made me miss the old days more.

The rest of the room looked like any number of dens I must have visited, but I felt I should have remembered it. I should have remembered who'd once lived here. I'd been in most houses in the subdivision, thanks to trick or treating and birthday parties. But that had been so long ago, and this place seemed alien.

I'd wasted too much time already, trying to avoid what had to be done.

I turned back to the dead man. I shoved my toe under one of his shoulders and, keeping my gun aimed at his head just in case, rolled the body over. His head hit the floor with a dull thud, but did not bounce.

The man's eyes were open but unfocussed. There was a hole torn into his cheek, as if the flesh had been bitten off, perhaps by the bite that had made him what he was. I stood over him, straddling his waist, looking into his face and trying to see in him the man he had been before, but I could not make that person out. Whoever that person had been seemed gone.

There was no reason I shouldn't just do what I had come to do and move on. Since he wasn't breathing, it wasn't as if I could fool myself into thinking that he was asleep. But still . . .

I began to kneel, to look more closely into those dead eyes, but before my knees hit the floor, the room roared with a gunshot – not mine, since the gun had not bucked in my hands – and the man's head exploded, his brains splattering my face. I turned to see my father standing in the hallway that led to the den. He shook his head.

"We don't have time to waste," he said quietly. He knew I always feared him more when he whispered. "Now, make up your mind. Are you a man? Or are you still a boy?"

He didn't wait for my answer, just turned and walked off.

I went to the window that I had broken earlier and watched him walk toward the house on the other side of the street. As he grew smaller and more distant, I tried to see in him the man he had been before, but though I watched him until he vanished inside, I could neither imagine nor remember that man.

As I tried to sleep that night, after a day spent doing my parents' – my father's – wishes, the faces of those I had killed filled my mind. I had moved on from that first house and tried to perform my assignment quickly – no dawdling, no pause for reflection, no second thoughts. I tried to feel proud again, as I had when we'd first set out that morning. But I couldn't make myself do it. Because even though my parents told me I had killed no one, had slapped my back and congratulated me, I still felt guilt. I still felt haunted.

In that twilight state that was not quite waking and not quite dream, I finally did see what I had been looking for as I'd begun to kneel. I finally did see them as they had been.

As I lay in the small back room that was more closet than bedroom, I tried to ignore both the moaning from outside the cabin and the sharp whispers from the next room. Eventually, I escaped them and found some temporary respite from both, but there was no true rest, for I kept seeing the faces, and they had become what I feared.

I was in a foggy neverworld, and the undead, now live again, rose up gigantic from the horizon, like suns. The teenaged girl I'd found fallen in the backyard, one arm missing so I could see the muscles of her shoulder, was now my long ago babysitter. The old woman lying twisted in the middle of the street, a dog, equally dead, hanging from a leash wrapped around her wrist, had become my kindergarten teacher. The man without pants who I'd found with fingers gnawed away was suddenly the one who'd once chased me from his yard after I'd sneaked in to get back a stray baseball. They hovered over me, eyes accusing, and spoke.

"How could you, Bobbie?" said Julie, who'd never seemed to tire of reading Dr Seuss to me.

"You were always my favourite," said Mrs Giordano, her fingers sending out clouds of chalk.

"Do you really think you accomplished anything today?" said Mr Baxter, a baseball gripped in the hands he once again had. "You're just wasting your time. Don't you already realise how this is going to end?"

I shouted at them to stop, and woke sitting up, having completely shaken off any possibility of sleep. Heart racing, I got out of my cot and went to the room's narrow window. It was night-time, *their* time, and I knew that those we had not killed were out there, awake again, hunting for us. I could vaguely make out the barbed wire off in the gloom, but the moon was not full enough for me to see it clearly.

I'd escaped the torture of my dreams, but now that I was up, there was no avoiding the acid commentary from the main room on the other side of the thin wall. Mom and dad were supposed to be sleeping, getting ready for what was to come the following day, but as usual, the opportunity to have at each other when they thought I was asleep was too much for them. Without witnesses (or so they assumed), now they could let the real venom flow.

"– don't think you're handling this right," I could hear Mom say, though I had not heard what it was she had been accusing dad of not handling right. She'd been keeping a list for as long as I could remember.

"Well, we're alive, aren't we?" said my father, almost hissing as he tried to keep his voice low. "Can't you at least give me that much? Shouldn't that count for something?"

"Do you really consider this being alive? I don't. We'd have been better off—"

"What? Dead? Like them? Like those on the other side of the fence I almost died building for you?"

"I'm sick of hearing about that fence. Sick of it!"

"But I know what you really mean, that *you'd* have been better off. This is about him, isn't it?"

"No, it's not about him. There *is* no him. It's about us."

"Admit it."

"*You're* the one who keeps fantasising about someone else. *You're* the one who keeps bringing it up."

"Admit it!"

By now, they were long past any pretence of whispering.

"All right, I think of him!" she shouted. "Is that what you wanted to hear? I think of him and how maybe if I had chosen differently I wouldn't be here, I'd—"

Mother screamed at him until she was silenced by a slap, and then there was another, less forceful blow, likely her also getting physical. It was obviously going to be another long night, and I couldn't bear it any longer, not this night. I unlocked the window, and slid out onto the cool, damp grass. The night smelled wonderful. It had been a long time since I had been allowed to walk freely beneath the stars. Much too long. But I was a man now. It was about time I made some decisions of my own.

I headed for the perimeter fence that dad had built so many years before, back when most still scoffed at what was to come.

The undead threw themselves against the barbed wire. There seemed to be no fewer of them for all the work we had done that day. At first they moved listlessly, half-heartedly, but then they must have sensed my approach, for they began congregating at the spot closest to me. I knew I was in no danger, though, for dad had built the fence well, back when life had still been normal. I tried to imagine it moved to around the home we had once shared, as my parents had been planning, and us living there again, but could not.

Mom thought it was time to be normal once again. I didn't remember normal. Not really. Mom thought it was time for us to move back to our old home in the heart of the subdivision, if only we could clean out the undead. I wasn't so sure. How could you go back to something you couldn't really remember?

"How about you?" I asked the half-dozen wanderers. "Do you remember when things were normal?"

None of them answered. They just kept thrusting at the fence, leaving pieces of themselves hanging behind on the barbed wire. I took a step closer. They were thrusting themselves at *me*.

"Robert!"

I tumbled back as dad shouted and grabbed my arm.

"What do you think you're doing?" he said as I looked up at him, scrambling backward through the mossy earth. "Are you crazy? What the hell's going on in that head of yours?"

He held a pistol in one hand, and he raised back his other as if to strike me. Mom leapt between us before he could, and I was able to get to my feet.

"What do you expect, Nathan?" she said. "What kind of life have you given us? How did you expect him to turn out?"

I was disgusted. All I'd succeeded in doing was moving their fighting outside. Let the undead be their witnesses. I turned, and as soon as I had, I heard gunfire. But I didn't let it stop me from walking back to the cabin.

When the echoing faded, I could hear dad bellowing—

"– a game, Robert. But it isn't. Snap out of it. This is all we've got. It's all we've got!"

Even though I tried to pull away from my parents on the next morning's march, we entered the subdivision together. Dad walked by my side while Mom hung back so we could speak privately. Also, she probably preferred being out of his reach as well. The looks that passed between them when in silence were as irritating as their words when they spoke. I could sense what was to come, and picked up my pace, but dad kept up with me. Mom glared at him, and finally he began to speak.

"Are you sure you're up for this today, Robbie?" he said, affecting a light tone that did not suit him. "Yesterday was a big day for you."

"I'm fine, dad."

"Your mother and I figured that you might want to hang back today, and let us do the heavy lifting. You could watch for the day if you . . . if you need time to process."

" 'Process' isn't your kind of word, dad."

He looked over his shoulder back at Mom. She frowned, which accentuated the puffiness of her cheek.

"You know what I mean," he said, his lips thin. I could tell how tough it was for him to appear jovial. "What you did last night was kind of weird, son, and –"

"This is all kind of weird, dad. And it's going to stay weird. Don't worry about me. Worry about yourself."

I broke into a run then, and neither of them tried to keep up. I doubted they could even if they'd wanted to.

I ignored the houses we'd visited the day before, ran deeper into the heart of the subdivision. I made random turns at each corner, hoping that they wouldn't see where I ended up. I didn't stop until I was sure that I'd lost them, in front of a home with a swing set in the yard.

This time, the front door was unlocked. I moved slowly through the home, hoping to find people there, ready to see another family, one that, unlike us, hadn't made it. I needed something to tell me that we had made the right choice. Were still making the right choice. A reminder I could hold onto. But as I moved through the pastel rooms empty of any sign of life . . . or death . . . the house seemed to hold nothing for me.

And then, just as I was about to abandon this home for the next, I saw that one of the closet doors had been locked shut. Not with anything that could have kept anyone out, no combination lock or keyhole, only two latches, one each at the top and bottom of the door. This was meant to keep something *in*.

I could see that I was going to be here for a while. So I went back to a window, opened it, and fired my shotgun once into the air. That should keep my parents happy, I thought, and might even keep dad from coming to check up on me. Let them think that all was well.

Back at the closet, I hesitated, reminding myself that no matter how dark the closet might be, it was still day-time. I flipped the latches, and then didn't even have to open the door – it slowly opened on its own and a body slumped to my feet.

It was a little boy. He couldn't have been more than five, maybe six. A dead little boy.

No, I told myself. If anything, he was a not-quite-dead little boy. His parents had probably locked him in when they went foraging on their own, to prevent him from wandering off and getting infected, back before the world was taught that all you had to do to become infected was to die, just die, and that was that. So once those loving parents I imagined died on their own, the son they'd meant to protect starved, and he died inside the place that was meant to save him. In fact, those same parents had probably prayed that even if he did die in that way, they'd at least stopped him from having to come back. But there was no escape, not from this.

The boy's fingernails were gone, but whether that had been done in life when he realised that his parents weren't returning and he was struggling to get free or after death when he was hoping to feed a different kind of hunger, I would never know.

That could have been me. That could still end up being me.

I put down the shotgun and cradled him in my arms. I'd never even thought of doing that to one of the undead before, but suddenly, it seemed right. He was heavier than I thought he'd be. I'd figured that he'd be a husk, dried out, light. But lifting him made me realise that what I'd intended to do might not be so easy.

I carried him to what had to have been his room. It looked not so much different from the one I'd had. The superheroes in the posters seemed silly now, though. I placed him in a chair by his desk, and pushed the chair in close so he couldn't fall out. I found one of his schoolbooks on a shelf, slid it open under one of his hands, and put a pencil in the other. I sat on his bed, and studied him. I tried to imagine a world in which he could still be sitting there, doing his homework.

But I didn't think I'd be allowed time to do that for long.

At the next home on the street, I found a man who'd dropped on the front lawn, as if he'd come home from a late night with his friends, and fallen asleep there drunk. His right arm spoiled the illusion, though, for it had been sliced through near the shoulder, and hung by only a thin strip of skin and muscle. It had been a clean cut, so someone must have attacked him with a machete, likely in self-defence. But whoever it was hadn't been wholly successful. The man's teeth gave that much away. Stuck between them was the second proof that this was something other than merely a sleeping man – trapped bits of rotting flesh.

I looked about nervously, expecting my parents to have sneaked up on me, but I was still unseen. I fired my shotgun into the air again, hoping that my parents would once more misinterpret the sound, and then placed it in the grass next to the man. I pulled him by his ankles across the lawn, out into the street, and back to the first house I had visited. I dragged him up to the boy's bedroom, then went back downstairs and found a dining room chair. I propped the man in it immediately next to the boy, bent forward, apparently helping with the homework. From the back, only the man's dangling arm gave away that this couldn't possibly be the case, so I laid that arm across the boy's shoulders, supported in such a way as to complete the illusion.

I sat back on the boy's bed and studied the tableau until I realised the one thing that was missing, and then I retrieved my gun and continued with my search.

I found that missing piece three houses down, floating in a swimming pool. She wasn't exactly what I needed – she was too old, looking more like a grandmother. But she would have to do. I'd been lucky, but I knew I was running out of time. I put my gun down again and used a pole with a net on the end to bring her closer to the side of the pool.

I pulled her up to the pebbled concrete lip of the pool, and began to drag her, just as I had dragged the man, but I stopped quickly when I saw the trail of flesh that I was leaving behind. The pool had left her soggy and soft. I imagined that she had been trapped in the water for quite a while. She'd probably stumbled in one night after she'd reanimated, and then spent each day sleeping and each night desperately trying to get out, but no longer had enough of either her brain-power or sense of balance to use the ladder.

At first I thought I'd have to hug her to be able to move her where I wanted without peeling flesh on the pavement, but I sure didn't feel like having one of the undead ooze all over me. But thinking back, I realised that maybe I wouldn't have to. I returned to the house where I had found the child, and as I expected, was able to locate a little red wagon in the garage. I wheeled it back by the pool and folded the woman into it as best as I could.

She was too big, and kept threatening to roll off. I had to leave my gun behind one more time, so I could walk along with my package, with one hand on the wagon's handle, the other steadying her head.

Back at the home, I carefully posed her at the bottom of the stairs, the banister tight in one armpit, her head tilted back. When I let go of her, she slipped slightly, but stayed there in position. It was dinnertime, and she was calling her family down so they'd all sit around the table and eat it together. I went back up to the bedroom and watched the father and son from one corner of the room, standing as far away as I could to preserve the illusion. I squinted to avoid seeing the mottled flesh and impossible posture. Yes. This was the way it was supposed to be.

I could have spent all day lingering there, watching them, but I was running out of time. I left the bedroom, pausing for last one moment at the top of the stairs to peer down at the carefully balanced woman below.

Coming, mother, I thought, and smiled.

Then I hurried back to where I'd last left my gun.

But there was no gun.

I stared at the edge of the pool where the gun had been, my first thought being, *What do I tell my father?*, when I realised that, of course, the person who had taken my gun had to have *been* my father.

The sound of gunfire told me I was right, as I heard first one shot, and then two others in close succession. I knew what that meant, in what order he had dispatched the family I had made. First the mother, then the father and son. I raced back to the house where I had posed the undead, and got to the front door just as my dad approached it from inside, a gun in each hand. He dropped them both and flung himself at me, and this time my mother was not there to intervene.

I ducked my chin to my chest and wrapped my arms over my head, but some of his punches still broke through. He shouted at me, but I couldn't really hear what he was saying because my ears were covered. It was as if I was underwater. But I'm sure I'd have recognised what he was saying. He'd said it all to me and to Mom so many times before, both with fists and without.

I dropped, not so much from the power of his blows as from having learned that a sign of surrender would make it stop. And the blows did stop, so I lowered my arms, and then one, last unexpected punch came in and caught me on the side of the jaw. I looked up at him, tasting blood. The sun was already high overhead, which gave my father a halo as he stood there. His mouth opened and closed, but it took a few moments before any words came out.

"I'm sorry, Robbie."

He always said he was sorry. But what did it mean? Being sorry didn't make it right.

I didn't have to say that out loud. He could tell easily enough what I was thinking. He knelt beside me so he could look me straight in the eye.

"Look, son, I want you to live," he said. "You're going to have to stop playing these games if you're going to make it. And we're all going to get through this, I promise. What I saw in there, Robbie, that was sick. It was disgusting. And if you keep at it, it will eventually kill you. Now, no more playing around. Agreed?"

He extended a hand to me. And I took it. That may have meant something to him, been some kind of symbol, but it didn't mean anything to me.

He helped me back to my feet. I wiped the blood from my mouth with the back of my hand.

"Can I have my gun back?" I asked.

He studied me for a moment, then shook his head. He turned and picked up both guns.

"Maybe tomorrow," he said, not looking at me. "For now, let's just go home."

Yes, I thought. *Let's*.

After dinner that night, dad wandered off, claiming he needed to check the perimeter fence, but I knew it was really so Mom could take me aside to speak to me privately. Usually, he took me with him, pointing out the areas in need of repair, instructing me in the ways of being a man. But that night, Mom and I sat alone on the porch, and as we talked – or rather, as she talked and I tried only to listen – I just stared off at the length of barbed wire as dad prodded each inch of it and eventually moved on beyond my line of sight.

As Mom spoke, I kept my mouth shut. That was from my personal set of survival skills, the ones dad taught me when he didn't think he was teaching me. Never give away too much of yourself. Especially not now, since Mom wasn't sounding like herself. Suddenly, she was sounding like dad.

She followed up a mix of apologies, concerns, and loving comments with a question.

"Is it really that bad?" she asked, words that would have enraged her coming from dad. So I didn't feel I had to answer that one, since she'd already answered it herself so many times before. I'm sure she filled the silence I offered her with the correct answer.

"You've got to stop acting out like this," she said. "I'm not sure where it's come from all of a sudden, but it doesn't accomplish anything. And it just makes your father mad."

Hearing her say that, with a bruise still darkening on her face, forced me to let down my guard.

"Mom, I don't think anything *makes* dad mad. You know that. You've got to know that. He just *is* mad."

"Oh, Robbie, you don't remember the man he used to be," she said, pulling her chair closer to me. "You were too young. How *could* you remember? It's all *this* that makes him mad. He loves us, Robbie, you've got to believe that. I can understand you wanting it all to be just like it was again, because that's what your father wants. But it can't be. We can never go back."

"But it's not just him. *You* want us to clean out down there. *You* want us to go back."

This time, she became the quiet one. I refused to look at her until I heard her begin to cry. When she finally spoke again, it was in a whisper.

"There is no back, Robbie. There probably never will be. But it would be nice to pretend for a while. Could you help me with that, Robbie? Could you stop fooling around so I can have that?"

"I'll try," I said, because saying I'd try felt like less of a lie than saying that I actually would.

She patted my shoulder, and then went back inside, leaving me to continue contemplating the barbed wire. She only came out twice more that night, first to give me a new damp cloth for my face that still pulsed from my father's beating, and then later, as the sun was setting, to tell me to come inside and go to bed, as we don't want to stir them up. Though at first, I thought she said "We don't want to stir *him* up."

I came to bed, but I wasn't going to get any sleeping done that night.

At least not there.

Mom and dad talked later into the night than usual, and it was a struggle to stay awake until they stopped. But eventually, even they had to give up, and once enough silence had passed, I went to the window out of which I had slipped the night before. I tried to yank it up, but it wouldn't open. I looked more closely and could see where dad must have nailed the window shut.

My exit from the cabin was going to have to be a little more daring. I tiptoed from my back room to where my parents were sleeping in the middle of the main room that served as kitchen, dining room and their bedroom. As I passed, I looked at them briefly, curled up on opposite sides of the bed, their backs to each other, and didn't have either the time or the strength of will to imagine them as they once had been. I wasn't entirely sure that I believed either of them ever had *been* anything different.

I took my gun from the foot of their bed and slowly opened the front door of the cabin. Out on the porch, I leapt over the railing to the ground beneath to avoid making the steps creak.

Walking the line for so many years with my dad, I knew the fence's weak spots. Not just where the undead might try to get in, but the ones where I could try to get out. On the south side of our enclosure stood a tree that was no more than a dozen feet on our side of the fence. High off the ground, one of its branches thrust toward the world outside, extending over the sharp wire of the fence.

I rushed to the tree before the undead could sense my presence, and tossed my gun over the fence. Then I shinnied into the upper branches, and crawled along the one that crossed over. It seemed a long way down, and I prayed as I flung myself into the air toward a pine on the other side of the fence. I climbed down, retrieved the gun, and dashed through the dark woods, back to the subdivision where I had been born, prepared to do what I had to do if one of the undead found me. If there was only one, I could probably outrun it, but if there were more, I'd have to fight. But I would not use the gun. Not until I was ready. I didn't want dad to hear.

I wandered the streets, searching for what had been my home. I'd thought that even after all this time that it was going to be easy to find – after all, it doesn't take *that* long to make a circuit of a hundred homes – but this was the first time I'd been here at night, and I'd forgotten that with the electricity gone, there were no streetlights. In the dark, each street, each home, looked pretty much like another. I had to return to a friend's house that was on the far corner of the subdivision, and close my eyes, and remember. I pretended that I was coming home for dinner. I counted off the grid in my mind. Then I heard shuffling in the grass behind me, so I opened my eyes and ran off quickly.

I recreated the route I had pictured, dashing left, then right, then left again, until I once more stood in the driveway of our old home. As I moved toward the front door, gun slick in my hands, I heard a rustling against the pavement. Crawling in the faint moonlight across what had been my street was what I at first took to be a dog. But it wasn't a dog. It was a man, the lower half of his torso gone, pulling himself along, aiming at me. I could have gone into the house and left him scratching fruitlessly at the front door. I could have let him live, as it were. But instead, I ran at him, surprised by my fury. I slammed the butt of my gun into the back of what remained of his head until his fingers stopped clutching at my pants. I didn't want him to exist any more, not on my street, not in front of my house. He wasn't someone I could look at and still pretend. And I needed to be able to pretend.

I rubbed the gun in the grass to wipe off the blood, and moved to the front door before others could find me. Dad had locked it, and what I had done had filled me with such an adrenaline rush that I would have sworn that I could have kicked it in. But then I smiled, remembering I didn't need to. I found the hollowed-out rock set in a line with other real rocks that edged the garden. The key was still there, and I let myself in the way I'd always done when I'd come home from school having forgotten to take mine along.

The house was smaller than I'd remembered it, the walls closer, the ceilings lower, and at first I thought that, key or no key, I'd somehow gotten in to the wrong house. If only it could have been that. It was just that I had grown. Too many years had passed. I moved through each room, trying to remember the way things had been, but found that I could not remember. I'd only been six years old, after all. All I could do was tell myself the endless things I *should* remember.

Here, take a look at the kitchen, isn't that where Mom made oatmeal raisin cookies? Through that door, in the garage, didn't dad fix your bicycle chain? Up in my bedroom, couldn't I recall the phosphorescent stars that had glowed on the ceiling, the ones that they had both helped me apply? But no, nothing. No matter how many times I tried to flesh out my memories, I could not make them become real to me.

Unfortunately, there was only one location in that house that brought back true memories.

I opened the door that led to the windowless basement and paused at the top of the stairs. Without electricity, it was total darkness, but that didn't bother me. That was exactly how I had liked it best so long ago. Darkness had offered escape. I shut the door behind me, and walked down the stairs, feeling the air grow cooler with each step. I felt my way to the alcove beneath the stairs, and crawled into the small opening there. I placed the gun beside me and wrapped my arms around my knees. The moment I bent my head down, all the memories I had been searching for but could not find suddenly came flashing back.

Plates breaking. Doors slamming. Holes being punched in walls. Slaps and kicks and shouts. Occasional police sirens, when the neighbours thought things had gotten bad enough and bothered to call them. I had sometimes stayed down here for hours, listening to the sounds of havoc above, praying for them to stop. How they started was always a mystery, and even though as I sat there now, I could remember those times before the mayhem even started, I still could not recall precisely the why of it. It was and probably always would be a mystery. Even as the exact details of my attempts to escape came back to me, all I could recall of catalysts was . . .

We'd be watching television, or playing a board game, or just talking about how the day had gone. And Mom or I would say something that would set dad off. Whatever that something was was out of reach now. But dad would get that familiar glazed look, and his eyes would unfocus. We'd see what was coming, and quickly try to apologise, but it was always too late, and a fist would fly out, and he'd begin to roar. However it started, it always ended with me down here.

If it began with something Mom said, I'd try to get between them at first, to stop it, but I was too small then, and eventually I'd get pushed to the side. I'd run here, tears streaming down my face. If it started with dad coming after me, it still ended the same way, because Mom would intervene, which would make dad even angrier, and when his focus would shift directly to her, I'd flee to the basement, too. As I sat there, I tried to remember what Mom had been talking to me about for years, the man dad had been before, but though this room brought back many memories, it could not bring back that.

But then, the sounds I was remembering became real. I heard movement across the floorboards overhead, and shouts. I could not make out what the voices were saying, but I momentarily thought that I had gone back in time, that I was a small boy again, and Mom and dad were at it again. A part of me realised that it was just that I had never shut the front door behind me, and the undead had wandered in, but though there was a reasonable explanation, in the dark, past and present melded. I knew that there was more than one up there, as I could hear steps coming from opposite ends of the house, but at the same time I could almost see Mom and dad up there, making those creaks, supplying those sounds. A table overturned, making yesterday more real than ever.

Eventually, the undead must have sensed me, for they came banging at the basement door. That, too, made the past more immediate. The grunts and moans I was hearing could have been dad demanding the key, and Mom withholding it for as long as she could. That memory had played out endlessly in the life before. I felt fear over whether the door would hold, but fear was not new to me down here. It had been my partner in the dark before. And the door had held against dad – he'd never gotten in until he had ripped the key from Mom – so it should hold now. It only had to last until dawn, and then they would tumble where they stood. I would rise out of the basement, and step over their bodies, and return . . . to where? To what?

I pressed my forehead more deeply into my knees and cried with an intensity I hadn't allowed myself to feel for years. The drumbeat of bodies against the door brought back fresh all of the yelling from before, all of the beatings, all of the frustration at being too small to fight back. I wailed so loud that I blotted out all sounds of the current struggle above. I was back in the past, only I was no longer a small child, I was as I am now. My tears were dried by anger, and I picked up my gun.

"No more," I screamed. "No more!"

I rushed to the bottom of the stairs and fired up at the doorway, screaming as I had been screamed at, cursing as I had been cursed at. I fired until I ran out of shells, and then threw myself up the stairs, holding my gun like a bat, ready to beat down whomever, whatever remained. But the house was now still. I climbed over the bodies piled on the other side of what remained of the door, and exited our house forever.

As I left the subdivision behind me, I was suddenly sure of two things.

That I would never live there again.

And that I would make sure that there would be no more fighting.

As I topped the ridge that separated the world that was from the world we had now, a shadow came toward me. I drew the shotgun back, ready to swing. But lucky for both of us, I realised that it was moving too quickly.

It was Mom.

"Where's your father?" she said, having trouble getting the words out between her sobs. "Have you seen your father?"

I was able to convince Mom to take refuge with me back at the cabin, but as soon as the sun rose, we returned to the subdivision to search for dad. Turns out I'd been premature when I'd sworn I would never be back. We split up to search for him, and while she wandered cluelessly, calling out dad's name, I headed straight to our old home, where I learned that I'd been correct in my second vow – dad would never again be the cause of rancour.

I found him dead by the basement door. He was in a pile with two of the undead, his skin shredded and his bones broken. I told myself that his death had been caused by those I'd found him with, and not by my gunfire. I tried not to look closely enough to tell.

But it didn't really matter. All that mattered was that it was over.

Mom and I buried him that same day, in a sunny spot within the perimeter of the fence. But before we covered him with earth, I did as he had instructed me and put the barrel of the gun in his mouth and fired, to make sure that he wasn't coming back.

Dad would have been proud of me. I didn't even have to turn away.

Mom and I dragged heavy stones over his grave, and once we were done, I felt as if we should say something. But I could think of nothing to say, so it was up to Mom to give his eulogy.

She spoke then of things she'd never spoken of before, at least not to me. She spoke of how they had begun, how she'd always hoped they'd eventually end up, and all things in between. She spoke of how she loved the good in him, and how she forgave him for the bad.

Her falling tears, however, could not erase the bruise under her eye.

But still, now that dad was gone, I finally let myself believe for the first time in the man he had been before.

DENNIS ETCHISON

Calling All Monsters

DENNIS ETCHISON HAS BEEN CALLED "the most original living horror writer in America" (*The Viking-Penguin Encyclopedia of Horror and the Supernatural*) and "the finest writer of psychological horror this genre has produced" (Karl Edward Wagner, *Year's Best Horror Stories*).

His fiction has appeared in numerous periodicals and anthologies since 1961. Some of his most best-known tales are included in the collections *The Dark Country*, *Red Dreams*, *The Blood Kiss*, *The Death Artist* and *Talking in the Dark*.

As a novelist his books include *The Fog*, *Darkside*, *Shadowman*, *California Gothic* and *Double Edge*, along with the novelizations *Halloween II*, *Halloween III* and *Videodrome*, the latter three titles written under the pseudonym "Jack Martin".

A World Fantasy and British Fantasy Award-winning editor of anthologies such as *Cutting Edge*, *Masters of Darkness I–III*,

MetaHorror, *The Museum of Horrors* and *Gathering the Bones* (with Ramsey Campbell and Jack Dann), Etchison also writes magazine articles, film reviews and screenplays (for John Carpenter and Dario Argento, amongst others), and was supervising editor for *Tapping the Vein*, a graphic novel series based on the *Books of Blood* by Clive Barker.

He served as staff writer for the HBO television series *The Hitchhiker*, and since 2002 he has adapted all 156 episodes of the original *Twilight Zone* TV series for broadcast world-wide on *The Twilight Zone Radio Dramas*.

President of the Horror Writers Association from 1992–94, Etchison's latest collections of short fiction, *Fine Cuts* and *Got to Kill Them All & Other Stories*, recently appeared from PS Publishing and Cemetery Dance Publications, respectively.

"This is a tribute to my love of old horror movies," reveals the author. "It's also an example of the way stories often occur to me in threes. Some people refer to this as one instalment of my 'Organ Transplant Trilogy', but I was not aware that 'Calling All Monsters', 'The Machine Demands a Sacrifice' and 'The Dead Line' were parts of a set when I wrote them.

"In each case I knew only that the story I had in mind needed to be told. In retrospect they do seem to fit together, presenting three self-contained variations on the same underlying concept.

"I had long been concerned – haunted is perhaps a better word – with the question of when exactly life ends. How do we determine that precisely? Is it the cessation of breathing? Heartbeat? Brainwaves? It's not an easy or comforting subject to consider; hence this particularly uncomfortable story.

"I hope it gives you something more to think about than the usual chills. I still don't have the answer, but I think this one poses a truly disturbing question."

THE FIRST THING I SEE is the white light.

And I think: so they have taken me to one of those places. I knew it. That was why the pain. My brain stops spinning like a cracked gyroscope long enough for me to relax. Then I get it, all of it. And I think I may go mad, if it is true.

A rubber hand closes my eyes and I see red again. Black lightning forks shimmer in a kind of bas-relief in front of me. Then the whirling stains settle in. I think they are Rorschach tests. The black shapes flow like ink on a blotter. I look into the first one. It seems to me to be an accident. I see a car, no, two cars, and the smaller one is jack-knifed over the big one. Then the pain starts again at the back of my head, not throbbing like before but only dull and steady like a hot light bulb so I try not to think any more about the ink blot.

The voices again over me. They drone, too slow, hurting my ears, trying to seep in through the hardening blockages I can feel there, especially the low one that sounds like the man has a greasy tongue. I want them to stop but they continue, the greasy tongue bending closer. Then I understand, but don't understand, because I know he must be speaking a foreign language. I want the sound to stop. They always speak in foreign languages or at least thick, oleaginous accents, slow and heavy until they give the orders, then harsh and guttural. I remember. I want it to stop because it hurts me. Don't they care? It hurts me!

"I'm sorry," says the man, slipping his hands into his coat pockets. "But it's too late for us to do anything."

But of course it hurts me. That is part of it. I remember now. It is always that way. They even called it the House of Pain once, didn't they? Yes, and the accent oppressive and stressed where you didn't expect it to be and he never bothered about anaesthesia. I believe he said it was a shortage of supplies on the island but I don't believe that. I think for him it was a House of Pleasure.

Yes, that is what they are doing. That is what they are doing. Maybe I keep forgetting, keep drifting off because it is less painful that way. My heart doesn't speed when I think of it. You would think it would. All I feel there is the hardness, cold and brassy and clammy, over my heart. I don't understand that part yet but somehow it seems to fit.

I am bound. I know that now. The cool pressure around my rib cage loosens like a mummy's fingers and the cold lifts from my heart, leaving a sticky spot there. I strain mightily to move my arms and legs but still they won't work. Strapped. I get it more clearly. Lifting, there was lifting right after the start of the pain, and even then I couldn't move, so I must have been bound even then, and more lifting, always higher. But I played it smart. I kept my eyes closed. I knew what was coming. I didn't need my eyes to tell me where they were taking me. It was up lots of stairs, almost always, the top of an old building, tons of sweating stone blocks crumbling in the mortar and piles of dust and powdered limestone in corners where the torches never reached, and the stairs wound in a spiral up and down, down to the dungeons but they took me up, up to the laboratory. They always take them up at first. To the skylight. But now it must be night, the light artificial. They always worked at night on the important experiments.

"I'm sorry" says the man in charge, hiding his powdered hands in his white coat. "But it's too late for us to do anything to save him. We've run all the standard tests, and so now . . ." He makes a helpless gesture.

Something smooth and lightly textured brushes my chin, my lips, my nose, my brow. Now the red darkens. I hear the swish of starched smocks. There are several of them. They move surely, impatiently. So this is a big one. Not just the ubiquitous assistant but others, experts from all over have come to observe. The low voices grind again, like old automobiles on cold mornings with the electrolyte low.

They hurry, I feel it in my skin more than hear it. It must be night. The air they stir toward me is cold. I grow colder. Even my head. Funny but as the cold spreads up from my neck the spot at the back of my head aches less and less. That is, I suppose, some kind of relief.

But still I am afraid.

I wait for the generators to start up. They always need them for electricity. I hear no lightning. So they must use the generators to rev up their particle chambers, their glowing vacuum tubes, their bubbling flasks of coloured fluids, their magnetic arcs jumping and sweeping up and up and up the conductor rods. Snapping and crackling, humming and spinning rotors that whirr and whine and buzz. I used to like them. I think of the lightning bugs I used to collect in mayonnaise jars. They sparked and jumped on the sill all night and it reminded me of their experiments, and the thought scared me a little but it was still pleasurable, a sublimely creepy game I played on myself that always slipped me off into a comfortable dream.

The difference now is that I can't wake up.

I hear a hum. They are ready.

"I'm sorry," says the man in charge, hiding his powdered hands in a wrinkled white coat. "But it's too late for us to do anything to save your husband. We've run all the standard tests, and so now . . ." He bares his hands nervously and moves them in a helpless gesture.

The woman bursts into tears. "But you can't! I showed you the will, notarised, carried with me all these years! And the copy in his pocket!"

The doctor fumbles through his papers. "I can show you his EKG. Here, see for yourself."

As the machinery is lowered over me on damped hinges, I can no longer feel the pain in my head. Sounds, sensations are receding. I wonder if it is the head they are after. I remember such a head, floating in a porcelain tray, clear tubes of nutrient running in through the nostrils, stained bandages pinned around the crown. The eyes were open, and so maybe it will not be so bad. And the head went on thinking. What did it think? Let me try – yes, the door, the one with the heavy bar in front. And the sliding window at the base for food. Another experiment. The head, released from physical demands, focused its powers to make contact and control. Even the deformed monster from the previous operation. He controlled the creature behind the door, calling it out to smash through the boards and—

But now they fit it over my abdomen. I can no longer feel there but I know that is where the instrument is clamping down. That is where they always start.

I wonder if my table is mounted to swivel, to turn me upright. I hear the sheet rustling down below. They may, since I am strapped so completely I can't move a toe or finger. I hear the clasping of surgical steel. It begins.

"I'm sorry," says the doctor in charge, quickly hiding his pale-powdered hands deep in his wrinkled, blood-smeared white coat. "But it's too late for us to do anything to save your husband. We've run the standard tests for death and there is just no response, nothing. I am sorry. So now . . ." He bares his shrivelled hands furtively and moves them in a helpless gesture of absolution.

The wife erupts in tears of frustration and rage. "But you can't operate yet! I showed you the will, notarised, carried with me all these years, since the first time. And the copy of the instructions in his wallet, and the neck chain, you found them at the accident tonight! What more does it take?"

The doctor ducks her freezing gaze and agitates his papers, moistening a finger. "Let me show you his EKG. Here, you can see for yourself, no activity whatever. I'm sorry, but we have to go ahead, do you see? We can't afford to risk any further deterioration. We have the other clause to consider, the main clause."

For the love of God I can't feel but I can hear it slicing away. Why can't I feel? They must use anaesthetic now but even so I know what fiends they are. I think I always knew. O now the obscene sucking sound growing fainter even as my hearing dissolves, wet tissue pulling apart. They suction my bood, the incision clamped wide like another mouth a monstrous Caesarean and I hear the shiny scissors clipping tissues clipping fat, the automated scalpels striking tictactoe on my torso and I know they are taking me, the blood in my head tingles draining down down and I am almost gone, O what is it what are they doing to me the monsters ME they must be it can't be that other nono my papers they couldn't do THAT they couldn't break the terms it says in blackandwhite NO so it has to be like those other times I have seen the altered specimen on the table the wrapped composite the sutured One Who Waits drifting in fluid for the new brain the shaved skin the transplanted claws the feral rictus the excised hump promised long ago the suddenly stripped subcutaneous map scarred creations I call you in

"The main clause."

"B-but that was conditional, you can read –!" She comes close to blowing it then, nearly falling all over herself in a quivering puddle right there in the hospital corridor, She tries one last time. "He–he wanted the contract, a kind of extra life insurance benefit for the children. But it meant more, a lot more to him. It was really the last chance for him to do something for others, for humanity. But he got to be obsessed with the technical question of dying, don't you understand? The exact moment of death. When? He was never sure. When is it? Can you prove it to me?"

"My dear lady, the heartbeat and respiration cease, the muscles go slack . . ."

"God damn it, you cold fish! He wanted an EEG!"

The doctor backs off, assuming a professional stance. "Your husband agreed to sell his usable internal organs to the transplant bank for the usual fee which you, as his beneficiary, will receive within 60 days. Neither you nor your husband made any move to break the contract prior to his, eh, demise this evening and so, I'm afraid . . . there is nothing further I am empowered to do. The standard tests of death have been administered in accordance with the laws of the state, and now his internal physical remains belong to the Nieborn Clinic. His personal effects, of course, remain yours – I'm sure they are at the front desk by now – as well as his, eh, other remains, which will be available to you for burial or cremation. In the morning. And now, if you'll excuse me, Mrs . . ."

She sobs. There is nothing else for her.

I call you now as always before you must return taste sweet revenge on these the true monsters break in now the floodgate opens the dam breaks the skylight shatters under deathlocked weight the torch is dropped the windmill collapses the trapdoor opens the tank splits and gushes controls are shortcircuited the surrogate returns the animal people cry ARE WE NOT MEN? at last the grafts rebel appendages reborn to murder I call you back I call you in now do not wait come as always to the laboratory

House of Pain operating room crypt castle tower NOW I call you where are you? now I call you I call you I call you ARE WE NOT MEN? O God what forgotten corner have I walled myself into what have I done FOR THE LOVE OF GOD

The vacutract unit is shut off. The organs are sealed and deposited in liquid nitrogen. The heavy insulated door is closed, and the chrome catch padlocked. Rubber gloves are stripped. Leave the remains for the orderlies. It goes to the morgue anyway. But for God's sake keep that sheet over the face, so curiously distorted at the end.

The operation is a success.

the last thing I see is the blackness

R. CHETWYND-HAYES

The Shadmock

RONALD CHETWYND-HAYES WAS KNOWN AS "Britain's Prince of Chill" at a time when horror fiction was a more genteel genre. During a publishing career that lasted more than forty years, he produced eleven novels, more than 200 short stories, and edited twenty-five anthologies.

He started writing fiction in the early 1950s, and his first published book was the science fiction novel *The Man from the Bomb* from Badger Books in 1959. While looking on a bookstall in the early 1970s, he noticed the profusion of horror titles and submitted a collection of his own stories simultaneously to two publishers. Much to his embarrassment, both publishers accepted the book, which eventually appeared in paperback as *The Unbidden.*

Chetwynd-Hayes decided to become a full-time writer and began producing a prolific number of ghost stories and sedate tales of terror, many tinged with his disarming sense of humour that led to the invention of such outlandish monstrosities as "The Hoppity-Jump", "The Jumpity-Jim", "The Slippity-Slop", "The Fly-by-Night", "The Gale-Wuggle", "The Humgoo", "The Cumberloo" and "The Gibbering Ghoul of Gomershal".

His stories were widely anthologised and collected in such volumes as *Cold Terror*, *Terror by Night*, *The Elemental* (*aka From Beyond the Grave*), *The Night Ghouls and Other Grisly Tales*, *The Monster Club*, *Tales of Fear and Fantasy*, *Shudders and Shivers*, *The Vampire Stories of R. Chetwynd-Hayes* (aka *Looking for Something to Suck and Other Vampire Stories*), *Phantoms and Fiends* and *Frights and Fancies*.

The author's stories were adapted for the screen in the anthology movies *From Beyond the Grave* (1973) and *The Monster Club* (1980). In the latter, based on probably his most famous and successful book, James Laurenson played the love-struck Shadmock, while the author himself was portrayed by veteran horror actor John Carradine.

In 1989 R. Chetwynd-Hayes was presented with Life Achievement Awards by both the Horror Writers of America and the British Fantasy Society, and he was the Special Guest of Honour at the 1997 World Fantasy Convention in London. He died in 2001.

The Basic Rules of Monsterdom

Vampires – sup; Werewolves – hunt; Ghouls – tear;
Shaddies – lick; Maddies – yawn; Mocks – blow;
Shadmocks – only whistle.

A CAR WAS DRIVING down a lonely country road.

Such a car could have only belonged to a man who was well endowed with this world's goods and had a subconscious desire to advertise the fact. The car must have been made by Messrs Rolls Royce in one of their off moments, for the paintwork was bright red, the headlamps gleamed with blue chromium plating and a naked brass lady sat on top of the radiator. The interior further proclaimed the affluent and original taste of the owner, for the seats were covered with rich, bright yellow leather, the switchboard was a mass of complicated gadgets and there was a faint aroma of expensive cigar smoke and aftershave lotion.

The man behind the steering wheel was easily recognisable as one of those streamlined wolves who lurk in air-conditioned offices perched on top of shoebox-shaped buildings, and roar their Napoleon-brandy-tainted rage over the chilly depths below. He was a large man, with a beefy, rather brutal face that was lit by a pair of small blue eyes and surmounted by a mass of iron-grey hair. His massive shoulders and heavy, bulky body were encased in an electric-blue suit that looked as if it had been tailored by a slightly mad artist, and all but screamed its defiance at the purple shirt and green tie.

The girl by his side had the blonde, brittle beauty of an expensive doll. Her pale, unlined face invited admiration rather than passion, her soft yellow hair defied anyone to disturb its perfectly arranged curls, and the full, red, but discontented mouth was clearly reserved for eating beautifully prepared dinners and dispensing exclusive kisses. Her green dress and open mink coat was a concession to titillation and good taste. The bosom promised but did not reveal: the hemline dared but never retreated above mid-thigh. Her long, red-tipped fingers toyed with a diamond ring, as she looked bad-temperedly out at the racing, grey-ribbon stretch of road.

"Why the hell you want to take a place in the sticks, is beyond me. We've got more houses now than we know what to do with."

The man grunted and switched on the headlights for the first shadows of night were falling across the open countryside.

"Sheridan," the cool, brittle voice rose sharply, "I do wish you would answer me sometimes. I'm not one of your junior executives to be ignored or grunted at."

"Caroline, your body talks, your tongue makes a noise, but you say little that is worth listening to, let alone answering."

Caroline creased her smooth forehead into an angry frown, and her large, hazel eyes became as chips of fire-tinted glass.

"You are taking me to a dead and alive hole called Wittering . . ."

"Withering," Sheridan Croxley corrected. "You may remember I was born there. The son of a cowherd and a kitchen maid. Both of my parents worked at the Grange. Now I have bought it. Do I have to say more?"

"No." The girl smiled derisively. "You've got a chip on your shoulder the size of Everest and this is one way of getting rid of it. Lord of the Manor where your old man shovelled cow-shit. I should have known."

The great head swung round and the little eyes glared at her, but she merely shrugged and deepened her mocking smile.

"You going to hit me now, or wait until you've stopped the car?"

The head jerked back and redirected its cold stare at the road, but Caroline saw the huge, hair-covered hands tighten their grip on the steering wheel.

Darkness had won its daily battle with the dying day when the large car roared between the twin rows of huddled cottages that made up the hamlet of Withering, and continued on under an avenue of trees that terminated where a massive iron gate barred the way. Sheridan hooted the horn twice and presently was rewarded by the sight of a bent figure that emerged very slowly from a stone-walled lodge that stood to the right of the gate. This apparition shuffled into the beam of light cast by the headlamps and Caroline saw the gross outline and the hideous bearded face.

"What an awful looking creature," she said. "I sincerely hope you intend getting rid of that."

"You'll find keeping servants down here is more than a problem – it's well nigh an impossibility. You keep what will stay." He lowered the offside window and leaned out. "I'm the new owner. Open the gates and get a move on."

The man nodded his head and the long, white hair writhed like a nest of bleached snakes; then he opened his mouth to reveal black, toothless gums, in which Caroline could only suppose to be a derisive grin.

"Come on, damn you. Open the gate," Sheridan roared.

Still nodding, still grinning, the grotesque figure reached out great, clawlike hands, that, in the fierce beam of light, seemed to grow to gigantic proportions – and gripped an upright bar of each gate, before pulling them apart. Then with an abrupt jerk of the powerful wrists it thrust the gates backwards and with a shriek of oil-starved hinges, they crashed against the flanking walls.

"Must have the strength of an elephant," Sheridan muttered as he eased the car forward. "One good thing, there's no need to worry about trespassers with him on the front gate."

Caroline turned her head as they drove past the terrifying figure with its gaping mouth, toothless gums and heavy, bowed shoulders. "He's got a dampening effect on me too. Honestly, Sheridan, if the rest of the staff are anything like that – that thing – I'm all for going back to town tonight."

"You'll do no such damn thing," Sheridan growled. "If people who work for me do their job, I couldn't give a monkey's curse what they look like."

They were racing along a tree-lined drive and the terrified eyes of a rabbit glittered momentarily in the headlights, before it scampered into the dense undergrowth. Then the trees slipped behind to be replaced by an overgrown lawn that lay like an uneven carpet before the great house. It had possibly begun life as a farmhouse, but over the centuries extensions had been added, until now it sprawled out as an untidy conglomeration of turrets, crouching chimneys, glimmering windows and weather-beaten brickwork. Sheridan braked the car before a wide porchway, then climbed out on to a gravelled drive and looked up at the house with evident satisfaction.

"What do you think of it?" he asked Caroline who had come round the car to join him.

"There's no lights anywhere," she complained. "It looks awfully desolate."

"Hell, what do you expect. There's only three of 'em in there. Mother, father and son – but they keep the place spotless. I expect they are in the kitchen at the back."

He scarcely finished speaking when the massive double doors slowly opened to reveal a brilliantly lit hall and a man dressed in a decent black suit, who respectfully inclined his head as Sheridan Croxley strode forward.

"You were on the ball, Grantley," he said genially. "We've only just this minute driven up."

The man again inclined his head and stood respectfully to one side.

"I have sharp ears, sir."

Caroline thought that if size were any criterion, his ears should have detected a pin drop in a thunderstorm. They resembled monstrous, tapered wings that stood up on either side of his narrow head and were not enhanced by the thick, black hair which was combed up into a thick pile, thus adding another four or five inches to the man's height. His face was deadly white and the slanted eyes ebony black. When he smiled – a respectful smirk – the unnaturally thin tips parted to uncover great yellow teeth though his appearance was repellent, even sinister, he was not unhandsome in a grotesque, nightmarish sort of way.

He gave Caroline one swift glance, then murmured with his husky voice: "Good evening, madam. May I take the liberty of welcoming you to Withering Grange?"

She could do no more than acknowledge this gracious greeting and was again rewarded by that yellow-toothed, but respectful smirk. When they had entered the large, oak-panelled hall, he clapped his hands and as if by magic, a green baize lined door opened and two persons entered.

"May I," requested Grantley, "present my wife, who combines the duties of housekeeper and cook?"

Mrs Grantley had all the attributes that are needed to make a beautiful woman – plus a little extra. She was tall, dark, with splendid brown eyes and a mass of black hair which she wore shoulder length, and her full, mature figure was calculated to excite any man's interest. But it was the little something extra which drew Caroline's wide-eyed attention and forced her to involuntarily cry out. Mrs Grantley was endowed with a full, rich, and very luxurious beard. It began as a drooping moustache and spread out over the pale cheeks and chin, to flow down over the shapely bosom, where it terminated in a few straggling hairs that quivered slightly when their owner spoke.

"I will endeavour to give satisfaction, madam."

Caroline was incapable of speech and could only stare at the housekeeper's unusual appendage, while unconsciously shaking her head in disbelief.

"Women of our kind are not permitted to shave," the butler said softly. "This," he motioned a young man to step forward, "is my son, Marvin. He can act as footman when the occasion demands, but is normally employed as odd job man."

Caroline switched her gaze from father to mother, then to the youth who stood a little in front of them, and instantly it changed to one of unstinted admiration. The expressions – good looking – handsome – flashed across her mind, then were dismissed as being totally inadequate. He was beautiful. There was no other word to describe the perfect, pale features, the wonderful blue eyes, the long, blond hair, the white, even teeth and the muscular, but slim, body. There was nothing feminine in that beautiful face; on the contrary, Caroline was aware of an animal magnetism that made her forget his bizarre parents and the presence of her husband who had been watching her previous discomfort with sardonic amusement.

"I think, Caroline, Mrs Grantley is waiting for your instructions regarding dinner."

"What!" She tore her gaze away from the beautiful face. "Oh, yes. Whatever is convenient. I . . ."

"For God's sake!" Sheridan broke in impatiently. "Not what – but when? I should imagine dinner is almost ready."

"Oh . . . in about an hour."

Grantley was the epitome of a perfect butler.

"Would eight o'clock be satisfactory, Madam?"

"Yes . . . that would be fine."

"Then permit me to show you to your room."

"Surely," she overcame her reluctance to address this strange creature, "you must have some help with the housework. It seems too much for three people. I mean the house is so big."

Grantley was leading them up the great staircase and answered without turning his head.

"We manage quite well, thank you, madam. It is simply a matter of keeping to a system and my father comes up from the lodge each day to do the heavy work."

"Your father!" She remembered the awful old man who had opened the front gates and shuddered to think that he would actually enter the house – perhaps even walk up these stairs. "Surely he's too old . . ."

"He's very strong, madam," Grantley stated suavely, as he

opened a door and stood to one side so that they could enter. "The blue room, sir. You expressed a preference for this one, I believe."

"Yes, this will do fine." Sheridan Croxley walked across the room and then turned and looked round with evident satisfaction. "Used to be old Sir Harry's room. Used to sleep his after dinner bottle of port off in here, while my old dad was pigging it down in the village."

"Will that be all, sir?" Grantley enquired.

"We would like a bath," Sheridan replied.

"Of course, sir. Marvin is running them now. The bathrooms are on the opposite side of the passage."

He went out and closed the door with respectful quietude and they heard his soft footsteps recede along the passage. Caroline sank down on the bed and mopped her forehead with a lace handkerchief.

"Good heavens, where did you find them?"

"I didn't." Sheridan removed his jacket and walked to the dressing-table. "They came with the house. Old Sir Harry Sinclair died some twenty years ago and I gather it has been empty off and on ever since, with this lot acting as caretakers. But I should say they are worth their keep. You can see how the place is kept and Mrs Grantley's cooking has to be sampled to be believed."

"But she looks like something that has escaped from a fair-ground," Caroline protested. "Did you hear what he said? 'Women of our kind are not permitted to shave.' Sheridan, we can't have a bearded lady about the place."

"I see no reason why not," Sheridan growled. "She's a good cook and can't help having an – an unusual growth. Don't suppose she enjoys it."

"But what about him? Grantley, for God's sake! Those ears and that great pile of hair! And that thing on the front gate!"

"Not to mention the young one," added Sheridan caustically. "I saw you giving him the once over."

"Now you're being ridiculous. Although how that pair produced a son like that is beyond me. Sheridan, this place gives me the willies. Let's get out of here."

"We will. On Monday morning. But not one minute sooner. So have your bath, put on some glad rags and make the best of it."

He was glaring at her with that cold, baleful stare she knew so well – and she flinched.

"If you say so. But surely we don't have to dress for dinner when there are only the two of us?"

He grinned and Caroline felt the familiar surge of loathing and desire that seemed to originate somewhere in the region of her stomach and set her brain on fire. She trembled and his grin broadend.

"Not now, my little slut. As my old man would have said – we have company coming. The local sky-pilot. Bloody old fool, but he's been here for over forty years and it'll be fun to let him know how the world has changed."

Caroline felt the blood drain from her face and thwarted passion curdled and became unreasoning rage.

"You bastard! You dirty, bombastic bastard. You haven't an ounce of decent feeling in your entire body."

He leaned over her and she had a close-up view of the veined cheeks, the pouched eyes and the small, brutal mouth. He playfully slapped her cheek.

"But you wouldn't have me any other way. Would you, little slut?"

She pushed him away and he went laughing into the dressing-room, to emerge a few minutes later wearing a towel dressing-gown and beaming with obvious delight.

"Look at this!" He spread out the skirts of the dressing-gown. "I found it in the wardrobe. Must have belonged to old Sir Harry. Little did he realise that one day the son of his cowherd would be wearing his dressing-gown."

"Big deal. If you rummage round, you might find a pair of his old socks."

She ducked as Sheridan flicked a towel at her, then relaxed when he left the room. Scarcely had the door closed when there was a soft tapping on the panels, then after an interval, it opened and Marvin entered carrying two large suitcases. Caroline felt her heart leap when she again saw that flawless face and sensed the strange magnetism that seemed to radiate from the clear eyes and slim, upright figure. He spoke in a low, beautifully modulated voice.

"Your bath is ready, madam."

"Thank you . . . Marvin."

"Where would you like me to put the luggage?"

"Oh," she managed to laugh, "on the bed will do."

She watched him as with effortless ease he laid the heavy cases on the bed, then turned to face her. "Would you like me to unpack, madam?"

"Eh . . . yes. Unpack my husband's – and lay out his dinner jacket."

"Very good, madam."

He worked silently, gracefully, every movement of his long-fingered hands was an act of poetry, and Caroline cursed herself for a fool when she found her legs were trembling.

"What does . . ." It was such an effort to speak clearly, ". . . a good-looking boy like you do in a dead and alive hole like this?"

Marvin looked back at her over one shoulder and she had a perfectly ridiculous feeling that he was peering into her soul. That clear, cool glance had ripped aside the silly pretensions, and the ugly sores of warped sensuality, the scars, the blemishes – all were revealed and she was as naked as a sinner on judgement day. He turned his head away and continued to unpack Sheridan's case.

"I read a lot. But mostly I like to work in the garden."

"Do you really?"

He held up Sheridan's dinner jacket and brushed out an imaginary crease with the back of his hand.

"Yes, madam. I like to make dead things grow."

Caroline got up and walked slowly towards him and no power on earth could have stopped her laying a hand on his arm. He expressed no surprise at this act of familiarity, or in fact gave any sign that he had noticed. Her undisciplined mind allowed the words to come tripping off her tongue.

"You are very handsome. You must know that."

He piled two shirts, two vests and a spare pair of pyjamas over one hand, then walked slowly to the tallboy.

"Thank you for the compliment, madam. But I have always understood that I am singularly plain."

"Who on earth told you that?"

"Those who have real beauty. The beauty that is born of darkness and suffering."

"You must be a poet. A beautiful, slightly mad poet."

He closed a drawer, gave one quick glance at Sheridan's dinner jacket and frilled shirt which was laid out on the bed, then backed gracefully to the door.

"You are very gracious, madam. Will that be all?"

"Yes . . . yes, that will be all. For the time being."

He inclined his head, then turned and quietly left the room.

Caroline went back to her chair and for some reason began to cry.

The Reverend John Barker was a scholar first and a clergyman second. A more bumbling, inarticulate, woolly-minded old man would have been hard to find, but he also had a built-in compass that directed him to the local houses that employed the best cook and kept a distinguished cellar. He rode up to Withering Grange on an ancient female bicycle, and having propped this under the nearest window, removed his trouser clips and pulled the massive bell-handle.

Caroline, eye-riveting in a silver dress that revealed more than it concealed, heard his high-pitched, rather squeaky voice, as he instructed Grantley as to the disposal of his outer garments.

"Hang the coat on a chairback near the kitchen fire, there's a good fellow. And wrap the muffler round one of the hot-water pipes. Delicate chest, you know."

Caroline advanced into the hall, looking like one of St Anthony's more difficult trials. She smiled sweetly, although the sight of this thin old man, with stooping shoulders and the face of an inquisitive rabbit, did not forecast an entertaining evening, and extended her hand.

"I am Mrs Croxley, you must be . . .?"

She paused as Sheridan had not bothered to inform her of the expected guest's name, but the clergyman hastened to repair this omission.

"John Barker, dear lady. Barker – canine proclamation – doggy chatter – Fido protest. John – as in – but alas – not divine."

Caroline said: "Good Lord!" then hastily composed her features into an expression of polite amusement.

"Both my husband and I are delighted you could come, Mr Barker. Would you care to wash your hands before dinner?"

The Reverend John Barker waved his hand in an impatient gesture.

"Good heavens, no. I had a bath before I came." He began to wander round the hall, peering at the panelling, fingering the scroll-work. "Wonderful old place this. Always wanted to see inside, but old Sir Harry never let anyone cross the door mat. I once tried to sneak in the back, but that bearded horror in the kitchen stopped me."

"Would you care for an aperitif before dinner?" enquired Caroline in a voice which suggested she was not far from desperation. "Cocktail or something?"

Mr Barker shook his head violently.

"Thank you, no. Rots the guts and ruins the palate. Which way to the dining-room?"

"First door to the left," said Caroline weakly.

"Right." He shuffled quickly in the direction indicated and presently Caroline heard his little cries of pleasure as fresh antiquarian delights attracted his attention. He poked his head round the door.

"Dear lady, do you realise that you have a genuine Jacobean sideboard?"

"No." Her smile was like a faulty neon sign. "How marvellous."

"And the dining-table is at least early Georgian."

"Really!" Caroline cast an anxious glance at the staircase. "Would you excuse me for a few minutes, Mr Barker?"

"Of course. I want to examine the fireplace. Take your time, dear lady."

Caroline found Sheridan in his dressing-room where he was adjusting the angle of his bow-tie.

"Sheridan, that clergyman is here. He's mad."

"Eccentric."

"Well, whatever he is, I can't control him. He keeps running about examining the furniture."

"Wait until I jog his memory and let him know who owns it."

When they entered the dining-room, Mr Barker was seated at the table with a napkin tucked in his shirt collar, and an expectant expression on his face. He beamed at his host and rose quickly to his feet.

"You've dressed, my dear fellow! Upon my soul, I did not realise that people still did that sort of thing. Haven't seen my monkey suit and boiled shirt for years."

"'Evening, Barker." Sheridan held the ecclesiastical hand for a brief second, then released it. "Glad you could come at such short notice. Sit down. Grantley tells me dinner is ready."

Indeed, at that moment the butler entered pushing a food trolley, followed by Marvin who assisted his father in piling dishes on to the sideboard. Mr Barker watched the operation with lively interest.

"First class staff you've got here, Mr Croxley. Efficient and unusual."

"They seem to know their job," Sheridan retorted briefly.

Mr Barker raised his voice and addressed Grantley.

"Passed your father by the front gate, Grantley. He seems hale and hearty."

Grantley watched his son serve each of the diners with iced melon before answering. "He keeps very well for his age, thank you, sir."

"Should think he does." The vicar sampled his melon, then nodded his approval. "The old chap looks now as he did twenty years ago. Come to think of it – you all do."

Grantley adjusted the flame under a hotplate and turned his head away so that his face was hidden from the old man's sharp-eyed gaze.

"It is very kind of you to say so, sir."

"Well, Barker," Sheridan filled his guest's glass with some fine old claret, "I don't suppose you ever expected to see me in this house."

The clergyman sipped his wine, then after reluctantly removing his gaze from Grantley, looked at his host with some astonishment.

"I must confess I had not given the matter any thought. I am sure you and your beautiful lady grace the Grange admirably."

"But damn it all," said Sheridan with some heat. "I told you who I was. My father was George Croxley – the cowherd. I went to the old church school. You used to come every Wednesday morning and put us through the catechism."

"So I did." The Reverend Barker smiled indulgently. "I gave up that pastime years ago. Doubt if I could recite the catechism meself now. 'Fraid I don't remember you. Remember your father though. Used to get drunk every Saturday night."

"Well, now I'm here," Sheridan insisted.

"So you are." The clergyman nodded gently. "Nothing extraordinary about that. I mean to say, we all sprang from humble origins. Goodness gracious, who would have thought that a species of monkey would take over the kingdom of the world?"

"Yes, but . . ." Sheridan tried to bring the conversation back to a mundane track, but the reverend gentleman was astride a hobby horse that was not easily checked.

"I cannot but help feel that the monkey was not a good choice. Surely one of the cat family would have been much more satisfactory. They have a much less emotional approach to life . . ."

"Grantley," Sheridan unceremoniously broke into the clergyman's discourse, "when you have served the first course, you may leave."

"Very good, sir."

The tall, oddly featured man and the handsome boy served the roast beef, placed the vegetable dishes in Caroline's vicinity, then silently departed. The Reverend Barker watched the door being slowly closed, then exploded into an excited torrent of words.

"Extraordinary! Fantastic! Unbelievable, but possible. Quite within the realms of possibility. Goodness gracious, yes. Thought so for years, but never dared believe. May I be forgiven for my lack of faith."

Sheridan glanced at his wife, then screwed his face up into a scowl.

"Don't follow you, Barker. You're not making sense, man."

"Really!" The long, lined face expressed surprise. "I would have thought the facts were clear to anyone of normal perception. But of course you are not a student of monstrumology."

"Say again," instructed Sheridan caustically.

"Monstrumology. A much neglected line of research which is unfortunately often treated with derision by the uninformed. As I said earlier it is most surprising that the kingdom of the world should have come under the sway of a species of monkey, and there is reason to suppose there were other claimants to the throne. I refer you to Astaste and his *Book of Forbidden Knowledge*, which devotes no less than six chapters to the *Caninus-fulk* and the *Vampr-Monstrum*. Many legends are based on his findings and I have often believed – now I know – that the old people – as they were known to the unlettered peasantry of medieval Europe – did not completely die out. Quite a large number must have continued to exist even to this day."

"I have never . . ." Sheridan began, but the vicar was leaning back in his chair, his eyes closed and hands folded across his stomach. His voice droned on – and on.

"Conrad von Leininstein, who disappeared mysteriously in 1831, stated categorically that they had started to crossbreed. Vampire to werewolf, ghoul to vampire, then crossbreed to crossbreed, thus producing terrifying hybrids. His illustrations are really most edifying. He also hinted they were moving up into high places, which has often led me to conject about the possibility of my bishop—"

"Look here," Sheridan roared, "this has gone quite far enough. You are alarming my wife and unnecessarily irritating me."

"But, my dear sir," Mr Barker opened his eyes, "I am only telling you all this for your own good. If my suspicions are well founded, then you have a shaddy on your front gate, a mock for a butler and a maddie in the kitchen. The first can lick the flesh from your bones, the second blow the skin from your face – if not something far worse – and the third kill or possess with a gaping yawn. They can all infect their victims with a transforming virus."

Sheridan Croxley did not bother to comment on these allegations, but emptied his wine glass and glared at the ceiling. Caroline decided to ask a question.

"Mr Barker, what is a shaddy and those other things you mentioned?"

Mr Barker sat back and prepared to deliver another lecture.

"A very good question, dear lady. A shaddy is the off-spring of a werevam and a weregoo, which in turn have sprung from the union of a vampire and a werewolf – or in some cases a common or churchyard ghoul. Whereas, a maddy is the fruit of a cohabitation – such unions are not of course blessed by mother-church –

between a weregoo and vamgoo – thus having ghoul connections on both sides . . ."

"Damnation hell," Sheridan muttered, but his exasperation appeared to be lost on the clergyman who continued his discourse.

"A mock – most naturally – is the seed of a shaddy and maddy, or in some cases a raddy, who, as will be supposed, has sprung from the loins of a werevam and vamgoo . . ."

"But," Caroline interrupted, her fear – disbelief, but – heavens above – growing doubts, overcome by a terrible curiosity, "the young man, the good-looking boy – surely he cannot be a monster?"

The Reverend John Barker sat upright and beamed with ghoulish pleasure. "But, dear lady, he is, if I might coin a phrase, the cherry on top of the trifle. If my calculations are correct, that young man – if indeed he is young – is the off-spring of a mock and a maddy, and therefore is the dreaded, the horrific – shadmock."

Sheridan lowered his head and sneered at the irritatingly enthusiastic clergyman.

"Surely among this phalanx of monsters, there is not much to choose between one or the other. What with – what was it? – yawning, licking, blowing and heaven knows what, there isn't much left for a milksop boy to do. What is his speciality? Spitting?"

Mr Barker shook his head in sad reproof.

"Do not, I beg of you, treat this matter lightly, my dear sir. The shadmock may be the lowest branch on the monsteral tree, and therefore been denied the more fearsome aspects of his sires – as for example the horns his father hides beneath that piled-up hair – but be has a gift that is said to be the most venomous in the entire family. He whistles."

"Whistles!" Sheridan repeated.

"Whistles," said Caroline dreamily.

Mr Barker tried to demonstrate by whistling himself, but a set of ill-fitting false teeth defeated his object.

"Yes, indeed. In none of the works which I have read, is there mention of the style of whistle, or what its immediate effect will be, but all unite in maintaining it is fearful to the extreme. I wonder if I can remember the old rhyming jingle that emphasised this fact."

And he screwed up his eyes and after some thought, began to recite the following words.

"Fall to your knees and pray out aloud,
When the moon hides her face behind stormy cloud,
Blame not the wind for the midnight shriek,
Or pretend 'tis the floorboard beginning to creak.
Wonder not why your hair stiffly bristles:
Just abandon all hope when the shadmock whistles."

Caroline screamed softly and Sheridan began to swear very loudly.

Sheridan's rage had not abated when they retired to bed.

"The old fool is as cracked as a fried egg. When I think that a maniac like that climbs up into a pulpit every Sunday and preaches to a lot of simple-minded yokels. I feel like going up the wall myself. Did you ever hear anything like it? Shaddies, mocks and what was it? – shamrocks?"

"Shadmock," Caroline corrected. "But, Sheridan, those three do look awful."

"Ninety-nine percent of the human race look bloody awful. Now, for heaven's sake, dismiss all this rubbish from your mind and go to sleep. I've come down here for relaxation – not to listen to the prattling of an old madman."

Sheridan slept. Caroline lay on her back looking up at the ceiling and listening to faraway sounds that were so faint as to be well-nigh indistinguishable, but could not be dismissed as imagination. A long, drawn-out howl, a scream that was choked in mid-note, and once, much nearer, the soft thud of running feet.

It was a long while before Caroline found the courage to climb out of bed and approach the window. That she finally did so was the result of necessity rather than desire. Imagination created terrifying mental pictures of what might be taking place in that moonlit, unkempt garden, and there was a burning need to be reassured that all was well. In fact, when she at last looked out over that expanse of grass-clad earth, and the still, naked trees that stood like giant sentinels beyond, the scene was one of surprising tranquillity. The moon had tinted every tree, bush and blade of grass with silver, and in those places where it was not permitted to stray, slabs of soft shadow lurked like sleeping ghosts waiting for the kiss of sunlight. A large tabby cat wandered out from beneath the trees and when it had reached a spot some twenty yards from the house, sat down and began to lick its fur. Caroline watched the dainty movements; the flickering pink tongue, the raised paw that slid round pointed ears; the grey streaked fur that glittered like polished steel in the cold moonlight. Suddenly the cat froze and became a study in still-life. Head to one side, yellow eyes staring with awful intensity at the glowering trees, one paw still held over erect ear, back arched, tail coiled like a grey, tapered spring. Then it was a blurred streak that sped across the garden, and with it went the tranquillity, the soft, melancholy stillness that reigns in places where animated life has ceased to walk. Fear stalked across the grass and breathed upon the house.

The old man from the front gate – the shaddy – came out from under the trees and shuffled into the centre of the garden. He was carrying a dead sheep over his shoulders, draped round his neck like a monstrous fur collar, and blood trickled down his shirt front in a red, glistening stream that sprinkled the grass with moonbright rubies. He stopped, then turned and Caroline heard a low, rumbling laugh as Grantley stepped out of the shadows bearing a brace of rabbits slung over one arm. The woman at the window whimpered when she saw the small shrivelled heads; all the fur burnt away, the ears crumpled into crisp curls – the teeth blackened stubs. Father and son stood side by side: two hunters home from the chase, each bearing the fruits of his own particular skill – both waiting for the third to put in an appearance.

Marvin came running across the garden, and Caroline caught her breath when she watched the long, graceful strides, the strange, almost animal, beauty of the youthful face and form. A hot wave of desire submerged the fear – the loathing – of the older creatures, making her clutch the window frame, until her fingers were like streaks of frozen snow.

Marvin carried a basket filled with some peculiar white vegetables.

Here surely was a beautiful Abel coming home to a pair of evil-visaged Cains? He held his basket out for their inspection, and the hideous old man laughed – a raucous bellow that savaged Caroline's ears – and Grantley shook his bead, so that the piled-up hair was disarranged and two black horns glittered in the moonlight. Then Marvin put his head to one side and his full lips parted – and instantly the laughter sank down to a rumbling gurgle. The elder men – creatures – became as still as stricken trees, and both stared at the handsome youth as though he was a cobra preparing to strike. Marvin jerked his head towards the house; a brief, imperious gesture, and they trotted away like two wild dogs before a thoroughbred stallion.

Caroline returned to the great double bed and after lying still for a few, heart-thudding minutes, reached out and nudged her sleeping husband.

"Sheridan."

He was dragged up from the slough of sleep. Came awake spluttering, voicing his irritation by a series of snorted words.

"What is it? Wassat matter?"

"Sheridan . . . I can't sleep."

"What!"

"I can't sleep."

The morning was clear and cold, with a wind-scoured sky and a frost-bright sun. The naked trees fought with a keen, east wind, and below the iron-hard earth was a graveyard for an army of dead leaves that seethed and rustled as though mourning the green-adorned summer of long ago. But Caroline was watching the old man from the front gate hoover the carpet.

As he worked, his bearded mouth opened and closed, and his red-black tongue darted between the thin lips in a most extraordinary and revolting way. Caroline was reminded of a snake looking for blowflies. When she passed him on her way to the stairs, he looked up and grinned, baring those obscene black gums, and a gurgling sound seeped up from this throat, which Caroline hopefully translated to mean good morning.

Down in the dining-room Sheridan was already seated at the breakfast table, and he greeted his wife's entrance with an irritated scowl.

"You might try to come down to breakfast on time. We haven't a houseful of servants."

Grantley, who was now his usual dapper self, with black hair piled high, white face a mask of solicitude, eased a chair under her legs and murmured.

"If I might be allowed, sir. We are so delighted that the old house has a master once again, there can be no trouble involved in serving both you and your gracious lady. Only pleasure."

"Damned decent of you," Sheridan growled. "Come to think of it, must have been lonely with no fresh faces all these years. How long have you been here?"

Grantley served devilled kidneys, then poured coffee from a silver pot.

"It must be a trifle over twenty years. I remember the old gentleman – Sir Harold Sinclair – was delighted when we offered our services. Servants are, apparently, loath to stay in this isolated place and our arrival was timely."

"How did you get on with the old devil?" Sheridan inquired.

"Unfortunately the poor old gentleman met with an accident soon after our installation. Fell over the banisters on his way to the bathroom. My father, who was but a few steps behind at the time, was inconsolable."

Sheridan said "Good God," and Caroline trembled.

Grantley deposited a toast-rack on the table, then added a dish of fresh butter.

"The poor gentleman had been so kind as to make provision for us, prior to his untimely end, so we have been able to stay on at the house which, if I might be so bold, we have come to love."

"Damned pleased you do," Sheridan grunted. "Your wife is an excellent cook, the place is run to perfection. I could wish the garden were in better shape – but then, I suppose you can't be expected to do everything."

"I am of the opinion, sir, that unbridled nature serves the house more adequately than mutilated grass and tortured plants. Which, regrettably, reminds me of a melancholy item of news it is my sad duty to impart."

"Sad news!" Sheridan paused, a fork holding a morsel of kidney half way to his mouth. "What is it?"

"The reverend gentleman, sir. Your guest of yesterday evening. He, like my late employer – met with a fatal accident. It appears that he was cycling past Devil's Point – a steep incline, which to my mind is inadequately fenced – and due possibly to a fainting fit, or some other mishap, fell over and broke his back."

"Good God!" Sheridan dropped his fork and Caroline slid down in her chair. "Broke his back?"

"Yes, sir. Between the second and third vertebrae."

Sheridan took up his knife and fork and quickly recovered from the shocking news.

"The old fool was a mad old windbag, but still, I'm sorry he came to a sticky end."

"He was, I believe, a knowledgeable gentleman," remarked Grantley urbanely. "And knowledge, when widely broadcast, can be disconcerting. Even – under some circumstances – dangerous."

Caroline felt sick with terror. She knew, with the same certainty that would have been hers had she witnessed the terrible act, that Mr Barker had been murdered. Or did one associate murder with these creatures? Could a lion, or any wild beast, commit murder? She would have screamed, yelled out the unthinkable truth, had not Marvin entered the room carrying a plate of bread and butter.

For a heart-stopping moment his eyes met hers and instantly Caroline became as a condemned gourmet who is looking forward to his last breakfast, and refuses to think about the grim ceremony that must follow. Terror was now a delicious excitement that blended with her deep-rooted masochistic urge and became almost unendurable pain-pleasure. He leaned over the table and her fevered gaze was rivetted on his smooth, round wrist. Sheridan looked up and grinned.

"Heard about what happened to our guest of last night, lad?"

The beautiful head nodded. "Yes, sir. Most regrettable."

Sheridan's grin broadened. "Well, he won't call you a mock again."

Marvin straightened up and smiled gently.

"With respect, sir. A shadmock. My father is a mock."

Caroline giggled when she saw the look of amazement spread over her husband's face and the spark of anger that made his little eyes gleam.

"I'm inclined to think that old Barker was not the only one with a screw loose. Perhaps all of you have been here too long. A change of scenery would be beneficial."

Grantley's voice was so gentle, so reasonable.

"I venture to suggest, sir – that would not be convenient."

Sheridan Croxley flung his napkin aside and rose so violently his chair went over. Marvin calmly pulled it upright, then stood to one side and waited for the storm to break. Sheridan's face turned to an interesting shade of purple and his voice rose to a full-throated roar that had made many senior executives tremble.

"Not convenient! Damn your blasted insolence. You may think you're indispensable, but this is not the only house I own. This place is only a weekend retreat – a whim – of which I may soon tire. So, guard your tongue."

Grantley appeared to be in no way put out by this tirade, but merely inclined his head, then motioned Marvin to remove the plates.

"I greatly regret if my words have given offence. I am well aware that your stay must, of necessity, be of short duration."

Sheridan's anger was further incensed by this roundabout apology and without saying another word, he strode abruptly from the room. Caroline seemed to have become glued to her chair. She had only eyes for Marvin, ears that had an insatiable hunger for the sound of his voice and hands that wanted to touch, rip – fondle.

"You must not mind my husband. He has alternating moods."

The words were addressed to Marvin, but it was Grantley who gave her a quick glance, and it seemed that the respectful mask was slipping. There was a hint of contempt in his eyes.

"Gentlemen have their little ways. More coffee, madam?"

She had lifted the cup to her lips when there was the sound of approaching footsteps, the door was flung open and Sheridan was back, roaring his anger.

"Grantley, not a telephone in the house works."

"That is correct, sir. They have not worked for over twenty years."

"What!" The tycoon shook his head in disbelief. "Why then in God's name haven't they been repaired?"

Grantley raised an eyebrow and permitted himself a pale smile.

"It was never considered needful, sir."

"Never considered . . .!" Caroline thought for a moment that her husband was about to suffer the – on her part – long-desired heart attack. "What sort of world have you damned people been living in? I am beginning to believe that that poor old fool was right. You are monsters . . . half-baked . . . addled-brained monsters."

Grantley did not reply to this accusation, but stood with bowed head, rather like a larch tree, bending before a particularly violent wind. Sheridan regained a measure of self-control.

"Well, I'd better drive down to the village and telephone from there."

Grantley coughed. A gentle, apologetic clearing of the throat.

"I regret to say, sir – that will not be possible."

Sheridan swung round and glared at the dark figure.

"Indeed! Why not?"

"Because – with respect, sir – we could not permit it."

The old man – the shaddy – moved into one doorway; his mouth was open, his long arms hung limply, but the stubby fingers were curved into menacing claws. At the same time the door leading to the back regions opened and Mrs Grantley, her beard quivering with frightful anticipation, entered and took up a position beside her husband.

Sheridan Croxley turned his head from left to right, then bellowed his rage and defiance.

"What the hell is going on here? I warn you, if that ugly old brute doesn't get out of my way, I'll knock him down."

Grantley shook his head as though he deplored this aggressive statement, then said softly: "I can promise, he will not lay a hand on you, sir."

Sheridan slowly approached the heavy, grotesque figure, and when he was within striking distance, shot out his massive fist, straight for the gaping mouth. Grandfather-Shaddy did not so much as flinch. His mouth opened even wider until his face was split in half by a great gaping, gum-lined hole – then the black tongue twisted and became a long, vicious whiplash, that flicked the threatening fist – then quickly withdrew. The mouth closed with a resounding snap and the shaddy began to chew with every sign of intense satisfaction. Sheridan roared with pain, then stepped back and stared at the raw gash that ran across his knuckles and up the back of his hand. In one place the bare bone glimmered softly like red-tinted ivory. The shaddy swallowed and growled some unintelligible words. Grantley translated.

"My father wishes to compliment you on your flesh, sir. He says it's very tasty."

With a roar of rage, Sheridan flung himself at the taunting figure; leaped across the intervening space with outstretched hands, motivated by an overwhelming urge to kill. Grantley tilted his head back and made a kind of subdued rumbling sound. Then when Sheridan's eyes came level with his own, he opened his mouth and – blew. It was not by any means a hard blow. A mere puff that might have extinguished a candle flame, but its effect on the big man was electrifying. He screamed and clasped shaking hands to his eyes, trying to claw away the burning agony that had come from a tainted breath. The voice of Grantley had not lost one iota of its respectful quality, as it spoke comforting words.

"Your discomfort is only temporary, sir. Nothing in the least to worry about."

Gradually Sheridan ceased to dance from one foot to the other; the time came when he was able to lower his hands and look, with red-rimmed eyes, at his tormentor.

"What the hell are you? In the name of sanity – what – who are you?"

Grantley parted his lips in a mirthless smile and looked thoughtfully over his victim's right shoulder. Caroline was watching Marvin. The handsome one . . . the dream-lover . . . the walker of the dark-ways . . . He was leaning against the wall staring aimlessly at the open door and it seemed as though nothing could ever disturb the quiet serenity of that beautiful face, or bring a flash of passion to the clear blue eyes. Then Grantley answered.

"We are you, sir, as you would be – without your clothes." Then his expression changed and he became once again the attentive, even, solicitous butler. "May I suggest, sir, that you go to your room and lie down. This has been an upsetting experience for you. If you wish, my father can accompany you."

"I'll see you damned," Sheridan roared. "Somehow, be you madmen, animals or monsters, I'll smash you. If you were wise you'd kill me."

They all shook their heads. "We couldn't do that, sir," Grantley explained. "We need you."

Sheridan rushed from the room and the sound of his heavy footsteps could be heard ascending the stairs. Caroline remained in her chair and watched Marvin who had now resumed his duties and was clearing the table. Once he threw her a smile-tinted glance and she was so happy she almost cried.

Sheridan barricaded himself in their bedroom.

Grantley and his father were polishing the dining-room furniture – the former with effortless ease, the latter with much gum-baring glee – and Caroline was following Marvin round the house to a plot of cultivated ground.

The shadmock – the designation was now firmly rooted in her mind – was carrying a spade and hoe and did not, despite an occasional plaintive whimper, acknowledge her presence, or bother to turn his head when she stumbled over a lump of concealed masonry and measured her length on the ground.

The cultivated plot was about twenty feet square and stood out from its unkept surroundings like a sheet of clear water in an arid desert. It had been lovingly fashioned and meticulously tended and presented neat rows of piled earth that curved gracefully down to rounded valleys. Marvin laid the hoe and spade down, then removed his jacket and rolled up his shirt sleeves. Caroline watched him like a puppy waiting for a kind word – or at least an encouraging whistle – and when it was not forthcoming, dared to make her presence known by timidly touching his arm.

"I want to help. Please let me help."

He smiled politely. A mere matter of parted lips, creasing of mouth, but she was as grateful as Lazarus for a sip of water.

"You are very kind, madam. If you would care to hoe the furrows, I would be greatly obliged. But, please do not tire yourself."

She seized the hoe – an instrument that to date she had only seen in an ironmonger's window – and began to worry the loose earth that lay between the mounds. Marvin watched her with evident anxiety.

"Be careful of the young shoots, madam. They are just germinating and a moment's carelessness could be fatal."

"I'll be careful." She was so happy that he was at last talking to her, but fearful that this frail contact might wither away before it had time to grow. "I didn't know anything grew at this time of year."

"My plants are all perennials, madam."

Caroline peered at the nearest mound and saw for the first time, little white shoots that were just beginning to peek coyly above the black earth. White, seemingly soft, they could have been sprouting tulip plants or maybe baby leeks.

"What are they?" she asked.

"Corpoties, madam."

"What on earth are they? A vegetable?"

He smiled at her childish ignorance and shook his head.

"Not quite, madam I suppose one could say they are a kind of meat-and-veg plant. They need a lot of careful attention. I use bone-manure in the early stages, then water them at regular intervals with a blood mixture. But of course the initial chopping up of the seed specimens is most important. If one chops too small, the result is a stringy and entirely inedible result. Too large," he shrugged and Caroline was delighted to see his face was alight with boyish enthusiasm, "means a soggy and flavourless plant. Are you keen on gardening, madam?"

'Absolutely," Caroline exclaimed. "Please go on, I could listen to you for hours."

Now his smile was wonderful to behold. All the icy reserve had gone and he was bubbling over with the joy of a stamp collector who has discovered an educated postman.

"I say, I'm so glad. You see, Father and Mother, and of course Grandfather, are all hunters. They have no appreciation of the intense satisfaction that comes from planting, then reaping the fruits of the earth. Sometimes I become quite irritated with them and worry most awfully in case I lose my temper and do something dreadful. But, dash it all, the earth is so generous. You get so much more from it than you put in."

"You're so right," Caroline agreed gushingly, grabbing his nearest arm between her two hands. "I expect you've got green fingers."

He frowned and she trembled. Had she said the wrong thing.

"No, I haven't. Only the long dead have green fingers. The ripe dead – the ready-for-planting dead."

Her hands dropped from his arm and she shook her head in token denial, while her brain screamed its fear and grief. Because of his face, his beautiful exterior, she had been thinking of him as a normal, if rather shy boy, who could be transformed into a passionate lover. But now she knew he was just as much – perhaps more – a monster as his hideous elders, but – and this was the real horror – it did not make the slightest difference to her feelings towards him. His boyish enthusiasm would not be denied.

"There have been three sets of new owners during the past fifteen years, but they were not all *just right*. They did not always keep and ripen in the way that is so important. And Father and Grandad are so rotten. They keep on about the essence which keeps us strong, and how the specimens must be drained, and no one will listen to me . . . and only give me the rubbish . . . the old, the sick . . . the ones that are almost dry . . ."

At last Caroline reached the frontier where she moved out of the shadows and met reality face to face. She turned and ran back to the house and Marvin's young voice called after her.

"Please don't go. I can't bear it when people go away, it makes me angry . . . y . . . y . . . y . . ."

The last word ended in a kind of drawn out whistle. Not a full-lipped whistle, just a suggestion of liquid vowels; a hint of what might follow. Caroline ran even faster.

Sheridan, at first, would not let her in. He shouted from behind the barricaded door: "You're on their side. Don't try to tell me any different. I saw you mooning over the young one and you did nothing to stop them. Nothing at all."

"Please, Sheridan. Let me in. We've got to help each other. My God, if you only knew."

"May I be of service, madam?"

She stifled a scream as the soft voice spoke behind her – and there was Grantley, grave of face, respectful of demeanour, standing a few feet away.

"The door . . ." She shrank back against the wall and allowed the first words that came to mind, to come tripping off her tongue. "The door . . . it's stuck."

"Kindly permit me, madam".

He placed one large hand on the left panel and after pausing for a moment, suddenly pushed. The door flew back and there was a resounding crash as a wardrobe went hurling back against the side wall. Caroline saw Sheridan sitting on the bed, his face a white mask of abject fear. Grantley bowed.

"Will you forgive the intrusion, sir. But I have to inform you that Mrs Grantley will be yawning in half an hour. I trust that this will be convenient."

Sheridan made a noise that was half way between a scream and a shout and Grantley bowed again.

"Thank you, sir. I am obliged."

He departed, closing the door behind him and from somewhere along the landing they heard a muted growl – a low, impatient sound that could have been menacing or enquiring. Caroline ran to her husband and clasped his arm.

"We must try to get away. Sheridan, listen to me, I am sane at this moment, but, God help me, if I see Marvin again, I will be helpless. Please do something."

He shook her off and all but snarled his rage-fear, looking so much like one of *them*, Caroline covered her eyes and sank down on the bed. Her husband watched her for a few minutes, then his lips curled up into a sneer and he beat his fists on to the bedside cabinet.

"I won't run. Do you hear me? I won't run from a set of degenerate madmen. I haven't got where I am by running. The entire set-up is one gigantic swindle. Grantley is not the first man to spit fire – acid – and the old man, not the last who will attach a length of wire to his tongue. Haven't you ever been to a fairground, for God's sake? But I won't be caught a second time. Once bitten . . ."

Caroline raised her head and screamed at him.

"Stop fooling yourself. They are monsters. MONSTERS. A different species – throwbacks – creatures we all know exist, but dare not think about. Try to remember and stop pretending you are not afraid. Remember the face in the crowd: the room you accidently entered: the howl you heard in the night: the thing that peeped round the corner – all the memories the mind chose to forget. Now – if you dare – say you do not believe."

He sat down beside her and was suddenly a tired, middle-aged man, who had forgotten how to relax.

"Perhaps you're right I wouldn't know. I have met so many monsters, I'd never be able to distinguish one from the other. But if what you say is true, what is the point of running? They must be everywhere. A vast freemasonry of tooth and claw, fur and fang. There can be no escape."

As they sat together and watched the morning grow old, there was peace between them for the first time in four years. Despair flattened the hills of contention, filled in the pits of derision and left free the plains of tolerance.

"I can't help myself," she whispered. "He . . . you know who I mean . . . has something that calls to me."

They did not speak again until a quiet knock on the door brought horror back and a muffled cry to Caroline's lips. The door opened and Grantley entered.

"Beg pardon, sir – madam. But Mrs Grantley is ready to yawn."

Sheridan Croxley climbed to his feet and after one quick glance at the bearded face that looked over the butler's shoulder, backed to the window.

"I warn you," he said quletly, "I will defend myself."

"That would not be wise," said Grantley suavely. "We have no wish to cause you discomfort and in any case resistance is useless. Please try to understand, sir, we only wish to help you. Fulfil your potential."

Mrs Grantley came into the room and never had she looked so grotesque. She walked with a strange stiff-legged gait; her eyes glittered and did not move, but stared at the, by now, terrified man with the cold intensity of a venomous snake. She strutted towards him and he made no move to defend himself, but became as still as a hypnotised rabbit; lower lip sagging, eyes bulging and face so white the erupted veins stood out like red streaks in polished marble. Then they were standing face to face, shoulders to shoulders, hips to hips, and they could have been lovers about to embrace. Then the maddy yawned.

Her mouth opened until the lower jaw hid her neck and the upper lip curled up over the nose, so that her mouth was one gaping cavern where discoloured teeth glimmered like two rows of weather-stained tombstones. A yawn – a shuddering rumble – began somewhere behind her heaving bosom, then rose up and became a body-shaking roar. Her shoulders qulvered, her buttocks and legs jerked, her arms flailed like wind tossed branches, but her head remained still. Then the yawning roar died. Was cut off a though a hidden switch had been pulled and at once all movement ceased. Both figures became as rigid statues. Croxley a study in frozen terror. The Maddy an awful automaton that is preparing to carry out a scheduled programme. Then she suddenly leaned forward and pressed her gaping mouth to that of Sheridan Croxley. Caroline heard the hiss of expelled breath and Sheridan gave one mighty shudder, before falling back, senseless against the wall. Mrs Grantley picked him up as though he were a child and laid his limp body on the bed.

The butler gave a little sigh of satisfaction.

"Pray do not distress yourself, madam. Mr Croxley's period of unconsciousness will be of short duration. When he is himself again, you will soon find a great change in his character. My wife has erased what is commonly called the soul and the gentleman will be able to develop his natural attributes without the hindrance of a conscience."

They both looked thoughtfully at Caroline who screamed once, thereby causing Grantley to shake his heed in sad reproof.

"There is no need for alarm, madam. We have no intention of – how shall I put it? – desouling you. This is not our normal practice. But Mr Croxley can be of great service to us – if I may be allowed to make such a bold statement. We have long wished for a representative in the upper strata of the business world. When the gentleman has fully matured – and I would remind you, madam, that he has been licked by a Raddy, blown on by a Mock and yawned upon by a Maddy – he will indeed be one of us and advance our interests to everyone's satisfaction. We may even put him up for parliament. It would be nice to have one of our number in the cabinet. We have several on the back benches, but that is not quite the same thing."

"What . . . what do you intend to do with me?" Caroline asked.

Grantley smiled and adjusted his bow tie.

"It is not always wise to ask leading questions, madam. Suffice to say, you will not be wasted."

They went out and Caroline was left to await the waking of her desouled husband.

The sun was setting when Sheridan stirred, then sat up and looked round the room with a slightly puzzled expression. Caroline could not see any alteration in his appearance, although there was a certain bleakness in the eyes that usually meant he was about to erupt into a fit of bad temper.

"What the hell happened?" he asked.

"Don't you remember?"

"I wouldn't ask if I remembered. We were sitting here frightened about something. And, oh yes, Grantley came in with that wife of his. Rather attractive in an odd sort of way."

"That . . . that thing . . . attractive!"

"I wouldn't expect another woman to agree. Now get out of here. I feel strange and probably another sleep will do me good."

"But, Sheridan," Caroline pleaded, "this is no time for us to be parted. That . . . woman yawned on you and . . ."

Sheridan was staring at her and there was a baleful gleam in his eye that reminded her of a vicious dog that has cornered an intruder and is now seriously considering attack. When she moved the cold, watchful stare followed her and soon an unreasoning flood of fear made her run to the door and go stumbling down the stairs.

Marvin was in the dining-room and looked up when Caroline entered and although he appeared to be pleased to see her, his first words were those of reproach.

"Why did you run away? I thought that I had at last found someone who liked gardening. I was so disappointed and almost became angry. And no one must make me angry."

Despite her fear, the awful knowledge, Caroline again came under the influence of that strange, animal charm, and suddenly he was a tree standing alone in a desert of madness. She ran to him and grabbed one limp hand and held it to her face.

"I am so frightened. Please help me."

He looked surprised – even alarmed.

"Why, madam? I am not angry."

"Please don't call me madam. I am afraid of your father – and the others. They have done something dreadful to my husband."

He nodded – almost cheerfully.

"I expect they have desouled him. Now he will be one of us and feel much better. Why, do you want to be desouled?"

"No." She shook her head violently and tried to bury her face in his shirt front, but he moved away.

"Just as well. I have never known a woman to be desouled. Father usually drains them and I plant what is left in the garden. Women make good corpoties. I expect that is what will happen to you."

"Nooo." She screamed her protest and tried to shake him in a frenzy of horror, but he was like a deeply rooted tree, or a rock that has its foundations deep down in the earth, for he did not move. "You must not let them touch me. Please . . . please protect me and I'll do anything you say. Anything at all."

He considered this proposal for some time. Then he put his head on to one side and asked: "Anything at all? Even help me all day in the garden?"

"Yes. I will . . . I will."

"Help me plant the little bits and pieces? Do the thinning out? Transplant? Water? Chop-up? Mince? Prepare the mixture?"

"Yes. Yes . . . oh God . . . yes."

He nodded his approval.

"That is very good. You have made me very happy."

"Then you will protect me from them?"

The beautiful, blue and so innocent eyes looked straight into hers.

"If they try to drain you, I will become angry."

"Yes . . . but will you protect me?"

He frowned and Caroline flinched.

"I have already promised. I will become angry."

He turned and walked away with that kind of hurt and resentful expression that one might expect to find on the face of a boy scout whose word of honour has been doubted. Caroline felt like a mouse who has taken refuge in a mousetrap from a herd of ill-intentioned cats. She sank down on to a chair and closed her eyes and instantly a crazy network of words spread across her brain. "Drain . . . desoul . . . mock . . . shaddy . . . mock . . . shadmock . . . lick . . . yawn . . . blow . . . whistle . . ." The voice of the lately departed Mr Barker came back as a haunting whisper.

> Wonder not why your hair stifly bristles.
> Just abandon all hope when the shadmock whistles.

Caroline giggled and pursed her lips and tried an experimental whistle. What was there so terrible about whistling. But – and now she could not suppress a shudder – who would have thought there could have been anything extraordinary about licking, yawning or, for that matter, blowing.

"What the hell are you doing?"

Her eyes snapped open and there was Sheridan standing by the door, his eyes cold mirrors of contempt. Already she could detect the subtle change. His face had that bleached, deathlike whiteness that was characteristic of *them*. A stubble of black beard darkened his chin, and it might have been the result of a fevered imagination, but were there not two little bumps rearing up through his hair?

She said: "I am waiting . . . For dinner . . . or something."

He grunted – or was it a growl? – then turned and went out through the door which led to the servants' quarters. About twenty minutes later Grantley entered pushing a trolley, and Caroline at once noticed a trifling alteration in his appearance. His hair was no longer piled-up to form a raven crest over his head, but was neatly combed around his pointed ears and parted in the centre. The two, gleaming ebony horns did not – if one could only view them dispassionately – seem out of place. They added an almost noble aspect to his long face, and drew attention to his rather well-shaped skull. But Caroline could not help screaming and clutching clenched fists to her mouth. Grantley ignored or did not notice her distress, and after depositing a number of covered dishes and a single plate on the table, bowed most respectfully.

"Mr Croxley presents his compliments, madam, and instructed me to inform you that he will be dining in the kitchen. He feels he should now be among his peers."

Caroline did not comment, but continued to stare at the horns which were causing her deep concern. Grantley gave one educated glance at the table, then walked with unruffled dignity back to the door. There he paused and coughed apologetically.

"There is one little matter. Will it be convenient for madam to be drained at eight o'clock?"

Caroline made a strange noise that terminated with the single word – drained! Grantley appeared to accept this sound to mean acquiescence, and inclined his head.

"I am deeply obliged, madam. I must apologise for this unseemly haste, but I find we are rather short of essential fluid and madam's contribution will be greatly appreciated."

Caroline groaned and slid from her chair and then rolled over on to the floor. She was not aware that Grantley came back into the room and without too much effort replaced her unconscious body back into its former position. By pushing the chair tight against the table, he was able to ensure that such an unfortunate mishap would not occur again.

There is absolutely no doubt that mocks – apart from a few distressing weaknesses – make excellent domestic servants.

The shaddy and the maddy came for her at eight o'clock.

Two bearded faces, two pairs of powerful hands, two muscle-corded backs; they lifted Caroline from her chair and carried her out of the dining-room and down a long passage. The prospect of imminent death is a great reviver, and she was wide awake when they entered the long, sparsely furnished room.

Sparsely furnished! A long table, a large galvanised iron bath, two plastic buckets, two carving knives, one saw and a roll of rubber tubing. Grantley was wearing a butcher's apron.

"If madam will lie down," he bowed in the direction of the table, "we will proceed."

Caroline struggled, kicked, screamed and did all in her power to break free from those iron-strong hands, but it was hopeless. Grantley looked on with an expression of shocked surprise.

"It is to be regretted that madam cannot see her way clear to cooperation."

She was being dragged closer to the table, with its straps and headclamp, and when she jerked her head round, there was

Sheridan standing by the window, tall, bulky, looking more like *them* by the minute, with lust gleaming in his eyes. He chuckled – a low, growling laugh – and rubbed his hands together with fiendish delight.

Caroline swung her head from side to side, but nowhere was there a sign of the protector, the beautiful one, the innocent with the fatal whistle. Her scream took on words.

"Marvin, help me! Marvin . . ."

She was on the table and the two bearded monsters were preparing to strap her down, when the door opened – and he was there. Blue eyes wide with alarm, full-lipped mouth slightly open, his blond hair tousled as though he had lately risen from a virginal bed. He said nothing, but looked enquiringly at his father.

Grantley frowned. "This does not concern you. When she has been drained, you may plant what remains."

"I want her to help me in the garden," the soft voice said.

The mock deepened his frown and shook his head angrily.

"You cannot always have what you want. There are others to consider. Her essence must be drained and stored, so that we may all be nourished during the winter months. You really must grow up and face your responsibilities."

"I want her to help in the garden," Marvin repeated.

"Marvin," the Maddy was trying the mother approach, "be a good boy. We let you have that stockbroker to play with before he was drained, and we did not interfere when you pulled the legs off that property speculator, even though he was useless for our purpose afterwards. But now the time has come for us to take a stand. There is no point in licking or yawning the humwoman, she has no monsteral qualities. She must therefore be drained, minced and planted. Then – if you are a good boy – you will be able to harvest the corpoties next spring."

Marvin opened and closed his hands, while his entire body became rigid. When he spoke his voice was very low – almost a growl.

"Let . . . her go."

Before Grantley or either of the other monsters could speak, Sheridan lurched forward, his great hands balled up into fists, his little eyes like tiny pits of blue fire.

"See here," he was spitting the words out, "it's all decided. All cut and dried. I gather I'm not completely one of you lot, until," he jerked his head in the direction of Caroline, "she has had the chop. I'm hungry, pretty boy. Hungry for more money, more power, and when I'm hungry, I smash anyone that gets in my way. So go and play in your garden, unless you want to get hurt."

Marvin's eyes were wide open and they gleamed with cold contempt. At the same time he looked so young and helpless, standing there before the bulky, powerful figure of Sheridan Croxley. Then he said softly: "A peasant should learn to guard his tongue."

Sheridan's fist caught the boy squarely under the chin and lifted him off the floor, before sending him hurling across the room and crashing against the closed door. The door trembled, the Maddy shrieked, the Shaddy roared and the Mock – Grantley – voiced his objections.

"In Satan's name, you should not have done that, newly acquired brother. Now he will be angry."

"I'm angry," Sheridan retorted. "Bloody angry."

"Yes," Grantley was watching his son with growing concern, "but the anger of a fly cannot be compared with the rage of a lion."

"A fly!"

"Quiet." Grantley waited until Marvin had regained his feet and stood upright against the door. "Now, son, control. Our newly acquired brother will be disciplined for this act, you may have no doubt about that. So don't get angry. Please practise some self-control. He alone was to blame, so there's no need to make us all suffer . . ."

Marvin took a deep breath, if that can describe the rumbling intake of air; the unnatural expanding of the chest, or the dilated cheeks which bulged like white walled tyres. Grantley hesitated for only a moment, then turned and made for the solitary window, where he arrived a bad third, his father and wife having been similarly motivated.

The lower sash had been raised – not before all the glass panes had been broken in the frantic struggle – and grand-father Shaddy had his head and shoulders out over the sill, when the whistle began.

Caroline had watched the eyes dilate, the head go back, the hands slowly turn, revealing the smooth, hairless backs, the fingers stiff and widely spread; the pink tongue coiled back until it resembled a tightly wound spring. Then the whistle. It was born somewhere deep down in the stomach and gradually rose up until it erupted from the throat as a single note of shrill sound.

Just abandon all hope when the shadmock whistles.

In the midst of her terror, Caroline thought: "It's not so bad. After all, what can a whistle do?" Then quickly changed her mind when the sound rose to a higher pitch.

A whistle – a shriek – a sound that went higher and higher until it reached a pitch that seemed to make the walls tremble and broke the remaining fragments of glass in the window. Then from the shadmock's mouth appeared a pencil-thin streak of light. It shot across the room and struck Sheridan in the base of the throat.

The big man screamed and for a moment clawed the air with convulsing fingers, before he crashed down across the table, his head hanging limply over the edge. Blood seeped from his open mouth and formed a pool on the floor.

The shadmock advanced slowly forward and the whistling sound rose to an even higher pitch, while the beam of light became a pulsating, white-whiplash that flicked across the conglomeration of bodies that were jammed in the window frame. Marvin moved his head from side to side and the three bodies jerked, quivered, bellowed and screamed. Only that of Sheridan remained still.

It was then that Caroline realised that the door was unguarded. She crept towards it like a mouse in a den of fighting wild-cats, and hardly daring to breathe, eased her way out into the passage.

The front door was not locked.

Caroline ran desperately down the drive. Running under trees that shook their naked branches as though in sinister merriment; stumbling over pot-holes, bowed down by the horrible fear that rode on her shoulders.

She staggered round a bend and there were the front gates, mercifully unguarded. The iron barrier that partitioned the world of everyday activity that men call sanity, from the bizarre realm of the unacceptable. She ran by instinct, not daring to think, prepared for disaster to strike at every step.

The gates were locked. A thick iron chain was wound several times round the rusty bars and this was secured by a massive padlock. The rough ironwork rasped her soft palms, when in a frenzy of despair, she shook the gates and cried out her hopeless appeal.

"Help me . . . help me."

Barely had the sound of her voice died away when running footsteps came crashing through the undergrowth and Marvin emerged from beneath the trees. Beautiful as Adonis, graceful as a golden snake, he came to her, and at once the fear, the urgent need for escape, was submerged under a blanket of slavish desire. His voice was gentle, but reproachful.

"Why did you run away? I was not angry with *you*."

"I was frightened."

He began to lead her back up the drive, talking all the while, like any enthusiast who has found a kindred soul to share his burning interest.

"There's no need to be frightened. My parents have decided to let me have my own way. They always do in the end. Now you can help me in the garden. Help me prepare your husband for planting. Will you do that?"

"Yes . . . yes, Marvin."

"Cut him up and watch him grow ripe?"

"Yes, Marvin."

"And you won't make me angry, will you?"

"No, Marvin."

"I expect I'll be angry with you sometimes. I just can't help myself. But I'll be awfully sorry afterwards. That should be a great comfort for you. I'm always sorry afterwards. Always . . . afterwards."

They disappeared round the bend in the drive and for a while peace reigned among the slumbering trees and the rolling hills beyond. Then a colony of rooks rose up with much flapping of wings and raucous cries and became black, wheeling shadows against the clouded sky.

CHRISTOPHER FOWLER

The Spider Kiss

CHRISTOPHER FOWLER'S BOOKS include the novels *Roofworld*, *Rune*, *Red Bride*, *Darkest Day*, *Spanky*, *Psychoville*, *Disturbia*, *Soho Black* and *Calabash*, and such short story collections as *City Jitters* (two volumes), *The Bureau of Lost Souls*, *Sharper Knives*, *Flesh Wounds*, *Personal Demons*, *Uncut*, *The Devil in Me* and *Demonized*.

Fowler's first "Bryant & May" mystery novel, *Full Dark House*, won the British Fantasy "August Derleth" Award for Best Novel and was also a finalist for the Crime Writer Association's Dagger Award. He has also won British Fantasy Awards for his short stories "Wageslaves" and "American Waitress", in 1998 and 2004 respectively, while his novella "Breathe" was recognised with the same award in 2005.

Most of the author's novels are in various stages of development as movies, and his story "The Master Builder" was filmed by CBS-

TV as *Through the Eyes of a Killer* (1992) starring Tippi Hedren. *Left Hand Drive*, based on his first short story, won Best Film in the 1993 British Short Film Festival.

Fowler's latest books include *White Corridor*, the fifth (and to date the darkest) Bryant & May novel, involving a killer who strikes on a blizzard-bound stretch of motorway, while *Old Devil Moon* is his first new collection of strange tales in five years.

"I had an idea ages ago about a less-than-benign form of Buddhism," explains the author, "in which, instead of coming back in a more evolved form or as a lesser creature, we entirely lost the right to move on and this transformation devolved to some humbler, more innocent species, who could move up to us. In which case there would be chaos (understandably), and we would need a specialised law enforcement unit to combat the problem.

"I imagined a TV series, *Karma Police*, with cars racing down alleys and people with the heads of flies, and really strong ant-girls. You can see how the networks would have passed on this one, can't you?

"Instead I wrote this short story. Still think it would make a good TV series though."

TWO DEAD, A HOUSE TRASHED, a trail of food, garbage and excrement. Jackson pushed back his baseball cap and scratched his sweating forehead. "It's going to be a long night, man. I don't know what we're dealing with here." He looked at the woman in the pink quilted housecoat and yellow plastic curlers. "Ask her again, Dooley." He didn't see why he should have to deal with witnesses when he had a new partner to break in for the job.

Dooley approached the frightened woman and eyed her with something approaching sympathy. "I don't know, Matt, maybe we should get her some counselling first. She looks pretty shaken up."

"Just fuckin' ask her, okay?"

Dooley tried to look official but he was wearing an XXL sunset-orange Hawaiian shirt. They had both been off-duty when the call had come through. "Tell us what you saw once more, Ma'am. Take your time."

"I told you, I was watching a rerun of *American Idol* when I heard a noise out in the yard. I thought it was an animal. We had a 'gator come through here last fall. I turned down the TV, put on the light and this guy came out—"

"Describe him?"

"Big, heavy, balding, fat belly, around forty. He'd been going through my garbage, had grass cuttings and doggy-doo all around his mouth, it was just gross. Stared right at me, but kind of didn't see me, like he was on drugs, you know?"

"And you say he was wearing—"

"That was the weirdest thing – he had no pants on, just a Miami Dolphins shirt. And then he squatted and took a dump. Right in front of me on the lawn. He took a dump and wandered off next door. That was when I called 911. And now I've missed the rest of the show."

"Nice," said Jackson, "glad I already had supper. Tell her to fuck off."

"Thank you Ma'am. We may need to talk to you again."

"No, we won't, she's a fucking moron, come with me." Jackson beckoned to his new partner, lowering an avuncular arm around him. "Then this guy walks – get this – *walks* – through the glass patio doors, bam, smash, into the next house where the victims are sleeping, and pulls 'em out of bed. And he kind of – *scratches* – at their faces in a frenzy. They got no features any more, Dan. Cocksucker didn't give a fuck about leaving traces or cutting himself, he just walked away. The woman's teeth are spread out there all over the fucking drive. He must be spouting blood, but no one saw where he went."

"I don't think anyone wanted to look too closely. You want to do a search before the rest of the department gets down here?"

"Fucking right I do. Was a time when the Miami PD would let Homicide take care of things themselves, without dragging every so-called fucking expert off the bench to take a look. Everybody's a fucking big shot. See that?" Matt Jackson pointed to the bedroom lights flicking on in the identical white clapboard houses on the other side of the road. "Gawkers'll be uploading the whole thing into blogs any second now. It'll be on fucking Yourspace or

Mytube or whatever the fuck it is before we get back. Let's get at it."

Heavy blood-spatters made the trail on the blacktop easy to follow. "He must have cut himself real bad," said Dooley.

"You mean like, when he tore the woman's teeth out of her head? No shit, Dooley." Jackson scratched his hairy belly and pulled at his shorts, hitching them higher. Everything he said was coated in layers of world-weariness that you had to be careful about unwrapping. "Hey, check this out." He waved his torch in the direction of the scarlet splashes. They turned into an unlit vacant lot, following the trail. "No way am I climbing over a fucking chicken-wire fence. My wife bought me this shirt. You go."

"Jesus, Matt, I know I'm new around here but why do I have to—"

"You're an African-American with ginger hair and an Irish name, you got some way to go before I start trusting you. Just get over there." Jackson cradled his hands, giving his partner a leg-up.

Dooley dropped to the other side and continued to follow the trail. He disappeared into an oleander bush, then called out. "Oh man, you're going to love this. He's buried himself."

"What do you mean?"

"I mean he's in the fucking ground."

"Then cuff him up and bring him out."

"I don't think I can do that. You'd better come and see."

Jackson snagged his shirt on the top of the fence and tore off a button. He was still cursing under his breath when he came upon Dooley and their quarry. His torch revealed a fat naked butt. The top half of the guy's body had been wedged into grass and earth.

"Christ, it looks like he dug himself a burrow using his head. Take a leg, let's get him out." They each grabbed an ankle and pulled. As the body emerged, they realised they were looking at a very dead man. He had bulldozed himself into the ground, grinding the flesh from his face and filling his mouth with hard dry soil.

"Another fucking crazy on crystal meth," said Jackson, turning away. "For this I missed the last quarter of the game?"

* * *

Next morning, he and Dooley were sweating beneath a wheezy air-conditioner in their Calle Ocho office, trying to concentrate on a bunch of forms the Miami Police Department required them to fill out. "It doesn't make sense," Dooley complained. "Everyone in the neighbourhood knew this guy. He never took a drug in his life, a regular churchgoer, a restaurant critic at the local paper, for Christ's sake, and suddenly he starts eating dogshit and leaves? What would make him go nuts like that?"

"You mean apart from the temperature and the fact that people spazz out all the time around here? You've already been working in this unit for long enough to know that nothing we deal with makes sense. That Baptist minister last week who thought he could fly, the one who threw himself off the AT&T building? He was supposed to be a regular kind of guy, but the medics had to lift him off the sidewalk with barbecue tongs. Who knows?"

"Well, something weird's going on, and it's not just because of the heat," said Dooley, wiping air-con dust from his computer screen. "We got another call coming in right now."

They arrived at the San Paulo Deli on 3rd to find the owner, a tiny Cuban guy called Jacinto, standing in the wreckage of his store, fending off a customer with an aluminium stool. Jackson knew Jacinto. He ate there sometimes, even though the food was awful. "What he hell's going on here, Jacko?" he asked. "What'd you do to this guy, poison him?"

"He was eating his lunch and just went crazy," Jacinto explained, setting aside the stool in relief. "Stuck his hands in the fish tank and started biting the heads off my crawfish."

"Okay," we'll take over now," said Dooley, drawing his gun from its holster.

"Hey Dan, don't overreact, okay? said Jackson. "Trust me, you don't want the fucking paperwork. Try giving him a verbal warning before you decide to blow his fucking head off."

They looked back at the angry diner, a skinny young Asian who was frothing bubbles from his nostrils and rocking back and forth. His white shirt was torn in half, he was wearing one black trainer, and his cheeks were smeared with blood from the sharp shells of the crustaceans he had bitten. Every few seconds he screamed like a seagull. "This one has definitely been smoking crack," said Jackson.

"No," Jacinto shook his head, "I know him, a good man, Mr Yuan is a teacher at my son's school for five years now."

Jackson scrunched up his eyes and tilted his head to one side, trying to square the foaming, squawking madman before them with Jacinto's ID. He was still considering the problem when Mr Yuan charged at them. He and Dooley braced themselves, preparing to fire warning shots, but the teacher leapt into the counter and soared over their heads, sending himself face-first through the deli's deafening plate-glass window.

"Fuck me," said Jackson, running out through the falling shards to the spot where the bloody body had touched down. "What the fuck is happening around here?"

"Like you said, when the heat rises this town goes postal," Dooley replied.

"Get the medics, no way am I touching this guy." Jackson tried to stuff his shirt back into his pants as he knelt, but he'd put on weight lately. "I'm getting too old for this shit. I spend my days sitting in a car that smells like a hot gym shoe, eating cow-parts from street vendors with names I can't even pronounce. South Beach PD is looking to set up new specialist units. The money's good. I could apply for a position there. Be a fucking sight easier stopping fags from bitch-slapping each other outside bars than staying here to act as pest control for the locals."

"Maybe this is just a blip," said Dooley. "It'll pass."

But it didn't pass. Over the next few days, things got much worse.

"You want to know how many crazies we've had in the last two weeks?" asked Jackson, throwing the remains of his hot dog in the nearest bin as they walked toward the Hong Kong Center. The temperature was soaring to record highs. Over a week had passed since Mr Yuan killed himself in the 3rd Street deli. "One hundred and seven reports of life-threatening behaviour, ten fatalities, and that's just between Bayshore Drive and the I–95. One woman out on Dodge Island chewed a hole through her husband's throat and sat on top of his body until they came to take her away. They found a naked old guy down on Beethoven who had broken his neck trying to lick his own balls."

"It's not just the heat. I think I'm starting to see a pattern here," said Dooley, eyeing his partner with distaste as Jackson noisily sucked mustard from his nicotine-stained fingers. "Check out this one." He pulled a page from his back pocket and unfolded it. "See, before I joined the force I trained to be a naturalist."

"You mean you ran around with no fucking clothes on?"

"That's a naturist, Matt. I studied endangered species of insect. This was in the local press yesterday. Some guy locked himself in his apartment, painted his entire body with black and orange stripes, wrapped himself in duct tape and then suffocated trying to get back out of it. The attending medic said he kept making a weird ratcheting noise as he was dying."

"What are you telling me here?"

"Okay, I know how this is going to sound." Dooley held up his hands and took a deep breath. "There's a rare bug that's nearly extinct, called the New Forest Cicada, something like that. It's black and orange. It spends eight years in a larval stage, and as it emerges from its cocoon it releases a shrill series of clicks."

"You telling me this guy thought he was a fucking *cicada*?"

Dooley looked sheepish. "The story just reminded me, is all."

"Take my advice and leave it to the detective division," said Jackson. "We're just here to clean up the shit, and I mean that – nearly everyone we've been called to take in has dropped a log in the street after killing someone. If that's a linking MO, it's pretty fucked up. Kill someone if you have to but use a fucking toilet, for Christ's sake."

"Maybe not so odd," said Dooley. "I need to talk to a guy I know."

"Okay, but remember what I said, it's not our problem. Let the other divisions sort their own shit out."

"Don't worry, this guy's not a detective, he's a Buddhist."

I knew Dooley was going to be trouble, Jackson thought as he took an incoming call and watched his young partner walking away.

Dooley went to see Jim Pentecost. Once they had been students together, but their careers had taken them in separate directions. Pentecost now ran a Buddhist centre from an art deco schoolhouse in South Beach. His long hair, beads and kaftan gave him the appearance of a neo-hippie, but he taught New Age philosophies even hippies would have found extreme. He clasped Dooley warmly to his chest. "Man, it's been a long time," he said, grabbing the cop's arm and pulling him into the building's cool interior. "I'd like to think this is a friendly call, but I guess you're here on business?"

"Kind of," Dooley admitted. "Remember you used to tell me your theories about man's relationship with the animal kingdom, life balance, all that kind of stuff? You still believe it?"

"More than ever, Dan, even though it's too late now."

"What do you mean?"

"Hell, the balance has been destroyed. Man's greed has won the day, my friend. They're ripping up the world's last unspoiled sites to make money for the stockholders."

The pair seated themselves in a shadowed courtyard, musky with the smell of incense. "The wars of the future will be about energy, water, religious control," Pentecost continued. "Capitalists are the new warmongers. They have destroyed the Earth's natural inhabitants, and now they will in turn be made extinct. The karmic equilibrium has been tipped against humans. It's like the ozone layer – once you pass a certain point, balance can never, ever be restored."

"Yeah, but what does all that mean?" asked Dooley. "I can only report from personal experience. We're seeing so much aberrant behaviour on the streets, we can't even begin to deal with it."

"What kind of behaviour exactly?" asked Pentecost, intrigued.

Dooley thought for a minute, then set about describing what he had seen.

Matt Jackson pushed back the door to the old *Sport World* warehouse and stepped inside. The heat was grotesque; the building had trapped the day's warmth. His partner had missed the call, and the only other squad cars in the area had been called to the airport, where a man was standing on the roof of his Toyota waving a rifle around and screaming his head off, blocking the intersection at Biscayne Boulevard.

Jackson walked through corridors of fierce light and back into patches so dark that his eyes were flooded with drifting orange spots. The call had warned that a naked woman had run amok in the pet shop of a local mall before fleeing into the warehouse. Jackson figured that at least she was unlikely to be armed, and moved through the empty hall with confidence. Ahead he thought he saw a human shape, swaying back and forth at the edge of the light. She looked young and pretty fit, even though she was probably insane. *That would make her a better bet than my old lady*, Jackson thought.

"Hey there, Miss," he called. "I'm a police officer, I'm here to help you." He placed his palm over the reassuring warmth of his gun. The figure remained fixed to the spot. Jackson could see now that she was, indeed, naked; tanned long legs, brown hair that fell to her shoulders in a glossy curtain, slender hips, flat belly, enhanced breasts. *Holy mama*, he thought, *maybe I'll get lucky even if she is crazy*. He advanced with confidence. "Tell you what, lady, I'm having a bad day. It's too fucking hot, I've got a case of jock itch you wouldn't believe and I could do with a cold beer." She circled him slowly, warily, tilting her head to one side. "What say we go outside and get one together?" he suggested with a smile.

It should have been easy after that, but he'd made a mistake, believing the woman was harmless because she was naked. Jackson got cocky and dropped his attention for a moment, just long enough for her to manoeuvre behind him with incredible speed, dropping slender, muscular arms around his chest that tightened like pincers, crushing the breath from his lungs. Even as he fought to draw air, he marvelled at her athleticism. How could she be so fast, so powerful?

As they toppled backwards, Jackson blacked out. *Shit*, he thought, *it feels like I'm having a fucking heart attack*.

When he came around, the woman had pinned his wrists together with her left hand, and was pinching his nostrils shut, smacking at his chin. Clearly, she was trying to open Jackson's mouth. She worked in silence, patiently and calmly, with great determination. Her perfumed hair brushed his sweating forehead as she drew her face close, studying Jackson carefully. She seemed to be searching for some sign of recognition. As she slowly opened her mouth, Jackson could see that there was something dark inside it, some kind of animal trying to get out. A thin black leg appeared, seeking purchase on the woman's shiny red lips, then another, and another. Her mouth widened further, and Jackson watched in mute horror as the first of the black funnel-web tarantulas tentatively emerged.

"Karmic imbalance," Pentecost repeated. "I was always taught that if all the animals on earth were wiped out tomorrow, the insects would survive. But now the chain has started to falter at the very basis of life, and even many of the hardiest species of insect are dying. Insects, birds, fish and animals all have souls, although they're not the same as human beings. When the souls of men become tainted, malnourished and weak, they can be replaced with purer, more driven-to-survive life forces. What you're seeing is the start of reincarnation's replacement program."

"You're telling me I have to go to my boss and warn him that insects' souls are coming back inside soulless people?" asked Dooley uncomfortably, remembering the woman who had killed her husband in the manner of a praying mantis devouring her mate.

"Yes, and there's nothing you can do about it." Pentecost sat back in shadow, resting his head against the wall. "Not this time around, anyway."

The woman drew close and placed her mouth directly over Jackson's, allowing the spider to extend its bristling black legs and climb across, feeling its way inside a new warm haven. Jackson felt something tickle his cheeks, but there was sweat in his eyes and he could not see clearly. The insect was wriggling desperately, its hairy legs splaying outward as it supported a bulbous venom-filled body. It tried to free itself, but the woman's full lips closed tightly over his, so that the creature was fully propelled from one mouth to the other.

The spider's torso-sac shifted back and forth across his tongue. It was large and heavy and pregnant, a species from Eastern Australia, and was followed by another, pushed in so hard by the woman's tongue that the first spider stung the inside of his cheek in distress. With horror, Jackson realised that she was feeding him. He gagged, the contents of his stomach rising to spray acidic vomit over the wriggling mass, but she kept her mouth clamped tightly over his. Jackson could feel the creatures writhing, the hairs on their legs pricking and scratching the back of his throat.

Then their poisonous *chelicerae* lowered into his soft red flesh, and they started to inject their lethal venom.

Who the hell is ever going to believe that the souls of dying life-forms are transmigrating to living humans? thought Dooley as he headed back into the fierce South Beach sunlight and hailed a cab. *Hey, Jackson wants to change his job. Maybe we can persuade PDHQ to let us set up a special unit; take a tip from the old Radiohead song and call it the Karma Police. Nah, that's way too whack. How do you prevent something happening if you don't know who it will get next?*

As he settled back in the taxi he watched a fat, juicy fly crawling up the window. Its iridescent wings caught the late Miami sunshine and reflected prismatic shards of rainbow light. The hairs on its legs were as glossy as needles. He had never noticed how beautiful they were before now.

Without thinking, he licked it off the window and swallowed.

NANCY HOLDER

Café Endless: Spring Rain

NANCY HOLDER HAS SOLD approximately eighty novels, many of them set in the *Buffy the Vampire Slayer* universe; and two hundred short stories, essays, and articles. She has received four HWA Bram Stoker Awards, and has been nominated for three more. She is a former trustee of the Horror Writers Association.

Holder has recently turned in the manuscript for her first short story collection, *Lady Madonna*, to be published by Babbage Press.

She lives in San Diego with her daughter and co-author Belle, their cats Kitten Snow Vampire and David, and their three hermit crabs, Mr Crabbypants, Athena and Kumquat. Despite wishing to sleep in her spare time, she is active in Belle's First Year Junior Girl Scout troop and helps out at Belle's school.

"There really is a Café Endless in Roppongi," explains Holder, "and I passed by it many times on my most recent trip to Japan. I never went inside, but I'm willing to bet it's a little bit different from how I've imagined it.

"I lived in Yokosuka during my middle school years and have been back a few times since then. I also wrote about the Harajuku street dancers in a novella set in the Buffverse."

IT WAS SPRING IN YOYOGI PARK, and not a rain, exactly. Cool mist floated in the air, drawn to the heat of the thousand milling bodies, clinging to all the things that lived: girl groups dressed in black lace and garters, thirty young boys dressed up as James Dean, pompadours and chains and black leather jackets. The perennial hippies in black velvet hats and tie-dyed dusters. Ointen Rose, the most popular Sunday street band in Harajuku, their pride and joy a black bass player who was actually quite good.

It would have been perfect day to go to the Empress's iris garden in the Meiji Shrine complex. If you stood still long enough and stared across the fish pond in a tranquil state, you could see Her Majesty's spirit shimmering in the mist that was not mist but gentle spring rain. But Satoshi's charge for the day was Buchner-san, the American agent for Nippon Kokusai Sangyo, and she had asked to be shown the famous street-dancing kids of Harajuku.

She had made the request boldly, knowing it wasn't the polite Japanese thing to do. That was no problem; no one in Ni-Koku-Sangyo expected Buchner-san to act Japanese, and they would never have hired her if she had. She was their American, their contact with the States, and they wanted her as bold and brassy and utterly unsubtle as she was.

"These are great! This is great!" she kept exclaiming as they traversed the closed-off boulevard. As they did each Sunday, the groups had set up as far apart as possible, which was not very far at all; and the din was so great that you couldn't hear the generators that powered their electric guitars. Satoshi had never heard the generators.

The fan clubs of the more popular groups invented gestures and little dances to accompany the songs of their heroes, and as they shouted and pointed and shoo-whopped, Buchner-san shouted in his ear, "It's like *Rocky Horror*! Do you know about *Rocky Horror*?"

"Oh, yes," he said politely. With the arrogance of her countrymen, which he found so charming, she always assumed his ignorance. That there was a fundamental lack in his country. In fact, he had seen the original stage play in London, and had owned a bootleg laser disc before Americans could even purchase laser disc players. "It is very interesting."

"I love Tim Curry." She flashed a smile at him. He was getting tired, but would never let her know. All the English, all her talking and questions. Her energetic curiosity. Not that he was complaining; he was happy to show her this amazing Tokyo phenomenon, and pleased if she enjoyed their Sunday afternoon together. He was Ni-Koku-Sangyo's representative today, and entertaining her was his responsibility. Satoshi was a Japanese man, and fulfilling responsibilities with good effort gave him a sense of pride and accomplishment.

After a while he steered her to the food booths and bought her some doughy snacks of octopus meat and a beer. When she discovered what she was eating, she laughed and said "I'm eating octopus balls!" and Satoshi laughed back, although other Americans had made the same joke. He didn't mind. He never found their humor offensive or insulting, as some of his colleagues did. Americans to him were like puppies, eager, alert, bounding and fun. Although not to be dismissed as unintelligent or lacking in shrewdness. They were tough businessmen. Business *people*.

"Do you believe in ghosts, Buchner-san?" he asked her after they finished their snack.

"Hmm. Do I believe in ghosts." She looked at him askance. "Why do you ask?"

"If you look across the iris garden at the Meiji Shrine, you can see a ghost."

"If you're Japanese." She grinned at him. "I'm afraid I'm far too earthbound for that, Nagai-san."

"No. Anyone can see it. Because it's there. No special abilities – or genetic traits – are required."

"Then let's go see it."

He inclined his head. "Unfortunately, it is now closed. But you must come back if you have free time before you go. Tell the taxi *Meiji-jingu*."

"And the subway stop?"

How he admired these American women! "*Meiji-jingu-mae*."

"Got it." She was writing it down. Abruptly she frowned and looked up. "God, it's raining harder."

Perhaps that was her way of hinting that she would like to go, and not an indirect rebuke that he had not thought to warn her that it might rain, or to bring umbrellas. Or neither; Americans didn't think like that. It might simply be a comment about the weather.

"Shall I take you to Roppongi? The Hard Rock Café is there." She had made mention to Satoshi's boss, Iwasawa-san, that she would like to buy a Tokyo Hard Rock Café T-shirt for her nephew. Although she was almost forty, she was not married. Iwasawa privately called her "Big Mama". Satoshi thought that was hilarious.

"Oh, the Hard Rock! That'd be great. I want to buy my nephew a souvenir." Obviously she had forgotten she'd told Iwasawa. A Japanese would not have. He – she – would have taken it for granted that the request had been made, and now was about to be fulfilled. And a small notch on the chart of indebtedness was now made in favor of Ni-Koku-Sangyo, to be be paid at the proper time.

They walked back down the boulevard, taking one last look at the bands. The rain was falling not harder, but more like gentle rain now, than mist. Perhaps the Harajuku kids would have to shut down; all that electricity could not be safe.

He began to hail a cab, but she asked to take the subway "if it's not too much trouble". Then she would know how to come back if she had time to "visit his ghost". He acquiesced, content to do as she wished, although he was a little disappointed. While with her he was on his expense account, and he far preferred cabs to crowded subways.

He showed her how to walk to the station, pointing out landmarks, and explained how to buy a ticket. In Japan there was no stigma attached to ignorance, only to not trying one's best. They went to the trains and he explained how she could tell she was boarding the correct one. With a sense of fearless joy she absorbed all he said. He was very sorry she would not meet Tsukinosuke.

But of course, she would have quite happily informed him that she didn't believe in vampires, either.

The ride was not long but it was crowded. He could remember a time years ago when Japanese people stared at Americans and Japanese men groped American women on the trains as everyone stood netted together like fish. Now it was Tokyo, London, New York, the three big cities of the world, and such days of primitive behavior were over.

As they ascended the Roppongi station, the rain was falling like the strands of spider webs catching dew. Satoshi's chest tightened. He took measured steps as they turned the corner past the big coffee house, Almond, pretending he was scanning for umbrellas. Resourceful Roppongi merchants kept supplies of cheap umbrellas on hand for sudden thundershowers.

People hurried into Almond, jamming the pink-and-white foyer and cramming into booths for hot coffee and pastries. Hordes of young Japanese girls, giggling and beautifully dressed. No other women on earth dressed with as much fashion and taste as Tokyoites. Although Satoshi was almost thirty, he was not married, either. He imagined his reasons were more compelling than Buchner-san's.

As they passed the windows resplendent with bright pink booths, he had to force himself not to look to the right and up to the leaded-glass windows on the third floor of the building. Still, he saw in his mind their exquisite, ancient beauty and his heart began to pound, much as he imagined Buchner-san's heart would if she saw the Empress's ghost. The throbbing traveled through his veins and arteries to his groin, a journey often taken in this vicinity.

Ignoring the growing, biting pleasure, Satoshi began to lead his American charge down the main street. Halfway between here and Tokyo Tower was the Hard Rock Café. Beers there currently went for eight hundred yen, about eight dollars. That would give her something to talk about back home.

His back was to the windows, but he felt the sudden heat of the spring rain, and he struggled not to turn around.

Buchner-san touched his arm, and he almost shouted. "Wait, Nagai-san, please. What's that place?"

Of course it had drawn her. How could it not? He replied, as evenly as he could, "Oh, that's Café Endless."

"Those windows are beautiful!"

As indeed they were, even in the grey light of spring rain: turquoise and emerald and ruby blood; lapis and onyx. There were no designs, no patterns, but one responded to the intention: enticement, seduction, promise.

She said "I wish I had my camera."

Immediately Satoshi began to scan for instant cameras as well as umbrellas. Buchner-san had no idea he was doing so. She was staring at the windows, unaware that washes of color were shifting over her face. Hypnosis; Satoshi felt only a fleeting pang of jealousy, for he was secure in his love.

And his need.

"Let's go there." She jabbed her finger toward the windows as if he might not know where she meant. "We could get some coffee."

He smiled. If that was what she wanted to do, that was what they would do. "As you wish."

"Oh. That is, if you have time." Now she looked concerned. She checked her watch. Americans were so unbelievably direct, yet they constantly put others in the most awkward of positions. How could he ever admit that yes, he was in a bit of a rush? For now he was beginning to sweat, so close were they to Café Endless. The scars on his neck burned; on his chest, burned; on his penis and testicles. Burned up.

"Of course we have plenty of time." He gestured for her to go first, although it made more sense for him to lead the way. She smiled at him, happy puppy, and with his guidance behind her, led the way to the plain grey elevator that opened onto the street.

They got in and he punched the button for the third floor. The doors opened and he shepherded her out, very politely. There was no sign, although it was not a private club.

"Do you think they'll have cappuccino?" she asked over her shoulder. So far they had not been able to find cappuccino for her. He had a feeling they called it something else in Japanese, although he didn't know what. That could have been a cause for embarrassment, but since she was American it was simply an amusing puzzle for them to solve.

"Perhaps they will," he said. Before he opened the swirling Art Nouveau doors of carved wood flowers and etched pastel glass, he smelled the blood that was for him the essence of Café Endless. He breathed in and dreamed of pain, and of *her*.

Café Endless.

He had first seen her in the winter, in a *kabuki* play, which was outrageous: even in ultra-modern Japan, women did not perform *kabuki*. It was the province of men, men playing men and men playing women and men believing in the women and men believing themselves to be women, so strong was their commitment and talent.

He had ducked into the *kabuki* theater only to get out of a driving winter rain. It was so odd, the streets icy, the sky liquid. It seemed that as soon as the rain hit the earth, it froze. He was loaded with parcels from his shopping expedition: this was the Ginza, the famous shopping district of Tokyo, and he was buying himself a new suit to celebrate his promotion. But he was loaded down, and it was rush hour; so he thought to buy a standing-room-only ticket for one act of *kabuki* until things calmed down.

Inexplicably (to this day), there had been plenty of seats, and he had been able to settle in and relax. The scrim had lifted; the musicians began to play.

Marvel.

She danced of a snow ghost, traveling sadly through a landscape of white. Shimmering white and blue, a figure of distinct and profound loneliness, a creature of tragedy.

And then a bride: moment of joy! Flashing snowflake instant!

And then a heron, a bird of majesty and delicacy. To him, a winged picture of fidelity and forbearance that flew away,

away,

over the snow.

Silence had blanketed the theater, then applause so overwhelming that Satoshi absorbed it as if for himself, and wept. Backstage he tried to find the actor, billed as Tsukinosuke. But no one saw Tsukinosuke then, nor ever again.

In that winter rain he had stumbled out of the theater, bereft. He was in love with that dancing creature. His new clothes, his promotion, his being were meaningless beside the beauty of that dance. As never before, he understood the vitality of tradition, the dignity of the worship of what had existed before one's own self had come into being. There was no shame in awe; there was exaltation.

The wonder was that *she* believed that, too.

Now, with Buchner-san, he sat at a wrought-iron table of leaves and sexual flowers topped with glass. After some discussion the waiter brought Satoshi some absinthe and – voila! – what they called *café au lait* in Japan, but in America was *cappuccino*.

"It's like finding the Holy Grail," Satoshi said as the waiter set the cup down before his charge. "I feel that I can die now." Buchner-san laughed long and hard and told him he was a card.

As they sipped their beverages, he couldn't help but look past her toward the doors on the other side of the café. She wasn't there; he would feel it if she were. But there was exquisite pain in the longing that made his body tight and hot and breathless.

And then:

Marvel.

As the weak sun began to sink and the windows washed orange, crimson, blood, blood red, the Chinese scarlet of dying birds. Voluptuous and ostentatious, free of restraint, smears and pools of red that transformed the rooms of Café Endless into the chambers of a beating heart.

"Oh," Buchner-san murmured, "look." She pointed at a mirror, and for a moment he panicked. Slowly he swiveled his head, and saw his reflection. And he knew in that moment that he did not fully trust *her*, and he was ashamed. Quickly he recovered himself and said nothing, waiting for a cue to reveal what Buchner-san was talking about.

"I look like I'm bleeding." She made a little face. "I look terrible!"

"Never." Satoshi picked up his absinthe and sipped the bitter liqueur. Discreetly he held it in his mouth so that the taste would linger when she kissed him.

"Oh, you're so gallant." She smiled at him and turned her head this way and that. "It's ghoulish."

"No, very lovely. Very *kabuki*."

She struck a pose, tilting her head and crossing her eyes. "*Banzai*!"

He liked her so very much. For a moment he considered sharing his situation with her, not in the sense of telling her about it but of inviting her to participate. But as she said, she was far too earthbound for that. And he was too selfish.

Then it was dark. "Jesus, we've been here for over an hour!" she said, glancing at her watch. "It seems like we just got here." She drained her cup. "I've got to get going." Satoshi let the last few drops of absinthe slide down his throat and signaled for the check. "No, no, you stay. I'll grab a cab."

"Your Hard Rock T-shirts. It will only take a minute," he said, and then: Marvel. Waves of pleasure, excitement, desire. The blood in his veins warmed, literally; he began to sweat, his organs to warm. Warm, endlessly warm, heat melting away the last snow, the first endless spring rain. His nipples hardened, his penis stiffened and throbbed, his testicles contracted and pulsated with semen.

"I'll have to get them later," she said breathlessly. "I have a dinner tonight."

"Oh, I'm so sorry." It was natural to apologise. He hadn't asked how long she could stay out. His forehead beaded with perspiration and he put his hands in his lap because they were shaking. If he left Café Endless now, he would probably fall to his knees in the street, reeling.

He got to his feet. "I'll take you back to your hotel."

"No, no, I'll grab a taxi." She held out a hand. "Don't worry about it, Nagai-san. It's really no problem."

The waiter silently glided over to their glass and metal table. Satoshi signed for the drinks. Moving cautiously, he got to his feet. His mouth was filled with absinthe and the memory of blood. His scars ached, and burned. He daubed his forehead with his handkerchief and put it back in his pocket.

"You really don't have to bother," Buchner-san assured him as they went to the elevator. "I'll just grab a cab on the street."

They got to the ground floor. Satoshi felt as if his penis were being pulled through the ceiling of the elevator and back to Café Endless, back to the rooms above Café Endless. She was there. She was there, and she was waiting, his blue snow goddess.

Buchner-san cried, "Look, there's one!" and waved her hand. Instantly a cab pulled over. Satoshi had been to New York many times, and realised that he would probably never see that loud, raucous place again.

"Thank you so much," Buchner-san told him as she climbed into the cab. Satoshi smiled and told the driver in Japanese exactly where her hotel was. "It's been so nice to see you. I'm really sorry I have to dash off like this."

"Oh, please excuse me," Satoshi replied. His English was beginning to go. "It was nothing." He would order a number of T-shirts from the Hard Rock and have them sent to her hotel. Different sizes and the two choices, white or black. But not too many to overwhelm her. Just enough to impress her and perhaps – if it were possible to so affect this brassy American lady – to make her feel indebted to him and therefore, to Nippon Kokusai Sangyo.

"*Ciao!*" she cried gaily, and the taxi took off, weaving her into the traffic and fabric of Roppongi.

He stumbled, wiping his forehead, and lurched back to the elevator. No one else was inside; he fell against the wall and closed his eyes, his penis fiery, found the buttons and hit the one not for the third floor and Café Endless, but for the fourth floor, where she was waiting.

He saw her as he opened the door, as she often appeared to him: *Tsukinosuke, kabuki* master in a *kimono* of ice blue, snowy white and golden herons whose embroidered wings were the long, floor-length sleeves of the fabulous gown. She twirled slowly in a circle, her face chalk white as if with *kabuki* make-up, her eyes black and liquid. Her hair, a long tail of smoke that reached her hips. Her mouth, tiny red flame. In her hands she held two white fans that she moved like heron's wings. The room was Japanese, spare and beautiful and natural, with paper *shoji* walls and straw *tatami* floors. Two pen and ink drawings of irises flanked her as she stood against the black-night window, the curtains pulled back.

"Good evening," he said, locking the door. She regarded him. She rarely spoke. Slowly she waved the fans, as if teasing the flames in his blood to rise.

He pulled off his shoes and clothes and went to her, facing her.

She moved her fans over him. He opened his mouth and she flicked one of the fans shut and held it sideways. He accepted it into his mouth. She pulled from the folds of her *kimono* sleeve two white silk sashes, came behind him, and tied it to the ends of the fan, brought it around, tied the other ends behind his head so that he was gagged with the fan. His eyes watered as if from smoke. His body quivered.

A slice across his buttocks. He almost ejaculated.

A slice over the nether part of his testicles. A pearl of semen blossomed on the tip of his penis as he moaned.

The blood, trickling.

Holding his penis, stroking with her frigid hands and long nails, she sliced his neck.

Drinking, drinking as he became a bonfire, taking more, draining more, and more and more as he began to suspect with mounting ecstasy that this was the night, tonight it was the fulfillment, and he groaned louder, fighting not to come.

Too late, almost too late, they fell to the *futon* that when he touched it, became a field of snow through which tiny iris buds shot. Her long black hair swirled like waves against the moon. She threw open her legs and Satoshi thrust himself into the iciness. From his penis rose steam that was not steam but spring mist.

Oh, he loved her, he loved her; and he filled her as she gave a hoarse growl deep in her chest. And still coming, as she came, he reached under the *futon* for the stake and pressed it between her breasts until droplets of blood burbled hot around the tip. Her eyes were wild with pleasure and fear; she threw back her head and convulsed around him. He pushed harder than he ever had before, piercing the skin. She gasped and reached out her hands to stop him.

He captured one of her arms and slipped the black velvet restraint around her white, cold wrist. Pulled on the rope through the hook in the wooden brace of the wall, taking up all the slack until she was stretched, hard. Restrained her other arm. She sobbed once, and he could see the question in her eyes as well: *Tonight*?

He looked past her eyes and into her hair that swirled and moved and made him see ghosts. Then he rose and went to the phone beside the alcove where he prayed to his ancestors. Chrysanthemums, not irises, stood in a black bowl. A scroll of a heron flapped gently against the wall.

He took the gag out of his mouth and called the Hard Rock Café and ordered the T-shirts, giving them the number of his Nippon Kokusai Sangyo Enterprises Visa card. Buchner-san's hotel address.

The joy of being Japanese was that each action existed for itself, and fulfillment was possible in infinite, discreet moments. He had been a good representative of Nippon Kokusai Sangyo. He had been a good host. He had been a good man.

He would be a good vampire.

"Satoshi," she whispered, and his heart seized inside him as if she were boiling the blood into a heart attack. Silently he returned to her. She was still bound, and she writhed. Opening her mouth, she beckoned him toward her. He covered her, closing his eyes, bracing himself.

Fire, fire and pain; he felt the blood stripped from his veins and arteries like gunpowder trails. Her white face beneath his as he hardened again and thrust inside her while she sucked and sucked. He wasn't afraid, and he was terrified.

Then it was happening, not as she had ever said it would, because she had never told him what it would be like. But his soul rose into the sky like a vapor and hovered with the stars above Café Endless. He had a sense that she was with him; together they soared through the exquisite night sky of Tokyo, lights and clouds and moon and spring rain dropping on umbrellas and upturned faces, the wings of herons.

On the roof garden of the New Otani Hotel, where Buchner-san lay.

In through her window. She stirred and moaned. Soft from a bath, and fragrant, and searing to his touch. She slept naked. Satoshi glided over her burning breasts and parted her burning legs. She protested mildly, asleep or enthralled; he bent over her. He was very, very cold and she was hot enough to melt metal. Where he touched her, steam rose. And smoke.

Then the vapor that was *she* guided him to Buchner-san's neck. Tears slid down his face and became sparkling icicles. He bent, and drank.

Ecstasy! Lava into his freezing loins, his penis, his heart. Warm candle wax, boiling *miso* soup. A bath among steaming rocks and bubbling hot springs. And pleasure of the most sensuous nature, hard and soft, pliant and conquering. It would be his last gift to Buchner-san, whom he admired greatly.

And *she* with him, taking also, then sharing with him, her hands on his body, inside his body.

Ecstasy! Beyond all imagining; the fulfillment of the dance she had promised short months before, indescribable wonder that set him to weeping.

And then:

On top of her body, on the *futon*, as she pulled her teeth from his neck and swallowed the last pearly drops. His eyes barely able to open. He whispered, "Was it just a dream?"

Her black eyes answered, "Wasn't it all just a dream?" And Satoshi was sorrowful for everything left behind, for this discrete, infinite moment that he would lose and for all the other moments that had been his life.

They regarded one another.

She whispered, in her real voice, "It will be soon. Hold me very tightly."

He did, arms around hers, legs around hers. He fought to keep his eyes open. Hers were drooping as well. He had thought they would be aware together.

Moments passed. As he drowsed, he listened to the rain.

Then he felt the heat on his shoulder first. He gasped and his eyes popped open. Beneath him, she took a sharp breath and tensed, and looked at him.

"I'm not afraid," he whispered. And truly as never before, he understood the vitality of tradition, the dignity of the worship of what had existed before one's own self had come into being. There was no shame in awe; there was exaltation.

"Nor I," she said. "Nor am I afraid."

Then at once he ignited. Flames and smoke; he heard the choked cry in his throat but then had no throat to express it. Hair, skin, bone, but no blood as the weak sun began to rise and the window washed orange, crimson, blood, blood red, the Chinese scarlet of dying birds. Forgiving and enduring, free of restraint, crackles and washes of red that transformed the rooms above Café Endless into the chambers of a burning, stilling heart.

And then, as she caught fire as well, a moment of joy! Flashing snowflake instant!

Writhing, they danced of ghosts traveling gloriously through a landscape of white. *Kabuki* masters, transcendent beings shimmering white and blue, figures of distinct and profound companionship, creatures of triumph.

And then, two simple herons, birds of majesty and delicacy. A winged picture of fidelity and forbearance that flew away,

away,

into the spring rain that was not rain exactly, but tears of exquisite emotion,

to the Empress's iris garden, where the ghosts of other herons lived.

THOMAS LIGOTTI

The Medusa

THOMAS LIGOTTI'S LATEST COLLECTION of stories is *Teatro Grottesco*, published in a deluxe edition by Durtro in 2006 and recently reprinted in a trade edition from Mythos Books.

Also scheduled to appear from the same publishers is a non-fiction book, *The Conspiracy Against the Human*. Subtitled *The Horror of Life and the Art of Horror*, this work comprises an excursion through the darker byways of literature, philosophy and psychology, approaching its themes in the uncompromisingly bleak and often blackly humorous manner familiar to readers of Ligotti's tales.

A short film of the author's story "The Frolic" has been completed and will be offered as a DVD with numerous bonus features. In addition, through an agreement with Fox Studios subsidiary Fox Atomic, a graphic novel based on works from Ligotti's 1996 collection *The Nightmare Factory* is due to be released for Halloween 2007.

As he reveals: "'The Medusa' had two inspirations: Arthur Machen's legend-based horror tales, with their sinister glamour and doomed protagonists, and the pessimistic philosophical writings of E. M. Cioran."

I

BEFORE LEAVING HIS ROOM Lucian Dregler transcribed a few stray thoughts into his notebook.

> The sinister, the terrible never deceive: the state in which they leave us is always one of enlightenment. And only this condition of vicious insight allows us a full grasp of the world, *all* things considered, just as a frigid melancholy grants us full possession of ourselves.
>
> We may hide from horror only in the heart of horror.
>
> Could I be so unique among dreamers, having courted the Medusa – my first and oldest companion – to the exclusion of all others? Would I have her respond to this sweet talk?

Relieved to have these fragments safely on the page rather than in some precarious mental notebook, where they were likely to become smudged or altogether effaced, Dregler slipped into an old overcoat, locked the door of his room behind him, and exited down a series of staircases at the back of his apartment building. An angular pattern of streets and alleys was his usual route to a certain place he now and then visited, though for time's sake – in order to *waste* it, that is – he chose to stray from his course at several points. He was meeting an acquaintance he had not seen in quite a while.

The place was very dark, though no more than in past experience, and much more populated than it first appeared to Dregler's eyes. He paused at the doorway, slowly but unsystematically removing his gloves, while his vision worked with the faint halos of illumination offered by lamps of tarnished metal, which were spaced so widely along the walls that the light of one lamp seemed barely to link up and propagate that of its neighbor. Gradually, then, the darkness sifted away, revealing the shapes beneath it: a beaming forehead with the glitter of wire-rimmed eyeglasses below, cigarette-holding and beringed fingers lying asleep on a table, shoes of shining leather which ticked lightly against Dregler's own as he now passed cautiously through the room. At the back stood a column of stairs coiling up to another level, which was more an appended platform, a little brow of balcony, than a section of the establishment proper. This level was caged in at its brink with a railing constructed of the same rather wiry and fragile material as the stairway, giving this area the appearance of a makeshift scaffolding. Rather slowly, Dregler ascended the stairs.

"Good evening, Joseph," Dregler said to the man seated at the table beside an unusually tall and narrow window. Joseph Gleer stared for a moment at the old gloves Dregler had tossed onto the table.

"You still have those same old gloves," he replied to the greeting, then lifted his gaze, grinning: "And that overcoat!"

Gleer stood up and the two men shook hands. Then they both sat down and Gleer, indicating the empty glass between them on the table, asked Dregler if he still drank brandy. Dregler nodded, and Gleer said "Coming up" before leaning over the rail a little ways and holding out two fingers in view of someone in the shadows below.

"Is this just a sentimental symposium, Joseph?" inquired the now uncoated Dregler.

"In part. Wait until we've got our drinks, so you can properly congratulate me."

Dregler nodded again, scanning Gleer's face without any observable upsurge in curiosity. A former colleague from Dregler's teaching days, Gleer had always possessed an open zest for minor intrigues, academic or otherwise, and an addiction to the details of ritual and protocol, anything preformulated and with precedent. He also had a liking for petty secrets, as long as he was among those privy to them. For instance, in discussions – no matter if the subject was philosophy or old films – Gleer took an obvious delight in revealing, usually at some advanced stage of the dispute, that he had quite knowingly supported some treacherously absurd school of thought. His perversity confessed, he would then assist, and even surpass, his opponent in demolishing what was left of his old position, supposedly for the greater glory of disinterested intellects everywhere. But at the same time, Dregler saw perfectly well what Gleer was up to. And though it was not always easy to play into Gleer's hands, it was this secret counter-knowledge that provided Dregler's sole amusement in these mental contests, for

> Nothing that asks for your arguments is worth arguing, just as nothing that solicits your belief is worth believing. The real and the unreal lovingly cohabit *in our terror*, the only "sphere" that matters.

Perhaps secretiveness, then, was the basis of the two men's relationship, a flawed secretiveness in Gleer's case, a consummate one in Dregler's.

Now here he was, Gleer, keeping Dregler in so-called suspense. His eyes, Dregler's, were aimed at the tall narrow window, beyond which were the bare upper branches of an elm that twisted with spectral movements under the floodlights fixed high upon the outside wall. But every few moments Dregler glanced at Gleer, whose babylike features were so remarkably unchanged: the cupid's bow lips, the cookie-dough cheeks, the tiny grey eyes now almost buried within the flesh of a face too often screwed up with laughter.

A woman with two glasses on a cork-bottomed tray was standing over the table. While Gleer paid for the drinks, Dregler lifted his and held it in the position of a lazy salute. The woman who had brought the drinks looked briefly and without expression at toastmaster Dregler. Then she went away and Dregler, with false ignorance, said: "To your upcoming or recently passed event, whatever it may be or have been."

"I hope it will be for life this time, thank you, Lucian."

"What is this, quintus?"

"*Quartus*, if you don't mind."

"Of course, my memory is as bad as my powers of observation. Actually I was looking for something shining on your finger, when I should have seen the shine of your eyes. No ring, though, from the bride?"

Gleer reached into the open neck of his shirt and pulled out a length of delicate chainwork, dangling at the end of which was a tiny rose-colored diamond in a plain silver setting.

"Modern innovations," he said neutrally, replacing the chain and stone. "The moderns must have them, I suppose, but marriage is still marriage."

"Here's to the Middle Ages," Dregler said with unashamed weariness.

"And the middle-aged," refrained Gleer.

The men sat in silence for some moments. Dregler's eyes moved once more around that shadowy loft, where a few tables shared the light of a single lamp. Most of its dim glow backfired onto the wall, revealing the concentric coils of the wood's knotty surface. Taking a calm sip of his drink, Dregler waited.

"Lucian," Gleer finally began in a voice so quiet that it was nearly inaudible.

"I'm listening," Dregler assured him.

"I didn't ask you here just to commemorate my marriage. It's been almost a year, you know. Not that that would make any difference to you."

Dregler said nothing, encouraging Gleer with receptive silence.

"Since that time," Gleer continued, "my wife and I have both taken leaves from the university and have been traveling, mostly around the Mediterranean. We've just returned a few days ago. Would you like another drink? You went through that one rather quickly."

"No, thank you. Please go on," Dregler requested very politely.

After another gulp of brandy, Gleer continued. "Lucian, I've never understood your fascination with what you call the Medusa. I'm not sure I care to, though I've never told you that. But through no deliberate efforts of my own, let me emphasise, I think I can further your, I guess you could say, pursuit. You are still interested in the matter, aren't you?"

"Yes, but I'm too poor to afford Peloponnesian jaunts like the one you and your wife have just returned from. Was that what you had in mind?"

"Not at all. You needn't even leave town, which is the strange part, the real beauty of it. It's very complicated how I know what I know. Wait a second. Here, take this."

Gleer now produced an object he had earlier stowed away somewhere in the darkness, laying it on the table. Dregler stared at the book. It was bound in a rust-colored cloth and the gold lettering across its spine was flaking away. From what Dregler could make out of the remaining fragments of the letters, the title of the book seemed to be: *Electro-Dynamics for the Beginner*.

"What is this supposed to be?" he asked Gleer.

"Only a kind of passport, meaningless in itself. This is going to sound ridiculous – how I know it! – but you want to bring the book to this establishment," said Gleer, placing a business card upon the book's front cover, "and ask the owner how much he'll give you for it. I know you go to these shops all the time. Are you familiar with it?"

"Only vaguely," replied Dregler.

The establishment in question, as the business card read, was BROTHERS' BOOKS: DEALERS IN RARE AND ANTIQUARIAN BOOKS, LIBRARIES AND COLLECTIONS PURCHASED, LARGE STOCK OF ESOTERIC SCIENCES AND CIVIL WAR, NO APPOINTMENT NEEDED, MEMBER OF MANHATTAN SOCIETY OF PHILOSOPHICAL BOOKDEALERS, BENJAMIN BROTHERS, FOUNDER AND OWNER.

"I'm told that the proprietor of this place knows you by your writings," said Gleer, adding in an ambiguous monotone: "He thinks you're a real philosopher."

Dregler gazed at length at Gleer, his long fingers abstractly fiddling with the little card. "Are you telling me that the Medusa is supposed to be a book?" he said.

Gleer stared down at the table-top and then looked up. "I'm not telling you anything I do not know for certain, which is not a great deal. As far as I know, it could still be anything you can imagine, and perhaps already have. Of course you can take this imperfect information however you like, as I'm sure you will. If you want to know more than I do, then pay a visit to this bookstore."

"Who told you to tell me this?" Dregler calmly asked.

"It seems better if I don't say anything about that, Lucian. Might spoil the show, so to speak."

"Very well," said Dregler, pulling out his wallet and inserting the business card into it. He stood up and began putting on his coat. "Is that all, then? I don't mean to be rude but—"

"Why should you be any different from your usual self? But one more thing I should tell you. Please sit down. Now listen to me. We've known each other a long time, Lucian. And I know how much this means to you. So whatever happens, or doesn't happen, I don't want you to hold me responsible. I've only done what I thought you yourself would want me to do. Well, tell me if I was right."

Dregler stood up again and tucked the book under his arm. "Yes, I suppose. But I'm sure we'll be seeing each other. Good night, Joseph."

"One more drink," offered Gleer.

"No, good night," answered Dregler.

As he started away from the table, Dregler, to his embarrassment, nearly rapped his head against a massive wooden beam which hung hazardously low in the darkness. He glanced back to see if Gleer had noticed this clumsy mishap. And after merely a single drink! But Gleer was looking the other way, gazing out the window at the tangled tendrils of the elm and the livid complexion cast upon it by the floodlights fixed high upon the outside wall.

For some time Dregler thoughtlessly observed the wind-blown trees outside before turning away to stretch out on his bed, which was a few steps from the window of his room. Beside him now was a copy of his first book, *Meditations on the Medusa*. He picked it up and read piecemeal from its pages.

> The worshipants of the Medusa, including those who clog pages with "insights" and interpretations such as these, are the most hideous citizens of this earth – and the most numerous. But how many of them *know* themselves as such? Conceivably there may be an inner cult of the Medusa, but then again: who could dwell on the existence of such beings for the length of time necessary to round them up for execution?
>
> It is possible that only the dead are not in league with the Medusa. We, on the other hand, are her allies – but always

against ourselves. How does one become her *companion* . . . and live?

We are never in danger of beholding the Medusa. For that to happen she needs our consent. But a far greater disaster awaits those who know the Medusa to be gazing at them and long to reciprocate in kind. What better definition of a marked man: one who "has eyes" for the Medusa, whose eyes have a will and a fate of their own.

Ah, to be a thing without eyes. What a break to be *born* a stone!

Dregler closed the book and then replaced it on one of the shelves across the room. On that same overcrowded shelf, leather and cloth pressing against cloth and leather, was a fat folder stuffed with loose pages. Dregler brought this back to the bed with him and began rummaging through it. Over the years the file had grown enormously, beginning as a few random memoranda – clippings, photographs, miscellaneous references which Dregler copied out by hand – and expanding into a storehouse of infernal serendipity, a testament of terrible coincidence. And the subject of every entry in this inadvertent encyclopaedia was the Medusa herself.

Some of the documents fell into a section marked "Facetious", including a comic book (which Dregler picked off a drugstore rack) that featured the Medusa as a benevolent superheroine who used her hideous powers only on equally hideous foes in a world without beauty. Others belonged under the heading of "Irrelevant", where was placed a three-inch strip from a decades-old sports page lauding the winning season of "Mr *(sic)* Medusa." There was also a meager division of the file which had no official designation, but which Dregler could not help regarding as items of "True Horror". Prominent among these was a feature article from a British scandal sheet: a photoless chronicle of a man's year-long suspicion that his wife was periodically possessed by the serpent-headed demon, a senseless little guignol which terminated with the wife's decapitation while she lay sleeping one night and the subsequent incarceration of a madman.

One of the least creditable subclasses of the file consisted of pseudo-data taken from the less legitimate propagators of mankind's knowledge: renegade "scientific" journals, occult-anthropology newsletters, and publications of various centers of sundry studies. Contributions to the file from periodicals such as *The Excentaur*, a back issue of which Dregler stumbled across in none other than Brothers' Books, were collectively categorised as "Medusa and Medusans: Sightings and Material Explanations". An early number of this publication included an article which attributed the birth of the Medusa, and of all life on Earth, to one of many extraterrestrial visitors, for whom this planet had been a sort of truckstop or comfort station en route to other locales in other galactic systems.

All such enlightening finds Dregler relished with a surly joy, especially those proclamations from the high priests of the human mind and soul, who invariably relegated the Medusa to a psychic underworld where she served as the image par excellence of romantic panic. But unique among the curiosities he cherished was an outburst of prose whose author seemed to follow in Dregler's own footsteps: a man *after his own heart*. "Can we be delivered," this writer rhetorically queried, "from the 'life force' as symbolised by Medusa? Can this energy, if such a thing exists, be put to death, crushed? Can we, in the arena of our being, come stomping out – gladiator-like – net and trident in hand, and, poking and swooping, pricking and swishing, *torment* this soulless and hideous demon into an excruciating madness, and, finally, annihilate it to the thumbs-down delight of our nerves and to our soul's deafening applause?" Unfortunately, however, these words were written in the meanest spirit of sarcasm by a critic who parodically reviewed Dregler's own *Meditations on the Medusa* when it first appeared twenty years earlier.

But Dregler never sought out reviews of his books, and the curious thing, the amazing thing, was that this item, like all the other bulletins and ponderings on the Medusa, had merely fallen into his hands unbidden. (In a dentist's office, of all places.) Though he had read widely in the lore of and commentary on the Medusa, none of the material in his rather haphazard file was attained through the normal channels of research. None of it was gained in an official manner, none of it foreseen. In the fewest words, it was all a gift of unforeseen circumstances, strictly unofficial matter.

But what did this prove, exactly, that he continued to be offered these pieces to his puzzle? It proved nothing, exactly or otherwise, and was merely a side-effect of his preoccupation with a single subject. Naturally he would be alert to its intermittent cameos on the stage of daily routine. This was normal. But although these "finds" proved nothing, rationally, they always did suggest more to Dregler's imagination than to his reason, especially when he poured over the collective contents of these archives devoted to his oldest companion.

It was, in fact, a reference to this kind of imagination for which he was now searching as he lay on his bed. And there it was, a paragraph he had once copied in the library from a little yellow book entitled *Things Near and Far*. "There is nothing in the nature of things," the quotation ran, "to prevent a man from seeing a dragon or a griffin, a gorgon or a unicorn. Nobody as a matter of fact has seen a woman whose hair consisted of snakes, nor a horse from whose forehead a horn projected; though very early man probably did see dragons – known to science as pterodactyls – and monsters more improbable than griffins. At any rate, none of these zoological fancies violates the fundamental laws of the intellect; the monsters of heraldry and mythology do not exist, but there is no reason in the nature of things nor in the laws of the mind why they should not exist."

It was therefore in line with the nature of things that Dregler suspended all judgements until he could pay a visit to a certain bookstore.

II

It was late the following afternoon, after he emerged from day-long doubts and procrastinations, that Dregler entered a little shop squeezed between a grey building and a brown one. Nearly within arm's reach of each other, the opposing walls of the shop were solid with books. The higher shelves were attainable only by means of a very tall ladder, and the highest shelves were apparently not intended for access. Back numbers of old magazines – *Black-*

wood's, *The Spectator*, the London and American *Mercurys* – were stacked in plump, orderless piles by the front window, their pulpy covers dying in the sunlight. Missing pages from forgotten novels were stuck forever to a patch of floor or curled up in corners. Dregler noted page two-hundred-and-two of *The Second Staircase* at his feet, and he could not help feeling a sardonic sympathy for the anonymous pair of eyes confronting an unexpected dead end in the narrative of that old mystery. Then again, he wondered, how many thousands of these volumes had already been browsed for the last time. This included, of course, the one he held in his own hand and for which he now succumbed to a brief and absurd sense of protectiveness. Dregler blamed his friend Gleer for this subtle aspect of what he suspected was a farce of far larger and cruder design.

Sitting behind a low counter in the telescopic distance of the rear of the store, a small and flabby man with wire-rimmed eyeglasses was watching him. When Dregler approached the counter and lay the book upon it, the man – Benjamin Brothers – hopped alertly to his feet.

"Help you?" he asked. The bright tone of his voice was the formal and familiar greeting of an old servant.

Dregler nodded, vaguely recognizing the little man from a previous visit to his store some years ago. He adjusted the book on the counter, simply to draw attention to it, and said: "I don't suppose it was worth my trouble to bring this sort of thing here."

The man smiled politely. "You're correct in that, sir. Old texts like that, worth practically nothing to no one. Now down there in my basement," he said, gesturing toward a narrow doorway, "I've got literally thousands of things like that. Other things too, you know. The *Bookseller's Trade* called it 'Benny's Treasurehouse'. But maybe you're just interested in *selling* books today."

"Well, it seems that as long as I'm here . . ."

"Help yourself, Dr Dregler," the man said warmly as Dregler started toward the stairway. Hearing his name, Dregler paused and nodded back at the bookdealer; then he proceeded down the stairs.

Dregler now recalled this basement repository, along with the three lengthy flights of stairs needed to reach its unusual depths. The bookstore at street-level was no more than a messy little closet in comparison to the expansive disorder down below: a cavern of clutter, all heaps and mounds, with bulging tiers of bookshelves laid out according to no easily observable scheme. It was a universe constructed solely of the softly jagged brickwork of books. But if the Medusa was a book, how would he ever find it in this chaos? And if it was not, what other definite form could he expect to encounter of a phenomenon which he had avoided precisely defining all these years, one whose most nearly exact emblem was a hideous woman with a head of serpents?

For some time he merely wandered around the crooked aisles and deep niches of the basement. Every so often he took down some book whose appearance caught his interest, unwedging it from an indistinct mass of battered spines and rescuing it before years rooted to the same spot caused its words to mingle with others among the ceaseless volumes of "Benny's Treasurehouse", fusing them all into a babble of senseless, unseen pages. Opening the book, he leaned a threadbare shoulder against the towering, filthy stacks. And after spending very little time in the cloistered desolation of that basement, Dregler found himself yawning openly and unconsciously scratching himself, as if he were secluded in some personal sanctum.

But suddenly he became aware of this assumption of privacy which had instilled itself in him, and the feeling instantly perished. Now his sense of a secure isolation was replaced, at all levels of creaturely response, by its opposite. For had he not written that "personal well-being serves solely to excavate within your soul a chasm which waits to be filled by a landslide of dread, an empty mold whose peculiar dimensions will one day manufacture the shape of your *unique* terror?"

Whether or not it was the case, Dregler felt that he was no longer, or perhaps never was, alone in the chaotic treasurehouse. But he continued acting as if he were, omitting only the yawns and the scratchings. Long ago he had discovered that a mild flush of panic was a condition capable of *seasoning* one's more tedious moments. So he did not immediately attempt to discourage this, probably delusory, sensation. However, like any state dependent upon the play of delicate and unfathomable forces, Dregler's mood or intuition was subject to unexpected metamorphoses.

And when Dregler's mood or intuition passed into a new phase, his surroundings followed close behind: both he and the treasure-house simultaneously crossed the boundary which divides playful panics from those of a more lethal nature. But this is not to say that one kind of apprehension was more excusable than the other; they were equally opposed to the likings of logic. ("Regarding dread, intensity in itself is no assurance of validity.") So it meant nothing, necessarily, that the twisting aisles of books appeared to be tightening around the suspicious bibliophile, that the shelves now looked more conspicuously swollen with their soft and musty stock, that faint shufflings and shadows seemed to be frolicking like a fugue through the dust and dimness of the underground treasurehouse. Could he, as he turned the next corner, be led to see that which should not be seen?

The next corner, as it happened, was the kind one is trapped in rather than turns – a cul-de-sac of bookshelves forming three walls which nearly reached the rafters of the ceiling. Dregler found himself facing the rear wall like a bad schoolboy in punishment. He gazed up and down its height as if contemplating whether or not it was real, pondering if one could simply pass through it once one had conquered the illusion of its solidity. Just as he was about to turn and abandon this nook, something lightly brushed against his left shoulder. With involuntary suddenness he pivoted in this direction, only to feel the same airy caress now squarely across his back. Continuing counterclockwise, he executed one full revolution until he was standing and staring at someone who was standing and staring back at him from the exact spot where he, a mere moment before, had been standing.

The woman's high-heeled boots put her face at the same level as his, while her turban-like hat made her appear somewhat taller. It was fastened on the right side, Dregler's left, with a metal clasp studded with watery pink stones. From beneath her hat a few strands of straw-colored hair sprouted onto an unwrinkled forehead. Then a pair of tinted eyeglasses, then a pair of unlipsticked lips, and finally a high-collared coat which descended as a dark, elegant cylinder down to her boots. She calmly withdrew a pad of paper from one of her pockets, tore off the top page, and presented it to Dregler.

"Sorry if I startled you," it said.

After reading the note, Dregler looked up at the woman and saw that she was gently chopping her hand against her neck, but only a few times and merely to indicate some vocal disability. Laryngitis, wondered Dregler, or something chronic? He examined the note once again and observed the name, address, and telephone number of a company that serviced furnaces and air-conditioners. This, of course, told him nothing.

The woman then tore off a second pre-written message from the pad and pressed it into Dregler's already paper-filled palm, smiling at him very deliberately as she did so. (How he wanted to see what her eyes were doing!) She shook his hand a little before taking away hers and making a silent, scentless exit. So what was that reek Dregler detected in the air when he stared down at the note, which simply read: "Regarding M."

And below this word-and-a-half message was an address, and below that was a specified time on the following day. The handwriting was nicely formed, the most attractive Dregler had ever seen.

In the light of the past few days, Dregler almost expected to find still another note waiting for him when he returned home. It was folded in half and stuffed underneath the door to his apartment. "Dear Lucian," it began, "just when you think things have reached their limit of ridiculousness, they become more ridiculous still. In brief – we've been had! Both of us. And by my wife, no less, along with a friend of hers. (A blond-haired anthropology prof whom I think you may know, or know of; at any rate she knows you, or at least your writings, maybe both.) I'll explain the whole thing when we meet, which I'm afraid won't be until my wife and I get back from another 'jaunt'. (Eyeing some more islands, this time in the Pacific.)

"I was thinking that you might be skeptical enough not to go to the bookstore, but after finding you not at home I feared the worst. Hope you didn't have your hopes up, which I don't think has ever happened to you anyway. No harm done, in either case. The girls explained to me that it was a quasi-scientific hoax they were perpetrating, a recondite practical joke. If you think you were taken in, you can't imagine how I was. Unbelievable how real they made the whole ruse seem to me. But if you got as far as the bookstore, you know by now that the punchline to the joke was a pretty weak one. The whole point, as I was told, was merely to stir your interest just enough to get you to perform some mildly ridiculous act. I'm curious to know how Mr B. Bros. reacted when the distinguished author of *Meditations on the Medusa* and other ruminative volumes presented him with a hopelessly worthless old textbook.

"Seriously, I hope it caused you no embarrassment, and both of us, all *three* of us, apologise for wasting your time. See you soon, tanned and pacified by a South Sea Eden. And we have plans for making the whole thing up to you, that's a promise."

The note was signed, of course, by Joseph Gleer.

But Gleer's confession, though it was evident to Dregler that he himself believed it, was no more convincing than his "lead" on a Bookstore Medusa. Because this lead, which Dregler had not credited for a moment, led further than Gleer, who no longer credited it, had knowledge of. So it seemed that while his friend had now been placated by a false illumination, Dregler was left to suffer alone the effects of a true state of unknowing. And whoever was behind this hoax, be it a true one or false, knew the minds of both men very well.

Dregler took all the notes he had received that day, paper-clipped them together, and put them into a new section of his massive file. He tentatively labelled this section: "Personal Confrontations with the Medusa, Either Real or Apparent".

III

The address given to Dregler the day before was not too far for him to walk, restive peripatetic that he was. But for some reason he felt rather fatigued that morning, so he hired a taxi to speed him across a drizzle-darkened city. Settling into the spacious dilapidation of the taxi's back seat, he took note of a few things. Why, he wondered, were the driver's glasses, which every so often filled the rear-view mirror, even darker than the day? Did she make a practice of thus "admiring" all her passengers? And was this backseat debris – the "L"-shaped cigarette butt on the door's armrest, the black apple core on the floor – supposed to serve as objects of *his* admiration?

Dregler questioned a dozen other things about that routine ride, that drenched day, and the city outside where umbrellas multiplied like mushrooms in the greyness, until he grew satisfied with his lack of a sense of well-being. Earlier he was concerned that his flow of responses that day would not be those of a man who was possibly about to confront the Medusa. He was apprehensive that he might look on this ride and its destination with lively excitement or as an adventure of some kind; in brief, he feared that his attitude would prove, to a certain extent, to be one of insanity. To be sane, he held, was either to be sedated by melancholy or activated by hysteria, two responses which are "always and equally warranted for those of *sound* insight." All others were irrational, merely symptoms of imaginations left idle, of memories out of work. And above these mundane responses, the only elevation allowable, the only valid transcendence, was a sardonic one: a bliss that annihilated the visible universe with jeers of dark joy, a *mindful* ecstasy. Anything else in the way of "mysticism" was a sign of deviation or distraction, and a heresy to the obvious.

The taxi turned onto a block of wetted brownstones, stopping before a tiny streetside lawn overhung by the skeletal branches of two baby birch trees. Dregler paid the driver, who expressed no gratitude whatever for the tip, and walked quickly through the drizzle toward a golden-bricked building with black numbers – two-oh-two – above a black door with a brass knob and knocker. Reviewing the information on the crumpled piece of paper he took from his pocket, Dregler pressed the glowing bell-button. There was no one else in sight along the street, its trees and pavement fragrantly damp.

The door opened and Dregler stepped swiftly inside. A shabbily dressed man of indefinite age closed the door behind him, then asked in a cordially nondescript voice: "Dregler?" The philosopher nodded in reply. After a few reactionless moments the man moved past Dregler, waving once for him to follow down the ground-floor hallway. They stopped at a door that was directly beneath the main stairway leading to the upper floors. "In here," said the man, placing his hand upon the doorknob. Dregler noticed the ring, its rosewater stone and silver band, and the disjunction between the man's otherwise dour appearance and this comparatively striking piece of jewelry. The man pushed open the door and, without entering the room, flipped a lightswitch on the inside wall.

To all appearances it was an ordinary storeroom cluttered with a variety of objects. "Make yourself comfortable," the man said as he indicated to Dregler the way into the room. "Leave whenever you like, just close the door behind you."

Dregler gave a quick look around the room. "Isn't there anything else?" he asked meekly, as if he were the stupidest student of the class. "This is it, then?" he persisted in a quieter, more dignified voice.

"This is it," the man echoed softly. Then he slowly closed the door, and from inside Dregler could hear footsteps walking back down the hallway.

The room was an average understairs niche, and its ceiling tapered downward into a smooth slant where angular steps ascended upward on the other side. Elsewhere its outline was obscure, confused by bedsheets shaped like lamps or tables or small horses; heaps of rocking chairs and baby-chairs and other items of disused furniture; bandaged hoses that drooped like dead pythons from hooks on the walls; animal cages whose doors hung open on a single hinge; old paint cans and pale turps speckled like an egg; and a dusty light fixture that cast a grey haze over everything.

Somehow there was not a variety of odors in the room, each telling the tale of its origin, but only a single smell pieced like a puzzle out of many: its complete image was dark as the shadows in a cave and writhing in a dozen directions over curving walls. Dregler gazed around the room, picked up some small object and immediately set it down again because his hands were trembling. He found himself an old crate to sit on, kept his eyes open, and waited.

Afterward he could not remember how long he had stayed in the room, though he did manage to store up every nuance of the eventless vigil for later use in his voluntary and involuntary dreams. (They were compiled into that increasingly useful section marked "Personal Confrontations with the Medusa", a section that was fleshing itself out as a zone swirling with red shapes and a hundred hissing voices.) Dregler recalled vividly, however, that he left the room in a state of panic after catching a glimpse of himself in an old mirror that had a hair-line fracture slithering up its center. And on his way out he lost his breath when he felt himself being pulled back into the room. But it was only a loose thread from his overcoat that had gotten caught in the door. It finally snapped cleanly off and he was free to go, his heart livened with dread.

Dregler never let on to his friends what a success that afternoon had been for him, not that he could have explained it to them in any practical way even if he desired to. As promised, they did make up for any inconvenience or embarrassment Dregler might have suffered as a result of, in Gleer's words, the "bookstore incident." The three of them held a party in Dregler's honor, and he finally met Gleer's new wife and her accomplice in the "hoax." (It became apparent to Dregler that no one, least of all himself, would admit it had gone further than that.) Dregler was left alone with this woman only briefly, and in the corner of a crowded room. While each of them knew of the other's work, this seemed to be the first time they had personally met. Nonetheless, they both confessed to a feeling of their prior acquaintance without being able, or willing, to substantiate its origins. And although plenty of mutually known parties were established, they failed to find any direct link between the two of them.

"Maybe you were a student of mine," Dregler suggested.

She smiled and said: "Thank you, Lucian, but I'm not as young as you seem to think."

Then she was jostled from behind ("Whoops," said a tipsy academic), and something she had been fiddling with in her hand ended up in Dregler's drink. It turned the clear bubbling beverage into a glassful of liquid rose-light.

"I'm so sorry. Let me get you another," she said, and then disappeared into the crowd.

Dregler fished the earring out of the glass and stole away with it before she had a chance to return with a fresh drink. Later in his room he placed it in a small box, which he labelled: "Treasures of the Medusa."

But there was nothing he could prove, and he knew it.

IV

It was not many years later that Dregler was out on one of his now famous walks around the city. Since the bookstore incident, he had added several new titles to his works, and these had somehow gained him the faithful and fascinated audience of readers that had previously eluded him. Prior to his "discovery" he had been accorded only a distant interest in scholarly and popular circles alike, but now every little habit of his, not least of all his daily meanderings, had been turned by commentators into "typifying traits" and "defining quirks". "Dregler's walks," stated one article, "are a constitutional of the modern mind, urban journeys by a tortured Ulysses *sans* Ithaca." Another article offered this back-cover superlative: "the most baroque inheritor of Existentialism's obsessions."

But whatever fatuosities they may have inspired, his recent books – *A Bouquet of Worms, Banquet for Spiders*, and *New Meditations on the Medusa* – had enabled him to "grip the minds of a dying generation and pass on to them his pain." These words were written, rather uncharacteristically, by Joseph Gleer in a highly favorable review of *New Meditations* for a philosophical quarterly. He probably thought that this notice would revive his friendship with his old colleague, but Dregler never acknowledged Gleer's effort, nor the repeated invitations to join his wife and him for some get-together or other. What else could Dregler do? Whether Gleer knew it or not, he was now one of them. And so was Dregler, though his saving virtue was an awareness of this disturbing fact. And this was part of his pain.

"We can only live by leaving our 'soul' in the hands of the Medusa," Dregler wrote in *New Meditations*. "Whether she is an angel or a gargoyle is not the point. Each merely allows us a gruesome diversion from some ultimate catastrophe which would turn us to stone; each is a mask hiding the *worst* visage, a medicine that numbs the mind. And the Medusa will see to it that we are protected, sealing our eyelids closed with the gluey spittle of her snakes, while their bodies elongate and slither past our lips to devour us *from the inside*. This is what we must never witness, except in the imagination, where it is a charming sight. And in the word, no less than in the mind, the Medusa fascinates much more than she appalls, and haunts us just *this side* of petrification. On the other side is the unthinkable, the unheard-of, that-which-should-not-be: hence, the Real. This is what throttles our souls with a hundred fingers – somewhere, perhaps in that dim room which caused us to forget ourselves, that place where we left ourselves behind amid shadows and strange sounds – while our minds and words toy, like playful, stupid pets, with *diversions* of an immeasurable disaster. The tragedy is that we must steer so close in order to avoid this hazard. *We may hide from horror only in the heart of horror.*"

Now Dregler had reached the outermost point of his daily walk, the point at which he usually turned and made his way back to his apartment, that *other* room. He gazed at the black door with the brass knob and knocker, then glanced down the street at the row of porchlights and bay windows, which were glowing madly in the late dusk. Looking skyward, he saw the bluish domes of streetlamps: inverted halos or open eyes. A light rain began to sprinkle down, nothing very troublesome. But in the next moment Dregler had already sought shelter in the welcoming brownstone.

He soon came to stand before the door of the room, keeping his hands deep in the pockets of his overcoat and away from temptation. Nothing had changed, he noticed, nothing at all. The door had not been opened by anyone since he had last closed it behind him on that hectic day years ago. And there was the proof, as he knew, somehow, it would be: that long thread from his coat still dangled from where it had been caught between door and frame. Now there was no question about what he would do.

It was to be a quick peek through a hand-wide crack, but enough to risk disillusionment and the dispersal of all the charming traumas he had articulated in his brain and books, scattering them like those peculiar shadows he supposed lingered in that room. And the voices – would he hear that hissing which heralded her presence as much as the flitting red shapes? He kept his eyes fixed upon his hand on the doorknob, turning it gently to nudge open the door. So the first thing he saw was the way it, his hand, took on a rosy dawn-like glow, then a deeper twilight crimson as it was bathed more directly by the odd illumination within the room.

There was no need to reach in and flick the lightswitch just inside. He could see quite enough as his vision, still exceptional, was further aided by the way a certain cracked mirror was positioned, giving his eyes a reflected entrance into the dim depths of the room. And in the depths of the mirror? A split-image, something fractured by a thread-like chasm that oozed up a viscous red glow. There was a man in the mirror; no, not a man but a mannikin, or a frozen figure of some kind. It was naked and rigid, leaning against a wall of clutter, its arms outstretching and reaching behind, as if trying to break a backwards fall. Its head was also thrown back, almost broken-necked; its eyes were pressed shut into a pair of well-sealed creases, two ocular wrinkles which had taken the place of the sockets themselves. And its mouth gaped so widely with a soundless scream that all wrinkles had been smoothed away from that part of the old face.

He barely recognised this face, this naked and paralyzed form which he had all but forgotten, except as a lurid figure of speech he once used to describe the uncanny condition of his soul. But it was no longer a charming image of the imagination. Reflection had given it charm, made it acceptable to sanity, just as reflection had made those snakes, and the one who wore them, picturesque and not petrifying. But no amount of reflection could have conceived seeing the thing itself, nor the state of being stone.

The serpents were moving now, coiling themselves about the ankles and wrists, the neck; stealthily entering the screaming man's mouth and prying at his eyes. Deep in the mirror opened another pair of eyes the color of wine-mixed water, and through a dark tangled mass they glared. The eyes met his, but not in a mirror. And the mouth was screaming, but made no sound. Finally, he was reunited, in the worst possible way, with the thing within the room.

Stiff inside of stone now, he heard himself think. *Where is the world, my words?* No longer any world, any words, there would only be that narrow room and its two inseparable occupants. Nothing other than that would exist for him, could exist, nor, in fact, had ever existed. In its own rose-tinted heart, his horror had at last found him.

GEMMA FILES

In The Poor Girl Taken by Surprise

A FREELANCE FILM CRITIC for more than ten years, Gemma Files lives in Toronto with her husband and son and teaches screenwriting and Canadian film history at the Toronto Film School. She wrote two episodes of Showtime's short-lived erotic horror anthology series *The Hunger*, and has screenplay credit on the feature film *By Night*.

She has published two short story collections through Prime Books, *Kissing Carrion* and *The Worm in Every Heart*, the latter containing her 1999 International Horror Guild Award-winning short story "The Emperor's Old Bones". More recently, her story "Spectral Evidence" won the Chiaroscuro's 2006 Short Story Contest.

Forthcoming is a novella, "Pen Umbra", in editor Richard Chizmar's *Thrillers 2*, and a second collection of poetry, *Dust*

Radio, from Kelp Queen Press. She is also working on a novel and a third collection of stories.

"I wrote the following story 'for' a magazine which, annoyingly enough, never ended up being published," recalls Files, "particularly so since it also featured a massive, ego-stroking 'Gemma Files, how are you so awesome?'-style interview with yours truly.

"So I kicked it over to my second collection, *The Worm in Every Heart*, instead. Since then, it's become hands-down my favourite story to read in public, structured as it is like an extended stage monologue. Though both my parents are actors, I rarely get to impersonate anyone except my characters . . . and *Grand-mère* Tessdaluye is just a real hoot, crappy grade-school *Franglais* and all. I often emerge feeling like *une vraie Canadienne*, which is always pleasant, if slightly inaccurate (since I was actually born in London, England, not London, Ontario).

"In terms of inspiration, meanwhile, the story draws from several sources: Grim fairy tales like 'Fitcher's Bird' and 'Mister Fox', Vincent Cassel's freakish performance in Christophe Gans' *Le pacte des loups* (*Brotherhood of the Wolf*), plus various Quebecois stories about the loups-garoux that I heard (or saw – a National Film Board of Canada short called *The Haunted Canoe* comes to mind) as a kid.

"For more on the Lykaian Zeus cult, I recommend Adam Douglas' essential *The Beast Within: Man, Myths and Werewolves*. Add some feminist deconstruction and serial killer lore (the Poor Girl staff remind me of the Bloody Benders), a dash of Tanith Lee's *Red As Blood*, stir; don't drink at night, let alone under a full moon."

> "Aren't you a little slut, to eat the flesh and drink the blood of your own grandmother?"
>
> —*Little Red Riding-Hood*, traditional

THIS IS AN OLD STORY. Most stories are. Anyone who says different is lying, or perhaps simply misinformed.

But thus, and even so:

Once upon a time, my darlings, these woods were full of wolves

– yes, even here in the wilds of Upper Canada, where the light which seeps between evergreens and maple trees alike is as brown and stinging as though it comes filtered through a thousand mosquitowings at once. Here where the sky is clogged with bark and cobwebs, where black biting flies hover thick under the branches and each step stirs the pine-needle loam up like hay, or sodden grey-brown snow; here amongst the tangle of crab-apple trees and blackthorn bushes, where even the quietest footfall is enough to send little toads hopping clear, like brown clumps of dirt with tiny, jewelled eyes . . .

Even here in these dim and man-empty places, where things leap from tree to tree far overhead, just out of sight. Where under the mulch and muck of dead leaves a veritable feast of dust lies waiting – a fine, dun carpet of ground and yellowed bones.

Which is why, if you hear footsteps behind you as you make your way along the forest's paths, it may be best to stop and hide and wait – as quietly as possible – until they pass you by. And if you see something high in the leaves above, something that looks like eyes travelling fast through the darkness, it may be best to ignore it, even if one is sure it can only be swamp gas – though in truth, there are few real swamps nearby, unless that sump of downed maples and frozen mud you struggled your way through to get to The Poor Girl Taken By Surprise tonight counts as such.

For there are so many things in these woods left still uncounted, even now: Trees whose branches rise high as church-spires, a perfect shape for the keels of bewitched canoes to scrape themselves upon. Caves in which squat the dried-out corpses of savages, hunted beyond endurance and sick with strange diseases, who starved to death rather than allow themselves to be captured and corralled like animals; their hungry ghosts may yet be heard keening at twilight, ill-wishing any whiteman whose shadow dares to cross their doorstep. A lake that goes up and a cathedral that goes down and a woman dressed all in birch-bark walking, rustling, with her left hand clutched tightly to her chest – that dead-white skeleton hand whose touch to the unwary forehead means madness, whose touch to the unwary back means death . . .

Yet here we sit snug and warm and dry nonetheless, traders and settlers and immigrants bound for even more distant places alike, before this open, welcoming fire; here we may eat and drink our fill and go 'round the circle in turn, each of we travellers swapping a story for our place beneath this roof 'till morning. And I will be more than glad to add my own contribution to that roster, if only it should please you to bend your ear and listen.

Might it be that you have a place already set at your table for a poor old woman such as I, *Monsieur? Madame?* A place at your sideboard for a starving, childless widow, *mesdames et messieurs, s'il vous plâit?*

Oh, no matter; I have walked far tonight, expecting to go yet farther, before I saw your sign and heard your merriment. But I am not yet so weak with hunger that I cannot seat myself.

Once upon a time, and a time it was . . .

. . . there were two sisters who lived all alone, with no mother and no father to care for them, in the very deepest and darkest part of the woods. They lived in the house of their grandmother, who was often away on long trips, but they were not lonely, these two; never so, not in each other's company. For they were used, from long experience, to making their own amusements.

And what brought this lopsided little family to the heart of the forest, *deux gamines* and one old woman, so far away from everything that is soft, feminine and civilised? Their property dated back to before the Plains of Abraham, before the French Revolution; granted land in perpetuity, as dowery and domain, 'till one of them might be inclined to sell or give it away – and if that sounds like a curse rather than a gift, then so be it. A not-so-self-imposed exile in the no longer-New World for reasons untold, or (at least) unspoken.

The name, *messieurs?* Ah, but our names have come to mean so very little here in this empty country of ours, have they not? Just as our definitions tend to . . . shift, down the centuries. *Tessedaluye, Tessedal'œil, Tête-de-l'œil* – "head of the eye," no? Or perhaps a misapprehension never corrected: Head of something very, very different. *L'œil, la luce, la loup . . .*

And so it was, after all: *Tête-du-loup*, "head of the wolf". Wolf's-head.

A strange name, certainly. And yet I know it was well as though it were – my own.

The savages who had occupied this particular plot of land began to shun it soon after the family first arrived to take possession of their new hunting-grounds. For they were ferocious hunters, these ones, male and female alike; from winter through spring, summer and fall, each season to its own sort of prey. In the old country, it had been whispered that the Tessedaluye kept their own calendar, and maybe even their own prayer-book too – had pledged themselves neither wholly to the Catholic nor the Hugenot faith, in those dark days after Catherine de'Medici and her brood split France limb from limb, twisting the wound so that it would never heal cleanly again. Which made them no sort of Christians at all, perhaps.

Or not *good* ones, at any rate.

And where was this house, you ask? Oh, not so very far from here at all. Not so very far that they were not often diverted by the light and noise of The Poor Girl Taken By Surprise which spilled towards them from across the lake, since they had never seen a public-house before, or travellers in such numbers: Music, laughter, the rumble of ox-carts, bright city-bought fabrics, men and women dancing like leaves in the wind. These things were mysteries and amazements to the two sisters, poor solitary bumpkins that they were!

For they knew many things, these girls, you see, though the ways of Man were not among them. How to trap a rabbit, and skin it. How to tell the track of stag from that of moose. How to cook a hedgehog under an earthenware bowl, peel its stinging quills free, and crack it for its tender meat. What parts of every creature may be dried for carrying, which must be hung awhile before they become palatable, which may be pickled, or otherwise preserved. And which parts are best eaten just as they are, raw and red and dripping, on the very spot where they were butchered.

The human animal, only, was one they had never hunted. Let alone . . .

. . . tasted.

* * *

Girls are curious creatures, a fact their grandmother was well acquainted with – fated to be wild in their season, just as she had been in hers. So even though she understood that her warnings would (in all probability) go unheeded, she was constrained to voice them anyway.

Come close, my darlings, come closer; listen to me a while, before I go where I must. We do not meddle with those we do not know, yes? Therefore keep always to the safest path, the well-trod road of needles rather than the easier-seeming road of pins – back and forth to Grandmother's house, where you may pull the bobbin and the latch will go up, open the door and come in.

And perhaps you should have stayed behind, old woman, if you feared so for their safety; this is what you may be thinking, and not without cause. But we cannot always choose the way things happen. I have my habits and my instincts, just as they . . . did.

A cry from the back, now: You, sir, *répétez-vous?* Ah, *were they pretty,* of course. For the most important questions must be answered first, naturally.

Well. We all know the tale of Rose Red and Snow White, do we not? From which one may gather that one was coarse and the other fine, one dark and the other fair. One might have been considered pretty, even in this company. The other –

– the other, not so much.

It was winter by then, which made things harder. Winter settles hard upon us all in this inhospitable place, am I mistaken? For when the light grows thin and the nights long, there is very little to amuse one's self with, aside from sleep. Or hunting when the hunger takes you, which is often enough.

The people at the inn, also hungry – some of you here amongst them, no doubt – tried their hand at hunting as well. But when one does not know the territory, *c'est difficile*. The girls watched their distress mount, counting down the days to their grandmother's return, and I think that it must have seemed to them that without their aid the men and women of The Poor Girl Taken By Surprise must surely pine and die like bear-cubs woken too early, beaver kits trapped in an icebound lodge . . . for they were tender-hearted creatures, as all girls are. Yes, indeed.

Almost as much so as they were also born hunters, long-used to watching and waiting while prey struggled deeper and deeper into its own trap. To check for signs of struggle in the snow or drops of blood in the underbrush, for the uneven prints of some weakened thing, for whatever Nature herself might have selected – pre-ordained, in her own magnanimous way – for them to cull.

The Feast of Stephen, Saint Stephen's Day, has long been set aside for charity. So that was the day our two sisters set out for the inn across the lake, bearing gifts with which to barter their welcome: Furs they had cured themselves, berries and fruits they had stored, a goodly portion of meat left over from their own store-room.

How they must have smiled when they drew within sight of these doors, as the moon rose and the snow began to fall – a night much like this one, come to think! For inside was light, warmth and singing, pedlars with their wares spread out on tables, all manner of strange and interesting folk from all manner of places they had never dreamed on, let alone been.

And how the inn's inhabitants must have smiled to see them coming, also: These two girls, unaccompanied, with their basket of goods and their gawky, gawping stares. Like veritable manna from Heaven.

I was far away by then, *mes amis*, following my quarry under a lead-coloured snow-storm sky. Yet I do believe, nevertheless, that I can reckon the very moment during which my granddaughters' rash actions led them somewhere they had never wanted to be.

You at the back – yes, you: I have no doubt you thought my Sylvie "pretty", when you knew her. And my Perrinette, with her puppyish ways; you must have thought her a bad bargain in comparison, though well worth the price of such company. When you fed them both grog and gin, played your fiddles and dared them to dance with each other, dressed them up in your cheap whores' cast-offs and rouged their lips and cheeks to make them look more . . . appetising?

Oui, madame, c'est véritable: I know for fact that you were there that night as chief inciter, if not ring-leader, in those drunken revels. And how, you may well ask?

Let us say that if I wrinkle my nose just so, I can – without a doubt – smell it on you.

Their only mistake – the "sin" that condemned them – was that they had never learned how men, too, prey on men, poor little ones. I had spared them that knowledge, foolishly, out of some vain hope of preserving their innocence; far too well, as it turns out. And for that I will no doubt have to make amends, in time.

This glittering mess-hall, this carbuncle, squatting over a field of shallow graves. This poisoned honeycomb, a nest to trap and drown flies in. This place where off-season travellers sometimes simply disappear, leaving nothing but their few sad treasures and a table or so of full bellies behind.

But you were surprised as well, I am sure, when – after the girls saw you, for the first time, in your true shapes – they let you see them, in theirs.

My Sylvie found a thin place in the ice with her paw as they broke from the inn, and sank like a stone to its bottom. But my poor Perrinette, hampered by her fine new clothing, was easily brought to ground. And though she snapped at you with her slavering jaws and tore at you with her clever, clawed hands, you shot her all the same: put a ball in her brain, tore her limb from limb, flayed her wolf's skin away from the man-skin still lurking below, then dragged what was left of her back inside.

For there is much meat to be had from a wolf, if one knows where to make the cuts. Almost as much, in the end, as there is on a poor girl, taken by surprise.

Yes, it is a sad story indeed. And though you do not seem eager to hear the end of it, I will tell it to you all the same.

These woods were full of wolves when we first came here, but we drove them out, hunting them almost to their extinction. For they knew the truth of our nature, just as the savages did: we are the sort who do not care to share what is ours, not even with our closest kin. So when the wolves had fled we hunted savages, and because we hunted them, the savages dressed up like us and prayed to us, prayed to us not to eat them. We became their gods for a time, until they fled as well, to find themselves others.

Or – perhaps – to seek out a place with none.

But we are not gods, and never have been. We are Wolf's-heads. Tessedaluye. We are . . .

. . . shall I really have to say the word aloud, my friends?

The primal sin of those like myself, *mes amis*, is that because we were once people who acted like beasts, we are forever cursed to be beasts who know they were once men. A wolf hunts in a pack, to eat, not to kill – it is a proponent of all those most wonderful, natural qualities: Liberty, loyalty, fraternity. But a *were*-wolf hunts to kill rather than eat, a creature whose unslaked hunger is only for blood and slaughter, defilement and degradation. It will prey even on its own family, for the bonds of kinship mean startlingly little to it; it can violate the families of others, and will, for much the same reason.

The were-wolf likes to play, to torture, and takes a grim humour in its continual masquerade, the toothy animal face beneath the gentle human mask. Perhaps this is because the oldest story behind the myth – one which those amongst us educated in the Classics may well recognise – is that of King Lykaon and his fifty sons; Lykaon, whose disgusting crimes caused the old god Zeus to flood the known world, washing it clean for future, less perverse occupants. Lykaon and his sons, who were transformed into wolves for profaning and denying the gods, for serving strangers human meat, for ravening the land they were supposed to protect like bandits rather than rulers.

And since sometimes Lykaon's name is linked with that of Tantalus, perhaps it follows that the rule he broke was the one which warns us not to share in the eating of our own children, or others'. For to force or trick others into sharing the flesh of your own line is always an evil sort of victory over them, a potential spreading of moral contagion.

Later, in Arcadia, followers of the cult of Lykaian Zeus believed that each year, one of their number would be doomed to turn into a wolf. If that person could only live for a year without tasting human flesh, he or she would return to human form; if not, he or she would remain a wolf forever. But to be a man turned wolf makes the hunger for human flesh a dreadful, and constant, temptation . . .

Ah, yes. Perhaps you have felt it too, by now: That very different sort of greed, aching in all your bones, at the root of every tooth. That itch beneath the skin, just where you can never quite reach. That song in your blood which calls out to the rising moon, dinning in your ears like some evil tide.

For we are all were-wolves here, make no mistake. Every parent who beats and rapes their own child, every man driven to eat his fellow's flesh – like a savage, though they most-times have better reason for it – by seasonal extremity. He, she, I, you; all of us who break the social compact by treating each other as something . . . less than human.

And the cry, the cry, echoing down unchanged throughout the ages: *It is not so, nor was not so, and God forbid that it should be so!*

But it is so. Is it not?

And still: *Calme-toi*. How could I possibly hurt you, *m'sieu* – an old woman like myself? Look at me. Look.

Yes, just that way.

Sit. Stay. *Asseyez-vous*, each and every one of you, before I am forced to let my – worse – nature slip.

. . . better.

Ah, and now I recall how when I was but a gay girl like my poor Perrinette, still foolish enough to risk myself for trifles, I wore nothing but scarlet velvet . . . scarlet, so the stains would not show so badly. You understand.

Yet how times change, and how they do not. How do they never.

But I do not blame you for her death, any of you – oh no, not I. How could I, and not count myself a hypocrite? For I, of all people, should know how very difficult it is to refuse fresh meat when it presents itself, especially out here in this bleak and denuded frontier landscape. Out here, where hunger rules.

After all, I, too, have been known to prey on the unwary, in my time. I, too, have followed close behind travelling families and used their love for one another to harry them to their doom. I, too, keep a cellar full of bones.

Yet I will give you this one thing for gift, *mesdames et messieurs* of The Poor Girl Taken By Surprise: This much, I will tell you for free. That there is more than one reason, traditionally, why a wolf who speaks – a wolf with human hands – should always be *burnt* rather than *eaten*.

You killed one of my children, and ate the other. But I do not begrudge you – since, in doing so, you have allowed yourselves to be eaten from inside-out by this same raging hunger that has always driven us, I and my kind, down all the long years before we came to this country, and after. In a way, you have *become* my children, my kin; Tessdaluye by nature, if not by name. And how could I harm my own kind, after all?

Well . . . easily enough, as I have explained already.

Nevertheless, I catch myself feeling generous, for now. For as a fellow hunter, I do so admire your arrangement here – this inn, sprung perpetually open like a trap disguised as providence; this fine, new trick of letting the little pigs come to be served and watching them serve themselves up, in turn. A steady stream of travellers lodging once, then moving on, and never being seen again: only tracks in the snow, covered over before the moon next rises, and (here and there, in the underbrush) the rustle of soft paws following. With nothing left behind but the hard, dark scat of some unseen thing, so concentrated it must surely eat nothing but meat.

Oh yes indeed, *ça marche, absolutement. Ça ira.*

But never forget whose sufferance you live by from this moment on, curs. As last of my line, I am first in the blood here – alpha and omega, the aleph and the zed. And so you will come to my call, heel at my command, because I am—

– ah, *ça phrase?*

"Top dog."

You may even call me grandmother, if you wish.

SYDNEY J. BOUNDS

Downmarket

PROLIFIC BRITISH AUTHOR Sydney J. Bounds joined the Science Fiction Association in 1937, where he met writers Arthur C. Clarke, William F. Temple and John Christopher (Sam Youd).

He founded the SF fan group, the Cosmos Club, during World War II, and his early fiction appeared in the club's fanzine, *Cosmic Cuts*. His first professional sale never appeared, but by the late 1940s he was contributing "spicy" stories to the monthly magazines published by Utopia Press.

Writing under a number of pseudonyms, he became a regular contributor to such SF magazines as *Tales of Tomorrow*, *Worlds of Fantasy*, *New Worlds Science Fiction*, *Other Worlds Science Stories* and *Fantastic Universe*, amongst other titles. When the magazine markets began to dry up, Bounds became a reliable contributor to various anthology series, including *New Writings in SF*, *The Fontana Book of Great Ghost Stories*, *The Fontana Book of Great Horror*

Stories, *The Armada Monster Book* and *The Armada Ghost Book*. His story "The Circus" was adapted by George A. Romero for a 1986 episode of the TV series *Tales of the Darkside*.

Other anthologies to feature Bounds' work include *Tales of Terror from Outer Space*, *Gaslight Tales of Terror*, *Frighteners*, *Keep Out the Night*, *The Mammoth Book of Vampires*, *The Mammoth Book of New Terror*, *Great Ghost Stories*, *Tales to Freeze the Blood* and Philip Harbottle's *Fantasy Adventure* series. In 2002, Harbottle edited the first-ever collections of Bounds' work, *The Best of Sydney J. Bounds: Strange Portrait and Other Stories* and *The Best of Sydney J. Bounds: The Wayward Ship and Other Stories*, for Cosmos Books.

The author died in November 2006, and "Downmarket" was one of his final stories.

METAL LINKS RATTLED as Jimmy tugged uselessly at the heavy chain shackling him to a railing in the market place. The padlock was big and heavy. Lifting his head he saw that the hands of the church clock stood at ten after three, so he'd been here for two hours.

Some joke.

A round moon glided the deserted square silver between shifting shadows. The breeze that disturbed autumn leaves and rustled a plastic bag chilled his thin teenaged body. At least it wasn't raining – and a good job winter hadn't arrived.

He'd seen no sign of life, apart from a ginger cat, since they'd chained him to the railing. The cat paused to sniff at his boots, then moved on. In summer, there might have been a pair of lovers to release him. The beat copper hadn't been testing doors either, and that was strange.

Jimmy looked past the shuttered stalls to the dark windows of shops and offices bordering the market. He still had hours to wait before the early workers arrived for breakfast at the café. And he was afraid.

He felt betrayed, and desperate, with only one aim: to survive the night. And he'd thought Mary liked him.

The Market House, where Clay the supervisor had his office, was a pale shape in the centre of the square. Jimmy raised his gaze to the plinth in a niche beneath the eaves, where a stone figure brooded over the market.

He'd never taken much notice before; who looks closely at some old statue? It was grey and tarnished. Now he saw that the figure was grotesque, tail as a man, with wings folded about a skeletal figure and hog-like snout. A single blank eye seemed to stare directly at him, and he shivered.

He gave a start: had it moved? That had to be his imagination.

Napoleon Jimson was a natural coward. When threatened, he relied on his long spindly legs to get him out of trouble.

He'd always been able to outrun the bullies at the Home; to dodge and swerve around his tormentors. His name had caused a lot of aggro; he hated it, and never forgave his mother for inflicting it on him. Not that he remembered her; soon after his father had unloaded her, she'd unloaded him.

Kids can be cruel, and it wasn't only boys who laughed as they chanted:

"Nap, Nap,
What a sap.
Takes the rap,
Gets the strap!"

He wanted only a quiet life, to be left alone, but this time he hadn't run fast enough.

The hands of the church clock moved slowly towards the quarter hour. It was going to be a long night. The wind had freshened, moaning through the branches of trees, bringing him the ripe smell of spoilt fruit.

Jimmy looked beyond the stalls to a row of old buildings sandwiched between the new; an ancient arcade cut between the pub and a pizza parlour. There came a small movement; only a rat at the rubbish.

He tugged ineffectually at the chain. Clay hadn't made any

mistake; the handcuffs dug into his skinny wrists and tightened as he struggled. The chain was solid and double-wrapped about the railing. He could move, but not far.

The clock chimed. He sensed the weight of the statue's gaze, heavy as granite, and looked up. The shadowed figure had unfurled its wings. He blinked, and a cloud passed across the face of the moon, blotting out the impossible.

He waited, shivering in the darkness, imagining the sound of beating wings.

When the cloud passed he saw that the niche was empty, the strange figure gliding in a circle on outstretched wings. He cried out in shock and it changed course, swooping towards him and growing larger.

When he ran away from the Home, he hitched a lift to London and moved into one of the cardboard cities. He called himself "Jimmy" if anyone challenged him. It was winter and the homeless huddled together.

He was never work-shy but all he could get was a part-time job minding a street barrow when the owner adjourned to the pub. He lived on pasties and chocolate bars; he'd always had a craving for chocolate.

The unemployed didn't bother him. It was the others: the winos and perverts, the addicts and pushers. And the muggers.

Three of them found him late one evening in a shopping mall. "You gotta chance to share a few quid with your old mates, Jim."

As they closed in, light flashed off a blade and he was off and running; he had strong legs and long strides. In the spring, he left London for the south.

The figure glided in to land no more than a few yards away, apparently as light as a feather. It had to be hollow. It furled its wings and stood motionless, watching him. Jimmy began to shake.

The thing, whatever it was, looked formidable, scaly, and the gaze of its single eye skewered him like a lance. Its smell reminded him of a cesspit he'd once almost stumbled into, and he stared in disbelief at the overlapping plates thick with bird droppings.

Then it moved towards him on short stubby legs, talons clicking on the cobblestones. It approached boldly, snout lifted, sniffing the air.

Disbelief gave way to terror as he failed to convince himself it was only someone wearing a mask. In a frenzy of fear he wrenched at the chain holding him prisoner. The cuffs tore his wrists and he ignored the pain and blood as he tried desperately to run away.

The figure waddled nearer, bringing its stench close, open snout within inches of his face.

Jimmy sobbed.

He didn't need to go far, only to a small town somewhere between London and the coast where a willing worker was appreciated. They called him a porter and worked him hard, fetching and carrying boxes and crates all day and clearing up afterwards.

The market stalls had gaudy awnings of red and white stripes and they were busy. He had little time to pause between errands. It was "Jim, more cauli here," and "Fetch another crate of bananas, quick."

By nightfall he was exhausted but happy. The job didn't pay much, but the stall-holders saw he didn't go hungry.

He came to like the smell of fresh fish and oranges, the sight of colourful fabrics snapping in the breeze. He enjoyed the cheerful market cries. "Sixty a pound mushrooms. Fresh today, best beetroot!"

The recession hadn't affected this market; the traders had a satisfied air of prosperity, raking in cash as fast as Jimmy could wheel up another barrowload of produce. And he made friends. At least, he thought of them as friends . . .

He backed away as far as the chain allowed and the stinking grey figure followed him. The smell was so strong it threatened to choke him, and he tried to hold his breath.

He tugged at his chain and dreamt for a moment that the whole railing moved.

Talons reached out to grasp him, the way a miser reaches for gold. Jimmy wished he'd never run away from the Home, never left London. He wished he'd accepted the chocolates Mary had offered, now scattered over the ground and out of reach. He wished for . . . anything but this.

He expelled his breath in a rush. "Get away – leave me alone!"

Clay, the market supervisor, was about thirty with a craggy face and surprised Jimmy with his subtle sense of humour. He gave the nod when Mary asked if he could be kept on as their regular porter.

Big Ernie, who ran the fish stall, treated him all right in spite of his size; he seemed a gentle giant.

Mary was older, perhaps forty. She ran a second-hand bookstall and took to Jimmy as if he were a long-lost son. She clucked over him and gave him comics to read.

"There's a shed, just off the square, where we keep barrows and stuff," she told him. "You could sleep there in the summer."

So he moved in, made himself a nest of old sacks, and everything was fine till the night they came for him.

It ignored his words. Talons drew him into a close embrace. He shuddered at their touch and, desperate, thrust at the figure with his hands in an attempt to push it away.

The scales felt cold and hard as stone, slimy with bird droppings. He couldn't budge it, and shuddered. The talons tightened as if intent on crushing his thin body. Jimmy screamed his despair.

During his last day, he'd noticed sly looks in his direction; traders exchanging a nudge and a wink. And overheard whispers that made him uneasy.

"After all, it's only once a year."

When the stalls closed and the clearing up began, Clay, Mary and Big Ernie surrounded him.

"Forget that today, Jimmy," Clay said. "Someone else can do it – we're taking you for a slap-up meal."

"You deserve it," Mary said quickly. "It's a sort of celebration."

"Yeah, an anniversary. For the market."

They took him to the pizza parlour. "Anything you like, Jimmy," Ernie said. "Anything at all. No limit."

He had three toppings on his pizza, chocolate gateau to follow and a large Coke. It was the best meal he'd ever had and when, later, he crawled into his bed in the shed, he quickly fell asleep with a smile on his face.

Stiff wings enfolded him, holding him close, and talons dug into his flesh. Jimmy thought wildly of comic book heroes but there was not one around to save him. The market square remained silent and empty; he was alone with his nightmare.

A scream was strangled in his throat. He tried to wipe his hands clean, made them into fists to beat on the scaly hide. He might as well have pummelled a cliff face.

The hog-like snout descended and, gently, grey lips touched his.

Perhaps it was the slight sound as the shed door opened that woke him. Or moonlight falling across his face. He was instantly alert, scrambling out of his nest and ready to run; he always slept in jeans and T-shirt.

"Take it easy, Jimmy," a familiar voice said. Clay's face showed pale in the cold light.

"What's wrong?" His pulse was beating faster.

"Nothing's wrong," Mary said, appearing behind the supervisor. "We want you to come outside, that's all."

Jimmy hesitated. He needed to trust his friends but he had a bad feeling about this visit. He started to run, swerving around them to reach the door, and Big Ernie's arms wrapped about him and he knew it was hopeless. Ernie had the strength of a bear.

"I haven't done anything wrong," he protested.

"Of course you haven't," Mary said quickly. "You're a good boy."

Ernie lifted him and carried him with ease, outside to the square, to one of the railings. Clay snapped on handcuffs and chained him to a railing.

"Why?" He was nearly in tears. "Why are you doing this?"

Mary looked sadly at him. "You'll be helping all of us. All the traders. All your friends."

She offered an open box of chocolates. "These will help."

He looked at her with suspicion. "What are they? Drugs?"

"Just something to help you."

"I don't do drugs." He knocked the box out of her hand, scattering loose chocolates over the cobblestones.

Clay let out a sigh. "That's it then. Come away, Mary."

The three of them left him chained to the railing, crossed the square and disappeared into the arcade. Their footfalls echoed and faded. Then he was alone in the silent market, waiting.

The lips felt rubbery and he gagged on a vile stench. His arms imprisoned, he was forced backwards over the iron railing until it seemed his spine would snap. He looked up into a single unblinking eye.

The thing sucked, like mouth-to-mouth resuscitation in reverse, slowly at first and then harder until Jimmy's tongue was pulled from its root, choking him. Pain disabled him and he was close to fainting.

As if tempted by a delicacy, the snout sucked greedily with the power of an industrial vacuum cleaner.

This can't be happening, Jimmy thought frantically, but the pain was real. His lungs tore loose and came up through his mouth, his last breath a ragged gasp, and still the suction increased.

"Like I once sucked out a bird's egg," the thought came before he blacked out.

Then his heart was in his mouth, his brain wrenched from its bony cage. Bones splintered and the marrow sucked out. When he was drained, the thing spread its wings ready for flight; gorged and heavy it wobbled on stumpy legs in the moonlight before it took off.

Pre-dawn, before anyone else was about, Clay removed the padlock and chain. Mary collected the discarded clothes, and Big Ernie pushed the empty skin into a plastic bag and tossed it into a waste bin.

They gazed up at the satisfied figure in its niche above the Market House, sure now that they could look forward to another good year.

ROBERT E. HOWARD

The Horror from the Mound

ROBERT ERVIN HOWARD was born and raised in rural Texas, where he lived all his life. The son of a pioneer physician, he began writing professionally at fifteen, and three years later sold his first story to the legendary pulp magazine *Weird Tales*.

A prolific and proficient author, he published Westerns, sports stories, horror tales, true confessions, historical adventures and detective thrillers while developing a series of heroic characters with whom he would forever be identified with: Solomon Kane, King Kull, Bran Mak Morn and, of course, Conan the Cimmerian. Between 1932 and 1935, Howard wrote twenty-one sword and sorcery adventures of Conan, ranging in length from 3,500 words to 75,000 words.

He tragically committed suicide at the age of thirty in June 1936.

The following vampire Western was originally published in the May 1932 issue of *Weird Tales* and subsequently adapted by writer Gardner F. Fox and artist Frank Brunner as "The Monster from the Mound!" in the second issue of Marvel Comics' *Chamber of Chills* (January, 1973).

STEVE BRILL DID NOT BELIEVE in ghosts or demons. Juan Lopez did. But neither the caution of the one nor the sturdy skepticism of the other was shield against the horror that fell upon them – the horror forgotten by men for more than three hundred years – a screaming fear monstrously resurrected from the black lost ages.

Yet as Steve Brill sat on his sagging stoop that last evening, his thoughts were as far from uncanny menaces as the thoughts of man can be. His ruminations were bitter but materialistic. He surveyed his farmland and he swore. Brill was tall, rangy and tough as bootleather – true son of the iron-bodied pioneers who wrenched West Texas from the wilderness. He was browned by the sun and strong as a long-horned steer. His lean legs and the boots on them showed his cowboy instincts, and now he cursed himself that he had ever climbed off the hurricane deck of his crank-eyed mustang and turned to farming. He was no farmer, the young puncher admitted profanely.

Yet his failure had not all been his fault. Plentiful rain in the winter – so rare in West Texas – had given promise of good crops. But as usual, things had happened. A late blizzard had destroyed all the budding fruit. The grain which had looked so promising was ripped to shreds and battered into the ground by terrific hailstorms just as it was turning yellow. A period of intense dryness, followed by another hailstorm, finished the corn.

Then the cotton, which had somehow struggled through, fell before a swarm of grasshoppers which stripped Brill's field almost over night. So Brill sat and swore that he would not renew his lease – he gave fervent thanks that he did not own the land on which he had wasted his sweat, and that there were still broad rolling ranges to the west where a strong young man could make his living riding and roping.

Now as Brill sat glumly, he was aware of the approaching form of his nearest neighbor, Juan Lopez, a taciturn old Mexican who lived in a hut just out of sight over the hill across the creek, and grubbed for a living. At present he was clearing a strip of land on an adjoining farm, and in returning to his hut he crossed a corner of Brill's pasture.

Brill idly watched him climb through the barbed-wire fence and trudge along the path he had worn in the short dry grass. He had been working at his present job for over a month now, chopping down tough gnarly mesquite trees and digging up their incredibly long roots, and Brill knew that he always followed the same path home. And watching, Brill noted him swerving far aside, seemingly to avoid a low rounded hillock which jutted above the level of the pasture. Lopez went far around this knoll and Brill remembered that the old Mexican always circled it at a distance. And another thing came into Brill's idle mind – Lopez always increased his gait when he was passing the knoll, and he always managed to get by it before sundown – yet Mexican laborers generally worked from the first light of dawn to the last glint of twilight, especially at these grubbing jobs, when they were paid by the acre and not by the day. Brill's curiosity was aroused.

He rose, and sauntering down the slight slope on the crown of which his shack sat, hailed the plodding Mexican.

"Hey, Lopez, wait a minute."

Lopez halted, looked about, and remained motionless but unenthusiastic as the white man approached.

"Lopez," said Brill lazily, "it ain't none of my business, but I just wanted to ask you – how come you always go so far around that old Indian mound?"

"No sabe," grunted Lopez shortly.

"You're a liar," responded Brill genially. "You savvy all right; you speak English as good as me. What's the matter – you think that mound's ha'nted or somethin'?"

Brill could speak Spanish himself and read it, too, but like most Anglo-Saxons he much preferred to speak his own language.

Lopez shrugged his shoulders.

"It is not a good place, *no bueno*," he muttered, avoiding Brill's eye. "Let hidden things rest."

"I reckon you're scared of ghosts," Brill bantered. "Shucks, if that is an Indian mound, them Indians been dead so long their ghosts 'ud be plumb wore out by now."

Brill knew that the illiterate Mexicans looked with superstitious aversion on the mounds that are found here and there through the Southwest – relics of a past and forgotten age, containing the moldering bones of chiefs and warriors of a lost race.

"Best not to disturb what is hidden in the earth," grunted Lopez.

"Bosh," said Brill. "Me and some boys busted into one of them mounds over in the Palo Pinto country and dug up pieces of a skeleton with some beads and flint arrowheads and the like. I kept some of the teeth a long time till I lost 'em, and I ain't never been ha'nted."

"Indians?" snorted Lopez unexpectedly. "Who spoke of Indians? There have been more than Indians in this country. In the old times strange things happened here. I have heard the tales of my people, handed down from generation to generation. And my people were here long before yours, Señor Brill."

"Yeah, you're right," admitted Steve. "First white men in this country was Spaniards, of course. Coronado passed along not very far from here, I hear-tell, and Hernando de Estrada's expedition came through here – away back yonder – I dunno how long ago."

"In 1545," said Lopez. "They pitched camp yonder where your corral stands now."

Brill turned to glance at his rail-fenced corral, inhabited now by his saddle-horse, a pair of work-horses and a scrawny cow.

"How come you know so much about it?" he asked curiously.

"One of my ancestors marched with de Estrada," answered Lopez. "A soldier, Porfirio Lopez; he told his son of that expedition, and he told *his* son, and so down the family line to me, who have no son to whom I can tell the tale."

"I didn't know you were so well connected," said Brill. "Maybe you know somethin' about the gold de Estrada was supposed to hid around here somewhere."

"There was no gold," growled Lopez. "De Estrada's soldiers bore only their arms, and they fought their way through hostile country – many left their bones along the trail. Later – many years later – a mule train from Santa Fe was attacked not many miles from here by Comanches and they hid their gold and escaped; so the legends got mixed up. But even their gold is not there now, because Gringo buffalo-hunters found it and dug it up."

Brill nodded abstractedly, hardly heeding. Of all the continent of North America there is no section so haunted by tales of lost or hidden treasure as is the Southwest. Uncounted wealth passed back and forth over the hills and plains of Texas and New Mexico in the old days when Spain owned the gold and silver mines of the New World and controlled the rich fur trade of the West, and echoes of that wealth linger on in tales of golden caches. Some such vagrant dream, born of failure and pressing poverty, rose in Brill's mind.

Aloud he spoke: "Well, anyway, I got nothin' else to do and I believe I'll dig into that old mound and see what I can find."

The effect of that simple statement on Lopez was nothing short of shocking. He recoiled and his swarthy brown face went ashy; his black eyes flared and he threw up his arms in a gesture of intense expostulation.

"Dios, no!" he cried. "Don't do that, Señor Brill! There is a curse – my grandfather told me—"

"Told you what?" asked Brill.

Lopez lapsed into sullen silence.

"I can not speak," he muttered. "I am sworn to silence. Only to an eldest son could I open my heart. But believe me when I say better had you cut your throat than to break into that accursed mound."

"Well," said Brill, impatient of Mexican superstitions, "if it's so bad why don't you tell me about it? Gimme a logical reason for not bustin' into it."

"I can not speak!" cried the Mexican desperately. "I *know!* – but I swore to silence on the Holy Crucifix, just as every man of my family has sworn. It is a thing so dark, it is to risk damnation even to speak of it! Were I to tell you, I would blast the soul from your body. But I have sworn – and I have no son, so my lips are sealed for ever."

"Aw, well," said Brill sarcastically, "why don't you write it out?"

Lopez started, stared, and to Steve's surprise, caught at the suggestion.

"I will! *Dios* be thanked the good priest taught me to write when I was a child. My oath said nothing of writing. I only swore not to speak. I will write out the whole thing for you, if you will swear not to speak of it afterward, and to destroy the paper as soon as you have read it."

"Sure," said Brill, to humor him, and the old Mexican seemed much relieved.

"*Bueno!* I will go at once and write. Tomorrow as I go to work I will bring you the paper and you will understand why no one must open that accursed mound!"

And Lopez hurried along his homeward path, his stooped shoulders swaying with the effort of his unwonted haste. Steve grinned after him, shrugged his shoulders and turned back toward his own shack. Then he halted, gazing back at the low rounded mound with its grass-grown sides. It must be an Indian tomb, he decided, what with its symmetry and its similarity to other Indian mounds he had seen. He scowled as he tried to figure out the seeming connection between the mysterious knoll and the martial ancestor of Juan Lopez.

Brill gazed after the receding figure of the old Mexican. A shallow valley, cut by a half-dry creek, bordered with trees and underbrush, lay between Brill's pasture and the low sloping hill beyond which lay Lopez's shack. Among the trees along the creek bank the old Mexican was disappearing. And Brill came to a sudden decision.

Hurrying up the slight slope, he took a pick and a shovel from the tool shed built on to the back of his shack. The sun had not yet set and Brill believed he could open the mound deep enough to determine its nature before dark. If not, he could work by lantern-light. Steve, like most of his breed, lived mostly by impulse, and his present urge was to tear into that mysterious hillock and find what, if anything, was concealed therein. The thought of treasure came again to his mind, piqued by the evasive attitude of Lopez.

What if, after all, that grassy heap of brown earth hid riches – virgin ore from forgotten mines, or the minted coinage of old Spain? Was it not possible that the musketeers of de Estrada had themselves reared that pile above a treasure they could not bear away, molding it in the likeness of an Indian mound to fool seekers? Did old Lopez know that? It would not be strange if, knowing of treasure there, the old Mexican refrained from disturbing it. Ridden with grisly superstitious fears, he might well live out a life of barren toil rather than risk the wrath of lurking ghosts or devils – for the Mexicans say that hidden gold is always accursed, and surely there was supposed to be some especial doom resting on this mound. Well, Brill meditated, Latin-Indian devils had no terrors for the Anglo-Saxon, tormented by the demons of drouth and storm and crop failure.

Steve set to work with the savage energy characteristic of his breed. The task was no light one; the soil, baked by the fierce sun, was iron-hard, and mixed with rocks and pebbles. Brill sweated profusely and grunted with his efforts, but the fire of the treasure-hunter was on him. He shook the sweat out of his eyes and drove in the pick with mighty strokes that ripped and crumbled the close-packed dirt.

The sun went down, and in the long dreamy summer twilight he worked on, almost oblivious of time or space. He began to be convinced that the mound was a genuine Indian tomb, as he found traces of charcoal in the soil. The ancient people which reared these sepulchers had kept fires burning upon them for days, at some point in the building. All the mounds Steve had ever opened had contained a solid stratum of charcoal a short distance below the surface. But the charcoal traces he found now were scattered about through the soil.

His idea of a Spanish-built treasure-trove faded, but he persisted. Who knows? Perhaps that strange folk men now called Mound-Builders had treasure of their own which they laid away with the dead.

Then Steve yelped in exultation as his pick rang on a bit of metal. He snatched it up and held it close to his eyes, straining in the waning light. It was caked and corroded with rust, worn almost paper-thin, but he knew it for what it was – a spur-rowel, unmistakably Spanish with its long cruel points. And he halted completely bewildered. No Spaniard ever reared this mound, with its undeniable marks of aboriginal workmanship. Yet how came that relic of Spanish caballeros hidden deep in the packed soil?

Brill shook his head and set to work again. He knew that in the center of the mound, if it were indeed an aboriginal tomb, he would find a narrow chamber built of heavy stones, containing the bones of the chief for whom the mound had been reared and the victims sacrificed above it. And in the gathering darkness he felt his pick strike heavily against something granite-like and unyielding. Examination, by sense of feel as well as by sight, proved it to be a solid block of stone, roughly hewn. Doubtless it formed one of the ends of the death-chamber. Useless to try to shatter it. Brill chipped and pecked about it, scraping the dirt and pebbles away from the corners until he felt that wrenching it out would be but a matter of sinking the pick-point underneath and levering it out.

But now he was suddenly aware that darkness had come on. In the young moon objects were dim and shadowy. His mustang nickered in the corral whence came the comfortable crunch of tired beasts' jaws on corn. A whippoorwill called eerily from the dark shadows of the narrow winding creek. Brill straightened reluctantly. Better get a lantern and continue his explorations by its light.

He felt in his pocket with some idea of wrenching out the stone and exploring the cavity by the aid of matches. Then he stiffened. Was it imagination that he heard a faint sinister rustling, which seemed to come from behind the blocking stone? Snakes! Doubtless they had holes somewhere about the base of the mound and there might be a dozen big diamond-backed rattlers coiled up in that cave-like interior waiting for him to put his hand among them. He shivered slightly at the thought and backed away out of the excavation he had made.

It wouldn't do to go poking about blindly into holes. And for the past few minutes, he realised, he had been aware of a faint foul odor exuding from interstices about the blocking stone – though he admitted that the smell suggested reptiles no more than it did any other menacing scent. It had a charnel-house reek about it – gases formed in the chamber of death, no doubt, and dangerous to the living.

Steve laid down his pick and returned to the house, impatient of the necessary delay. Entering the dark building, he struck a match and located his kerosene lantern hanging on its nail on the wall. Shaking it, he satisfied himself that it was nearly full of coal oil, and lighted it. Then he fared forth again, for his eagerness would not allow him to pause long enough for a bite of food. The mere opening of the mound intrigued him, as it must always intrigue a man of imagination, and the discovery of the Spanish spur had whetted his curiosity.

He hurried from his shack, the swinging lantern casting long distorted shadows ahead of him and behind. He chuckled as he visualised Lopez's thoughts and actions when he learned, on the morrow, that the forbidden mound had been pried into. A good thing he opened it that evening, Brill reflected; Lopez might even have tried to prevent him meddling with it, had he known.

In the dreamy hush of the summer night, Brill reached the mound – lifted his lantern – swore bewilderedly. The lantern revealed his excavations, his tools lying carelessly where he had dropped them – and a black gaping aperture! The great blocking stone lay in the bottom of the excavation he had made, as if thrust carelessly aside. Warily he thrust the lantern forward and peered into the small cave-like chamber, expecting to see he knew not what. Nothing met his eyes except the bare rock sides of a long narrow cell, large enough to receive a man's body, which had apparently been built up of roughly hewn square-cut stones, cunningly and strongly joined together.

"Lopez!" exclaimed Steve furiously. "The dirty coyote! He's been watchin' me work – and when I went after the lantern, he snuck up and pried the rock out – and grabbed whatever was in there, I reckon. Blast his greasy hide, I'll fix him!"

Savagely he extinguished the lantern and glared across the shallow, brush-grown valley. And as he looked he stiffened. Over the corner of the hill, on the other side of which the shack of Lopez stood, a shadow moved. The slender moon was setting, the light dim and the play of the shadows baffling. But Steve's eyes were sharpened by the sun and winds of the wastelands, and he knew that it was some two-legged creature that was disappearing over the low shoulder of the mesquite-grown hill.

"Beatin' it to his shack," snarled Brill. "He's shore got somethin' or he wouldn't be travelin' at that speed."

Brill swallowed, wondering why a peculiar trembling had suddenly taken hold of him. What was there unusual about a thieving old Greaser running home with his loot? Brill tried to drown the feeling that there was something peculiar about the gait of the dim shadow, which had seemed to move at a sort of slinking lope.

There must have been need for swiftness when stocky old Juan Lopez elected to travel at such a strange pace.

"Whatever he found is as much mine as his," swore Brill, trying to get his mind off the abnormal aspect of the figure's flight. "I got this land leased and I done all the work diggin'. A curse, heck! No wonder he told me that stuff. Wanted me to leave it alone so he could get it hisself. It's a wonder he ain't dug it up long before this. But you can't never tell about them Spigs."

Brill, as he meditated thus, was striding down the gentle slope of the pasture which led down to the creek-bed. He passed into the shadows of the trees and dense underbrush and walked across the dry creek-bed, noting absently that neither whippoorwill nor hoot-owl called in the darkness. There was a waiting, listening tenseness in the night that he did not like. The shadows in the creek bed seemed too thick, too breathless. He wished he had not blown out the lantern, which he still carried, and was glad he had brought the pick, gripped like a battle-ax in his right hand. He had an impulse to whistle, just to break the silence, then swore and dismissed the thought. Yet he was glad when he clambered up the low opposite bank and emerged into the starlight.

He walked up the slope and onto the hill, and looked down on the mesquite flat wherein stood Lopez's squalid hut. A light showed at the one window.

"Packin' his things for a getaway, I reckon," grunted Steve. "Ow, what the—"

He staggered as from a physical impact as a frightful scream knifed the stillness. He wanted to clap his hands over his ears to shut out the horror of that cry, which rose unbearably and then broke in an abhorrent gurgle.

"Good God!" Steve felt the cold sweat spring out upon him. "Lopez – or somebody—"

Even as he gasped the words he was running down the hill as fast as his long legs could carry him. Some unspeakable horror was taking place in that lonely hut, but he was going to investigate if it meant facing the Devil himself. He tightened his grip on his pick-handle as he ran. Wandering prowlers, murdering old Lopez for the loot he had taken from the mound, Steve thought, and forgot his wrath. It would go hard for any one he caught molesting the old scoundrel, thief though he might be.

He hit the flat, running hard. And then the light in the hut went out and Steve staggered in full flight, bringing up against a mesquite tree with an impact that jolted a grunt out of him and tore his hands on the thorns. Re-bounding with a sobbed curse, he rushed for the shack, nerving himself for what he might see – his hair still standing on end at what he had already seen.

Brill tried the one door of the hut and found it bolted. He shouted to Lopez and received no answer. Yet utter silence did not reign. From within came a curious muffled worrying sound, that ceased as Brill swung his pick crashing against the door. The flimsy portal splintered and Brill leaped into the dark hut, eyes blazing, pick swung high for a desperate onslaught. But no sound ruffled the grisly silence, and in the darkness nothing stirred, though Brill's chaotic imagination peopled the shadowed corners of the hut with shapes of horror.

With a hand damp with perspiration he found a match and struck it. Besides himself only old Lopez occupied the hut – old Lopez, stark dead on the dirt floor, arms spread wide like a crucifix, mouth sagging open in a semblance of idiocy, eyes wide and staring with a horror Brill found intolerable. The one window gaped open, showing the method of the slayer's exit – possibly his entrance as well. Brill went to that window and gazed out warily. He saw only the sloping hillside on one hand and the mesquite flat on the other. He started – was that a hint of movement among the stunted shadows of the mesquites and chaparral – or had he but imagined he glimpsed a dim loping figure among the trees?

He turned back, as the match burned down to his fingers. He lit the old coal oil lamp on the rude table, cursing as he burned his hand. The globe of the lamp was very hot, as if it had been burning for hours.

Reluctantly he turned to the corpse on the floor. Whatever sort of death had come to Lopez, it had been horrible, but Brill, gingerly examining the dead man, found no wound – no mark of knife or bludgeon on him. Wait! There was a thin smear of blood on Brill's questing hand. Searching, he found the source – three or four tiny punctures in Lopez's throat, from which blood had oozed sluggishly. At first he thought they had been inflicted with a stiletto – a thin round edgeless dagger – then he shook his head. He had seen stiletto wounds – he had the scar of one on his own body. These wounds more resembled the bite of some animal – they looked like the marks of pointed fangs.

Yet Brill did not believe they were deep enough to have caused death, nor had much blood flowed from them. A belief, abhorrent with grisly speculations, rose up in the dark corners of his mind – that Lopez had died of fright, and that the wounds had been inflicted either simultaneously with his death, or an instant afterward.

And Steve noticed something else; scattered about on the floor lay a number of dingy leaves of paper, scrawled in the old Mexican's crude hand – he would write of the curse on the mound, he had said. There were the sheets on which he had written, there was the stump of a pencil on the floor, there was the hot lamp globe, all mute witnesses that the old Mexican had been seated at the rough-hewn table writing for hours. Then it was not he who opened the mound-chamber and stole the contents – but who was it, in God's name? And who or what was it that Brill had glimpsed loping over the shoulder of the hill?

Well, there was but one thing to do – saddle his mustang and ride the ten miles to Coyote Wells, the nearest town, and inform the sheriff of the murder.

Brill gathered up the papers. The last was crumpled in the old man's clutching hand and Brill secured it with some difficulty. Then as he turned to extinguish the light, he hesitated, and cursed himself for the crawling fear that lurked at the back of his mind – fear of the shadowy thing he had seen cross the window just before the light was extinguished in the hut. The long arm of the murderer, he thought, reaching for the lamp to put it out, no doubt. What had there been abnormal or inhuman about that vision, distorted though it must have been in the dim lamplight and shadow? As a man strives to remember the details of a nightmare dream, Steve tried to define in his mind some clear reason that would explain why that flying glimpse had unnerved him to the extent of blundering headlong into a tree, and why the mere vague remembrance of it now caused cold sweat to break out on him.

Cursing himself to keep up his courage, he lighted his lantern, blew out the lamp on the rough table, and resolutely set forth, grasping his pick like a weapon. After all, why should certain seemingly abnormal aspects about a sordid murder upset him? Such crimes were abhorrent, but common enough, especially among Mexicans, who cherished unguessed feuds.

Then as he stepped into the silent starflecked night he brought up short. From across the creek sounded the sudden soul-shaking scream of a horse in deadly terror – then a mad drumming of hoofs that receded in the distance. And Brill swore in rage and dismay. Was it a panther lurking in the hills – had a monster cat slain old Lopez? Then why was not the victim marked with the scars of fierce hooked talons? *And who extinguished the light in the hut?*

As he wondered, Brill was running swiftly toward the dark creek. Not lightly does a cowpuncher regard the stampeding of his stock. As he passed into the darkness of the brush along the dry creek, Brill found his tongue strangely dry. He kept swallowing, and he held the lantern high. It made but faint impression in the gloom, but seemed to accentuate the blackness of the crowding shadows. For some strange reason, the thought entered Brill's chaotic mind that though the land was new to the Anglo-Saxon, it was in reality very old. That broken and desecrated tomb was mute evidence that the land was ancient to man, and suddenly the night and the hills and the shadows bore on Brill with a sense of hideous antiquity. Here had long generations of men lived and died before Brill's ancestors ever heard of the land. In the night, in the shadows of this very creek, men had no doubt given up their ghosts in grisly ways. With these reflections Brill hurried through the shadows of the thick trees.

He breathed deeply in relief when he emerged from the trees on his own side. Hurrying up the gentle slope to the railed corral, he held up his lantern, investigating. The corral was empty; not even the placid cow was in sight. And the bars were down. That pointed to human agency, and the affair took on a newly sinister aspect. Some one did not intend that Brill should ride to Coyote Wells that night. It meant that the murderer intended making his getaway and wanted a good start on the law, or else – Brill grinned wryly. Far away across a mesquite flat he believed he could still catch the faint and far-away noise of running horses. What in God's name had given them such a fright? A cold finger of fear played shudderingly on Brill's spine.

Steve headed for the house. He did not enter boldly. He crept clear around the shack, peering shudderingly into the dark windows, listening with painful intensity for some sound to betray the presence of the lurking killer. At last he ventured to open a door and step in. He threw the door back against the wall to find if any one were hiding behind it, lifted the lantern high and stepped in, heart pounding, pick gripped fiercely, his feelings a mixture of fear and red rage. But no hidden assassin leaped upon him, and a wary exploration of the shack revealed nothing.

With a sigh of relief Brill locked the doors, made fast the windows and lighted his old coal oil lamp. The thought of old Lopez lying, a glassy-eyed corpse alone in the hut across the creek, made him wince and shiver, but he did not intend to start for town on foot in the night.

He drew from its hiding-place his reliable old Colt .45, spun the blue steel cylinder and grinned mirthlessly. Maybe the killer did not intend to leave any witnesses to his crime alive. Well, let him come! He – or they – would find a young cowpuncher with a six-shooter less easy prey than an old unarmed Mexican. And that reminded Brill of the papers he had brought from the hut. Taking care that he was not in line with a window through which a sudden bullet might come, he settled himself to read, with one ear alert for stealthy sounds.

And as he read the crude laborious script, a slow cold horror grew in his soul. It was a tale of fear that the old Mexican had scrawled – a tale handed down from generation to generation – a tale of ancient times.

And Brill read of the wanderings of the caballero Hernando de Estrada and his armored pikemen, who dared the deserts of the Southwest when all was strange and unknown. There were some forty-odd soldiers, servants, and masters, at the beginning, the manuscript ran. There was the captain, de Estrada, and the priest, and young Juan Zavilla, and Don Santiago de Valdez – a mysterious nobleman who had been taken off a helplessly floating ship in the Caribbean Sea – all the others of the crew and passengers had died of plague, he had said, and he had cast their bodies overboard. So de Estrada had taken him aboard the ship that was bearing the expedition from Spain, and de Valdez joined them in their explorations.

Brill read something of their wanderings, told in the crude style of old Lopez, as the old Mexican's ancestors had handed down the tale for over three hundred years. The bare written words dimly reflected the terrific hardships the explorers had encountered – drouth, thirst, floods, the desert sandstorms, the spears of hostile redskins. But it was of another peril that old Lopez told – a grisly lurking horror that fell upon the lonely caravan wandering through the immensity of the wild. Man by man they fell and no man knew the slayer. Fear and black suspicion ate at the heart of the expedition like a canker, and their leader knew not where to turn. This they all knew: among them was a fiend in human form.

Men began to draw apart from each other, to scatter along the line of march, and this mutual suspicion, that sought security in solitude, made it easier for the fiend. The skeleton of the expedition staggered through the wilderness, lost, dazed and helpless, and still the unseen horror hung on their flanks, dragging down the stragglers, preying on drowsing sentries and sleeping men. And on the throat of each was found the wounds of pointed fangs that bled the victim white; so that the living knew with what manner of evil they had to deal. Men reeled through the wild, calling on the saints, or blaspheming in their terror, fighting frenziedly against sleep, until they fell with exhaustion and sleep stole on them with horror and death.

Suspicion centered on a great black man, a cannibal slave from Calabar. And they put him in chains. But young Juan Zavilla went the way of the rest, and then the priest was taken. But the priest fought off his fiendish assailant and lived long enough to gasp the demon's name to de Estrada. And Brill, shuddering and wide-eyed, read:

". . . And now it was evident to de Estrada that the good priest had spoken the truth, and the slayer was Don Santiago de Valdez, who was a vampire, an undead fiend, subsisting on the blood of the living. And de Estrada called to mind a certain foul nobleman who had lurked in the mountains of Castile since the days of the Moors, feeding off the blood of helpless victims which lent him a ghastly immortality. This nobleman had been driven forth; none knew where he had fled but it was evident that he and Don Santiago were the same man. He had fled Spain by ship, and de Estrada knew that the people of that ship had died, not by plague as the fiend had represented, but by the fangs of the vampire.

"De Estrada and the black man and the few soldiers who still lived went searching for him and found him stretched in bestial sleep in a clump of chaparral; full-gorged he was with human blood from his last victim. Now it is well known that a vampire, like a great serpent, when well gorged, falls into a deep sleep and may be taken without peril. But de Estrada was at a loss as to how to dispose of the monster, for how may the dead be slain? For a vampire is a man who has died long ago, yet is quick with a certain foul unlife.

"The men urged that the Caballero drive a stake through the fiend's heart and cut off his head, uttering the holy words that would crumple the long-dead body into dust, but the priest was dead and de Estrada feared that in the act the monster might waken.

"So they took Don Santiago, lifting him softly, and bore him to an old Indian mound near by. This they opened, taking forth the bones they found there, and they placed the vampire within and sealed up the mound – *Dios* grant until Judgment Day.

"It is a place accursed, and I wish I had starved elsewhere before I came into this part of the country seeking work – for I have known of the land and the creek and the mound with its terrible secret, ever since childhood; so you see, Señor Brill, why you must not open the mound and wake the fiend –"

There the manuscript ended with an erratic scratch of the pencil that tore the crumpled leaf.

Brill rose, his heart pounding wildly, his face bloodless, his tongue cleaving to his palate. He gagged and found words.

"That's why the spur was in the mound – one of them Spaniards dropped it while they was diggin' – and I mighta knowed it's been dug into before, the way the charcoal was scattered out – but, good God—"

Aghast he shrank from the black visions – an undead monster

stirring in the gloom of his tomb, thrusting from within to push aside the stone loosened by the pick of ignorance – a shadowy shape loping over the hill toward a light that betokened a human prey – a frightful long arm that crossed a dim-lighted window. . .

"It's madness!" he gasped. "Lopez was plumb loco! They ain't no such things as vampires! If they is, why didn't he get me first, instead of Lopez – unless he was scoutin' around, makin' sure of everything before he pounced? Aw, hell! It's all a pipe-dream—"

The words froze in his throat. At the window a face glared and gibbered soundlessly at him. Two icy eyes pierced his very soul. A shriek burst from his throat and that ghastly visage vanished. But the very air was permeated by the foul scent that had hung about the ancient mound. And now the door creaked – bent slowly inward. Brill backed up against the wall, his gun shaking in his hand. It did not occur to him to fire through the door; in his chaotic brain he had but one thought – that only that thin portal of wood separated him from some horror born out of the womb of night and gloom and the black past. His eyes were distended as he saw the door give, as he heard the staples of the bolt groan.

The door burst inward. Brill did not scream. His tongue was frozen to the roof of his mouth. His fear-glazed eyes took in the tall, vulture-like form – the icy eyes, the long black finger nails – the moldering garb, hideously ancient – the long spurred boot – the slouch hat with its crumbling feather – the flowing cloak that was falling to slow shreds. Framed in the black doorway crouched that abhorrent shape out of the past, and Brill's brain reeled. A savage cold radiated from the figure – the scent of moldering clay and charnel-house refuse. And then the undead came at the living like a swooping vulture.

Brill fired point-blank and saw a shred of rotten cloth fly from the Thing's breast. The vampire reeled beneath the impact of the heavy ball, then righted himself and came on with frightful speed. Brill reeled back against the wall with a choking cry, the gun falling from his nerveless hand. The black legends were true then – human weapons were powerless – for may a man kill one already dead for long centuries, as mortals die?

Then the claw-like hands at his throat roused the young cow-puncher to a frenzy of madness. As his pioneer ancestors fought hand to hand against brain-shattering odds, Steve Brill fought the cold dead crawling thing that sought his life and his soul.

Of that ghastly battle Brill never remembered much. It was a blind chaos in which he screamed beast-like, tore and slugged and hammered, where long black-nails like the talons of a panther tore at him, and pointed teeth snapped again and again at his throat. Rolling and tumbling about the room, both half enveloped by the musty folds of that ancient rotting cloak, they smote and tore at each other among the ruins of the shattered furniture, and the fury of the vampire was not more terrible than the fear-crazed desperation of his victim.

They crashed headlong into the table, knocking it down upon its side, and the coal oil lamp splintered on the floor, spraying the walls with sudden flame. Brill felt the bite of the burning oil that spattered him, but in the red frenzy of the fight he gave no heed. The black talons were tearing at him, the inhuman eyes burning icily into his soul; between his frantic fingers the withered flesh of the monster was hard as dry wood. And wave after wave of blind madness swept over Steve Brill. Like a man battling a nightmare he screamed and smote, while all about them the fire leaped up and caught at the walls and roof.

Through darting jets and licking tongues of flame they reeled and rolled like a demon and a mortal warring on the fire-lanced floors of hell. And in the growing tumult of the flames, Brill gathered himself for one last volcanic burst of frenzied strength. Breaking away and staggering up, gasping and bloody, he lunged blindly at the foul shape and caught it in a grip not even the vampire could break. And whirling his fiendish assailant bodily on high, he dashed him down across the uptilted edge of the fallen table as a man might break a stick of wood across his knee. Something cracked like a snapping branch and the vampire fell from Brill's grasp to writhe in a strange broken posture on the burning floor. Yet it was not dead, for its flaming eyes still burned on Brill with a ghastly hunger, and it strove to crawl toward him with its broken spine, as a dying snake crawls.

Brill, reeling and gasping, shook the blood from his eyes, and staggered blindly through the broken door. And as a man runs from the portals of hell, he ran stumblingly through the mesquite and chaparral until he fell from utter exhaustion. Looking back he saw the flame of the burning house and thanked God that it would burn until the very bones of Don Santiago de Valdez were utterly consumed and destroyed from the knowledge of men.

JAY LAKE

Fat Man

JAY LAKE LIVES IN PORTLAND, OREGON, with his books and two inept cats, where he works on numerous writing and editing projects, including the World Fantasy Award-nominated *Polyphony* anthology series from Wheatland Press.

His current novels are *Trial of Flowers* from Night Shade Books and *Mainspring* from Tor Books, with sequels to both books planned.

Lake is the winner of the 2004 John W. Campbell Award for Best New Writer and a multiple nominee for the Hugo and World Fantasy Awards.

" 'Fat Man' was written about five years after I'd relocated to the Pacific Northwest," the author explains. "I've always been fascinated by Forteana, and especially cryptozoology. Bigfoot is perhaps the world's second most famous cryptozooid, after Nessie.

"This is of course Bigfoot country up here, a land where history is still quite young and the kingdom of the trees still holds sway. There are patches of the Old Forest – you know the one – within a few miles of my house. I asked myself the question, what if Bigfoot isn't Bigfoot? What if he's the Old Forest talking back to the scars of history Westerners have only recently begun to blaze?

"'Fat Man' is my answer to that question."

CLINT AMOS AND HIS FRIEND Barley John Dimmitt stalked through the Mt. Hood National Forest, not far from Timothy Lake in southeast Clackamas County. They stalked quietly so as not to disturb the elk they hunted, but more to the point, so as not to disturb the forest rangers. Clint didn't hold with tags nor permits. Barley John generally agreed with Clint on most things. It made life easier for everyone involved.

The two of them hunted this division of the forest because most people avoided it. Hikers and campers had disappeared over the years; unlucky accidents befell loggers. There had been more than one lost child never found, even by legions of search-and-rescue trail runners. The Forest Service had quietly closed down the last of the managed trails about three years earlier, killing what little tourism their town of Sweden, Oregon, had still received. Even the most die-hard independent loggers now looked elsewhere for their cutting permits.

No trails was okay with Clint, though, because it meant fewer rangers, and no tourists messing up his hunt. No loggers was hard on the job situation, but he couldn't fix that.

They moved silently amid ranks of hemlocks and lodgepole pines. Rhododendrons grew in the burn breaks, and at the edges of the shadow along the ridges, but deeper in only the smaller plants struggled alongside the doomed offspring of their tall parents. The forest smelled of loam and tingly pine scent and the cold greyness of the mountain rock buried not far beneath their feet. Snow would be there soon, which made the elk easier to find but more difficult to hunt.

Barley John held out his hand, fingers spread down.

He'd heard something.

Clint would allow that while Barley John didn't have the sense God granted to a Canada goose, the man could hear grass growing. It made Barley John a hell of a hunting partner.

Clint crouched, his Ruger Deerfield carbine loose and ready in his hands. The position folded his substantial gut, but it was the only way he could pop up for a clean shot. He could hold it still for a while. Barley John might spot their prey, but Clint always got first shot. He usually got the clean kill, too.

Let it be a big mama elk, he thought, with some good meat for the coming months. They ain't either of them had a job in over a year, since Barger's Sawmill had closed, and his wife's pay had been cut twice at that auto parts place up in Estacada.

He didn't kill, they didn't eat.

Hell, no one in the whole town of Sweden had enough to eat without they went out and shot first. It was like to make a man mad at the government, raising taxes and taking jobs away all at the same time. Clint wasn't sure whether it was the Japs, the Chinese or the al-Qaeda, but somebody that had snuggled up to those damned Democrats had gone and stolen his job. Made his life hell, too.

He hadn't been old enough to serve, but he remembered Vietnam. This country should be so strong again. Sometimes taking a clean shot felt good. He could pretend it was someone whose death would make his life better.

Barley John made a clicking noise to get Clint's attention, then waved his hand to the right, two fingers now up. Clint swung his carbine to the four o'clock position relative to their line of travel and watched for movement. Barley John stepped quietly away, disappearing among the pines to find a covering position. Clint's partner would flush the elk, Clint would take his first shot, then Barley John would drop the animal if need be.

The light was pearly grey, prophesying snow. Clint felt time slow down like it always did when his finger was right on the trigger. Meat, sausage and steaks for the winter. Jobs. Slick Willie in his sights. He shouldered the carbine and slowed his breathing.

Somewhere further off to the right Barley John clicked again, louder this time, then tossed a rock. There was a flash of fur as the elk bolted and Clint took his shot, the old Ruger bucking against his shoulder even as he realised something was wrong.

He must have hit, because there was an unholy screech, like the sound of a really big eagle or hawk. Whatever it was – no elk, he was already certain – it went down in a thrashing of rhododendrons at the edge of a clearing.

"Damn!" shouted Barley John, breaking cover and sprinting toward the bushes. Clint was close behind him, moving fast for a big guy. They both pulled up short, thirty or forty feet from whatever they had hit.

"That weren't no elk," Clint said. "Bear, maybe."

"No. Looked more like an ape."

"Ain't no apes out—"

They stared at each other for a moment.

"Bigfoot," breathed Barley John, real quiet.

Clint nodded. It couldn't be true, could it? "Cover me," he whispered. "If it moves, plug it." Keeping the Ruger low and close to his body, he approached the bushes where a watery beam of sunlight had stabbed downward.

It was big, lying on its side, belly large as a bear's. Clint studied what he'd shot. Belly or not, it couldn't be a bear. Didn't have no fur as such. Rather, it was covered with stringy hair. There were hands and feet instead of paws. This thing also had ropy ridges of scar tissue on its knees and elbows, all around its fingers and toes.

This was the biggest fat man he'd ever seen. But no man was that huge. Clint estimated it at eight feet or more, at least five hundred pounds. Slowly he reached out and nudged it in the belly with the carbine's barrel.

No reaction.

He walked around the thing, noticing out of the corner of his eye that Barley John was still covering him.

"Big fella," Barley John said.

"Bigfoot. Like you figured." Clint poked its head with the carbine, just behind the ear. Nothing. Not even a twitch.

"Think he's still breathing?"

Clint snorted. "Think I'm putting my hands down there to find out? Bastard could fit a melon inside those damned jaws." He shouldered his carbine, his aim point wavering.

Barley John hefted his own weapon. "What you doing?"

"Checking," said Clint, and shot the enormous creature in the butt. It didn't twitch at all.

"Friend," Clint breathed, "I believe we may be on our way to fame and riches. This here's a real live Bigfoot."

"Actually," said Barley John in a rare show of independence, "this here's a real dead Bigfoot. I got just one question."

Clint was already imagining himself being interviewed on Jerry Springer or *20/20*, describing their arduous days-long hunt of the killer ape. "What's that?"

"How we going to haul this thing out here without we cut it up first?"

In the end they got the body back to Clint's old Wagoneer with a travois, a comealong, a hundred feet of rope and hours upon hours of cursing to cover four miles of trail with such a damned big deadweight load. An elk they'd have just skinned and field-dressed, hauling out in pieces.

It was dark by the time Clint wheeled the Jeep off the unmaintained Forest Service track and on to State Highway 224, the road that ran through the town of Sweden. Sweden's only road, in fact, except for some gravel lanes running back into the woods on each side of the highway. He pulled over and got out to unlock the front hubs and put the vehicle back into two-wheel drive. It was cold, with no moon, and his breath steamed in the starlight.

They'd lashed Bigfoot to the roof. Glancing up, Clint saw the wind stirring his kill's fur. Looked like the fingers had curled up on the drive out of the forest. Reflex action, he thought. Nobody and no thing took a bullet in the butt without flinching, not even knocked out cold.

Up and back into the truck, where Barley John was smoking a joint and staring into the woods.

"Put that thing away before we get home," Clint said. "Margie'll hate the smell on me as it is. She sees that joint flaring in the Jeep she'll lay into me like crows on summer wheat."

"You ain't the one smoking," Barley John answered mildly.

"Don't make no difference to her. Says we set a bad example for the kids."

Barley John took a deep drag, then carefully stubbed the joint out on the dashboard before slipping it into a pocket of his fatigue jacket. "Clint."

"Yeah?"

"I got a question."

"Shoot." Clint held on through a tight curve on 224. The load on the roof was so heavy the metal creaked, and it pulled the Jeep off balance.

"Did we do the right thing?"

"Does the Pope shit in the woods?" Clint glanced over at Barley John. His hunting partner looked positively distressed. That was unusual. "What do you mean?"

"It was like . . . shooting a man or something."

Clint laughed. "Just tell yourself he was a damned liberal traitor. You'll feel shitloads better."

Somehow explaining that to Barley John made *him* feel worse. They drove on into the darkness. After a few minutes, Clint said, "Mind if I take a quick pull off that joint?"

Sweden was a town of three hundred people, with a post office not much larger than a gas station restroom, and gas station not much bigger than that. There was an old truck stop, diesel pumps long since shut down and ripped out, that hosted Sweden's one halfway thriving business, the Fish Creek Café. Operating in a well-lit corner near the doors, the Café always seemed lost in the immensity of its own building, but it still had the huge walk-in coolers from busier days.

Clint pulled up in front of the restaurant to drop his load. Shelley Mendes who ran the place let folks use her coolers in exchange for a few cuts when someone made a run in to Estacada to have their meat processed. Sometimes people got ambitious and finished dressing their own kills on the concrete apron outside, but that tended to draw bears, so Shelley discouraged the practice.

It was almost nine o'clock when they lurched to a halt outside the Café. The lights were on within, with a few folks scattered around in the dozen booths or along the service counter. Clint noticed a Clackamas County sheriff's cruiser parked out front, the big Ford Crown Victoria gleaming among the collection of primer-coloured pickups and rusting Subarus normal for rural Oregon.

"Hell. Damerow's in there."

Clint and Barley John had gone to high school with Elise Damerow. Elise had been a hard-playing jockette then, who never seemed to date any of the boys, and had harboured an intense and dedicated dislike for Clint and his friends. All he ever did was tease her a little.

She hadn't changed much over the years, except for acquiring the badge and the gun and, recently, a tattooed girlfriend who lived in a tree house out in the National Forest somewhere. Certainly her dislike of Clint hadn't diminished at all.

"What are we going to do with him?" asked Barley John, thumping on the roof. "We ain't got no permits."

Clint grinned. "Ain't no such thing as a Bigfoot permit. But I'll park out back. We can go in, talk to Shelley, maybe *Deputy* Damerow will be on her way by the time we need to unload."

He killed the lights and drove around behind the Fish Eagle's building, stopping next to the dumpster. Then he and Barley John went inside.

"Evening, boys," said Shelley. She was a handsome girl, blonde streaking to silver over a comfortable figure a man could admire, widowed in Desert Storm and not much interested in close personal company after that. Clint had thrown a pass or two, times when Margie had been out of state visiting her sister. Shelley been nice enough about it, but there were some pass returns even Clint had little trouble receiving.

"Shelley." Clint nodded. Barley John just bobbed his head along with Clint, a silent echo.

She swiped at an imaginary dust spot on the counter. "What can I do for you? Coffee?"

"Yes, ma'am. Both our usuals." Barley John nodded again, though his lips moved slightly this time. "Might want to use your freezer." Clint leaned a little closer. "*Later*," he whispered, nodding toward the deputy who was getting up from her booth.

"You boys ever heard of permits?" Shelley asked with a smile.

Damerow walked up, hip slung out so her pistol was the most prominent part of her. Not that she had much else of prominence, in Clint's opinion. Thin as a fence rail and half as good looking. He had to admit, when the chips were down far enough to actually *need* a cop, he'd rather have Damerow coming around to help than anyone else, but otherwise he didn't have much use for the woman.

"See you had to park out back. Lot too crowded?" Her grey eyes glinted.

Clint shrugged. "You know how it is."

"Shoot something in season, it ought to have a tag. Shoot something out of season, well . . ." She laid some money down on the counter, pushed it toward Shelley. "Lucky for you boys I'm no game warden. Get it out of sight before I have to notice it."

"M-m-man's got to eat," said Barley John with the stutter Damerow always seemed to induce in him.

She smiled, chucked him under the chin. "What you eat should make you happy, Johnnie." With another glare at Clint, she headed out the door.

He watched until the cruiser pulled out on to 224, then turned back to pick up his coffee. Barley John was blushing red as Shelley's ketchup bottles.

"I do declare," Shelley said, closing Barley John's fingers around the second Styrofoam cup, "that woman likes you."

"He's always had a thing about dykes," said Clint.

Barley John stuttered into life again. "C-c-c-can't use that word n-n-no more."

"Women, then. You got a thing for manly women."

Shelley walked off, laughing into her dishrag.

Outside with Shelley's flatcar dolly, they unlashed the Bigfoot. Clint wasn't willing to cut or dress it, figuring the carcass was worth a lot more whole. The fingers had curled into a fist, he noticed. Clint rigged a comealong to one of the roof stanchions of the building, then used the Jeep's bumper winch to pull the Bigfoot off the roof, Barley John guiding the load onto the dolly.

After that they wheeled him inside.

Somebody in one of the booths yelped and Shelley turned to look. Her eyes narrowed to about the same degree Damerow had employed to glare Clint down. "What in the Nathan Hale is *that*, Clinton Amos?"

"Game we shot," he said, glancing around the Fish Creek. Walter Arnason had gotten up from his booth to get a better look, as had the Koiichi brothers. Clint was damned glad Damerow was gone.

"Game. Huh." She flicked her towel back and forth, thinking. "You been shooting gorillas in the mist, maybe. Whatever *that* is, I don't want no steaks off it."

Barley John grinned. "Ain't gonna be no steaks."

"John," Clint said with a warning lift in his voice.

"That's no bear," said Freddie Koiichi.

The six or seven people left in the Café were crowding around the flatbed dolly now.

"Bigfoot," Clint confessed.

Walter Arnason laughed. "Duh shit, Clint. You boys are gonna be famous."

"You called anybody yet?" That was Franky Koiichi putting his oar in.

"No, and I ain't gonna until I had time to think it over good. Don't none of you do me no favours in the mean time, okay?"

They all stared for a while at the massive body on the dolly. Shelley finally spoke up again. "You shoot it, Clint?"

He swelled with pride. "Yeppers."

"I spotted it," said Barley John.

What *had* gotten into that boy? Clint wondered. "Our kill," he said with a generosity he didn't feel.

"Sweden's kill," said Shelley. Her voice was decisive. "You put this thing in my freezer, the whole town has to stand to profit. I don't want your sorry fat ass running off to Portland or Seattle with the evidence. Folks are going to come here, eat my food, buy Koiichi's gas, and mail home postcards from our little post office. That all right with you, Mr Bigfoot Bigshot?"

Clint didn't have anywhere else to store the creature. He sure as hell wasn't taking it home to Margie. He looked around the room. Seven pairs eyes looked back. None of them made much money, half of them didn't have jobs at all. Himself included.

"Damn, I hate being public spirited without a reward in the bargain," Clint said slowly, enjoying his moment. "But I'll hold title – I mean, me and Barley John will hold title. I promise, whatever we make of this stays in Sweden."

Everybody in the Fish Creek Café shook on that, like a round of toasts at New Year's. They wheeled the dolly into the number three freezer, which Shelley turned way down cold just for the occasion before sharing out celebratory beers on the house.

Around midnight Clint dropped Barley John off at the little rusted-out Airstream trailer tucked in the freezing damp woods, Then he went home to his huge, rotting A-frame at the edge of town – a converted visitor's lodge from the 1940s – to explain to his wife what he had done.

Breakfast was tense. Margie slapped down Krust-Eze hotcakes and glared Clint Junior, Suzanne and no-longer-baby Hobson out the door to the school bus while Clint groaned through a headache composed of equal parts mild hangover and lack of sleep from being kicked out of bed at six in the morning. He managed a kiss for Hobson and quick hug for Suzanne. Clint Junior just dodged a punch on the arm, too old for his dad.

Then Margie pulled up a chair for herself and tucked into another stack of hotcakes with the same two strips of bacon the family economy allowed each of the children. Clint listened to the clink of her fork and smelled the cloying smudge of her syrup in wounded silence. They never had spoken last night.

That made him a little sad.

"Elise called," Margie finally said. The tines of her fork were squeaking on the empty plate now, pushing dollops of syrup around. "Yesterday evening."

Elise? Damerow, he realised. She was talking about the deputy.

"Said you and Johnnie had been out poaching again."

"You want to eat this winter?" he asked mildly, though angry words boiled inside of him. He was too tired to let them out. "Besides, it wasn't poaching."

"What the hell was it, then? You find enough religion to get honest with a hunting license?"

"No. I shot . . . something that ain't covered by the Department of Fish and Wildlife."

Margie stared at him, her face somewhere between angry and desperate. He remembered how pretty she'd been twenty years back. Hell, she was still pretty now under all the weight and chopped-short easy-to-care-for hair and them ugly, stretchy Wal-Mart clothes bought up in the city.

"What," she finally asked. "You shoot a space alien or something?"

"Bigfoot," he said proudly.

"Bigfoot?" She sounded like she'd never heard the word before.

"Bigfoot. And I do mean *big*."

"Jesus, Clint." Margie shook her head, tears standing in her eyes. "You were either drunk or stupid, or both. For the love of God, if you're gonna go poach, poach something I can cook."

"Barley John was there when I killed it," he said, defensive. "Shelley seen it when I brought it in. Walter Arnason and the Koiichis too."

"A real Bigfoot?"

"Real as they come."

"What are you going to do?"

"Call a press conference." He grinned. "Go big. Charge admission. Make some money." Clint reached across the table, took his wife's hand. "Big money, Margie. This'll be bigger than . . . than . . . I don't know. It will be like the Super Bowl come to Sweden, Oregon, and we'll own the winning team."

She burst into tears, somehow looking prettier than ever.

There were a lot of people at the Fish Creek Café that afternoon when Clint pulled up to check on his kill. A whole lot of people.

He had to park out back for real.

Every booth was full inside, and most of the seats taken at the counter. Some of the folks were regulars, but a lot were people he saw only once in a while, at Koiichi's buying gas, or maybe passed by on the road to Estacada to do some city shopping. A few he didn't recognise at all.

Shelley was flying back and forth behind the counter. She actually had help, which she hadn't been able to afford since the mill closed and took the last of Sweden's steady jobs with it. Clint stared at the cook, who looked familiar but out-of-place, until he realised it was Damerow's tree-hugger girlfriend, skinnier than Damerow was, her head shaved, with sea-green tattoos on her face and a big silver barbell coming out of both sides of her nose.

"Damn lot of people in here," he grumbled at Shelley when she stopped in front of his seat at the counter.

"Three people can't keep a secret unless two of them are dead," she said. "Besides, this is good for business. Whole town profits, right? We shook on it."

"Yeah, we did." He shook his head. "Coffee, when you get a minute. I came by to have a look, but I don't want to crack open number three freezer with all these folks here."

She sounded exasperated, just like Margie. "What do you think these folks are here *for*?"

He sipped at his coffee and thought that one over for a little while. Publicity was good, but they couldn't just start letting mobs in.

This wasn't a mob, though. Maybe he could do something. Definitely no cameras. The photo rights would be worth a lot. Millions.

Could he trust Shelley? Clint really wanted to ask her to let him put a lock on the number three freezer, but he had a good idea what she'd say to him. He wouldn't like having to find a new home for the Bigfoot.

Trust.

"Alrightie," Clint said, standing up and stretching. He felt as fake as he had the first time he'd oh-so-casual-like put his arm around Margie, back in the day. The diner had gone quiet as a schoolhouse in summer. "I'm gonna check on number three."

He walked around the counter and into the kitchen.

"Clint."

It was Shelley.

He turned to see a whole crowd standing behind her, massed at the counter as if waiting to start a race.

"You want to come look," he said, uncomfortable but knowing he had to play it Shelley's way, "come look. Two rules." He stuck up his fingers. "Only if I know you. And no talking to the press. The whole town's got to be together on this one."

There was some muttering, but Shelley nodded.

He went back to number three. The handle was popped loose. Somebody had opened the freezer before he got here, sometime since last night. Clint almost said something, but he didn't want to lose the goodwill of the moment. Besides, it had to be Shelley. She wouldn't have let anyone else in back here, except maybe that little slip of a cook she'd suddenly hired.

Which meant Damerow knew, he realised.

Clint tugged the handle open. The lights flickered on inside. Bigfoot lay where they'd left him last night, still on the dolly, his hair all frosty. People pushed in behind Clint, filing into the freezer like they were going to a funeral home viewing. He stopped one man, a big redhead in a chequered shirt.

"Do I know you, friend?" Clint asked. "We ain't open for the public yet."

"Worked the mill together back in ninety-two, ninety-three," the redhead said. "I drove the log lifter out in the loading yard. Moved on downstate."

"Why you back today?"

The redhead grinned, nodded at the Bigfoot. "Wouldn't you come back for this?"

After that, Clint gave up checking people. He just watched for cameras in their hands, or flashes going off.

They were all crowded around the body in a circle, still in that funeral way, when the comments began. Just like a memorial.

"Big fella," said Janie Watkins who lived with her deaf husband a couple of mileposts northwest of town in a cabin older than anything else in this part of the county.

"Didn't die happy," observed the redhead from downstate.

"Didn't live happy, neither." That was Walter Arnason, back for more after the previous night. "Look at them scars. Like someone worked him over with a k-bar a long time ago."

They went on that way, commenting on his size, details of his body, like high school students dissecting their class frog. Finally Clint cleared his throat. "It's cold in here, folks. Let's let him rest while me and Shelley work out our press strategy." He was proud of that line.

"What are you going to call him?" asked Janie.

"Swedish Steve," said Clint without even thinking about it.

"Goodbye, Swedish Steve," she said before leaving. Everyone else repeated the line on their way out, until it was only Clint and Shelley left.

"I guess half the state knows now," he said.

Her smile was hard. "Better get to work on your *press strategy* then, Clint."

Clint looked back at Swedish Steve. The corpse's hands were open flat now. He was certain they'd been fists the night before.

He spent all afternoon at home trying to write out his pitch. Clint knew he'd have to find someone pretty big, fast, to get behind this. Michael Jackson would dig it, but no way he was going near that cross-raced freak. There were some good Oregon conservatives he liked, like that hotel guy Hemstreet, but Clint figured he needed someone from the press, or Hollywood.

No matter who, he had to have a good pitch to deliver when he got his prospective sponsor on the phone. Clint had seen enough TV shows about people who won the lottery or whatever then lost it all on investment scams and greedy relatives. He didn't want to just go to the papers or the TV stations. He needed his Mr Big.

Margie wouldn't get off work until seven, be home until later, so Clint was by himself with the kids came in around four. Clint Junior – a junior in high school – banged open the door and flopped out on the couch with a burp. Suzanne – seventh grade – followed him in with a flip of her hair and a drama queen sigh before disappearing into her room.

Clint waited for Hobson, but his youngest – third grade – didn't follow.

"Where's your brother?" he asked Clint Junior.

"What brother?"

"*Junior.*"

"Oh, you mean my baby *bother*." Clint Junior grinned. "He got off the bus same us up by the Fish Creek. Went kiting off into the woods with that freakazoid friend of his."

The "freakazoid" was Barley John's nephew, Tyler Dimmitt Stephens. Tyler was a chip off the old barleycorn, which Clint didn't figure was good for the kid's future, but Barley John's nephew got along with Hobson like kerosene and matches.

"He's supposed to come home first," Clint grumbled. "House rules."

"I ain't his keeper." Clint Junior flopped open a math book and pretended to study.

Clint didn't feel like arguing the point. He fetched his coat and stepped out the front door to go look for his youngest son. Hobson and Tyler had no more sense of time than a jaybird did, and it was close to dark.

Outside had the crisp, clear feeling of snow about to fall. The sky was pearly grey again, and the wind worried at the collar of his corduroy coat. Clint briefly wished he'd grabbed his field jacket instead, but he figured a quick walk up to the Fish Creek Café to shout into the woods would serve. He lived about half-a-mile southeast of the town centre, so the distance was just right for a warm-up. As he walked, he hollered, "Tyler! Hobson! Come on in, boys."

There was no sign of the kids by the time he'd made it to the Café, so he stuck his head in the door. Shelley wasn't there, but Damerow's weirdo girlfriend still was working behind the counter. It was still busier than normal.

Was she showing people the freezer? He wondered how much profit Shelley could pull into her own pocket off Swedish Steve without him knowing it. Clint realised he'd have to start spending his days down at the Café, have the kids meet him here when they got off the bus.

"You seen Tyler and Hobson?" he asked the girlfriend.

"Nope."

"Two little kids," he added. "Got off the bus maybe half an hour ago."

"Nope."

"Shelley here?"

"Nope."

"You know how to say anything else?"

She shot him the finger. "Nope."

He fingered her back, then went stomping around in the woods that lined the Fish Creek's huge parking lot on the southeast side.

On the northwest, it kind of gravelled over to Koiichi's gas station, then to the Post Office. If they'd run into the woods, as Clint Junior had said, it was here.

Twenty minutes later, after a stop at Tyler's house confirmed Barley John's sister hadn't seen the boys either, Clint was back at the Fish Creek Café. It was already getting twilight, and he was worried. He banged open the door again. There were a bunch of people inside, maybe half of them locals.

"I don't mean to raise a panic," he said "but there's a couple of boys missing out there, and I'm hoping some of you folks can come walk the woods and help me search."

"Aw, shit," someone groaned, but the vinyl booths creaked as everyone in the restaurant got up in a hurry. The girlfriend went for the telephone. Calling Damerow, Clint figured, but right about now that was probably a good idea.

"Any of you got flashlights in your trucks, please get 'em out," he called. "It's darker than the inside of a racoon's ass out there once the sun goes down."

The girlfriend brought him a Mag-Lite from behind the counter, one of those five-battery police special skullbreakers.

"Thanks."

"I called Elise, and Shelley," she said. Then, "Sorry about your kid."

"What do you mean, *sorry*?" he asked, instantly suspicious. And where the hell was Shelley, anyway? a little voice in the back of his head wondered.

She shot him the finger again. "Sorry he's lost. Sorry he's got a loser fuckface like you for a dad."

Clint was shaking with rage then, all in a moment, but he knew better than to slap her down in a room full of worried people. "Come on," he shouted. "We got to go."

They poured out of the café, splitting up in different directions, calling the kids' names. Clint's heart felt like a fist in his chest, straining to get out. When he ran into Clint Junior in the parking lot, he gave his older son a bone-cracking hug.

"Easy, dad," Clint Junior said in a soft voice. "Little bother's just off playing with a bird's nest or something."

Neither of them believed it.

* * *

By the time Margie's old Plymouth Arrow came straining up the highway, around 7:40 pm, the whole town was out. Damerow had arrived shortly after the search was launched, and tried to call for back-up, but a bank robbery at the other end of the country in Portland's outskirts had tied up all available units. She did get the fire district people out, and a promise from the Forest Service to send rangers. They hadn't shown yet.

Clint didn't want to talk to the Forest Service, not one tiny bit, but he wanted his boy back a whole lot more. It was already below freezing out here and people were starting to say the word "bodies" when they should have been saying "kids".

Margie's Arrow slowed as it passed the Post Office and Koiichi's, then pulled over in front of the Fish Creek Café. The lot was completely full. Clint watched her get out, ask someone what was going on, and be pointed toward him.

He wanted to run away, right then, more than anything he'd ever wanted in his life. He couldn't face his wife and tell her he'd lost their baby boy. Clint knew that all Margie's toughness would be gone like piss in the wind with the news.

He knew he'd be the one to kill her with the words.

Margie walked up to where Clint stood in the glare of one of the Café's security lights. Her face was already a crumpled mess, like God's laundry basket.

"Honey," he said slowly. "We'll find him."

"I . . . he . . ." Her words wouldn't come, stuck in her mouth like taffy.

"Everyone's on it," Clint told her, his voice tightening as he spoke. "We've been stopping every car that passes through, getting them to help. The whole damned town of Sweden's out here, Margie."

"Hob . . . Hob . . ." She gulped for air, dying as surely as any hard-landed rainbow trout. "Hobson."

He opened up his arms and folded in her tears. They stood in the frigid air, bodies shaking together, while people shouted and called and played lights in the trees all around them, as far as Clint could see. Farther, he hoped. All the way to the end of the world.

Half-an-hour or so later, Margie was inside having coffee and crying with Shelley. Clint stayed out in the cold. He wanted to search, badly, but Damerow had ordered him to remain at the Fish Creek. "We've got to find *you* when we find him," she'd said.

Clint had done fire district search-and-rescue work off and on since he was a teenager. He knew the rules. Still he punished himself by waiting in the cold, refusing Shelley's coffee, as uncomfortable as any of the searchers.

As uncomfortable as Hobson or Tyler.

Barley John came sidling up out of the darkness, a fading flashlight in his hand. In the distance, people were shouting. "Clint," he said. "You'd better come on."

Clint knew without asking that this wasn't good.

He followed Barley John into the woods, onto the gravel track where Barley John's sister's trailer was, and maybe another dozen families beyond her. Further down they cut off the track into wooded darkness marked only by a swarm of flashlights. From behind him, Clint heard the grumble of the fire district's old Power Wagon rescue truck.

Whatever it was, they needed the truck for it. That was even worse than not good.

Barley John led Clint to a little crowd of people pointing their flashlights up into a Douglas fir. The lowest branches were forty feet off the ground. A little higher, there was something pale.

"The dog was barking," someone said, the crowd beginning to tell Clint the story in dozens of voices. "My boy heard something." "She never comes out here." "It was like wind said my name." "Who looks up in the woods?" "Walked past here a dozen times." "How would anyone get up there?" "Blood dripping down the tree trunk." "Must have been a wolf." "An eagle." "Bigfoot's revenge."

Then the Dodge was there, easing between the trees, and men were unbolting a ladder and laying it against the tree and strapping on climbing spikes and arranging safety ropes and ascending the bark and shouting and calling for the stretcher and it was like all the time in Clint's life had collected in this one moment, a huge bank of time teetering on the edge of a cliff, an avalanche that would sweep away all the rest of his days in a tide of grief and rage and pain.

The rope came down with the stretcher and there was one tiny body strapped in tight under blankets and people caught it. Clint pushed forward, but it was Stephanie Dimmitt who never would marry Bart Stephens because she didn't want to be Stephanie Stephens who threw herself on the bloodied blankets and wailed. Tyler Dimmitt Stephens lay there, his face swollen, his scalp torn, the colour of a ice cube with lips as dark blue as Clint's jeans.

"What about Hobson?" he asked, but nobody heard.

Tyler's eyes fluttered open, a blue as icy as his lips though Clint would have sworn they were brown like his uncle's, and Tyler said in a clear, piercing voice, "Monkey, it was the monkey." He threw up on the blankets, a mix of bile and blood, and began to shiver violently.

The fire district people shoved Tyler in the back of the Power Wagon and backed out, already shouting into their radio for a medevac flight.

A few minutes later, Clint was almost alone. With a dull echo of surprise, he realised he was standing next to Damerow.

"Hobson's close by," she told him. "Whatever sick fuck did this, he can't have gone too far. You started the search quickly enough." Damerow put her arm across his shoulders, which didn't even feel weird to Clint even though she was dyke or whatever he was supposed to call her now. "You did the right thing, Clint. You didn't do anything wrong."

Then the steam of her breath carried her away, chattering into a walkie-talkie, redirecting people and equipment like Eisenhower at Normandy.

After a while, Clint walked back to the Fish Creek Café. He wanted to look inside number three, see if Swedish Steve was still there. He really wanted to see if there was blood on Swedish Steve's hands.

When he got there, Damerow was standing outside the big aluminium door with a digital camera in her hand.

"Figured you'd be along," she said. "I want a look. Care to fess up?"

Clint nodded, tugged open the door. They stepped inside, and he began to tell the story. It was clear Damerow had already heard it, but he told her everything he knew anyway, except the part about the freezer door being loose and the hands changing around. He didn't want to sound crazy.

There was no blood on Swedish Steve's hands, but the right one had two fingers extended, like a V-for-victory. Clint figured it was Damerow's girlfriend mindfucking him, but he wasn't about to say that to the deputy either.

The Fish Creek Café stayed open all night, as home base for the search for Hobson. Clint finally decided to keep indoors, to watch the number three freezer, he told himself. But there was coffee, and company, and occasional kindness. Margie was long gone, swallowed up in that mysterious sisterhood of grieving women. Clint wondered half-seriously if he was ever going to see her again, either.

Clint Junior insisted on staying out with the search parties, while Suzanne had ridden off to the hospital in Portland in the helicopter with Stephanie and Tyler.

That left Clint alone, even when a group bustled in for coffee and burgers and a restroom stop. He gathered from the gossip that Damerow had split the searchers, keeping one half on a wide-ranging spiral, while the other half worked close around the tree where Tyler had been found. They'd maybe located a blood slick near the tree, but it would be tomorrow at the earliest before there could be any reliable crime lab work on that.

Damerow came in around 3:00 am. She was tired, pale, her skin almost green. "Bad news, Clint," she said, sitting down opposite him and blowing on her hands to warm them.

"What isn't?"

"Hospital called. They did typing on the blood on Tyler's face and clothes. Not real forensics work, mind you, but there was plenty to go around, you should pardon my bluntness. Mix of two types. Tyler's a B negative. You wouldn't happen to know if Hobson's an AB positive, would you?"

"Hello no," said Clint, "I've got no idea. Margie might know." He sighed, a long, shuddering sob of a sigh. "But I'd bet both nuts it's his blood. Whose else would it be?"

"An attacker's," she said, but her face was almost frozen in her lack of expression. Damerow wasn't giving much away right now. "The book says you're suspect number one, but you've got no cuts or bruises, sure as hell not enough to bleed as much as Tyler had on him. Besides which, I've known you longer than I've had my tits. You're a jerk, and an oaf, and you're mean to your wife and shiftless in the bargain, but you'd no more kill a kid than you would fly to the moon on gossamer wings. Beyond that, you'd *have* to be able to fly to put Tyler fifty feet up a Doug fir."

"Well, I can't fly." Clint's voice was flat as an old tire.

"Neither can anyone else. It's what we call a little forensics problem. More to the point, you've got an alibi tight as anyone else's. You left your other kids at home ten minutes before people here saw you hollering for help. No way you ran around in the woods, slaughtered two kids, climbed a tree, cleaned up and got back here that fast."

It didn't surprise him that she'd been talking to witnesses. It shouldn't – it was her job. "So who put him up that tree?"

"Some psycho with a ladder and a hell of a lot of nerve. If I knew who," Damerow said "I'd know where Hobson is."

"Hobson's body," said Clint.

"That's still Hobson." She stood up, patted him on the shoulder, then leaned over and kissed his head.

"Wait."

"What? You going to confess and ruin all my good police-work?"

"No. But it was him. Swedish Steve."

"The *Bigfoot*? He's dead, Clint. You've been up too long."

"He got out before. I found the door loose this morning, on number three. And his hands . . . they're different every time I look at them."

"Come on, big boy." She grabbed Clint's shoulder, dragged him to his feet. "Let's go look."

The fingers of Swedish Steve were still in a vee. Damerow took more pictures, then got some Scotch tape from beneath the counter and sealed the door at the top, middle and bottom, taping one of her business cards on the handle. "Somebody sneaks in, they'll miss the top tape," she told Clint.

"What have you told the sheriff about Swedish Steve?" he asked.

"Nothing, yet. I don't want to come off like a loony tune here. But the County Attorney's going to be all over this child abduction as soon as it hits the paper in Portland, and I'm going to have to come clean before it looks like I've been hiding evidence." She grimaced. "You want a big score, you've got another eight to twelve hours to make it. In the mean time, keep your sorry ass in here where plenty of people can see you."

She went back outside, to the miserable cold of the search for whatever was left of his youngest. He went back to his booth and cried for a while.

Later, the kid-sized hole in his heart was really getting to Clint, and the coffee had stopped helping much. He figured a little cold air would brace him up, so with a nod to the girlfriend behind the counter, he stepped outside.

There were still lights in the woods, and people calling his son's name. Every direction, both sides of the highway, like little fireflies. He stood shivering, wondering what he could do. Should do. Should have done.

It couldn't be the damned Bigfoot. It had to be, but it couldn't. Who got up from a freezer, with three bullets in them, and ran around behind everybody's back?

He should be out there, should be one of them fireflies. Hobson would hear his daddy's voice instead of some strangers'. Clint knew the kid like no one else but Margie did. He'd recognise the kind of hidey-hole that would appeal to Hobson, running from whatever fucking psycho had sliced up Tyler so bad.

Dead or alive, no one could find Clint's kid better than Clint could.

Tugging his cap down over his forehead, Clint lurched off into the woods, heading toward where Tyler had been found. Damerow had been right. Stood to reason the kid would have run from that point. He was so tired he nearly stumbled with every step, and the cold cramped him up something fierce, but Clint figured that was God's way of telling him he should have kept a better eye on the boy.

What else could he have done?

Clint wasn't sure where he was any more. He'd lived in Sweden all his life, never been lost once, but this was different. One second he'd swear he was waist-deep in snow that hadn't come yet, the next he was almost summer warm. He didn't recognise the trees, either.

There were still voices, though. He tried to follow them. He couldn't quite make them out. Some funny singsong language – the Koiichi brothers talking Japanese to each other?

"Hobson," he croaked. Maybe it was his son.

Then he heard that eagle screech again, just like it had before he'd shot the Bigfoot. Clint stumbled, throwing out one hand against a pine to catch himself, and had a vision of a little skiff on a river, a huge bearded man firing some old-fashioned pistol up at him, as if he was in the air. A campsite burned along the riverbank, people in furs lying faced-down in the water.

He stumbled again, collapsed into some blackberry canes that tore at his clothes. The bearded man was screaming now, cursing in some other language, while the skiff turned sideways and his pistol tumbled away to the river below and the biggest God-damned osprey Clint had ever imagined in his life beat great, slow wings that sounded like a dying man's heart, its enormous claws dug deep into the bearded man's shoulders.

Right where Swedish Steve had big scars.

Clint gasped as flat-faced women smeared with bear grease sawed at his joints and tendons with sharpened clamshells, then woke up screaming to a flashlight in his face.

"Buddy, we'd better get you back inside," said Barley John, looking sadder than Clint had ever seen him.

Someone shook Clint's shoulder, hard. His head jerked violently. A cup tumbled with the motion. Cold coffee sprayed in his face and hair.

"I'm awake," he said, almost shouting.

"Are you Clinton Gerald Amos?"

Sitting up, Clint rubbed his eyes. A tall man in a trench coat, with a narrow black tie and Ray Bans, stared down at him. Early morning sunlight glared in the windows of the Fish Creek Café, making Clint squint. The guy was a near ringer for Agent Mulder from that TV show.

"What the hell are you?"

The tall man frowned. "I'm with the Paranormal Investigation Bureau."

"Para . . ." Clint rubbed his eyes again. "What the fuck? Get away from me, you fruitcake."

The tall man knelt, bringing him almost face to face with Clint. "We're a private foundation sir, investigating paranormal incidences. Ah, *X Files* material, if you will. Except in real life. We also compensate handsomely for verifiable information."

"Do you *compensate handsomely* for missing children?" Clint asked, his voice getting nasty. This was the first person he'd spoken with since Hobson had disappeared who he could legitimately punch out.

"Children?" The Paranormal guy looked surprised. "I'm here about your Bigfoot."

Clint jumped up out of the booth, grabbed the glass cylinder of sugar, and took a hard swing. His visitor ducked the punch and began backing off, as a couple of other people came up out of their booths, intent on stopping the fight.

The door banged open so hard the glass cracked. "Clint Amos, get your ass out here *now*!"

It was Damerow, another deputy with her who Clint didn't recognise, big fella with a red face and beefy lips. Franky Koiichi and Bob Watkins were already backing Paranormal guy into a corner as Clint walked out into the frigid morning.

Damerow stabbed him in the chest with her fingertip. "Do you have *any* fucking idea where Stacey Kamerone is right now?"

"What?" Stacey Kamerone was the teenaged daughter of the postmistress.

"She was missing from her room when her mother went to wake her up this morning. Window was open, a little blood on the sill." The finger stabbed again. "*Three* fucking kids in less than twenty-four hours, in *my* town, and you started it somehow. And Sunfire tells me you fucking left the café last night after I fucking told you to stay the fuck *put*!"

"Elise," said the other deputy, grabbing her elbow.

Damerow took her finger off Clint's chest. "Where the hell is she, Clint?"

"You check the freezer?"

"God damn it, Clint, I will shoot you where you stand if you are fucking with—"

"*Deputy* Damerow!" barked the other deputy in a voice southern as corn pone. "That is *enough*!"

"It wasn't me and you know it," Clint said, his voice low and urgent. "Check the Goddamned freezer. Take Deputy Dawg here with you."

She looked ready to slug him, but she kept her voice down. "I know it wasn't you, shithead, but I can't prove it because you left the Goddamned café!"

"So what's in the freezer, Damerow?" asked the other deputy.

"You wouldn't believe it if you saw it," muttered Damerow, "but it doesn't have anything to do with these kids."

"I'd like to judge that for myself."

Damerow shot Clint a look that probably should have wounded him, then the trio trailed back to the number three freezer.

"Got your card on the door," said the new deputy, Rohan – Clint had finally puzzled out his name tag.

"Tape's broken," Damerow said in a smaller voice. She glanced at Clint. "Who's been in here?"

"Hell if I know. I fell asleep."

"Some fucking father you—"

"*Damerow!*" shouted Rohan. "Enough!"

Damerow got quiet, tugged her digital camera out of her coat pocket, and took shots of the snapped open tape on the freezer door. Whoever it had been hadn't even tried to set the tape back in place.

When they walked in, Swedish Steve's right hand had three fingers extended.

Damerow was somewhere else, and Rohan was sweating Clint inside Shelley's tiny office.

"Listen to me," the big deputy said. "I know you've got alibis. I know you've been in here since yesterday. But you walked out last night, which means all that good cover is gone.

"You're friends with half this shithole town, and anyone of them could lie their asses off for you and I'll never know. But you listen to me, Amos. When they realise exactly what you've done, what kind of person you really are, they're going to stop covering for you. Give it up now, and maybe this nightmare will be over sooner. Because I promise you, it will end one way or the other."

Clint stared up at Rohan, his eyes red and rimmed with hot, sandy crap. "You can keep asking me the questions, but the truth ain't changing. It's my fucking kid that's missing, Deputy. What am I covering for? What the hell am I hiding?"

"You tell me, Amos. You're the one hiding the kids from us."

Clint jumped up, banging his head on a shelf and sending a row of computer and food service manuals flying. "How the *fuck* did I kidnap Stacy Kamerone, smart guy? Am I identical twins? Did I fucking hypnotise everybody in this town? Sure I was out for a while, but I came back. I was sleeping in the restaurant booth until Paranormal boy woke me up. Right in plain sight of everybody."

Rohan grabbed Clint's shirt front, murder in his piggy eyes, when the office door opened. "A word with you, deputy," said a tall Hispanic woman in civilian clothes. She laid one hand on Rohan's arm, showing him a badge with the other.

Rohan dropped Clint and backed out. His face promised further retribution. Another civilian, a small black guy in a fruity sweater with reindeer woven into the pattern, stepped into the door. "Agent Moran, FBI, from the Portland field office," he said.

"Thanks for pulling that maniac off me."

"Deputy Rohan was doing what he thought best, I'm sure," said Moran.

Clint was suddenly bone-tired. Soul tired. "And what do you think best?"

"Walk the ground with me, Mr Amos, if you would."

Clint followed Moran out, past Deputy Rohan being read the riot act by Moran's partner, and into the cold morning of a world without his son.

They walked without talking until they reached the tree where Tyler had been found. It was surrounded by police tape, which Moran brushed past. He and Clint stared upward.

"Don't do a lot of tree forensics," Moran said. "Except once in a while on logging cases. Spiking and what all."

His tone was conversational, even friendly, but Clint refused to be drawn in. "I guess not."

"How would you climb this tree, Mr Amos?"

Clint stared up forty feet of branchless trunk to where the canopy began to spread wide. It wasn't even all that high, as Douglas firs went. "I wouldn't."

"But if you had to."

He shrugged. "Get a bucket truck, I guess."

"Climbing spikes, ropes . . .?" The agent's voice was gentle.

"Look at me, Moran." Clint patted his belly. "I'm seventy, eighty pounds overweight, well past forty. I couldn't climb this tree if my butt was on fire and there was water at the top."

"I believe you, Mr Amos. That's the sad part."

"Sad?"

"Because if you *could* climb this tree, this whole nasty business would be over."

"Damerow said as much last night."

"Deputy Damerow's well past the end of her rope right now. However, I have already developed considerable respect for that woman." Moran paused, as if considering his words. "But you know, don't you?"

"Yes." Clint's shoulders shook as sobs overtook him again. The scars on Swedish Steve matched the places where those Indian women had been cutting on him in his dream. Matched where the osprey had grabbed that great bear of a man. "Bigfoot. I shot the Bigfoot, and somehow he's doing this in return."

"The body in the freezer? He has more witnesses to his good behaviour than you do to yours, Mr Amos. In a bulky coat, you might pass unremarked. That person, thing, whatever it is, would be noticed by a blind man."

"You'd think," said Clint quietly. "But Tyler said something about monkeys. And that's what Swedish Steve is. A big, giant, killer monkey."

Something rattled behind them, that Clint belatedly recognised as gunfire. He was only two or three steps after Moran in heading back for the Fish Creek Café.

* * *

"It was a monkey," shouted Freddie Koiichi. "Outside Walter's house. Just like the kid said."

There was a group of people in the parking lot, angry, a lot of them with pistols and rifles. Deputy Rohan and the Hispanic FBI agent were there, looking very unhappy.

"What the hell happened?" Clint said.

The crowd crystallised around him. Most of them were from Sweden, most of them knew him, knew that his kid had been the first to go. "A monkey," Freddie repeated. "Trying to climb into Walter Arnason's back bedroom."

"His kid Bobby was in there getting ready for school," someone else shouted.

"Well," asked Clint, "did you hit it?"

Somebody laughed, sharp and nervous. "Shot at it," muttered Freddie. "So did a couple of the guys."

Rohan looked disgusted. "They blew out the window and winged the kid."

Damerow stalked out of the Fish Creek Café, walked over to Clint and Agent Moran. She looked like hammered shit, and sounded like it too as she said "I've got to show you something."

"Not now," said Clint.

"It's something that means I believe you."

He glanced at Moran, whose face was impassive. "Fine," Clint said, and stepped away from the crowd as Deputy Rohan began to harangue them, threatening the whole lot with arrest.

She pulled out her digital camera and flipped it over to the little preview screen. "Look here," Damerow said. "I just took this picture."

It showed Swedish Steve lying in the freezer.

The deputy flipped the little menu button a number of times. "Now look here. My first picture."

Swedish Steve again.

"What's the point?" asked Clint.

Moran frowned. "He looks different."

"He's *thinner* now."

Clint was ready to explode. "How the *fuck* is that possible?" He whirled, charged at Freddie Koiichi. "Give me your pistol, Freddie, *now*!"

Unnerved, Freddie handed the Glock 9 mm to Clint.

"Is this thing ready to fire?" Clint asked.

"Hey there," said Rohan, but Moran touched his arm.

Freddie took the pistol back, worked the slide, and returned it to Clint. Clint headed for the Fish Creek Café, trailing Moran, Damerow, Rohan, the other FBI agent and a dozen of his fellow Swedes. Gun in front, he moved through the door, past the girlfriend back at the counter and back to the number three freezer.

He stopped there, taking a deep breath. "Somehow that fucker in there is doing this to our kids," Clint announced. "I'm going to put four or five into his head and stop him for good and all."

Rohan really didn't like that, but Moran had a firm hand on the deputy now. Damerow looked ready to shoot either Clint or the Bigfoot. Everyone else just looked scared.

Not knowing what else to do, Clint yanked the freezer door open.

Swedish Steve lay inside, right where they'd left him. His left hand had four fingers up now. "Somebody else is missing," Clint said with sick certainty.

"Rohan," barked Moran and Damerow almost in unison.

Clint heard the deputy's footfalls echoing away. He lifted the Glock, pointed it at Swedish Steve's temple, and rested his finger on the trigger.

Something was wrong, he realised. He had a flashback to the Indian women, cutting away by firelight at the soft places of some man's body. His body, at least in that dream or vision or whatever it had been.

This wasn't the right thing to do. Somehow, Clint knew that. Then he thought of Hobson, and realised he didn't care. He took a deep breath and pulled the trigger.

All hell broke loose and then some. The bullet shattered Swedish Steve's frozen left temple, spraying Clint and Moran with crunchy pinkish-grey goo. Then the great body split at the seams.

The hair rippled, carrying skin with it, twisting off like a nuclear sunburn. Little monkey men, tiny versions of Swedish Steve perhaps three feet tall, jumped free from his body, sloughing off as if they had escaped from a prison. There were two, then four, then a dozen.

Someone began screaming. Clint wasn't sure, it might have been him. A lot of people began shooting, which wasn't too smart in the enclosed, metal-walled space of the walk-in freezer. There was a lot more screaming as the little doubles of Swedish Steve jumped up on people's chests, gnawed at fingers and crotches, leapt for exposed ears, noses and lips.

Bullets rang and whizzed in a spray of blood and painful shouts, while Damerow shouted for people to get down and stop shooting.

The door, Clint thought, don't let them get the fuck out, and he tried to wade through the press of panicked bodies, but too many of his fellow townsmen were already crowding the exit and the little bastards were running across their heads, tearing bits of scalp as they went, and he could hear screaming outside in the dining room of the Fish Creek Café.

Someone, or something, tripped him. Clint went down as a shotgun roared, hearing another screech from some big-ass bird. The floor was cold, but the blood pooling on it was warm, so he waited until it was safe to move.

Twenty minutes later Clint was in a circle of people out in the parking lot. Every one of them had a gun in their hand. Damerow and Moran were there with Clint. Keeping an eye on him, maybe. A lot of folks were missing. Including Freddie Koiichi, whose pistol he still held.

Moran was talking into a hand-held radio. "Clackamas County Deputy Rohan's dead. Special Agent Martinez is dead. We have at least three civilian deaths and a large number of casualties." He glanced up at the clouds. "Confirm that. Highway is closed at both ends. Give us at least twenty-five miles of separation. No one comes in here without my say-so." There was a long pause. "Well if that happens, send in the Army. Hell if I know what else to do. Moran out."

The FBI agent slipped the radio into a pocket of his parka. "We're on our own, people," he announced. "After that honkie firing squad in there, I'm not endangering any more lives until we know exactly what the hell is going on here. I've got a cop or an armed parent standing watch over every child that's still here. What do we do now? This is your town, what the hell was that?"

"Swedish Steve," said Clint. "What I've been saying since yesterday. That Bigfoot fucker did this."

"Nobody splits into a dozen killer monkeys," said Moran. His voice quivered toward panic. "That shit just doesn't happen."

Clint stared him down. "You were standing there."

Nothing had been left of Swedish Steve except the tiny, contorted body of a very old white man, his head blown to pieces by Clint's bullet. What Clint had glimpsed of his body had unnervingly familiar scars. They'd killed two of the monkeys, or whatever they were. At least those little beasts *could* be killed.

Of course, nobody had seen a single one of them since the survivors had swarmed out of the Fish Creek Café and disappeared into the woods.

"So what was that? Or they?"

Damerow's girlfriend spoke up. She'd been cooking out front when the swarm had come out, fought them with a scoop of flaming grease. That's how one of the two dead monkeys had died, though there were a couple of dicey minutes with a fire extinguisher afterward. "They're his fetches."

"Fetch?" asked Clint.

"Fetch. Double. There's probably a Northwest Native American term for it, but I don't know the word. They're parts of him, like, reflections."

"How do you know this?" Moran demanded.

"You have a better theory?"

A horrible idea dawned on Clint. "I want to see one of these fetches," he said. He glanced at Damerow. "Can I go back inside? With her?" He inclined his head at the girlfriend.

"My name is Sunfire."

Right, thought Clint, Damerow had mentioned that name earlier.

"Go with them, Damerow," Moran ordered

Damerow, Sunfire and Clint went back into the Café, Clint and Damerow with weapons drawn.

"Sunfire?" Clint asked. "Really? Is that what is says on your birth certificate?"

"Shut *up*, fuckwad."

"Shut up you both," growled Damerow. "There might be more of them in here."

There were certainly more dead people in here, Clint thought. It made him sick. How many of them had shot each other? How many had died from the fetches, as Sunfire had called them? He could see Freddie Koiichi lying outside freezer number three, throat torn open.

"I'd rather look at the one Sunfire killed," Clint whispered. He really, really didn't want to go back into the freezer.

They walked slowly across the Café. Tables were overturned, blood spattered on the floor, with flecks of white extinguisher goo everywhere, along with spilled salt, sugar and ketchup. The effect was unnerving.

Sunfire's dead fetch lay curled up between the counter and the kitchen area, its furry back facing them. Clint handed his pistol to Sunfire, who shook her head, so Damerow took it. He grabbed a twelve-inch knife off the prep counter, leaned out and poked the fetch with the point of the blade.

It was too familiar, and too weird. Just as he'd done to Swedish Steve, back in the woods. Clint had an image of the fetch dissolving into a dozen tinier fetches, and so on, until Sweden was overrun with microscopic, hellish imps.

If he was right, that wasn't true.

The fetch rolled over. Its front was horribly damaged where Sunfire had burned it.

"Nice work, girlfriend," Clint breathed. He worked the tip of the knife into the bubbly flesh, wiggled it in, then tried to saw back and forth without actually laying a steadying hand upon the fetch.

The fetch slid back and forth on the fire-scarred linoleum floor of Shelley's kitchen, but the knife caught and dug in deeper, with a scent like fried bacon wafting up from the hairy little body.

"What the hell—" Damerow began, but Sunfire shushed her.

Then something popped and the skin slid open, just as Swedish Steve's had, curling back to reveal a withered, pale body wrapped within the hairy fat.

One of the women behind him began to retch, then threw up.

"All the victims," said Clint hoarsely over the choking and spattering. "Over the years, the missing hikers and vanished kids. He, somehow, he took them in. Each of these fetches is a little bit of Swedish Steve wrapped around one of . . . one of . . . us."

Then he began to cry in earnest, because Clint knew where Hobson was.

"Now what?" Moran had gone into the restaurant alone after listening to their report, and come back out again looking pale and determined.

"We lure them in," said Clint. "They're still human under that monkey skin. That's must be why Swedish Steve went after the kids. We need my Margie, and Kathy Kamerone, and any other parents those lost kids might know, and we need all the kids, and we need them in a big circle, out here in the parking lot where the fetches can see them. And we call to Stacey and Hobson and whoever's in there, bring them out to us." He paused, breath caught in his throat. "Then we kill them. Our lost children."

"No," said Sunfire. "We don't kill them. We set them free."

Clint was just sick. "How?

"We bring that old man out here, the one you said was still in the freezer, and those two dead fetches. The curse, or monster, or whatever it is, it's about him. He was the first. He pulled the others in. We lay him to rest, heal his soul, the others will follow."

"Heal his soul?" Moran asked, his voice incredulous.

Clint turned on the FBI agent. Maybe, somehow, he could have Hobson back, if he could keep Moran from exterminating the damned fetches. "What's your plan, Efrem Zimbalist Junior? You've got the highway closed. Going to napalm us all to death? Destroy the village in order to save it?"

"If I have to," said Moran quietly. "This is, in my terms, a hot biohazard of the worst kind. I'm willing to give her idea a little time before I go nuclear. So to speak."

Clint grinned. He could feel his lips tight back across his teeth. Anything for his son. Anything. "So to speak. Her idea is mine, Special Agent."

When Clint looked around, he was surprised to see Damerow smiling at him. "I'll go in and get Swedish Steve," he said. Amazingly, his voice didn't squeak with terror. "If two of you will get the other fetches. We'll still need the children here, too."

"And a battalion of shrinks," muttered Moran, "assuming any of them live through this."

"It ain't like the fucking movies," Clint told the agent. He uncocked the slide on the Glock, stuck it into his belt loop, took a big stretch, and headed once more for the bloody interior of the Fish Creek Café.

Sunfire and Moran followed him in. Sunfire split off immediately to retrieve the fetch that she had killed, while Moran and Clint walked very lightly to the door of number three freezer.

It was still standing open.

Clint glanced down at Freddie Koiichi, and said a prayer to a God he didn't believe in anyway. Then he stepped around the corner and into the freezer.

Rohan was there, face down in a substantial pool of blood which was already a dark, goopy mess. Martinez was slumped against the wall by the door, her pistol in her lap, three bullet holes on her face and neck. Walter Arnason was there too, though Clint could only tell who he was by his clothes.

And a fetch, its head blown almost free of its neck, along with Swedish Steve.

Clint walked over to Swedish Steve, who looked very tiny indeed coiled up on a mass of bloody gobbets on the Shelley's flatbed dolly. He was a very old man, his skin wrinkled and loose on tiny bones. The scars were still familiar. Clint thought briefly of Hobson, then lifted what was left of Swedish Steve in his arms like a baby.

On the way out the door, the body flexed. Clint looked down to see the lips moving. He almost dropped Swedish Steve as the old man whispered something unintelligible.

In the parking lot, they laid out the three bodies they had gathered. Sunfire began to walk a circle around them, chanting, as the children of Sweden were herded into place in a wider circle by frightened men and women with guns. Clint looked up to see Margie staring at him, her eyes so deeply ringed that she looked as if she'd been beaten. She shook her head slightly, then stared down at her feet.

He was profoundly glad that Suzanne had gone on the helicopter. At least his daughter would survive.

Sunfire motioned for the circle to open a pathway facing the woods. She kept walking, chanting, waving, her voice sing-songing up and down in a language Clint didn't understand. It was cold as hell, and flurries began to whip down from higher elevations.

They all stood there, their breath hanging in the air heavy as their hopes, listening to some New Age hippie sing.

Then the first fetch crept out of the woods.

"Pray for him," Sunfire said, working the words into her song as she kept circling the bodies. "Pray for them."

Clint found himself wondering exactly how many fetches there had been. Around him, people began to say the Lord's Prayer.

"Our Father, who art in Heaven, hallowed be Thy name."

Sunfire still circled and sang, her voice and hands and body inviting the fetch into the circle. Another came out of the shadows to witness the fate of the first.

"Thy kingdom come, Thy will be done, on Earth as it is in Heaven."

Two more now, and the first fetch crouched next to the old man's body. The snow flurries were picking up. Clint found himself wondering which of these fetches had been his son.

"Hobson," he said quietly, melding his voice in with the prayer. "Hobson Bernard Amos."

"Give us this day our daily bread, and forgive us our trespasses, as we forgive those who trespass against us."

There were nine of them now, moving into the circle one by one. Had there been twelve back in the freezer? With the two dead, was there only one left outside the circle? Still saying his son's name over and over again, Clint couldn't tell which was Hobson.

"And lead us not into temptation, but deliver us from evil."

A tenth fetch appeared. Clint thought maybe there had been thirteen all told, that one more was missing. He wasn't sure how he knew, but he knew.

Hobson had not yet come.

Clint laid his Glock upon the ground, broke the circle, went to sit among the fetches gathered by the body of Swedish Steve, and opened up his arms.

"For Thine is the kingdom, and the power, and the glory, for ever and ever, amen."

"Hobson Bernard Amos," said Clint as his son, twisted and small, wrapped in fur and rage, came into his arms.

Sunfire closed the circle around them, the children holding hands, the adults ranked behind them, and sang a song of sunsets and leaping salmon and birds vanishing over the mountaintops. He heard that familiar raptor screech, then that same enormous osprey Clint had seen in his dream dropped from the clouds, straight toward them. Its claws spread wide as the massive wings spilled air for the bird to come tight inside the circle where Clint sat.

The fetches climbed on to the body of Swedish Steve, like scorpions on their mother's back. In his arms, the fetch that had been Hobson struggled to join its new brothers even as the osprey dug its claws into Swedish Steve's body and beat its wings to gain altitude again.

Clint hung on to the body, not willing to lose his son one last time. Across from him, in the adult circle, Margie's face was twisted, tears streaming from her bruised eyes. Sunfire looked down on him, pitying but hard. Hobson twisted, trying to escape.

He finally looked to Damerow. The deputy shook her head.

Clint let go of his son.

Clint Amos and Barley John Dimmitt were fishing on the Willamette River, off of Sauvie Island. Neither one of them lived in Sweden any more. Nobody did, not since the fire last fall had raked the town completely out of season, against all odds burning in the snow. Fire was a clean end, the problem of missing bodies neatly handled as long as Moran tied up the forensics.

Margie was with her sister in Idaho, saying she might come back some day. She had Clint Junior and Suzanne with her. Clint figured he'd never see any of them again.

He and Barley John were still together because they had nobody else. They talked less than ever. Clint liked being on the water, in part because every now and then he'd see or hear an osprey. The centre of the river was also far away from any trees.

Clint cast his line, but the float popped loose, and the weight took his hook too deep. Pulling it back in, he felt a snag. "Damn."

"Probably," Barley John agreed.

Clint worked the line a little, unwilling to cut it without making some minimal effort. It came back toward him, still weighted, but dead weight, not a fish. Curious, he reeled it in.

Crusted in mud and some little shellfish was an old pistol. Real old. The handle was curved back a bit, and when he rubbed at it with his thumb, Clint could see an octagonal barrel.

"What do you think?" he asked, showing the thing to Barley John.

"It's damned, too. Just like us."

Clint shrugged and stared across the water. Something screeched, maybe an osprey, maybe a lesser bird. He hefted the mud-encrusted grip. He knew who had shot from here, and what they had been shooting at.

"You belong to the river now," he told it, then threw the weapon back in. "We all do," he added, watching his reflection in the ripples of the splash. Something big flying overhead cast a shadow on the water that made Clint close his eyes and think of Hobson.

BRIAN LUMLEY

The Thin People

HAVING "RETIRED" FROM THE BRITISH ARMY in December 1980, Brian Lumley's breakthrough book was the horror novel *Necroscope*, featuring Harry Keogh, the man who can talk to dead people.

It was followed by *Necroscope II: Wamphyri!*, and with the first two volumes having seen initial paperback publication in the UK, the series was eventually picked up by Tor Books in the USA. *Necroscope III: The Source*, took only five months to complete in 1987, and such was the appeal of the *Necroscope* books that Tor published the perceived trilogy in the space of just twelve months. By that time, however, Lumley had already written *Necroscope IV: Deadspeak* and *V: Deadspawn*.

Such had been the success of the first five volumes, and such was the demand from readers, that Lumley went straight on to write the *Vampire World Trilogy* and further sequels and spin-offs, the most recent being *Necroscope: The Touch*. Thirteen countries and counting have now published, or are in the process of publishing, these and others of Lumley's novels and short story collections, which in the USA alone have sold well over three million copies.

His vampire short story "Necros" was adapted for the Showtime series *The Hunger*, and in 1998 he received the genre's prestigious Grand Master Award at the World Horror Convention in Phoenix, Arizona.

"For three years I lived in Crouch End, in the north of London," Lumley recalls. "Do you remember the Stephen King story? I think that one came out of a visit he paid to Peter Straub, when Straub was living in Crouch End.

"We used to have a saying, my wife and I: 'All roads lead to Crouch End.' Peter Tremayne lived not far away (and still does); Clive Barker did one of his plays up there (those were the early days, before his books started bleeding); Douglas Hill lived there. Others whose names escape me now . . .

"Up there in Crouch End, you'd bump into some weird people. And there were these weird, thin houses. On my way back from the pub one night, I found myself looking at a thin house and wondering who in the world could live in such a cramped, concertinaed sort of place. The answer seemed obvious . . ."

I

FUNNY PLACE, BARROWS HILL. Not *Barrow's* Hill, no. Barrows without the apostrophe. For instance: you won't find it on any map. You'll find maps whose borders approach it, whose corners impinge, however slightly, upon it, but in general it seems that cartographers avoid it. It's too far out from the centre for the tubes, hasn't got a mainline station, has lost much of its integrity by virtue of all the infernal demolition and reconstruction going on around and within it. But it's still there. Buses run to and from, and the older folk who live there still call it Barrows Hill.

When I went to live there in the late seventies I hated the place. There was a sense of senility, of inherent idiocy about it. A damp sort of place. Even under a hot summer sun, damp. You could feel blisters of fungus rising even under the freshest paint. Not that the

place got painted very much. Not that I saw, anyway. No, for it was like somewhere out of Lovecraft: decaying, diseased, inbred.

Barrows Hill. I didn't stay long, a few months. Too long, really. It gave you the feeling that if you delayed, if you stood still for just one extra moment, then it would grow up over you and you'd become a part of it. There are some old, old places in London, and I reckoned Barrows Hill was one of the oldest. I also reckoned it for its *genius loci*; like it was a focal point for secret things. Or perhaps not a focal point, for that might suggest a radiation – a spreading outwards – and as I've said Barrows Hill was ingrown. The last bastion of the strange old things of London. Things like the thin people. The very tall, very thin people.

Now nobody – but nobody *anywhere* – is ever going to believe me about the thin people, which is one of the two reasons I'm not afraid to tell this story. The other is that I don't live there any more. But when I did . . .

I suspect now that quite a few people – ordinary people, that is – knew about them. They wouldn't admit it, that's all, and probably still won't. And since all of the ones who'd know live on Barrows Hill, I really can't say I blame 'em. There was one old lad lived there, however, who knew *and* talked about them. To me. Since he had a bit of a reputation (to be frank, they called him "Barmy Bill of Barrows Hill") I didn't pay a deal of attention at first. I mean, who would?

Barrows Hill had a pub, a couple of pubs, but the one most frequented was The Railway. A hangover from a time when there really was a railway, I supposed. A couple of years ago there had been another, a serious rival to The Railway for a little while, when someone converted an old block into a fairly modern pub. But it didn't last. Whoever owned the place might have known something, but probably not. Or he wouldn't have been so stupid as to call his place The Thin Man! It was only open for a week or two before burning down to the ground.

But that was before my time and the only reason I make mention of pubs, and particularly The Railway, is because that's where I met Barmy Bill. He was there because of his disease, alcoholism, and I was there because of mine, heartsickness – which, running at a high fever, showed all signs of mutating pretty soon into Bill's problem. In short, I was hitting the bottle.

Now this is all incidental information, of course, and I don't intend to go into it other than to say it was our problems brought us together. As unlikely a friendship as any you might imagine. But Barmy Bill was good at listening, and I was good at buying booze. And so we were good company.

One night, however, when I ran out of money, I made the mistake of inviting him back to my place. (My place – hah! A bed, a loo and a typewriter; a poky little place up some wooden stairs, like a penthouse kennel; oh, yes, and a bonus in the shape of a cupboard converted to a shower.) But I had a couple bottles of beer back there and a half-bottle of gin, and when I'd finished crying on Barmy Bill's shoulder it wouldn't be far for me to fall into bed. What did surprise me was how hard it was to get him back there. He started complaining the moment we left the bar – or rather, as soon as he saw which way we were headed.

"Up the Larches? You live up there off Barchington Road? Yes, I remember you told me. Well, and maybe I'll just stay in the pub a while after all. I mean, if you live right up *there* – well, it's out of my way, isn't it?"

"Out of your way? It's a ten-minute walk, that's all! I thought you were thirsty?"

"Thirsty I am – always! Barmy I'm not – they only say I am 'cos they're frightened to listen to me."

"They?"

"People!" he snapped, sounding unaccustomedly sober. Then, as if to change the subject: "A half-bottle of gin, you said?"

"That's right, Gordon's. But if you want to get back on down to The Railway . . ."

"No, no, we're halfway there now," he grumbled, hurrying along beside me, almost taking my arm in his nervousness. "And anyway, it's a nice bright night tonight. They're not much for light nights."

"They?" I asked again.

"People!" Despite his short, bowed legs, he was half a pace ahead of me. "The thin people." But where his first word had been a snarl, his last three were whispered, so that I almost missed them entirely.

Then we were up Larches Avenue – *the* Larches as Barmy Bill had it – and closing fast on 22, and suddenly it was very quiet. Only the scrape of dry, blown leaves on the pavement. Autumn, and the trees half-naked. Moonlight falling through webs of high, black, brittle branches.

"Plenty of moon," said Bill, his voice hushed. "Thank God – in whom I really don't believe – for that. *But no street lights*! You see that? Bulbs all missing. That's them."

"Them?" I caught his elbow, turning him into my gateway – if there'd been a gate. There wasn't, just the post, which served as my landmark whenever I'd had a skinful.

"Them, yes!" he snapped, staring at me as I turned my key in the lock. "Damn young fool!"

And so up the creaky stairs to my little cave of solitude, and Barmy Bill shivering despite the closeness of the night and warmth of the place, which leeched a lot of its heat from the houses on both sides, and from the flat below, whose elderly lady occupier couldn't seem to live in anything other than an oven; and in through my own door, into the "living" room, where Bill closed the curtains across the jutting bay windows as if he'd lived there all of his life. But not before he'd peered out into the night street, his eyes darting this way and that, round and bright in his lined, booze-desiccated face.

Barmy, yes. Well, maybe he was and maybe he wasn't. "Gin," I said, passing him the bottle and a glass. "But go easy, yes? I like a nip myself, you know."

"A nip? A nip? Huh! If I lived here I'd need more than a nip. This is the middle of it, this is. The very middle!"

"Oh?" I grinned. "Myself, I had it figured for the living end!"

He paced the floor for a few moments – three paces there, three back – across the protesting boards of my tiny room, before pointing an almost accusing finger at me. "Chirpy tonight, aren't you? Full of beans!"

"You think so?" Yes, he was right. I did feel a bit brighter. "Maybe I'm over it, eh?"

He sat down beside me. "I certainly hope so, you daft young sod! And now maybe you'll pay some attention to my warnings and get yourself a place well away from here."

"Your warnings? Have you been warning me, then?" It dawned

on me that he had, for several weeks, but I'd been too wrapped up in my own misery to pay him much heed. And who would? After all, he was Barmy Bill.

"Course I have!" he snapped. "About them bloody—"

"Thin people," I finished it for him. "Yes, I remember now."

"Well?"

"Eh?"

"Are you or aren't you?"

"I'm listening, yes."

"No, no, *no*! Are you or aren't you going to find yourself new lodgings?"

"When I can afford it, yes."

"You're in danger here, you know? They don't like strangers. Strangers change things, and they're against that. They don't like anything strange, nothing new. They're a dying breed, I fancy, but while they're here they'll keep things the way they like 'em."

"Okay," I sighed. "This time I really am listening. You want to start at the beginning?"

He answered my sigh with one of his own, shook his head impatiently. "Daft young bugger! If I didn't like you I wouldn't bother. But all right, for your own good, one last time . . . just listen and I'll tell you what I know. It's not much, but it's the last warning you'll get . . ."

II

"Best thing ever happened for 'em must have been the lamp-posts, I reckon."

"Dogs?" I raised my eyebrows.

He glared at me and jumped to his feet. "Right, that's it. I'm off."

"Oh, sit down, sit down!" I calmed him. "Here, fill your glass again. And I promise I'll try not to interrupt."

"Lamp-posts!" he snapped, his brows black as thunder. But he sat and took the drink. "Yes, for they imitate 'em, see? And thin, they can hide behind 'em. Why, they can stand so still that on a dark night you wouldn't know the difference! Can you imagine that, eh? Hiding behind or imitating a lamp-post!"

I tried to imagine it, but: "Not really," I had to admit. Now, however, my levity was becoming a bit forced. There was something about his intensity – the way his limbs shook in a manner other than alcoholic – which was getting through to me. "Why should they hide?"

"Freaks! Wouldn't you hide? A handful of them. Millions of us. We'd hound 'em out, kill 'em off!"

"So why don't we?"

"'Cos we're all smart young buggers like you, that's why! 'Cos we don't *believe* in 'em."

"But you do?"

Bill nodded, his three- or four-day growth of hair quivering on jowls and upper lip. "Seen 'em," he said "and seen . . . *evidence* of them."

"And they're real people? I mean, you know, human? Just like me and you, except . . . thin?"

"And tall. Oh – *tall*!"

"Tall?" I frowned. "Thin and tall. How tall? Not as tall as—"

"Lamp-posts," he nodded, "yes. Not during the day, mind you, only at night. At night they—" (he looked uncomfortable, as if it had suddenly dawned on him how crazy this all must sound) "—they sort of, well, kind of *unfold* themselves."

I thought about it, nodded. "They unfold themselves. Yes, I see."

"No, you don't see," his voice was flat, cold, angry now. "But you will, if you hang around here long enough."

"Where do they live," I asked, "these tall, thin people?"

"In thin houses," he answered, matter-of-factly.

"Thin houses?"

"Sure! Are you telling me you haven't noticed the thin houses? Why, this place of yours very nearly qualifies! Thin houses, yes. Places where normal people wouldn't dream of setting up. There's half-a-dozen such in Barchington, and a couple right here in the Larches!" He shuddered and I bent to turn on an extra bar in my electric fire.

"Not cold, mate," Bill told me then. "Hell no! Enough booze in me to keep me warm. But I shudder every time I think of 'em. I mean, what *do* they do?"

"Where do they work, you mean?"

"Work?" he shook his head. "No, they don't work. Probably do a bit of tea-leafing. Burglary, you know. Oh, they'd get in anywhere, the thin people. But what do they *do*?"

I shrugged.

"I mean, me and you, we watch telly, play cards, chase the birds, read the paper. But them . . .?"

It was on the tip of my tongue to suggest maybe they go into the woods and frighten owls, but suddenly I didn't feel half so flippant. "You said you'd seen them?"

"Seen 'em sure enough, once or twice," he confirmed. "And weird! One, I remember, came out of his thin house in Barchington; I could show you it some time in daylight. Me, I was behind a hedge sleeping it off. Don't ask me how I got there, drunk as a lord! Anyway, something woke me up.

"Down at its bottom the hedge was thin where cats come through. It was night and the council men had been round during the day putting bulbs in the street-lights, so the place was all lit up. And directly opposite, there's this thin house and its door slowly opening; and out comes this bloke into the night, half of him yellow from the lamplight and half black in shadow. See, right there in front of the thin house is a street lamp.

"But this chap looks normal enough, you know? A bit stiff in his movements; he sort of moves jerky, like them contortionists who hook their feet over their shoulders and walk on their hands. Anyway, he looks up and down the street, and he's obviously satisfied no one's there. Then . . .

"He slips back a little into the shadows until he comes up against the wall of his house, and he – unfolds!

"I see the light glinting down one edge of him, see it suddenly split into two edges at the bottom, sort of hinged at the top. And the split widens until he stands in the dark there like a big pair of dividers. And then one half swings up until it forms a straight line, perpendicular – and now he's ten feet tall. Then the same again, only this time the division takes place in the middle. Like . . . like a joiner's wooden three-foot ruler, with hinges so he can open it up, you know?"

I nodded, fascinated despite myself. "And that's how they're built, eh? I mean, well, hinged?"

"Hell, no!" he snorted. "You can fold your arms on your

elbows, can't you? Or your legs on your knees? You can bend from the waist and touch your toes? Well I sure can! Their joints may be a little different from ours, that's all – maybe like the joints of certain insects. Or maybe not. I mean, their science is different from ours, too. Perhaps they fold and unfold themselves the same way they do it to other things – except it doesn't do them any harm. I dunno . . ."

"What?" I asked, puzzled. "What other things do they fold?"

"I'll get to that later," he told me darkly, shivering. "Where was I?"

"There he was," I answered, "all fifteen foot of him, standing in the shadows. And then—?"

"A car comes along the street, sudden like!" Bill grabbed my arm.

"Wow!" I jumped. "He's in trouble, right?"

Barmy Bill shook his head. "No way. The car's lights are on full, but that doesn't trouble the thin man. He's not stupid. The car goes by, lighting up the walls with its beam, and where the thin man stood in shadows against the wall of his thin house—"

"Yes?"

"A drainpipe, all black and shiny!"

I sat back. "Pretty smart."

"You better believe they're smart. Then, when it's dark again, out he steps. And *that's* something to see! Those giant strides – but quick, almost a flicker. Blink your eyes and he's moved – and between each movement his legs coming together as he pauses, and nothing to see but a pole. Up to the lamp-post he goes, seems almost to melt into it, hides behind it. And *plink*! – out goes the light. After that . . . in ten minutes he had the whole street black as night in a coal mine. And yours truly lying there in somebody's garden, scared and shivering and dying to throw up."

"And that was it?"

Barmy Bill gulped, tossed back his gin and poured himself another. His eyes were huge now, skin white where it showed through his whiskers. "God, no – that wasn't it – there was more! See, I figured later that I must have got myself drunk deliberately that time – so's to go up there and spy on 'em. Oh, I know that sounds crazy now, but you know what it's like when you're mindless drunk. Jesus, these days I can't *get* drunk! But these were early days I'm telling you about."

"So what happened next?"

"Next – he's coming back down the street! I can hear him: *click*, pause . . . *click*, pause . . . *click*, pause, stilting it along the pavement – and I can see him in my mind's eye, doing his impression of a lamp-post with every pause. And suddenly I get this feeling, and I sneak a look round. I mean, the frontage of this garden I'm in is so tiny, and the house behind me is—"

I saw it coming. "Jesus!"

"A thin house," he confirmed it, "right!"

"So now *you* were in trouble."

He shrugged, licked his lips, trembled a little. "I was lucky, I suppose. I squeezed myself into the hedge, lay still as death. And *click*, pause . . . *click*, pause, getting closer all the time. And then – behind me, for I'd turned my face away – the slow creaking as the door of the thin house swung open! And the second thin person coming out and, I imagine, unfolding him or herself, and the two of 'em standing there for a moment, and me near dead of fright."

"And?"

"*Click-click*, pause; *click-click*, pause; *click-click* – and away they go. God only knows where they went, or what they did, but me? – I gave 'em ten minutes start and then got up, and ran, and stumbled, and forced my rubbery legs to carry me right out of there. And I haven't been back. Why, this is the closest I've been to Barchington since that night, and too close by far!"

I waited for a moment but he seemed done. Finally I nodded. "Well, that's a good story, Bill, and—"

"I'm not finished!" he snapped. "And it's not just a story . . ."

"There's more?"

"Evidence," he whispered. "The evidence of your own clever-bugger eyes!"

I waited.

"Go to the window," said Bill, "and peep out through the curtains. Go on, do it."

I did.

"See anything funny?"

I shook my head.

"Blind as a bat!" he snorted. "Look at the street-lights – or the absence of lights. I showed you once tonight. They've nicked all the bulbs."

"Kids," I shrugged. "Hooligans. Vandals."

"Huh!" Bill sneered. "Hooligans, here? Unheard of. Vandals? You're joking! What's to vandalise? And when did you last see kids playing in these streets, eh?"

He was right. "But a few missing light bulbs aren't hard evidence," I said.

"All *right*!" he pushed his face close and wrinkled his nose at me. "Hard evidence, then." And he began to tell me the final part of his story . . .

III

"Cars!" Barmy Bill snapped, in that abrupt way of his. "They can't bear them. Can't say I blame 'em much, not on that one. I hate the noisy, dirty, clattering things myself. But tell me: have you noticed anything a bit queer – about cars, I mean – in these parts?"

I considered for a moment, replied: "Not a hell of a lot of them."

"Right!" He was pleased. "On the rest of the Hill, nose to tail. Every street overflowing. 'Specially at night when people are in the pubs or watching the telly. But here? Round Barchington and the Larches and a couple of other streets in this neighbourhood? Not a one to be seen!"

"Not true," I said. "There are two cars in this very street right now. Look out the window and you should be able to see them."

"Bollocks!" said Bill.

"Pardon?"

"Bollocks!" he repeated. "Them's not *cars*! Rusting old bangers. Spoke-wheels and all. Twenty, thirty years they've been trundling about. The thin people are *used* to them. It's the big shiny new ones they don't like. And so, if you park your car up here overnight – trouble!"

"Trouble?" But here I was deliberately playing dumb. Here I knew what he meant well enough. I'd seen it for myself: the occasional shiny car, left overnight, standing there the next morning with its tyres slashed, windows smashed, lamps kicked in.

He could see it in my face. "You know what I mean, all right. Listen, couple of years ago there was a Flash Harry type from the city used to come up here. There was a barmaid he fancied in The Railway – and she was taking all he could give her. Anyway, he was flash, you know? One of the gang lads and a rising star. And a flash car to go with it. Bullet-proof windows, hooded lamps, reinforced panels – the lot. Like a bloody tank, it was. But –" Bill sighed.

"He used to park it up here, right?"

He nodded. "Thing was, you couldn't threaten him, you know what I mean? Some people you can threaten, some you shouldn't threaten, and some you mustn't. He was one you mustn't. Trouble is, so are the thin people."

"So what happened?"

"When they slashed his tyres, he lobbed bricks through their windows. And he had a knowing way with him. He tossed 'em through thin house windows. Then one night he parked down on the corner of Barchington. Next morning – they'd drilled holes right through the plate, all over the car. After that – he didn't come back for a week or so. When he did come back . . . well, he must've been pretty mad."

"What did he do?"

"Threw something else – something that made a bang! A damn big one! You've seen that thin, derelict shell on the corner of Barchington? Oh, it was him, sure enough, and he got it right, too. A thin house. Anybody in there, they were goners. And *that* did it!"

"They got him?"

"They got his car! He parked up one night, went down to The Railway, when the bar closed took his lady-love back to her place, and in the morning—"

"They'd wrecked it – his car, I mean."

"Wrecked it? Oh, yes, they'd done that. They'd *folded* it!"

"Come again?"

"Folded it!" he snapped. "Their funny science. Eighteen inches each way, it was. A cube of folded metal. No broken glass, no split seams, no splintered plastic. Folded all neat and tidy. An eighteen-inch cube."

"They'd put it through a crusher, surely?" I was incredulous.

"Nope – folded."

"Impossible!"

"Not to them. Their funny science."

"So what did he do about it?"

"Eh? Do? He looked at it, and he thought, 'What if I'd been sitting in the bloody thing?' Do? He did what I would do, what you would do. He went away. We never did see him again."

The half-bottle was empty. We reached for the beers. And after a long pull I said: "You can kip here if you want, on the floor. I'll toss a blanket over you."

"Thanks," said Barmy Bill, "but no thanks. When the beer's gone I'm gone. I wouldn't stay up here to save my soul. Besides, I've a bottle of my own back home."

"Sly old sod!" I said.

"Daft young bugger!" he answered without malice. And twenty minutes later I let him out. Then I crossed to the windows and looked out at him, at the street all silver in moonlight.

He stood at the gate (where it should be) swaying a bit and waving up at me, saying his thanks and farewell. Then he started off down the street.

It was quiet out there, motionless. One of those nights when even the trees don't move. Everything frozen, despite the fact that it wasn't nearly cold. I watched Barmy Bill out of sight, craning my neck to see him go, and—

Across the road, three lamp-posts – where there should only be two! The one on the left was OK, and the one to the far right. But the one in the middle? I had never seen that one before. I blinked bleary eyes, gasped, blinked again. Only *two* lamp-posts!

Stinking drunk – drunk as a skunk – utterly boggled!

I laughed as I tottered from the window, switched off the light, staggered into my bedroom. The barmy old bastard had really had me going. I'd really started to believe. And now the booze was making me see double – or something. Well, just as long as it was lamp-posts and not pink elephants! Or thin people! And I went to bed laughing.

. . . But I wasn't laughing the next morning.

Not after they found him, old Barmy Bill of Barrows Hill. Not after they called on me to identify him.

"Their funny science," he'd called it. The way they folded things. And Jesus, they'd folded him, too! Right down into an eighteen-inch cube. Ribs and bones and skin and muscles – the lot. Nothing broken, you understand, just folded. No blood or guts or anything nasty – nastier by far *because* there was nothing.

And they'd dumped him in a garbage-skip at the end of the street. The couple of local youths who found him weren't even sure what they'd found, until they spotted his face on one side of the cube. But I won't go into that . . .

Well, I moved out of there just as soon as I could – do you blame me? – since when I've done a lot of thinking about it. Fact is, I haven't thought of much else.

And I suppose old Bill was right. At least I hope so. Things he'd told me earlier, when I was only half listening. About them being the last of their sort, and Barrows Hill being the place they've chosen to sort of fade away in, like a thin person's "elephant's graveyard," you know?

Anyway, there are no thin people here, and no thin houses. Vandals aplenty, and so many cars you can't count, but nothing out of the ordinary.

Lamp-posts, yes, and posts to hold up the telephone wires, of course. Lots of them. But they don't bother me any more.

See, I know *exactly* how many lamp-posts there are. And I know exactly *where* they are, every last one of them. And God help the man who ever plants a new one without telling me first!

TANITH LEE

The Hill

TANITH LEE BEGAN WRITING at the age of nine. After leaving school, she worked variously as a library assistant, shop assistant, filing clerk and waitress before spending a year at art college. She published three children's books in the early 1970s, but it was only after DAW Books issued her novel *The Birthgrave* in 1975 that she became a full-time writer.

Since then she has written and published around sixty novels, nine collections and over 200 short stories. Her radio plays have been broadcast by the BBC, and she also scripted two episodes of the cult TV series *Blakes 7*.

Tanith Lee has twice won the World Fantasy Award for short fiction and was awarded the British Fantasy Society's August Derleth Award in 1980 for her novel *Death's Master*. In 1998 she was short-listed for the Guardian Award for Children's Fiction for her novel *Law of the Wolf Tower*, the first book in the

"Claidi Journal" series. Her latest titles include the YA novel *Piratica III*.

"Maybe it would be nice to say, 'When I was a child ghost stories, horror films and bad dreams could keep me awake all night – but I grew out of that'," muses the author. "Only I didn't grow out of it, and through my so far fifty-nine years I have often disturbed those around me and resident cats with my unease/terror/ wanting to turn on a light.

" 'The Hill' came in a dream. And in my dream I saw exactly what the heroine sees on that final evening. This time I didn't wake anyone else though. Cowering I thought: 'That's going to make a story'."

LONG AGO, WHEN I WAS ABOUT FIFTEEN YEARS OF AGE, I looked out at the familiar sea, and saw that on the horizon, and without warning, it had grown into a tall and rounded hill. I mean that I saw a hill, made of the deep milky blue summer sea, standing up, far out and *motionless*, from the rest of the water. I stopped in astonishment. Part of my surprise was caused by the fact that no one else among the many people on the cliff path seemed to see what *I* did. This impossible, wondrous, terrifying thing. For if the liquid ocean could form a solid hill, surely the fabric of the world, and everything else we believe in, came into question. I confess too, I had at that time no doubts either about my eyesight, or my sanity.

I Chazen's Beasts

I am an independent woman. Daughter of a handsome, feckless father, a pretty and foolish mother, I grew up into a plain, intelligent adult. I make no bones about the intelligence, despite its limits. I have nothing else to boast of. My person is quite tall, neat and inclined to be thin. While at the age of twenty-two, my hair had already begun to grey. Several have asked me why this happened so early; had I received some severe shock? I had to shock them by replying I had not. For, at that time, I hadn't.

I live alone, but not always in my own apartment, three rooms at the top of a large old house near London. At other times I live in the houses of my employers. I am a librarian. My task is to sort and regulate the libraries of others far less able, and normally far more wealthy than Miss Alice June Constable: myself.

The invitation to Northerham House, which I had been expecting some while, finally arrived on a late summer morning.

Used to such trips I was packed and on the train in less than five hours, reaching my destination at six o'clock that evening.

A warm strong wind was blowing as I walked up the lane. The trees shook their huge, tired green leaves, and through the rocking boughs I glimpsed the village of Northerham – which locals pronounce *North'rum* – below. It appeared the usual pastoral place, small houses with gardens, an inn, a pub, and a Saxon church with rambling graveyard.

The house of my employer stood off the lane, at the end of a short, curving, heavily tree-hung drive. This was no mansion either, but a pleasant two-storey building with an arch over the front door, and recently cut lawns. To the back extended long gardens ultimately swathed in woods. There was a scent of wall-flowers, and zoos. I'd been told, in a letter from the master of the house, Professor Chazen, that by the time I arrived he would be away again on his travels. The housekeeper was off too. Only a manservant, a Mr Swange, and a maid of all work (Doris), were in residence. Aside that was from the professor's collection of exotic beasts. All of these lived, I had been assured, among the back premises, sheds, enclosures and pens. Chazen travelled widely, and tended to bring back curios, often of the animal kind. I can recall I had thought that his library should prove very interesting, and looked forward to reading some of the material I was to catalogue.

My knocks on the front door got no reply. I therefore went round to the back by the gravel path.

A small garden cordoned off the kitchen. Washing flapped vigorously on a line and two or three hens strutted about. The kitchen door was open, but no one in sight.

I peered over the hedge, and so came face-to-face as it were with the first of the animal pens about ten yards away. Eight or nine cat creatures – large for a domestic cat certainly but smaller than most of the wild variety – were prowling or snoozing in the wire-fronted box. This container was some sixteen feet by six feet high. It's true I have never left England, but I have seen many collections and read thousands of books, and never had I seen or heard of anything quite like these cats. They were a dirtyish white in colour, their fur or pelt tufted, and streaked with faint brown mottles. Their eyes glowed a pale, embered blue.

As I stared, I heard a woman's step on the gravel.

"Oh, Miss – did you knock? I never heard you—"

Doris the maid was all apologies. She led me inside and presently we were sharing the teapot at the scrubbed table. (I have never thought it necessary to keep servants at a "correct" distance. One can learn a lot from them, and in any case I am, after all, a sort of intermittant servant myself. Besides, where needful, I can usually assert my authority.)

"Then shall I show you the animals, Miss?" inquired Doris after I had mentioned them, some quarter of an hour later.

I was curious. Also I disapproved of the cage which held the tufted cats. I asked her if all the cages were as restricted.

"Oh no, Miss. Some are very enormous. But the cats are let out at night in summer, and in winter they're moved with the others to warmer pens in the sheds."

"Let *out*?"

"Well, there's half a mile of woods at the end of the gardens that Professor Chazen owns with the house. They're fenced and netted right over, with small places left to let birds and mice and suchlike in and out. His cats are noctual really – they prefer night-time. You may hear a bit of squawking down along the woods after dark. Take no notice, Miss."

"Noctual" having been explained (nocturnal), I envisioned nights pierced by weird cries, as small English rodents and fowls were rent by Chazen's felines. But I sleep well. Probably it was no worse dying like that than by the fangs of a fox, or some neighbouring tabby.

"What other beasts are there?" I asked her, as she conducted me through the hedge by the gate.

"All sorts. There's them—" (the cats) "—and some badgery things, sort of bears I think he says – and ratty things – ugh!" (a shudder, though I noticed it was more ritual than impassioned) "snakes – great big beetles, all hairy – lizards – the professor says they're very intelligent."

The cats growled as we passed them, lazy and bored. They had a meaty smell, and looked healthy. Their blue eyes were neither friendly or disarming, but Doris clucked at them. Favourites? A sort of netted tunnel, at present closed off from the cage, ran to the dark green woods that frothed up beyond the lawn, shrubs and sheds. I had been wondering how the "letting-out" was managed.

Under the shade of oak and apple trees, we skirted other imprisoned animals, some of these, as she'd told me, in huge enclosures. I recognised none of the species. The snakes meanwhile were invisible, and the beetles shut in a large long shed to the side. I kept up my questions, now as to where the menagerie came from. "Oh, all sorts of countries," exclaimed Doris. "Africa – the Indies – America even. And some of them are trained, he says, to do clever things—" but when she said this her face fell suddenly. I considered why. Perhaps she did not like the idea of performing animals.

I began to see the netting running right over the woods, a roof and walls, glinting as the sun sank behind us on the orchards and fields of Kent. Birds were calling and singing in the trees, impervious or stoical about the cat-tunnel leading to their sanctuary.

Our shadows long before us, Doris pointed out the padlocked gate reserved for human entry. I saw too scattered bronze feathers and a stripe of red – which I took for the remains of a slain pheasant – just inside the man-made boundary.

"Blett has charge of maintaining the netting," said Doris. "Or he's supposed to. He's off on his honeymoon. Too taken up with it, if you ask me. He got sacked – nearly got himself sacked. It was just the day the professor left. There was a great hole in the fencing Blett'd missed. The professor didn't half take on. In a right two-and-six he was," (surprising me by her Cockney rhyming slang: two-and-six: fix). "Blett said to me the animals get restless and tear holes, trying to get out. He said things *frighten* them. I ask you, what things, *here* . . . not like the jungle, is it? But you should hear how they go on sometimes."

"The animals?"

"No, people in the village."

"Do they?"

"Really silly I calls it. So does my gentleman friend." She blushed and looked slyly at me, I, the elderly spinster. I smiled. Doris added, "It's the old ones mostly. Professor Chazen, well he doesn't go to church, doesn't believe in God, you see. And then all this stuff he's collected in the house, and the garden – the villagers like to say the professor's tempting the Devil himself."

"Do you believe in the Devil?" I asked Doris. I am a modern-minded old maid, so thought I had better let her know it.

A grim pause resulted.

"Yes," she said at last, fearfully.

I was then sorry, and chided myself.

And so found we had stopped, and stood staring at a decidedly gigantic pen.

"What's in here?"

"That's the lizards."

Roused maybe by a sympathetic awareness of her words, one of these just then emerged from a sort of bothy of twigs and stones. It straddled a piece of floor, and turned its reptillian head to see us through a swivelling, sidelong eye. It was itself very big, the size of a small spaniel, with grey scales that seemed highly polished, gleaming in the last sunlight, and purplish claws reminiscent of those of a fowl. A spiny crest, which had been lowered, now rose high. Magnified by a power of about six, one could imagine it tramping the prehistoric plains.

I preferred the lizard greatly to the furry cat-beasts. It looked soulless, dull, intemperate and not pretty. You could mistake it for nothing that it was not.

"And these? Are they African?"

"I can't remember, Miss." And then, "Oh! I must run – I left my cake in the oven—"

My first days at Northerham began as have a score of other employments.

The library was large and impressive in structure and layout; a total muddle with regard to contents. Many of the tall book-stacks reared quite empty, apart from dust – one needed a ladder to ascend. Such an item had been ordered from London, it seemed, but not yet arrived. Crates massed in awkward places, savagely undone, their edges all bent nails and splinters. Some wonderful books might lie inside, unsorted and liable to be torn if not removed with extreme care.

I set to work as I always do, devizing first the best system, only then unpacking. A huge old mahogany table provided help with this. In the late morning I'd lay out some appealing tome, and after lunch read for an hour at least. I am a fast reader. Little escapes me that way. And I wasn't unhappy otherwise. My room was kept clean and orderly, its bed comfortable. There was a small private bathroom next door. The view looked off down the back garden to the wood, over the pens and netting, from which, as was inevitable, uncanny warbles and squeaks would frequently sound after dark. Meals were prepared by Doris, a very good – if rather eccentric – cook. I had met Mr Swange the first evening, when he attended the bringing in of my dinner to the dining room. Unlike rose-and-cream Doris, he was a skulking iron man with a bleak expression. As so often with manservants I've met, he treated me to a polite condescension amounting to insolence. I have generally found it useless to waste time on that. Aside from exchanging a few acid civilities, we had little to do with each other.

One of Swange's tasks was, however, to inspect the outside of the pens at sunset, and let out the corracats, as it transpired they were called.

That Swange did not like either the task or the cats was plain enough. But I became used to seeing his angular figure stalking over the back lawn as I tidied myself in my room before dinner. Sometimes he was softly cursing in the way only an aristocrat or a criminal is allowed to. My hearing is good, but I had heard all such words before, and now and then in other tongues. It meant nothing to me except that the flit of his electric torch returning was as regular as seven o'clock.

On Saturday Doris, with whom I'd kept up the teatime chat in the kitchen, asked if next day I'd be going to church. I said I would not, though would visit the church some other time, as historically it might interest me. Doris seemed sorry I wasn't a church-goer in the theosophic sense. (Just like the professor.) It seemed Swange didn't attend either, Doris told me crisply. He preferred the new hotel at Hodcieux (pronounced locally as *Hoed-Say*) where probably he sometimes met his fancy woman, ten years his senior.

If Doris was offended by her present position in a house of atheists, she had managed herself. She stayed pleasant and obliging to me, and from what I saw, timidly flirtatious with Mr Swange. Perhaps she respected too the shape of a pistol I had noted in his jacket when he went out to check the pens and release the corracats. We all retain means to protect ourselves, if wise. I took no offence at his gun.

As to the house, it was curiously rambling and shadowy for its size. Certain bigger rooms had been partitioned to make two or even three chambers out of one. Some of these lacked windows. Stairs went up and down, twining behind the rooms in obscure ways, to which, fairly quickly, I became accustomed. But it was something of a maze, if a tiny example.

Everywhere one came on statuettes and fetishes from foreign climes. The majority of these were exceptionally horrible to look at, leering with pointed teeth often daubed with painted blood, garlanded by carven heads, (severed, obviously) and clutching in their claws clubs and other more spiky weapons. Doris, whom I had met now and then cleaning the rooms, refused to touch these icons.

"They're not to be disturbed, he" (she would mean the professor) "says. And I – well, I wouldn't *care* to touch them, Miss A."

"Whyever not? Are they so valuable?"

"He says," said she, "they can – invogle things. *Bring* things on – bad wishes, curses."

I queried inwardly what her "*invogle*" meant – *invoke*? "But they're made of wood or stone," I suggested. She said then something else I was later to recall.

"People – witches – heathen priests – can call up spirits, Professor Chazen told me. Oh, he's often given me such a turn with his tales of those places – my blood ran cold. And such bad dreams I had. He said he'd seen as much, in the dark jungles . . . they use wooden images – even animals – as a – what did he say? – a focus – can that be right? Focus . . . and they can summon the *dead*."

I refrained now from saying anything. This litany of necrotic return seemed significant to Doris, a kind of valued other-side-of-the-coin to her religious belief. I have noted similar fancies among pious persons before.

It was the next Thursday evening, about seven-thirty, as I was going down to drink a glass of sherry before dinner, that I heard the crabby voice of Swange complaining to Doris in the main hall below.

I stopped on the stairs to listen. I make no excuse for such a habit. Sometimes it's proved a sensible precaution.

"Those damn beasts are acting oddly," I had heard Swange say.

"Oh, but – they're all so queer. You know he always says" (again, I could assume, I thought, she referred to Chazen) "some of them have odd ways. You'd only have to look at them twice to know it. And they often act up, don't they?"

"It's worse than usual, tonight. Plenty of them are scratch-scratching away at that netting. As for those cats – they've having a fight fit for the *Dog and Pullet* at turn-out time—" At which I heard Doris giggle.

Nevertheless, "Maybe it's just," she said "the heat."

"They're from blinking *Africa*, Dorry!"

So he called her "Dorry", did he?

She said softly, I only just caught it, "Don't take on so. It won't be for much longer, will it, de—"

She broke off as *he* hissed: "Keep it down. That old bat'll be about in a minute."

On her cue, the old bat gave a subdued cough, measured out to sound as if she were slightly further off up the stair than she was, and resumed her passage down to prove him right.

After dinner, I allowed myself half an hour of Mozart on the rather fine if out-of-tune piano. Then I decided on a brief stroll around the grounds at the back. I'd done this once or twice before to get some air, while it was cooler. No one made any comment. Of course, I was wanting to see if Chazen's beasts were as restive as Swange had said.

Nothing however seemed much altered, at least to me.

The corracats had already sprinted off along their tunnel into the fenced woodland. (In their vacant daytime cage, a few clumps of fur added evidence to Swange's account of a fight. But animals often fight, especially when cooped up.) Other animals were out of sight in the sleeping quarters of their pens. Nocturnals paced along the perimeters, but their sentry-go activity was also quite normal, or so I thought. Only the badger-bears, whose name I hadn't learned, seemed at all apparently disturbed. On previous walks here I had seen them lying down, grooming or playing. Tonight all three were up in the pair of trees that grew inside their pen. Blett was supposed, I had gathered, also to trim such enclosed trees down and back from the wire, both here and in the wood. He had signally failed in this. The bears had climbed as high up as they could get indeed, to where the boughs strained against the netting roof that sealed them in. Two of the animals were cuddled together. The third, alone in the second tree, gave the clear impression of their watchman. It uttered a soft, brittle chittering as I went by. And six pale narrow eyes, catching the glim of a rising half moon, observed me with intense uneasy indifference.

I reached the edge of the caged woods, and glanced at the avenues inside. But the woodland was black, and the trace of starlight here and there gave only misleading information – mirages of water, a huge black clump that might be anything, and seemed slightly to move in the windless atmosphere. Of the cats there was no sign. They would be far off down among the trees, no doubt, as distant from the habitat of man as they could get.

I turned from the wood, and looked at the lizard enclosure. This was in the same blackness, just a trickle of starlight on a stone, a leaf – seeming to be other things – a gem, an *eye*. On other evenings, I had seen four or five of the creatures moving about. Now, despite the illusions, none was visible. They must be asleep, or hiding, in their bothy.

Returning to the house, whose curtained lampshine fell dimly on the lawn, I was struck by a peculiar something about the night.

I couldn't at first have said what it was. Certainly, as I have remarked, the evening was hot and airless. That brisk wind combing the trees on my arrival had perished days ago.

Eventually I stopped still once more. I listened. There was not a sound.

Those who live in towns and cities always suppose the country-side to be quiet. In the mechanical way it probably is, aside from the chug of a tractor or the chuffing of a periodic train. But by day *and* night a constant barrage of *natural* noises goes on. Birds flute or shrill alarms. Unseen animal movements cause rustlings and bustle. Frogs croak from ponds, insects buzz, and crickets whirr. After sunset, the volume seems increased. Dogs bark to each other from the hamlets, farms and villages, mice and rabbits squeal, foxes offer eerie banshee screams, owls and night-jars sew up any silent seams of darkness with the stitches of their peculiar music.

Tonight, there was nothing. The motionless, empty air was heavy, and *charged*, as if before a storm. Yet the sky was very clear, deep blue with stars and lifting moonlight.

Back in the house I made myself tea. Bidding Doris goodnight, I went back to the library. I worked and read for another hour, then retreated to bed.

I am not unduly fanciful. Nor am I quite insensitive.

About three in the morning, according to my clock at the bedside, I woke; without a start, but fully and totally. It was as if I had not been asleep at all, so absolute was my awareness of myself and everything about me. None of the usual brief cloudiness of sleep remained. Nor had I been dreaming. My eyes had opened on the nearer of the two windows of my room.

I tend to leave my bedroom casement ajar and the curtains undrawn, when there is the privacy for it. Here I had done so. Framed between the drapes lay the sky. The moon had gone over, but the night still was not at all dark, far less so than the bedroom. I saw very clearly. Nothing was there, looking in at the window.

And yet, along with the unusual sudden waking clarity of my brain, was a sort of definite knowledge that, a second or so before I opened my eyes – *something had been.*

II Rising Up

Now and then in my later life, or rather this later middle part of life I now occupy, odd things have come my way. To say I'm always inured to such amazements would be to lie. But generally I take a (perhaps foolish) interest in them.

After the window incident, decidedly I grew more alert. (Nor did I doubt some visitor had been there. A daylight inspection from said window showed the damaged creeper outside, which bore witness to something quite hefty having *dragged* itself up the brickwork, and then slithered back.)

When I went down to breakfast that morning, Doris was in that mood she had referred to before as a two-and-six.

"Excuse me, Miss A. It's them – those cats again. Poor Mr Swange went to get them back in their pen – as a rule they're already in the tunnel, and soon as they seen him they rush down like anything – it's when he feeds them, you see. Only today they wouldn't budge. Ran about along the edge of the net, and then straight back in the woods. He says they might have the rabbis—"

"The rabb—do you mean *rabies*, Doris?"

"That illness where they froth pink at the mouth, Miss A."

"Doris, that would be very serious. Has he – have you – had contact with them?"

"Oh, we weren't bitten, Miss. And Mr Swange *never* goes into the woods without the professor going with him."

I knew that with rabies, a bite wasn't necessary to cause fatal infection. Infected dogs have frequently licked a human hand before the madness became apparent in them. This hand having one small open cut, the poisonous saliva does its work. Even if not going into the woods, Swange *had* entered the cats' tunnel. A smear of fresh spit on the net—

It seemed best not to frighten Doris worse. She was already in her two-and-six.

"I'm sure it isn't rabies, Doris. How long have the animals been here, it's quite some time, isn't it?"

"About eight months for the cats, Miss A."

"Then rabies is most unlikely. Symptoms present themselves inside a few days, or weeks at the most."

Swange didn't appear. Doris seemed upset. When she produced her basket and got ready to walk down to the village, I offered to go with her. I could do, I said, with the exercise.

She cheered up on the way. Between the fields and hedgerows she chattered about her family, even adding that her "friend" and she planned one day to open a pub or hotel, and be "independent".

I left her in the village street to do her shopping for the house, and took myself over to the church. It was the typical Saxon model, its tower pointed and thatched. But outside I noticed the graveyard was excessively neglected. The old stones, romantic enough in high grass, weeds, moss and ivy, leaned, here and there the stagnant earth actually overturned. In some spots the tilting of the slabs had become precarious, and fallen urns massed in the grass like skulls.

Then I rounded a corner. Between two massive old yew trees another little scene was going on.

From his dress, I recognised the vicar at once. He, and a group of men more roughly clad, were frowning and peering at a solid patch of chaos.

The yews were, from my point of view, quite concealing. In their shade I paused.

"This is too dreadful," said the vicar.

"Yes, sir. An' it's the same business as yesterday, sir, so it is. Plain as my nose."

"Truly, Robert. But yesterday was never so bad as this."

"Well, sir, I blame that bas—I blame that feller Blett."

The other men rumbled. It seemed they did too.

Without doubt, someone appeared to have acted the vandal here. Worked on in a coarse, uneven circle, the old graves were riven, and in places whole slabs had been heaved upward, like unnerving trap doors. The smell of antique, hot moist earth and wetly-dried death filtered through the summer air.

I considered the name, Blett. He was the man who maintained Professor Chazen's animal pens.

"But to do such a sacriligious thing – why would *Blett* do this, in the very graveyard he cared for less than two weeks ago?"

"We seen how he cared for it. If he scythed the grass five times this year, I'm the Prince of Wales."

"I find it hard to think so ill of him." The vicar was an elderly little man of twenty-seven or eight. He plainly wanted to practise Christ's marvellous and ordinarily impossible teaching to love all men as himself. The difficulty, one could see, was constantly painful, but manfully he stayed at it. Believe or disbelieve as one may, the courage of such fragile warriors deserves to be saluted.

"Well, sir," someone patiently said "Blett never did much about the yard here. And if he's had one sober day since I known him I'd doubt. And when he gets got the sack—"

"A rank drunkard he is," vowed one of the others. "And a – well, he's a bad 'un—"

"See, Vicar, he comes back after the sacking, and he spoils the graves – that were yesterday. Then last night he gets another skinful and back he comes and does worse. Allays bin a revengeful bas—a revengeful feller, Blett."

Doris had told me Blett was off on his honeymoon. Had she lied to spare me the more sordid details? I sensed Chazen too must have sacked the revengeful feller.

"Don't fret, sir," the men were now reassuring the vicar, like several kind fathers with a worried little boy. "We'll see to it. Make it proper. Then you come and bless the place over. That'll make all fine."

As they dispersed, I slunk away. Sunday fell the day after tomorrow. I hoped everything would be tidy in time for Doris's next church attendance. Though I doubted village gossip would spare her the news of a disturbance of graves.

She looked decidedly wan at lunch but volunteered nothing, so I too pretended ignorance.

During the afternoon, just as I had set a tenement of uncrated books on the mahogany sorting table, a loud crash resounded below in the core of the house, followed at once by Doris's scream.

I descended swiftly to the ground floor and found her in a gloomy, seldom-used old drawing-room. Partitioned off from another bigger room, it had only one window, facing towards the back lawn, draped either side by thick brocade curtains. Dusty yellow afternoon rayed in, showing the clustering mamoths of dark furniture, and Doris with both hands still clamped to her mouth. Her broom leaned on a chair and on the floor lay her dusters and can of polish. With one more thing.

"It fell, Miss – it just rocked and fell."

An example of the hideous fetish statues was in pieces on the wooden floor beyond the carpet. To my mind its breakage involved no great aesthetic loss. The head had sprawled away intact under a sideboard, where it grinned its nacred, "blood"-splotched fangs.

"I swear, Miss A – I never touched it. I never *do* touch the horrible things – I was over there, polishing that cabinet. And there's this scraping and scratching, and I looks round – and there it goes! Oh Miss!"

In countries prone to major, or minor, earth tremors, this would be a commonplace. But earthquakes are rare, if not unheard of, in Kent.

"Never mind it, Doris. Of course it wasn't your fault."

I'd noticed the single window had been opened wide, perhaps to air the mustiness of the room, for there was a quite nasty smell, dirty and distracting. The windowsill had been scored with a little mark. I went over and saw something had scratched the sill. This had a very recent look, but that might be deceiving. Doris screamed again.

"*There! There!*"

I glared back, and under the sideboard beheld the fetish's grinning head rattling from side to side, its fangs seeming to gnash in a flutter of something white –

"Doris, stay completely still – and silent!"

At my command she froze.

Moving forward I seized her broom and thrust its bristled end directly in under the sideboard.

Something squalled and rolled out, kicking and spitting.

It was not the severed wooden head, but one of the corracats, as I had already deduced from the flutter of its tail.

With a few more irresistible shoves, I broomed the creature back across the room and up against the wall beneath the window, the window through which it must have entered. As I did so I also ripped the nearer curtain from its rings. The heavy brocade plunged down across the cat, and in a series of moments of clawing, rolling and wailing, it had thoroughly enmeshed itself beyond all hope of voluntary exit.

"Fetch Swange!" I shouted, guarding my well-wrapped trophy with the broom.

Doris ran out and was back with him inside five minutes.

In spite of his aversion, as I'd trusted Swange knew, or had been instructed how to cope. He had on thick gauntlets, and soon bundled the shrieking corracat outside and into its pen by the kitchen garden.

There it cowered alone, since the rest of its kind still ran free in the wood. Swange had found meanwhile, he said, another wide open place in the woodland fencing. He set to mending the hole, cursing Blett.

"That's how kitty will have got out," said Doris, explaining needlessly. "And I reckon that Blett done it before he left, to get back at us . . . to be truthful," she went on, hanging her head at the grave error of an earlier lie, "Blett isn't on honeymoon – who'd have him? No, the professor sacked him good and proper, like he said he would to Mr Swange. Oh, I heard the professor shouting, right down in the woods – Blett and the professor were in the wood, you see. It was just after the trap came to take the professor's bags to the train – Anyway, Blett must have slung his hook, as they say. Then come back later and mucked with the fences. And the professor was in such a rage. He went off without a word. But, well—" having raised her head she lowered her eyes. I had a sudden distinct impression she neither liked nor trusted Chazen, perhaps even feared him. She added softly, "I didn't want to burden you, Miss, with all that tale when you'd just arrived. I thought you might think bad of us all and leave."

I smiled and told her I understood.

However, in a while I too went up to inspect the damaged barrier around the wood. Indeed it had been mutilated, but if from the outside, indicating an aggressor no longer in possession of a key to the gate, I was unsure. I pondered if Swange, or Doris, had been at all perturbed by the strange track leading, both inside the wire and out to the scene of the crime. It was a cumbersome and dragging course Blett had made – perhaps due to more than usual drunkenness. Torn leaves and smashed shrubs described it. Yet also, surely, it was too *low* a path for a man to create – though unnecessarily wide for the progress of any animal I had seen here. Had he been crawling all the way on his knees?

Doris said nothing on this. Nor did she question why the escaped cat come into the house. Maybe she put it down to mischief. But it seemed to me that a wild creature would prefer the wild, if it could have it. Only very great eagerness, or fright, would drive it into a human habitation.

Whatever the cause, for our various reasons, we three persons Doris, Swange and I, now seemed to generate a muted tension.

As the evening drew on, Doris was exceptionally quiet at her work. Swange had vanished, but later, as always, I noted his torch flitting back housewards through the seven o'clock dark.

He had checked the pens presumably, but not allowed the one recaptured corracat its routine nightly access to the wood. Presently it began to give off rapid short screeches. These went on and on. The sound was like that of a violin rasped by the bow of a madman. Inevitably, others among the animal prisoners soon added an intermittent chorus.

As I went down, once more I heard Doris speaking very low to Swange. "Couldn't you let it out, Sidney? The fence is all mended now." But apparently Sidney, (were they so intimate?) could not. For the frantic cries went on, and only ceased, one and all, about eleven-thirty that night.

What woke me on this occasion was a noise at least as old as the Dark Ages; in other forms much older. It was the ominous clanging of a church bell – since Christian times a tocsin, the signal of invasion, or some worse calamity.

I'm not entirely unused to emergencies. I sprang up and put on my walking boots and buttoned my coat, which carried some extra protection, over my nightgown. Downstairs I found the lights all on, Doris huddling in her nightclothes and Swange fully dressed. From the smell of whisky I had the feeling he might not anyway have gone to bed.

"It's in the village," he loftily told me, "that bell."

"Yes of course. The church. Hadn't we better go and see?"

"That isn't part of my work," he replied.

"Someone may need assistance."

"I'm not a village man. They can look after themselves."

I shrugged. "Well, Swange, you can let me out, if you will. I intend to find out what's happened."

Swange swore, not very foully. Doris caught his arm. "Mr Swange! You can't let Miss A go on her own—"

"Of course he can. I'm quite well able to look after myself. Open the front door at once, man."

With an iron fist for a face, he obeyed me, and slammed the door shut again as soon as I was on the drive.

The bell was yet ringing for all it was worth, much louder and more alarming in the open air and under the hanging swags of black moonless foliage. I set off down the drive and along the lane at a brisk trot. It was generally a dawdle of twenty minutes, but I covered the ground in ten.

There were plenty of lights on in the village too, and in the church. People stood out on the street along the graveyard wall, or leaned from cottage windows. I noted the pub had opened up again too, and was now serving drinks at three twenty-five in the morning. In just over an hour the sun would rise.

As I entered the main street, the clangour of the bell suddenly ended.

The whole landscape now rang with silence. Everyone ceased to move, myself included. While from the church tower came a faint shout. The crowd repeated the message to itself and so to me. "They've got 'un – it's Jim Hardy, is it? What's he at? Has he gone off his onion?"

Presently two men and the little vicar, all in dressing-gowns, appeared in the church door, supporting another man of sturdy middle years. He was dressed for the day in labourer's clothes, but all awry, his hair over his face and his coat trailing half off. As they tried to bring him out of the door, he started to roar. It seemed he would fight them all rather than leave the church. But then abruptly his legs gave. He stopped roaring, and they partly carried him up the path between the graves, to the gate in the wall, and so through groups of people to the welcoming pub.

I stood decorously with a bundle of women outside. We looked in on the lighted saloon bar. Everything that was said in there we all heard clearly enough.

After the second brandy, the man called Hardy responded to the oft-asked question "What were up with you, Jim, ringing the bell like that?"

"I see it," he said. "Plain as I see you."

"See *what*, Jim?"

"Like it says," said Jim Hardy, "in the Bible. The graves giving them up, and the dead a-walking."

* * *

It seemed Jim was a decent, hard-working labourer, who could turn his hand to various tasks, and he had been promised three days employment, with board, at a farm by Low Cob, a hamlet some thirteen miles from Northerham. There was only a single car in the village, this not owned by Jim, naturally. The cart-ride he had hoped for fell through. As he was expected in Cob by five-thirty that morning he had therefore had to set out on foot in the middle hours of the night.

His road took him through the village about 2:00 am. The moon was sinking as he paused by the graveyard wall to light his pipe.

"That was when I seen 'em."

Unlike many older rural people, Jim Hardy was not unduly superstitious about graves. At first, he said, he thought what he was seeing was foxes or badgers, playing about there under the trees and among the tall, uncut grass. There seemed quite a few of them, a whole family, he thought, and he was asking himself what the local hunt would make of running any of them to earth on sacred ground, when something in the whole movement and method of the animals struck him as quite odd. "They were seeming," he said, shuddering, "to be slinking along slow, all of 'em, on their bellies. And in a kind of – like – a circle."

So then he'd got the notion it was *men* in the churchyard – after all, weren't these uncertain forms too big-looking for foxes? And carrying on like that – they must be up to no good. There were solid silver candle-sconces in the church that were said to date back to the days of King Henry V. Though locked in a cupboard in the vestry, the church door itself was always left undone.

Jim Hardy was perfectly brave on this score. He put down his bag of work tools and selected a fine strong hammer. This in hand, he slipped through the gate, and crept by the trees and the leaning stones . . . towards the spot where the robbers were cavorting in their peculiar, lurching circle.

He took his stand where I had, between those two vast yew trees, safe from detection as he thought in their coal-black shadow.

And then one last shaft of the sinking moon struck helpfully between the graves. And he saw.

At first – as one might not – he didn't believe his eyes. "Was like a dream," he said "like some joke som'un played on me."

But he found he couldn't move. His limbs had changed to lead, and his eyes frozen in a stare, unable to turn away. He went cold too, he told us all, as if winter snow came down on the summer land.

"They was circling, right enough, going around and around. Like *worms* they was, great, huge worms, crawling on their bellies, but their necks and heads raised up – and their *chests* raised up clear of the ground – like snakes I see in a book – and their hollow eyes – they looked at me, they looked and the eyes shone! There was white fire in them eyes, though they was all dead hollow sockets, and the broken ribs showed through their chest-cases and the round bone showed through the scalp of their heads like old yeller felt caps."

His perverse acuity of description held us riveted. But having said all this, Jim Hardy lapsed. He began to shake, to stamp his feet, and to pull at something invisible in the air – I came to realise he was enacting his breaking loose from paralysis, his flight into the unlocked church, his climb up the tower, and his ringing of the harsh old bell.

From the scatter of his now gasping words, we made out that from the window above, before starting to ring, he had also seen the circle of corpses, still with heads and upper torsos raised, (ribs starting through the flesh as if through unmended waistcoats) the arms and legs dragging *boneless* behind them, the glint of white hell-fire in the cores of dead eye-sockets, but each and all slithering round and round atop the wreckage of their undone graves, aimless or determined, he could not know which, in this ritual of their living resurrection.

The pub had become very still.

Finally the vicar, meaning well, put his slender hand gently on Jim's shoulder. Then Jim grew totally dumb. He sat rigid, only his head tilted back on the chair, his eyes fixed unblinking, locked again in the frozen stare he had described. He was very white, and his hands were very cold I should think, as if from the summer snow he had mentioned.

He would, or could, say no more. He would not move either, though they coaxed him.

Then the doctor arrived. Sent for long since, he'd been delayed by delivering a baby to the policeman's wife – which was why, of course, the policeman too had arrived with the doctor. Unfairly the doctor berated the men in the pub, saying that giving brandy had not been a sensible idea in a case of such extreme shock. The doctor informed us all too that corpses pushing out of their tombs and slithering in the churchyard by "*walking*" on their chests was all "tosh. Did any of the rest of you see anything like that? *No*? And does it anyway seem like the Last Day to you? Is the moon turned red as blood?" The policeman was more civilised, pleased perhaps at the healthy son with which his wife had presented him. He led the party of muttering men to inspect the ruin of the graves. Their torchlight – not electric but lit on sticks from a kitchen range – soon began to fade with the coming of dawn.

I myself went down and took a surreptitious look at the site of Jim Hardy's horror. It was the exact place, obviously, the vicar and the men had been troubled at yesterday. And there could be no doubt now, doctor or no, that the graves were fully upheaved, headstones and slabs flung headlong. The soil and other debris which had also come up, including, doubtless, pieces of bone, had poured off everywhere. The ground richly stank, the terrible odour of ancient mortal decay, and one man had turned away to vomit.

Nevertheless, no one else had seen what Jim Hardy claimed to have done.

I noted however, elsewhere in the churchyard, runnels where the grass was mashed and flattened, the ivy torn in trails, and on the old dark roots, or even in some cases quite far up the trunks over my head, were peeled green wounds. Very likely, Jim rushing in his panic, and now the nervous searchers, had caused this further damage.

III The Apocalypse

They were tender to Jim Hardy, but the hard-tongued doctor whisked him off to the hospital.

Later the policeman, augmented by two more senior others from Hodcieux, interviewed the village, and subsequently the three of us at the house.

I have no clue what Swange said, or Doris, (though I suspect it was very little.) I merely told the truth, which is usually the easiest way, where one can.

The village man nodded when I said I too had afterwards gone to look at the broken graves, and seen how the grass and ivy were disturbed. One of the senior officers, he who had already demanded why I had gone to the village at all in the middle of the night – my answer, to see what was wrong, made him snort – now commented sternly that for so curious and prying a woman, I appeared unnmoved. I replied that in my work, curiosity is not a fault, but that also I had learned some self-control.

(Doris told me after, with a strange momentary pride in me, that she had heard the village policeman remark to the less favourable other that I was, "The best type of Englishwoman". I had gone fearlessly to the village in order to help, and confronted by horror had not lost my nerve. With the aid of such "handmaidens, young or old" the Empire had been forged. This amused me rather. My ancestry is mixed, and certainly I do not regard myself as particularly British, let alone English.)

The police departed and we were left alone.

The scalding day passed uncomfortably. The animals of Chazen's menagerie seemed all of them unsettled. The cats in the wood were shrilling, the other cat, for which at last the tunnel had been unlocked in daylight, skulked and now refused to leave the pen for the trees. Neither would the small bears come down from their high perches, even when tempted with food. The beetles, rats and snakes kept intransigently to inner refuges of the cages from which they could not be seen. Various other species, including the lizards, appeared to have dug pits in the earth of their pens and hidden. Swange was in a stiff, cold rage. One could see it from his stalking about the lawns. He was like a guardian forced to take charge of unruly children he disliked. Later he too disappeared, as he so often did. Doris, when I met her, was pale and anxious.

By now I had abandoned my efforts on the library. Instead I'd searched among the crates of books, attempting to find anything that would throw light on those travels the professor had previously made, and so on the collections of curios, and animals, thereby accumulated.

I did locate certain texts relating at least to some of these. The corracats, for example, hailed from South Africa, where they were known to live in prides. Hunters and carrion-eaters both, sometimes they would climb trees, and in the heart of certain jungles, they were said to be the servants of a particular god, who, taking cat-shape, troubled the afterlife of men.

The snakes meanwhile were allegedly capable of swallowing whole cows, which I doubted, judging not by their size alone, but from the formation of their jaws.

The beetles were especially treasured. Asian in origin, they had evolved a means of attaching gems to their hairy carapaces, sealing emeralds and rubies in; but why or how was not properly explained. Nor had I spotted any jewels cemented on Chazen's beetles.

I could find nothing written about the badger-bears, or on any other beast, apart from the lizards. There was a slim pamphlet devoted to them, slipped between the pages of another book. It seemed they could be discovered in Indonesia. Select temples maintained them as pets, and their intelligence put them under the jurisdiction of yet another god or goddess, (according to the author, rather a cruel one) in whose honour they would perform funeral rites, including, of all things, "morbidly clowning, to inspire and agitate the dead."

Aside from this book, I picked up another small volume, its title being: *Raising the Dead: Ceremonies of An Elder World.*

On these pages I found engravings which depicted several of the nightmarish fetishes and icons physically represented in Chazen's house. The "instructions", if so they may be termed, were by stages stupid, insane, risible and disgusting. On the last page of the delicious tome I came across a scrawl I recognised. It was Chazen's own handwriting, familiar to me from our earlier exchange of letters. It said only this: *The eternal and unalterable secret of animation, or re-animation, is the presence of life – how can it be any other thing than that*?

By evening, every single animal in the garden-menagerie had escaped.

Immersed in my studies, I'd ceased to hear either birdsong of wailing from the back premises of the house. Nor that both had ended. The first I knew of any break-out was the very different noise of Swange shouting and swearing in the hall below. (Those who contend only women become hysterical are in error. Neither female nor male necessarily needs internal possession of a womb to lose their *head*.)

I decided to go down when Doris's high frightened voice joined his.

"What is the matter?"

"Miss A – Oh Miss—"

"Don't start telling *that* old hen," bellowed Swange. "What can *she* do? She's an old meddler. She'll only make the whole mess worse." Swange was not himself. High-coloured and ranting, at his wits' end.

And it was *my* fault? I descended the last stair and trod squarely on his foot. (A slap in the face is seldom essential.) He blundered back, then in again, so I detected a past history of unfortunate developments. He collected himself just in time.

"I do beg your pardon, Mr Swange," I said. "A misstep. At my age . . . my balance, you know. But whatever is wrong?"

He gaped, then replaced his iron mask. It was Doris who told me.

"They've all got out, Miss. All those animals. They must've been that scared – you could see they were – all bristly and hiding – and digging – even the little cat in the pen, he's gone too – Oh! What shall we do?"

I asked if any were very dangerous? Could they be inveigled to return? What precisely had so alarmed them?

Doris twittered and Swange interruptively boomed, "None that dangerous, except to ducks and chickens. But they're valuable to *him*. And no, we can't lure them back – haven't I been trying? As for what they're scared of—" here he broke off. The hot metal of his face cooled to pallor. "That business in the village. What was *that*?"

"I don't know, Mr Swange. Something certainly. But there have been incidents of grave-robbery before here and there—"

"Oh spare me silly women! It's never that. I went and took a look myself. I spoke to some of the blokes. The graves are *empty*. No one took them, but those corpses are out and away. It's against God."

I was quite startled to find Swange after all superstitious, and at least an affiliate believer.

"Yes, I imagine God might take a poor view of such a spiritually distasteful resurrection. But what do *you* believe has happened?"

"It's Chazen. He's a bloody devil. We've meant to get away from here this twelvemonth. Me and her – Doris. Saving up. The old girl at the hotel – I put it about here I'm her fancy man. But it isn't that. I've known her for years. She needs some persuasion, but I'm going to buy the place, then Dorry and me can be independent." (So Swange was indeed, incredibly, Doris's "gentleman friend"!) But Swange plunged on. "Him, with all his so-called learning and his funny ways, and all this mumbo-jumbo – *fascinates* Chazen it does, the rotten fool. The Devil himself'll carry him off, mark my words."

"So you believe the professor is responsible—"

"I *know* the bastard is. *Know* it. We have to get away – like those animals of his – cleverer than us, eh? I'd even bet Chazen might be around the place, somewhere, watching to see how it all goes. Easy enough to get his stuff put on the train and stay behind. He's at the back of this unholy filth." He gave an angry laugh, then swallowed it. Approvingly I saw he had done that because Doris had started to cry.

Beyond the windows, a thick brassy dusk was quickly coming down. No bird sang or flew over the trees. From the narrow window at the back, I could see the edge of the cats' deserted pen, the netting wrenched up. And night was on its way.

"Is this the real reason why Blett left Chazen's employment?" I inquired, keeping my back turned to Swange and Doris, who were clinging together in the gloaming.

"Him, that soaker? He *helped* Chazen. Blett was loony."

"Helped him in what way?"

"You don't want to know, Miss Constable."

"I do."

"Every single one of those animals and insects – they're all to do with heathen death rites – raising the dead. And Chazen and Blett, they'd do the rituals in the woods, and now and then they'd kill one of the animals – a rat, a lizard, a bear, a cat. Meant to make the jungle magic happen. Stir it all up, after dark—"

"Ritual sacrifices."

Swange only swore, vividly now. Doris's sobs became loud.

I waited, then turned and said calmly, "What shall we do then, Mr Swange?"

He gave me a look, but in the end, in the gathering dimness, I was only a fragile ageing woman, the weaker sex, deferential at last, needing his protection. To his credit, he gave it.

"That's all right, Miss Constable. We'll be safe enough till morning if we keep inside. But we'll fasten all the doors and windows. Better start now."

I began this narrative with a reminiscence – about the day when I was barely out of childhood; the day I saw the static hill that had grown out of the fluid of the sea.

Probably it is quite apparent that, not doubting my sight or my sanity (at fifteen years it is sometimes easier not to), I was afraid. The phenomenon of the hill, to me, indicated a rent in the fabric of the organised world.

No one was with me. I've said, my father was feckless, (and liked alcohol more than it cared for him) and my mother a ninny. I was alone, and the holiday people on the cliff, passing to and fro, evidently hadn't perceived anything out of the ordinary.

I began to cry – by which I mean water ran uncontrollably out of my eyes – tears, I presume, though in fact it was not like crying at all. Perhaps it was only a flag run up reading *Help! Help!*

Eventually an elderly couple, a man and lady, halted by me.

When I look back, I grasp that undoubtedly they were only a handful of years older than I am now. Not elderly then, in the precise sense, though his hair at least was grey. But generous they were. And wise.

Neither said to me demandingly, *What is it, girl*? Or worse, floodingly, *Oh dear, dear child, whatever is wrong*?

The gentleman bowed and lifted his hat. He said "May my wife and I be of service, young lady?"

And when I turned my streaming eyes on them, she solemnly said "My husband is always to be trusted."

What a wonder! A sober yet gallant male, a level-headed female who utterly approved of him. Oh, yes, others might have been suspicious. But I was not, nor had I need to be. They were as genuine as new-minted gold.

I wiped my eyes and they cleared. I said "Look there, out at sea – that hill! It has never been there before. How *can* it be there?"

They turned and stared, as I did then, out across the blue plains of the Atlantic ocean, to the sea-blue hill rising steeply up from it.

"Upon my word," said he, "what a thing. What do you think—?" to his wife – "Is it some island?"

"But the young lady would know if it was an island. She has told us. It was never there, before."

That they too saw it, *perused* it, discussed it, this extended to me great reassurance.

While – for the first time in my life – I found myself no longer alone. I had finally successfully communicated with two other sentient and thinking things. I am well aware those moments on the cliff secured in me for ever a hopeful *liking* for strangers, and a wish toward independence and – perhaps – the desire to grow up – not into some bloom of womanhood, but straight into my middle years. It's possible, I suppose, even my hair turned grey at such an early age because of this desire, rather than because of some shock or failing.

On the cliff then we three watched the mystery of the hill. And so shortly thereafter, the three of us also observed how it started to bulge, to topple, and to change—

At midnight, it began.

The doors and windows of Northerham House had been locked and bolted. Had there been bars, such as a mediaeval castle or manor boasted, they would have been lowered into their slots. Swange oversaw all. That is, he followed me about, at least, to be sure the silly old maid had got things right. She had. Mr Swange had no notion, perhaps luckily, of the number of times she had been called upon for accuracy.

Presumably he knew Doris had also fulfilled her duty. I imagine that she had.

That evening she catered for our communal meal – pretence at separation was now extraneous. We ate cold meat, pickles, hot potatoes, cheese and biscuits, with a fine claret I think Swange had liberated from the cellar, caring not much by now for his "Master" Chazen's possessions.

Night itself descended with slight incident. But it was very overcast and black, starless, moonless and stormy, yet no thunder sounded, no lightning irritated the sky. Swange had decided every electric lamp in the house should be switched on, and this was seen to. To me then it seemed we had made of the house a livid fiery beacon. Nevertheless, all approaches – front and back – the empty sheds and encloures, woods both fenced and adjacent to the property, the lane which led up to the drive and the drive itself, were blankly illumined by a cold, flat yellow.

Swange refused Doris's request to close the curtains.

"We must *see*," he said.

He meant *see what draws near*. He had become a sergeant in an ancient fort.

After our amalgamated meal, I went upstairs and, so far as I could, readied myself.

How should any of us know what might be abroad? A thrill of dismay went through me at the memory of the village, probably unprepared – yet even so it was by now far too late to venture into the dark. For the dark surrounded us, and we were only this small lighthouse perched on a rock.

Having gone up, I gazed from the library. From here I could see the tree-hung drive, and the curve of the lane beyond which led into Northerham.

No warning church bell sounded.

Hours were shed like heavy leaves, from a tree that did not mind whether spring would follow autumn and winter. Who, in like circumstance, has never felt the awful indifference of natural things? *They* know but too well they must first go down into the abyss. But we, the animals abroad on the world's face, accept nothing, and so struggle.

At five minutes to midnight I heard the large, always belated, library clock strike the quarter hour behind me among the book-stacks. Perhaps despite myself I had been dozing a little, seated there at the window. For sure, it seemed to me that all at once everything had altered.

I got up, walked about, and looked once more from the window.

Nothing anywhere moved, not even the massed clouds above.

But again I became aware of that dense tremble of silence I had noted before. The room, the whole house, was smothered by it. It occurred to me that this silence was in fact not *merely* an absence of all sound. Human things have sharper faculties than they credit. There is nothing particularly supernatural in this, save in the most literal sense – for they are primal instincts that long ago moved in us freely, and doubtless many times saved the lives of our remotest ancestors. Now and then such talents surface again. This *silence* then was my own animal faculty, which told me unerringly the moment of terror was upon us.

I concentrated my gaze along the drive. In all that motionless light and dark of shadows and electric beams, after all – *movement.* The leaves and boughs there, low-hanging to the path, were dipping, shaking. Something approached.

A twig snapped like a pistol shot. The sound seemed to splinter the night.

Out on to the drive the creature emerged. It pushed foward, in a jerky slithering. Unmistakable; it was just as Jim Hardy had recounted: a dead thing once living and mortal. Both sets of its limbs dragged bonelessly alongside and behind it, but it *walked* forward on its chest, which arched up from the driveway, so displaying the broken ribs of the body cavity among the quivering flags of mummified, cloth-like skin. Some rags of hair too fluttered over its skull and down its back. Maybe, when formerly alive, it had been female. The head and neck reared craningly upwards, turning a little, stiffly, as if it glanced constantly and carefully from left to right. And in the broad light of the house, the hollow black caves of its eyes flashed with a cold white sparkle.

Undeniably, it seemed to have the definite purpose of *reaching* the house. But as it drew very near, suddenly it swung itself, with a ghastly, ungainly, almost-grace, away. Like any familiar or tradesman, it rounded the corner, apparently going round toward the kitchen door.

By then another of them had crawled out on to the drive, proceeding exactly as had the first of its kind. To judge by the now-continuous jostle of the lower boughs and bushes in the lane, there were many more close behind.

At this moment Doris shrieked, not once, but three times, very loudly and very near. Running out, I found her on the landing, standing there rigid, and Swange not five feet away from her. They must have retreated here from the ground floor. Now they were staring in petrified horror down the staircase, at something I could not yet see.

My eyes flew to the main door. It had stayed fast shut, as had all windows. Had the creatures then discovered some way in at the back? Was one of them already below in the hall?

Brushing by Doris, I went to the head of the stair-case. And looked straight down into the face of death.

If there had been any doubt – I had had none – denial would no longer be possible. The thing which now came sliding, awkward and inexorable, with a quietly scraping thumping drumbeat up the broad stairs – was dead as any corpse could be. And if it was not as ancient and decayed as the others I'd witnessed outside, this one had been made dilapidated in other ways. Whole chunks had been wrenched from it, and certainly its eyes had been gouged out, for the pits were fairly fresh and still a little sticky with blood. Inside them nevertheless some kind of eyelight glared up at me, glittering. On the front of the head there clung a dense mane of blackish hair, though this was knotted and twisted too with blood, and with soil, and decorated with chips of what must be bone. Unlike the other corpses too, it wore clothing, or the remnants, modern enough, even to the stained and frayed silk tie still knotted round its torn throat. Beside all that, it was sufficiently fresh it ripely stank. It had the rich dirty meaty smell I had in error previously thought belonged only to the corracat in the drawing-room.

The corpse was by now about halfway up the stair. It showed no wish to halt its advance. And as each step was attempted and achieved, a sinister scratching sounded.

"No, Sidney," quavered Doris in a tiny whisper behind me. "Can't you see – it's *him*!"

Him? I turned to her for a split second. "*Who* is it, Doris?"

"The professor—" she whispered, before stepping back and dropping on the landing in a dead faint.

This was when Swange fired his handgun.

I spun about again to watch a vase shatter in the hall below. He had missed. Besides – if the creature were already dead, what use was there in firing at it?

And yet – do the dead walk? Do hills form from the sea? I can't say decidedly, but I will suggest, not very often.

My own little pistol was already in my hand, small and dainty as a toy, quite suitable for a silly old maid.

I raised my arm, aiming for the space between the dead man's eyes, judged the swinging of the head, and fired point blank.

The thing on the staircase leaped. Affrontedly it reared right up, so that first it balanced on its knees and then swiftly rose to its feet – after which it tumbled slowly over backward and plummeted down to the foot of the stairs. There it writhed once, oddly as if trying to become comfortable. After that it grew immobile, and stayed so.

Swange and I also stayed where we were a while, each one of us with our smoking gun. Doris lay motionless on the carpet behind us.

Silence had come again. It was unlike the silence I had twice been aware of. This was simply the absence of any noise.

Swange spoke very low.

"He was in the house. All the time. He came out of the old drawing-room, from behind the dresser. Doris'd smelled a smell in there. We thought a rat had died in the wall. But he just came out. I said to him, Are you all right Professor Chazen? Stupid bloody thing to say. His head like that, and crawling – he was dead, wasn't he. Doris ran straight up here, and I can tell you, I came after her. They were all round the house by then. They still are—"

I started to go down. "*Don't!*" cried Swange.

"It's all right, Mr Swange. I just need to see – ah, yes," I said, reaching the stairfoot, standing over the corpse of my previously unmet employer, and finding what I *thought* I had in the moment he fell.

Unpleasant shrieks were beginning outside, and growls, thuds and grunting. Something slammed against the door and Swange gave a yell. But I could already make out what took place through the nearest window. "Come and look, Mr Swange. We have some most unlikely allies."

He bounded down, and together we watched from the security behind the glass, as three corracats scrambled among the two last corpses to have reached the drive. The cats were tearing them in pieces, and as they did this, like a macabre conjuring trick, we beheld what lay behind the façade of each of the slithering undead.

Swange spoke his most blistering oath to date.

"When the corpse of the professor reared up and fell, I could see its claws," I said mildly, "poking through the chest, and another set from the lower torso. That was how they could move. They'd eaten their way in, tunnelled through each corpse. Their heads were pushed up into the skull cavity. It must have been like donning a helmet, once the hindrance of any brains were either eaten or discarded."

Swange made a stifled sound.

I said "As for seeing out, no doubt they could spy well enough from each side through chinks in the skull. And what glittered so brightly through the eye-holes of the dead when catching any light, was not an eye at all, in fact only their *scales*."

Outside now the five cats were very busy, ripping away the dry old flesh to come at those same shining scales, and so to the more succulent living lizard flesh beneath. A further two cats burst from around the side of the house, involved in a vicious tug-of-war over a single dead lizard already pulled from its cadaver. Similar hunting screams came now from every direction. It seemed the cats meant to complete their hunt on all sides of the house.

Doris called feebly from above, "Sidney, Sidney—"

I went up at once and helped her to rise.

"Did Sidney shoot it?" she whimpered, pointing at Chazen's body in the hall. Though dim with faintness, her eyes strayed to my own pistol. "Or was it *you*, Miss?"

I told her firmly, "I'm afraid *I* shot the vase, Doris. But Mr Swange luckily has a steady hand. He killed the thing with one shot."

Below, Swange gave me a scowl. Then winked. "You're too hard on yourself, Miss A. You were just rattled, that was all, and no wonder. At any other time I'm sure you could shoot like a regular trooper."

No newspaper carried this story. It was, I assume, kept quiet for fear the grisly facts cause more upset than interest.

The police of course were for some days ever-present. After them came people to do with collecting and reinstating the disturbed remains – what survived of them. The graveyard was tidied and resanctified to holy ground.

The rest of Chazen's animals were rounded up and removed to a well-run zoo – aside from a pair of corracats and one snake, which eluded the searchers, and perhaps still roam the Kentish fields and woods, stealing the odd chicken or sheep. Even given the reputation of the snakes, probably no cows go missing.

Despite the bullet I had fired into the dead professor's head, experts soon enough discovered he had been killed by a savage blow to the *back* of the cranium, delivered some days earlier, and administered by a torn-up stake from the fence. Blett was the inevitable suspect. Inside a week he had been traced to a lodging house in Plymouth, and on apprehension, confessed. He had murdered Chazen in a fit of drunken wrath, fed up, he said, with Chazen's constant complaints about poor upkeep of the grounds.

Seeing what he had done, Blett had hastily dug a grave and tipped Chazen in. But this bodge was no match either for the heat or Chazen's cats. Unrealizing, Blett had bolted with drunk optimimism for the coast. He had also been drunk enough, prior to the argument and homicide, deliberately to have damaged every cage and shed, in what he afterwards termed "cunning ways" not immediately obvious. He intended all the precious collected animals the professor used for study (or slaughter during trials of black magic), to escape. Swange's lack of interest in the menagerie, and frequent trips to Hodcieux and the hotel, had also no doubt aided the sabotage, which went mainly undetected. Blett's subsequent fate was the usual miserable one prescribed in such circumstances. He hanged.

As for the rest, while Chazen's servants had thought he caught the train – which even Swange had ultimately doubted – the professor's body lying summer-rotting in his wood enticed the corracats to devour parts of him. For that reason they refused to return into the pen, while one which had got out through one of Blett's holes in the wood-fencing, followed Chazen's corpse into the house, once it was transported there. Mostly, the *freshness* of

Chazen's death had stirred up the great lizards to their original function.

For these animals had really taken a rôle in mystic funereal rites of certain temples. The professor had never learned, beyond foolish guesswork, what this rôle was. But it was one of the temples' deeper mysteries.

Only some years after did I come across a volume on the sacred death practices of eastern Asia, which, in half a page, enlightened me as to why the lizards acted as they had. They were, it seemed, trained to enter the corpses of the dead, scouring out as they did so any impeding bodily matter. Then, once in full possession of a body, they would make the cadaver "dance". This dance then was the appalling reared-up slither-crawl Jim Hardy, Doris, Swange and I had seen at first-hand. To the initiates of the temples, however, it was neither a horrific nor a profane act. Let alone the "morbid clowning" Chazen's own ignorant book claimed it to be. By showing the unopposed animal possession of every corpse, otherwise empty and lacking any motive power of its own, the "dance" displayed that the human spirit had gone far away to a place of joy and safety, where its happiness was so sure, it no longer cared what became of the cast-off flesh.

Able to get out, the lizards had quickly located Chazen's body. One served him as it had been trained to do, finally conveying its ceremonial corpse into the privacy and dark of the drawing-room, through a wide open window. (It had previously tried entry via a smaller casement without success – that of my bedroom.) The other lizards, now all questing to fulfil their purpose, found the graveyard. Perhaps a keen sense of smell assisted them, and their formerly honorable task was soon accomplished. Why did all of them return to the house? It was no doubt part of the rite to seek their temple. The house by now stood for this temple. Alas for them. None of them survived the onslaught of the corracats – nor my single pistol shot.

Ironically, no one was abroad that night in the village. The concluding journey of the lizards, in their pantomime costumes of death, went unseen. Jim Hardy therefore remains the sole village witness, and once released from hospital drank free of charge for a month on the story.

Doris and Swange are by this time long married, and thrive in their hotel at Hodcieux, which the locals pronounce Hoed-Say. I receive a postcard every year. And so have learned there are now also three little Swanges too, and one little Doris.

Chazen's house has become, I gather, a select school for young ladies. The books from the library were sold for a small fortune. I can't think why. Though decent enough, they were scarcely the best of their type I have catalogued.

And so. The hill.

The hill in the ocean became for me my credo, just as the two kind strangers who watched with me the hill's metamorphosis, channeled my unhappy youth quickly into a satisfactory, premature middle-age.

I've said, we saw the impossible hill begin to bulge and topple. And then it sank sidelong – and floated with a slow swiftness, away over the horizon. Other hills very like it soon followed after. They were all the same blue as the sea, and drifted now in a lifting wind, like a fleet of ships. They were clouds.

Yes. My hill, so solid and static and inexplicable, had been a cloud, placed strangely by a freak of calm weather, darker than the upper sky and matching the colour of the water, seeming therefore to be *made* of the water, upright and uncanny. A rent in the world that threatened to reveal the surrounding abysm of chaos.

We laughed, the couple and I. Less with relief than with wonder at the trick a string of coincidences of the elements had played. The gentleman thanked me too, for giving him an interesting tale to tell that night at dinner in their boarding-house. We parted, never to meet again.

A cloud. It isn't, however, that I believe that chaos does *not* lie on all sides of us. Evidently it does, and well we know it, in our innermost hearts. But it is the *fear* of the chance of *stumbling* on that chaos that makes us start at shadows. The dead at Northerham were animated by a purely physical possession. The hill in the sea was built from a cloud the wind left to lie just long enough to deceive.

If I have any hope for anything, I trust we are eternally protected from the naked view of chaos – while in this world.

And if at last we must confront it, we shall then be in some other greater form, well able to contend with blasting light or shattering darkness. Like the souls of the dead who never care what is done with their cast-off flesh.

JOE R. LANSDALE

Godzilla's Twelve Step Program

TEXAS-BORN MOJO STORYTELLER and scriptwriter Joe R. Lansdale is the author of more than thirty novels in all genres, including crime, Western, horror and pulp adventure.

The author of *Act of Love*, *Dead in the West*, *The Night-runners*, *Cold in July*, *The Bottoms*, *Lost Echoes* and the *Drive-In* series, he is also known for his seven novels about two unlikely friends, Hap Collins and Leonard Pine, who live in a town in East Texas and find themselves solving a variety of often violent or macabre mysteries. The series began with *Savage Season* in 1990 and has continued through *Mucho Mojo*, *Two-Bear Mambo*, *Bad Chili*, *Rumble Tumble*, *Veil's Visit* and *Captains Outrageous*.

His short fiction has been collected in *By Bizarre Hands*,

Bestsellers Guaranteed, *Writer of the Purple Rage*, *High Cotton*, *Bumper Crop* and *The Shadows Kith and Kin*.

Lansdale has also written scripts for various comic books and animated television shows, and his Bram Stoker Award-nominated novella *Bubba Ho-Tep*, about an aged Elvis Presley and black John F. Kennedy battling the eponymous soul-sucking Egyptian mummy, was filmed by Don Coscarelli in 2002. His short story, "Incident On and Off a Mountain Road" was also adapted by Coscarelli as the premier episode of the first season of Showtime's *Masters of Horror* series.

Lansdale is the winner of six HWA Bram Stoker Awards, the British Fantasy Award, the MWA Edgar Award, the American Mystery Award, the Horror Critics Award and the "Shot in the Dark" International Crime Writer's Award. In 2007 he was voted the World Horror Convention's Grand Master winner with the highest number of votes ever cast in the history of the seventeen-year-old award.

"'Godzilla's Twelve Step Program' came to me in a flash," recalls the author. "I think I had seen in the news about a half-dozen different twelve-step programmes – alcohol, drugs, sex addiction, etc. – and I thought, you know, you could apply this to anything.

"There may have been something about Godzilla in the air as well. I know I had at one time a blow-up dinosaur that had led to my writing 'Bob the Dinosaur Goes to Disneyland', and it may well have influenced this one along with those twelve steps. Whatever, it's a favourite of mine."

I: Honest Work

GODZILLA, ON HIS WAY TO WORK at the foundry, sees a large building that seems to be mostly made of shiny copper and dark, reflecting solar glass. He sees his image in the glass and thinks of the old days, wonders what it would be like to stomp on the building, to blow flames at it, kiss the windows black with his burning breath, then dance rapturously in the smoking debris.

One day at a time, he tells himself. One day at a time.

Godzilla makes himself look at the building hard. He passes it by. He goes to the foundry. He puts on his hard hat. He blows his fiery breath into the great vat full of used car parts, turns the car parts to molten metal. The metal runs through pipes and into new moulds for new car parts. Doors. Roofs. Etc.

Godzilla feels some of the tension drain out.

II: Recreation

After work Godzilla stays away from downtown. He feels tense. To stop blowing flames after work is difficult. He goes over to the BIG MONSTER RECREATION CENTER.

Gorgo is there. Drunk from oily seawater, as usual. Gorgo talks about the old days. She's like that. Always the old days.

They go out back and use their breath on the debris that is deposited there daily for the center's use. Kong is out back. Drunk as a monkey. He's playing with Barbie dolls. He does that all the time. Finally, he puts the Barbies away in his coat pocket, takes hold of his walker and wobbles past Godzilla and Gorgo.

Gorgo says, "Since the fall he ain't been worth shit. And what's with him and the little plastic broads anyway? Don't he know there's real women in the world?"

Godzilla thinks Gorgo looks at Kong's departing walker-supported ass a little too wistfully. He's sure he sees wetness in Gorgo's eyes.

Godzilla blows some scrap to cinders for recreation, but it doesn't do much for him, as he's been blowing fire all day long and has, at best, merely taken the edge off his compulsions. This isn't even as satisfying as the foundry. He goes home.

III: Sex and Destruction

That night there's a monster movie on television. The usual one. Big beasts wrecking havoc on city after city. Crushing pedestrians under foot.

Godzilla examines the bottom of his right foot, looks at the scar there from stomping cars flat. He remembers how it was to have people squish between his toes. He thinks about all of that and changes the channel. He watches twenty minutes of *Mr Ed*, turns off the TV, masturbates to the images of burning cities and squashing flesh.

Later, deep into the night, he awakens in a cold sweat. He goes to the bathroom and quickly carves crude human figures from bars of soap. He mashes the soap between his toes, closes his eyes and imagines. Tries to remember.

IV: Beach Trip and the Big Turtle

Saturday, Godzilla goes to the beach. A drunk monster that looks like a big turtle flies by and bumps Godzilla. The turtle calls Godzilla a name, looking for a fight. Godzilla remembers the turtle is called Gamera.

Gamera is always trouble. No one liked Gamera. The turtle was a real asshole.

Godzilla grits his teeth and holds back the flames. He turns his back and walks along the beach. He mutters a secret mantra given him by his sponsor. The giant turtle follows after, calling him names.

Godzilla packs up his beach stuff and goes home. At his back he hears the turtle, still cussing, still pushing. It's all he can do not to respond to the big dumb bastard. All he can do. He knows the turtle will be in the news tomorrow. He will have destroyed something, or will have been destroyed himself.

Godzilla thinks perhaps he should try and talk to the turtle, get him on the twelve step program. That's what you're supposed to do. Help others. Maybe the turtle could find some peace.

But then again, you can only help those who help themselves. Godzilla realises he can not save all the monsters of the world. They have to make these decisions for themselves. But he makes a mental note to go armed with leaflets about the twelve step program from now on.

Later, he calls in to his sponsor. Tells him he's had a bad day. That he wanted to burn buildings and fight the big turtle. Reptilicus tells him it's okay. He's had days like that. Will have days like that once again.

Once a monster always a monster. But a recovering monster is where it's at. Take it one day at a time. It's the only way to be happy in the world. You can't burn and kill and chew up humans and their creations without paying the price of guilt and multiple artillery wounds.

Godzilla thanks Reptilicus and hangs up. He feels better for awhile, but deep down he wonders just how much guilt he really harbors. He thinks maybe it's the artillery and the rocket-firing jets he really hates, not the guilt.

V: Off the Wagon

It happens suddenly. He falls off the wagon. Coming back from work he sees a small doghouse with a sleeping dog sticking halfway out of a doorway. There's no one around. The dog looks old. It's on a chain. Probably miserable anyway. The water dish is empty. The dog is living a worthless life. Chained. Bored. No water.

Godzilla leaps and comes down on the doghouse and squashes dog in all directions. He burns what's left of the doghouse with a blast of his breath. He leaps and spins on tip-toe through the wreckage. Black cinders and cooked dog slip through his toes and remind him of the old days.

He gets away fast. No one has seen him. He feels giddy. He can hardly walk he's so intoxicated. He calls Reptilicus, gets his answering machine. "I'm not in right now. I'm out doing good. But please leave a message, and I'll get right back to you."

The machine beeps. Godzilla says, "Help."

VI: His Sponsor

The doghouse rolls around in his head all the next day. While at work he thinks of the dog and the way it burned. He thinks of the little house and the way it crumbled. He thinks of the dance he did in the ruins.

The day drags on forever. He thinks maybe when work is through he might find another doghouse, another dog.

On the way home he keeps an eye peeled, but no doghouses or dogs are seen.

When he gets home his answering machine light is blinking. It's a message from Reptilicus. Reptilicus' voice says, "Call me."

Godzilla does. He says, "Reptilicus. Forgive me, for I have sinned."

VII: Disillusioned. Disappointed.

Reptilicus' talk doesn't help much. Godzilla shreds all the twelve step program leaflets. He wipes his butt on a couple and throws them out the window. He puts the scraps of the others in the sink and sets them on fire with his breath. He burns a coffee table and a chair, and when he's through, feels bad for it. He knows the landlady will expect him to replace them.

He turns on the radio and lies on the bed listening to an Oldies station. After a while, he falls asleep to Martha and the Vandellas singing "Heat Wave".

VIII: Unemployed

Godzilla dreams. In it God comes to him, all scaly and blowing fire. He tells Godzilla he's ashamed of him. He says he should do better. Godzilla awakes covered in sweat. No one is in the room.

Godzilla feels guilty. He has faint memories of having awakened to go out and destroyed part of the city. He really tied one on, but he can't remember everything he did. Maybe he'll read about it in the papers. He notices he smells like charred lumber and melted plastic. There's gooshy stuff between his toes, and something tells him it isn't soap.

He wants to kill himself. He goes to look for his gun, but he's too drunk to find it. He passes out on the floor. He dreams of the devil this time. He looks just like God except he has one eyebrow that goes over both eyes. The devil says he's come for Godzilla.

Godzilla moans and fights. He dreams he gets up and takes pokes at the devil, blows ineffective fire on him.

Godzilla rises late the next morning, hung over. He remembers the dream. He calls into work sick. Sleeps off most of the day. That evening, he reads about himself in the papers. He really did some damage. Smoked a large part of the city. There's a very clear picture of him biting the head off of a woman.

He gets a call from the plant manager that night. The manager's seen the paper. He tells Godzilla he's fired.

IX: Enticement

Next day some humans show up. They're wearing black suits and white shirts and polished shoes and they've got badges. They've got guns, too. One of them says, "You're a problem. Our government wants to send you back to Japan."

"They hate me there," says Godzilla. "I burned Tokyo down."

"You haven't done so good here either. Lucky that was a coloured section of town you burned, or we'd be on your ass. As it is, we've got a job proposition for you."

"What?" Godzilla asks.

"You scratch our back, we'll scratch yours." Then the men tell him what they have in mind.

X: Choosing

Godzilla sleeps badly that night. He gets up and plays the monster mash on his little record player. He dances around the room as if he's enjoying himself, but knows he's not. He goes over to the BIG MONSTER RECREATION CENTER. He sees Kong there, on a stool, undressing one of his Barbies, fingering the smooth little slot between her legs. He sees that Kong has drawn a crack there, like a vagina. It appears to have been drawn with a blue ink pen. He's feathered the central line with ink-drawn pubic hair. Godzilla thinks he should have got someone to do the work for him. It doesn't look all that natural.

God, he doesn't want to end up like Kong. Completely spaced. Then again, maybe if he had some dolls he could melt, maybe that would serve to relax him.

No. After the real thing, what was a Barbie? Some kind of form of Near Beer. That's what the debris out back was. Near Beer. The foundry. The Twelve Step Program. All of it. Near Beer.

XI: Working for the Government

Godzilla calls the government assholes. "All right," he says. "I'll do it."

"Good," says the government man. "We thought you would. Check your mailbox. The map and instructions are there."

Godzilla goes outside and looks in his box. There's a manila envelope there. Inside are instructions. They say: "Burn all the spots you see on the map. You finish those, we'll find others. No penalties. Just make sure no one escapes. Any rioting starts, you finish them. To the last man, woman and child."

Godzilla unfolds the map. On it are red marks. Above the red marks are listings: *Nigger Town. Chink Village. White Trash Enclave. A Clutch of Queers. Mostly Democrats.*

Godzilla thinks about what he can do now. Unbidden. He can burn without guilt. He can stomp without guilt. Not only that, they'll send him a check. He has been hired by his adopted country to clean out the bad spots as they see them.

XII: The Final Step

Godzilla stops near the first place on the list: *Nigger Town.* He sees kids playing in the streets. Dogs. Humans looking up at him, wondering what the hell he's doing here.

Godzilla suddenly feels something move inside him. He knows he's being used. He turns around and walks away. He heads toward the government section of town. He starts with the governor's mansion. He goes wild. Artillery is brought out, but it's no use, he's rampaging. Like the old days.

Reptilicus shows up with a megaphone, tries to talk Godzilla down from the top of the Great Monument Building, but Godzilla doesn't listen. He's burning the top of the building off with his breath, moving down, burning some more, moving down, burning some more, all the way to the ground.

Kong shows up and cheers him on. Kong drops his walker and crawls along the road on his belly and reaches a building and pulls himself up and starts climbing. Bullets spark all around the big ape.

Godzilla watches as Kong reaches the summit of the building

and clings by one hand and waves the other, which contains a Barbie doll.

Kong puts the Barbie doll between his teeth. He reaches in his coat and brings out a naked Ken doll. Godzilla can see that Kong has made Ken some kind of penis out of silly putty or something. The penis is as big as Ken's leg.

Kong is yelling, "Yeah, that's right. That's right. I'm AC/DC, you sonsofabitches."

Jets appear and swoop down on Kong. The big ape catches a load of rocket right in the teeth. Barbie, teeth and brains decorate the greying sky. Kong falls.

Gorgo comes out of the crowd and bends over the ape, takes him in her arms and cries. Kong's hand slowly opens, revealing Ken, his penis broken off.

The flying turtle shows up and starts trying to steal Godzilla's thunder, but Godzilla isn't having it. He tears the top off the building Kong had mounted and beats Gamera with it. Even the cops and the army cheer over this.

Godzilla beats and beats the turtle, splattering turtle meat all over the place, like an overheated poodle in a microwave. A few quick pedestrians gather up chunks of the turtle meat to take home and cook, 'cause the rumour is it tastes just like chicken.

Godzilla takes a triple shot of rockets in the chest, staggers, goes down. Tanks gather around him.

Godzilla opens his bloody mouth and laughs. He thinks: If I'd have gotten finished here, then I'd have done the black people too. I'd have gotten the yellow people and the white trash and the homosexuals. I'm an equal opportunity destroyer. To hell with the twelve step program. To hell with humanity.

Then Godzilla dies and makes a mess on the street. Military men tip-toe around the mess and hold their noses.

Later, Gorgo claims Kong's body and leaves.

Reptilicus, being interviewed by television reporters, says, "Zilla was almost there, man. Almost. If he could have completed the program, he'd have been all right. But the pressures of society were too much for him. You can't blame him for what society made of him."

On the way home, Reptilicus thinks about all the excitement. The burning buildings. The gunfire. Just like the old days when he and Zilla and Kong and that goon-ball turtle were young.

Reptilicus thinks of Kong's defiance, waving the Ken doll, the Barbie in his teeth. He thinks of Godzilla, laughing as he died.

Reptilicus finds a lot of old feelings resurfacing. They're hard to fight. He locates a lonesome spot and a dark house and urinates through an open window, then goes home.

KARL EDWARD WAGNER

.220 Swift

KARL EDWARD WAGNER DIED IN 1994 at the age of forty-eight. He is remembered at the insightful editor of fifteen volumes of *The Year's Best Horror Stories* series from DAW Books (1980–94) and an author of superior horror and fantasy fiction.

While still attending medical school, Wagner set about creating his own character, Kane, the Mystic Swordsman. After the first book in the series, *Darkness Weaves with Many Shades*, was published in 1970 Wagner relinquished his chance to become a doctor and turned to writing full-time. *Death Angel's Shadow*, a collection of three original Kane novellas, was followed by the novels *Bloodstone* and *Dark Crusade* and the collections *Night Winds* and *The Book of Kane*. More recently, these books have been reissued in the omnibus volumes *Gods in Darkness* and *Midnight Sun* from Night Shade Books.

Wagner's horror fiction appeared in a variety of magazines and anthologies, and was collected in *In a Lonely Place*, *Why Not You and I?*, *Author's Choice Monthly Issue 2: Unthreatened by the Morning Light* and the posthumous *Exorcisms and Ecstasies*.

"In the summer of 1969 I lived in a cabin in Haywood County, North Carolina," recalled Wagner, "while working in a medical clinic there. The cabin and mountain settings are those in which I was living during this time.

"The legends of the Lost Mines of the Ancients, as described in '.220 Swift', are not pseudo-history as one critic suggested, but are historical fact – or mystery. Manly Wade Wellman, a noted writer and scholar of southern history and folklore, kindly gave me the use of his own research material regarding this archeological mystery, and over the years I was able to include some research of my own.

"The books and sources referred to in this regard are all actual materials, as are the legends and Indian myths. As Wellman for many years demonstrated in his own writing, history and folklore often propose mysteries far greater than any writer's imagination can provide."

I

WITHIN, THERE WAS MUSTY DARKNESS and the sweet-stale smell of damp earth.

Crouched at the opening, Dr Morris Kenlaw poked his head into the darkness and snuffled like a hound. His spadelike hands clawed industriously, flinging clods of dirt between his bent knees. Steadying himself with one hand, he wriggled closer to the hole in the ground and craned his neck inward.

He stuck out a muddy paw. "Give me back the light, Brandon." His usually overloud voice was muffled.

Brandon handed him that big flashlight and tried to look over Kenlaw's chunky shoulder. The archeologist's blocky frame completely stoppered the opening as he hunched forward.

"Take hold of my legs!" came back his words, more muffled still.

Shrugging, Brandon knelt down and pinioned Kenlaw's stocky legs. He had made a fair sand-lot fullback not too many years past, and his bulk was sufficient to anchor the overbalanced archeologist. Thus supported, Kenlaw crawled even farther into the tunnel. From the way his back jerked, Brandon sensed he was burrowing again, although no hunks of clay bounced forth.

Brandon pushed back his lank white hair with his forearm and looked up. His eyes were hidden behind mirror sunglasses, but his pale eyebrows made quizzical lines toward Dell Warner. Dell had eased his rangy denim-clad frame onto a limestone knob. Dan made a black-furred mound at his feet, tail thumping whenever his master looked down at him. The young farmer dug a crumpled pack of cigarettes out of his shirt pocket, watching in amused interest.

"Snake going to reach out, bite his nose off," Dell ventured, proffering the cigarettes to Brandon, selecting one himself when the other man declined.

The cool mountain breeze whisked his lighter flame, whipped the high weeds that patchworked the sloping pasture. Yellow grass and weed – cropped closely here, there a verdant blotch to mark a resorbed cow-pie. Not far above them dark pines climbed to the crest of the ridge; a good way below, the slope leveled to a neat field of growing corn. Between stretched the steep bank of wild pasture, terraced with meandering cow paths and scarred with grey juts of limestone. The early summer breeze had a cool, clean taste. It was not an afternoon to poke one's head into dank pits in the ground.

Kenlaw heaved convulsively, wriggling back out of the hole. He banged down the flashlight and swore; dirt hung on his black mustache. "Goddamn hole's nothing but a goddamn groundhog burrow!" Behind his smudged glasses his bright-black eyes were accusing.

Dell's narrow shoulders lifted beneath his blue cotton work shirt. "Groundhog may've dug it out, now – but I remember clear it was right here my daddy told me granddad filled the hole in. Losing too much stock, stepping off into there."

Kenlaw snorted and wiped his glasses with a big handkerchief. "Probably just a hole leading into a limestone cave. This area's shot through with caves. Got a smoke? Mine fell out of my pocket."

"Well, my dad said Granddad told him it was a tunnel mouth of some sort, only all caved in. Like an old mine shaft that's been abandoned years and years."

Ill-humoredly snapping up his host's cigarette, Kenlaw scowled. "The sort of story you'd tell to a kid. These hills are shot through with yarns about the mines of the ancients, too. God knows how many wild goose chases I've been after these last couple days."

Dell's eyes narrowed. "Now all I know is what I was told, and I was told this here was one of the mines of the ancients."

Puffing at his cigarette, Kenlaw wisely forbore to comment.

"Let's walk back to my cabin." Brandon suggested quickly. "Dr. Kenlaw, you'll want to wash up, and that'll give me time to set out some drinks."

"Thanks, but I can't spare the time just now," Dell grunted, sliding off the rock suddenly. The Plott hound scrambled to its feet. "Oh, and Ginger says she's hoping you'll be down for supper this evening."

"I'd like nothing better," Brandon assured him, his mind forming a pleasant image of the farmer's copper-haired sister.

"See you at supper then, Eric. So long, Dr Kenlaw. Hope you find what you're after."

The archeologist muttered a goodbye as Warner and his dog loped off down the side of the pasture.

Brandon recovered his heavy Winchester Model 70 in .220 Swift. He had been looking for woodchucks when he'd come upon Dell Warner and his visitor. From a flap pocket of his denim jacket he drew a lens cover for the bulky Leupold 3 × 9 telescopic sight.

"Did you say whether you cared for that drink?"

Kenlaw nodded. "Jesus, that would be good. Been a long week up here, poking into every groundhog hole some hillbilly thinks is special."

"That doesn't happen to be one there," Brandon told him, hefting the rifle. "I've scouted it several times for chucks – never anything come out."

"You just missed seeing it – or else it's an old burrow," Kenlaw judged.

"It's old," Brandon agreed, "or there'd be fresh-dug earth scattered around. But there's no sign of digging, just this hole in the hillside. Looks more like it was dug out from below."

II

The cabin that Eric Brandon rented stood atop a low bluff about half a mile up a dirt road from the Warner farmhouse. Dell had made a show of putting the century-old log structure into such state of repair that he might rent it out to an occasional venturesome tourist. The foot-thick poplar logs that made its roughhewn walls were as solid as the day some antebellum Warner had levered them into place. The grey walls showed rusty streaks where Dell had replaced the mud chinks with mortar, made from river sand hauled up from the Pigeon as it rushed past below the bluff. The massive riverrock fireplace displayed fresh mortar as well, and the roof was bright with new galvanized sheet metal. Inside was one large puncheon-floored room, with a low loft overhead making a second half-storey. There were no windows, but a back door opened onto a roofed porch overlooking the river below.

Dell had brought in a power line for lighting, stove and refrigerator. There was cold water from a line to the spring on the ridge above, and an outhouse farther down the slope. The cabin was solid, comfortable – but a bit too rustic for most tourists. Occasionally someone less interested in heated pools and color television found out about the place, and the chance rent helped supplement the farm's meager income. Brandon, however, had found the cabin available each of the half-dozen times over the past couple years when he had desired its use.

While the archeologist splashed icy water into the sink at the cabin's kitchen end, Brandon removed a pair of fired cartridges from the pocket of his denim jacket. He inspected the finger-sized casings carefully for evidence of flowing, then dropped them into a box of fired brass destined for reloading.

Toweling off, Kenlaw watched him sourly. "Ever worry about ricochets, shooting around all this rock like you do?"

"No danger," Brandon returned, cracking an ice tray briskly. "Bullet's moving too fast – disintegrates on impact. One of the nice things about the .220 Swift. Rum and Coke okay?" He didn't care to lavish his special Planter's Punch on the older man.

Moving to the porch, Kenlaw took a big mouthful from the tall glass and dropped onto a ladderback chair. The Jamaican rum seemed to agree with him; his scowl eased into a contemplative frown.

"Guess I was a little short with Warner," he volunteered.

When Brandon did not contradict him, he went on. "Frustrating business, though, this trying to sort the thread of truth out of a snarl of superstition and hearsay. But I guess I'm not telling you anything new."

The woven white-oak splits of the chair bottom creaked as Kenlaw shifted his ponderous bulk. The Pigeon River, no more than a creek this far upstream, purled a cool, soothing rush below. Downstream the Canton papermills would transform its icy freshness into black and foaming poison.

Brandon considered his guest. The archeologist had a sleek roundness to his frame that reminded Brandon of young Charles Laughton in *Island of Lost Souls*. There was muscle beneath the pudginess, judging by the energy with which he moved. His black hair was unnaturally sleek, like a cheap toupee, and his bristly mustache looked glued on. His face was round and innocent; his eyes, behind round glasses, round and wet. Without the glasses, Brandon thought they seemed tight and shrewd; perhaps this was a squint.

Dr Morris Kenlaw had announced himself the day before with a peremptory rap at Brandon's cabin door. He had started at Brandon's voice behind him – the other man had been watching from the ridge above as Kenlaw's dusty Plymouth drove up. His round eyes had grown rounder at the thick-barrelled rifle in Brandon's hands.

Dr Kenlaw, it seemed, was head of the Department of Anthropology at some Southern college, and perhaps Brandon was familiar with his work. No? Well, they had told him in Waynesville that the young man staying at the Warner's cabin was studying folklore and Indian legends and such things. It seemed Mr Brandon might have had cause to read this or that article by Dr Kenlaw . . . No? Well, he'd have to send him a few reprints, then, that might be of interest.

The archeologist had appropriated Brandon's favorite seat and drunk a pint of his rum before he finally asked about the lost mines of the ancients. And Brandon, who had been given little chance before to interrupt his visitor's rambling discourse, abruptly found the other's flat stare fixed attentively on him.

Brandon dutifully named names, suggested suggestions; Kenlaw scribbled notes eagerly. Mission accomplished, the archeologist pumped his hand and hustled off like a hound on a scent. Brandon had not expected to see the man again. But Dell Warner's name was among those in Kenlaw's notes, and today Brandon had run into them – Kenlaw, having introduced himself as a friend of Brandon, had persuaded Dell to show him his family's version of the lost mines. And that trail, it would seem, had grown cold again.

The chunky reddish-grey squirrel – they called them boomers – that had been scrabbling through the pine needle sod below them, suddenly streaked for the bushy shelter of a Virginia pine. Paying no attention, Dan romped around the corner of the cabin and bounded onto the porch. Brandon scratched the Plott hound's black head and listened. After a moment he could hear the whine and rattle as a pickup lurched up the dirt road.

"That'll be Dell," he told Kenlaw. "Dan knew he was headed here and took the short-cut up the side of the ridge. Dog's one of the smartest I've seen."

Kenlaw considered the panting black hound. "He's a bear hound, isn't he?"

"A damn good one," Brandon asserted.

"A bear killed young Warner's father, if I heard right," Kenlaw suggested. "Up near where we were just now. How dangerous are the bears they have up here?"

"A black bear doesn't seem like much compared to a grizzly," Brandon said "but they're quite capable of tearing a man apart – as several of these stupid tourists find out every summer. Generally they won't cause trouble, although now and then you get a mean one. Trouble is, the bears over in the Smokies have no fear of man, and the park rangers tend to capture the known troublemakers and release them in the more remote sections of the mountains. So every now and then one of these renegades wanders out of the park. Unafraid of man and unaccustomed to foraging in the wild, they can turn into really nasty stock killers. Probably what killed Bard Warner that night. He'd been losing stock and had the bad sense to wait out with a bottle and his old 8-mm. Mannlicher. Bolt on the

Mannlicher is too damn slow for close work. From what I was told, Bard's first shot didn't do it, and he never got off his second. Found what was left pulled under a rock ledge the next morning."

Dell's long legs stuck out from the battered door of his old Chevy pickup. He emerged from the cab balancing several huge tomatoes in his hands; a rolled newspaper was poked under one arm.

"These'll need to go into the refrigerator, Eric," he advised. "They're dead ripe. Get away, Dan!" The Plott hound was leaping about his legs.

Brandon thanked him and opened the refrigerator. Finger-combing his wind-blown sandy hair, Dell accepted his offer of a rum and Coke. "Brought you the Asheville paper," he indicated. "And you got a letter."

"Probably my advisor wondering what progress I've made on my dissertation," Brandon guessed, setting the letter with no return address carefully aside. He glanced over the newspaper while his friend uncapped an RC and mixed his own drink. Inflation, Africa, the Near East, a new scandal in Washington, and, in New York, a wave of gang-land slayings following the sniping death of some syndicate kingpin. In this century-old cabin in the ancient hills, all this seemed distant and unreal.

"Supper'll be a little late," Dell was saying. "Faye and Ginger took off to Waynesville to get their hair done." He added: "We'd like to have you stay for supper too, Dr Kenlaw."

The redhead's temper had cooled so that he remembered mountain etiquette. Since Kenlaw was still here, he was Brandon's guest, and a supper invitation to Brandon must include Brandon's company as well – or else Brandon would be in an awkward position. Had Kenlaw already left, there would have been no obligation. Brandon sensed that Dell had waited to see if the archeologist would leave, before finally driving up.

"Thanks, I'd be glad to," Kenlaw responded, showing some manners himself. Either he felt sheepish over his brusque behavior earlier, or else he realised he'd better use some tact if he wanted any further help in his research here.

Brandon refilled his and Kenlaw's glasses before returning to the porch. Dell was standing uncertainly, talking with the archeologist, so Brandon urged him to take the other porch chair. Taking hold with one hand of the yard-wide section of white-oak log that served as a low table, he slid it over the rough planks to a corner post and sat down. He sipped the drink he had been carrying in his free hand, and leaned back. It was cool and shady on the porch, enough so that he would have removed his mirror sunglasses had he been alone. Brandon, a true albino, was self-conscious about his pink eyes.

As it was, Kenlaw was all but gawking at his host. The section of log that Brandon had negligently slewed across the uneven boards probably weighed a couple hundred pounds. Dell, who had seen the albino free his pickup from a ditch by the straightforward expedient of lifting the mired rear wheel, appeared not to notice.

"I was asking Dr Kenlaw what it was he was looking for in these mines," Dell said.

"If mines they are," Brandon pointed out.

"Oh, they're mines, sure enough," the archeologist asserted. "You should be convinced of that, Brandon." He waved a big hand for emphasis. Red clay made crescents beneath untrimmed nails.

"Who were the 'ancients' who dug them?" Dell asked. "Were they the same Indians who put up all those mounds you see around here and Tennessee?"

"No, the mound builders were a lot earlier," Kenlaw explained. "The mines of the ancients were dug by Spaniards – or more exactly, by the Indian slaves of the conquistadors. We know that de Soto came through here in 1540 looking for gold. The Cherokees had got word of what kind of thieves the Spaniards were, though, and while they showed the strangers polite hospitality, they took pains not to let them know they had anything worth stealing. De Soto put them down as not worth fooling with, and moved on. But before that he sank a few mine shafts to see what these hills were made of."

"Did he find anything?" Dell wanted to know.

"Not around here. Farther south along these mountains a little ways, though, he did find some gold. In northern Georgia you can find vestiges of their mining shafts and camps. Don't know how much they found there, but there's evidence the Spaniards were still working that area as late as 1690."

"Must not have found much gold, or else word would have spread. You can't keep gold a secret."

"Hard to say. They must have found something to keep coming back over a century and a half. There was a lot of gold coming out of the New World, and not much of it ever reached Spain in the hands of those who discovered it. Plenty of reason to keep the discovery secret. And, of course, later on this area produced more gold than any place in the country before the Western gold rush. But all those veins gave out long before the Civil War."

"So you think the Spaniards were the ones that dug the mines of the ancients," Dell said.

"No doubt about it," stated Kenlaw, bobbing his head fiercely.

"Maybe that's been settled for northern Georgia," Brandon interceded, "although I'd had the impression this was only conjecture. But so far as I know, no one's ever proved the conquistadors mined this far north. For that matter, I don't believe anyone's ever made a serious study of the lost mines of the ancients in the North Carolina and Tennessee hills."

"Exactly why I'm here," Kenlaw told him impatiently. "I'm hoping to prove the tie-in for my book on the mines of the ancients. Only, so far I've yet to find proof of their existence in this area."

"Well, you may be looking for a tie-in that doesn't exist," Brandon returned. "I've studied this some, and my feeling is that the mines go back far beyond the days of the conquistadors. The Cherokees have legends that indicate the mines of the ancients were here already when the Cherokees migrated down from the north in the thirteenth century."

"This is the first I've heard about it then," Kenlaw scoffed. "Who do you figure drove these mines into the hills, if it wasn't the conquistadors? Don't tell me the Indians did it. I hardly think they would have been that interested in gold."

"Didn't say it was the Indians," Brandon argued.

"Who was it then?"

"The Indians weren't the first people here. When the Cherokees migrated into the Tellico region not far from here, they encountered a race of white giants – fought them and drove the survivors off, so their legends say."

"You going to claim the Vikings were here?" Kenlaw snorted.

"The Vikings, the Welsh, the Phoenicians, the Jews – there's good evidence that on several occasions men from the Old World reached North America long before Columbus set out. Doubtless there were any number of pre-Columbian contacts of which we have no record, only legends."

"If you'll forgive me, I'll stick to facts that are on record."

"Then what about the Melungeons over in Tennessee? They're not Indians, though they were here before the first pioneers, and even today anthropologists aren't certain of their ancestry."

Brandon pressed on. "There are small pockets of people all across the country – not just in these mountains – whose ethnic origins defy pinning down. And there are legends of others – the Shonokins, for example . . ."

"Now you're dealing with pure myth!" Kenlaw shut him off. "That's the difference between us, Brandon. I'm interested in collecting historical fact, and you're a student of myths and legends. Science and superstition shouldn't be confused."

"Sometimes the borderline is indistinct," Brandon countered.

"My job is to make it less so."

"But you'll have to concede there's often a factual basis for legend," Brandon argued doggedly. "And the Cherokees have a number of legends about the caves in these mountains, and about the creatures who live within. They tell about giant serpents, like the Uktena and the Uksuhi, that lair inside caves and haunt lonely ridges and streams, or the intelligent panthers that have town-houses in secret caves. Then there's the Nunnehi, an immortal race of invisible spirits that live beneath the mounds and take shape to fight the enemies of the Cherokee – these were supposedly seen as late as the Civil War. Or better still, there's the legend of the Yunwi Tsunsdi, the Little People who live deep inside the mountains."

"I'm still looking for that 'factual basis,'" Kenlaw said with sarcasm.

"Sometimes it's there to find. Ever read John Ashton's *Curious Creatures in Zoology*? In his chapter on pygmies he quotes from three sources that describe the discovery of entire burying grounds of diminutive stone sarcophagi containing human skeletons under two feet in length – adult skeletons, by their teeth. Several such burial grounds – ranging upwards to an acre and a half – were found in White County, Tennessee, in 1828, as well as an ancient town site near one of the burials. General Milroy found similar graves in Smith County, Tennessee, in 1866, after a small creek had washed through the site and exposed them. Also, Weller in his *Romance of Natural History* makes reference to other such discoveries in Kentucky as well as Tennessee. Presumably a race of pygmies may have lived in this region before the Cherokees, who remember them only in legend as the Yunwi Tsunsdi. Odd, isn't it, that there are so many Indian legends of a pygmy race?"

"Spare me from Victorian amateur archeology!" Kenlaw dismissed him impatiently. "What possible bearing have these half-baked superstitions on the mines of the ancients? I'm talking about archeological realities, like the pits in Mitchell County, like the Sink Hole mine near Bakersville. That's a pit forty feet wide and forty feet deep, where the stone shows marks of metal tools and where stone tools were actually uncovered. General Thomas Clingman studied it right after the Civil War, and he counted three hundred rings on the trees he found growing on the mine workings. That clearly puts the mines back into the days of the conquistadors. There's record of one Tristan de Luna, who was searching for gold and silver south of there in 1560; the Sink Hole mine contained mica, and quite possibly he was responsible for digging it and the other mines of that area."

"I've read about the Sink Hole mine in Creecy's *Grandfather's Tales*," Brandon told him. "And as I recall the early investigators there were puzzled by the series of passageways that connected the Sink Hole with other nearby pits – passageways that were only fourteen inches wide."

The archeologist sputtered in his drink. "Well, Jesus Christ, man!" he exploded after a moment. "That doesn't have anything to do with Indian legends! Don't you know anything about mining? They would have driven those connecting tunnels to try to cut across any veins of gold that might have lain between the pits."

Brandon spread his big hands about fourteen inches apart. He said: "Whoever dug the passageways would have had to have been rather small."

III

Afternoon shadows were long when Dell drove the other two men down to the house in his pickup. The farmhouse was a two-storey board structure with stone foundation, quite old, but in neat repair. Its wide planks showed the up-and-down saw marks that indicated its construction predated the more modern circular sawmill blade. The front was partially faced with dark mountain stone, and the foundation wall extended to make a flagstone veranda, shaded and garlanded by bright-petaled clematis.

Another truck was parked beside Kenlaw's Plymouth – a battered green 1947 Ford pickup that Brandon recognised as belonging to Dell's father-in-law, Olin Reynolds. Its owner greeted them from the porch as they walked up. He was a thin, faded man whose bony frame was almost lost in old-fashioned overalls. His face was deeply lined, his hair almost as white as Brandon's. Once he had made the best moonshine whiskey in the region, but his last stay in Atlanta had broken him. Now he lived alone on his old homestead bordering the Pisgah National Forest. He often turned up about dinner time, as did Brandon.

"Hello, Eric," Olin called in his reedy voice. "You been over to get that 'chuck that's been after my little girl's cabbages yet?"

"Hi. Olin," Brandon grinned. "Shot him yesterday morning from over across by that big white pine on the ridge."

"That's near a quarter-mile," the old man figured.

Brandon didn't say anything because Ginger Warner just then stepped out onto the porch. Dell's younger sister was recently back from finishing her junior year at Western Carolina in nearby Cullowhee. She was tall and willowy, green-eyed and quick to smile. Her copper hair was cut in a boyish shag instead of the unlovely bouffant most country women still clung to. Right now she had smudges of flour on her freckled face.

"Hi, Eric," she grinned, brushing her hands on her jeans. "Supper'll be along soon as the biscuits go in. You sure been keeping to yourself lately."

"Putting together some of my notes for the thesis," he apologised, thinking he'd eaten dinner here just three nights ago.

"Liar. You've been out running ridges with Dan."

"That's relaxation after working late at night."

Ginger gave him a skeptical look and returned to her biscuits.

With a ponderous grunt, Dr Kenlaw sank onto one of the wide-armed porch rockers. He swung his feet up onto the rail and gazed thoughtfully out across the valley. Mist was obscuring the hills beyond, now, and the fields and pasture closer at hand filled with hazy shadow. Hidden by trees, the Pigeon River rushed its winding course midway through the small valley. Kenlaw did not seem at ease with what he saw. He glowered truculently at the potted flowers that lined the porch.

"What the hell!" Kenlaw suddenly lurched from his rocker. The other three men broke off their conversation and stared. Balancing on the rail, the archeologist yanked down a hanging planter and dumped its contents into the yard.

"Where the hell did this come from!" he demanded, examining the rusted metal dish that an instant before had supported a trailing begonia.

Dell Warner bit off an angry retort.

"For god's sake, Kenlaw!" Brandon broke the stunned reaction.

"Yeah, for god's sake!" Kenlaw was too excited to be nonplussed. "This is a Spanish morion! What's it doing hanging here full of petunias?"

Ginger stepped onto the porch to announce dinner. Her freckled face showed dismay. "What on earth . . .?"

Kenlaw was abashed. "Sorry. I forgot myself when I saw this. Please excuse me – I'll replace your plant if it's ruined. But, where did you get this?"

"That old bowl? It's lain around the barn for years. I punched holes along the rim, and it made a great planter for my begonia." She glanced over the rail and groaned.

"It's a morion – a conquistador's helmet!" Kenlaw blurted in disbelief. Painstakingly he studied the high-crested bowl of rusted iron with its flared edges that peaked at either end. "And genuine too – or I'm no judge. Show me where this came from originally, and I'll buy you a pickup full of begonias."

Ginger wrinkled her forehead. "I really don't know where it came from – I didn't even know it was anything. What's a Spanish helmet doing stuck back with all dad's junk in our barn? There's an old iron pot with a hole busted in it where I found this. Want to look at it and tell me if it's Montezuma's bullet-proof bathtub?"

Kenlaw snorted. "Here, Brandon. You look at this and tell me I'm crazy."

The albino examined the helmet. It was badly pitted, but solid. It could not have lain outside, or it would have rusted entirely away centuries ago. "It's a morion, of course," he agreed. "Whether it dates to conquistador days or not, I'm not the one to tell. But it does seem equally unlikely that a careful reproduction would be lying around your barn."

"Hell, I know where that come from," Olin cut in, craning his long neck to see. "I was with your-all's daddy time he found it."

Kenlaw stared at the old mountain man – his eyes intent behind thick glasses. "For god's sake – where?"

Olin worked his pointed chin in a thoughtful circle, eying Dell questioningly. The younger man shrugged.

"Place up on Old Field Mountain," Olin told him, "near Tanasee Bald in what's now Pisgah National Forest. There's a sort of cave there, and I guess it won't do no harm now telling you a couple of old boys named Brennan used to make a little blockade from a still they'd built back inside. Me and Bard used to stop up there times and maybe carry wood and just set around. Well, one time Bard goes back inside a ways, and we worried some because he'd had a little – and after a while he comes back carrying that thing there and calling it an Indian pot 'cause he found it with a lot of bones way back in there. He liked to keep arrowheads and axe-heads and such-like when he found them, and so he carried that there back and put it with some other stuff, and I guess it's all just laid there and been scattered around the barn since."

"You can find the place still?" Kenlaw pounced. "Can you take me there tomorrow? Who else knows about this?"

"Why, don't guess there's nobody knows. The Brennans is all out of these parts now and gone – never did amount to much. Hardin Brennan got hisself shot one night arguing with a customer, and they said his brother Earl busted his head in a rock fall back there in the cave. Earl's wife had left him, and there was just his boy Buck and a daughter Laurie. She was half-wild and not right in the head; young as she was, she had a baby boy they said must've been by her own kin, on account everybody else was half afraid of her. They all went up north somewheres – I heard to live with their mother. There's other Brennans still around that might be distant kin, but far as I know nobody's gone around that cave on Old Field

Mountain since Buck and his sister left here better than twenty years back."

Kenlaw swore in excitement. "Nobody knows about it, then? Fantastic! What time tomorrow do you want to go? Better make it early. Seven?"

"Say about six instead," Olin suggested. "You'll need the whole day. How about coming up to the cabin – if that's all right with you, Eric? Shouldn't go back in there by yourself, and Lord knows my old bones are too brittle for scrambling around such places."

"Sure, I'll go along," Brandon agreed. "Sounds interesting."

"No need to," Kenlaw told him. "I've done my share of spelunking."

"Then you know it's dangerous to go in alone. Besides, I'm intrigued by all this."

"You all coming in to eat?" Faye Warner pushed open the screen. "Ginger, I thought you'd gone to call them. Everything's ready."

IV

There was chicken and ham, cornbread and gravy, tomatoes and branch lettuce, bowls of field peas, snap beans, corn and other garden vegetables. Kenlaw's scowl subsided as he loaded his plate a second time. Shortly after dinner the archeologist excused himself. "Been a long day, and we'll be up early enough tomorrow."

Olin drove away not long after, and when Dell went off to see to some chores, Brandon had the porch to himself. He was half-asleep when Ginger came out to join him.

"Did I startle you?" she apologised, sliding onto the porch swing beside him. "You're jumpy as a cat. Is that what living in the city does to your nerves?"

"Keeps you alert, I guess," Brandon said sheepishly.

Coppery hair tickled his shoulder. "Then you ought to get out of New York after you finish your project or whatever it is. Sounds like you must spend most of your time travelling around from one place to another as it is."

"That's known as field research."

"Ha! Dell says you don't do anything but laze around the cabin, or go out hunting. No wonder you still don't have your doctorate. Must be nice to get a government grant to run around the country studying folklore."

"Well, part of the time I'm organizing my notes, and part of the time I'm relaxing from the tension of writing."

"I can see how lugging that cannon of a rifle around would be exercise. Why don't you use that little air pistol instead?"

"What air pistol?"

"You know. You use it sometimes, because once I saw you shoot a crow with it that was making a fuss in the apple tree in front of the cabin. I saw you point it, and there wasn't a sound except the crow gave a squawk, and then feathers everywhere. My cousin has an air pistol too, so I knew what happened."

"Little spy." His arm squeezed her shoulder with mock roughness.

"Wasn't spying," Ginger protested, digging her chin into his shoulder. "I was walking up to help Dell chop tobacco."

When Brandon remained silent, she spoke to break the rhythmic rasp of the porch swing. "What do you think of Dr Kenlaw?"

"A bit too pig-headed and pushy. They raise them that way up north."

"That's one, coming from a New Yorker! Or are you from New York originally? You have less accent than Dr Kenlaw."

"Hard to say. I grew up in a foster home; I've lived a lot of places since."

"Well, folks around here like you well enough. They don't much like Dr Kenlaw."

"I expect he's too aggressive. Some of these obsessive researchists are like that."

Ginger lined her freckles in a frown. "You're a researcher. Is Dr Kenlaw?"

Brandon went tense beneath her cheek. "What do you mean?"

"I mean, have you ever heard of him? If you're both studying the same subjects pretty much . . .?"

"I don't know his work, if that's what you mean." Brandon's muscles remained steel-tight. "But then, he knows his subject well enough. Why?"

"He seems to be more interested in gold than in archeology,"

Ginger told him. "At least, that's the way his questions strike most folks he talks to."

Brandon laughed and seemed to relax again. "Well, there's more acclaim in discovering a tomb filled with gold relics than in uncovering a burial of rotted bones and broken pot shards, regardless of the relative value to archeological knowledge. That's why King Tutankhamen's tomb made headlines, while the discovery of a primitive man's jawbone gets squeezed in with the used car ads."

"There was a curse on King Tut's tomb," Ginger reminded him dourly.

"Even better, if you're fighting for a grant."

"Grants!" Ginger sniffed. "Do you really mean to get that degree, or do you just plan to make a career of living off grants?"

"There's worse ways to make a living," Brandon assured her.

"Somehow I can't see you tied down to some university job. That's what you'll do when you get your doctorate, isn't it? Teach?"

"There's a lot of PhD's out there looking for jobs once the grants dry up," Brandon shrugged. "If there's an opening somewhere, I suppose so."

"There might be an opening at Western Carolina," Ginger hinted.

"There might."

"And why not?" You like it down here – or else you wouldn't keep coming back. And people like you. You seem to fit right in – not like most of these loud New York types."

"It does feel like coming home again when I get back here," Brandon acknowledged. "Guess I've never stayed in one place long enough to call it home. Would you like for me to set up shop in Cullowhee?"

"I just might."

Brandon decided she had waited long enough for her kiss, and did something about it. Shadows crept together to form misty darkness, and the cool mountain breeze carried the breath of entwined clematis and freshly turned earth. The creak of the porch swing measured time like an arthritic grandfather's clock, softened by the rustle of the river. A few cows still lowed, and somewhere a chuck-will's-widow called to its mate. The quiet was dense enough so that they could hear Dan gnawing a bone in the yard below.

Ginger finally straightened, stretched cozily from her cramped position. "Mmm," she purred; then: "Lord, what is that dog chewing on so! We didn't have more than a plate of scraps for him after dinner."

"Maybe Dan caught himself a rabbit. He's always hunting."

"Oh! Go see! He killed a mother rabbit last week, and I know her babies all starved."

"Dan probably saw that they didn't." Brandon rose to go look. "What you got there, boy?"

Ginger saw him stiffen abruptly. "Oh, no! Not another mamma bunny!"

She darted past Brandon's arm before he could stop her.

Dan thumped his tail foolishly and returned her stare. Between his paws was a child's arm.

V

Olin Reynolds shifted his chaw reflectively. "I don't wonder Ginger came to carry on such a fit," he allowed. "What did you figure it was?"

"Certainly not a child's arm," Brandon said. "Soon as you got it into good light you could see it was nothing human. It had to have been some type of monkey, and the resemblance gave me a cold chill at first glance, too. Pink skin with just a frost of dirty white fur, and just like a little kid's arm except it was all muscle and sinew instead of baby fat. And it was a sure enough hand, not a paw, though the fingers were too long and sinewy for any child's hand, and the nails were coarse and pointed like an animal's claws."

"Wonder where old Dan come to catch him a monkey," Olin put in.

"Somebody's pet. Tourists, maybe – they carry everything they own in those damn campers. Thing got away; or more likely, died and they buried it, and Dan sniffed it out and dug it up. He'd been digging, from the look of him."

"What did you finally do with it?"

"Dell weighted it down in an old gunny sack and threw it into a deep hole in the river there. Didn't want Dan dragging it back again to give the ladies another bad start."

"Just as well," Olin judged. "It might have had somebody come looking for to see what come of it. I suspect that'll be Dr Kenlaw coming up the hill now."

Kenlaw's Plymouth struggled into view through the pines. Brandon glanced at his watch, noted it was past seven. He stretched himself out of Olin's ladderback chair and descended the porch steps to greet the archeologist.

"Had a devil of a time finding the turn-off," Kenlaw complained, squeezing out from behind the wheel. "Everything set?"

"Throw your stuff in my pickup, and we'll get going," Olin told him. "Where we're headed, ain't no kind of road any car can follow up."

"Will that old bucket make it up a hill?" Kenlaw laughed, opening his trunk to take out a coil of rope and two powerful flashlights.

"This here old Ford's got a Marmon-Herrington all-wheel-drive conversion." Olin said coldly. "She can ride up the side of a bluff and pull out a cedar stump while your feet are hanging straight out the back window of the cab."

Kenlaw laughed easily, shoving spare batteries and a geologist's pick into the ample pockets of the old paratrooper's jacket he wore. Brandon helped him stow his gear into the back of the truck, then climbed into the cab beside Reynolds.

It was a tight squeeze in the cab after Dr Kenlaw clambered in, and once they reached the blacktop road the whine of the gears and fan made conversation like shouting above a gale. Olin drove along in moody silence, answering Kenlaw's occasional questions in few words. After a while they left the paved roads, and then it was a long kidney-bruising ride as the dual-sprung truck attacked rutted mountain paths that bored ever upward through the shouldering pines. Kenlaw cursed and braced himself with both arms. Brandon caught a grin in Olin's faded eyes.

The road they followed led on past a tumbledown frame house, lost within a yard that had gone over to first-growth pine and scrub. A few gnarled apple trees made a last stand, and farther beneath the encroaching forest, Brandon saw the hulking walls of a log barn – trees spearing upward past where the roof had once spread. He shivered. The desolation of the place seemed to stir buried memories.

Beyond the abandoned farmhouse the road deteriorated into little more than a cow path. It had never been more than a timber road, scraped out when the lumber barons dragged down the primeval forest from the heights half a century or more ago. Farm vehicles had kept it open once, and now an occasional hunter's truck broke down the young trees that would otherwise have choked it.

Olin's pickup strained resolutely upward, until at length they shuddered into an overgrown clearing. Reynolds cut the engine. "Watch for snakes," he warned, stepping down.

The clearing was littered beneath witch's broom and scrub with a scatter of rusted metal and indistinct trash. A framework of rotted lumber and a corroded padlock faced against the hillside. Several of the planks had fallen inward upon the blackness within.

Olin Reynolds nodded. "That's the place. Reckon the Brennans boarded it over before they moved on to keep stock from falling in. Opening used to just lie hidden beneath the brush."

Dr Kenlaw prodded the eroded timbers. The padlock hasp hung rusted nails over the space where the board had rotted away. At a bolder shove, the entire framework tore loose and tumbled inward.

Sunlight spilled in past the dust. The opening was squeezed between ledges of rock above and below, wide enough for a man to stoop and drop through. Beyond was a level floor, littered now with the debris of boards.

"Goes back like that a ways, then it narrows down to just a crack," Olin told them.

Kenlaw grunted in a self-satisfied tone and headed back for the pickup to get his equipment.

"Coming with us?" Brandon asked.

Olin shook his head firmly. "I'll just wait here. These old bones are too eat up with arthuritis to go a-crawling through that snaky hole."

"Wait with him, Eric, if you like," Kenlaw suggested. "I probably won't be long about this. No point you getting yourself all dirty messing around on what's likely to be just another wild goose chase."

"I don't mind," Brandon countered. "If that morion came out of this cave, I'm curious to see what else lies hidden back there."

"Odds are, one of those Brennans found it someplace else and just chucked it back in there. Looks like this place has been used as a dump."

Kenlaw cautiously shined his light across the rubble beneath the ledge. Satisfied that no snakes were evident, the archeologist gingerly squeezed his corpulent bulk past the opening and lowered himself to the floor of the cavern. Brandon dropped nimbly beside him.

Stale gloom filled a good-sized antechamber. Daylight trickled in from the opening, and a patch of blackness at the far end marked where the cavern narrowed and plunged deeper into the side of the mountain. Brandon took off his mirror sunglasses and glanced about the chamber – the albino's eyes were suited to the dank gloom.

The wreckage of what had once been a moonshine still cluttered the interior of the cavern. Copper coil and boiler had long ago been carried off, as had anything else of any value. Broken barrels, rotted mounds of sacks, jumbles of firewood, misshapen sculptures of galvanized metal. Broken bits of Mason jars and crockery shards crunched underfoot; dead ashes made a sodden raisin pudding. Kenlaw flung his light overhead and disclosed only sooty rock and somnolent bats.

"A goddamn dump," he muttered petulantly. "Maybe something farther back in."

The archeologist swung his light toward the rear of the chamber. A passage led farther into the mountain. Loose stones and more piled debris half blocked the opening. Pushing his way past this barricade, Kenlaw entered the narrow tunnel.

The passage was cramped. They ducked their heads, twisted about to avoid contact with the dank rock. Kenlaw carefully examined the walls of the cavern as they shuffled on. To Brandon's eye, there was nothing to indicate that man's tools had shaped the shaft. After a time, the sunlight from behind them disappeared, leaving them with their flashlights to guide them. The air grew stale with a sourness of animal decay, and as the passage seemed to lead downward, Brandon wondered whether they might risk entering a layer of noxious gases.

"Hold on here!" Kenlaw warned, stopping abruptly.

Darkness met their probing flashlight beams several yards ahead of their feet, as the floor of the passage disappeared. Kenlaw wiped his pudgy face and caught his breath, as they shined their lights down into the sudden pit that confronted them.

"Must be thirty-forty feet to the bottom," Kenlaw estimated. "Cavern's big enough for a high school gym. The ledge we're standing on creeps on down that fault line toward the bottom. We can make it if you'll just watch your step."

"Is the air okay?" Brandon wondered.

"Smells fresh enough to me," Kenlaw said. He dug a crumpled cigarette pack from his pocket, applied his lighter. The flame fanned outward along the direction they had come. Kenlaw dropped the burning wad of paper over the edge. It fell softly through the blackness, showering sparks as it hit the floor.

"Still burning," the archeologist observed. "I'm going on down."

"Nice if that was natural gas down there," Brandon muttered.

"This isn't a coal mine. Just another natural cavern, for my money."

Clinging to the side of the rock for support, they cautiously felt their way down the steep incline. Although an agile climber could negotiate the descent without ropes, the footing was treacherous, and a missed step could easily mean a headlong plunge into the darkness.

They were halfway down when Kenlaw paused to examine the rock wall. Switching hands with his flashlight, he drew his geologist's pick and tapped against the stone.

"Find something?" Brandon turned his light onto the object of the archeologist's scrutiny, saw a band of lighter stone running along the ledge.

"Just a sample of stratum," Kenlaw explained, hastily breaking free a specimen and shoving it into one of his voluminous pockets. "I'll have to examine it back at my lab – study it for evidence of tool marks and so on."

The floor of the pit appeared little different from the chamber through which they had entered the cavern, save that it lacked the accumulated litter of human usage. The air was cool and fresh enough to breathe, although each lungful carried the presence of a sunless place deep beneath the mountains.

"Wonder when the last time was anyone came down here?" Brandon said, casting his light along the uneven floor. The bottom was strewn with broken rock and detritus, with a spongy paste of bat guano and dust. Footprints would be hard to trace after any length of time.

"Hard to say," Kenlaw answered, scooping up a handful of gravel and examining it under his light. "Sometimes the Confederates worked back into places like this after saltpetre. Maybe Bard Warner came down here, but I'm betting that morion was just something some dumb hillbilly found someplace else and got tossed onto the dump."

"Are these bones human?" Brandon asked.

Kenlaw stuffed the gravel into a jacket pocket and scrambled over to where Brandon crouched. There was a fall of broken rock against the wall of the pit opposite their point of descent. Interspersed with the chunks of stone were fragments of mouldering bone. The archeologist dug out a section of rib. It snapped easily in his hand, showing whiteness as it crumbled.

"Dead a long time," Kenlaw muttered, pulling more of the rocks aside. "Maybe Indian."

"Then it's a human skeleton?"

"Stone burial cairn, at a guess. But it's been dug up and the bones scattered about. These long bones are all smashed apart."

"Maybe he was killed in a rock slide."

Kenlaw shook his head. "Look how this femur is split apart. I'd say more likely something broke open the bones to eat the marrow."

"An animal?"

"What else would it have been?"

Kenlaw suddenly bent forward, clawed at the detritus. His thick fingers locked onto what looked to be the edge of a flat rock. Grunting, he hauled back and wrenched forth a battered sheet of rusted iron.

"Part of a breastplate! Damned if this isn't the original skeleton in armor! Give me a hand with the rest of these rocks."

Together they dragged away the cairn of rubble – Kenlaw puffing energetically as he flung aside the stones and fragments of bone. Brandon, caught up in the excitement of discovery himself, reflected with a twinge that this was hardly a careful piece of excavation. Nonetheless, Kenlaw's anxious scrabbling continued until they had cleared a patch of bare rock.

The archeologist squatted on a stone and lit a cigarette. "Doesn't tell me much," he complained. "Just broken bones and chunks of rust. Why was he here? Were there others with him? Who were they? What were they seeking here?"

"Isn't it enough that you've found the burial of a conquistador?"

"Can't prove that until I've run some tests," Kenlaw grumbled. "Could have been a Colonial – breastplates were still in use in European armies until this century. Or an Indian buried with some tribal heirlooms."

"There's another passage back of here," Brandon called out.

He had been shining his light along the fall of rock, searching for further relics from the cairn. Behind where they had cleared away some of the loose rocks, a passageway pierced the wall of the pit. Brandon rolled aside more of the stone, and the mouth of the passage took shape behind the crest of the rock pile.

Kenlaw knelt and peered within. "Not much more than a crawl space," he announced, "but it runs straight on for maybe twenty or thirty feet, then appears to open onto another chamber."

Brandon played his flashlight around the sides of the pit, then back to where they stood. "I don't think this is just a rock slide. I think someone piled all these rocks here to wall up the tunnel mouth."

"If they didn't want it found, then they must have found something worth hiding," the archeologist concluded. "I'll take a look. You wait here in case I get stuck."

Brandon started to point out that his was the slimmer frame, but already Kenlaw had plunged headfirst into the tunnel – his thick buttocks blocking Brandon's view as he squeezed his way through. Brandon thought of a fat old badger ducking down a burrow. He kept his light on the shaft. Wheezing and scuffling, the other man managed to force his bulk through the passage. He paused at the far end and called back something, but his words were too muffled for Brandon to catch.

A moment later Kenlaw's legs disappeared from view, and then his flushed face bobbed into Brandon's light. "I'm in another chamber about like the one you're standing in," he called back. "I'll take a look around."

Brandon sat down to wait impatiently. He glanced at his watch. To his surprise, they had been in the cavern some hours. The beam of his flashlight was yellowing; Brandon cut the switch to save the batteries, although he carried spares in his pockets. The blackness was as total as the inside of a grave, except for an occasional wan flash as Kenlaw shined his light past the tunnel mouth from the pit beyond. Brandon held his hand before his face, noted that he could dimly make out its outline. The albino had always known he could see better in the dark than others could, and it had seemed a sort of recompense for the fact that bright light tormented his pink eyes. He had read that hemeralopia did not necessarily coincide with increased night vision, and his use of infrared rifle scopes had caused him to wonder whether his eyes might not be unusually receptive to light from the infrared end of the spectrum.

Kenlaw seemed to be taking his time. At first Brandon had heard the sharp tapping of his geologist's pick from time to time. Now there was only silence. Brandon flipped his light back on, consulted his watch. It had been half an hour.

"Dr Kenlaw?" he called. He thrust his shoulders into the passage and called again, louder. There came no reply.

Less anxious than impatient, Brandon crawled into the tunnel and began to wriggle forward, pushing his light ahead of him. Brandon was stocky, and it was a tight enough squeeze. The crawl space couldn't be much more than two feet square at its widest point. Brandon reflected that it was fortunate that he was not one of those bothered by claustrophobia.

Halfway through the tunnel, Brandon suddenly halted to study its walls. No natural passage; those were tool marks upon the stone – not even Kenlaw could doubt now. The regularity of the passage had already made Brandon suspicious. Cramped as it was, it reminded him of a mine shaft, and he thought again about the mention in Creecy's *Grandfather's Tales* of the interconnecting tunnels found at the Sink Hole pits.

The tunnel opened onto another chamber much like the one he had just quitted. It was a short drop to the floor, and Brandon lowered himself headfirst from the shaft. There was no sign of Kenlaw's light. He stood for a moment uneasily, swinging his flash about the cavern. Perhaps the archeologist had fallen into a hidden pit, smashed his light.

"Dr Kenlaw?" Brandon called again. Only echoes answered.

No. There was another sound. Carried through the rock in the subterranean stillness. A sharp tapping. Kenlaw's geologist's pick.

Brandon killed his flash. A moment passed while his eyes adjusted to the blackness, then he discerned a faint haze of light – visible only because of the total darkness. Switching his own light back on, Brandon directed it toward the glimmer. It came from the mouth of yet another passageway cut against the wall opposite.

He swung his light about the pit. Knowing what to look for now, Brandon thought he could see other such passages, piercing the rock face at all levels. It came to him that they began to run a real risk of losing their way if they were able to progress much farther within these caverns. Best to get Kenlaw and keep together after this, he decided.

The new shaft was a close copy of the previous one – albeit somewhat more cramped. Brandon scraped skin against its confines as he crawled toward the sound of Kenlaw's pick.

The archeologist was so engrossed in what he was doing that he hadn't noticed Brandon's presence, until the other wriggled out onto the floor of the pit and hailed him. Spotlighted by Brandon's flash, Kenlaw glowered truculently. The rock face where he was hammering threw back a crystalline reflection.

"I was worried something had happened," Brandon said, approaching.

"Sorry. I called to you that I was going on, but you must not have heard." Kenlaw swept up handfuls of rock samples and stuffed them into the already bulging pockets of his paratrooper's jacket. "We'd best be getting back before we get lost. Reynolds will be wondering about us."

"What is this place? Don't tell me all of this is due to natural formation!" Brandon swept his light around. More diminutive tunnels pierced the sides of this pit also. He considered the broken rock that littered the floor.

"This *is* a mine of some sort, isn't it. Congatulations, Dr Kenlaw – you really *have* found one of the lost mines of the ancients! Christ, you'll need a team of spelunkers to explore these pits if they keep going on deeper into the mountain!"

Kenlaw laughed gruffly. "Lost mines to the romantic imagination, I suppose – but not to the trained mind. This is a common enough formation – underground streams have forced their way through faults in the rock, hollowed out big chambers wherever they've encountered softer stone. Come on, we've wasted enough time on this one."

"Soft rock?" Brandon pushed past him. "Hell, this is quartz!"

He stared at the quartz dike where Kenlaw had been working. Under the flashlight beam, golden highlights shimmered from the chipped matrix.

"Oh my god." Brandon managed to whisper.

These were good words for a final prayer, although Kenlaw probably had no such consideration in mind. The rush of motion from the darkness triggered some instinctive reflex. Brandon started to whirl about, and the pick of the geologist's hammer only tore a furrow across his scalp instead of plunging into his skull.

The glancing blow was enough, Brandon went down as if poleaxed. Crouching over him, Kenlaw raised the hammer for the *coup de grâce*.

When Brandon made no move, the murderous light in the other man's eyes subsided to cunning. Brandon was still breathing, although bare bone gleamed beneath the blood-matted hair. Kenlaw balanced the geologist's pick pensively.

"Got to make this look like an accident," he muttered. "Can't risk an investigation. Tell them you took a bad fall. Damn you, Brandon! You would have to butt in the one time I finally found what I was after! This goddamn mountain is made out of gold, and that's going to be my secret until I can lock up the mining rights."

He hefted a rock – improvising quickly, for all that his attack had been born of the moment. "Just as well the pick only grazed you.

Going to have to look like you busted your head on the rocks. Can't have it happen in here, though – this has to be kept hidden. Out there on the ledge where we first climbed down – that's where you fell. I'll block the tunnel entrance back up again. All they'll know is that we found some old bones in a cave, and you fell to your death climbing back up."

He raised the rock over Brandon's head, then threw it aside. "Hell, you may never wake up from that one there. Got to make this look natural as possible. If they don't suspect now, they might later on. Push you off the top of the ledge headfirst, and it'll just be a natural accident."

Working quickly, Kenlaw tied a length of rope to Brandon's ankles. The man was breathing hoarsely, his pulse erratic. He had a concussion, maybe worse. Kenlaw debated again whether to kill him now, but considered it unlikely that he would regain consciousness before they reached the ledge. An astute coroner might know the difference between injuries suffered through a fatal fall and trauma inflicted upon a lifeless body – they always did on television.

Brandon was heavy, but Kenlaw was no weakling for all his fat. Taking hold of the rope, he dragged the unconscious body across the cavern floor – any minor scrapes would be attributed to the fall. At the mouth of the tunnel he paused to pay out his coil of rope. Once on the other side, he could haul in Brandon's limp form like a fish on a line. It would only take minutes to finish the job.

The tunnel seemed far more cramped as he wriggled into it. The miners must have had small frames, but then people were smaller four centuries ago. Moreover, the Spaniards, who almost certainly would have used slave labor to drive these shafts, weren't men to let their slaves grow fat.

It *was* tighter, Kenlaw realised with growing alarm. For a moment he attempted to pass it off to claustrophobia, but as he reached a narrower section of the tunnel, the crushing pressure on his stout sides could not be denied. Panic whispered through his brain, and then suddenly he understood. He had crammed his baggy jacket pockets with rock samples and chunks of ore from the quartz dike; he was a good twenty pounds heavier and inches bulkier now than when he had crawled through before.

He could back out, but to do so would lose time. Brandon might revive; Reynolds might come looking for them. Gritting his teeth against the pressure on his ribs, Kenlaw pushed his light on ahead and forced his body onward. This was the tightest point, and beyond that the way would be easier. He sucked in his breath and writhed forward another foot or more. His sides ached, but he managed yet another foot with all this strength.

No farther. He was stuck.

His chest aching, Kenlaw found scant breath to curse. No need to panic. Just back out and take off the jacket, push it in ahead of him and try again. He struggled to work his corpulent body backward from the tunnel. The loose folds of his paratrooper's jacket rolled up as he wriggled backward, bunching against the bulging pockets. Jammed even tighter against his flesh and against the rock walls, the laden coat bunched up into a wedge. Kenlaw pushed harder, setting his teeth against the pain, as rock samples gouged into his body.

He couldn't move an inch farther. Backward or forward.

He was stuck midway in the tunnel.

Still Kenlaw fought down his panic. It was going to cost him some bruises and some torn skin, no doubt, but he'd work his way free in good time. He must above all else remain calm, be patient. A fraction of an inch forward, a fraction of an inch backward. He would take his time, work his way loose bit by bit, tear free of the jacket or smooth out its bunched-up folds. At worst, Reynolds would find him, bring help. Brandon might be dead by then, or have no memory of the blow that felled him; he could claim he was only trying to drag his injured companion to safety.

Kenlaw noticed that the light from his flash was growing dim. He had meant to replace the batteries earlier; now the spares were part of the impedimenta that pinioned him here. No matter; he didn't need light for this – only to be *lighter*. Kenlaw laughed shakily at his own joke, then the chuckle died.

The flashlight was fast dwindling, but its yellowing beam was enough to pick out the pink reflections of the many pairs of eyes that watched him from the mouth of the tunnel – barely glimpsed shapes that grew bolder as the light they feared grew dim.

And then Kenlaw panicked.

VI

The throbbing ache in his skull was so intense that it was some time before Brandon became aware that he was conscious. By gradual increments, as one awakens from a deep dream, he came to realise that something was wrong, that there was a reason for the pain and clouded state of awareness. An elusive memory whispered of a treacherous attack, a blow from behind . . .

Brandon groaned as he forced himself to sit up, goaded to action as memory returned. His legs refused to function, and after a moment of confusion, he realised that his ankles were tied together. He almost passed out again from the effort to lean forward and fumble with the knots, and more time dragged past as he clumsily worked to free his ankles.

His brain refused to function clearly. He knew that it was dark, that he could see only dimly, but he could not think where his flashlight might be, nor marvel that his albino eyes had so accommodated to give him preternatural vision in a lightless cavern. Remembering Kenlaw's attack, he began to wonder where the other man had gone; only disjointedly did he understand the reasons behind the archeologist's actions and the probable consequences of his own plight.

The knots at last came loose. Brandon dully considered the rope – his thoughts groping with the fact that someone had tied it to his ankles. Tied him to what? Brandon pulled on the rope, drew coils of slack through the darkness, until there was tension from the other end. He tugged again. The rope was affixed to something beyond. With great effort, Brandon made it to his feet, staggered forward to lean against the rock face beneath which he had lain. The rope was tied to the wall. No, it entered the wall, into the tunnel. It was affixed to something within the narrow passage.

Brandon knelt forward and followed the rope into the crawl space. Dimly he remembered that this was the shaft by which he had entered – or so he hoped. He had hardly crawled forward for more than a body-length, when his fingers clawed against boots. Brandon groped and encountered damp cloth and motionless legs – the rope pressing on beneath their weight.

"Kenlaw?" he called out in a voice he scarcely recognised. He shook the man's feet, but no response came. Bracing himself against the narrow passage, Brandon grasped the other man's ankles and hauled back. For a moment there was resistance, then the slack body slid backward under his tugging. Backing out of the tunnel, Brandon dragged the archeologist's motionless form behind him. The task was an easy one for him, despite that the pain in his skull left Brandon nauseated and weak.

Emerging from the shaft, he rested until the giddiness subsided. Kenlaw lay where he had released him, still not moving. Brandon could only see the man as a dim outline, but vague as that impression was, something seemed wrong about the silhouette. Brandon bent forward, ran his hands over the archeologist's face, groping for a pulse.

His fingers encountered warm wetness across patches of slick hardness and sticky softness, before skidding into empty eye sockets. Most of the flesh of Kenlaw's face and upper body had been stripped from the bone.

Brandon slumped against the wall of the cavern, trying to comprehend. His brain struggled drunkenly to think, but the agony of his skull kept making his thoughts tumble apart again just as understanding seemed to be there. Kenlaw was dead. He, Brandon, was in a bad way. This much he could hold in his mind, and with that, the recognition that he had to get out of this place.

That meant crawling back through the narrow shaft where Kenlaw had met his death. Brandon's mind was too dazed to feel the full weight of horror. Once again he crawled into the tunnel and inched his way through the cramped darkness. The rock was damp, and now he knew with what wetness, but he forced himself to wriggle across it.

His hands encountered Kenlaw's flashlight. He snapped its switch without effect, then remembered the fresh batteries in his pockets. Crawling from the tunnel and onto the floor of the chamber beyond, he fumbled to open the flashlight, stuff in new batteries. He thumbed the switch, again without result. His fingers groped across the lens, gashed against broken glass. The bulb was smashed, the metal dented; tufts of hair and dried gore caked the battered end. Kenlaw had found service from the flashlight as a club, and it was good for little else now. Brandon threw it away from him with a curse.

The effort had taxed his strength, and Brandon passed from consciousness to unconsciousness and again to consciousness without really being aware of it. When he found himself capable of thought once again, he had to remember all over again how he had come to this state. He wondered how much time had passed, touched his watch, and found that the glare from the digital reading hurt his eyes.

Setting his teeth against the throbbing that jarred his skull, Brandon made it to his feet again, clutching at the wall of the pit for support. Olin, assuming he was getting anxious by now, might not find the passage that led from the first pit. To get help. Brandon would have to cross this cavern, crawl through the shaft back into the first pit, perhaps climb up along the ledge and into the passageway that led to the outer cavern. In his condition it wouldn't have been easy even if he had a light.

Brandon searched his pockets with no real hope. A nonsmoker, he rarely carried matches, nor did he now. His eyes seemed to have accommodated as fully to the absence of light as their abnormal sensitivity would permit. It was sufficient to discern the shape of objects close at hand as shadowy forms distinct from the engulfing darkness – little enough, but preferable to total blindness. Brandon stood with his back to the shaft through which he had just crawled. The other tunnel had seemed to be approximately opposite, and if he walked in a straight line he ought to strike the rock face close enough to grope for the opening.

With cautious steps, Brandon began to cross the cavern. The floor was uneven, and loose stones were impossible for him to see. He tried to remember if his previous crossing had revealed any pitfalls within this chamber. A fall and a broken leg would leave him helpless here, and slowly through his confused brain was creeping the shrill warning that Kenlaw's death could hardly have been from natural causes. A bear? There were persistent rumors of mountain lions being sighted in these hills. Bobcats, which were not uncommon, could be dangerous under these circumstances. Brandon concentrated on walking in a straight line, much like a drunk trying to walk a highway line for a cop, and found that the effort demanded his entire attention.

The wall opposite loomed before him – Brandon was aware of its darker shape an instant before he blundered into it. He rested against its cool solidity for a moment, his knees rubbery, head swimming after the exertion. When he felt stronger once again, he began to inch his way along the rock face, fumbling for an opening in the wall of the pit.

There – a patch of darkness less intense opened out of the stone. He dared not even consider the possibility that this might not be the shaft that was hidden behind the cairn. Brandon fought back unconsciousness as it surged over him once more, forced his muscles to respond. Once through this passage, Olin would be able to find him. He stopped to crawl into the tunnel, and the rock was coated with a musty stickiness.

Brandon wriggled forward across the moist stone. The sensation was already too familiar, when his out-thrust fingers clawed against a man's boot. Kenlaw's boot. Kenlaw's body. In the shaft ahead of him.

Brandon was too stunned to feel terror. His tortured mind struggled to comprehend. Kenlaw's body lay in the farther chamber, beyond the other passage by which he had returned. And Brandon knew a dead man when he came upon one. Had he circled the cavern, gone back the way he had come? Or was he delirious, his injured brain tormented by a recurring nightmare?

He clutched the lifeless feet and started to haul them back, as he had done before, or thought he had done. The boots were abruptly dragged out of his grasp.

Brandon slumped forward on his face, pressing against the stone to hold back the waves of vertigo and growing fear. Kenlaw's body disappeared into the blackness of the tunnel. How serious was his head injury? Had he imagined that Kenlaw was dead? Or was it Kenlaw ahead of him now in this narrow passage?

Brandon smothered a cackling laugh. It must not be Kenlaw. Kenlaw was dead, after all. It was Olin Reynolds, or someone else, come to search for him.

"Here I am!" Brandon managed to shout. "In here!"

His lips tasted of blood, and Brandon remembered the wetness he had pressed his face against a moment gone. It was too late to call back his outcry.

New movement scurried in the tunnel, from either end. Then his night vision became no blessing, for enough consciousness remained for Brandon to know that the faces that peered at him from the shaft ahead were not human faces.

VII

Olin Reynolds was a patient man. Age and Atlanta had taught him that. When the sun was high, he opened a tin of Vienna sausages and a pack of Lance crackers, munched them slowly, then washed them down with a few swallows from a Mason jar of blockade. Sleepy after his lunch, he stretched out on the seat and dozed.

When he awoke, the sun was low, and his joints complained as he slid from the cab and stretched. Brandon and Kenlaw should have returned by now, he realised with growing unease. Being a patient man, he sat on the running board of his truck, smoked two cigarettes and had another pull from the jar of whiskey. By then dusk was closing, and Reynolds decided it was time for him to do something.

There was a flashlight in the truck. Its batteries were none too fresh, but Reynolds dug it out and tramped toward the mouth of the cave. Stooping low, he called out several times, and, when there came no answer to his hail, he cautiously let himself down into the cavern.

The flashlight beam was weak, but enough to see that there was nothing here but the wreckage of the moonshine still that had been a going concern when he last set foot within the cavern. Reynolds didn't care to search farther with his uncertain light, but the chance that the others might have met with some accident and be unable to get back was too great for him to ignore. Still calling out their names, he nervously picked his way along the passage that led from the rear of the antechamber.

His batteries held out long enough for Reynolds to spot the sudden drop-off before he blundered across the edge and into space. Standing as close to the brink as he dared, Reynolds pointed his flashlight downward into the pit. The yellow beam was sufficient to pick out a broken heap of a man on the rocks below the ledge. Reynolds had seen death often enough before, and he didn't expect an answer when he called out into the darkness of the pit.

As quickly as his failing light permitted, Reynolds retraced his steps out into the starry darkness of the clearing. Breathing a prayer that one of the men might have survived the fall, he sent his truck careening down the mountain road in search of help.

Remote as the area was, it was well into the night before rescue workers in four-wheel-drive vehicles were able to converge upon the clearing before the cavern. Men with lights and emergency equipment hurried into the cave and climbed down into the pit beyond. There they found the broken body of Dr Morris Kenlaw – strangely mutilated, as if set upon by rats after he fell to his death. They loaded his body onto a stretcher, and continued to search for his companion.

Eric Brandon they never found.

They searched the cavern and the passageway and the pit from corner to crevice. They found the wreckage of an old still and, within the pit, Kenlaw's body – and that was all. Later, when there were more lights, someone thought he saw evidence that a rock fall against the far wall of the pit might be a recent one; but after they had turned through this for a while, it was obvious that only bare rock lay underneath.

By morning, news of the mystery had spread. One man dead, one man vanished. Local reporters visited the scene, took photographs, interviewed people. Curiosity seekers joined the search. The day wore on, and still no sign of Brandon. By now the State Bureau of Investigation had sent men into the area in addition to the local sheriff's deputies – not that foul play was suspected so much, but a man had been killed and his companion had disappeared. And since it was evident that Brandon was not to be found inside the cavern, the mystery centered upon his disappearance – and why.

There were many conjectures. The men had been attacked by a bear, Brandon's body carried off. Brandon had been injured, had crawled out for help after Olin Reynolds had driven off; had subsequently collapsed, or become lost in the forest, or was out of his mind from a head injury. Some few suggested that Kenlaw's death had not been accidental, although no motive was put forward, and that Brandon had fled in panic while Reynolds was asleep. The mountainside was searched, and searched more thoroughly the next day. Dogs were brought in, but by now too many people had trampled over the site.

No trace of the missing man was discovered.

It became necessary that Brandon's family and associates be notified, and here the mystery continued. Brandon seemed to have no next-of-kin, but then, he had said once that he was an orphan. At his apartment in New York, he was almost unknown; the landlord could only note that he paid his rent promptly – and often by mail, since he evidently travelled a great deal. The university at which he had mentioned he was working on his doctorate (when asked once) had no student on record named Eric Brandon, and no one could remember if he had ever told them the name of the grant that was supporting his folklore research.

In their need to know *something* definite about the vanished man, investigators looked through the few possessions and personal effects in his cabin. They found no names or addresses with which Brandon might be connected – nothing beyond numerous reference works and copious notes that showed he had indeed been a serious student of regional folklore. There was his rifle, and a handgun – a Walther PPK in .380 ACP – still nothing to excite comment (the Walther was of pre-War manufacture, its serial number without American listing), until someone forced the lock on his *attache* case and discovered the Colt Woodsman. The fact that this .22-calibre pistol incorporated a silencer interested the FBI, and, after fingerprints had been sent through channels, was of even greater interest to the FBI.

"They were manufactured for the OSS," the agent explained, indicating the Colt semiautomatic with its bulky silencer. "A few of them are still in use, although the Hi-Standard HD is more common now. There's no way of knowing how this one ended up in Brandon's possession – it's illegal for a private citizen to own a silencer of any sort, of course. In the hands of a good marksman, it's a perfect assassination gun – about all the sound it makes is that of the action functioning, and a clip of .22 hollow points placed right will finish about any job."

"Eric wouldn't have killed anyone!" Ginger Warner protested angrily. The FBI agent reminded her of a too-scrubbed Bible salesman. She resented the highhanded way he and the others had appropriated Brandon's belongings.

"That's the thing about these sociopathic types; they seem perfectly normal human beings, but it's only a mask." He went on: "We'll run ballistics on this and see if it matches with anything on file. Probably not. This guy was good. Real good. What we have on him now is purely circumstantial, and if we turn him up, I'm not sure we can nail him on anything more serious than firearms violations. But putting together all the things we know and that won't stand up in court, your tenant is one of the top hit men in the business."

"Brandon – a hit man!" scoffed Dell Warner.

"Brandon's not his real name," the agent went on, ticking off his information. "He's set up other identities too, probably. We ran his prints; took some looking, but we finally identified him. His name was Ricky Brennan when he was turned over to a New York state foster home as a small child. Father unknown; mother one Laurie Brennan, deceased. Records say his mother was from around here originally, by the way – maybe that's why he came back. Got into a bit of trouble in his early teens; had a fight with some other boys in the home. One died from a broken neck as a result, but since the others had jumped Brennan, no charges were placed. But out of that, we did get his prints on record – thanks to an institutional blunder when they neglected to expunge his juvenile record. They moved him to another facility, where they could handle his type; shortly after that, Brennan ran away, and there the official record ends."

"Then how can you say that Eric is a hired killer!" Ginger demanded. "You haven't any proof! You've said so yourself."

"No proof that'll stand up in court, I said," the agent admitted. "But we've known for some time of a high-priced hit man who likes to use a high-powered rifle. One like this."

He hefted Brandon's rifle. "This is a Winchester Model 70, chambered for the .220 Swift. That's the fastest commercially loaded cartridge ever made. Factory load will move a 48-grain bullet out at a velocity of over 4100 feet per second on a trajectory flat as a stretched string. Our man has killed with head shots from distances that must have been near three hundred yards, in reconstructing some of his hits. The bullet virtually explodes on impact, so there's nothing left for ballistics to work on.

"But it's a rare gun for a hit man to use, and that's where Brandon begins to figure. It demands a top marksman, as well as a shooter who can handle this much gun. You see, the .220 Swift has just too much power. It burned out the old nickel steel barrels when the cartridge was first introduced, and it's said that the bullet itself will disintegrate if it hits a patch of turbulent air. The .220 Swift may have fantastic velocity, but it also has a tendency to self-destruct."

"Eric used that as a varmint rifle," Dell argued. "It's a popular cartridge for varmint shooters, along with a lot of other small-calibre high-velocity cartridges. And as for that silenced Colt, Eric isn't the first person I've heard of who owned a gun that's considered illegal."

"As I said, we don't have a case – yet. Just pieces of a puzzle, but more pieces start to fall into place once you make a start. There's more than just what I've told you, you can be sure. And we'll find out a lot more once we find Brandon. At a guess, he killed Kenlaw – who may have found out something about him – then panicked and fled."

"Sounds pretty clumsy for a professional killer," Dell commented.

The agent frowned, then was all official politeness once more. These hillbillies were never known for their cooperation with Federal agents. "We'll find out what happened when we find Brandon."

"If you find him."

VIII

Brandon seemed to be swirling through pain-fogged delirium – an endless vertigo in which he clutched at fragments of dream as a man caught in a maelstrom is flung against flotsam of his broken ship. In rare moments his consciousness surfaced enough for him to wonder whether portions of the dreams might be reality.

Most often, Brandon dreamed of limitless caverns beneath the mountains, caverns through which he was borne along by partially glimpsed dwarfish figures. Sometimes Kenlaw was with him in this maze of tunnels – crawling after him, his face a flayed mask of horror, a bloody geologist's pick brandished in one fleshless fist.

At other times Brandon sensed his dreams were visions of the past, visions that could only be born of his obsessive study of the folklore of this region. He looked upon the mountains of a primeval age, when the boundless forest was untouched by the iron bite and poisoned breath of white civilization. Copper-hued savages hunted game along these ridges, to come upon a race of diminutive white-skinned folk who withdrew shyly into the shelter of hidden caverns. The Indians were in awe of these little people, whose origins were beyond the mysteries of their oldest legends, and so they created new legends to explain them.

With the successive migrations of Indians through these mountains, the little people remained in general at peace, for they were wise in certain arts beyond the comprehension of the red man – who deemed them spirit-folk – and their ways were those of secrecy and stealth.

Then came a new race of men: white skins made bronze by the sun, their faces bearded, their flesh encased in burnished steel. The conquistadors enslaved the little folk of the hills as they had enslaved the races of the south, tortured them to learn the secrets of their caves beneath the mountains, forced them to mine the gold from its driven deep into the earth. Then followed a dream of mad carnage, when the little people arose from their tunnels in unexpected force, to entrap their masters within the pits, and to drive those who escaped howling in fear from that which they had called forth from beneath the mountains.

Then came the white settlers in a wave that never receded, driving before them the red man, and finally the game. Remembering the conquistadors, the little people retreated farther into their hidden caverns, hating the white man with his guns and his settlements. Seldom now did they venture into the world above, and then only by night. Deep within the mountains, they found sustenance from the subterranean rivers and the beds of fungoid growths they nourished, feeding as well upon other cave creatures and such prey as they might seek above on starless nights. With each generation, the race slipped farther back into primordial savagery, forgetting the ancient knowledge that had once been theirs. Their stature became dwarfish and apelike, their faces brutish as the devolution of their souls; their flesh and hair assumed the dead pallor of creatures that live in eternal darkness, even as their vision and hearing adapted to their subterranean existence.

They remembered their hatred of the new race of men. Again and again Brandon's dreams were red with visions of stealthy ambush and lurid slaughter of those who trespassed upon their hidden domain, of those who walked mountain trails upon nights when the stars were swallowed in cloud. He saw children snatched from their blankets, women set upon in lonely places. For the most part, these were nightmares from previous centuries, although there was a recurrent dream in which a vapid-faced girl gave herself over willingly to their obscene lusts, until the coming of men with flashlights and shotguns drove them from her cackling embrace.

These were dreams that Brandon through his comatose delirium could grasp and understand. There were far more visions that defied his comprehension.

Fantastic cities reeled and shattered as the earth tore itself apart, thrusting new mountains toward the blazing heavens, opening vast chasms that swallowed rivers and spat them forth as shrieking steam. Oceans of flame melted continents into leaden seas, wherein charred fragments of a world spun frenziedly upon chaotic tides and whirlpools, riven by enormous bolts of raw energy that coursed like fiery cobwebs from the cyclopean orb that filled the sky.

Deep within the earth, fortress cities were shaken and smashed by the Hell that reigned miles above. From out of the ruins, survivors crept to attempt to salvage some of the wonders of the age that had died and left them exiles in a strange world. Darkness and savagery stole from them their ideals, even as monstrous dwellers from even greater depths of the earth drove them from their buried cities and upward through caverns that opened onto an alien surface. In the silent halls of vanished greatness, nightmarish shapes crawled like maggots, while the knowledge of that godlike age was a fading memory to the degenerate descendants of those who had fled.

How long the dreams endured, Brandon could not know. It was the easing of the pain in his skull that eventually convinced Brandon that he had passed from dream into reality, although it was into a reality no less strange than that of delirium.

They made a circle about where he lay – so many of them that Brandon could not guess their number. Their bodies were stunted, but lacking the disproportion of torso to limbs of human dwarves. The thin white fur upon their naked pink flesh combined to give them something of the appearance of lemurs. Brandon thought of elves and of feral children, but their faces were those of demons. Broad nostrils and outthrust, tusked jaws stopped just short of being muzzles, and within overlarge red-pupiled eyes glinted the malign intelligence of a fallen angel.

They seemed in awe of him.

Brandon slowly raised himself on one arm, giddy from the effort. He saw that he lay upon a pallet of dried moss and crudely cured furs, that his naked body seemed thin from long fever. He touched the wound on his scalp and encountered old scab and new scar. Beside him, water and what might be broth or emollients filled bowls which might have been formed by human hands, and perhaps not.

Brandon stared back at the vast circle of eyes. It occurred to him to wonder that he could see them; his first thought was that there must be a source of dim light from somewhere. It then came to him to wonder that these creatures had spared him; his first thought was that as an albino they had mistakenly accepted him as one of their race. In the latter, he was closer to the truth than with the former.

Then slowly, as his awakening consciousness assimilated all that he now knew, Brandon understood the truth. And, in understanding at last, Brandon knew who he was, and why he was.

IX

There was only a sickle of moon that night, but Ginger Warner, feeling restless, threw on a wrap and slipped out of the house.

On some nights sleep just would not come, although such nights came farther apart now. Walking seemed to help, although she had forgone these nocturnal strolls for a time, after once when she realised someone was following her. As it turned out, her unwelcome escort was a Federal agent – they thought she would lead them to where her lover was hiding – and Ginger's subsequent anger was worse than her momentary fear. But in time even the FBI decided that the trail was a cold one, and the investigation into the disappearance of a suspected hired killer was pushed into the background.

It was turning autumn, and the thin breeze made her shiver beneath her dark wrap. Ginger wished for the company of Dan, but her brother had taken the Plott hound off on a weekened bear hunt. The wind made a lonely sound as it moved through the trees, chattering the dead leaves so that even the company of her own footsteps was denied her.

Only the familiarity of the tone let her stifle a scream, when someone called her name from the darkness ahead.

Ginger squinted into the darkness, wishing now she'd brought a light. She whispered uncertainly: "Eric?"

And then he stepped out from the shadow of the rock outcropping that overhung the path along the ridge, and Ginger was in his arms.

She spared only a moment for a kiss, before warning him in one breathless outburst: "Eric, you've got to be careful! The police – the FBI – they've been looking for you all summer! They think you're some sort of criminal!"

In her next breath, she found time to look at him more closely. "Eric, where have you been? What's happened to you?"

Only the warm pressure of his arms proved to her that Brandon was not a phantom of dream. The wind whipped through his long white hair and beard, and there was just enough moonlight for her to make out the streak of scar that creased his scalp. He was shirtless; his only attire a ragged pair of denim jeans and battered boots. Beneath his bare skin, muscles bunched in tight masses that were devoid of fleshy padding. About his neck he wore a peculiar amulet of gold, and upon his belt hung a conquistador's sword.

"I've been walking up and down in the earth," he said. "Is summer over, then? It hadn't seemed so long. I wonder if time moves at a different pace down there."

Both his words and his tone made her stare at him anew. "Eric! God, Eric! What's happened to you?"

"I've found my own kind," Brandon told her, with a laugh that gave her a chill. "But I was lonely among them as well, and so I came back. I knew there must be an open passageway somewhere on your land here, and it didn't take me long to find it."

"You've been hiding out in some caves?" Ginger wondered.

"Not hiding out. They recognised me for who I am, don't you understand? They've forgotten so much over the ages, but not all of the old wisdom has left them. They're not quite beasts yet!"

Ginger considered the scar on his head, and remembered that he must have been wandering in some undiscovered system of caverns for many weeks, alone in the darkness.

"Eric," she said gently, "I know you've been hurt, that you've been alone for a long time. Now I want you to come back with me to the house. You need to have a doctor look at your head where you hurt it."

"It's certain to sound strange to you, I realise," Brandon smiled. "I still sometimes wonder if it isn't all part of my dreams. There's gold down there – more gold than the conquistadors ever dreamed – and hoards of every precious stone these mountains hold. But there's far greater treasure than any of this. There's a lost civilization buried down below, its ruins guarded by entities that transcend any apocalyptic vision of Hell's demons. It's been ages since any of my people have dared to enter the hidden strongholds – but I've dared to enter there, and I've returned."

Ginger compressed her lips and tried to remember all she'd learned in her psychology course last year.

"Eric, you don't have to be worried about what I said about the police. They know you weren't to blame for Dr Kenlaw's death, and they admitted to us that they didn't have any sort of evidence against you on all that other nonsense."

She hoped that was all still true. Far better to have Eric turn himself in and let a good lawyer take charge, than to allow him to wander off again in this condition. They had good doctors at the center in Morganton who could help him recover.

"Come back?" Brandon's face seemed suddenly satanic. "You'd

have me come back to the world of men and be put in a cell? I think instead I'll rule in Hell!"

Ginger did not share in his laughter at his allusion. There were soft rustlings among the leaves alongside the trail, and the wind was silent.

She cried out when she saw their faces, and instinctively pressed against Brandon for protection.

"Don't be afraid," he soothed, gripping her tightly. "These are my people. They've fallen far, but I can lead them back along the road to their ancient greatness.

"Our people," Brandon corrected himself, "Persephone."

ROBERT SILVERBERG

Our Lady of the Sauropods

ROBERT SILVERBERG IS A MULTIPLE WINNER of both the Hugo and Nebula Awards and he was named a Grand Master by the Science Fiction/Fantasy Writers of America in 2004.

He began submitting stories to science fiction magazines in his early teens, and his first published novel, a children's book entitled *Revolt on Alpha C*, appeared 1955. Silverberg won his first Hugo Award the following year.

Always a prolific writer – for the first four years of his career he reputedly wrote a million words a year – his numerous books include such acclaimed novels as *To Open the Sky*, *To Live Again*, *Dying Inside*, *Nightwings* and *Lord Valentine's Castle*. The latter became the basis for his popular "Majipoor" series, set on the eponymous alien planet.

"I abandoned short story writing in 1973," reveals Silverberg, "and felt only relief, no regret, at giving it up. Short stories were just too much trouble to do.

"But then came a magazine called *Omni.*

"It was printed on slick, shiny paper and its publishers understood a great deal about the techniques of promotion, and it started its life with a circulation about six times as great as any science fiction magazine had ever managed to achieve, along with dozens of pages of expensive advertising. It could, therefore, afford to pay a great deal of money for its material.

"After some comings and goings in the editorial chair the job of fiction editor for *Omni* went to my old friend Ben Bova, who began to hint broadly that it would be a nice idea if I wrote a short story for him. He mentioned a sum of money. It was approximately as much as I had been paid for each of my novels prior to the year 1968.

"The amount of money Bova mentioned was at least capable of causing me to rethink my antipathy to short story writing. By the time I was through rethinking, however, Bova had moved upstairs to become *Omni*'s executive editor. The new fiction editor was another old friend of mine, the veteran science fiction writer Robert Sheckley, who also thought I ought to be writing stories for *Omni.*

"In the first month of the new year I gave in. I phoned Sheckley somewhat timidly and told him I was willing to risk my nervous system on one more short story after all.

"For me it was a big thing indeed: at that moment short story writing seemed to me more difficult than writing novels, more difficult than learning Sanskrit, more difficult than winning the Olympic board-jump. Though in an earlier phase of my career I had thought nothing of turning out three or four short stories a week, it took me about five working days to get the opening page of this one written satisfactorily and I assure you that that week was no fun at all.

"But then, magically, the barriers dissolved, the words began to flow, and in a couple of days toward the end of January 1980 the rest of the story emerged. 'Our Lady of the Sauropods', I called it, and when *Omni* published it in the September 1980 issue, the cover announced, ROBERT SILVERBERG RETURNS!

"I imagined the puzzled readers, who surely were unaware that it was seven years since I had deigned to write short stories, turning to each other and saying, 'Why, wherever has he been?' "

21 AUGUST. 07:50 HOURS. Ten minutes since the module meltdown. I can't see the wreckage from here, but I can smell it, bitter and sour against the moist tropical air. I've found a cleft in the rocks, a kind of shallow cavern, where I'll be safe from the dinosaurs for a while. It's shielded by thick clumps of cycads, and in any case it's too small for the big predators to enter. But sooner or later I'm going to need food, and then what? I have no weapons. How long can one woman last, stranded and more or less helpless, aboard a habitat unit not quite five hundred meters in diameter that she's sharing with a bunch of active, hungry dinosaurs?

I keep telling myself that none of this is really happening. Only I can't quite convince myself of that.

My escape still has me shaky. I can't get out of my mind the funny little bubbling sound the tiny powerpak made as it began to overheat. In something like fourteen seconds my lovely mobile module became a charred heap of fused-together junk, taking with it my communicator unit, my food supply, my laser gun and just about everything else. And but for the warning that funny little sound gave me, I'd be so much charred junk now, too. Better off that way, most likely.

When I close my eyes, I imagine I can see Habitat Vronsky floating serenely in orbit a mere 120 kilometers away. What a beautiful sight! The walls gleaming like platinum, the great mirror collecting sunlight and flashing it into the windows, the agricultural satellites wheeling around it like a dozen tiny moons. I could almost reach out and touch it. Tap on the shielding and murmur, "Help me, come for me, rescue me." But I might just as well be out beyond Neptune as sitting here in the adjoining Lagrange slot. No way I can call for help. The moment I move outside this cleft in the rock I'm at the mercy of my saurians and their mercy is not likely to be tender.

Now it's beginning to rain – artificial, like practically everything else on Dino Island. But it gets you just as wet as the natural kind. And clammy. Pfaugh.

Jesus, what am I going to do?

08:15 hours. The rain is over for now. It'll come again in six hours. Astonishing how muggy, dank, thick, the air is. Simply breathing is hard work, and I feel as though mildew is forming on my lungs. I miss Vronsky's clear, crisp, everlasting springtime air. On previous trips to Dino Island I never cared about the climate. But, of course, I was snugly englobed in my mobile unit, a world within a world, self-contained, self-sufficient, isolated from all contact with this place and its creatures. Merely a roving eye, traveling as I pleased, invisible, invulnerable.

Can they sniff me in here?

We don't think their sense of smell is very acute. Sharper than a crocodile's, not as good as a cat's. And the stink of the burned wreckage dominates the place at the moment. But I must reek with fear-signals. I feel calm now, but it was different as I went desperately scrambling out of the module during the meltdown. Scattering pheromones all over the place, I bet.

Commotion in the cycads. *Something's coming in here!*

Long neck, small birdlike feet, delicate grasping hands. Not to worry. Struthiomimus, is all – dainty dino, fragile, birdlike critter barely two meters high. Liquid golden eyes staring solemnly at me. It swivels its head from side to side, ostrichlike, click-click, as if trying to make up its mind about coming closer to me. *Scat!* Go peck a stegosaur. Let me alone.

The struthiomimus withdraws, making little clucking sounds.

Closest I've ever been to a live dinosaur. Glad it was one of the little ones.

09:00 hours. Getting hungry. What am I going to eat?

They say roasted cycad cones aren't too bad. How about raw ones? So many plants are edible when cooked and poisonous otherwise. I never studied such things in detail. Living in our antiseptic little L5 habitats, we're not required to be outdoors-wise, after all. Anyway, there's a fleshy-looking cone on the cycad just in front of the cleft, and it's got an edible look. Might as well try it raw, because there's no other way. Rubbing sticks together will get me nowhere.

Getting the cone off takes some work. Wiggle, twist, snap, tear – *there*. Not as fleshy as it looks. Chewy, in fact. Like munching on rubber. Decent flavor, though. And maybe some useful carbohydrate.

The shuttle isn't due to pick me up for thirty days. Nobody's apt to come looking for me, or even think about me, before then. I'm on my own. Nice irony there: I was desperate to get out of Vronsky and escape from all the bickering and maneuvering, the endless meetings and memoranda, the feinting and counterfeinting, all the ugly political crap that scientists indulge in when they turn into administrators. Thirty days of blessed isolation on Dino Island! An end to that constant dull throbbing in my head from the daily infighting with Director Sarber. Pure research again! And then the meltdown, and here I am cowering in the bushes wondering which comes first, starving or getting gobbled.

09:30 hours. Funny thought just now. Could it have been sabotage?

Consider. Sarber and I, feuding for weeks over the issue of opening Dino Island to tourists. Crucial staff vote coming up next month. Sarber says we can raise millions a year for expanded studies with a program of guided tours and perhaps some rental of the island to film companies. I say that's risky both for the dinos and the tourists, destructive of scientific values, a distraction, a sellout. Emotionally the staff's with me, but Sarber waves figures around, showy fancy income-projections, and generally shouts and blusters. Tempers running high, Sarber in lethal fury at being opposed, barely able to hide his loathing for me. Circulating rumors – designed to get back to me – that if I persist in blocking him, he'll abort my career. Which is malarkey, of course. He may outrank me, but he has no real authority over me. And then his politeness yesterday. (*Yesterday?* An aeon ago.) Smiling smarmily, telling me he hopes I'll rethink my position during my observation tour on the island. Wishing me well. Had he gimmicked my powerpak? I guess it isn't hard if you know a little engineering, and Sarber does. Some kind of timer set to withdraw the insulator rods? Wouldn't be any harm to Dino Island itself, just a quick, compact, localized disaster that implodes and melts the unit and its passenger, so sorry, terrible scientific tragedy, what a great loss. And even if by some fluke I got out of the unit in time, my chances of surviving here as a pedestrian for thirty days would be pretty skimpy, right? Right.

It makes me boil to think that someone's willing to murder you over a mere policy disagreement. It's barbaric. Worse than that: it's tacky.

11:30 hours. I can't stay crouched in this cleft forever. I'm going to explore the island and see if I can find a better hideout. This one simply isn't adequate for anything more than short-term huddling. Besides, I'm not as spooked as I was right after the meltdown. I realise now that I'm not going to find a tyrannosaur hiding behind every tree. And tyrannosaurs aren't going to be much interested in scrawny stuff like me.

Anyway I'm a quick-witted higher primate. If my humble mamalian ancestors seventy million years ago were able to elude dinosaurs well enough to survive and inherit the earth, I should be able to keep from getting eaten for the next thirty days. And with or without my cozy little mobile module, I want to get out into this place, whatever the risks. Nobody's ever had a chance to interact this closely with the dinos before.

Good thing I kept this pocket recorder when I jumped from the module. Whether I'm a dino's dinner or not, I ought to be able to set down some useful observations.

Here I go.

18:30 hours. Twilight is descending now. I am camped near the equator in a lean-to flung together out of tree-fern fronds – a flimsy shelter, but the huge fronds conceal me, and with luck I'll make it through to morning. That cycad cone doesn't seem to have poisoned me yet, and I ate another one just now, along with some tender new fiddleheads uncoiling from the heart of a tree-fern. Spartan fare, but it gives me the illusion of being fed.

In the evening mists I observe a brachiosaur, half-grown but already colossal, munching in the treetops. A gloomy-looking triceratops stands nearby and several of the ostrichlike struthiomimids scamper busily in the underbrush, hunting I know not what. No sign of tyrannosaurs all day. There aren't many of them here, anyway, and I hope they're all sleeping off huge feasts somewhere in the other hemisphere.

What a fantastic place this is!

I don't feel tired. I don't even feel frightened – just a little wary.

I feel exhilarated, as a matter of fact.

Here I sit peering out between fern fronds at a scene out of the dawn of time. All that's missing is a pterosaur or two flapping overhead, but we haven't brought those back yet. The mournful snufflings of the huge brachiosaur carry clearly even in the heavy air. The struthiomimids are making sweet honking sounds. Night is falling swiftly and the great shapes out there take on dreamlike primordial wonder.

What a brilliant idea it was to put all the Olsen-process dinosaur-reconstructs aboard a little L5 habitat of their very own and turn them loose to recreate the Mesozoic! After that unfortunate San Diego event with the tyrannosaur, it became politically unfeasible to keep them anywhere on earth, I know, but even so this is a better scheme. In just a little more than seven years Dino Island has taken on an altogether convincing illusion of reality. Things grow so fast in this lush, steamy, high-CO_2 tropical atmosphere! Of course, we haven't been able to duplicate the real Mesozoic flora, but we've done all right using botanical survivors, cycads and tree ferns and horsetails and palms and gingkos and auracarias, and thick carpets of mosses and selaginellas and liverworts covering the ground. Everything has blended and merged and run amok: it's hard now to recall the bare and unnatural look of the island when we first laid it out. Now it's a seamless tapestry in green and brown, a dense jungle broken only by streams, lakes and meadows, encapsulated in spherical metal walls some two kilometers in circumference.

And the animals, the wonderful fantastic grotesque animals—

We don't pretend that the real Mesozoic ever held any such mix of fauna as I've seen today, stegosaurs and corythosaurs side by side, a triceratops sourly glaring at a brachiosaur, struthiomimus contemporary with iguanodon, a wild unscientific jumble of Triassic, Jurassic and Cretaceous, a hundred million years of the dinosaur reign scrambled together. We take what we can get. Olsen-process reconstructs require sufficient fossil DNA to permit the computer synthesis, and we've been able to find that in only some twenty species so far. The wonder is that we've accomplished even that much: to replicate the complete DNA molecule from battered and sketchy genetic information millions of years old, to carry out the intricate implants in reptilian host ova, to see the embryos through to self-sustaining levels. The only word that applies is *miraculous*. If our dinos come from eras millions of years apart, so be it: we do our best. If we have no oterosaur and no allosaur and no archaeopteryx, so be it: we may have them yet. What we already have is plenty to work with. Some day there may be separate Triassic, Jurassic and Cretaceous satellite habitats, but none of us will live to see that, I suspect.

Total darkness now. Mysterious screechings and hissings out there. This afternoon, as I moved cautiously, but in delight, from the wreckage site up near the rotation axis to my present equatorial camp, sometimes coming within fifty or a hundred meters of living dinos, I felt a kind of ecstasy. Now my fears are returning, and my anger at this stupid marooning. I imagine clutching claws reaching for me, terrible jaws yawning above me.

I don't think I'll get much sleep tonight.

22 August. 06:00 hours. Rosy-fingered dawn comes to Dino Island, and I'm still alive. Not a great night's sleep, but I must have had some, because I can remember fragments of dreams. About dinosaurs, naturally. Sitting in little groups, some playing pinochle and some knitting sweaters. And choral singing, a dinosaur rendition of *The Messiah* or maybe Beethoven's Ninth.

I feel alert, inquisitive, and hungry. Especially hungry. I know we've stocked this place with frogs and turtles and other small-size anachronisms to provide a balanced diet for the big critters. Today I'll have to snare some for myself, grisly though I find the prospect of eating raw frog's legs.

I don't bother getting dressed. With rain showers programmed to fall four times a day, it's better to go naked anyway. Mother Eve of the Mesozoic, that's me! And without my soggy tunic I find that I don't mind the greenhouse atmosphere half as much.

Out to see what I can find.

The dinosaurs are up and about already, the big herbivores munching away, the carnivores doing their stalking. All of them have such huge appetites that they can't wait for the sun to come up. In the bad old days when the dinos were thought to be reptiles, of course, we'd have expected them to sit there like lumps until daylight got their body temperatures up to functional levels. But one of the great joys of the reconstruct project was the vindication of the notion that dinosaurs were warm-blooded animals, active and quick and pretty damned intelligent. No sluggardly crocodilians these! Would that they were, if only for my survival's sake.

11:30 hours. A busy morning. My first encounter with a major predator.

There are nine tyrannosaurs on the island, including three born in the past eighteen months. (That gives us an optimum predator-to-prey ratio. If the tyrannosaurs keep reproducing and don't start eating each other, we'll have to begin thinning them out. One of the problems with a closed ecology – natural checks and balances don't fully apply.) Sooner or later I was bound to encounter one, but I had hoped it would be later.

I was hunting frogs at the edge of Cope Lake. A ticklish business – calls for agility, cunning, quick reflexes. I remember the technique from my girlhood – the cupped hand, the lightning pounce – but somehow it's become a lot harder in the last twenty years. Superior frogs these days, I suppose. There I was, kneeling in the mud, swooping, missing, swooping, missing; some vast sauropod snoozing in the lake, probably our diplodocus; a corythosaur browsing in a stand of gingko trees, quite delicately nipping off the foul-smelling yellow fruits. Swoop. Miss. Swoop. Miss. Such intense concentration on my task that old T. rex could have tiptoed right up behind me, and I'd never have noticed. But then I felt a subtle something, a change in the air, maybe, a barely perceptible shift in dynamics. I glanced up and saw the corythosaur rearing on its hind legs, looking around uneasily, pulling deep sniffs into that fantastically elaborate bony crest that houses its early-warning system. *Carnivore alert!* The corythosaur obviously smelled something wicked this way coming, for it swung around between two big gingkos and started to go galumphing away. Too late. The treetops parted, giant boughs toppled, and out of the forest came our original tyrannosaur, the pigeon-toed one we call Belshazzar, moving in its heavy, clumsy waddle, ponderous legs working hard, tail absurdly swinging from side to side. I slithered into the lake and scrunched down as deep as I could go in the warm oozing mud. The corythosaur had no place to slither. Unarmed, unarmored, it could only make great bleating sounds, terror mingled with defiance, as the killer bore down on it.

I had to watch. I had never seen a kill.

In a graceless but wondrously effective way, the tyrannosaur dug its hind claws into the ground, pivoted astonishingly, and, using its massive tail as a counterweight, moved in a ninety-degree arc to knock the corythosaur down with a stupendous sidewise swat of its huge head. I hadn't been expecting that. The corythosaur dropped and lay on its side, snorting in pain and feebly waving its limbs. Now came the coup de grace with hind legs, and then the rending and tearing, the jaws and the tiny arms at last coming into play. Burrowing chin-deep in the mud, I watched in awe and weird fascination. There are those among us who argue that the carnivores ought to be segregated into their own island, that it is folly to allow reconstructs created with such effort to be casually butchered this way. Perhaps in the beginning that made sense, but not now, not when natural increase is rapidly filling the island with young dinos. If we are to learn anything about these animals, it will only be by reproducing as closely as possible their original living conditions. Besides, would it not be a cruel mockery to feed our tyrannosaurs on hamburger and herring?

The killer fed for more than an hour. At the end came a scary moment: Belshazzar, blood-smeared and bloated, hauled himself ponderously down to the edge of the lake for a drink. He stood no more than ten meters from me. I did my most convincing imitation of a rotting log; but the tyrannosaur, although it did seem to study me with a beady eye, had no further appetite. For a long while after he departed, I stayed buried in the mud, fearing he might come back for dessert. And eventually there was another crashing and bashing in the forest – not Belshazzar this time, though, but a younger one with a gimpy arm. It uttered a sort of whinnying sound and went to work on the corythosaur carcass. No surprise: we already knew that tyrannosaurs had no prejudices against carrion.

Nor, I found, did I.

When the coast was clear, I crept out and saw that the two tyrannosaurs had left hundreds of kilos of meat. Starvation knoweth no pride and also few qualms. Using a clamshell for my blade, I started chopping away.

Corythosaur meat has a curiously sweet flavor – nutmeg and cloves, dash of cinnamon. The first chunk would not go down. You are a pioneer, I told myself, retching. You are the first human ever to eat dinosaur meat. *Yes, but why does it have to be raw?* No choice about that. Be dispassionate, love. Conquer your gag reflex or die trying. I pretended I was eating oysters. This time the meat went down. It didn't stay down. The alternative, I told myself grimly, is a diet of fern fronds and frogs, and you haven't been much good at catching the frogs. I tried again. Success!

I'd have to call corythosaur meat an acquired taste. But the wilderness is no place for picky eaters.

23 August. 13:00 hours. At midday I found myself in the southern hemisphere, along the fringes of Marsh Marsh about a hundred meters below the equator. Observing herd behavior in sauropods – five brachiosaurs, two adult and three young, moving in formation, the small ones in the center. By "small" I mean only some ten meters from nose to tail-tip. Sauropod appetites being what they are, we'll have to thin that herd soon, too, especially if we want to introduce a female diplodocus into the colony. *Two* species of sauropods breeding and eating like that could devastate the island in three years. Nobody ever expected dinosaurs to reproduce like rabbits – another dividend of their being warm-blooded, I suppose. We might have guessed it, though, from the vast quantity of fossils. If that many bones survived the catastrophes of a hundred-odd million years, how enormous the living Mesozoic population must have been! An awesome race in more ways than mere physical mass.

I had a chance to do a little herd-thinning myself just now. Mysterious stirring in the spongy soil right at my feet, and I looked down to see triceratops eggs hatching! Seven brave little critters, already horny and beaky, scrabbling out of a nest, staring around defiantly. No bigger than kittens, but active and sturdy from the moment of birth.

The corythosaur meat has probably spoiled by now. A more pragmatic soul very likely would have augmented her diet with one or two little ceratopsians. I couldn't do it.

They scuttled off in seven different directions. I thought briefly of catching one and making a pet out of it. Silly idea.

25 August. 07:00 hours. Start of the fifth day. I've done three complete circumambulations of the island. Slinking around on foot is fifty times as risky as cruising around in a module, and fifty thousand times as rewarding. I make camp in a different place every night. I don't mind the humidity any longer. And despite my skimpy diet, I feel pretty healthy. Raw dinosaur, I know now, is a lot tastier than raw frog. I've become an expert scavenger – the sound of a tyrannosaur in the forest now stimulates my salivary glands instead of my adrenals. Going naked is fun, too. And I appeciate my body much more, since the bulges that civilization puts there have begun to melt away.

Nevertheless, I keep trying to figure out some way of signaling Habitat Vronsky for help. Changing the position of the reflecting mirrors, maybe, so I can beam an SOS? Sounds nice, but I don't even know where the island's controls are located, let alone how to run them. Let's hope my luck holds out another three and a half weeks.

27 August. 17:00 hours. The dinosaurs know that I'm here and that I'm some extraordinary kind of animal. Does that sound weird? How can great dumb beasts *know* anything? They have such tiny brains. And my own brain must be softening on this protein-and-cellulose diet. Even so, I'm starting to have peculiar feelings about these animals. I see them *watching* me. An odd knowing look in their eyes, not stupid at all. They stare and I imagine them nodding, smiling, exchanging glances with each other, discussing me. I'm supposed to be observing them, but I think they're observing me, too, somehow.

This is crazy. I'm tempted to erase the entry. But I'll have it as a record of my changing psychological state if nothing else.

28 August. 12:00 hours. More fantasies about the dinosaurs. I've decided that the big brachiosaur – Bertha – plays a key role here. She doesn't move around much, but there are always lesser dinosaurs in orbit around her. Much eye contact. *Eye contact between dinosaurs?* Let it stand. That's my perception of what they're doing. I get a definite sense that there's communication going on here, modulating over some wave that I'm not capable of detecting. And Bertha seems to be a central nexus, a grand totem of some sort, a – a switchboard? What am I talking about? What's happening to me?

30 August. 09:45 hours. What a damned fool I am! Serves me right for being a filthy voyeur. Climbed a tree to watch iguanodons mating at the foot of Bakker Falls. At climactic moment the branch broke. I dropped twenty meters. Grabbed a lower limb or I'd be dead now. As it is, pretty badly smashed around. I don't think anything's broken, but my left leg won't support me and my back's in bad shape. Internal injuries too? Not sure. I've crawled into a little rock-shelter near the falls. Exhausted and maybe feverish. Shock, most likely. I suppose I'll starve now. It would have been an honor to be eaten by a tyrannosaur, but to die from falling out of a tree is just plain humiliating.

The mating of iguanodons is a spectacular sight, by the way. But I hurt too much to describe it now.

31 August. 17:00 hours. Stiff, sore, hungry, hideously thirsty. Leg still useless and when I try to crawl even a few meters, I feel as if I'm going to crack in half at the waist. High fever.

How long does it take to starve to death?

1 Sep. 07:00 hours. Three broken eggs lying near me when I awoke. Embryos still alive – probably stegosaur – but not for long. First food in forty-eight hours. Did the eggs fall out of a nest somewhere overhead? Do stegosaurs make their nests in trees, dummy?

Fever diminishing. Body aches all over. Crawled to the stream and managed to scoop up a little water.

13:30 hours. Dozed off. Awakened to find haunch of fresh meat within crawling distance. Struthiomimus drumstick, I think. Nasty sour taste, but it's edible. Nibbled a little, slept again, ate some more. Pair of stegosaurs grazing not far away, tiny eyes fastened on me. Smaller dinosaurs holding a kind of conference by some big cycads. And Bertha Brachiosaur is munching away in Ostrom Meadow, benignly supervising the whole scene.

This is absolutely crazy.

I think the dinosaurs are taking care of me.

2 Sep. 09:00 hours. No doubt of it at all. They bring eggs, meat, even cycad cones and tree-fern fronds. At first they delivered things only when I slept, but now they come hopping right up to me and dump things at my feet. The struthiomimids are the bearers – they're the smallest, most agile, quickest hands. They bring their offerings, stare me right in the eye, pause as if waiting for a tip. Other dinosaurs watching from the distance. This is a coordinated effort. I am the center of all activity on the island, it seems. I imagine that even the tyrannosaurs are saving choice cuts for me. Hallucination? Fantasy? Delirium of fever? I feel lucid. The fever is abating. I'm still too stiff and weak to move very far, but I think I'm recovering from the effects of my fall. With a little help from my friends.

10:00 hours. Played back the last entry. Thinking it over. I don't *think* I've gone insane. If I'm insane enough to be worried about my sanity, how crazy can I be? Or am I just fooling myself? There's a terrible conflict between what I think I perceive going on here and what I know I ought to be perceiving.

15:00 hours. A long, strange dream this afternoon. I saw all the dinosaurs standing in the meadow and they were connected to one another by gleaming threads, like the telephone lines of olden times, and all the threads centered on Bertha. As if she's the switchboard, yes. And telepathic messages were traveling. An extrasensory hookup, powerful pulses moving along the lines. I dreamed that a small dinosaur came to me and offered me a line and, in pantomime, showed me how to hook it up, and a great flood of delight went through me as I made the connection. And when I plugged it in, I could feel the deep and heavy thoughts of the dinosaurs, the slow rapturous philosophical interchanges.

When I woke, the dream seemed bizarrely vivid, strangely real, the dream-ideas lingering as they sometimes do. I saw the animals about me in a new way. As if this is not just a zoological research station, but a community, a settlement, the sole outpost of an alien civilization – an alien civilization native to earth.

Come off it. These animals have minute brains. They spend their days chomping on greenery, except for the ones that chomp on other dinosaurs. Compared with dinosaurs, cows and sheep are downright geniuses.

I can hobble a little now.

3 Sep. 06:00 hours. The same dream again last night, the universal telepathic linkage. Sense of warmth and love flowing from dinosaurs to me.

Fresh tyrannosaur eggs for breakfast.

5 Sep. 11:00 hours. I'm making a fast recovery. Up and about, still creaky but not much pain left. They still feed me. Though the struthiomimids remain the bearers of food, the bigger dinosaurs now come close, too. A stegosaur nuzzled up to me like some Goliath-sized pony, and I petted its rough scaly flank. The diplodocus stretched out flat and seemed to beg me to stroke its immense neck.

If this is madness, so be it. There's community here, loving and temperate. Even the predatory carnivores are part of it: eaters and eaten are aspects of the whole, yin and yang. Riding around in our sealed modules, we could never have suspected any of this.

They are gradually drawing me into their communion. I feel the pulses that pass between them. My entire soul throbs with that strange new sensation. My skin tingles.

They bring me food of their own bodies, their flesh and their unborn young, and they watch over me and silently urge me back to health. Why? For sweet charity's sake? I don't think so. I think they want something from me. I think they need something from me.

What could they need from me?

6 Sep. 06:00 hours. All this night I have moved slowly through the forest in what I can only term an ecstatic state. Vast shapes, humped monstrous forms barely visible by dim glimmer, came and went about me. Hour after hour I walked unharmed, feeling the communion intensify. Until at last, exhausted, I have come to rest here on this mossy carpet, and in the first light of dawn I see the giant form of the great brachiosaur standing like a mountain on the far side of Owen River.

I am drawn to her. I could worship her. Through her vast body surge powerful currents. She is the amplifier. By her are we all connected. The holy mother of us all. From the enormous mass of her body emanate potent healing impulses.

I'll rest a little while. Then I'll cross the river to her.

09:00 hours. We stand face to face. Her head is fifteen meters above mine. Her small eyes are unreadable. I trust her and I love her.

Lesser brachiosaurs have gathered behind her on the riverbank. Farther away are dinosaurs of half a dozen other species, immobile, silent.

I am humble in their presence. They are representatives of a dynamic, superior race, which but for a cruel cosmic accident would rule the earth to this day, and I am coming to revere them.

Consider: they endured for a hundred forty million years in ever-renewing vigor. They met all evolutionary challenges, except the one of sudden and catastrophic climatic change against which nothing could have protected them. They multiplied and proliferated and adapted, dominating land and sea and air, covering the globe. Our own trifling, contemptible ancestors were nothing next to them. Who knows what these dinosaurs might have achieved if that crashing asteroid had not blotted out their light? What a vast irony: millions of years of supremacy ended in a single generation by a chilling cloud of dust. But until then – the wonder, the grandeur—

Only beasts, you say? How can you be sure? We know just a shred of what the Mesozoic was really like, just a slice, literally the bare bones. The passage of a hundred million years can obliterate all traces of civilization. Suppose they had language, poetry, mythology, philosophy? Love, dreams, aspirations? No, you say, they were beasts, ponderous and stupid, that lived mindless bestial lives. And I reply that we puny hairy ones have no right to impose our own values on them. The only kind of civilization we can understand is the one we have built. We imagine that our own trivial accomplishments are the determining case, that computers and spaceships and broiled sausages are such miracles that they place us at evolution's pinnacle. But now I know otherwise. Humanity has done marvelous things, yes. But we would not have existed at all had this greatest of races been allowed to live to fulfill its destiny.

I feel the intense love radiating from the titan that looms above me. I feel the contact between our souls steadily strengthening and deepening.

The last barriers dissolve.

And I understand at last.

I am the chosen one. I am the vehicle. I am the bringer of rebirth, the beloved one, the necessary one. Our Lady of the Sauropods am I, the holy one, the prophetess, the priestess.

Is this madness? Then it is madness.

Why have we small hairy creatures existed at all? I know now. It is so that through our technology we could make possible the return of the great ones. They perished unfairly. Through us, they are resurrected aboard this tiny glove in space.

I tremble in the force of the need that pours from them.

I will not fail you, I tell the great sauropods before me, and the sauropods send my thoughts reverberating to all the others.

20 September. 06:00 hours. The thirtieth day. The shuttle comes from Habitat Vronsky today to pick me up and deliver the next researcher.

I wait at the transit lock. Hundreds of dinosaurs wait with me, each close beside the nest, both the lions and the lambs, gathered quietly, their attention focussed entirely on me.

Now the shuttle arrives, right on time, gliding in for a perfect docking. The airlocks open. A figure appears. Sarber himself! Coming to make sure I didn't survive the meltdown, or else to finish me off.

He stands blinking in the entry passage, gaping at the throngs of placid dinosaurs arrayed in a huge semicircle around the naked woman who stands beside the wreckage of the mobile module. For a moment he is unable to speak.

"Anne?" he says finally. "What in God's name—"

"You'll never understand," I tell him. I give the signal. Belshazzar rumbles forward. Sarber screams and whirls and sprints for the air-lock, but a stegosaur blocks the way.

"No!" Sarber cries, as the tyrannosaur's mighty head swoops down. It is all over in a moment.

Revenge! How sweet!

And this is only the beginning. Habitat Vronsky lies just 120 kilometers away. Elsewhere in the Lagrange belt are hundreds of other habitats ripe for conquest. The earth itself is within easy reach. I have no idea yet how it will be accomplished, but I know it will be done and done successfully, and I will be the instrument by which it is done.

I stretch forth my arms to the mighty creatures that surround me. I feel their strength, their power, their harmony. I am one with them, and they with me.

The Great Race has returned, and I am its priestess. Let the hairy ones tremble!

BASIL COPPER

The Flabby Men

BASIL COPPER'S FIRST STORY in the horror field, "The Spider", was published in 1964 in *The Fifth Pan Book of Horror Stories*, since when his short fiction has appeared in numerous anthologies, been extensively adapted for radio and television, and collected in *Not After Nightfall*, *Here Be Daemons*, *From Evil's Pillow*, *And Afterward, the Dark*, *Voices of Doom*, *When Footsteps Echo*, *Whispers in the Night*, *Cold Hand on My Shoulder* and *Knife in the Back*.

Along with two non-fiction studies of the vampire and werewolf legends, his other books include the novels *The Great White Space*, *The Curse of the Fleers*, *Necropolis*, *The Black Death* and *The House of the Wolf*. Copper has also written more than fifty hardboiled thrillers about Los Angeles private detective Mike Faraday, and has continued the adventures of August Derleth's Sherlock Holmes-like consulting detective Solar Pons in several volumes of short stories and the novel *Solar Pons versus The Devil's Claw* (actually written in 1980, but not published until 2004).

The late American literary critic and teacher Edward Wagenknecht said about the following story: "In 'The Flabby Men' we do learn at last what has caused everything that has terrified us from the beginning, but through most of the tale (though the specific expressions of the terror are always concrete enough), we are kept guessing, so that we come to fear that nature herself has become corrupted, which would be far more terrible than any particular evil could possibly be."

I

I DID NOT LIKE THE LOOK OF THE ISLAND from the very first. I had come from the capital along an undulating, scree-strewn beach road on the mainland, that circled around great outcrops of splintered firs and pine, and the Switzer was beginning to run out of fuel when I sighted the ferry in the gathering dusk. The lava-like rubble of the shore stretched drearily to an oily, slime-washed sea and against the dark yellow of this sullen background foul, scummy pustules burst and reformed.

The piles of the ferry-landing were red with rust, I noticed, as the machine purred onto the metallized surface of the pier, and a heap of old-fashioned petrol containers lay huddled together on the shingle like the husks of some giant fruit or the whorled shells of monstrous land-crabs.

The wind was rising, bringing with it drifts of cold, pungently tainted spume from farther out, and the harshly striated mass of the island, black, brown, and sickly yellow, gashed the sea about two miles offshore. My ring brought no one from the dusty glass and steel office so badly needing paint and upkeep. I waited and then tried the electric klaxon on the Switzer; it stirred the echoes and sent a few broken-winged birds scuttering clumsily among the rocks. I tried once more and then gave up; batteries were too precious to waste in this fashion.

Rort should have met me at the landing. I had a vision-tube check on that just before I started, and they knew I was arriving about six. Now it was after seven and the crowd on the island should be alerted. Test conditions were said to be ideal for the next two weeks and I was eager to get ahead with the first. There was little sound in the cove, though farther out white was beginning to show among the folds of yellow; nothing but the slap of foul water, wind strumming over splintered wood, and, for a few brief seconds, a startled buzz as a weather helicopter flapped its way hesitantly southwards.

I had not expected the ferry to be working; that would have been too much, but Rort had said they had got a power launch going which would take me and my traps out. The Switzer would have to take its chance on the jetty with a tarpaulin over it; the swarms of voracious vermin that had been infesting the shore for the past few months might have a go at it, but I doubted whether they would make much impression on its tracks, the only nonmetal component likely to prove edible. Even so I had stripped the machine down to essentials; it looked as though I might have some trouble in getting fuel for the trip back.

The darkness was growing, blurring the outline of rocks and the distant island; the jetty shuddered under the impact of the undertow, and there was a sharp scrabbling and muffled squeaks from the rusting debris at the side of the pier, which I didn't like. Whole parties of people had been devoured by a debased form of giant rat which haunted the seashore, and it was said that the plague of land-crabs had increased of late.

I went to the end of the jetty and winked my flash seawards a few times and then unloaded my cases of equipment and personal gear. While I was clipping the rubberized tarpaulin over the Switzer I heard the shrill whine of a jet, and a short while after I made out the dim shape of a turbo-launch creaming out from the direction of the island. That would be Rort.

The soughing of the wind had increased and water was slapping stealthily along the filthy foreshore, stirring uneasily among the crumbling rubbish that littered the marge. It was a sad inheritance, I thought, this debilitated world; an aftermath of violence that would have to be painfully reknitted by the industry of a few patient men and women, self-dedicated and working with poor, worn-out tools.

There was a crunch from the shadows and I stabbed the flash beam into the dusk, outlined the slavering, grey, depraved jawline, red-rimmed, white-filmed eyes, and slit-nostrilled mask of a large creature like the caricature of a hare, which went hopping off with a clatter among the oil cans. I went over to the Switzer and something else scurried away. There were the marks of sharp teeth on the half-tracks, where the creatures had been tearing the covering. I sprayed the area round the vehicle with a powerful poison I had brought from the stores, which I felt would discourage all but the hardiest and hungriest.

When I had finished, the noise of the jet filled the cove and then eased off as someone throttled down; I went to the edge of the jetty and saw a familiar, grey-hulled Ministry launch bearing the hieroglyphics of the Central Committee. Rort came out of the wheelhouse.

"Sorry to keep you waiting. I came earlier but had to go back over. They get worried if I'm away long. This is the only transport to and from the island you know, and Future knows what things are in the water."

Rort was a tall, thin man with a tangled stubble of beard; he had been a research worker in one of the innumerable project teams set up by the Central Committee, and had been seconded for special duties. He had always been the worrying kind, but now I seemed to detect an even greater nervousness in his manner, as he helped me get the equipment stowed aboard; I set this down to the location of the island and the forsaken atmosphere of this part of the coast.

He told me something of the situation as we put off. There was an oily swell running now, with what would have been whitecaps in years gone by, before poisons clogged the earth, and I sat on a bench in the charthouse with him while he steered. Rort was definitely uneasy but when I questioned him, he shrugged it off as an indefinable something. One concrete occurrence had rattled him though, which was partly a cause of his unease. Unloading the group's equipment a few weeks before, he had slipped on the slime-covered landing and a case of radio energy cells – their only supply – had gone to the bottom.

That meant the sending of test data over the transmitter to base was strictly limited, to conserve energy; and fuel for the launch was short. The relief helicopter was not due for a month; in another week or two there might be difficulties in communications. I asked Rort about the island; he cleared his throat with a rasping noise, a sign of dislike with him, but I was surprised when I heard there was actually some sort of settlement, on the lines of the old-style village, in a cove on the seaward side, somewhere over the other shoulder of the flinty hill which was beginning to climb up the dark sky as we approached the shore.

Rort said there were about sixty people; fifty men and a few breeders, and they had a miserable existence growing vegetables on imported unsoured soil and fishing far out; cleansing and sterilizing conditions were fantastic, of course, but I gathered they had worked out a satisfactory and safe system. Their rations were supplemented by the Central Committee at various times of the year, and I remembered seeing somewhere that the experiment was one likely to be encouraged in various places.

At all events they had welcomed the group and had been pathetically eager to provide labour and materials from their own scanty stores; they felt that the survey, even though organised only to carry out research on conditions, would improve their lot immediately, though there was something in their reasoning when looked at as a long-term policy. Research groups set up by the Central Committee were constantly on the move as the cloud moved round, and though we still got the same reaction, there were hopes in higher circles that the effects might wear off in our lifetime.

But most of this would not, of itself, have been enough to cause this uneasiness. It sprang from something other than the sombre environment into which every pulse of the boat's progress was bearing us. When I put this thought into the form of a direct statement Rort did not immediately reply. Then his tall body uncoiled itself from over the wheel.

"I don't know," he said. "But there's something deadly in the wind. You can laugh, but you haven't been here these weeks like the rest of us. Later, you'll know what I mean."

I was still chewing over this infuriatingly vague answer when we began the run into the jetty. The shingle was harsh, black clinker, something like volcanic ash, and the vessel grated unpleasantly against it as Rort let the water slowly take us in. He steadied the boat, holding a corroded handrail that jutted out from the concrete slipway, and after we had unloaded we pulled the craft farther up the shore.

Back from the beach the wind suddenly plucked at one, as though it were buffeting down from the black bulk of the hill which rose into the misty dusk above us; we slipped and floundered on the yellow clay pathway that wound through black, slippery rocks, covered with sickly smelling encrustations, and once a shimmering, black and yellow creature like a toad flopped away soggily down the hillside, leaving a trail of crimson slime behind it.

I was winded long before we had reached the lower shoulder of the hill; the air seemed calmer here and looking down I could see the faint smudge of the launch beside the jetty and farther out, the tired, grey wrinkle of the sea, changing to the ghostly green glow it always assumed after dark. To my relief Rort suddenly turned aside from the pathway, and went through two sloping wet shoulders of stone that breasted across the face to the right.

Hesitantly I followed; it was an oppressive place, wet underfoot, the encrusted walls exuding moisture and overhead the sweep of rock toppling forward until it met in a dizzy arch. We were using our flashes now but presently the walls fell away, and we walked across an undulating upland slashed with the gentian, scarlet and black of the parasitical fungi that sometimes grew to two or three feet across. Along a gully and up another slope and then Rort halted. He pointed through a gap between groups of stunted trees. I was looking at K4 Research Station.

II

K4 had been constructed some two years before, at a time when the drive for economy and the need for a chain of observation stations had been at the height of conflict; the result was an amalgam of extravagances and sterilities. The Central Committee had felt that the scientific needs of establishments overrode those of expediency and comfort so that at K4 primitive concrete constructions like the old-fashioned blockhouses had been left without proper proofing and finish, while the expensive and elaborate equipment housed within began to deteriorate for want of protection and proper maintenance.

The life there was a peculiar blend of crowded discomfort and brooding loneliness; the days were given over to exhaustive examination of the content of the soil, the air, and the sea surrounding the island, while the evenings were spent in writing up notebooks, in conducting analytical experiments among the crazy cackle of geiger counters in the tall, lighthouse-like building overlooking the rocky coast, and in limited social intercourse among our colleagues.

Of these some are worthy of more than passing mention: Dr Fritzjof, a Swede who had lost an arm as a result of nuclear experiments; Masters, the Director of the station, a tall, handsome-looking man in his late forties with hair inclining to silver; sober, careful-minded, and good-humoured, a pleasant man to work with; Professor Lockspeiser, a young, tawny-bearded Australian who had done astonishing work on the degeneration of atomized structures and the causes of sterility in contaminated females; Pollock, despite his name, a West Indian physicist; and a breeder, officially C2147, but known to us as Karla.

A tall, blonde girl with a well-made body and prominent breasts and buttocks, she was ostensibly there as laboratory assistant, but really to be near Fitzwilliams, one of the physicists, by whom she was pregnant. This made no difference to the usual emergency regulations then in force and she was still expected to carry out her obligations to other members of the staff, which she did with energy. It was my turn to enjoy her on the third or fourth evening after my arrival and a very fine experience it was, she being, as I said, a very passionate, well-built girl, most willing and inventive and with a most attractive smile and white teeth; Polish, I think. We all thought Fitzwilliams a lucky man as permanent possession of her was vested in him; he showed me the papers he had taken out on one occasion in which C2147 was specifically mentioned. I knew then it was correct as I had seen the same symbols, branded in the usual place for all breeders of her class.

If I record this in some detail it was because the monotony and aridity of the life made such occurrences assume the emotional and significant impact of a sunburst on a person blind from birth; it irradiated a glow that lasted for days and certainly Karla's presence and the amenities she afforded lent the little garrison some degree of contentment.

It was about a week after my arrival that the first of a long procession of events occurred, which were later to assume a quite disproportionate significance when they began to fall into place. It had been a day of storm and violence; shards of rain beat savagely at the transparent slits of the observation tower, almost drowning the discontented chatter of the instruments.

I had been out in the early afternoon, the weather abating, to draw off fluid from a particular form of fungi whose formation rather interested us, and when I turned up along the cliff, my cases full of specimens and cuttings, I was suddenly struck by the fact that since my arrival I had seen so little of the island. The clouds were still lowering and the harsh chumble of the sea on the slimy rocks did not form a background of any great charm, but a beam of sickly, dusty "sunlight" – an archaic term I use for want of a better word – suddenly pricked out a path to the sea's edge and against this metallic sheen I saw the filigree work of a pier and what looked like a cluster of huts and buildings.

I assumed this was the village Rort had spoken of and having some time in hand thought I would take a look, but an hour's stumble among foul rocks and dripping, cave-like formations along the shore made me realise that I could not hope to regain K4 before darkness. The afternoon was already deepening to early dusk when I came out on a primitive path and found myself near the spot. Though the greenish twilight and the slop of the waves among the pebbles of the foreshore gave the place a somewhat eerie aspect, I could not say I was particularly conscious of this, interested as I was to see the village.

I say village, but it was little more than the most primitive kind of settlement, framed in two gigantic spits of rock which made a sort of notch in the black sand. The wind had risen and the stench of decay was in the twilight. Dead matter and poisonous dribbles of spume whirled about the dark strand.

The green luminosity of the sea bathed the area in its pale, unearthly light though it had not yet assumed the intensity it would reveal with the coming of full darkness. I felt like a creature as unsubstantial as mist as I drifted, like a lost soul in a latter-day inferno. I was minded of a reproduction – on the vision-tube, of course – of an ancient illustration; one of the mimes on the celluloid strips I believe it was. It concerned the legend of the vampire and the scene depicted a man in a broad-brimmed hat and cloak wandering, much as I did tonight, through a landscape of mist and nightmare, to what strange adventure I never discovered, for the remainder of the strip was beyond preserving and some had been lost.

What did seem strange here was the lack of any life; a light, a figure, a footfall, an electric signal – anything would have broken that blank aridity. Now I was among the round, dome-like dwellings these people had improvised for themselves, and the bulbous openings were, I hazarded, some form of double air-lock in which they would remove their polluted clothing before going inside.

I could not help thinking that they had made the best of their bleak conditions though; unless one were completely underground, there was very little difference where one lived on the surface of the world today. Having completed a circuit of the buildings without seeing any sign of life and the darkness now being almost total, I decided to return along the shore the way I had come. As I swung round, shifting my cases to my left hand to ease my cramped fingers, I was conscious out of the corner of my eye, of a blurred shadow that seemed to flit across the dim phosphorescence of the water and flicker behind a boulder.

I am not a particularly courageous man but my curiosity was aroused. I had come a long way to set eyes on the people of this place and though I did not want to disturb them in their houses – a a formal visit would have taken up too much of my time that night – I would have liked to establish relations, preparatory to returning another day.

Among the boulders the atmosphere was foetid and the overhanging rocks and moss-like creepers made it dark. I soon began to regret my decision, but I had to go on as I could not now see properly to return and it was all uphill. The place appeared to be some sort of tunnel and I hoped it would lead towards the sea again.

Ahead of me there was a slight scratching noise that might have been metal-shod feet on rock, but I could not be certain. I paused to listen but the sound was not repeated. The place was beginning to get on my nerves. The walls were getting narrower and then the rocky, overhanging cliffs began to split into different passages and alleyways which made consistent direction impossible.

This was confusing, but as I stopped again for breath I felt a faint stirring of the hairs on my spine as there was another furtive movement – this time behind me. Then there followed a noise that I didn't particularly like. It was a sort of slithering, scratching sound, and I had the unpleasant simile of a blind person spring suddenly into my mind. I was in a cleft of rock by the side of the track, a nasty place in which to be trapped, and there was little time to lose.

Whoever – or whatever it was, could barely be a dozen feet away. I ducked down and with a quick flash of wild fear slithered, as quietly as I could, out of the blind alley and round the next corner which was about six feet away. I paused a few feet back from the entrance of another gully; here at least, I had a clear line of retreat. Nothing happened for a few moments and I thought that perhaps my imagination had been too much.

But the tapping began again after a bit and now it was much nearer. A pause and more sounds, another pause then a few more steps. There was a long period of hesitation as the thing gained the entrance to the passage where I crouched with the flash I had hastily eased out of my hip-pocket.

It would serve both to see the creature I faced and also as a weapon if need be. As the seconds went past I resolved on a bold move. Without wasting any more time I gave a loud and somewhat quavery shout which sounded deafening in the confined, echoing space, sprang out into the main gully, and stabbed on my flashlight.

A great shadow crept across the rock, my scream was echoed by a high, shrill cry, even louder than mine, and I fell down in a blind panic mixed up with some soft, yielding shape that blundered against me. The saviour of both was the flashlight which fortunately fell upwards, spreading its beams evenly and illuminating both faces. Which of us was the more frightened I cannot tell. It was a breeder from the village who had seen me prowling about and had come to investigate, at first thinking it was one of her own community.

We laughed in sickly relief and then she put me on the right road for home, glad of some company in those dark ravines. I was the first man of the outside world she had ever seen, and she was pathetically eager for knowledge; it was evident that she regarded the Central Committee and its scientific officers and other employees as the only hope for mankind, and she made me promise to visit the village again in the daylight and do what I could for its people.

This I readily agreed and noted down her number for future reference. Visits to the village and additional research here would give some variety to life on the island, and I was interested to see how these people made out in their hard and lonely struggle. This girl – she was little more than nineteen – was not unattractive but her hair was already going grey and she appeared to be suffering from debilitation. She stumbled many times along the track but always declined my assistance. When we gained the open shore again she was plainly exhausted and I stayed with her a bit after she had put me on my road; I offered to accompany her back to her people but she would not hear of this.

Her dark eyes seemed to have a world of experience in them and she was always looking first seaward and then over her shoulder, but I put this down to the strange environment and the hard life she led. As I waved her goodbye and set off along the stony track, she called me back. The thin cry in the wind again caused me some uneasiness, I could not say why, and when I reached her the dark eyes were closed and the hollows under them seemed full of pain.

Then she beckoned and urged me towards the shore where the baleful light from the sea was beating on the dark sand and against the worn white boulders of the cove. I had told her of my qualifications coming down the ravine, but I could not at first grasp what she wanted of me. But in broken sentences she at last made me understand her needs.

Before I could stop her she had unbuttoned the smock-like overall she was wearing and stood stripped to the waist. I had seen many strange things in my thirty-five years and was inured to most sights that have become a commonplace of these times, but I could not resist an exclamation.

The girl had what would have been a magnificent figure under normal circumstances. But across her abdomen and over her breasts were only what I could describe as a mass of devilish green fungi; beneath it the skin glowed faintly luminous, cicatriced and crisscrossed with vein-like cuts and striations. The whole mass seemed to have a life of its own, independent of the girl's body, and I felt it must be a trick of the twilight when I saw the growth – I can call it nothing else – begin to stir and twitch, sluggishly at first, and then almost imperceptibly to expand, flowing outwards gently but inexorably, a fraction of an inch before it settled down to a slow pulsation – or was it the girl's own breathing?

Fear settled on me as I looked at this. I could do nothing for the wretched child then, but as she dressed I told her I would do what I could. I would bring medicines, instruments, the next time I came . . . perhaps injections would help. She seemed infinitely relieved at this and clung to my arm for a moment as though I were her benefactor and she already cured.

She would not, or could not, tell me how she had contracted this malignant condition, but I gathered that hers was not the only case in the village. I was not disposed to linger; my encounter with the girl, the atmosphere of the island, and now this last shock had put a blight on my spirits, and I was eager to be off. As I went up the path I was almost inclined to break into a run. There was something else – something that defied analysis and yet gave me the greatest foreboding of all. For as I had crouched over the girl, attempting to diagnose something entirely outside my experience, there had been a strange perfume from her body.

I am, of course, familiar with the odours given off by the human body under various conditions of illness and decay, but I use the term perfume in its true sense. Whether it emanated from the girl herself or from the thing from which she suffered, I did not know. For a few moments, as I stood on that lonely shore, my mind was drenched with images; the drowned face of a girl I had once known, a melody playing somewhere long ago – something that I recalled as a treasured, recorded fragment of the past, on old archaic instruments by people playing together; what was it? Violins – that was it; violins and the perfume seemed somehow to symbolize all these things and above all the wild despair of regret.

But worst of all was the almost overmastering longing to reach the source of the perfume; there was wild delight in it and I caught myself, for one mad second, contemplating the frightful action of burying my mouth and face in the loathsome thing that was devouring the girl's body. Sanity came back like a blast of cold air as sand whipped by the night wind stung my eyes – and with it a black fear; I knew now what Rort meant. There was something devilish about the island, something which as scientists we had to unravel. I knew also that I had to go back to the village and find out what it was.

But for the moment while the wind buffeted me as I breasted a spur of rock and came back off the foreshore to the preferable loneliness of the downlands that led to K4, I forgot the nostalgia and remembered only the sickly horror of that degenerate moment. Then black fear took possession of me and I was running, slipping, and sliding across the slimy turf to the comparative peace and sanctuary symbolized by the tiny spark that was the light of K4's observation tower, piercing the smoky darkness like a torch.

III

I am ashamed to say it was almost three weeks before I felt able to go back to the village, and even then it was in the early morning so that I should have time to return before nightfall. Much of the interval had been spent in research on obscure radiation conditions and my companions at K4 had not been as helpful as they might. The night I arrived back, panting, muddy, my cases lost down some pothole, there had been roars of laughter from the steadier-nerved, though I noticed Rort looked considerably pale as I told my story.

Fitzwilliams, a short, stocky figure was particularly humorous at my expense; his dark brown moustache seemed to bristle as he exploded with laughter and he pounded his fist on the table as he elaborated his ideas.

"By Future, this is rich," he spluttered – we had given up using the term "God" since the nature of creation had been discovered – and then went on to embellish his fancy with some bawdy and outrageous trimmings. I well remember the laughing faces at the supper table that night; it was almost the last time that our little group had anything to be happy about, and that a feeble excuse at best. Looking back, I suppose it was ludicrous. I, a grown man, bounding across the slimy hillocks, completely out of control, my gear flying this way and that until I fetched up against the blockhouse entrance of K4.

That my first encounter with the girl was absurd, I was prepared to admit; my foolish fancies about the village and ravines; even my headlong flight. But the girl's condition was real enough; that was serious indeed and concerned us all if it were due to atmospheric conditions – and about that I was not prepared to laugh. I am afraid I got rather angry as the evening continued. But one man at least had not been amused.

"What do you think, Rort?" I asked.

His answer was a long time coming and when it did it was, for him, a strange one. He tapped nervously with his thin, tapering fingers, now stained and torn like most of our hands, and did not look at me directly.

"I prefer not to think – in this instance," he said quietly and then got up and went quickly out of the bantering atmosphere of the mess-room.

I was wrong though, about one thing. There was one other man who took my story seriously. That was Commander Masters, the person most likely to be able to do something about it. He buzzed for me to go up to his private room two evenings later. I could relax with him; he was a man I liked and trusted. Immensely capable, Masters looked more distinguished, more serious than usual, as he faced me across the gleaming metallized surface of his desk, his dusty silver hair outlined against the warm glow of the wall lamps, so that he seemed to resemble one of those ancient "saints" I had seen in a printed book preserved in a museum.

"You think this could be some new mutation that we haven't come up against?" he asked. I shrugged. There might be much more to it than that.

"I don't know. I should have to make some pretty exhaustive tests on the girl to be able to come to any real conclusion. I'd like to have her up here so that we could make some proper lab checks, but that wouldn't be fair to the others."

Masters's eyes narrowed and he shifted uneasily in his chair. "Meaning . . .?"

"Meaning that we don't know exactly what we're dealing with, sir. This condition – an unknown factor at the moment – may be peculiar to this one girl; it may or may not be malignant. Again, there's always the possibility it might be environmental or spread by contact."

"Hmm." Masters's nose wrinkled and he lay back in his chair, hands straight on the desk before him, and contemplated his nails for what seemed like minutes.

"What would you want in the way of gear and assistance to sort this out?"

"Little out of the ordinary. Laboratory facilities, of course; a few days uninterrupted study, someone to help me. This may be a false alarm, but it won't take long to establish the nature of the problem, one way or the other."

Masters straightened himself behind the desk. "Tell Fitzwilliams to give you everything you want from the lab. Make out the usual indent and credit the material to 'extracurricular investigation.' I don't know who you'll want to pair with you on the job."

He frowned again and consulted a panel inset into the desk which gave detailed breakdowns of each man on the station, with his duty rota, rest periods, and other information. He scanned rapidly down the columns, humming quietly to himself, while I waited, my mind half absorbed by the problem that the girl had set, half ashamed by my panic flight of such a short while ago. I wondered if Masters was secretly amused by my adventure and whether he considered this little extra assignment a means of testing my efficiency under stress.

Probably nothing of the kind. He understood well the loneliness and occasional strangeness of our work in remote places; it was a more likely possibility that he had discounted the fiasco from the start and knew that absorption in my self-allotted task would outweigh any possible dangers that might present themselves.

"Yes . . ." His fingers made calculations as he chopped at various names. "I can't spare Pollock" – and here he mentioned half a dozen names – ". . . that leaves you with Channing, Sinclair, and Rort. You'd better ask one of them if he wants a few days off."

Masters smiled briefly, for he knew as well as I that the trip might turn out unpleasantly. He stood up abruptly, with the swift, alert movements that often surprised his staff, and waved me to my feet with a suave but decisive gesture of the hand.

"Report to me before you go. And let me know if there's anything you need. If there is something down there we haven't seen before, we may not be able to help if we don't know what we're up against."

Reassuring words, that echoed in my mind long after I had gone back to my cabin.

IV

Fitzwilliams, of course, was frankly sceptical of the value of the whole business when I discussed the question of equipment with him; even the angle of the bristles in his moustache looked derisive, but when he heard that it was a direct priority from Masters he changed his manner and became instantly helpful.

"What do you expect to find?" he asked, laughing, though there was the beginning of doubt in his eyes. That was a question they were all asking during the next twenty-four hours and indeed it was a question I did not really like to ask myself. Karla seemed to be the one person who had taken my story to an extreme; perhaps it was because she was a woman, but nevertheless my description of the unfortunate girl at the cove had filled her with an unnameable terror; and my earlier uneasiness returned a day or two afterwards when we were talking the situation over.

We were sitting in the observation tower, where I had just completed a tour of duty. Karla had been taking part in an experiment that afternoon, acting alternately as assistant and subject. As we were both free for an hour or two we stayed on in the tower, idly chatting, while our reliefs busied themselves as they took over.

We sat on steel-backed chairs in a bay of one of the observation ports looking out over a dreary waste of uplands, even more forlorn in the dusk, pricked out here and there with the steel reflection of a mere that gave back the purple-tinted cloud that served for sky. Farther out, the green phosphorescence of the sea glowed menacing and wearily as it always did at dusk.

Karla had been silent, her mind overborne by this now familiar scene, which affected each of us to a certain extent, even though we had been trained to check emotion. Now she put her hand on my arm and her eyes were dark and troubled.

"This girl . . . will she die?"

"I don't know." I spoke honestly, for who could say? She looked even more distraught and turned again to the green and purple vista outside the observation port. Swirls of mist were even now heralding such a night as followed one after the other in this place.

"This is a dreadful spot," she said, and shuddered. Her remark surprised me, for she was an unusually steady and sober-minded girl whose position with the unit had been attained by those very qualities.

"Take care," she said, as we went down the stairway to our own quarters. "I have the strangest feeling that there is some harm in this for me."

She clutched my arm as she turned to go, and despite myself the expression in her face almost unnerved me for the fraction of a second.

Then I laughed: "Don't be silly," and gently pushed her towards the gallery leading to her own cabin. They were almost the last words on a serious topic Karla ever addressed to me but I had good cause to remember them, as later events will show.

To my relief Rort, whom I proposed to take along as my companion, was not only glad but even enthusiastic when I indicated my choice to him. His sombre face lit up at the thought of doing something more physically positive than the statistical work he was engaged on at that moment. For him, his manner was almost breathlessly hilarious as we checked over the instruments and other gear Masters's generous list had secured for us.

It had seemed to me the best plan not to base ourselves in the village but in a small observation post or blockhouse about two miles out, along the cliffs, so that we might make the best of ourselves in the event of any emergency. This commanded long stretches of jagged cliff in either direction and gave us an admirable control of the situation; for we could not be surprised, either by the villagers, by animals, or anything else.

Although the blockhouse, which we called No. 1 Post, was a good distance from K4, we had wireless communication and behind it were undulating uplands which afforded us, for the most part, with an unimpeded retreat to base should we need it. Masters had some of the team carry stores and gear over for us a few days before we moved in, so that we would have an easy walk over the first day. We were to report night and morning, in between trips to the village. I did not know how long the investigation would take me, but I hoped that we would have the situation in hand inside a week.

Rort was more optimistic than I had seen him since my arrival at the island, but I put this down to the fact that we had our own small adventure to play. He was an introspective type and long laboratory sessions coupled with even longer sojourns in his own cabin had worked upon his nerves. So I was even more surprised when I saw him packing a murderous-looking flash-gun in its heavy composition case the night before our departure. It was an action that was to mean a great deal to our two-man party before many days were over.

V

A short while before Rort and I were due to move into No. 1 Post, I set off in the early morning to make contact with the village once more and prepare them for our arrival. It was a day of wild beauty with ragged cloud whirled by a boisterous wind over the downlands and far below the yellow spume of the oily breakers achieved a slow-motion spectacle that seemed almost poetic, divorced of the stench that polluted the foreshore when one arrived at closer quarters. I saw nothing in my solitary walk – nothing living that is – save for a large, hawk-like bird that plummeted downwards into the tangle of underbrush, an action followed by the chilling shriek of some unfortunate creature.

As matters turned out I did not have to go the whole way, for on the rough track about a couple of miles from the village I met a gnarled man called McIver gathering pieces of wood which he was loading on a sort of primitive sledge. A wild, red-bearded man with staring eyes he was, and he turned out to be the leader of the local collective – headman it would have been in bygone times. When I explained what I wanted he was immediately cooperative. I told him about the girl and the possible dangers to the community, and he assured me that everything would be ready for our arrival at the end of the week.

Greatly excited and embarrassingly grateful for our offer of help, he would not stop for his wood but hurried back to the village as fast as his legs would carry him down the stony path. I retraced my steps to No. 1 Post to see that the provisioning was satisfactory. This was in a commanding position some little way inland but with a fine view in both directions along the coast from a stone and metal observation tower. Something unusual distracted my attention shortly after my arrival.

After a while spent putting some of my more personal kit in order, I thought I would go up the tower to see what the view was like and also to find out what we would need in the form of special gear. There was a nasty echo from the metallized stairplates as I went up the narrow passageway. Through the ports that let in a sickly light I could gradually see the winding, stony track that led away towards the west and then, eventually, the panoramic view both east and west along the rocky cliffs and beach.

This post had been carefully sited and provided a valuable link in the island's observation points. I had some trouble with the sliding door of the platform at the top as the fastenings had become corroded with time, but I was pleased to see that the equipment had suffered little, protected as it was by thick, transparent plating. It was a small chamber, the centre clear, the circular walls lined with benches and machinery. The large, elongated ports had become obscured by salt sea-spume and would need cleaning, but even so it was an impressive view afforded. Towards the south-east, even with glasses I could not see K4, but it was reassuring to think that its tower was not far off beyond the ridged higher ground that sloped up from the marshes.

As I turned to go down again I became aware of a darkening of the sky towards the west and then saw that it was a large cluster of sea birds hovering at a point in the cove. I do not know what made me put the glasses to my eyes as such sights were common along here. As first I concentrated on the birds and then, lowering the lenses, I became aware that something on the foreshore was attracting their attention. It was a long way off, too far for me to make out any detail, even with glasses, and there were rocks in between but I had the vague impression that something was crawling across the blackness of the sand.

There was a small, sharply defined object that was outlined against the dull shimmer of the sea and then a greater mass which vaguely undulated; or it may have been a trick of the sea-shimmer. But the overall impression was faintly repellent and reminded me unpleasantly of the sheen I had noticed on the body of the girl.

The incident lasted only a moment because whatever it was flowed over behind a larger spur of rock, apparently impelled by the surge of the tide, and there remained only the birds. Uneasy, I went down the stairs and turned back towards the comforting reality of K4.

VI

I did not tell anyone at the station of my uneasiness, as I had already made something of a spectacle of myself, but I followed Rort's example and made certain that my personal effects included my heaviest flash-gun. One or two of our colleagues still affected to smile at our little expedition, but the majority were more serious and, I think, half envious of the small independent command Rort and I had achieved.

Masters had us in for final instructions and I could not help reflecting that he must have supervised many such investigations as ours over the past few years – new mutations, fresh parasitic forms, strange debased creatures appearing round the coasts; these were the aftermath of radiation, each presenting him and many other research heads like him, with a new problem wherever encountered. Though it could never become just routine with him, his easy, genial manner concealed a complete lack of nerves; his was the kind of will and organizing brain it was comfortable to fall back upon and I was glad he was the directing force at K4.

Those on duty in the observation tower crowded to the windows to wave us off as Rort and I set out with our packs, and two or three of those off duty accompanied us for the first mile or so, before starting back with waves and an occasional joking remark. As we breasted the first rise after leaving base, I had given a last look behind and had seen Karla's white, anxious face staring towards us from the observation port of her own cabin. Her rigid attitude jarred oddly on my sensibilities and though I waved to her cheerily again and again, she never acknowledged the salute or made any flicker of recognition.

We walked in silence, both weighed down by the strange, indefinable atmosphere of the afternoon, weird even for this island and for these sombre circumstances. Rort was, I knew, content to leave the operational details of the "expedition" to myself, but he was a man who could be absolutely relied upon in an emergency, for all his worrying, which was why I had chosen him. Again, he was a quiet companion which was a boon when two people had to be cramped up in close proximity for some time, as we would be at No. 1 Post.

We had to make a wide detour round the marshes which even now occasionally claimed a victim, though the villagers always avoided them whenever possible. The greenish, stagnant water exuded a strange, flickering miasma, which writhed purple, green, and red, forming a fiendish backdrop all the while our walk skirted them.

I planned a fortnight's stay as the maximum at No. 1, as fresh stores were then due and, like a child, I wished to be on hand when news and contact with a larger world would brighten K4 for a little while. Besides, the investigations should last only a few days. I could have the breeder up to the post for medical examination; I had her number and McIver was making all the other arrangements.

These and other thoughts, notably the increasing uneasiness of all at K4, linked with the personal fears of Karla and Rort, were filtering through my mind as we stumbled and slithered painfully across the rough ground rising from the marshes and came out onto the downs and eventually to the post.

All was as I had left it. The last of the stores had been stowed and the observation tower showed blind red and green eyes east and west into the darkening landscape as we came down the track towards it. I stopped by the entrance a moment longer as Rort went inside and looked once again across the wild landscape of jagged cliffs and pale green sea, which never failed to impress and awe me.

There was nothing unusual in sight and no smoke or other indication of the village round the cove.

As I went in over the smooth flagged approach to the door I slipped and only my hand on the metal guard rail saved me from a nasty fall. As it was I bumped the wall and grazed my shin. I swore loudly which brought Rort out. When I turned to see what had caused the mishap, I was surprised to observe little patches of jelly-like substance on the ground and then noticed that there were other traces of it; in fact the whole area was dotted with slimy fragments. I had not noticed them on my last visit and was puzzled to account for the phenomena. There was also an unusual smell hanging on the air – musty, choking, and putrescent. Rort's eyes narrowed when I pointed this out to him. He said nothing but looked keenly around in the gathering dusk and a quarter of an hour later went out with a portable flame-thrower and thoroughly scorched the area. The slime seemed to shrivel into spores which went dancing off to seaward in the wind which was now springing up.

Inside our own quarters all had been made clean and cheerful and a few minutes later I was on the transmitter to Masters. His calm voice out of the darkness, only a few miles away across the ridge, provided a comforting reality in our lonely situation and gave the necessary life-line we needed. I told him nothing but routine matters. In any case my thoughts made no sense even to myself and there was no point in putting doubts into his mind as to the advisability of letting me loose on my own.

When I had switched off the radio – we were to have a vision-tube link-up when Rort got the tower apparatus in working order – we ate a huge supper with an appetite born of our long walk. The wind, which had been rising steadily, began an unpleasant buffeting against the plate-glass ports. Our living room and bedrooms were on the second floor which was fairly high up, and the ground floor was given up to stores, a factor which was to have some importance later.

Soon afterwards Rort slipped quietly out and I heard the squeak on the metal treads of the staircase, though whether he went up or down I couldn't make out. There was a short pause and then a rasping noise as he shot the massive bolts of the main door which led into the post, an eminently sensible precaution which I should have thought of myself. Then he was in the room again, a wry smile on his face, which needed no explanation. After we had stowed the supper things, he unpacked and reassembled his flash-gun and carried it with him when he went up to look at the tower.

He whistled as he saw the state of some of the instruments and then rubbed at the observation panels so that we could see out into the palely green, writhing darkness before us. To the south and eastwards and westwards there was nothing but a misty blackness but the sea always had light, except when there was rain or thick fog.

There was obviously little we could do that night but we lingered up there in the eyrie, reluctant to go lower down. It was not only the wind, which was making ugly, fanciful noises as it roistered about the cliffs and the tower, but something in our minds, like a shadow vaguely seen out of the corner of one's eye, which made us uneasy and a prey to slight scalp crawl – another of the research man's occupational diseases. Though we strained our eyes seaward and landward we could see nothing. Eventually we went down at a late hour, brewed some coffee, and went to bed. We had an uneventful night and both slept well.

VII

The next morning was cold and Rort and I spent almost two hours getting the heating system working, nearly missing our early contact with K4 in our absorption. I was particularly anxious to get the whole place up to scratch so that I could start on my work without delay; once we had achieved that I could leave routine matters to Rort; he had generously given up his own research projects in order to accompany me as general assistant, as he felt that a more active life for a week or two would do him good.

As for myself, I had been deeply impressed by the extraordinary condition of the breeder I had seen by the seashore; in all my experience I had never encountered anything like it and though the circumstances surrounding the episode were far from natural, I still had the feeling that there was some perfectly logical explanation, medical or environmental – possibly a combination of both.

We had a late breakfast and then went up to the tower to unsheath some of the instruments and inspect their general condition. They included a powerful telescope on a gyro-operated stand which I was particularly anxious to get into action. This would be most useful in both directions along the coast and its infrared twin in the same housing would help guard against surprise by night.

The landscape was normal when we looked out of the tower observation panels and there was nothing unusual; no movement except that of the sea and the flutter of an occasional bird. We did not get outside until almost midday and the door had remained bolted during that time. We then reconnoitred for a while along the rocky cliff path towards the eastwards in a region I had not seen before, but there was little of interest; the same rugged landscape, the same black sand and rocks, the same oily, sullen sea. It was almost an hour later when we returned and I was annoyed to see, as we made to enter the main door, a recurrence of the slime patches on the ground outside.

I made some comment to Rort and was about to go inside when he grasped my arm and brought me to a stop. I then saw a similar outbreak of the peculiar patches on the metal guard rail. The large door of the tower was of an old-fashioned pattern. It had been firmly secured by the authorities to guard against any incursion by the local inhabitants, but that special sealing had been removed when we took up our duties there.

Instead, the door was opened from the outside merely by a large metal ring operating a conventional latch. The door was now ajar. With an incredibly swift movement Rort's gun was unsheathed and in the aim position. I just had time to see that the metal ring was covered in slime before the panels went screaming back on their hinges at his kick and Rort had bounded over the sill. I followed, breathing fast, and our feet made a great deal of unnecessary noise as we took the metal stairs two at a time. There was nothing in the storeroom but more slime on the floor and similar patches on the treads.

The marks continued to the ramp outside the observation room and then ceased in a large patch on the floor, with the same sickening stench I had smelled before. There was no one – or rather I should say, nothing – in the tower and the other rooms were empty. I deliberately use the word nothing, because I think we both had a feeling that whatever came up those stairs was not human in the sense that we understood it.

We looked at one another and then Rort turned to the windows and gazed out across the bleak landscape of the island. He then stated something which I found difficult to dislodge from my mind for the rest of the day.

"Whatever it was," he said "could have seen us coming back and made its escape before we arrived."

Lunch was an uneasy meal and the big door remained locked, though it was full daylight . . .

VIII

It was early afternoon when we went down to the village. I felt we had spent enough time that day on restoration work and No. 1 Post was fully operational so far as my own sphere was concerned. We had neither of us said much about the happenings of the morning and Rort had carefully expunged the slime left by our visitor with a chemical solution. Neither had we informed K4 of the position by radio. There was no sense in raising an unnecessary alarm, and we could incorporate the information with our report of the day's doings during the evening call.

It was an interesting trip for us both. Rort had not been so far afield since arriving at the island, and I had not seen the village by daylight. It grew lighter or rather seemed to, as we came down the rough extent of track to that strange corner of land squeezed in between sky and sea. My eternal impression of this place was of the far off, long ago, extinct Eskimo villages that existed in former times; here again were the igloo dwellings domed, humped, and whorled, but instead of blocks of ice, concrete, presenting a ghastly, bleached effect from the constant action of the weather.

Here too were fungoid forms like fibroids overgrowing them and green, leprous stains that striated their surfaces into fantastic shapes. I supposed, correctly as it happened, that the government had erected these houses, for the technical problems involved were beyond the reach of these people. The domes were approached through a sliding metal door which led into a short corridor beyond which were two other doors, forming air-locks. Once inside, protective clothing was discarded and left in the last chamber before the house proper, chemical action automatically cleansing the material.

I had expected some activity on the village track and in what passed for its streets, but once again the place seemed to be deserted. There were the screams of sea-birds, the chumble of the sea between the massive shoulders of rock that descended from the hills, and the yellow-green foam thundering up the black sand, but nothing more. We bore straight up the street for a large building that looked like a meeting place or village seat of government. The method of entry into this type of dwelling is by the conventional way – that is, by the insertion of a finger or any other obstruction into a metal slot alongside the door, which operates a solenoid and slides back the entrance.

The method is repeated, with variations, on the air-locks, except that these can be controlled from the inside and anyone in the interior can lock the doors by instrument control and prevent another person from entering. On this occasion we were unlucky; we were stopped at the entrance to the middle chamber but the telescreen over the second door, which was operating, showed us that the council chamber or conference room it depicted was empty. This meant that the occupants were away but had locked the doors. The method of gaining entry from the outside would be known only to them and we had no means of discovering the combination. It would be little use to us if we were inside, as we had come to see the people of the village and could make no investigations until we had spoken with them.

Rort said nothing as we came out from the main porch, but his eyes turned back to seawards and after a moment he pointed. Then I saw what had caught his attention. It seemed as though the entire population of the village had gone down to the beach. There were small knots of figures clustered about the shore and others were spread out towards the eastwards, disappearing towards a cape which depended from the shoulder of black rock on the seaward side. The remainder of the villagers, if there were any more, were hidden from us by the shoulder of the hill.

As we skirted the shingle away from the village and gritted our way onto the sand, I wondered idly what had brought them all down there at that time of the afternoon. They were not fishing, that was certain, for many of their boats, ponderous metal affairs with painted numbers on their bows, were winched up towards the foreshore or riding heavily alongside the dusty red pier that contrasted so vividly with the glowing green and yellow of the sea.

It was this pier which first attracted my attention, as a great mass of people I now saw were striding up and down its length, some like ants upon the metal ladders that depended from the spindly legs into the water itself, while still more were busied about the boats. They did nothing with the cables which secured them but poked about under canvas covers or scuttled in and out of the doors of the larger craft. As we came closer we were unconsciously veering towards the east. The people had not been aware of our presence, but now some of them hastened forward with shrill cries of welcome and a few kept pace with us as we walked.

They were clustered more thickly along the foreshore here, among the black rocks between which the sea was riding sombrely with an awe-inspiring swell, and I could see still more men and women, with long hooked poles fishing about aimlessly in pools and among the rocks, sometimes sliding precariously about until they were arrested by a fissure or projection which prevented them from falling into the water. The centre of attraction seemed to be a region of even darker sand and rock which compressed itself into a narrow wedge bounded by the sea on one side and an almost perpendicular wall of rock on the other.

Where one's eye looked for the narrow passage thus formed to end in the cliff face, instead there was a large curved archway of solid rock, perhaps a hundred feet wide, and the path of black sand, already beginning to be washed by the sea, veered away around a corner and disappeared towards the east. As though an invisible line had been drawn across the area, the groups of people from the village had halted about a quarter of a mile from the arch and were standing gazing intently across the sand. As we came up we could see that McIver and other village elders were the centre of the group and that they had evidently been directing the afternoon's activity.

There was, it must be said, something foreboding and repellent about this quarter of the shore, even more so than the remainder. A curious stench borne on the wind had little to do with the clean wholesomeness of salt and there were strange dragging marks in the sand at this point, stretching away towards the rock archway, which even as we watched were being quietly erased by the action of the water. I soon saw that this entire area must be submerged at high tide.

McIver came up as soon as he heard we had arrived and his large, sombre face looked worried. His red beard and wild eyes reminded me of some pagan god of the dawn of the world as he stood there in the grey light of that weird shore, surrounded by his people, many of whom were as fantastically dressed and outré in their appearance as he.

As Rort and I hurried towards him, McIver gestured towards the great arch in the distance and his companions commenced to draw back a little, keeping pace with the rise of the tide. They seemed to take heart from our presence, though why I cannot say, as Rort and I were only mortal men like themselves; but to these poor souls we seemed armed with all the authority of the Central Committee and in those days the Committee represented law and hope for beings who had lived too long on the edge of the dark unknown.

McIver explained as we walked towards the tide-line; the village had been aroused because of the disappearance of one of the women. She had been traced as far as this wild shore. The area was a bad one and the people of the village kept away from it. McIver shook his head as we continued to question him; he feared the worst. The woman – she in fact was no more than a girl – had left trails in the sand. There were other things also; McIver preferred not to go into detail.

Rort and I soon saw what he meant. Across the sand, in bizarre and fantastic patterns, the girl's imprints – I would not say footsteps, as they were more like drag-marks – were accompanied on either side by great swathes of disturbed sand. I hesitate to be more fanciful than need be, but they resembled nothing so much as huge tracks such as a slug might make. The surface of the sand glittered dully in the light of the dying day and once again we saw traces of the nauseous jelly which had so disturbed us at No. 1 Post. The wind was rising and it cut to the bone as McIver, Rort, and I stood on the black sand and gazed towards the arch of the vast cave, whose entrance was aswirl with the incoming tide.

The tracks disappeared into the dark water. It was useless to follow and the place was such that I would have hesitated to enter with the Central Committee itself at my back. I already knew the answer to the next question I put to McIver. Though I compared the breeder's number in my notebook with the one McIver gave me, I was not at all surprised to hear it was my girl – the one I had already met on the path in such dramatic fashion a short while earlier; who was afflicted with the curious green fungi; and on whose behalf we had really mounted the small expedition of Rort and myself to No. 1 Post.

I knew, as I looked towards the arch, that the secret of her disease had disappeared with her, most likely forever, and that apart from the humanitarian considerations involved, a promising line of research had been lost to us. Rort swore savagely when I told him and McIver's face was downcast. I gave him instructions to prepare the whole village for medical examination. I was anxious to check whether there were any further manifestations of this unusual disease among the inhabitants. In the meantime Rort and I had a manifest duty to radio K4 with our report immediately. I knew Masters would place great importance on this.

I warned McIver to make certain all in the village was secured at night and told him to place lookouts if that were at all possible. He promised, with a touching degree of faith in our omniscience, to carry out such precautions as we thought necessary. I asked him to send a man with us to collect a portable radio transmitter from No. 1, so that Rort and I could keep in touch with the village after dark. We all felt this to be a good idea; after two visits to the post by unknown intruders and now the disappearance of the girl, it was obvious that there was something gravely wrong on the island. McIver went off to give the necessary orders. After another look at the black mouth of that uninviting cave, Rort and I, together with one of the villagers, started back en route to our post. Though neither of us said anything about it, we both wanted to get the heavily bolted door of the post behind us well before the advent of nightfall.

IX

For a long time that night I sat in the tower of No. 1 Post, looking out over the grey-greenish ocean whose glow seemed to symbolize the half-life in which the peoples of the world were living. Rort had radioed to K4 immediately on our return from the village and Masters had ordered a general watch kept throughout the night, both at our post and at the main station. According to Rort, the Commander had placed great importance on our information and was reacting with typical vigour. I could imagine the activity which was currently going on at K4. He had approved our action of supplying the village with a transmitter and McIver had already been through experimentally a quarter of an hour before.

There was nothing to report, but I had asked him to check with us three times a day in future. Rort was in the living quarters below, checking on the specialised equipment. I had the first watch, until midnight when Rort was to relieve me. Blown spume obscured the windows and the wind made a keening noise among the rusting antennae of the old post. Both Rort and I were thankful for the thick walls and heavy bolts on the main door. The traces of jelly-substance which our visitors had twice left behind them filled us both with a vague foreboding.

Though it was easy to become obsessed with sombre thoughts. This was why the Central Committee had decreed that research workers in the field, particularly in such spots as this, should be relieved after a year. Some of our colleagues at K4 would not be affected by such an atmosphere. I felt that Masters himself would have been posted to Hell and have felt only scientific curiosity at the prospect.

And the Australian, Lockspeiser, was a tough character; unimaginative and strong-minded, he could have worked at K4 for years without knowing such a word as “atmosphere”. Fritzjof too was a man to be relied upon. The others I was not so certain about. And though Rort’s nerves were not all they should be – he had gone through experiences enough to shake the strongest over the past few years – there were few companions I would have rather been with in a tight corner.

With these reflections and others, I drank the coffee Rort had left me and then, lulled by the faint rustle of the gusting wind round the tower, I must have dozed for a few minutes. When I awoke it was just before eleven. I rose yawning, for I had certain instrument checks to make. I went out onto the rusted steel platform which airily circled the tower, in the manner of an old-fashioned lighthouse. We had some trouble with the sliding door some days previously but now it had been greased and moved back smoothly beneath my hands.

I stood looking idly at the green sea reflected on the underside of the dark, louring clouds; green sky and green sea made a fantastic sight for those experiencing the phenomena for the first time, but these were old scenes for such workers as ourselves and I was watching for other signs. I made a few notes, checked the instrument levels on the delicately calibrated machines in their lead-lined boxes on the windy perch, and withdrew into the central chamber. I relocked the door. This undoubtedly saved my life.

It was just a quarter past eleven when the slithering began. I could hear it even above the faint mumble of the surf and the echoing sigh of the wind. The noise resembled an unpleasant suction process; swamp water boiled in it and blown spume and a nauseous tang like corruption on the high wind. And with the rotting perfume, which I had smelled before, freedom of action returned to me. I picked up my flash-gun and buzzed for Rort. He had already heard the sounds too.

"Main doors secure!" he yelled and then I heard his feet pounding on the metal-plated stairs. Something screamed from outside, freezing blood and bone, inhibiting action, paralyzing the will. A girl's face grew at the window, distorted; it gazed in at us fearfully, hair streaming in the wind. The thing was an impossibility; we were more than forty feet from the ground – unless she could scale perpendicular walls, wet with sea-spray, in semidarkness. I recognised the girl I had met on the cliff-path, the girl we had supposed sea-drowned in the cave.

She screamed again and as Rort flung himself to the outer platform door, I pinioned his arms; we struggled silently and the air was filled with a sickly, nauseous perfume. Something like squid-ink purpled the thick plate-glass of the outer ports; suckers waved hideously in the night. A face like an old sponge, oozing corruption, looked in at us; the girl disappeared.

"Great Future!" Rort swore. He sprang to the rocket lever and bright stars of fire burst over the tower, bringing writhing daylight to the ground below, where vast forms slithered and slid and shuddered worm-like. Rort screamed like a woman then and we both made for the stairs. On the ground floor, the great door was already bulging inwards. The smell of corruption flowed under the panels. Sanity returned in this extremity; wood roasted, metal burned white-hot, and the gelid mass mewed like a cat as Rort fried the door with his flash-gun.

Sinews cracking, we levered casks, metal boxes, anything with weight into the gap cut in the door, avoiding the mewing, dying thing which dabbled beyond the threshold. I seized a coil of rope. Upstairs, in the central tower, plate-glass shattered like doomsday. Instruments fell to the ground with a clatter. Rort at the stairhead blasted fire into the central chamber. Again the bleating cries, the nauseous stench repeated. I opened a casemate on the landward side, secured the rope, hurled it into the dying darkness. I prayed none of the creatures were on this side. I called to Rort, walked down the wall on the rope, flash-gun cocked. Something shuffled, the bushes whispered in the wind. Chaos in the tower and at the central door. Rort joined me; he was crying under his breath. His flame-gun made a bloody arc through the bushes and something scuttered with a squamous step. Then we were clear of the bushes, running strong, slithering and falling and leaping again until we were splashing into the less frightening terror of the swamp.

Rort was sobbing. "By Future!" he panted. "Did you see their eyes, man? Did you see their eyes?"

Blinded by sweat, elbows tucked into my side, I had no breath left to answer. With straining lungs we flew onwards to the safety of K4.

X

Masters looked grim. Once again the silver of the lamplight on his hair reminded me of a long-gone saint. Those not on watch by the heavy-duty radiation-units sat in a semicircle and listened to his instructions. There were about a dozen of us and we had absorbed what he had to say with the utmost attention for we all knew our lives most probably depended on it. McIver had been warned; the Central Committee alerted. But we could depend on no help from outside.

Masters had questioned Rort and myself minutely, both when we had made our first somewhat incoherent reports in the privacy of his office, and then in general conference.

"What creatures could scale walls like that and still have weight to break down such doors?" asked Fitzwilliams, with that mocking touch of scepticism which I found so exasperating. It was the fourth time he had asked the question in the last hour. Rort turned a flushed face to him. Anger trembled in his voice.

"Would you care to go out there now and find out for yourself?" he asked quietly.

Fitzwilliams blew out the air from his lungs with a loud noise in the silence of the conference room. His eyes appeared suddenly uneasy. He looked away awkwardly and said nothing.

"Matters in hand, gentlemen," said Masters succinctly. Everyone gave him attention.

"Nature of creatures, unknown. Appearance of girl at window; physical impossibility under normal circumstances. Circumstances not normal. We'll leave that for the moment. Possible source of emanations; cave near the village. Correct?"

He inclined his head towards me. I nodded. Masters got up and went over to the duty chart.

"General situation: emergency, lady and gentlemen" – the use of the female singular was a courtesy due to Karla's presence. "So far as we can tell K4 is immune from any possible attack. Two first priorities. The manning of No. 1 and No. 2 posts by adequate force. This means equipping with heavy radiation-units. Two: the investigation, tracking down, and destruction of these creatures. Now, I want to see you and Rort again, when this conference is over."

The meeting continued in Masters's brisk, inimitable manner. Rort and I, sitting facing the Commander in the bright lamplight, felt the first comfort since we had emerged from the depths of the swamp the previous night.

XI

Nothing happened for a week. Rort and I were among the strong party which had reconnoitred No. 1 Post the following morning. The burst door and windows, the smashed instruments, above all certain remains among the debris were enough to silence the strongest doubters. I noticed, maliciously, that Fitzwilliams had not volunteered to accompany the party.

A tractor vehicle with a heavy radiation-unit mounted on it, led the way. With the power available, this would be enough to deal with any known dangers. Fritzjof, who had volunteered to head the manning of No. 1 under the changed circumstances, led the party. He seemed as disappointed as Rort and myself at the lack of any tangible evidence on the nature of our visitors. There was the stench, it is true, and traces of jelly on the stairs, in front of the door and in the upper chamber. But of the creatures which Rort had certainly destroyed, there was not so much as a fragment of bone or a silver of hide.

Part of the problem was solved by careful examination of the walls of the tower. They had been scaled by some form of suction. Fritzjof smoked his pipe silently and pondered this; the grey light of the cliff-top seemed to flicker across his strong, square face. His empty sleeve, pinned to the front of his leather jacket, flapped in the wind.

He grunted. "Flying octopuses, that's what we're dealing with," he said jocularly. He strode confidently into the tower. His remark broke the tension and the remainder of the party followed in a relaxed atmosphere.

The next few days were occupied in putting things in order at the two posts and certain precautions were also taken in the village. No. 2 Post was on the far side of the island, on a point commanding all directions, both inland and to the seaward side. Masters felt it imperative to get both posts in full working trim; we did not know what we might have to face and early warning was necessary, especially if K4 itself were attacked.

Masters held another conference a few days afterwards, when he asked for volunteers to man the forward posts. I am ashamed to say so, but both Rort and I were relieved when Masters decided to second us to duties at K4. He felt that we had done our share and it was perhaps cowardice on our part to agree with him, but there was much sense in what he said; our nerves had been strained almost beyond endurance and we might perhaps have been weak links in a chain of new and untried personnel.

Masters had decided to detail four people for each post, which would leave twelve for K4, an adequate margin. Each post had two radio links and they were to report at regular intervals. The heavy radiation-units commanded the main doors and if necessary the parties could escape mounted on the tractor vehicles. Needless to say, each party member was heavily armed. Two flash-guns at least were to be mounted on the outer platforms of the towers to repel any attempt at invasion by the things, and powerful floodlights encircled the buildings.

The damaged equipment was repaired and after a while Masters expressed himself satisfied that everything possible had been done to ensure the safety of the personnel and the success of the arrangements. McIver's people were keeping watch near the cave entrance in daylight hours, but they had reported nothing. This did not mean that the things were not at large on the island; if they could swim – and there was no reason to believe they could not – they might well make their way to and from their lair unobserved at high tide, when most of the cave area was submerged.

Lockspeiser was to command No. 2 and Karla had volunteered for No. 1, much to my surprise; this in turn had changed to astonishment when Masters had agreed without demur. But then I thought things over and saw the sense of the arrangements; Karla was as expert as a man with flash-gun or radiation-unit and was quite without fear; these were the things which would count at the forward posts, whereas those with high scientific qualifications would be needed for the more exacting work at K4 and as post commanders.

The week passed quickly, in a feverish chaos of work, calculations, and hard physical labour. Masters inspected both posts and expressed himself satisfied; the radio links were tested. Early on a grey afternoon of wind-scoured sky the two groups marched out in opposite directions; it was a brave little show, though pitiful enough under the circumstances, and one or two of the hardier spirits raised a ragged cheer to encourage them on their way.

Rort and I sat in the main instrument chamber of K4 at the power telescopes and saw No. 2 party out of sight. Then we changed round to the other side. Fritzjof's small expedition were but faint dots on the high uplands now, Karla walking behind. Then a dip hid them from view. Rort and I did not know that we had seen our colleagues for the last time.

XII

I woke out of a dreamless sleep to find alarm bells ringing through the corridors of K4. The lights in the room where Rort and I were sleeping had come on automatically and it was only a moment or two before we had drawn on our night-duty overalls and were on our way to the main Control Room. Though there were only a dozen people left in the headquarters building it felt like a fort manned by thousands of men, as footsteps echoed, magnified, and distorted along the metal corridors.

Masters was already at the infrared periscope in the Control Dome, with Fitzwilliams operating the scanner. Rort and I sat in front of our own instrument panels and switched on.

"No. 2 Post reports Condition Normal," said Rort after a moment or two.

"McIver reports Condition Normal," I called out to Masters.

The night air was heavy with static and distorted human voices as technician after technician made his Condition Normal report. The operators of the heavy radiation-units, on the galleries above, overlooking the outer air; the men at the radar and other instrument panels; even those on visual lookout with flash-guns, all had their individual reports to make. A red light flashed on a control panel the other side of the Control Dome, indicating an abnormal state of affairs. Someone had failed to answer.

"No. 1 Post not replying," said the operator.

Rort and I exchanged tense glances.

"Radio failure?" someone conjectured aloud, hopefully. "Both sets?" replied Masters succinctly, his voice muffled from the Dome. No one replied. The uneasy silence was broken by the faint hum of the instruments.

The man at the No. 1 Post panel consulted a time capsule. "Nearly half an hour overdue in reporting," he said.

Nothing happened throughout the long night. Negative reports from stations operating; silence from No. 1 Post. It continued like this until dawn.

When daylight broke, misty and sulphurous, Masters had already made his plans. He personally led the four-man party, which included Rort and myself, out of K4. He had concluded, after some thought, that there was little danger during daylight as the creatures which had attacked No. 1 on the previous occasion had never been seen during the light hours. And if they inhabited the cave area on the shore by the village, their irruption into the world of men may have been governed in some way by the tides. But the overmastering desire of everyone at the moment was to discover the reason for the radio silence at No. 1.

We had not long to wait. No. 1 Post was a deserted shell. The remains of the door hung askew on its hinges as Rort and I had left it; the radiation-unit had been overturned but not damaged. The instruments and equipment of the post had been left intact. But of our colleagues there was no sign. Masters sniffed the air with distasteful curiosity. Once again that sickly sweet pungency polluted the atmosphere. Footsteps clattered on the metal stairs as the party searched the building. All they found was the clothing of our companions; it was soaked in the jelly-substance.

I walked over to the window at the top of the tower and looked out at the grey, sullen sea; of all the places in the world this was one for which I would always feel a high priority of hatred. As I moved to come away my foot kicked against something. I bent down and using the tongs supplied picked up something small and black. It was Fritzjof's official logbook.

Back at K4 that evening Masters buzzed for me at about half-past seven. I had sterilized the logbook in accordance with standing instructions and I took it in to his office with me. Matters rested as they had the previous night; K4 was at emergency and hourly reports came through from No. 2 and from McIver normally.

The book made curious reading but Fritzjof's devotion to the cause of science combined with his iron nerve did much to explain the nature of the phenomena with which we were faced. The first entries for the previous night were normal and dealt merely with technical matters. For reasons which later became obvious there was a long blank and then Fritzjof's next entry in the journal was timed 11:50 pm.

It read: "We have been under attack. At 10:02 precisely Fitzwilliams reported unusual disturbances around the tower. I at once activated the floodlights and rocket flares. At the same moment the main door of the post came under attack from some beings I shall attempt to describe later. Mazel immediately brought the radiation-unit into play, with some success. As soon as I saw that things were under control on the ground floor I hurried to the radio console but before I could establish contact with K4 was called at once to the tower, where Fitzwilliams and Karla were engaged with flare guns. There appeared to be dozens of invertebrate creatures of the octopus family attacking the post.

"They are immensely tall and armed with three long antennae equipped with suckers, on each side of what I will call the body, for want of a better word. Eyes or centres of intelligence, I can see none. But a hit at the top of the body where a man's head would normally be seems to affect the brain area. I am alarmed at our position for still more of them are gathering round the tower. Morale good.

"12:15. Another attack has been beaten off but I cannot get back to the radio console. There is a strange perfume coming up the stairs. The radiation-unit has ceased firing. Mazel cried out once but we have not been able to see what has happened. I have to stay here to defend the staircase. The tower has been under attack again. Fitzwilliams and Karla are handling themselves well.

"Later – 01:00 I think. The incredible has happened. I am now alone. I am not afraid but I wish K4 to know the truth. At about half-past twelve I detected a nauseous odour coming from the top of the tower and then my two colleagues called out. I was able to distinguish that the creatures had squirted something over them. I looked from the window and saw one of the great masses eject some form of dark ink from a sac at the top of the body, much as a squid does when disturbed. I could not believe what I next saw. Karla and Fitzwilliams, who had dropped their ray-guns, were forced to divest themselves of their clothes. The creature's sac then discharged again; the perfume had an incredible effect on my two companions. I was not able, myself, to detect it on this occasion.

"Its function was apparently to attract them. Both walked to the edge of the railing and were absorbed in the jelly-like substance of the creature's body. Their faces were happy!

"01:56. I may be mad but I do not think so. My colleagues have not died but have been swallowed, for want of a better word, as still-living organisms! On the evidence of tonight and of what we have discussed earlier at K4, I believe them eventually to become similar organisms themselves . . . Warn Masters. The cave area must be destroyed . . . the only way.

"Later. I am not sure of the time. Great Future help me. The things are at the window again . . . I must go . . . there is a nauseous stench.

"02:05. Not long now . . . back again . . . masks the only ans [a passage was then illegible] . . . Imperative . . . tell Masters . . ."

The logbook ended there. The Commander turned a tight-lipped face to me.

He voiced the thought finally. "This hardly seems possible."

"I agree," I said. "But Fritzjof's report seems incontrovertible. And there is this further evidence."

I passed over to him something which I had picked up from the floor of No. 1 Post. It had been embedded in congealed jelly and after the labs had carried out the usual cleansing tests it had been turned over to me.

It was a piece of circular discoloured metal, pitted and marked with green and yellow stains. It was my opinion that it formed part of an old-fashioned wristwatch, such as people used in the last century to denote the passing of time.

An inscription on the back read: CHARLES EVINRUDE. 1995.

"You really believe what you have written in your report?" said Masters. He was neither disbelieving nor believing, merely sifting facts.

I nodded. "It would explain the reappearance of the face of the missing girl from the village at the post window. It's my belief that people are 'digested' by these creatures, as Fritzjof described, and themselves become similar living organisms, revolting as this idea may seem to us. This wristwatch was worn by one of the creatures killed by the radiation-unit. After death the whole thing dissolved away."

Masters looked out of the port at the writhing green sky beyond.

"And Fritzjof and his colleagues are somewhere alive out there," he said simply, but with great weight. "It barely seems possible that in three generations, human beings should degenerate to that."

"The effect of radiation on humans long exposed to it, is largely unknown, sir," I said. "With long inbreeding and . . ."

Masters cut me short. His face was still pale.

"Fritzjof is right," he said crisply, his old manner returning. "We must make preparations at once to destroy these creatures in their lair."

He smiled in a strained manner. "And we shall take advantage of Fritzjof's forethought. What he was trying to tell us at the end of the log was, 'Masks the only answer.' A sensible precaution against the perfume ejected by these beings. See to it at once."

XIII

The box-shaped, square-bowed boat thundered in the surf, sending a shower of greenish, phosphorescent spray cascading down the metal decking. I found it difficult to breathe in the ponderous mask, and clutched the flash-gun to my side while I steadied myself with my other hand. The cave entrance before us grew ominously large, danced in mocking circles with the movement of the boat, receded briefly with the surge of the tide, and then grew again as the motor urged the unwieldy craft onwards.

Rort, unfamiliar in the black rubber suit which fitted him like a sheath, nodded reassuringly. One hand tapped lightly on the transparency of my facepiece as though to impart confidence. I glanced to left and right. There were six boats in our small invasion fleet; dawn burnt smokily across the green-yellow surge of water, bathed the black sand. I could see Masters in the bows of the nearest vessel; somewhere a radio speaker crackled unintelligibly. The canvas-sheathed stub of a radiation-unit poked from the bow of the nearest craft on my left, like the horn of a cow I had once seen depicted in a book.

Upwards, on the slopes of cliff were the minute figures of

McIver's men; they were waiting for the rocket-flare which was to signal the part they had been assigned. There were more than eighty people engaged in this all-out assault effort, almost every person on the island; even the women had been pressed into service, though few except the most able-bodied had been assigned the boats. Most made up the cliff force where they would be of the greatest use, with little danger to themselves.

McIver himself was assisting Masters; his must be the bulky figure I could see just behind the Commander. He wore some strange rig-out of his own, but topped by the mask and special equipment supplied by K4, looked just as individual as he always did. The strength of the current was very fierce here and the helmsman had anxious moments as we passed a belt of ragged rocks closing the entrance. Masters had deliberately chosen dawn and high tide for the assault. The tide had in fact turned and had been an hour on the ebb.

This way the assault party could be delivered to the very cave entrance, dawn affording the element of surprise. Masters had also argued that in the event of things going wrong it would be quicker and easier for the force to withdraw on the ebb. Later, if it became necessary we could stand off in good order across the sand at low tide. The radiation-units were to be debarked on the wings of the landing area to command the cave entrance, in case the creatures surprised the first wave before they were properly ashore.

Rort and myself were among those detailed to cover the landing of the heavy units by going ashore first to hold the beach. The sea slapped heavily on the sides of the big fishing boat and spume whipped by a needle-sharp wind blew over the fleet as we came inshore. Fortunately the prevailing wind was blowing off the beach which would mask the sound of the engines. We had no means of knowing whether these mollusc-like beings were able to hear in the human sense, but Masters, with his usual tactical reasoning, had decided not to take any unnecessary risk.

Rort's hand was on my shoulder and the helmsman's shout came a split second later as the boat bottom grated on the harsh black sand. The outlines of the beach and cliffs loomed more clearly out of the faint morning mist. Then Rort and I were over the side. The coldness of the water met us with a shock, but it was not more than three feet deep and we splashed wildly ashore, followed by two of the villagers. The small party went flat on the sand, flash-guns at the ready and pointed towards the cave. All along the beach the unwieldy fishing boats were splashing heavily through the shallows, minute figures, black against the green shimmer of the surf, detaching themselves from the craft and merging into the blackness of the sand.

We fanned out in a semicircle to protect the radiation-unit on our left which was just coming ashore, the tractor inching it down the ramp. The beach seemed alive with figures though we were in reality a modest task-force for the situation with which we were faced. I glanced from the cave back to our right and could see the other big weapons coming off the ramps. So far all had gone well and we were excellently placed to deliver attacks. The scheme was that once the radiation-units were well established, the advance parties would rendezvous near the cave entrance in order to pen up whatever creatures were within; this would ensure maximum slaughter with a minimum of danger to those on foot.

The big units would deal with any creatures which broke through the cordon and then, when they had been moved forward, would liquidate everything within the cavern. Or at least that was the scheme. I saw Masters in the middle of the groups on the beach and then his hand went up. I hurried along the shore towards him and the unit leaders from the six boats debouched from their groups at the same time. Masters drew everyone off to the right, where we were concealed by a hump of sea-drenched rock, while he held his briefing.

His instructions were, as always, succinct and to the point. Each of us knew what to do; everything within the cavern was to be destroyed, no matter what we might feel about the semihuman aspect of these creatures. Under no circumstances were face masks to be removed. Masters waved us off peremptorily and we all thudded back along the beach to take up position. The radiation-units were now ashore and in situ, the gunners hunched over the control panels on the heavy metal-railed platforms. They waved to Masters as a check. Rort and the other two men with us scrambled to their feet as I approached. I looked back. The cave entrance was menacing and blank in the cold light of dawn. Then the electric klaxon on one of the fishing boats sounded off. Masters waved us forward and twenty-four pairs of feet were gritting up the sand into the unknown.

XIV

There was a silence after the klaxon sounded and then a confused murmur down at the beach. One of the radiation-units shot pink flame and the sea boiled at our backs. Something mewed with a heart-chilling intensity we had experienced before. Rort spun on his heel. We were almost at the cave entrance now and vast shapes were stirring on the black sand. Down on the beach a huge form which had emerged from the sea was staining the green water in its death agonies. This was something no one could have foreseen. The things were returning to their lair after a night spent on land.

I saw the radiation-units swivel to cover the seaward side of the landing area, and Masters gesticulate as he mustered a force to repel this menace at our rear. The sea boiled again and several monstrous humps began to emerge, but we had no time to watch them. There were about a dozen of us within reach of the cave and it was obvious that we should have to deal with the things until such time as the main force could be deployed.

Rort's flash-gun erupted, and sand and gravel at the cave entrance glowed with heat; we were almost within the arch now. I was thankful for the mask when I saw the abominations which were stirring within. A humped form reared in the dying light and then others and yet others beyond. Rort fired again and again and then we were within the cave; our companions followed and jets of flame turned the vast cavern into which the advance was penetrating, into a lurid scene from hell.

Again the mewing cries and purple ink shot across in a wide arc, staining the dank sea walls. A grey, wrinkled form which seemed to detach itself from the background, a vague, amorphous shape ascended from the depths of the pit, stirred in front of me. Three long, whip-like antennae with whitish suckers thrashed the sand; the skin was glowing with soft inner fire and shimmered and sparkled in the light as though coated with mucus. Low mewing calls emanated from the mass like the sensuous purrs of a cat; the rounded hump at the top of the structure was bisected by a long slit which opened and closed as though taking in air.

Someone knelt at my elbow and fired a flare into the interior; the star-burst revealed a cavern of the proportions of a cathedral leading away into Future knew what unspeakable depths. The great mass in front of me swayed and pulsated and purple ink drenched our small group. I wiped my mask clear and saw Rort spraying fire into other forms beyond. I felt sick at heart for, as the great form had turned, I saw what appeared to be a human shape down within the jelly. A moment of madness then which turned to sick loathing and horror.

Cleansing flame burned from the jet of my gun into the heart of the abortion before me and the mewing changed into eldritch screams; the mass crumpled before my eyes, disintegrated in black oily smoke and flame. I fired again and again until the sickness and horror were dispersed in healing fire and nothing was left on the dark sand but minute lumps of jelly which dispersed in the rising wind.

More of the creatures appeared from the tunnels which now opened up before us; they moved with alarming speed and the antennae which had formerly been lethargic and leisurely in their movements now sliced the air like whips so that one had to exercise extreme caution. A man on my right screamed suddenly and I turned to find two of the antennae about him; one round the waist, the other pinioning his arm. His flame-gun clattered to the rock floor and he was drawn inexorably towards the pulsating mass of jelly. Rort then blotted out man and jelly in a white-hot spirt of merciful fire.

The cries had changed their note to that of alarm and anger; the air was filled with smoke through which we groped with difficulty. Bodies blundered against me in the murk and there was real danger that my companions might mistake each other for the creatures, with fatal results. The very floor of the rock cathedral seemed to tremble at the ponderous tread of these viscous monsters.

We stopped, fired, paused to strain our eyes through the fog of smoke; moved on, fired again in a nightmare of noise and high-pitched cries. A mass of the creatures were blocked in a narrow part of the tunnel ahead of us; it was a dangerous place. They were baffled at the failure of their previously successful tactics and I knew that if we were drawn into that place within reach of their antennae, the dangers were incalculable.

I waved my nearest companions back and then turned, on hearing an agonized cry; it was Rort. His beard bristled in the light of the dying flares and I saw that he had somehow fallen so that his mask had been knocked aside. Purple ink from the creatures' sacs drenched his clothing; he threw away the flashgun, held his hands wide, and marched towards the creatures, whose tentacles reached out to embrace him. I saw his face just before the flares died; it was something I had to live with for the rest of my life. It was radiant with happiness as the gelid mass closed over it.

I performed the same mercy for Rort then as I should myself have been grateful for. Discharge after discharge of purifying flame reduced my old friend to cinders and incinerated with him the pulsating excrescence that was devouring him alive. Sickened then, we fell back in the smoke and flame as the note of a klaxon pierced the depth of the cavern. The eight or nine survivors of our bloody sortie regained the open beach to full daylight.

The remaining monsters from the sea were being slaughtered in the shallows as Masters's inexorable ring of attackers closed round them. It was evident that we had gained the day here, but at our warning cries our rearmost companions faced about to find a solid wave of grey, fungoid beings pouring out of the cave onto the sand. I tripped on the soft beach and caught myself against a rock; pain stabbed through my side and the daylight faded before my eyes. Strong hands sustained me as a radiation-unit fried a mass of squirming creatures jammed in the cave entrance. A rocket burned then against the sky and as jet after jet of flame convulsed the fungoids that vainly tried to make their way over the black sand, the watchers on the headland detonated the explosive charges laid two days before and brought the whole of the cliffside down on the cave of horror, blotting out the creatures from the sight of man forever. I fainted as I was being carried to the boat and when I regained my senses briefly, saw that sinister shoreline recede for the last time.

XV

All that was long ago and is now the distant history of these awful times in which we live. What the vision-tube commentators and news bulletin readers called the invasion of the Flabby Men lasted but a brief period, but for that time the future of the world and with it that of humankind trembled in the balance. For the irruption into the world of men of the debased creatures who had taken so many of our companions, was not confined to our island alone. It was part of a large-scale general invasion by these creatures along many parts of the coast and it was only through the mustering of volunteer forces and extreme efforts by the Central Committee, that the attempt was defeated.

But many died and the campaigns lasted many months before the creatures which had ascended from the sea and from the depths of sea-caves were annihilated or driven back to whence they came. And who knows whether their survivors, possibly breeding at a fearful rate, may not yet mount another, more successful attack upon the last bastions of mankind? How they came, how they lived and bred, and why they took our companions we were never able to discover. In death they returned to a state of liquescence which defied the analysis of our laboratories. And what intelligence animated them and how they were able to communicate over long distances in order to synchronize their attacks upon the whole of our coastline – that again was beyond the analysis of our finest scientists and scholars.

Years have come and rolled away again; I am a senior administrator now, wise and calm after decades of decision and strife, but my sleep is still troubled by remembrance of my companions.

Fritzjof and Karla and Rort, my old friend, are those I particularly remember, of course, and the terrible and inexplicable manner of their going. It was many weeks and only a few days before I left the island forever, that I was able to piece together an overall picture of the chaos the Flabby Men had wrought upon our flimsy and ill-founded civilization. And even today, when the cloud still hangs over the earth, and radiation sickness and mutations are still with us, I find it difficult to blot out the final horror of the scenes we witnessed on that beach and in that cave.

It was found that I had two cracked ribs on my return to K4; long after the battle was over and the expedition had returned to headquarters, I lay ill with some sort of fever. I was not up for more than two weeks and it was another two still before I felt something of my old self again. I sat once more in Masters's office and answered questions put by that kindly and most resolute of men. We often discussed the implications of what was perhaps the strangest adventure that ever befell mankind, but we were never able to arrive at any logical answer. Perhaps it is better so. An odd conclusion, perhaps, for a scientist, but the result may be more acceptable for the world's peace of mind.

It was not until my last night at K4 that I told Masters what I had seen in the cave. The relief boat was coming back to pick me up the following day and I was to have the company of others on my return journey to the capital, where I was to stay for the next year, to allow my shattered nerves a chance to recover. The faint luminosity of the sea stirred uneasily, greenish-grey outside the great plated windows of the Commander's office, and blown spume dribbled across the glass in the light wind.

For in my last burst of anger and horror, in the dying flare I had seen, just before I killed the jelly-creature, the anguished face of Fritzjof, still alive, ingested by the fungoid mass and completely absorbed by it. His eyes seemed to implore me to destroy the still-living abomination which he had become, and his face was at peace before the final kiss of the flame effaced it for all time.

An even more fearful question had haunted my mind ever since, haunts it still.

"Supposing," I asked Masters, "the mountain did not destroy them when it fell? All the creatures, I mean. And that Karla and the others are still alive somewhere down there? If you can call it life . . ."

There was a long silence between us. Then my old chief drummed with his fingers on the desk before him. The brittle sound seemed to conceal great emotion.

"It is best not to ask such questions or to think such thoughts," he said gently.

Masters turned to face the ghastly green phosphorescence of the sea. When he spoke again his voice seemed to come from a great distance.

"Who knows, my friend, who knows?" he said.

ROBERT HOLDSTOCK

The Silvering

AN ESCAPEE FROM A medical research project into the immune response to parasitic worms, Rob Holdstock published his first SF novel (*Eye Among the Blind*) in 1975.

He has written science fiction, fantasy (both of the heroic and mythological types) and supernatural tales, as well as a clutch of film and TV tie-ins and "coffee table" books.

His novel *Mythago Wood* was a World Fantasy Award winner. Its sequel, *Lavondyss*, features ten palaeolithic "masks", one of which is "The Silvering", an animal totem and one of the Oldest Animals (the salmon). It is the author's intention to write a story about each of the ten masks. The score so far is four.

The "Mythago Cycle" of books also currently stands at four, with a fifth volume planned. The author has recently completed three volumes of "The Merlin Codex" with *The Broken Kings*, concerning Merlin's encounter with Jason and his new Argonauts.

"'The Silvering' was written after a particularly jolly Burns Night for the hosts, Chris Donaldson and Paul Oldroyd, who had enthused about 'Selkies'," explains Holdstock.

"The challenge was to write a Selkie story with a difference – a challenge not to be missed! Peter Crowther had already asked for a story for a new collection, and he published the tale in *Narrow Houses*, a volume of stories about superstitions.

"Asked to supply a personal supersitition, this un-superstitious author remembered his father saluting a single magpie as a sign of 'warding off bad luck'. Having set the superstition on record, as a joke, the author now salutes every damned magpie he sees, having managed to *make* himself superstitious!"

IT WAS NINE O'CLOCK and the croft was in darkness. Selka was late and Peterson was impatient for her, his anticipation subliming into frustration. He rose from his chair and peered moodily through the small window. The image of the moon was distorted by the coarse glass. The waves, breaking on the shore, were flashes of restless white. He could hear the murmuring rush of the sea, an unbroken sound.

Nothing, yet, was struggling ashore.

He went out into the night, glad of the clear air, the salt-sharp wind. He prowled the sea's edge, kicking through driftwood and weed, staring through the band of silver light on the dark water, below the waning moon. She would follow that light, he knew, swimming from the deep towards the rolling skin of her world.

Back in the croft he cut the cheese and chewed quietly, standing by the window, shivering. Selka liked the croft to be cold. She was uncomfortable in the warmth of a fire.

Peterson was hungry, and he served himself a plate of the cold fish stew that he had prepared for the woman, a concoction of conger eel, crab and codling heads, razor shells, mussels, cockles and periwinkles. There was weed in there too, the softened strands of bladderwrack, and the hearts of anenomes, their stings drawn. To help his own taste there was garlic and wine, and a pinch of sea herbs which grew wild on the high ground of the island. He drank some of the wine and became heady. He started to jump nervously at movement and moonshadow in the croft, and took to flashing his torch at the low ceiling, at the rusting metal panels and the dark rugs, nets and harnessings that hung on the cold stone walls.

The sea surged. The monotonous crash and hiss of the breakers was interrupted by the unmistakable sound of a beaching. He heard the driftwood disturbed and the eerie cry of Selka as she rolled on to the land. He smiled, relaxed, and poured two glasses of the chilled Macon. Five minutes later Selka screamed, three short, intense cries of pain, and Peterson blocked his ears. But the shedding of her seal-skin was successful, for a few minutes later she was darkly framed in the low doorway, wet with blood and sea, naked and trembling. She was carrying nothing, no fragment of the wrecked plane, and Peterson was disappointed.

The selkie hesitated, looking quickly round the small room. She seemed disorientated, the same as the first time she had come to the croft. Puzzled by this, Peterson invited her in, reaching his hand for her. She approached cautiously, the merest trace of light in her wide, soft eyes. The smell of the sea was strong on her and water suddenly gushed on to the floor, surprising them both. Reassuringly, Peterson stroked her arm.

"I have a bath ready for you."

The feel of her was both unpleasant and sensuous. She was slick with the ooze from below the discarded skin, but also firm, muscled. When the slime was washed away she would be slightly scaly, a tickling shagreen, and salt would crystallise in her creases. But with regular baths she could maintain herself in comfort on the land.

Selka knew the routine of washing, but tonight she was behaving strangely, as if unaware of the bath, or the toilet bowl. Instead, she dropped to a crouch and voided her stomach on the floor, alarming the man. The stench of fish and weed was overpowering. Selka wailed and whined as she incontinenced the remnants of her sea life. Peterson filled a bucket with water and mopped up the mess. At last, the woman found the bath and crawled in head first, twisting in the narrow tub and laughing.

Standing watching her, Peterson felt his despair grow into anguish. This was not Selka, of course, despite the similarity of looks. He stared apprehensively at the calm sea, the moon now set and no light available to attract the selkie who had become his lover. This "new-one" did not appeal. He needed the familiarity of his shared life with Selka, the communication that had so painstakingly evolved throughout the long summer and the bitter autumn nights of the last years, the memories in common.

As the new-one bathed, wallowing and watching with vision that could easily penetrate the Orcadian dark, Peterson walked to the sea's edge and followed the scent trail of the selkie until he found the carefully folded and hidden skin. She had wedged it below an outcrop of granite, high on the shore, and filled the entrance with pebbles and wood. The marine stench would attract flies in the morning, and already tiny hopping creatures were fussing at the part of the skin that she had left exposed.

Peterson carefully withdrew the soft pelt and carried it back to the house. The new-one thrashed in the bath and leapt out, standing shivering in the dark, watching anxiously as Peterson unfurled her marine protection.

"It's all right," he whispered soothingly. "If the strand fauna get to this they'll destroy it and weaken you. I'll keep it safe."

He held the skin towards her, then showed her the cupboard where he placed it, immersed in the deep bowl of sea water he had prepared for Selka.

The new-one relaxed. She was smaller than Selka, Peterson realised now. His eyes were wide as he stared at the slim, angular shape of the creature. He felt the first signs of desire, not as powerful as when Selka had bathed, undressed him and hugged him to the floor, but strong enough for him to discard his clothes. The new-one watched curiously, then grinned.

"Where is Selka?" Peterson asked. "Where is the one from before?"

The new-one cocked her head. Weed fragments fell from her hair, which was spidery and greyish. Selka's woman-hair had been silver and very tightly curled, covering half of her face and growing, too, from across her upper lip, an odd moustache that had tickled Peterson when they'd kissed. Selka, as human, had been very hairy, and her scales small, almost unnoticeable. This one was different, but when he touched her it was only at her creases that the skin grated in that fish-scale way. Her breasts were tiny, flattened to her prominent rib cage. The nipples, unlike Selka's, were blanched white and didn't react to his touch.

Peterson couldn't decide whether the new-one was young or old.

"Do you have a name?"

As if she understood the selkie grinned and murmured a series of vowels.

"I thought so," Peterson responded, referring both to the anticipated incomprehensibility of the name and the fact that the new-one understood him. It had been the same with Selka and the previous ones; all had shed the marine skin and at once seemed to intuit his language. Would it be the same in other countries, he had wondered?

"I can't pronounce your Neptunian sibilants, so I'll opt for Seela. That's clever, you see? Almost a human name, and refers to your primary morphological form. Except that you're not seals, really. Are you?"

He had seen selkies come ashore many times, watching them roll and scream as they had split themselves open to shed the marine skin. They were far uglier than seals, and the human shapes encased within the thin blubber had flexed and forced against the flesh, a bizarre and revolting prey struggling in the grey-blue stomach of the selkie itself. For that was what a selkie looked like: a stomach with an oddly, ugly human face, and matted hair that ran in streaks along the distended carcase.

He knew they were good swimmers, though. He had seen Selka water-dancing in the moon-channel once, and she could leap higher than any dolphin he had ever seen. The dance was old, he knew, but he had never understood the meaning behind the cavorting on tail flippers and the elaborate leaps and dives.

"Seela," he repeated and the selkie said the name, followed by the word "Peterson."

"Ah. You know me then."

Seela laughed.

"Selka told you. Where is Selka? Why hasn't she come?"

The new one – Seela – ran to the door of the croft and ducked out into the cold Scottish night. Peterson chased after her and grazed his head on the lintel, swearing loudly. The slim figure of the selkie was standing a few yards away, hunched. Seela had her back to the man, and seemed to be shaking.

Peterson approached her but when he touched the dry, cool skin, the woman darted back into the croft. The wind was increasing and the shore was awash with the noise of the surf. The darkness deepened, but he knew that to use a light would distress the creature this soon after its shedding.

Seela was crouched in a corner, eyes wider now, mouth tightly pinched. Her arms were around her frame and the wet marine skin was unfurled before her. But she had not gone ahead and returned to her marine form. She seemed unsettled, indecisive.

"Are you afraid?" Peterson asked. Seela's teeth chattered.

"I miss Selka," he went on, "please tell me why she hasn't come."

The selkie drew the skin to her and found the thinner fat of the face. She unfurled the skin and covered her head, crying out as the marine skin began to penetrate her flesh, to renew itself. Peterson was shocked, watching the anguish on the ugly face as the jaw opened and closed and the strange eyes stared steadily into the gloom.

"I won't ask about Selka any more. Come to bed. Come to bed? You'll be cool. You'll be touched. Selka liked my touch. She liked to feel me inside her. She always said that. Come to bed."

The selkie stopped its mourning sound, peeled off the mask. When Peterson had lain quietly in his rough bed for half an hour, the woman came to him, buried herself into his shape, curled up against him, her hand straying to his pubic hair and gripping the wiry tangle, finding an oddly and painfully secure grip. If she had wanted to love him he would have been prepared for it, but she spent the night half awake and shaking, and at dawn she slept, her mouth open, the smell of shellfish effusing from between the silvery, sharp teeth. She sang in her sleep, the faint sea-songs of her race, just as Selka had done. She sang of the island . . .

Selka had told him that her kin had first come to the island when a sailing ship had foundered, a *long* time before. From her brief description – all that her selkie folklore could summon – he thought it might have been a Viking war galley, blown against the rocks after its long, North Atlantic journey. With that sinking the selkies had come. But they had declined over the centuries, although the skins of two of them had remained on the grave-ledge, cold but still living.

Then the bomber, a Lancaster, had plunged into the deep. Attracted as they were to wrecks, the selkies had returned to the island. They had been present in profusion soon after the crash. Peterson remembered watching them sea-dance as he had converted the ruined croft, incorporating bits of metal and canvas that the sea had washed ashore for those first few months after the drowning. The croft was a shrine to the dead airmen, and Selka always brought him a gift from the deep, some piece of instrumentation, or leather, or harnessing. From other expeditions to the mainland he had collected the rugs, chairs and supplies that made the croft comfortable, and life tolerable on this remote patch of sea rock.

A hard rain freshened the shore just after dawn, stippling the heaving ocean and running from the dark granite above the littoral zone. Wearing only goggles and a thin layer of animal fat, Peterson walked to the sea and plunged in. His senses screamed with shock as the cold assaulted him, but he shivered warm again as he struck out strongly, away from the island and towards the deep pool where Selka used to swim before beaching. The sea was grey and heavy when he peered into its body, but he could see fish there, and the shadows of bigger, darker creatures. They moved close to the falling face of the cliff that widened to deep water where the selkies lived, near to the skeleton of the warplane.

When he was above the pool he drew a deep breath and plunged, long white hair streaming, beard flowing around him, swimming down vigorously through the hard current and into the warmer stillness. Here he somersaulted to stop himself rising and called for Selka with half the breath he held. In pain, and with his ears threatening to burst, he shot to the surface again and crawled energetically back towards the shore against the drag of the tide. In this way he returned to the pool.

Twice more he plunged to call. The fat was slowly stripped from his skin and the chill began to build in his tissues. He was too old.

His seventy years had seen him shrivel and become hard, like an abandoned skin. Cold penetrated fast. He did not like the cold inside him.

It was time to go back.

As he swam for the shore he saw Seela standing at the water's edge, watching him curiously. Before he reached the land she had turned and run beyond the croft, over the grim, stony earth and towards the scrubby trees that grew over the high hill in the centre of the island.

When the rain stopped she returned, screaming. The light hurt her, the day brighter now that the clouds had cleared. She wanted her skin, but Peterson locked the cupboard. The selkie walked backwards around the cluttered room, eyes on his, mouth working silently. She became entangled in nets, and thrashed helplessly and frantically until he released her.

"What happened to Selka?" he asked. Seela covered her face. "Please tell me."

She walked out into the day, shining and silver, arms wrapped around her. Her bones were prominent and through her flesh he could see the crushed shape of another creature. Peterson suddenly realised that this selkie was *old*. And with that particular understanding came an awareness of what she wanted from the island. She was not here to be with him, but for her own strange purpose, something that Selka had told him about.

Suddenly she came back into the room, pushing past Peterson with a quick glance that showed him moist eyes. She struggled at the cupboard where her marine skin was being stored, but the lock held fast. She watched him angrily.

"Not ready," she said. "Return to sea. Skin please."

"You want your skin? Then you must tell me where Selka is. Why didn't she come?"

"Please?" Seela ran her hands down the cupboard. Her nails were soft and made no sound, but the flesh whitened with the pressure. Through her skin Peterson could see the wood-form writhing, urgent for release. Its arms in hers were gnarled, its body hard-edged and unpleasant, pushing knobbily through the thinning fat of the woman. Its head, at the top of her chest, seemed to turn and open its mouth, like a child in the womb, flexing and kicking to develop its muscles.

It became quiescent and Seela accepted that Peterson had trapped her.

"Please . . ." she said, the word long and drawn out. "Luck . . . bad . . . no . . . skin . . ."

"I know about the legend. I know the superstition. I haven't *stolen* your skin, I'm just . . . protecting it. You can have it back when I have the answer to my question. Where is Selka? What has happened to her?"

"Selka went deep," the new-one whispered. "Silvering." She shrank slightly and backed away into the corner. Peterson stepped forward his heart racing. He had heard this expression, but he couldn't remember when or why. One of them, one of the selkies who had attended upon him over the years, one of them had mentioned this. There was a place, over the shelf, over the edge, where the selkies went when they were dying, following the moon down.

"No!" he said. "Selka was young. She was healthy. She wouldn't have gone deep."

"Big Tooth," Seela said. "Silvering." Moisture smelling of the sea trickled from her eyes.

Peterson felt his head spin and his legs shake. He leaned against the table, displacing the plates and glasses. "What do you mean? What do you mean?"

"Went deep," Seela said. "Big Tooth. We remember her skin on the ledge."

"I don't believe you. She was too fast. She could easily outswim a killer whale. I don't believe you. She can't be dead."

Seela cocked her head. "Big Tooth," she insisted. "Selka went deep."

Peterson cried out, sitting down hard. He could see his lover so clearly, so svelte, so lovely compared to this scrawny creature. He could feel her hair, the cool skin, the pressure of her teeth in his flesh, her grip, her tenderness. He could hear her laughter. He could hear the clink of glasses, drinking white Burgundy wines, her favourite drink with the cold fish and seaweed stew that was all she could eat.

"Not eaten. No. Not eaten. She can't have been."

"Not eaten," Seela said. "We remember her skin."

"You have her skin?"

Seela nodded. "Some. A piece."

Peterson stared at the selkie through blurring eyes. Did they keep the skin as a memorial? Did they rebirth the selkie? He struggled to remember the conversations with Selka, the night-long murmurings after love in which he had begun to piece together the beliefs and life cycle of the ubiquitous marine creature.

Life is in the skin. Each skin remembers the marine life which is why it is so precious. New-ones come from old skins. They are the same life, although part of the memory is gone. There is a shelf, in the deep water, near to the wreck of the bombing plane. At that shelf the skins are kept. Some of them are very old, waiting for the new-one to emerge and occupy it. This is our island. There has always been a beach here, and the calling of the Beautiful Voice. We cannot resist that voice. We must all go to it at some time in our lives. The Beautiful Voice still calls to me. But I am not ready yet.

The new-one would grow inside the old skin. If Selka was dead she could be brought back, the creature that he loved, the look of her, the feel of her, and part of the memory of her. They could rebuild their occasional life. He could have her back.

"Will you bring me her skin?" Peterson asked. The selkie before him seemed shocked, shaking her head.

"I must have that skin. I need Selka. She has been coming to me for three years. She's a part of me. I love her. Her life is in *my* skin. Please try to understand. Without her . . ."

Seela shivered. The wood-form inside her flexed and stretched and caused her pain. The time of the shedding was close. She would either have to return to the sea or proceed with the cycle. She looked anxiously at the locked cupboard. Peterson, grimly, walked away from her and went out to the beach.

They called it the Island of the Gone Away Ones. It was a magic place to the selkies. There was a call from the island, a Beautiful Voice, and occasionally the call was irresistible. Some who went to the island returned. Some didn't. No selkie knew the fate of those who had gone Away, but it was assumed they had called down bad luck upon themselves. Selkie superstitions were legion, and told Peterson much about their fear of humankind, which over the centuries had trapped the woman-form after the shedding, or taken the male-form into slavery. *Never shed skin by day. Always swim to the shore along the silver channel of the moon. Selkie blood shed in anger raises the storm from the deep . . .*

And most important of all: *Never let other hands touch the living skin on the shore.*

Peterson had done that to Selka, and now Seela. And Selka was lost . . .

There was a harsh cry from the croft, then the sound of glass breaking. Peterson ran towards the shack, listening to the frantic banging of metal against wood. Seela was shrieking like a seal, a mammalian cry of terror and rage. He knew the reason at once.

She swung round and hurled the hammer at him as he stepped through the door. The cupboard was dented but intact. Where she had dragged the rugs from the wall, the old selkie skins shone in the half-light, the stretched shapes translucently grey where he had pinned them out. She had found all five, and perhaps recognised the distorted faces of some or all of her kin.

"Gone Away Ones!" she howled. "You!" And then, almost crying, puzzled, "The Beautiful Voice."

She knew who he was, now, and her terror was ripe in the air, a salt stink emanating from her.

"My skin," she hissed. "Give back my skin."

"No. Not until I have your promise of Selka's skin. Fetch me Selka's skin."

"Need skin for fetch."

She was right, of course. He thought about it, then hardened his heart. "I'll cut one hand from your skin. You can swim easily enough without it. Do you agree?"

The selkie shuddered at the thought of such mutilation. "No. Selka gone deep. *Mustn't* touch skin."

"I want her back. You must help me."

"Cannot."

"No skin, then. No skin for you. I'll keep it. I'll keep it safe."

He already had another idea. It made his witnessing of the

selkie's desperation easier to handle. He was not a cold man, he believed, nor heartless, but now he was ruthless in a way he could not have imagined. This was what heartbreak could do to him.

Seela dissolved into despair before him and he let her run from the croft, compassionlessly watching her, heart beating hard as he knew what had to be done for his own satisfaction, for the love of Selka.

She tried to get back to the croft but Peterson barred the door against her. He stood in the half-light, leaning against the cupboard where her skin soaked in brine. He thought of Selka's laughter as the new-one hammered and cried beyond the wood.

At dusk she was crouched by the sea, and as the moon rose she swam out along the silver channel and barked and called in the hard tide until moonset brought her back. She was a miserable shape, huddled and dying, curled behind the croft during the long night, and in the morning the wood-form began to split her open.

Peterson followed the trail of pale blood over the rocky ground and into the heart of the island. Seela was limping. She was translucent, but the flexing green and brown of the wood-form gave her an oddly dynamic shape, as if green fire swirled within her. Every so often a grinning face bulged from between her shoulders and Seela's arms flapped as elongated fingers tried to prod and point towards the pursuer. The thing was watching Peterson, which was of no real consequence.

She had come from deep water to the shore, and there she had shed her marine skin to become the woman. Now she had travelled to the tree line and here the human was shed to become the wood-form. It squeezed from her, an insect struggling from its pupa. It chattered and shrieked. It used long nails to shred and tear at the throat and thighs of the skin, parting the fatty fabric, letting its twisted limbs find release. It was human in form and Peterson, watching from the rocks as the shedding occurred in a hollow among the thorns, was revolted by the distended, glistening crotch of the thing. He was reminded at once of the grotesque carvings in stone of the female entity from an earlier, pagan time, the grinning, womb-gaping horror that some called the nagig, or nagigtha, others kali. The consuming, spewing form of woman as nature, or nature as woman. A goblin, a dwarf, a female aspect of the violent reproduction of the world.

She rose from the discarded flesh of the selkie-woman, chattered through tiny teeth and yellow lips, shivered, shuddered, then defaecated where she stood, a stenchpile that voided her of the fish of her previous incarnation.

She saw Peterson. The squat form straightened, the eyes were piercing, dark below folds of flesh. She laughed as she hurled three stones at the watching human. All three projectiles struck him glancing but painful blows. When he emerged from hiding, a piece of granite the size of an egg bounced off his shoulder. She was aware of him, accurate, deadly, and no nonsense. Peterson withdrew to a more discreet position.

The nagigtha sighed and stretched. Her lank hair was troublesome and she wound it into braids, then folded the braids into a tall, odd top-knot. More comfortable, she picked up the skin of the marine-form, Seela, and scurried towards the shore, stopping at a rock pool at the head of a deep inlet. The water here was clean from the late tide. She crouched and scrubbed with her fingers at the skin, looking around her defensively, a witch washing the clothes of the dead. Finally, she beat the living fabric against a rock before rolling it tightly, squeezing it out and carrying it up to the trees.

With long fingers she hollowed out a hiding place among the roots of a thorn, wedged Seela into the hole and covered it with stones. Aware of Peterson she flung a stone and drew blood from his chin, but caught in the pattern of ritual events the nagigtha was helpless; she ran among the trees and curled up in shade, melding with the colours of the scrub wood.

Protected against the cold of the sea, he swam out to the pool, then struck back against the tide until his chest ached and his arms threatened to break. He crawled to the shore and collapsed among the driftwood and hard stones, his hand clutching at the beach-dried weed as if it could help drag him to safety. But he was aware of the small shape on the skyline. He watched, from his prone position, and saw the nagigtha slink away from her point of observation.

Each day for a week he swam at dusk. Each time he entered the water the nagigtha watched him, but she could not gain access to the croft, and had disappeared by the time he crawled ashore. She was weakening, he knew that. The cycle, at this phase of a selkie's life, was occurring fast. The nagigtha wanted to take back its marine skin, but there was no breaking the turmoil of hormonal and physical changes that was drawing the creature towards the deep part of the land.

On the eighth day the creature did not appear on the skyline and Peterson ran quickly over the island, crouching on the rise and staring into the thin woods. A pale autumn sun made watching difficult because of the shadowplay of trunks and branches in the gentle wind, but soon he saw the nagigtha. She was sluggish. She looked sick and sad. She crawled to a place in the wood where she burrowed and scooped, perhaps refreshing herself with soil. She leaned back and howled, then moved like an ape lumbering slowly through an oppressive enclosure, walking on hands and knees back to the shade.

In the morning she was shedding. Peterson approached cautiously, wet with dew from his night's vigil. The creature moaned as she saw him coming, but she was already rooted, and the wood-skin was peeling. Her legs were spread and covered with bark, the toes stretching to dig into the hard earth. Her arms were still supple, despite the sprouting of branches, and as Peterson crouched, smiling in triumph, she flicked a stone at him and cracked the enamel on one of his teeth.

He fell back on to his haunches, cursing. "Damn! Why do you have to be so accurate?"

He massaged his mouth and the pain ebbed. The nagigtha chattered, a last laughter, a defiant gesture now that she knew she was lost. The crusty skin split up to her forehead, dividing the face, but the eyes in the skin – and there was life in the skin, even after it was shed – seemed to watch him. The thorn that was emerging glistened with a resinous material and already flies were arriving to sample the temporary sap. They were caught and died, but the fragrance of the material was strong and pleasant.

"As soon as I have Selka I'll return your skins," Peterson said. He reached forward to help tug her wood-form away from the new tree. "I've kept your friends. I don't know why. Impulse, I suppose.

I've been here a long time. I like this wood. It gives me shade, it gives me pleasure. It reminds me of home. I love thorns. The mayflower is lovely. It comes late here. I hope you'll blossom for me beautifully . . ." He playfully prodded the trunk and the tree seemed to quiver, but it was beyond movement now. The selkie had rooted and was now at the mercy of nature. If the skin of the wood-form remained among the roots, one day it would grow back over the tree and the nagigtha shape would be regained. But Peterson would perform the role of the occasional animal, stealing the skin, taking it away so that this phase of the creature's life would become permanent, and it would grow and die and shed berries, and spread in a more natural way.

What *did* come of the berries of a nagigtha tree? It was something, an aspect of the selkie lore, that he had never asked Selka. He ought to do so as soon as she was reborn.

He had brought a large can of water to the wood and he poured this around the roots of the new thorn, helping the creature. But he tugged the wood-form skin out of its protecting hole and folded it.

"I don't need this, but I'll look after it for you. When I have Selka back again I'll bring it back to you. This is a promise. But you see, I can't have you running about the island while I'm away. You're too dangerous. So I have to root you for the moment. I need the other skins, the woman, the selkie, but I'll be careful with them. This is my promise. Enjoy the weather. The forecast is good for the next two weeks."

He hid the nagigtha skin in dry, wormless earth, wrapped around with muslin to keep it safe and cool. It would remain usable for a long time. There was not enough light from the moon to make the right channel, so for two days and nights he drank wine and ate cold fish, sitting in the darkness of the croft, the door open, watching the dark sea, listening to the waves, smelling the salt air. When the moon waxed, when the channel of silver drew his passion again to the task ahead of him, he unfurled the woman-skin and spread it out upon the cold rocks.

When he lay upon it, nude and shivering, the life began to kindle. He clenched his fists and teeth as the pain began, but soon relaxed into a howl of pain, flexing and writhing as his body was invaded.

The skin furled around him, probing deeply through his pores, working into his organs, drawing blood into the cold dermis, padding up the fat in an attempt to shape itself to the hard and unfamiliar shape below. It had been expecting the wood-form, something small, something angular; it struggled long and hard to accommodate Peterson.

For a while he felt strangled as the female head stretched and agonized around his chest. His hands were white and puffy as the arms tried to encapsulate them. The skin shuddered and shivered, its own life frustrated by the attempt to enclose him, to find its form, and he felt the breath being squeezed from his lungs, then his anus was probed and stretched, making him arch and kick.

By relaxing, the pain diminished, but for hours he had to cry against the growth and stretching of the woman-form. It crept to his extremities, agonizingly tight against his genitals. The vagina could not open into him, but he felt bruised by the attempt.

By the evening, below a dull sun and a warm breeze, he felt at peace. He was enclosed by Seela's skin and the pain had reduced to the feeling of thorns scraping over his body. He stood unsteadily, feeling weak and propping himself against the house. He stared down at the body he had become and saw his corpse, like a pupa, vaguely outlined below the fatty curves.

Worst of all was his mouth. The sharp teeth of the woman had pushed his own teeth out of their sockets. He had swallowed them all. They rested in his stomach. He was still swallowing blood. His jaws ached, and the new teeth pricked the flesh of his mouth.

He slept for a long time, drank water and scooped cold fish from the stewpot using hands that shook violently. His male face was twisted behind the stretched and hideous mask of the female; he was not orientated correctly, so that his mouth could be seen slightly to the right of the thin yet shapely mouth of the woman. His eyes made shadow-eyes behind the slanted sockets of the creature.

He slept for a long time, four days, perhaps, it was hard to tell. In that time his body was digested. Now, when he looked in the mirror, he could see only Seela. Peterson was dormant, down below, hidden; he would hatch out later, when his mission was accomplished.

* * *

Again, the skin rolled over him, consuming him. This skin was large, though, and encompassed him instantly, suffocating him in fat, swamping him in images of the deep.

And of men . . . the sound of screaming . . . the look of fear in eyes . . . the cold wind and the long fall to the land . . .

There was salt in his lungs, and the flux of cold and warm currents on his flanks. He rolled on the beach, barking and crying, feeling stones and driftwood snag at his back, letting dry weed tangle with his face. The croft door was open. The trees on the hill were silent, stark against the dusk sky. The sea rushed at him, water sucked and tugged at him, then withdrew quietly before surging back. He twisted round and the surge covered his face, cold and welcoming, calling to him. The moon-silver channel was wide.

He eased himself into the water and swam to the pool. There he circled once, then plunged, and having dived deep he kept on going, down along the underwater cliff, towards the ledge where the selkie skins were tied to weeds, their place of remembrance of the dead.

The spars of the bomber's metal hull were weed-racked and corroded. The old plane reached out across the very deep, angled down. It would one day slip from the ledge, broken apart by the weight of water acting upon the corruption of its joints. For the moment, the stub of its starboard wing was wedged in the rock, the port wing long-since vanished below. It was a monstrous and terrifying shape, reaching obscenely from the living cliff. Peterson's mind cleared, a clear-sight leading back forty years to his time in the plane, to the time when he had been human.

He swam through the bomber's empty windows, over the digested leather of the crew seats, through the wires that waved like threads of sea-life. The bones were long gone, long eaten. His friends were in the selkie skins, nourishing the creatures. Perhaps that was why they came ashore, his friends coming home to Peterson, the one survivor.

He had let them die to save his own life. But now, in this place of his sins, his guilt returned, mixed with cold memories of a deeper sea than he could comprehend, of fish, and a freezing emptiness. And selkie memories, too, of the island where the Beautiful Voice sang, his own voice, attracting the selkies before destroying them, all save Selka who had touched his heart, his actions unconscious, perhaps, guilt assuaged with violence after the siren call to the creatures who had consumed his friends. Although the hulk overshadowed everything, although it dominated the grave ledge and its covering of the shreds of skin of the selkies who had fed here, it was not the great and terrifying tomb that he had dreamed of all these years. He saw it with selkie vision. It was rotting iron, drifting wire, and the home of conger eels. He snapped and shredded one such homesteader, gulping down the screeching flesh, enjoying the meal not for its taste but for the pleasure in the anger he had taken in the killing.

Memories of men faded as he thought of the creature he loved. Which skin, on the ledge, was Selka's?

He returned to the surface to take breath. He had been without air for a day or more, he realised, and a sluggishness had begun to inhibit him. Male selkies breathed more frequently than the females, but they also swam more deeply, for purposes as yet unknown to Peterson. The female selkies rested for most of their days in a vertical hover against the cliff, slowly turning. Only when danger threatened did they break this pattern and dart into shadow. Peterson swam down among the slowly turning seal-shapes, nudged and nuzzled one to awaken her, but had no success.

One morning the males came swimming frantically from the deep, a fan of creatures fleeing from danger. The females broke from their drifting trance and scurried across the cliff. The sea pulsed with sound. Peterson was drawn by the frenzy and by the current, and found himself surfacing towards the pool and the dawn sun.

A killer whale had appeared. Its vast form shadowed the shore for an hour or so, then drifted away. Normality returned.

He beached for a while, relaxing in the air, tempted to shed his skins and drink wine, but the thought of the pain was too much. Another selkie came ashore and watched him. The woman below the skin was plump and ripe, clearly young. But the creature signalled to Peterson and he followed her, slipping back into the waves and meeting in the deep pool.

"Who are you?" she asked him. "I know your face, but you are not the One who went Away."

"What happened to Selka?"

As they swam around each other, he realised that his own name for his lover would mean nothing. He tried to articulate the selkie name for the creature whom he loved, and after a while the sound pulses registered on his companion's consciousness.

"She went deep. Big Tooth."

"But you have a part of her skin. Isn't that right?"

"The skin must never be touched. There is life in the skin—"

"I know. And I want that life back. I want her on the shore."

The selkie seemed puzzled. "Don't touch the skin. You must know this. She can never come back if you touch the skin."

"She is *in* the skin," Peterson said in the selkie language. "I know that her life is there. She must come back."

"I don't understand," the plump female said. "You know she has gone deep—"

"Into the Big Tooth. Yes. I know."

He hated the thought of Selka being eaten by the whale. It was good to feel the human response, the masculine feeling below the seal blubber.

"Then don't touch the skin," the young one urged him. "You know what will happen."

"Just show me the skin. Then leave the decision to me. Please?"

"Who are you? I recognise you. But your deeper beings are unfamiliar. Are you male? But you seem to be like me, female. You frighten me."

"I'm a friend, a dear friend, of your lost companion." Again, he articulated Selka's marine name. "There is nothing to fear from me."

"I'll show you the skin. But if you love your friend, don't touch it."

She led him down to the grave-ledge, showed him the dull grey fabric that was all that remained of Selka, then spiralled upwards and away, as if fleeing the scene of a crime. Her last words were, "*Are* you a female?"

"I'm a Gone Away One," Peterson said, aware that he would create confusion, yet feeling satisfaction in the simple truth.

"A ghost, then," his companion said, and for a long time her keening song was poignant in the half-deep waters.

Peterson reached for the skin. He noticed how clean it was, how straight its edges. He had expected tear marks, tooth marks, the signs of the death struggle. This skin seemed to have been cut carefully, someone preserving it. He bit gently into the flesh, loosened it from its tie around the root of a strand of thick weed, and carried it to the cockpit of the drowned bomber.

Memories overwhelmed him again, drawn out of his closed mind by the living presence of his friends in the selkie skin. Names came back to him.

Jackson. Murray. Mitchell. Stevens. He remembered the names clearly. He could see each man, hear each voice, hear the shouts, hear the calm, hear the moment of death, the moment of prayer. Mitchell had prayed. All the way down, Mitchell had spoken words from the bible. Stevens had yelled abuse. Murray had sung a funny song. Jackson had cried and shouted out a message of everlasting love for his wife, Mary, and his children. They had hit the water and gone down, struggling for release, all failing to escape, as Peterson had drifted down to the island on his silk, sobbing and screaming as the thought of what he had done to save his skin began to haunt him, even as the lives were being crushed from his friends.

The sea had claimed them, then the ridge, then the ledge. The great bomber had settled, wedged, and the creatures of the dark had moved in to feed. The skin, the flesh, the bone, the sinew, the codes, the life, the minds and memories of the men had been greedily and avidly sucked into the hungry jaws of the feeding lifeforms of this shelf by the island.

The selkie that had absorbed them had become the community, days on, reproducing fast, and they lived here, tied to the bomber and the island by the human life that thrived and burgeoned in their pulpy, blubbered bodies.

In Selka, Peterson had recognised the humour of Murray and the passionate family man that had been Jackson. She had even reminded him of Jackson, in her human looks, as if she had been his sister. He and Jackson had always been close. He had found it so easy to form a close relationship with the woman-form of the selkie that had contained so much of that lost essence of friendship.

What to do with the skin?

As he swam lazily through the skeleton of the bomber, Peterson realised that he could not access enough of the selkie Seela's memories to intuit the process by which Selka might reform from the skin. If the skin was the life, and if skin, kept for centuries below the shallow water, could in time regenerate the life that had once inhabited it, then Selka would return.

But how to do it?

There was a disturbance in the water. The iron bones of the plane shuddered, then slipped. Peterson twisted in the cold water and peered into the deep, and his seal-senses made him dart away as the savage features of the whale struck at him. The huge body glided downwards, then struck up again, dislodging the steel girders of the craft. It began to tumble, slipping away from the grave-ledge, dragging the skins of the selkies with it. Peterson struggled out of the frame, grazing his skin and shedding blood. The pale liquid rose in a stream of droplets, up through the murk to the silver surface above.

Blood in the water . . . a storm coming from the deep . . .

He swam furiously upwards, aware that above him the rest of the selkies were small, slim shapes, even now darting into the shallows, to safety. As he rose, as he struggled against the tide, he felt the turbulence around him, the eddying of something monstrous closing fast. He screamed as he twisted, tried to hide his gaze from the maw of the killer. It clamped around him and swept him dizzyingly out of his path, shaking him and savaging him as it plunged down again, into the great darkness.

And yet the teeth had not penetrated his skin, though blood still seeped in bubbles from his cut.

Inside the whale, something flexed, something called to him. In pain, terrified that at any moment the jaws would saw their way shut and sever him, Peterson stared through the skin of the whale . . .

He saw the selkie below, the serene features, the smile. She had her own eyes open, watching him through the eyes of the killer.

Suddenly her face changed – a harder jawline, a narrow look, and Jackson grinned at him, startling him. Jackson's lean features dissolved again and the thick-set face of Edward Mitchell glowered for a moment, replaced by Murray, pursing his lips in silent admonition. Then Selka again, swallowing back the human lives that had nourished her and formed her, as they would have nourished and formed all the selkies at the Island of the Beautiful Voice.

"Why did you follow me?" she seemed to say.

"Because I love you. I thought you had been killed. I thought going deep meant you had died. I came to find your skin, to bring you back to life."

"There is no coming back. This is the end of my life. This is the silvering. But you can be with me forever. If you've come this far, you must certainly want that."

Peterson twitched and flexed in the jaws. He wasn't so sure, now. His doubt must have been as transparent to Selka as the whale's flesh was translucent to the selkie soul beneath. It was angry. It turned and swam further down, into a great mass of silent, silver-grey weed.

The killer basked against the gleaming weed mass, stirring the giant fronds with its tail, using Peterson's struggling carcase to whip the strands and suckers into a frenzy of motion.

The life in the weed was awakened suddenly, and like some great squid its fronds stretched, quivered and rapidly enclosed the whale and Peterson. Slowly, Selka was absorbed into the weed, the fronds enclosing her, fusing with her, becoming her main form. Peterson, trapped outside the transformation, understood with clear terror and uninvited irony what he had missed in the life cycle of the selkie . . . that not only did they come to land and shed to become silent, for many years, in the form of a tree, drawing earth into their bodies, experiencing the sky and the storms of the above-water, but also that they went deep, to take on further outer forms, to become the vastest creatures of the sea. Perhaps then they would return to the seal-like creatures that were so familiar to mythology. Or perhaps, this was their final form, and Peterson would never see his lover again.

Selka, the weed-mass, drifted slowly towards the surface.

The whale was consumed, enclosed, and hard, tight fronds gripped the quiescent selkie that contained the aging human.

"I enjoyed you, Peterson," Selka whispered from the frond-mass. "I'm glad you followed me. I want you inside me again. I always did."

As Peterson screamed and struggled, as they surfaced towards the silver channel of the moon, the horny parts of the frond mass began to cut down to the Peterson-skin inside the seal, to bring him out, to bring him in.

MICHAEL MARSHALL SMITH

Someone Else's Problem

MICHAEL MARSHALL SMITH IS A WINNER of the Philip K. Dick, August Derleth, British Fantasy and International Horror Guild awards for his horror and science fiction stories, and he was a Guest of Honour at the World Horror Convention 2007 in Toronto, Canada.

He is also the author of the internationally best-selling *Straw Men* thriller trilogy, under the name "Michael Marshall". A new novel, *The Intruders*, is published in 2007. He is currently writer/producer on a feature adaptation of one of his own short stories, and working on his eighth novel. He lives in London with his wife, son and two cats.

"I used to have a job very like the protagonist in this story," admits Smith. "In fact, it was while working at a company much like the one described, that I met the writer Nicholas Royle, who became a great friend and inspiration – and was instrumental in my selling my very first short story.

"The character of Egerton crops up in a few of Nick's stories too, and even provided the inspiration for the name of the press under which he published his *Darklands* and *Darklands II* anthologies.

"Of course when I look back now, that time seems so very straightforward and simple. There's probably a moral in there somewhere, but I'll leave that as an exercise for the reader."

BY THE TIME JOHN TROTTED out of the ticket office he'd basically given up hope, and was already speculating on how long he'd have to wait for the next train to Cambridge. A panting scan of the departure board told him he had less than a minute to catch the 3:30 pm, and that it was due to depart from platform 10a.

10a? Where the hell was that? What was the difference between it and 10b? Platforms 2 to 6 were clearly visible, and John felt that he could take an educated guess as to where 1, 7 and 8 might be. The whereabouts of 10a was a complete mystery, however, not least to those in charge of sign-posting within the station.

Shouldering his bag and pocketing his wallet, John charged in what he judged the most likely direction, trying to fumble a cigarette out the packet at the same time. He was surprised to find that platform 10a was not the expected short bus ride away, but in fact just around the corner – and that there was a train sitting at the far end of it, chugging, its doors open and ready for someone just like him.

He leapt onto it at 3:30 precisely, after a headlong dash down the platform that had clearly made the attendant's day. He dropped the cigarette out the door as he made it aboard, having barely been able to take a couple of drags on it.

The carriage was dark, the lights off either as some penny-saving manoeuvre or perhaps because they just didn't work. The good news was the train was a lot less crowded than usual. One table was completely occupied by men slumped forward onto their forearms, but many others only had a single person in residence, meaning John could score a double seat to himself – the Holy Grail of train travel. He'd have to sit opposite someone, but he could live with that.

He chose a table a little way from the men, in case they all suddenly woke up and started shouting. Sliding his bag into the rack above, he dropped into the seat by the aisle and sent urgent placatory messages to his heart. He didn't intend to run like that again soon, if ever.

Work. Bloody work. *Work*. Why did people go to work? Wasn't there enough unhappiness in the world already? If not for Carolyn's inability to come to terms with the utter basics of using the computer network, coupled with a dogged insistence on not listening to *a single word John said* – even when she'd asked him for help in the first place – he could have been at the station forty minutes ago. He could have grabbed a *latte*, calmed himself down, and wouldn't have been driven into speechless fury at the slowness with which the old woman in the ticket hall had processed his credit card.

He could have had a proper cigarette, too. Probably more than one. The journey to Cambridge wasn't long. It wasn't like the nicotine withdrawal would kill him. But what non-smokers don't understand is there's nothing like telling someone they can't have a cigarette, to make them really, really want one.

It wasn't actually Carolyn's fault of course, not really – the computers at work didn't like *anyone* very much. Not even John, and he was nice to them, all the time. Bottom line, Egerton was to blame, because he was the one who'd insisted the company get this system from Hell against semi-expert advice (John's, mainly).

An office manager with a ten-word job title, Egerton was extremely skilled at recognising something as a problem but incapable of doing any of the donkey-work required to sort it out. The limit of his participation towards "forging a solution" was standing around with his hands on his hips and brow furrowed, as if war had broken out in some distant colony for which he felt somewhat responsible – though he did sometimes bark out suggestions which left John open-mouthed at their irrelevance.

John had never understood how being Press Officer made the

computers his responsibility, but somehow it was always he who coaxed the damn things into working. It was the same every time. Whenever he started on a little problem he found another – which had to be solved first – and this lead him onto still others, appearing from nowhere, lateral branches of confusion: until suddenly he was neck-deep in nested grief, circling some inner core of inexplicability, getting none of his own work done . . . and then nearly missing his bloody train. *Again*.

Perhaps, as Debs always said, it was time he learned how to tell people to piss off. Maybe there was even a course you could take: "Telling Co-Workers To Stuff It" – a residential weekend in Slough, priced at £395.00 + VAT (light refreshments included).

There was an inarticulate howl from the other end of the platform, presumably from the guard, and the train hissed, lurched and then started to pull slowly out of the station. As always, John felt his heart lift as he watched the edificial pillars and concrete slabs going backwards: taking the train out of London was like leaving a bad dream behind.

A brief thought wondered into his mind, a reminder that he hadn't sorted out some ad space that needed to be done by Monday. It could wait. He wasn't going to waste a train journey worrying about it, and Deborah, thank God, would beat him round the head if he tried worrying about work over the weekend.

And it really *was* the weekend, with an early start at that. Egerton had looked at him with distant concern when John had asked to leave mid-afternoon, clearly saddened by his evident abdication of responsibility towards the current office crisis of membership renewals, but had let him go in the end. Though not, John fully realised, out of any appreciation of the fact that the renewals were in no sense John's problem, and that he'd only been helping with them because – well, because he always had to.

The carriage lights flickered on as John stood up, extricated his drink and book from his bag and took his jacket off. Ice-cold can of Coke open, he sat back and found his place in his book. It was all over for the week. He was on a train with a good book, and he was on his way to see Debs. All in all, things could be a lot worse.

Before settling down to read, he took a glance around the carriage. The four men round the fully occupied table were still comatose, more drunk than John would have believed possible by this time in the afternoon. Maybe they'd been up all night, or all week. The other travellers were a disparate scattering of old people, swaddled in dark blue coats or zip-up beige jackets and peering stoically into space.

The only other young-ish person was sitting opposite John. A moderately attractive woman in her early thirties, she was assimilating the latest gripping developments in the marketing world from a trade magazine, making notes in an alarmingly neat hand on a lilac pad, concentrating with the gravity of a serious schoolgirl revising for an unimportant test.

John smiled to himself and settled down to his book.

A chapter slipped quickly away before he next looked up. Corporate Woman opposite had relinquished her magazine and was referring to a sheaf of papers as she roughed out a business letter. As John sat marvelling at the fact that her handwriting had got even *neater* for this, she glanced up, and he had to divert his gaze quickly out of the window.

On the other side of the glass, acres of green and genuinely quite pleasant land were rushing by. It all looked very nice, and he bore it no particular ill will, but he couldn't help wishing there were fewer miles of it between him and Deborah. She had a job in Cambridge she couldn't leave, and John had his stress factory back down in London, and there didn't seem to be any way of getting the twain to meet. The voyage from London to Cambridge was not exactly an epic quest, but weekends of camping out in each other's flats were not ideal, and the arrangement wasn't cheap either, now that John's senile Ford had lost the struggle against planned obsolescence.

John had thought several times about resigning, and with increasing fervency, but he knew he couldn't. Finding another job was never easy, and a wretched part of him knew that leaving would drop Egerton in the shit. They told him often enough he was indispensable, supposedly as a compliment. Actually it was just a warning as to how unpopular he'd be – and how guilty he'd feel – if he tried to escape.

Noticing that his view seemed a little blurred, John adjusted his focus to the window itself, rather than what lay beyond. He had become concerned that hours spent in front of word processors and databases would sooner or later damage his eyesight, and was relieved to see the problem was due to a smudge on the glass. It was a peculiar shape, like a baby's handprint. That was almost certainly what it was, in fact, though there was something about it that didn't look right. After a moment he lost interest, and seeing that the eye-contact coast was clear, he turned down to his book.

By the time he'd finished another chapter the steady rhythm of the train and the warmth of the carriage was beginning to make him feel drowsy. The sentences made less and less sense each time he read them, and he decided to doze instead. After a week spent chained behind her own desk, Deborah would want to go out and do some hardcore revelling, and he'd need all the energy he could muster to keep up with her.

Finding a long-forgotten mint in his jacket pocket, he unwrapped it and popped it into his mouth. He settled back into his seat with his legs out-stretched and his arm hanging slightly out over the aisle, achieving the modicum of comfort that was possible – despite, he suspected, the best efforts of the seats' designers. Eyelids drooping, he scrunched the mint wrapper in his hand and dropped it into the aisle, which was filthy, in stark similarity to the rest of the carriage. Amidst the crisp packets, beer cans and general debris, he felt that a sweet wrapper would go unnoticed.

To his surprise, he heard a quiet *tutting* sound.

Opening one eye, he looked at the woman opposite. She was still agonising over her letter, doubtless trying to project the level of assertiveness *Cosmopolitan* currently believed to be good for her.

John opened the other eye, and saw the remaining occupants of the carriage were still either prostrate or knitting. But then he heard the tutting noise again.

This time it was louder, and seemed to be coming from next to him, on his right-hand side. He turned to look across the aisle. The seats there were empty.

Puzzled, he'd started to return his eyes to the front when something made him look down into the aisle instead.

A monkey was standing there.

Something like a monkey, anyway. It was about eighteen inches high, and covered with short, dark brown hair, and stood steadily on rather spindly back legs.

The creature glared back up at him balefully before stalking up the aisle, and through the automatic door at the end of the carriage, leaving John with a strong after-image of hard blue eyes.

Closing his mouth slowly, his own eyes wide now, John turned to look at the woman opposite. She had shelved her business communication and now appeared to be writing a personal letter, her tongue peeking out of the corner of her mouth.

Maybe she's on her way to see someone too, John thought: *funny to think of other people having lives.*

In any event, the woman had the unmistakable air of someone who has *not* just witnessed a minor contretemps between a fellow passenger and a passing primate. John considered asking her it she'd seen it, spent about two seconds trying to work out how he'd phrase such an enquiry so as not to sound like he was barking mad (Excuse me – did you just see a monkey?), and rapidly decided against it. A quick glance around showed that everyone else in the carriage was asleep, even the ones with their eyes open.

There had to be a simple explanation, and it wasn't hard to come up with one. Some zoo-keeper or zoologist taking his work home with him. Or someone's quirky choice of pet: the look on the creature's face, and the tutting noise it had made, had seemed too human not to have been the result of training. Either way, what John had seen remained explicable. A monkey on an Intercity was odd, certainly (what fare did you have to pay for it? A child's? Could you toilet-train a monkey?), but only anecdotal odd.

Surely not odd enough to make his hands shake, and he held them together for a moment, to stop them.

But then there was another tutting sound.

John looked up quickly, but it was only the woman opposite, crossing a sentence of her letter out.

He looked back down at the table.

The problem was . . . he wasn't completely convinced it had been a monkey. The more he ran over the image in his mind, the less it tallied: and it hadn't even felt right when he'd first seen it. He should have thought "Monkey", immediately and conclusively, like a child dropping a square brick through a square hole. That's what brains were for – recognising known things. But his hadn't recognised it. He'd *told* himself that's what it was. When he tried to apply the term now his mind wouldn't settle on it, as if it didn't name it properly. No matter how he turned it around in his head, this brick wouldn't go in that hole.

No, his brain was saying. *That word is not correct. Find something else.*

The creature's eyes, for a start – shouldn't they have been brown? Didn't all monkeys have brown eyes? Maybe not – John wasn't really sure. He could conjure up a very clear picture of those eyes, and the way they'd stared at him, and decided that was probably what was spooking him. The creature's gaze had simply seemed too intelligent, too directed. And too unfriendly.

Too blue, basically. The more he remembered the eyes, the more he believed that's what had spooked him. Like seeing a cat with round pupils.

So there was a blue-eyed monkey on the train. End of story. An anecdote for Debs, now only about half-an-hour away, unless the train elected to sit outside Royston for twenty minutes for no apparent reason. Nothing more.

John sipped his now tepid Coke and reached again for his book, but he didn't pick it up. He didn't feel relaxed enough. Instead he looked out of the window. The sky was now a leaden grey, the trees unnaturally vivid against the clouds. It was going to rain soon, and hard by the look of it, which meant a taxi from the station.

Then he noticed the handprint on the glass again, and this time knew immediately what was wrong with it.

The fingers and the palm were too thin.

Babies had chubby hands. Whatever had made this mark had a hand the size of a baby's, but a narrow palm and long, thin fingers. Bony, strong-looking. The kind of hand you might find on a . . .

John looked quickly around the carriage.

Had it been on the table? If so – when? John had leapt onto the train at the very last minute, but he would have bet big money that Ms. Organised opposite had been ready at the gate before it opened. And the guys at the table in the corner: they *had* to have been on the train for a while, to have been so resolutely asleep by the time John got on. They'd have noticed a monkey on the table, surely? And been acting differently to the way John had observed them, as a result. Unless . . . it *could* be the print had been made when the train was on the way *down* to London from Cambridge, the first half of the return journey it was now completing.

The state of the aisle suggested the train hadn't been cleaned while turning round in London, and he doubted the windows got cleaned more than once a day (or week) anyway. Yes, good. But . . . Didn't that skewer the "zookeeper/someone's pet" line of reasoning? Why would someone travel down to London (bringing along their blue-eyed monkey pet), and then turn around and travel straight back?

The more he thought about it, the more the print made the problem bigger rather than smaller. The more concerned it made him, and still – probably – for no very good reason. The more he tried to picture the creature's hand, the harder he found to remember whether it had been covered in fur after all. He *thought* it had, remembered thinking that it was, but the picture that came into his head now was that of a hairless creature, its skin dark, somewhat gnarled and blotchy . . .

This was ridiculous. Maybe he should just *ask* someone else in the carriage if they'd seen anything . . .

He couldn't.

Breathing out heavily, he decided to go buy a coffee instead. While he remained seated, his mind was evidently determined to keep jumping at shadows. He should take a break, come back, forget about it. Reboot.

He stood and side-stepped into the aisle. The woman opposite glanced up. She had nice eyes, and looked kind, as well as tired. He hoped she had someone nice to spend the weekend with. She looked like she could do with some time off. A month or two, preferably. Maybe she was "indispensable" in some stress factory of her own, forever the person expected to solve other people's problems.

You and me both, sister.

The buffet car was in the next carriage, and empty of other customers. Unfortunately this desertion was mirrored behind the counter, so John stood in front of it, tapping a coin on the Formica. When no-one appeared after a few moments he turned and wandered across the carriage to the window. As he watched the trees and fields rush darkly by in front of charcoal grey, the first spots of rain spattered across the pane.

There was a noise behind him, and he turned, pausing only to don an expression of long-suffering patience.

There was nobody there.

Puzzled, he took a step, leaning forward to look around the compartment. There was flicker in the corner of his eye and he turned back to the window in time to see a thread of pale lightening outside, fragmented by the now heavy rain on the glass.

He looked back at the counter. Still no-one.

Then the sound came again. This time it was more of a rustling. John unconsciously ducked, his body coming alert before his mind realised why.

A human wouldn't make that kind of sound. They were too big. This was a small sound. A small, odd sound. Made by a small, odd . . .?

He looked quickly around the carriage again, this time scaling down his expected size of object, and searching higher and lower than before.

The sound came again, this time followed by a quiet clank, and John was able to pinpoint its source to behind the counter.

Shoulders slumping, he relaxed. The attendant must be crouched behind there, sorting stuff. That was all.

John leaned on the counter, and tapped a coin on its surface again. There was no response.

Then there was more rustling and John continued to move his head forward, concerned that maybe it was the monkey after all.

There was a quick scrabbling noise, and John realised it must be. Probably it was gambolling behind the counter, tucking into a sandwich. Rather him than me, John thought – having tried the food available on this train before – and wished he had a camera.

He moved forward again, until his eyes could just see over the counter. Then he stopped very suddenly.

Sitting on the floor behind the counter was the creature. Along with five others.

John stared. One monkey he could rationalise. A pair if necessary. But *six*?

This wasn't a group of monkeys, either. Seeing them *en masse* convinced him of that. Whatever they were, they weren't monkeys. He didn't even think they were animals.

Just then one of them looked up and saw his face.

John was struck motionless by its eyes and could only stare, as the creature reached over and tapped the shoulder of one of its companions – without ever moving his gaze from John. The other creatures stopped ripping a sandwich apart and turned to look up at John, their heads swivelling as if pulled on the same string.

No, they weren't animals.

John felt strangely vindicated by this realisation, though he wasn't sure what it meant, or how he knew. Animals just didn't sit like that, didn't turn like that. Perhaps they could have skin that looked this scarred, and oddly metallic, but they certainly didn't have *eyes* like that. *Humans* didn't have eyes like that.

These were the eyes of every madman under every bridge, of every shouter in the street combined. But they were clear, and they saw him.

John wasn't going to hang around and puzzle this one out, let himself get drawn into staying and solving this particular problem. Like all problems, it would lead to others – like where they'd *come* from, and where the buffet attendant was – and John didn't want to solve those either.

As he stood, quickly coming to this resolution, one of the creatures picked a can of mixer from the piles scattered over the floor, fingers clicking over the others as he made his selection, like an assaying spider. Then he suddenly hurled it at John's face.

Still mesmerised by the pairs of staring eyes, John failed to realise the implications of this until the can struck him hard on the bridge of the nose.

He snapped his head back, dismayed, and then all hell broke lose.

A barrage of cutlery and cans looped viciously over the counter, raining down onto John's head and neck, their accuracy too good to be true. The creatures seemed to slip their missiles onto hidden tracks in the air, hurtling them towards John far too quickly to avoid. One hit him squarely on the temple and he staggered back towards the window – as first one creature, then all the others, sprang up onto the counter, hurling anything within reach – and all completely and utterly silent.

Years of habit, years of hanging on in there, fell away from John's mind in a moment.

Fuck this, he thought. *Count me out*.

The creatures all coiled simultaneously, getting ready to leap, but John spun round and ran out of the compartment door into the space between the carriages.

He slipped and fell down on one knee, but quickly turned to slam the door shut and brace it with his legs, closing it just in time to hear six hard bodies slam into it from the other side.

He waited, heedless of the fact that he was lying down in the space between carriages, tensed like iron, prepared to have his legs broken rather than let them through.

The second impact never came.

After thirty seconds or so he stood up, breathing rapidly. Very cautiously he leaned forward to look through the glass in the upper half of the door.

The buffet carriage was empty, and there was nothing on the floor.

He stumbled backwards into one of the toilets, shutting and locking the door behind him. For a while he simply leaned back against it.

No, he told to himself firmly. *No*.

He fumbled into his shirt pocket and lit a very shaky cigarette, perching on the edge of the toilet seat. It was some moments before he could get it into his mouth first time, and as he smoked he looked at himself in the mirror.

There was a small red mark on his forehead, already fading, and another on the bridge of his nose. When he sluiced cold water over his face with one hand his skin felt bruised. Closing his eyes, he scrubbed at it viciously. When he looked again the mark was gone, had blended in with the pink of his rubbed skin. He dropped the cigarette in the toilet bowl before it could set off the smoke alarm.

As he dabbed the water off his face with the wet rag provided, John stared at himself with wide eyes. He wasn't crazy, he knew that. So *something* had happened. But he was going to leave it at that.

Something had happened, and now it was over.

He knew that when he stepped out he was going to look towards the door to the buffet. That was to be expected. But when he saw nothing there – and he *would* see nothing there – that was it. It was over.

He opened the door and stepped out.

He walked over to the glass door and looked through it.

The carriage beyond was deserted. His heart missed a beat when he thought he saw a small can on the floor, but when he looked closer he realised that it was just a shadow. There was nobody in there. Nothing in there.

No things in there.

He turned and walked stiffly back into his own carriage, foolishly trying to look normal in front of sleeping people. He sat down, feeling terribly at odds with the normality of his book, his bag, his jacket.

He avoided looking at the woman opposite, and almost jumped out of his skin when she spoke to him.

"Would you mind keeping an eye on my stuff?"

John looked up at her. The woman was smiling at him cautiously, wary of addressing someone she didn't know.

"No," he said. "No, that's fine."

"Do you want anything?"

John frowned in incomprehension.

"From the buffet," she explained.

John stared at her, wondering what to say. She was looking at him. He had to say something. But what?

"I've just been in there. There was no one serving."

"I'll wait," she smiled. "What did you want?"

If he told her not to go, he'd have to explain. He'd have to say something. She raised her eyebrow. He was taking too long to answer.

"A coffee would be great, thanks," he said, and she got up and went.

He watched her go. She'd be all right, surely.

He stared through the window at the rain for a while, and then found his place in his book.

* * *

It took another twenty minutes to get to Cambridge. John waited a little while longer, though he could see Debs' patiently waiting face beyond the barrier, and he wanted very much to be with her.

Finally he put his jacket on, pulled his bag down and headed towards the exit, leaving the address book and the handbag and the lilac pad and the copy of *Marketing Week* on the table in the empty carriage. He wondered what would happen to them. Thrown away, probably, after a suitable period in some storeroom.

He was the last person off the train, so he shut the door behind him with a *clunk* and walked slowly towards Debs and the weekend.

CLIVE BARKER

Rawhead Rex

CLIVE BARKER WAS BORN IN LIVERPOOL, England, but now lives and works in Hollywood, California.

An author, playwright, film director and visual artist, he exploded upon the horror scene in the mid-1980s with his six-volume collection of stories, *Books of Blood*, and the novel, *The Damnation Game*. Since then he has published such international bestsellers as *Weaveworld*, *The Great and Secret Show*, *Imajica*, *The Thief of Always*, *Everville*, *Sacrament*, *Galilee*, *Coldheart Canyon: A Hollywood Ghost Story* and the illustrated *Abarat* series. Forthcoming is *The Scarlet Gospels*, which features both his iconic characters Pinhead and Harry D' Amour.

Following a career in the theatre, Barker made his film directorial debut in 1987 with the influential *Hellraiser*, based on his novella "The Hellbound Heart". He followed that with *Nightbreed* and *Lord of Illusions*, and he was executive producer on the

Oscar-winning *Gods and Monsters*. *Hellraiser* has spawned a number of sequels, and the *Candyman* trilogy is inspired by his short story "The Forbidden".

"Rawhead Rex" was filmed in 1986 by director George Pavlou, starring the late David Dukes. It was also adapted as a graphic novel for Eclipse Books by writer Steve Niles and artist Les Edwards in 1993.

"I wrote the screenplay," says Barker about the film version. "I'm sure it wasn't a brilliant screenplay – it was my second screenplay – but I think it was probably marginally better than the movie.

"I followed the process of the book. I wrote a screenplay which was set in England, in the height of the summer, so you could really get the full drama out of this strange, dark, child-eating monster lurking in the pleasant countryside of Kent in mid-summer.

"They called me up and said 'Well, we're going to make the movie, but we're going to make it in Ireland, and we're going to make it in February.' So immediately, a whole counterpoint of this blazing English summer and this ravaging monster just went out of the window.

"They also didn't spend enough money on the special effects, so you end up with this rubber mask. I didn't actually think the design for the monster itself was bad at all, and I love the poster, but I wasn't comfortable with the picture. The picture tried, but didn't get there . . ."

OF ALL THE CONQUERING ARMIES that had tramped the streets of Zeal down the centuries, it was finally the mild tread of the Sunday tripper that brought the village to its knees. It had suffered Roman legions, and the Norman conquest, it had survived the agonies of Civil War, all without losing its identity to the occupying forces. But after centuries of boot and blade it was to be the tourists – the new barbarians – that bested Zeal, their weapons courtesy and hard cash.

It was ideally suited for the invasion. Forty miles south-east of London, amongst the orchards and hop-fields of the Kentish

Weald, it was far enough from the city to make the trip an adventure, yet close enough to beat a quick retreat if the weather turned foul. Every weekend between May and October Zeal was a watering-hole for parched Londoners. They would swarm through the village on each Saturday that promised sun, bringing their dogs, their plastic balls, their litters of children, and their children's litter, disgorging them in bawling horders on to the village green, then returning to "The Tall Man" to compare traffic stories over glasses of warm beer.

For their part the Zealots weren't unduly distressed by the Sunday trippers; at least they didn't spill blood. But their very lack of aggression made the invasion all the more insidious.

Gradually these city-weary people began to work a gentle but permanent change on the village. Many of them set their hearts on a home in the country; they were charmed by stone cottages set amongst churning oaks, they were enchanted by doves in the churchyard yews. Even the air, they'd say as they inhaled deeply, even the air smells fresher here. It smells of England.

At first a few, then many, began to make bids for the empty barns and deserted houses that littered Zeal and its outskirts. They could be seen every fine weekend, standing in the nettles and rubble, planning how to have a kitchen extension built, and where to install the jacuzzi. And although many of them, once back in the comfort of Kilburn or St John's Wood, chose to stay there, every year one or two of them would strike a reasonable bargain with one of the villagers, and buy themselves an acre of the good life.

So, as the years passed and the natives of Zeal were picked off by old age, the civil savages took over in their stead. The occupation was subtle, but the change was plain to the knowing eye. It was there in the newspapers the Post Office began to stock – what native of Zeal had ever purchased a copy of "Harpers and Queen" magazine, or leafed through "The Times Literary Supplement"? It was there, that change, in the bright new cars that clogged the one narrow street, laughingly called the High Road, that was Zeal's backbone. It was there too in the buzz of gossip at "The Tall Man", a sure sign that the affairs of the foreigners had become fit subject for debate and mockery.

Indeed, as time went by the invaders found a yet more permanent place in the heart of Zeal, as the perennial demons of their hectic lives, Cancer and Heart Disease, took their toll, following their victims even into this newfound-land. Like the Romans before them, like the Normans, like all invaders, the commuters made their profoundest mark upon this usurped turf not by building on it, but by being buried under it.

It was clammy the middle of that September; Zeal's last September.

Thomas Garrow, the only son of the late Thomas Garrow, was sweating up a healthy thirst as he dug in the corner of the Three Acre Field. There'd been a violent rainstorm the previous day, Thursday, and the earth was sodden. Clearing the ground for sowing next year hadn't been the easy job Thomas thought it'd be, but he'd sworn blind he'd have the field finished by the end of the week. It was heavy labour, clearing stones, and sorting out the detritus of out-of-date machinery his father, lazy bastard, had left to rust where it lay. Must have been some good years, Thomas thought, some pretty fine damn years, that his father could afford to let good machinery waste away. Come to think of it, that he could have afforded to leave the best part of three acres unploughed; good healthy soil too. This was the Garden of England after all: land was money. Leaving three acres fallow was a luxury nobody could afford in these straitened times. But Jesus, it was hard work: the kind of work his father had put him to in his youth, and he'd hated with a vengeance ever since.

Still, it had to be done.

And the day had begun well. The tractor was healthier after its overhaul, and the morning sky was rife with gulls, across from the coast for a meal of freshly turned worms. They'd kept him raucous company as he worked, their insolence and their short tempers always entertaining. But then, when he came back to the field after a liquid lunch in "The Tall Man", things began to go wrong. The engine started to cut out for one, the same problem that he'd just spent £200 having seen to; and then, when he'd only been back at work a few minutes, he'd found the stone.

It was an unspectacular lump of stuff: poking out of the soil perhaps a foot, its visible diameter a few inches short of a yard, its surface smooth and bare. No lichen even; just a few grooves in its face that might have once been words. A love-letter perhaps, a "Kilroy was here" more likely, a date and a name likeliest of all. Whatever it had once been, monument or milestone, it was in the way now. He'd have to dig it up, or next year he'd lose a good three yards of ploughable land. There was no way a plough could skirt around a boulder that size.

Thomas was surprised that the damn thing had been left in the field for so long without anyone bothering to remove it. But then it was a long spell since the Three Acre Field had been planted: certainly not in his thirty-six years. And maybe, now he came to think of it, not in his father's lifetime either. For some reason (if he'd ever known the reason he'd forgotten it) this stretch of Garrow land had been left fallow for a good many seasons, maybe even for generations. In fact there was a suspicion tickling the back of his skull that someone, probably his father, had said no crop would ever grow in that particular spot. But that was plain nonsense. If anything plant life, albeit nettles and convolvulus, grew thicker and ranker in this forsaken three acres than in any other plot in the district. So there was no reason on earth why hops shouldn't flourish here. Maybe even an orchard: though that took more patience and love than Thomas suspected he possessed. Whatever he chose to plant, it would surely spring up from such rich ground with a rare enthusiasm, and he'd have reclaimed three acres of good land to bolster his shaky finances.

If he could just dig out that bloody stone.

He'd half thought of hiring in one of the earth movers from the building site at the North End of the village, just to haul itself across here and get its mechanical jaws working on the problem. Have the stone out and away in two seconds flat. But his pride resisted the idea of running for help at the first sign of a blister. The job was too small anyhow. He'd dig it out himself, the way his father would have done. That's what he'd decided. Now, two and a half hours later, he was regretting his haste.

The ripening warmth of the afternoon had soured in that time, and the air, without much of a breeze to stir it around, had become stifling. Over from the Downs came a stuttering roll of thunder, and Thomas could feel the static crawling at the nape of his neck, making the short hairs there stand up. The sky above the field was empty now: the gulls, too fickle to hang around once the fun was over, had taken some salt-smelling thermal.

Even the earth, that had given up a sweet-sharp flavour as the blades turned it that morning, now smelt joyless; and as he dug the black soil out from around the stone his mind returned helplessly to the putrefaction that made it so very rich. His thoughts circled vacuously on the countless little deaths on every spadeful of soil he dug. This wasn't the way he was used to thinking, and the morbidity of it distressed him. He stopped for a moment, leaning on his spade, and regretting the fourth pint of Guinness he'd downed at lunch. That was normally a harmless enough ration, but today it swilled around in his belly, he could hear it, as dark as the soil on his spade, working up a scum of stomach-acid and half-digested food.

Think of something else, he told himself, or you'll get to puking. To take his mind off his belly, he looked at the field. It was nothing out of the ordinary; just a rough square of land bounded by an untrimmed hawthorn hedge. One or two dead animals lying in the shadow of the hawthorn: a starling; something else, too far gone to be recognisable. There was a sense of absence, but that wasn't so unusual. It would soon be autumn, and the summer had been too long, too hot for comfort.

Looking up higher than the hedge he watched the mongol-headed cloud discharge a flicker of lightning to the hills. What had been the brightness of the afternoon was now pressed into a thin line of blue at the horizon. Rain soon, he thought, and the thought was welcome. Cool rain; perhaps a downpour like the previous day. Maybe this time it would clear the air good and proper.

Thomas stared back down at the unyielding stone, and struck it with his spade. A tiny arc of white flame flew off.

He cursed, loudly and inventively: the stone, himself, the field. The stone just sat there in the moat he'd dug around it, defying him. He'd almost run out of options: the earth around the thing had been dug out two feet down; he'd hammered stakes under it, chained it and then got the tractor going to haul it out. No joy. Obviously he'd have to dig the moat deeper, drive the stakes further down. He wasn't going to let the damn thing beat him.

Grunting his determination he set to digging again. A fleck of rain hit the back of his hand, but he scarcely noticed it. He knew by experience that labour like this took singularity of purpose: head down, ignore all distractions. He made his mind blank. There was just the earth, the spade, the stone and his body.

Push down, scoop up. Push down, scoop up, a hypnotic rhythm of effort. The trance was so total he wasn't sure how long he worked before the stone began to shift.

The movement woke him. He stood upright, his vertebrae clicking, not quite certain that the shift was anything more than a twitch in his eye. Putting his heel against the stone, he pushed. Yes, it rocked in its grave. He was too drained to smile, but he felt victory close. He had the bugger.

The rain was starting to come on heavier now, and it felt fine on his face. He drove a couple more stakes in around the stone to unseat it a little further: he was going to get the better of the thing. You'll see, he said, you'll see. The third stake went deeper than the first two, and it seemed to puncture a bubble of gas beneath the stone, a yellowish cloud smelling so foul he stepped away from the hole to snatch a breath of purer air. There was none to be had. All he could do was hawk up a wad of phlegm to clear his throat and lungs. Whatever was under the stone, and there was something animal in the stench, it was very rotten.

He forced himself back down to the work, taking gasps of the air into his mouth, not through his nostrils. His head felt tight, as though his brain was swelling and straining against the dome of his skull, pushing to be let out.

"Fuck you," he said and beat another stake under the stone. His back felt as though it was about to break. On his right hand a blister had bust. A cleg sat on his arm and feasted itself, unswatted.

"Do it. Do it. Do it." He beat the last stake in without knowing he was doing it.

And then, the stone began to roll.

He wasn't even touching it. The stone was being pushed out of its seating from beneath. He reached for his spade, which was still wedged beneath the stone. He suddenly felt possessive of it; it was his, a part of him, and he didn't want it near the hole. Not now; not with the stone rocking like it had a geyser under it about to blow.

Not with the air yellow, and his brain swelling up like a marrow in August.

He pulled hard on his spade: it wouldn't come.

He cursed it, and took two hands to the job, keeping at arm's length from the hole as he hauled, the increasing motion of the stone slinging up showers of soil, lice, and pebbles.

He heaved at the spade again, but it wouldn't give. He didn't stop to analyse the situation. The work had sickened him, all he wanted was to get his spade, *his* spade, out of the hole and get the hell out of there.

The stone bucked, but still he wouldn't let go of the spade, it had become fixed in his head that he had to have it before he could leave. Only when it was back in his hands, safe and sound, would he obey his bowels, and run.

Beneath his feet the ground began to erupt. The stone rolled away from the tomb as if feather-light, a second cloud of gas, more obnoxious than the first, seemed to blow it on its way. At the same time the spade came out of the hole, and Thomas saw what had hold of it.

Suddenly there was no sense in heaven or earth.

There was a hand, a living hand, clutching the spade, a hand so wide it could grasp the blade with ease.

Thomas knew the moment well. The splitting earth: the hand: the stench. He knew it from some nightmare he'd heard at his father's knee.

Now he wanted to let go of the spade, but he no longer had the will. All he could do was obey some imperative from underground, to haul until his ligaments tore and his sinews bled.

Beneath the thin crust of earth, Rawhead smelt the sky. It was pure ether to his dulled senses, making him sick with pleasure. Kingdoms for the taking, just a few inches away. After so many years, after the endless suffocation, there was light on his eyes again, and the taste of human terror on his tongue.

His head was breaking surface now, his black hair wreathed with worms, his scalp seething with tiny red spiders. They'd irritated him a hundred years, those spiders burrowing into his marrow, and he longed to crush them out. Pull, pull, he willed the human, and Thomas Garrow pulled until his pitiful body had no strength left, and inch by inch Rawhead was hoisted out of his grave in a shroud of prayers.

The stone that had pressed on him for so long had been removed, and he was dragging himself up easily now, sloughing off the grave-earth like a snake its skin. His torso was free. Shoulders twice as broad as a man's; lean, scarred arms stronger than any human. His limbs were pumping with blood like a butterfly's wings, juicing with resurrection. His long, lethal fingers rhythmically clawed the ground as they gained strength.

Thomas Garrow just stood and watched. There was nothing in him but awe. Fear was for those who still had a chance of life: he had none.

Rawhead was out of his grave completely. He began to stand upright for the first time in centuries. Clods of damp soil fell from his torso as he stretched to his full height, a yard above Garrow's six feet.

Thomas Garrow stood in Rawhead's shadow with his eyes still fixed on the gaping hole the King had risen from. In his right hand he still clutched his spade. Rawhead picked him up by the hair. His scalp tore under the weight of his body, so Rawhead seized Garrow round the neck, his vast hand easily enclosing it.

Blood ran down Garrow's face from his scalp, and the sensation stirred him. Death was imminent, and he knew it. He looked down at his legs, thrashing uselessly below him, then he looked up and stared directly into Rawhead's pitiless face.

It was huge, like the harvest moon, huge and amber. But this moon had eyes that burned in its pallid, pitted face. They were for all the world like wounds, those eyes, as though somebody had gouged them in the flesh of Rawhead's face then set two candles to flicker in the holes.

Garrow was entranced by the vastness of this moon. He looked from eye to eye, and then to the wet slits that were its nose, and finally, in a childish terror, down to the mouth. God, that mouth. It was so wide, so cavernous it seemed to split the head in two as it opened. That was Thomas Garrow's last thought. That the moon was splitting in two, and falling out of the sky on top of him.

Then the King inverted the body, as had always been his way with his dead enemies, and drove Thomas head first into the hole, winding him down into the very grave his forefathers had intended to bury Rawhead in forever.

By the time the thunderstorm proper broke over Zeal, the King was a mile away from the Three Acre Field, sheltering in the Nicholson barn. In the village everyone went about their business, rain or no rain. Ignorance was bliss. There was no Cassandra amongst them, nor had "Your Future in the Stars" in that week's "Gazette" even hinted at the sudden deaths to come to a Gemini, three Leos, a Sagittarian and a minor star-system of others in the next few days.

The rain had come with the thunder, fat cool spots of it, which rapidly turned into a downpour of monsoonal ferocity. Only when the gutters became torrents did people begin to take shelter.

On the building site the earth-mover that had been roughly landscaping Ronnie Milton's back garden sat idling in the rain, receiving a second washdown in two days. The driver had taken the downpour as a signal to retire into the hut to talk race-horses and women.

In the doorway of the Post Office three of the villagers watched the drains backing up, and tutted that this always happened when it rained, and in half an hour there'd be a pool of water in the dip at the bottom of the High Street so deep you could sail a boat on it.

And down in the dip itself, in the vestry of St Peter's, Declan Ewan, the Verger, watched the rain pelting down the hill in eager rivulets, and gathering into a little sea outside the vestry gate. Soon be deep enough to drown in, he thought, and then, puzzled by why he imagined drowning, he turned away from the window and went back to the business of folding vestments. A strange excitement was in him today: and he couldn't, wouldn't, didn't want to suppress it. It was nothing to do with the thunderstorm, though he'd always loved them since he was a child. No: there was something else stirring him up, and he was damned if he knew what. It was like being a child again. As if it was Christmas, and any minute Santa, the first Lord he'd ever believed in, would be at the door. The very idea made him want to laugh out loud, but the vestry was too sober a place for laughter, and he stopped himself, letting the smile curl inside him, a secret hope.

* * *

While everyone else took refuge from the rain, Gwen Nicholson was getting thoroughly drenched. She was still in the yard behind the house, coaxing Amelia's pony towards the barn. The thunder had made the stupid beast jittery, and it didn't want to budge. Now Gwen was soaked and angry.

"Will you come on, you brute?" she yelled at it over the noise of the storm. The rain lashed the yard, and pummelled the top of her head. Her hair was flattened. "*Come on! Come on!*"

The pony refused to budge. Its eyes showed crescents of white in its fear. And the more the thunder rolled and crackled around the yard the less it wanted to move. Angrily, Gwen slapped it across the backside, harder than she strictly needed to. It took a couple of steps in response to the blow, dropping steaming turds as it went, and Gwen took the advantage. Once she had it moving she could drag it the rest of the way.

"Warm barn," she promised it; "Come on, it's wet out here, you don't want to stay out here."

The barn-door was slightly ajar. Surely it must look like an inviting prospect, she thought, even to a pea-brained pony. She dragged it to within spitting distance of the barn, and one more slap got it through the door.

As she'd promised the damn thing, the interior of the barn was sweet and dry, though the air smelt metallic with the storm. Gwen tied the pony to the crossbar in its stall and roughly threw a blanket over its glistening hide. She was damned if she was going to swab the creature down, that was Amelia's job. That was the bargain she'd made with her daughter when they'd agreed to buy the pony: that all the grooming and clearing out would be Amelia's responsibility, and to be fair to her, she'd done what she promised, more or less.

The pony was still panicking. It stamped and rolled its eyes like a bad tragedian. There were flecks of foam on its lips. A little apologetically Gwen patted its flank. She'd lost her temper. Time of the month. Now she regretted it. She only hoped Amelia hadn't been at her bedroom window watching.

A gust of wind caught the barn-door and it swung closed. The sound of rain on the yard outside was abruptly muted. It was suddenly dark.

The pony stopped stamping. Gwen stopped stroking its side. Everything stopped: her heart too, it seemed.

Behind her a figure that was almost twice her size rose from beyond the bales of hay. Gwen didn't see the giant, but her innards churned. Damn periods, she thought, rubbing her lower belly in a slow circle. She was normally as regular as clockwork, but this month she'd come on a day early. She should go back to the house, get changed, get clean.

Rawhead stood and looked at the nape of Gwen Nicholson's neck, where a single nip would easily kill. But there was no way he could bring himself to touch this woman; not today. She had the blood-cycle on her, he could taste its tang, and it sickened him. It was taboo, that blood, and he had never taken a woman poisoned by its presence.

Feeling the damp between her legs, Gwen hurried out of the barn without looking behind her, and ran through the downpour back to the house, leaving the fretting pony in the darkness of the barn.

Rawhead heard the woman's feet recede, heard the housedoor slam.

He waited, to be sure she wouldn't come back, then he padded across to the animal, reached down and took hold of it. The pony kicked and complained, but Rawhead had in his time taken animals far bigger and far better armed than this.

He opened his mouth. The gums were suffused with blood as the teeth emerged from them, like claws unsheathed from a cat's paw. There were two rows on each jaw, two dozen needle-sharp points. They gleamed as they closed around the meat of the pony's neck. Thick, fresh blood poured down Rawhead's throat; he gulped it greedily. The hot taste of the world. It made him feel strong and wise. This was only the first of many meals he would take, he'd gorge on anything that took his fancy and nobody would stop him, not this time. And when he was ready he'd throw those pretenders off his throne, he'd cremate them in their houses, he'd slaughter their children and wear their infants' bowels as necklaces. *This place was his*. Just because they'd tamed the wilderness for a while didn't mean they owned the earth. It was his, and nobody would take it from him, not even the holiness. He was wise to that too. They'd never subdue him again.

He sat cross-legged on the floor of the barn, the grey-pink intestines of the pony coiled around him, planning his tactics as best he could. He'd never been a great thinker. Too much appetite: it overwhelmed his reason. He lived in the eternal present of his hunger and his strength, feeling only the crude territorial instinct that would sooner or later blossom into carnage.

The rain didn't let up for over an hour.

Ron Milton was becoming impatient: a flaw in his nature that had given him an ulcer and a top-flight job in Design Consultancy. What Milton could get done for you, couldn't be done quicker. He was the best: and he hated sloth in other people as much as in himself. Take this damn house, for instance. They'd promised it would be finished by mid-July, garden landscaped, driveway laid, everything, and here he was, two months after that date, looking at a house that was still far from habitable. Half the windows without glass, the front door missing, the garden an assault-course, the driveway a mire.

This was to be his castle: his retreat from a world that made him dyspeptic and rich. A haven away from the hassles of the city, where Maggie could grow roses, and the children could breathe clean air. Except that it wasn't ready. Damn it, at this rate he wouldn't be in until next spring. Another winter in London: the thought made his heart sink.

Maggie joined him, sheltering him under her red umbrella.

"Where are the kids?" he asked.

She grimaced. "Back at the hotel, driving Mrs Blatter crazy."

Enid Blatter had borne their cavortings for half a dozen week-ends through the summer. She'd had kids of her own, and she handled Debbie and Ian with aplomb. But there was a limit, even to her fund of mirth and merriment.

"We'd better get back to town."

"No. Please let's stay another day or two. We can go back on Sunday evening. I want us all to go to the Harvest Festival Service on Sunday."

Now it was Ron's turn to grimace.

"Oh hell."

"It's all part of village life, Ronnie. If we're going to live here, we have to become part of the community."

He whined like a little boy when he was in this kind of mood. She knew him so well she could hear his next words before he said them.

"I don't want to."

"Well we've no choice."

"We can go back tonight."

"Ronnie—"

"There's nothing we can do here. The kids are bored, you're miserable . . ."

Maggie had set her features in concrete; she wasn't going to budge an inch. He knew that face as well as she knew his whining.

He studied the puddles that were forming in what might one day be their front garden, unable to imagine grass there, roses there. It all suddenly seemed impossible.

"You go back to town if you like, Ronnie. Take the kids. I'll stay here. Train it home on Sunday night."

Clever, he thought, to give him a get-out that's more unattractive than staying put. Two days in town looking after the kids alone? No thank you.

"Okay. You win. We'll go to the Harvest-bloody-Festival."

"Martyr."

"As long as I don't have to pray."

Amelia Nicholson ran into the kitchen, her round face white, and collapsed in front of her mother. There was greasy vomit on her green plastic mackintosh, and blood on her green plastic wellingtons.

Gwen yelled for Denny. Their little girl was shivering in her faint, her mouth chewing at a word, or words, that wouldn't come.

"What is it?"

Denny was thundering down the stairs.

"For Christ's sake—"

Amelia was vomiting again. Her face was practically blue.

"What's wrong with her?"

"She just came in. You'd better ring for an ambulance."

Denny put his hand on her cheek.

"She's in shock."

"Ambulance, Denny . . ." Gwen was taking off the green mackintosh, and loosening the child's blouse. Slowly, Denny stood up. Through the rain-laced window he could see into the yard: the barn door flapped open and closed in the wind. Somebody was inside; he glimpsed movement.

"For Christ's sake – ambulance!" Gwen said again.

Denny wasn't listening. There was somebody in his barn, on his property, and he had a strict ritual for trespassers.

The barn door opened again, teasing. Yes! Retreating into the dark. Interloper.

He picked up the rifle beside the door, keeping his eyes on the yard as much as he could. Behind him, Gwen had left Amelia on the kitchen floor and was dialling for help. The girl was moaning now: she was going to be okay. Just some filthy trespasser scaring her, that's all. On his land.

He opened the door and stepped into the yard. He was in his shirt-sleeves and the wind was bitingly cold, but the rain had stopped. Underfoot the ground glistened, and drips fell from every eave and portico, a fidgety percussion that accompanied him across the yard.

The barn door swung listlessly ajar again, and this time stayed open. He could see nothing inside. Half wondered if a trick of the light had—

But no. He'd seen someone moving in here. The barn wasn't empty. Something (not the pony) was watching him even now. They'd see the rifle in his hands, and they'd sweat. Let them. Come into his place like that. Let them think he was going to blow their balls off.

He covered the distance in a half a dozen confident strides and stepped into the barn.

The pony's stomach was beneath his shoe, one of its legs to his right, the upper shank gnawed to the bone. Pools of thickening blood reflected the holes in the roof. The mutilation made him want to heave.

"All right," he challenged the shadows. "Come out." He raised his rifle. "You hear me you bastard? Out I said, or I'll blow you to Kingdom Come."

He meant it too.

At the far end of the barn something stirred amongst the bales.

Now I've got the son of a bitch, thought Denny. The trespasser got up, all nine feet of him, and stared at Denny.

"Jee-sus."

And without warning it was coming at him, coming like a locomotive smooth and efficient. He fired into it, and the bullet struck its upper chest, but the wound hardly slowed it.

Nicholson turned and ran. The stones of the yard were slippery beneath his shoes, and he had no turn of speed to outrun it. It was at his back in two beats, and on him in another.

Gwen dropped the phone when she heard the shot. She raced to the window in time to see her sweet Denny eclipsed by a gargantuan form. It howled as it took him, and threw him up into the air like a sack of feathers. She watched helplessly as his body twisted at the apex of its journey before plummetting back down to earth again. It hit the yard with a thud she felt in her every bone, and the giant was at his body like a shot, treading his loving face to muck.

She screamed; trying to silence herself with her hand. Too late. The sound was out and the giant was looking at her, straight at her, its malice piercing the window. Oh God, it had seen her, and now it was coming for her, loping across the yard, a naked engine, and grinning a promise at her as it came.

Gwen snatched Amelia off the floor and hugged her close, pressing the girl's face against her neck. Maybe she wouldn't see: she mustn't see. The sound of its feet slapping on the wet yard got louder. Its shadow filled the kitchen.

"Jesus help me."

It was pressing at the window, its body so wide that it cancelled out the light, its lewd, revolting face smeared on the watery pane. Then it was smashing through, ignoring the glass that bit into its flesh. It smelled child-meat. It wanted child-meat. It would *have* child-meat.

Its teeth were spilling into view, widening that smile into an obscene laugh. Ropes of saliva hung from its jaw as it clawed the air, like a cat after a mouse in a cage, pressing further and further in, each swipe closer to the morsel.

Gwen flung open the door into the hall as the thing lost patience with snatching and began to demolish the window-frame and clamber through. She locked the door after her while crockery smashed and wood splintered on the other side, then she began to load all the hall furniture against it. Tables, chairs, coat-stand, knowing even as she did it, that it would be matchwood in two seconds flat. Amelia was kneeling on the hall floor where Gwen had set her down. Her face was a thankful blank.

All right, that was all she could do. Now, upstairs. She picked up her daughter, who was suddenly air-light, and took the stairs two at a time. Halfway up, the noise in the kitchen below stopped utterly.

She suddenly had a reality crisis. On the landing where she stood all was peace and calm. Dust gathered minutely on the window-sills, flowers wilted; all the infinitesimal domestic procedures went on as though nothing had happened.

"Dreaming it," she said. God, yes: dreaming it.

She sat down on the bed Denny and she had slept in together for eight years, and tried to think straight.

Some vile menstrual nightmare, that's what it was, some rape-fantasy out of all control. She lay Amelia on the pink eiderdown (Denny hated pink, but suffered it for her sake) and stroked the girl's clammy forehead.

"Dreaming it."

Then the room darkened, and she looked up, knowing what she'd see.

It was there, the nightmare, all over the upper windows, its spidery arms spanning the width of the glass, clinging like an acrobat to the frame, its repellent teeth sheathing and unsheathing as it gawped at her terror.

In one swooping movement she snatched Amelia up from the bed and dived towards the door. Behind her, glass shattered, and a gust of cold air swept into the bedroom. It was coming.

She ran across the landing to the top of the stairs but it was after her in a heart's beat, ducking through the bedroom door, its mouth a tunnel. It whooped as it reached to steal the mute parcel in her arms, huge in the confined space of the landing.

She couldn't out-run it, she couldn't out-fight it. Its hands fixed on Amelia with insolent ease, and tugged.

The child screamed as it took her, her fingernails raking four furrows across her mother's face as she left her arms.

Gwen stumbled back, dizzied by the unthinkable sight in front of her, and lost balance at the top of the stairs. As she fell backwards she saw Amelia's tear-stained face, doll-stiff, being fed between those rows of teeth. Then her head hit the bannister, and her neck broke. She bounced down the last six steps a corpse.

The rain-water had drained away a little by early evening, but the artificial lake at the bottom of the dip still flooded the road to a depth of several inches. Serenely, it reflected the sky. Pretty, but inconvenient. Reverend Coot quietly reminded Declan Ewan to report the blocked drains to the County Council. It was the third time of asking, and Declan blushed at the request.

"Sorry, I'll . . ."

"All right. No problem, Declan. But we really must get them cleared."

A vacant look. A beat. A thought.

"Autumn fall always clogs them again, of course."

Coot made a roughly cyclical gesture, intending a sort of observation about how it really wouldn't make that much difference when or if the Council cleared the drains, then the thought disappeared. There were more pressing issues. For one, the Sunday Sermon. For a second, the reason why he couldn't make much sense of sermon writing this evening. There was an unease in the air today, that made every reassuring word he committed to paper curdle as he wrote it. Coot went to the window, back to Declan, and scratched his palms. They itched: maybe an attack of eczema again. If he could only speak; find some words to shape his distress. Never, in his forty-five years, had he felt so incapable of communication; and never in those years had it been so vital that he talk.

"Shall I go now?" Declan asked.

Coot shook his head.

"A moment longer. If you would."

He turned to the Verger. Declan Ewan was twenty-nine, though he had the face of a much older man. Bland, pale features: his hair receding prematurely.

What will this egg-face make of my revelation? thought Coot. He'll probably laugh. That's why I can't find the words, because I don't want to. I'm afraid of looking stupid. Here I am, a man of the cloth, dedicated to the Christian Mysteries. For the first time in forty odd years I've had a real glimpse of something, a vision maybe, and I'm scared of being laughed at. Stupid man, Coot, stupid, stupid man.

He took off his glasses. Declan's empty features became a blur. Now at least he didn't have to look at the smirking.

"Declan, this morning I had what I can only describe as a . . . as a . . . visitation."

Declan said nothing, nor did the blur move.

"I don't quite know how to say this . . . our vocabulary's impoverished when it comes to these sorts of things . . . but frankly I've never had such a direct, such an unequivocal, manifestation of—"

Coot stopped. Did he mean God?

"God," he said, not sure that he did.

Declan said nothing for a moment. Coot risked returning his glasses to their place. The egg hadn't cracked.

"Can you say what it was like?" Declan asked, his equilibrium absolutely unspoiled.

Coot shook his head; he'd been trying to find the words all day, but the phrases all seemed so predictable.

"What was it like?" Declan insisted.

Why didn't he understand that there were no words? I must try, thought Coot, I *must*.

"I was at the Altar after Morning Prayer . . ." he began, "and I felt something going through me. Like electricity almost. It made my hair stand on end. Literally on end."

Coot's hand was running through his short-cropped hair as he remembered the sensation. The hair standing bolt upright, like a field of grey-ginger corn. And that buzzing at the temples, in his lungs, at his groin. It had actually given him a hard-on; not that he was going to be able to tell Declan that. But he'd stood there at the Altar with an erection so powerful it was like discovering the joy of lust all over again.

"I won't claim . . . I *can't* claim it was our Lord God—"

(Though he wanted to believe that; that his God was the Lord of the Hard-on.) "—I can't even claim it was Christian. But something happened today. I felt it."

Declan's face was still impenetrable. Coot watched it for several seconds, impatient for its disdain.

"Well?" he demanded.

"Well what?"

"Nothing to say?"

The egg frowned for a moment, a furrow in its shell. Then it said: "God help us," almost in a whisper.

"What?"

"I felt it too. Not quite as you describe: not quite an electric shock. But something."

"Why God help us, Declan? Are you afraid of something?"

He made no reply.

"If you know something about these experiences that I don't . . . please tell me. I want to know, to understand. God, I *have* to understand."

Declan pursed his lips. "Well . . ." his eyes became more indecipherable than ever; and for the first time Coot caught a glimpse of a ghost behind Declan's eyes. Was it despair, perhaps?

"There's a lot of history to this place you know," he said "a history of things . . . on this site."

Coot knew Declan had been delving into Zeal's history. Harmless enough pastime: the past was the past.

"There's been a settlement here for centuries, stretches back well before Roman occupation. No one knows how long. There's probably always been a temple on this site."

"Nothing odd about that." Coot offered up a smile, inviting Declan to reassure him. A part of him wanted to be told everything was well with his world: even if it was a lie.

Declan's face darkened. He had no reassurance to give. "And there was a forest here. Huge. The Wild Woods." Was it still despair behind the eyes? Or was it nostalgia? "Not some tame little orchard. A forest you could lose a city in; full of beasts . . ."

"Wolves, you mean? Bears?"

Declan shook his head.

"There were things that owned this land. Before Christ. Before civilisation. Most of them didn't survive the destruction of their natural habitat: too primitive I suppose. But strong. Not like us; not human. Something else altogether."

"So what?"

"One of them survived as late as the fourteen hundreds. There's a carving of it being buried. It's on the Altar."

"On the Altar?"

"Underneath the cloth. I found it a while ago: never thought much of it. Till today. Today I . . . tried to touch it."

He produced his fist, and unclenched it. The flesh of his palm was blistered. Pus ran from the broken skin.

"It doesn't hurt," he said. "In fact it's quite numb. Serves me right, really. I should have known."

Coot's first thought was that the man was lying. His second was that there was some logical explanation. His third was his father's dictum: "Logic is the last refuge of a coward."

Declan was speaking again. This time he was seeping excitement.

"They called it Rawhead."

"What?"

"The beast they buried. It's in the history books. Rawhead it was called, because its head was huge, and the colour of the moon, and raw, like meat."

Declan couldn't stop himself now. He was beginning to smile.

"It ate children," he said, and beamed like a baby about to receive its mother's tit.

It wasn't until early on the Saturday morning that the atrocity at the Nicholson Farm was discovered. Mick Glossop had been driving up to London, and he'd taken the road that ran beside the farm, ("Don't know why. Don't usually. Funny really.") and Nicholson's Friesian herd was kicking up a row at the gate, their udders distended. They'd clearly not been milked in twenty-four hours. Glossop had stopped his jeep on the road and gone into the yard.

The body of Denny Nicholson was already crawling with flies, though the sun had barely been up an hour. Inside the house the only remains of Amelia Nicholson were shreds of a dress and a casually discarded foot. Gwen Nicholson's unmutilated body lay at the bottom of the stairs. There was no sign of a wound or any sexual interference with the corpse.

By nine-thirty Zeal was swarming with police, and the shock of the incident registered on every face in the street. Though there were conflicting reports as to the state of the bodies there was no doubt of the brutality of the murders. Especially the child, dismembered presumably. Her body taken away by her killer for God knows what purpose.

The Murder Squad set up a Unit at "The Tall Man", while house to house interviews were conducted throughout the village. Nothing came immediately to light. No strangers seen in the locality; no more suspicious behaviour from anyone than was normal for a poacher or a bent building merchant. It was Enid Blatter, she of the ample bust and the motherly manner, who mentioned that she hadn't seen Thom Garrow for over twenty-four hours.

They found him where his killer had left him, the worse for a few hours of picking. Worms at his head and gulls at his legs. The flesh of his shins, where his trousers had slid out of his boots, was pecked to the bone. When he was dug up families of refugee lice scurried from his ears.

The atmosphere in the hotel that night was subdued. In the bar Detective Sergeant Gissing, down from London to head the investigation, had found a willing ear in Ron Milton. He was glad to be conversing with a fellow Londoner, and Milton kept them both in Scotch and water for the best part of three hours.

"Twenty years in the force," Gissing kept repeating, "and I've never seen anything like it."

Which wasn't strictly true. There'd been that whore (or selected highlights thereof) he'd found in a suitcase at Euston's left luggage department, a good decade ago. And the addict who'd taken it upon himself to hypnotise a polar bear at London Zoo: he'd been a sight for sore eyes when they dredged him out of the pool. He'd seen a good deal, had Stanley Gissing—

"But this . . . never seen anything like it," he insisted. "Fair made me want to puke."

Ron wasn't quite sure why he listened to Gissing; it was just something to while the night away. Ron, who'd been a radical in his younger days, had never liked policemen much, and there was some quirky satisfaction to be had from getting this self-satisfied prat pissed out of his tiny skull.

"He's a fucking lunatic," Gissing said "you can take my word for it. We'll have him easy. A man like that isn't in control, you see. Doesn't bother to cover his tracks, doesn't even care if he lives or dies. God knows, any man who can tear a seven-year-old girl to shreds like that, he's on the verge of going bang. Seen 'em."

"Yes?"

"Oh yes. Seen 'em weep like children, blood all over 'em like they was just out of the abattoir, and tears on their faces. Pathetic."

"So, you'll have him."

"Like that," said Gissing, and snapped his fingers. He got to his feet, a little unsteadily, "Sure as God made little apples, we'll have him." He glanced at his watch and then at the empty glass.

Ron made no further offers of refills.

"Well," said Gissing," I must be getting back to town. Put in my report."

He swayed to the door and left Milton to the bill.

Rawhead watched Gissing's car crawl out of the village and along the north road, the headlights making very little impression on the night. The noise of the engine made Rawhead nervous though, as it over-revved up the hill past the Nicholson Farm. It roared and coughed like no beast he had encountered before, and somehow the homo sapiens had control of it. If the Kingdom was to be taken back from the usurpers, sooner or later he would have to best one of these beasts. Rawhead swallowed his fear and prepared for the confrontation.

The moon grew teeth.

In the back of the car Stanley was near as damnit asleep, dreaming of little girls. In his dreams these charming nymphettes were climbing a ladder on their way to bed, and he was on duty beside the ladder watching them climb, catching glimpses of their slightly soiled knickers as they disappeared into the sky. It was a familiar dream, one that he would never have admitted to, not even drunk. Not that he was ashamed exactly; he knew for a fact many of his colleagues entertained peccadilloes every bit as offbeat as, and some a good deal less savoury than, his. But he was possessive of it: it was his particular dream, and he wasn't about to share it with anyone.

In the driving seat the young officer who had been chaffeuring Gissing around for the best part of six months was waiting for the old man to fall well and truly asleep. Then and only then could he risk turning the radio on to catch up with the cricket scores. Australia were well down in the Test: a late rally seemed unlikely. Ah, now there was a career, he thought as he drove. Beats this routine into a cocked hat.

Both lost in their reveries, driver and passenger, neither caught sight of Rawhead. He was stalking the car now, his giant's stride easily keeping pace with it as it navigated the winding, unlit road.

All at once his anger flared, and roaring, he left the field for the tarmac.

The driver swerved to avoid the immense form that skipped into the burning headlights, its mouth issuing a howl like a pack of rabid dogs.

The car skidded on the wet ground, its left wing grazing the bushes that ran along the side of the road, a tangle of branches lashing the windscreen as it careered on its way. On the back seat Gissing fell off the ladder he was climbing, just as the car came to the end of its hedgerow tour and met an iron gate. Gissing was flung against the front seat, winded but uninjured. The impact took the driver over the wheel and through the window in two short seconds. His feet, now in Gissing's face, twitched.

From the road Rawhead watched the death of the metal box. Its tortured voice, the howl of its wrenched flank, the shattering of its face, frightened him. But it was dead.

He waited a few cautious moments before advancing up the road to sniff the crumpled body. There was an aromatic smell in the air, which pricked his sinuses, and the cause of it, the blood of the box, was dribbling out of of its broken torso, and running away down the road. Certain now that it must be finished, he approached.

There was someone alive in the box. None of the sweet child-flesh he savoured so much, just tough male-meat. It was a comical face that peered at him. Round, wild eyes. Its silly mouth opened and closed like a fish's. He kicked the box to make it open, and when that didn't work he wrenched off the doors. Then he reached and drew the whimpering male out of his refuge. Was this one of the species that had subdued him? This fearful mite, with its jelly-lips? He laughed at its pleas, then turned Gissing on his head, and held him upside down by one foot. He waited until the cries died down, then reached between the twitching legs and found the mite's manhood. Not large. Quite shrunk, in fact, by fear. Gissing was blathering all kinds of stuff: none of it made any sense. The only sound Rawhead understood from the mouth of the man was this sound he was hearing now, this high-pitched shriek that always attended a gelding. Once finished, he dropped Gissing beside the car.

A fire had begun in the smashed engine, he could smell it. He was not so much a beast that he feared fire. Respected it yes: but not feared. Fire was a tool, he'd used it many times: to burn out enemies, to cremate them in their beds.

Now he stepped back from the car as the flame found the petrol and fire erupted into the air. Heat balled towards him, and he smelt the hair on the front of his body crisp, but he was too entranced by the spectacle not to look. The fire followed the blood of the beast, consuming Gissing, and licking along the rivers of petrol like an eager dog after a trail of piss. Rawhead watched, and learned a new and lethal lesson.

In the chaos of his study Coot was unsuccessfully fighting off sleep. He'd spent a good deal of the evening at the Altar, some of it with Declan. Tonight there'd be no praying, just sketching. Now he had a copy of the Altar carving on his desk in front of him, and he'd spent an hour just staring at it. The exercise had been fruitless. Either the carving was too ambiguous, or his imagination lacked breadth. Whichever, he could make very little sense of the image. It pictured a burial certainly, but that was about all he was able to work out. Maybe the body was a little bigger than that of the mourners, but nothing exceptional. He thought of Zeal's pub, "The Tall Man", and smiled. It might well have pleased some Mediaeval wit to picture the burial of a brewer under the Altar cloth.

In the hall, the sick clock struck twelve-fifteen, which meant it was almost one. Coot got up from his desk, stretched, and switched off the lamp. He was surprised by the brilliance of the moonlight streaming through the crack in the curtain. It was a full, harvest moon, and the light, though cold, was luxuriant.

He put the guard in front of the fire, and stepped into the

darkened hallway, closing the door behind him. The clock ticked loudly. Somewhere over towards Goudhurst, he heard the sound of an ambulance siren.

What's happening? he wondered, and opened the front door to see what he could see. There were car headlights on the hill, and the distant throb of blue police lights, more rhythmical than the ticking at his back. Accident on the north road. Early for ice, and surely not cold enough. He watched the lights, set on the hill like jewels on the back of a whale, winking away. It was quite chilly, come to think of it. No weather to be standing in the—

He frowned; something caught his eye, a movement in the far corner of the churchyard, underneath the trees. The moonlight etched the scene in monochrome. Black yews, grey stones, a white chrysanthemum strewing its petals on a grave. And black in the shadow of the yews, but outlined clearly against the slab of a marble tomb beyond, a giant.

Coot stepped out of the house in slippered feet.

The giant was not alone. Somebody was kneeling in front of it, a smaller, more human shape, its face raised and clear in the light. It was Declan. Even from a distance it was clear that he was smiling up at his master.

Coot wanted to get closer; a better look at the nightmare. As he took his third step his foot crunched on a piece of gravel.

The giant seemed to shift in the shadows. Was it turning to look at him? Coot chewed on his heart. No, let it be deaf; please God, let it not see me, make me invisible.

The prayer was apparently answered. The giant made no sign of having seen his approach. Taking courage Coot advanced across the pavement of gravestones, dodging from tomb to tomb for cover, barely daring to breathe. He was within a few feet of the tableau now and he could see the way the creature's head was bowed towards Declan; he could hear the sound like sandpaper on stone it was making at the back of its throat. But there was more to the scene.

Declan's vestments were torn and dirtied, his thin chest bare. Moonlight caught his sternum, his ribs. His state, and his position, were unequivocal. This was adoration – pure and simple. Then Coot heard the splashing; he stepped closer and saw that the giant was directing a glistening rope of its urine onto Declan's upturned face. It splashed into his slackly opened mouth, it ran over his torso. The gleam of joy didn't leave Declan's eyes for a moment as he received this baptism, indeed he turned his head from side to side in his eagerness to be totally defiled.

The smell of the creature's discharge wafted across to Coot. It was acidic, vile. How could Declan bear to have a drop of it on him, much less bathe in it? Coot wanted to cry out, stop the depravity, but even in the shadow of the yew the shape of the beast was terrifying. It was too tall and too broad to be human.

This was surely the Beast of the Wild Woods Declan had been trying to describe; this was the child-devourer. Had Declan guessed, when he eulogised about this monster, what power it would have over his imagination? Had he known all along that if the beast were to come sniffing for him he'd kneel in front of it, call it Lord (before Christ, before Civilisation, he'd said), let it discharge its bladder on to him, and smile?

Yes. Oh yes.

And so let him have his moment. Don't risk your neck for him, Coot thought, he's where he wants to be. Very slowly he backed off towards the Vestry, his eyes still fixed on the degradation in front of him. The baptism dribbled to a halt, but Declan's hands, cupped in front of him, still held a quantity of fluid. He put the heels of his hands to his mouth, and drank.

Coot gagged, unable to prevent himself. For an instant he closed his eyes to shut out the sight, and opened them again to see that the shadowy head had turned towards him and was looking at him with eyes that burned in the blackness.

"Christ Almighty."

It saw him. For certain this time, it saw him. It roared, and its head changed shape in the shadow, its mouth opened so horribly wide.

"Sweet Jesus."

Already it was charging towards him, antelope-lithe, leaving its acolyte slumped beneath the tree. Coot turned and ran, ran as he hadn't in many a long year, hurdling the graves as he fled. It was just a few yards: the door, some kind of safety. Not for long maybe, but time to think, to find a weapon. Run, you old bastard. Christ the race, Christ the prize. Four yards.

Run.

The door was open.

Almost there; a yard to go—

He crossed the threshold and swung round to slam the door on his pursuer. But no! Rawhead had shot his hand through the door, a hand three times the size of a human hand. It was snatching at the empty air, trying to find Coot, the roars relentless.

Coot threw his full weight against the oak door. The door stile, edged with iron, bit into Rawhead's forearm. The roar became a howl: venom and agony mingled in a din that was heard from one end of Zeal to the other.

It stained the night up as far as the north road, where the remains of Gissing and his driver were being scraped up and parcelled in plastic. It echoed round the icy walls of the Chapel of Rest where Denny and Gwen Nicholson were already beginning to degenerate. It was heard too in the bedrooms of Zeal, where living couples lay side by side, maybe an arm numbed under the other's body; where the old lay awake working out the geography of the ceiling; where children dreamt of the womb, and babies mourned it. It was heard again and again and again as Rawhead raged at the door.

The howl made Coot's head swim. His mouth babbled prayers, but the much needed support from on high showed no sign of coming. He felt his strength ebbing away. The giant was steadily gaining access, pressing the door open inch by inch. Coot's feet slid on the too-well-polished floor, his muscles were fluttering as they faltered. This was a contest he had no chance of winning, not if he tried to match his strength to that of the beast, sinew for sinew. If he was to see tomorrow morning, he needed some strategy.

Coot pressed harder against the wood, his eyes darting around the hallway looking for a weapon. It mustn't get in: it mustn't have mastery over him. A bitter smell was in his nostrils. For a moment he saw himself naked and kneeling in front of the giant, with its piss beating on his skull. Hard on the heels of that picture, came another flurry of depravities. It was all he could do not to let it in, let the obscenities get a permanent hold. Its mind was working its way into his, a thick wedge of filth pressing its way through his memories, encouraging buried thoughts to the surface. Wouldn't it ask for worship, just like any God? And wouldn't its demands be plain, and real? Not ambiguous, like those of the Lord he'd served up 'til now. That was a fine thought: to give himself up to this certainty that beat on the other side of the door, and lie open in front of it, and let it ravage him.

Rawhead. Its name was a pulse in his ear – Raw. Head.

In desperation, knowing his fragile mental defences were within an ace of collapsing, his eyes alighted on the clothes stand to the left of the door.

Raw. Head. Raw. Head. The name was an imperative. Raw. Head. Raw. Head. It evoked a skinned head, its defences peeled back, a thing close to bursting, no telling if it was pain or pleasure. But easy to find out—

It almost had possession of him, he knew it: it was now or never. He took one arm from the door and stretched towards the rack for a walking-stick. There was one amongst them he wanted in particular. He called it his cross-country stick, a yard and a half of stripped ash, well used and resilient. His fingers coaxed it towards him.

Rawhead had taken advantage of the lack of force behind the door; its leathery arm was working its way in, indifferent to the way the door jamb scored the skin. The hand, its fingers strong as steel, had caught the folds of Coot's jacket.

Coot raised the ash stick and brought it down on Rawhead's elbow, where the bone was vulnerably close to the surface. The weapon splintered on impact, but it did its job. On the other side of the door the howl began again, and Rawhead's arm was rapidly withdrawn. As the fingers slid out Coot slammed the door and bolted it. There was a short hiatus, seconds only, before the attack began again, this time a two-fisted beating on the door. The hinges began to buckle; the wood groaned. It would be a short time, a very short time, before it gained access. It was strong; and now it was furious too.

Coot crossed the hall and picked up the phone. Police, he said, and began to dial. How long before it put two and two together, gave up on the door, and moved to the windows? They were leaded, but that wouldn't keep it out for long. He had minutes at the most, probably seconds, depending on its brain power.

His mind, loosed from Rawhead's grasp, was a chorus of fragmented prayers and demands. If I die, he found himself thinking, will I be rewarded in Heaven for dying more brutally than any country vicar might reasonably expect? Is there compensation in paradise for being disembowelled in the front hall of your own Vestry?

There was only one officer left on duty at the Police Station: the rest were up on the north road, clearing up after Gissing's party. The poor man could make very little sense of Reverend Coot's pleas, but there was no mistaking the sound of splintering wood that accompanied the babbles, nor the howling in the background.

The officer put the phone down and radioed for help. The patrol on the north road took twenty, maybe twenty-five seconds to answer. In that time Rawhead had smashed the central panel of the Vestry door, and was now demolishing the rest. Not that the patrol knew that. After the sights they'd faced up there, the chauffeur's charred body, Gissing's missing manhood, they had become insolent with experience, like hour-old war veterans. It took the officer at the Station a good minute to convince them of the urgency in Coot's voice. In that time Rawhead had gained access.

In the hotel Ron Milton watched the parade of lights blinking on the hill, heard the sirens, and Rawhead's howls, and was besieged by doubts. Was this really the quiet country village he had intended to settle himself and his family in? He looked down at Maggie, who had been woken by the noise but was now asleep again, her bottle of sleeping tablets almost empty on the bedside cabinet. He felt, though she would have laughed at him for it, protective towards her: he wanted to be her hero. She was the one who took the self-defence night classes however, while he grew overweight on expense account lunches. It made him inexplicably sad to watch her sleep, knowing he had so little power over life and death.

Rawhead stood in the hall of the Vestry in a confetti of shattered wood. His torso was pin-pricked with splinters, and dozens of tiny wounds bled down his heaving bulk. His sour sweat permeated the hall like incense.

He sniffed the air for the man, but he was nowhere near. Rawhead bared his teeth in frustration, expelling a thin whistle of air from the back of his throat, and loped down the hall towards the study. There was warmth there, his nerves could feel it at twenty yards, and there was comfort too. He overturned the desk and shattered two of the chairs, partly to make more room for himself, mostly out of sheer destructiveness, then threw away the fire guard and sat down. Warmth surrounded him: healing, living warmth. He luxuriated in the sensation as it embraced his face, his lean belly, his limbs. He felt it heat his blood too, and so stir memories of other fires, fires he'd set in fields of burgeoning wheat.

And he recalled another fire, the memory of which his mind tried to dodge and duck, but he couldn't avoid thinking about it: the humiliation of that night would be with him forever. They'd picked their season so carefully: high summer, and no rain in two months. The undergrowth of the Wild Woods was tinder dry, even the living tree caught the flame easily. He had been flushed out of his fortress with streaming eyes, confused and fearful, to be met with spikes and nets on every side, and that . . . *thing* they had, that sight that could subdue him.

Of course they weren't courageous enough to kill him; they were too superstitious for that. Besides, didn't they recognise his authority, even as they wounded him, their terror a homage to it? So they buried him alive: and that was worse than death. Wasn't that the very worst? Because he could live an age, ages, and never die, not even locked in the earth. Just left to wait a hundred years, and suffer, and another hundred and another, while the generations walked the ground above his head and lived and died and forgot him. Perhaps the women didn't forget him: he could smell them even through the earth, when they came close to his grave, and though they might not have known it they felt anxious, they persuaded their men to abandon the place altogether, so he was left absolutely alone, with not even a gleaner for company. Loneliness was their revenge on him, he thought, for the times he and his brothers had taken women into the woods, spread them out, spiked and loosed them again, bleeding but fertile. They would die having the children of those rapes; no woman's anatomy could survive the thrashing of a hybrid, its teeth, its anguish. That was the only revenge he and his brothers ever had on the big-bellied sex.

Rawhead stroked himself and looked up at the gilded reproduction of "The Light of the World" that hung above Coot's mantelpiece. The image woke no tremors of fear or remorse in him: it was a picture of a sexless martyr, doe-eyed and woe-begone. No challenge there. The true power, the only power that could defeat him, was apparently gone: lost beyond recall, its place usurped by a virgin shepherd. He ejaculated, silently, his thin semen hissing on the hearth. The world was his to rule unchallenged. He would have warmth, and food in abundance. Babies even. Yes, baby-meat, that was the best. Just dropped mites, still blind from the womb.

He stretched, sighing in anticipation of that delicacy, his brain awash with atrocities.

From his refuge in the crypt Coot heard the police cars squealing to a halt outside the Vestry, then the sound of feet on the gravel path. He judged there to be at least half a dozen. It would be enough, surely.

Cautiously he moved through the darkness towards the stairs.

Something touched him: he almost yelled, biting his tongue a moment before the cry escaped.

"Don't go now," a voice said from behind him. It was Declan, and he was speaking altogether too loudly for comfort. The thing was above them, somewhere, it would hear them if he wasn't careful. Oh God, it mustn't hear.

"It's up above us," said Coot in a whisper.

"I know."

The voice seemed to come from his bowels not from his throat; it was bubbled through filth.

"Let's have him come down here shall we? He wants you, you know. He wants me to—"

"What's happened to you?"

Declan's face was just visible in the dark. It grinned; lunatic.

"I think he might want to baptise you too. How'd you like that? Like that would you? He pissed on me: you see him? And that wasn't all. Oh no, he wants more than that. He wants everything. Hear me? Everything."

Declan grabbed hold of Coot, a bear-hug that stank of the creature's urine.

"Come with me?" he leered in Coot's face.

"I put my trust in God."

Declan laughed. Not a hollow laugh; there was genuine compassion in it for this lost soul.

"He *is* God," he said. "He was here before this fucking shit-house was built, you know that."

"So were dogs."

"Uh?"

"Doesn't mean I'd let them cock their legs on me."

"Clever old fucker, aren't you?" said Declan, the smile inverted. "He'll show you. You'll change."

"No, Declan. Let go of me—"

The embrace was too strong.

"Come on up the stairs, fuck-face. Mustn't keep God waiting."

He pulled Coot up the stairs, arms still locked round him. Words, all logical argument, eluded Coot: was there nothing he could say to make the man see his degradation? They made an ungainly entrance into the Church, and Coot automatically looked towards the altar, hoping for some reassurance, but he got none. The altar had been desecrated. The cloths had been torn and smeared with excrement, the cross and candlesticks were in the middle of a fire of prayer-books that burned healthily on the altar steps. Smuts floated around the Church, the air was grimy with smoke.

"You did this?"

Declan grunted.

"He wants me to destroy it all. Take it apart stone by stone if I have to."

"He wouldn't dare."

"Oh he'd dare. He's not scared of Jesus, he's not scared of . . ."

The certainty lapsed for a telling instant, and Coot leapt on the hesitation.

"There's something here he *is* scared of, though, isn't there, or he'd have come in here himself, done it all himself . . ."

Declan wasn't looking at Coot. His eyes had glazed.

"What is it, Declan? What is it he doesn't like? You can tell me—"

Declan spat in Coot's face, a wad of thick phlegm that hung on his cheek like a slug.

"None of your business."

"In the name of Christ, Declan, look at what he's done to you."

"I know my master when I see him—"

Declan was shaking.

"—and so will you."

He turned Coot round to face the south door. It was open, and the creature was there on the threshold, stooping gracefully to duck under the porch. For the first time Coot saw Rawhead in a good light, and the terrors began in earnest. He had avoided thinking too much of its size, its stare, its origins. Now, as it came towards him with slow, even stately steps, his heart conceded its mastery. It was no mere beast, despite its mane, and its awesome array of teeth; its eyes lanced him through and through, gleaming with a depth of contempt no animal could ever muster. Its mouth opened wider and wider, the teeth gliding from the gums, two, three inches long, and still the mouth was gaping wider. When there was nowhere to run, Declan let Coot go. Not that Coot could have moved anyway: the stare was too insistent. Rawhead reached out and picked Coot up. The world turned on its head—

There were seven officers, not six as Coot had guessed. Three of them were armed, their weapons brought down from London on the order of Detective Sergeant Gissing. The late, soon to be decorated posthumously, Detective Sergeant Gissing. They were led, these seven good men and true, by Sergeant Ivanhoe Baker. Ivanhoe was not an heroic man, either by inclination or education. His voice, which he had prayed would give the appropriate orders when the time came without betraying him, came out as a strangled yelp as Rawhead appeared from the interior of the Church.

"I can see it!" he said. Everybody could: it was nine feet tall, covered in blood, and it looked like Hell on legs. Nobody needed it pointed out. The guns were raised without Ivanhoe's instruction: and the unarmed men, suddenly feeling naked, kissed their truncheons and prayed. One of them ran.

"Hold your ground!" Ivanhoe shrieked; if those sons of bitches turned tail he'd be left on his own. They hadn't issued him with a gun, just authority, and that was not much comfort.

Rawhead was still holding Coot up, at arm's length, by the neck. The Reverend's legs dangled a foot above the ground, his head lolled back, his eyes were closed. The monster displayed the body for his enemies, proof of power.

"Shall we . . . please . . . can we . . . shoot the bastard?" One of the gunmen inquired.

Ivanhoe swallowed before answering. "We'll hit the vicar."

"He's dead already." said the gunman.

"We don't know that."

"He must be dead. Look at him—"

Rawhead was shaking Coot like an eiderdown, and his stuffing was falling out, much to Ivanhoe's intense disgust. Then, almost lazily, Rawhead flung Coot at the police. The body hit the gravel a little way from the gate and lay still. Ivanhoe found his voice—

"Shoot!"

The gunmen needed no encouragement; their fingers were depressing the triggers before the syllable was out of his mouth.

Rawhead was hit by three, four, five bullets in quick succession, most of them in the chest. They stung him and he put up an arm to protect his face, covering his balls with the other hand. This was a pain he hadn't anticipated. The wound he'd received from Nicholson's rifle had been forgotten in the bliss of the blood-letting that came soon after, but these barbs hurt him, and they kept coming. He felt a twinge of fear. His instinct was to fly in the face of these popping, flashing rods, but the pain was too much. Instead, he turned and made his retreat, leaping over the tombs as he fled towards the safety of the hills. There were copses he knew, burrows and caves, where he could hide and find time to think this new problem through. But first he had to elude them.

They were after him quickly, flushed with the ease of their victory, leaving Ivanhoe to find a vase on one of the graves, empty it of chrysanthemums, and be sick.

Out of the dip there were no lights along the road, and Rawhead began to feel safer. He could melt into the darkness, into the earth, he'd done it a thousand times. He cut across a field. The barley was still unharvested, and heavy with its grain. He trampled it as he ran, grinding seed and stalk. At his back his pursuers were already losing the chase. The car they'd piled into had stopped in the road, he could see its lights, one blue, two white, way behind him. The enemy was shouting a confusion of orders, words Rawhead didn't understand. No matter; he knew men. They were easily frightened. They would not look far for him tonight; they'd use the dark as an excuse to call off the search, telling themselves that his wounds were probably fatal anyhow. Trusting children that they were.

He climbed to the top of the hill and looked down into the valley. Below the snake of the road, its eyes the headlights of the enemy's car, the village was a wheel of warm light, with flashing blues and reds at its hub. Beyond, in every direction, the impenetrable black of the hills, over which the stars hung in loops and clusters. By day this would seem a counterpane valley, toytown small. By night it was fathomless, more his than theirs.

His enemies were already returning to their hovels, as he'd known they would. The chase was over for the night.

He lay down on the earth and watched a meteor burn up as it fell to the south-west. It was a brief, bright streak, which edge-lit a cloud, then went out. Morning was many long, healing hours in the future. He would soon be strong again: and then, then – he'd burn them all away.

Coot was not dead: but so close to death it scarcely made any difference. Eighty per cent of the bones in his body were fractured or broken: his face and neck were a maze of lacerations: one of his hands was crushed almost beyond recognition. He would certainly die. It was purely a matter of time and inclination.

In the village those who had glimpsed so much as a fragment of the events in the dip were already elaborating on their stories: and the evidence of the naked eye lent credence to the most fantastic inventions. The chaos in the churchyard, the smashed door of the Vestry: the cordoned-off car on the north road. Whatever had happened that Saturday night it was going to take a long time to forget.

There was no harvest festival service, which came as no surprise to anyone.

Maggie was insistent: "I want us all to go back to London."

"A day ago you wanted us to stay here. Get to be part of the community."

"That was on Friday, before all this . . . this . . . There's a maniac loose, Ron."

"If we go now, we won't come back."

"What are you talking about; of course we'll come back."

"If we leave once the place is threatened, we give up on it altogether."

"That's ridiculous."

"You were the one who was so keen on us being visible, being seen to join in village life. Well, we'll have to join in the deaths too. And I'm going to stay – see it through. You can go back to London. Take the kids."

"No."

He sighed, heavily.

"I want to see him caught: whoever he is. I want to know it's all been cleared up, see it with my own eyes. That's the only way we'll ever feel safe here."

Reluctantly, she nodded.

"At least let's get out of the hotel for a while. Mrs Blatter's going loopy. Can't we go for a drive? Get some air—"

"Yes, why not?"

It was a balmy September day: the countryside, always willing to spring a surprise, was gleaming with life. Late flowers shone in the roadside hedges, birds dipped over the road as they drove. The sky was azure, the clouds a fantasia in cream. A few miles outside the village all the horrors of the previous night began to evaporate and the sheer exuberance of the day began to raise the family's spirits. With every mile they drove out of Zeal Ron's fears diminished. Soon, he was singing.

On the back seat Debbie was being difficult. One moment "I'm hot daddy", the next: "I want an orange juice daddy"; the next: "I have to pee".

Ron stopped the car on an empty stretch of road, and played the indulgent father. The kids had been through a lot; today they could be spoiled.

"All right, darling, you can have a pee here, then we'll go and find an ice-cream for you."

"Where's the la-la?" she said. Damn stupid phrase; mother-in-law's euphemism.

Maggie chipped in. She was better with Debbie in these moods than Ron. "You can go behind the hedge," she said.

Debbie looked horrified. Ron exchanged a half-smile with Ian. The boy had a put-upon look on his face. Grimacing, he went back to his dog-eared comic.

"Hurry up, can't you?" he muttered. "Then we can go somewhere proper."

Somewhere proper, thought Ron. He means a town. He's a city kid: its going to take a while to convince him that a hill with a view *is* somewhere proper. Debbie was still being difficult.

"I can't go here, mummy—"

"Why not?"

"Somebody might see me."

"Nobody's going to see you, darling," Ron reassured her. "Now do as your mummy says." He turned to Maggie, "Go with her, love."

Maggie wasn't budging.

"She's okay."

"She can't climb over the gate on her own."

"Well you go, then."

Ron was determined not to argue; he forced a smile. "Come on," he said.

Debbie got out of the car and Ron helped her over the iron gate into the field beyond. It was already harvested. It smelt . . . earthy.

"Don't look," she admonished him, wide-eyed, "you ***mustn't*** look."

She was already a manipulator, at the ripe old age of nine. She could play him better than the piano she was taking lessons on. He knew it, and so did she. He smiled at her and closed his eyes.

"All right. See? I've got my eyes closed. Now hurry up, Debbie. Please."

"Promise you won't peek."

"I won't peek." My God, he thought, she's certainly making a production number out of this. "Hurry up."

He glanced back towards the car. Ian was sitting in the back, still reading, engrossed in some cheap heroics, his face set as he stared into the adventure. The boy was so serious: the occasional half-smile was all Ron could ever win from him. It wasn't a put-on, it wasn't a fake air of mystery. He seemed content to leave all the performing to his sister.

Behind the hedge Debbie pulled down her Sunday knickers and squatted, but after all the fuss her pee wouldn't come. She concentrated but that just made it worse.

Ron looked up the field towards the horizon. There were gulls up there, squabbling over a tit-bit. He watched them awhile, impatience growing.

"Come on, love," he said.

He looked back at the car, and Ian was watching him now, his face slack with boredom; or something like it. Was there something else there: a deep resignation? Ron thought. The boy looked back to his comic book "Utopia" without acknowledging his father's gaze.

Then Debbie screamed: an ear-piercing shriek.

"Christ!" Ron was clambering over the gate in an instant, and Maggie wasn't far behind him.

"Debbie!"

Ron found her standing against the hedge, staring at the ground, blubbering, face red. "What's wrong, for God's sake?"

She was yabbering incoherently. Ron followed her eye.

"What's happened?" Maggie was having difficulty getting over the gate.

"It's all right . . . it's all right."

There was a dead mole almost buried in the tangle at the edge of the field, its eyes pecked out, its rotting hide crawling with flies.

"Oh God, Ron." Maggie looked at him accusingly, as though he'd put the damn thing there with malice aforethought.

"It's all right, sweetheart," she said, elbowing past her husband and wrapping Debbie up in her arms.

Her sobs quietened a bit. City kids, thought Ron. They're going to have to get used to that sort of thing if they're going to live in the country. No road-sweepers here to brush up the run-over cats every morning. Maggie was rocking her, and the worst of the tears were apparently over.

"She'll be all right," Ron said.

"Of course she will, won't you, darling?" Maggie helped her pull up her knickers. She was still snivelling, her need for privacy forgotten in her unhappiness.

In the back of the car Ian listened to his sister's caterwauling and tried to concentrate on his comic. Anything for attention, he thought. Well, she's welcome.

Suddenly, it went dark.

He looked up from the page, his heart loud. At his shoulder, six inches away from him, something stooped to peer into the car, its face like Hell. He couldn't scream, his tongue refused to move. All he could do was flood the seat and kick uselessly as the long, scarred arms reached through the window towards him. The nails of the beast gouged his ankles, tore his sock. One of his new shoes fell off in the struggle. Now it had his foot and he was being dragged across the wet seat towards the window. He found his voice. Not quite *his* voice, it was a pathetic, a silly-sounding voice, not the equal of the mortal terror he felt. And all too late anyway; it was dragging his legs through the window, and his bottom was almost through now. He looked through the back window as it hauled his torso into the open air and in a dream he saw daddy at the gate, his face looking so, so ridiculous. He was climbing the gate, coming to help, coming to save him but he was far too slow. Ian knew he was beyond salvation from the beginning, because he'd died this way in his sleep on a hundred occasions and daddy never got there in time. The mouth was wider even than he'd dreamed it, a hole which he was being delivered into, head first. It smelt like the dustbins at the back of the school canteen, times a million. He was sick down its throat, as it bit the top of his head off.

Ron had never screamed in his life. The scream had always belonged to the other sex, until that instant. Then, watching the monster stand up and close its jaws around his son's head, there was no sound appropriate but a scream.

Rawhead heard the cry, and turned, without a trace of fear on his face, to look at the source. Their eyes met. The King's glance penetrated Milton like a spike, freezing him to the road and to the marrow. It was Maggie who broke its hold, her voice a dirge.

"Oh . . . please . . . no."

Ron shook Rawhead's look from his head, and started towards the car, towards his son. But the hesitation had given Rawhead a moment's grace he scarcely needed anyway, and he was already away, his catch clamped between his jaws, spilling out to right and left. The breeze carried motes of Ian's blood back down the road towards Ron; he felt them spot his face in a gentle shower.

Declan stood in the chancel of St Peter's and listened for the hum. It was still there. Sooner or later he'd have to go to the source of that sound and destroy it, even if it meant, as it well might, his own death. His new master would demand it. But that was par for the course; and the thought of death didn't distress him; far from it. In the last few days he'd realised ambitions that he'd nurtured (unspoken, even unthought) for years.

Looking up at the black bulk of the monster as it rained piss on him he'd found the purest joy. If that experience, which would once have disgusted him, could be so consummate, what might death be like? Rarer still. And if he could contrive to die by Rawhead's hand, by that wide hand that smelt so rank, wouldn't that be the rarest of the rare?

He looked up at the altar, and at the remains of the fire the police had extinguished. They'd searched for him after Coot's death, but he had a dozen hiding places they would never find, and they'd soon given up. Bigger fish to fry. He collected a fresh armful of *Songs of Praise* and threw them down amongst the damp ashes. The candlesticks were warped, but still recognisable. The cross had disappeared, either shrivelled away or removed by some light-fingered officer of the law. He tore a few handfuls of hymns from the books, and lit a match. The old songs caught easily.

Ron Milton was tasting tears, and it was a taste he'd forgotten. It was many years since he'd wept, especially in front of other males. But he didn't care any longer: these bastard policemen weren't human anyway. They just looked at him while he poured out his story, and nodded like idiots.

"We've drafted men in from every division within fifty miles, Mr Milton," said the bland face with the understanding eyes. "The hills are being scoured. We'll have it, whatever it is."

"It took my child, you understand me? It killed him, in front of me—"

They didn't seem to appreciate the horror of it all.

"We're doing what we can."

"It's not enough. This thing . . . it's not human."

Ivanhoe, with the understanding eyes, knew bloody well how unhuman it was.

"There's people coming from the Ministry of Defence: we can't do much more 'til they've had a look at the evidence," he said. Then added, as a sop: "It's all public money, sir."

"You fucking idiot! What does it matter what it costs to kill it? It's not human. It's out of Hell."

Ivanhoe's look lost compassion.

"If it came out of Hell, sir," he said "I don't think it would have found the Reverend Coot such easy pickings."

Coot: that was his man. Why hadn't he thought of that before? Coot.

Ron had never been much of a man of God. But he was prepared to be open-minded, and now that he'd seen the opposition, or one of its troops, he was ready to reform his opinions. He'd believe anything, anything at all, if it gave him a weapon against the Devil.

He must get to Coot.

"What about your wife?" the officer called after him. Maggie was sitting in one of the side-offices, dumb with sedation, Debbie asleep beside her. There was nothing he could do for them. They were as safe here as anywhere.

He must get to Coot, before he died.

He'd know, whatever Reverends know; and he'd understand the pain better than these monkeys. Dead sons were the crux of the Church after all.

As he got into the car it seemed for a moment he smelt his son: the boy who would have carried his name (Ian Ronald Milton he'd been christened), the boy who was his sperm made flesh, who he'd had circumcised like himself. The quiet child who'd looked out of the car at him with such resignation in his eyes.

This time the tears didn't begin. This time there was just an anger that was almost wonderful.

It was half past eleven at night. Rawhead Rex lay under the moon in one of the harvested fields to the south-west of the Nicholson Farm. The stubble was darkening now, and there was a tantalising smell of rotting vegetable matter off the earth. Beside him lay his dinner, Ian Ronald Milton, face up on the field, his midriff torn open. Occasionally the beast would lean up on one elbow and paddle its fingers in the cooling soup of the boy-child's body, fishing for a delicacy.

Here, under the full moon, bathing in silver, stretching his limbs and eating the flesh of human kind, he felt irresistible. His fingers drew a kidney off the plate beside him and he swallowed it whole.

Sweet.

Coot was awake, despite the sedation. He knew he was dying, and the time was too precious to doze through. He didn't know the name of the face that was interrogating him in the yellow gloom of his room, but the voice was so politely insistent he had to listen, even though it interrupted his peace-making with God. Besides, they had questions in common: and they all circled, those questions, on the beast that had reduced him to this pulp.

"It took my son," the man said. "What do you know about the thing? Please tell me. I'll believe whatever you tell me—" Now *there* was desperation. "Just explain—"

Time and again, as he'd lain on that hot pillow, confused thoughts had raced through Coot's mind. Declan's baptism; the embrace of the beast; the altar; his hair rising and his flesh too. Maybe there was something he could tell the father at his bedside.

". . . in the church . . ."

Ron leaned closer to Coot; he smelt of earth already.

". . . the altar . . . it's afraid . . . the altar . . ."

"You mean the cross? It's afraid of the cross?"

"No . . . not—"

"Not—"

The body creaked once, and stopped. Ron watched death come over the face: the saliva dry on Coot's lips, the iris of his remaining eye contract. He watched a long while before he rang for the nurse, then quietly made his escape.

There was somebody in the Church. The door, which had been padlocked by the police, was ajar, the lock smashed. Ron pushed it open a few inches and slid inside. There were no lights on in the Church, the only illumination was a bonfire on the altar steps. It was being tended by a young man Ron had seen on and off in the village. He looked up from his fire-watching, but kept feeding the flames the guts of books.

"What can I do for you?" he asked, without interest.

"I came to—" Ron hesitated. What to tell this man: the truth? No, there was something wrong here.

"I asked you a frigging question," said the man. "What do you want?"

As he walked down the aisle towards the fire Ron began to see the questioner in more detail. There were stains, like mud, on his clothes, and his eyes had sunk in their orbits as if his brain had sucked them in.

"You've got no right to be in here—"

"I thought anyone could come into a church," said Ron, staring at the burning pages as they blackened.

"Not tonight. You get the fuck out of here." Ron kept walking towards the altar.

"You get the fuck out, I said!"

The face in front of Ron was alive with leers and grimaces: there was lunacy in it.

"I came to see the altar; I'll go when I've seen it, and not before."

"You've been talking to Coot. That it?"

"Coot?"

"What did the old wanker tell you? It's all a lie, whatever it was; he never told the truth in his frigging life, you know that? You take it from he. He used to get up there—" he threw a prayer-book at the pulpit "—and tell fucking lies!"

"I want to see the altar for myself. We'll see if he was telling lies—"

"*No, you won't!*"

The man threw another handful of books on to the fire and stepped down to block Ron's path. He smelt not of mud but of shit. Without warning, he pounced. His hands seized Ron's neck, and the two of them toppled over. Declan's fingers reaching to gouge at Ron's eyes: his teeth snapping at his nose.

Ron was surprised at the weakness of his own arms; why hadn't he played squash the way Maggie had suggested, why were his muscles so ineffectual? If he wasn't careful this man was going to kill him.

Suddenly a light, so bright it could have been a midnight dawn, splashed through the west window. A cloud of screams followed close on it. Firelight, dwarfing the bonfire on the altar steps, dyed the air. The stained glass danced.

Declan forgot his victim for an instant, and Ron rallied. He pushed the man's chin back, and got a knee under his torso, then he kicked hard. The enemy went reeling, and Ron was up and after him, a fistful of hair securing the target while the ball of his other hand hammered at the lunatic's face 'til it broke. It wasn't enough to see the bastard's nose bleed, or to hear the cartilage mashed; Ron kept beating and beating until his fist bled. Only then did he let Declan drop.

Outside, Zeal was ablaze.

Rawhead had made fires before, many fires. But petrol was a new weapon, and he was still getting the hang of it. It didn't take him long to learn. The trick was to wound the wheeled boxes, that was easy. Open their flanks and out their blood would pour, blood that made his head ache. The boxes were easy prey, lined up on the pavement like bullocks to be slaughtered. He went amongst them demented with death, splashing their blood down the High Street and igniting it. Streams of liquid fire poured into gardens, over thresholds. Thatches caught; wood-beamed cottages went up. In minutes Zeal was burning from end to end.

In St Peter's, Ron dragged the filthied cloth off the altar, trying to block out all thoughts of Debbie and Margaret. The police would move them to a place of safety, for certain. The issue at hand must take precedence.

Beneath the cloth was a large box, its front panel roughly carved. He took no notice of the design; there were more urgent matters to attend to. Outside, the beast was loose. He could hear its triumphant roars, and he felt eager, yes eager, to go to it. To kill it or be killed. But first, the box. It contained power, no doubt about that; a power that was even now raising the hairs on his head, that was working at his cock, giving him an aching hard-on. His flesh seemed to seethe with it, it elated him like love. Hungry, he put his hands on the box, and a shock that seemed to cook his joints ran up both his arms. He fell back, and for a moment he wondered if he was going to remain conscious, the pain was so bad, but it subsided, in moments. He cast around for a tool, something to get him into the box without laying flesh to it.

In desperation he wrapped his hand with a piece of the altar cloth and snatched one of the brass candleholders from the edge of the fire. The cloth began to smoulder as the heat worked its way through to his hand. He stepped back to the altar and beat at the wood like a madman until it began to splinter. His hands were numb now; if the heated candlesticks were burning his palms he couldn't feel it. What did it matter anyhow? There was a weapon here: a few inches away from him, if only he could get to it, to wield it. His erection throbbed, his balls tingled.

"Come to me," he found himself saying, "come on, come on. Come to me. Come to me." Like he was willing it into his embrace, this treasure, like it was a girl he wanted, his hard-on wanted, and he was hypnotising her into his bed.

"Come to me, come to me—"

The wood façade was breaking. Panting now, he used the corners of the candlestick base to lever larger chunks of timber away. The altar was hollow, as he'd known it would be. And empty.

Empty.

Except for a ball of stone, the size of a small football. Was this his prize? He couldn't believe how insignificant it looked: and yet the air was still electric around him; his blood still danced. He reached through the hole he'd made in the altar and picked the relic up.

Outside, Rawhead was jubilating.

Images flashed before Ron's eyes as he weighed the stone in his deadened hand. A corpse with its feet burning. A flaming cot. A dog, running along the street, a living ball of fire. It was all outside, waiting to unfold.

Against the perpetrator, he had this stone.

He'd trusted God, just for half a day, and he got shat on. It was just a stone: just a fucking *stone*. He turned the football over and over in his hand, trying to make some sense of its furrows and its mounds. Was it meant to *be* something, perhaps; was he missing its deeper significance?

There was a knot of noise at the other end of the church; a crash, a cry, from beyond the door a whoosh of flame.

Two people staggered in, followed by smoke and pleas.

"He's burning the village," said a voice Ron knew. It was that benign policeman who hadn't believed in Hell; he was trying to keep his act together, perhaps for the benefit of his companion, Mrs Blatter from the hotel. The nightdress she'd run into the street wearing was torn. Her breasts were exposed; they shook with her sobs; she didn't seem to know she was naked, didn't even know where she was.

"Christ in Heaven help us," said Ivanhoe.

"There's no fucking Christ in here," came Declan's voice. He was standing up, and reeling towards the intruders. Ron couldn't see his face from where he stood, but he knew it must be near as damn it unrecognisable. Mrs Blatter avoided him as he staggered towards the door, and she ran towards the altar. She'd been married here: on the very spot he'd built the fire.

Ron stared at her body entranced.

She was considerably overweight, her breasts sagging, her belly overshadowing her cunt so he doubted if she could even see it. But it was for this his cock-head throbbed, for this his head reeled—

Her image was in his hand. God yes, she was there in his hand, she was the living equivalent of what he held. A woman. The stone was the statue of a woman, a Venus grosser than Mrs Blatter, her belly swelling with children, tits like mountains, cunt a valley that began at her navel and gaped to the world. All this time, under the cloth and the cross, they'd bowed their heads to a goddess.

Ron stepped off the altar and began to run down the aisle, pushing Mrs Blatter, the policeman and the lunatic aside.

"Don't go out," said Ivanhoe, "It's right outside."

Ron held the Venus tight, feeling her weight in his hands and taking security from her. Behind him, the Verger was screeching a warning to his Lord. Yes, it was a warning for sure.

Ron kicked open the door. On every side, fire. A flaming cot, a corpse (it was the postmaster) with its feet burning, a dog skinned by fire, hurtling past. And Rawhead, of course, silhouetted against a panorama of flames. It looked round, perhaps because it heard the warnings the Verger was yelling, but more likely, he thought, because it knew, knew without being told, that the woman had been found.

"Here!" Ron yelled, "I'm here! I'm here!"

It was coming for him now, with the steady gait of a victor closing in to claim its final and absolute victory. Doubt surged up in Ron. Why did it come so surely to meet him, not seeming to care about the weapon he carried in his hands?

Hadn't it seen, hadn't it heard the warning?

Unless—

Oh God in Heaven.

—Unless Coot had been wrong. Unless it *was* only a stone he held in his hand, a useless, meaningless lump of stone.

Then a pair of hands grabbed him around the neck.

The lunatic.

A low voice spat the word "Fucker" in his ear.

Ron watched Rawhead approaching, heard the lunatic screeching now: "Here he is. Fetch him. Kill him. Here he is."

Without warning the grip slackened, and Ron half-turned to see Ivanhoe dragging the lunatic back against the Church wall. The mouth in the Verger's broken face continued to screech.

"He's here! Here!

Ron looked back at Rawhead: the beast was almost on him, and he was too slow to raise the stone in self-defence. But Rawhead had no intention of taking him. It was Declan he was smelling and hearing. Ivanhoe released Declan as Rawhead's huge hands veered past Ron and fumbled for the lunatic. What followed was unwatchable. Ron couldn't bear to see the hands take Declan apart: but he heard the gabble of pleas become whoops of disbelieving grief. When he next looked round there was nothing recognisably human on ground or wall—

—And Rawhead was coming for him now, coming to do the same or worse. The huge head craned round to fix on Ron, its maw gaping, and Ron saw how the fire had wounded Rawhead. The beast had been careless in the enthusiasm for destruction: fire had caught its face and upper torso. Its body hair was crisped, its mane was stubble, and the flesh on the left hand side of its face was black and blistered. The flames had roasted its eyeballs, they were swimming in a gum of mucus and tears. That was why it had followed Declan's voice and bypassed Ron; it could scarcely see.

But it must see now. It must.

"Here . . . here . . ." said Ron, "Here I am!" Rawhead heard. He looked without seeing, his eyes trying to focus.

"Here! I'm here!"

Rawhead growled in his chest. His burned face pained him; he wanted to be away from here, away in the cool of a birch-thicket, moon-washed.

His dimmed eyes found the stone; the homo sapien was nursing it like a baby. It was difficult for Rawhead to see clearly, but he knew. It ached in his mind, that image. It pricked him, it teased him.

It was just a symbol of course, a sign of the power, not the power itself, but his mind made no such distinction. To him the stone was the thing he feared most: the bleeding woman, her gaping hole eating seed and spitting children. It was life, that hole, that woman, it was endless fecundity. It terrified him.

Rawhead stepped back, his own shit running freely down his leg. The fear on his face gave Ron strength. He pressed home his advantage, closing in after the retreating beast, dimly aware that Ivanhoe was rallying allies around him, armed figures waiting at the corners of his vision, eager to bring the fire-raiser down.

His own strength was failing him. The stone, lifted high above his head so Rawhead could see it plainly, seemed heavier by the moment.

"Go on," he said quietly to the gathering Zealots. "Go on, take him. Take him . . ."

They began to close in, even before he finished speaking.

Rawhead smelt them more than saw them: his hurting eyes were fixed on the woman.

His teeth slid from their sheaths in preparation for the attack. The stench of humanity closed in around him from every direction.

Panic overcame his superstitions for one moment and he snatched down towards Ron, steeling himself against the stone. The attack took Ron by surprise. The claws sank in his scalp, blood poured down over his face.

Then the crowd closed in. Human hands, weak, white human hands were laid on Rawhead's body. Fists beat on his spine, nails raked his skin.

He let Ron go as somebody took a knife to the backs of his legs and hamstrung him. The agony made him howl the sky down, or so it seemed. In Rawhead's roasted eyes the stars reeled as he fell backwards on to the road, his back cracking under him. They took the advantage immediately, overpowering him by sheer weight of numbers. He snapped off a finger here, a face there, but they would not be stopped now. Their hatred was old; in their bones, did they but know it.

He thrashed under their assaults for as long as he could, but he knew death was certain. There would be no resurrection this time, no waiting in the earth for an age until their descendants forgot him. He'd be snuffed out absolutely, and there would be nothingness.

He became quieter at the thought, and looked up as best he could to where the little father was standing. Their eyes met, as they had on the road when he'd taken the boy. But now Rawhead's look had lost its power to transfix. His face was empty and sterile as the moon, defeated long before Ron slammed the stone down between his eyes. The skull was soft: it buckled inwards and a slop of brain splattered the road.

The King went out. It was suddenly over, without ceremony or celebration. Out, once and for all. There was no cry.

Ron left the stone where it lay, half buried in the face of the beast. He stood up groggily, and felt his head. His scalp was loose, his fingertips touched his skull, blood came and came. But there were arms to support him, and nothing to fear if he slept.

It went unnoticed, but in death Rawhead's bladder was emptying. A stream of urine pulsed from the corpse and ran down the road. The rivulet steamed in the chilling air, its scummy nose sniffing left and right as it looked for a place to drain. After a few feet it found the gutter and ran along it awhile to a crack in the tarmac; there it drained off into the welcoming earth.

KIM NEWMAN

The Chill Clutch of the Unseen

KIM NEWMAN IS THE AUTHOR of *The Night Mayor*, *Anno Dracula*, *The Bloody Red Baron*, *Dracula Cha Cha Cha* (aka *Judgment of Tears: Anno Dracula 1959*) and *Life's Lottery*, amongst other novels. His short stories are collected in *The Original Dr Shade and Other Stories*, *Famous Monsters*, *Seven Stars*, *Unforgivable Stories*, *Where the Bodies Are Buried*, *Dead Travel Fast* and *The Man from the Diogenes Club*.

A winner of two HWA Bram Stoker Awards, the British Science Fiction Award, the British Fantasy Award, the Children of the Night Award, the Fiction Award of the Lord Ruthven Assembly and two International Horror Guild Awards, he has also written and edited a number of non-fiction books, including *Horror: 100 Best Books* and *Horror: Another 100 Best Books* (both with Stephen Jones).

"The late, enormously-prolific Charles L. Grant wrote three books – *The Long Night of the Grave*, *The Soft Whisper of the Dead* and *The Dark Cry of the Moon* – as tributes to the vintage Hollywood monster movies he loved," explains Newman, "in which a mummy, a vampire and a werewolf visited Oxrun Station, the haunted small town that recurs in Charlie's work, and bothered successive generations of the community's leading law-enforcement family.

"When asked to contribute something to a book published as a tribute to Charlie, I remembered these short, sharp, fun little books and wanted to pay homage to that small section of his output.

"When they first came out, Charlie said he wanted to get away from the then-modish introspection of many thick novels about monsters and get back to the idea that vampires, werewolves and the like were scary bastards. This little piece is a post-script to his trilogy, using one of the few major Universal Studios monsters left alone.

"Now the enormously gracious, funny, gifted and genuinely heroic Charlie is no longer with us, the story has an added melancholy. I wrote it at the age (mid-forties) when those spared tragedies in early life have to get used to the idea that people we love won't be around forever. Like many people I know, I was starting to suffer bereavements – parents, older friends, colleagues, even some contemporaries. That's why this story is a fond meditation on all manner of meanings of the expression 'passing on' as much as it is a monster yarn – though, make no mistake, the monster here is one of the worst in the pantheon.

"As a footnote, it took me longer to come up with a title to fit Charlie's 'The Adjective Noun of the Noun' template than it did to write the story."

IT WAS AUTUMN, KISSING CLOSE TO WINTER; late November, early December; the daytime a few dim drab moments between elongated hours of heavy, cold dark. The last of the unswept leaves were dull orange, frost-crispy under his boots. He could not feel his toes. But the other aches were all there, in his leg-bones, his knuckles, his *face*. Your pains calling in, all present and correct,

Chief Stockton, sir. Hell, any day without blood in the toilet bowl was a good one. He was so old that the boy who'd taken over his job was retired (and buried). Someone he didn't know had sat in his old seat down at the police station for as long as most folks could remember. Someone with his name was on the highway patrol, so he supposed that the family tradition was being carried on. Stocktons had helped police this stretch of Connecticut since witch-hanging times. The family had been there for all the things worse than witches that came down the pike or stepped off the train.

Usually, it was the train.

That was why he kept his routine, trudging early to the railroad station and taking his chair – out on the platform in the balmy days of spring and summer, in the waiting room close to the black iron stove as winter's shroud descended – so he could keep to his watch. He knew most folks saw him as an old-timer who liked to get out of his empty house and be among people coming and going. Plenty were willing to stop and pass the time with him, talking about TV shows he'd never watch – *Ex-Flies* or somesuch. The town had long-time residents he thought of as "incomers", whose names he needn't learn. Always, he kept a lazy eye out for movements. Most of the town had forgotten. Things that couldn't be explained by light of day, it was most comfortable to tidy up and dismiss as imaginings of the night. It had been a long time since the worst of it. But he knew it wasn't over. The things he watched out for were like him, and took the long view. They could afford to wait it out. In the end, they'd be drawn to this place, to this station, to him.

And then . . .?

"Mornin'?" said the station-master's daughter Irene, who turned everything into a question. Or was it "Mournin'?"

"Ayup," he responded.

It was and he was. No further editorial needed.

Irene rattled the scuttle into the stove. The embers of yesterday's fuel were buried under fresh black coal. Smoke soon curled and she dropped the lid. The fire in the station waiting room stove had been burning since before she was born, never dying overnight even when snow lay three or four-feet deep and tears turned to frost on your face. It was a phenomenon, he supposed. One of the many tiny things about the place no one even questioned.

Irene wore heavy boots, work-jeans and a check shirt. Her hair was done in two thick rope-braids like a storybook child. She might be pretty, and he hoped someone would find out. Then again, the joke was that when she got married she'd even make "I do" into a question. "I do?"

He settled in his seat.

The next stopping train was due at 7:12 am. A commuter crawl, picking up fellows (and ladies, these days) in suits, snaking them off to work in the city. He needn't pay it much attention. That train started up North and collected people as it wound through the state; the rare people who ever got off were day visitors from one or two towns up the line. It was the 7:32 he needed to pay mind to, the empty train coming the other way, from the city – the last train of yesterday, sent back to the terminus so it could return mid-morning and scoop up those who didn't need to be in the city until after the working day started, the shoppers-and-lunchers and the work-at-homes with meetings to make.

Almost no one came in on the 7:32. But it was a bad one. It came from New York, and the city was a stage most things passed through on their way here. He wondered sometimes why they didn't stop there, where they could hide among – how had folks once put it? – the "teeming millions". Up here, no matter how subtle their ways, they'd eventually be noticed. But a giant octopus could get lost in the concrete canyons. Let alone a shroud-thin tatter which could as easily have been a tangle of discarded newspapers as what it was.

Today, there'd be something.

Stockton *knew* this, the way some old folks knew the weather. The quality of his pain changed. He'd learned to read the signs.

Others had known, but they were gone. Their kids had never believed the yarns or had closed their minds firmly. There weren't such things. Not any more. And especially not here. Think of what it'd mean for property values. And we've got too much else on our plates. There are enough real dangers to worry about, in these times of terror and disgrace, without being troubled by yesterday's phantasms, by the outgrown nightmares of generations past.

They weren't fools. They were just children.

Kids.

"Coffee?"

That genuinely was a question.

"Thank you, Irene, yes."

She kept a percolator in the office. Her father had maintained a coffee-pot in the same manner as he kept the stove burning, continually topping up sludge built up over decades. Irene had put an end to that, carefully losing the pot and buying a new, complicated machine with her own money.

Stockton took a gulp. He was expecting the coffee taste, but something else swarmed into his mouth.

"Hazelnut and rum?" Irene question-explained.

To which he would have said "no, thank you," but it was too late.

Some commuting fellow brought back these mutant concoctions from a place in the city. Coffee polluted with *flavours*. Stockton believed potato chips should taste of salt and nothing else. He had little time for any product described as "French" or with an acute accent in the brand-name.

Still, the warmth in his throat was welcome.

And the coffee taste was still there, underneath.

Irene left him and busied herself in the office. Stockton didn't see her father around much any more. It occurred to him that she might have inherited the job of station-master – station-mistress? – while he was paying attention to what might be coming into town as opposed to what was happening right here. The last-but-one police chief had been a woman, and nobody seemed to mind. She'd looked like a little girl dressed up for Trick or Treat in the bulky padded jacket and baseball cap that passed for a uniform these days, but her watch had been quiet. He'd have liked to see how she'd have handled the run of things he and his family had coped with.

The memories – the *stories* – crept unbidden into his mind.

Late, Late Show names. Totemic words and symbols.

Beast. Bat. Bandage.

Moon. Dead. Grave.

They didn't even have a *Late, Late Show* any more. Turn on the TV after midnight and it was all infomercials for exercise equipment.

Twenty years back, when a bulky crate had been unloaded from the train, he had thought it was the last of them. He'd been waiting for the fourth asphalt-spreader's boot to drop. He had known what lay inside.

A monster. The Monster.

The crate was delivered to Doc Stone's place. Doc, whose medical records were hard to track down and who went by an Ellis Island name. His well-equipped basement workroom drained a power surge and put the lights out all over the county just as the thing in his crate broke loose. Doc had tried to get between the party of Stockton's men and the thing he said was his child. Now, he lay at the bottom of the river in the embrace of a skeleton with yard-long arm-bones.

That had been the Big One. After that, the others who knew how things were around here thought it was over and drifted away or died. Only he knew it wasn't over.

Would never be over.

On the *Late, Late Show*, there was always next week and a sequel.

Tune in again to *Shock Theater*.

Bodies were rarely found. Fur, dust, bones. That meant nothing. There were always ways. Curses could be passed on with a bite or a legacy. Another electrical storm, a parchment translated aloud, a scientific breakthrough with unexpected consequences.

They would be back.

Something would be here. Soon.

Beast. Bat. Bandage. Body.

The casually-interested thought that was the Full House. Those four were all there was, all there would be. The famous names, the face cards.

Stockton thought of the others, the ones who had passed through or ended up. The ones who weren't head-liners.

The Amazon Manfish, broken out of a research institute in '56, gulping air through gills unequipped to process anything but warm water, shocked dead or comatose by a plunge through ice into Williamson's Kill. The madman's brain, disembodied in its jar, bubbling and flashing party lights as its mentacles kept the hump-backed surgeon in thrall, using his rheumy eyes to see and his warty hands to throttle. The roadhouse singer who exactly resembled a great-grandmother whose picture lay forgotten in the *Herald* archives, and whose bell-clear high notes stayed in the minds of men who found themselves ageing decades overnight. The long-nailed Chinaman with his platoon of silent servants, hatchets inside their sleeves, and his hothouse menagerie of exotic and deadly fauna. The slithering stretch of rancid greenery which sometimes took the form of a man of muck and root and opened huge, lucid eyes in its face of filth. The quiet, violet-eyed Christian family who spoke in even monotones and kept to themselves until someone noticed that if you told one of the children something then its parents – all the way across town – suddenly knew it too. The travelling freakshow and its too-tall, too-clever ringmaster. The lights in the sky and mysterious livestock fatalities. The experiments gone wrong in neglected houses outside the town limits. The grey-faced motorcycle gang whose fingers clicked to a rockin' beat as they tore apart the succession of ugly fast-food outlets thrown up on the site of the diner where they were ambushed and apparently wiped out in 1965, whose arrival was always prefaced by teenage death songs of the '60s coming unbidden from every radio and jukebox in town. The gentle murderer whose skull was swollen with acromegaly and whose heart pulsed only for the beautiful blind piano virtuoso whose short-tempered teachers tended to show up with their spines snapped. The extreme aesthete who could only paint masterworks if his subjects were beautiful and bloodless. The sheeted ghosts who were really scheming heirs, or vice versa. The neon-eyed swami who was always in plain view of a dozen witnesses, performing his mind-reading act, as the professors who once profaned a temple in a far-off land were struck down one by one with distinctive wavy daggers in their chests. The clever ape.

Most of them were buried out of the way, and hushed up. The bound back-numbers of the *Herald* in the town library were full of neatly clipped holes, sometimes extending to entire editions but for the weather reports. For one month in 1908, *only* the weather reports were clipped – which often made Stockton ponder what had passed through back then, making itself known only through climatic influence.

A clatter, and he was out of his reverie.

A train, pulling out. The 7:12, leaving for the city.

He hadn't noticed who got on, hadn't cared, but it disturbed him that his vigilance had clouded even for a minute. The past, the old stories, had swarmed in on him, settling on his brain. He had been running through a medley of monsters.

He focused.

On the 7:32.

It would be a bad one.

And then everyone would remember. The yarns their parents and grand-parents had told him. They were *true*! Eventually, they'd remember him, thank him for standing watch, need his advice. His hands couldn't wrap round a shotgun and his legs weren't up to a hike through the woods holding up a flaming torch, but his mind was still sharp. He still had the expertise.

There'd be bodies, of course.

He regretted that, but knew it was a stage. Before he'd be believed, before people paid attention, someone had to die. And die ugly, die strange. Two ragged holes in the throat of a woman bled whiter than virgin snow. A child torn to pieces as if by a wild animal but with clearly scratched gypsy signs in his tattered skin. A succession of elderly academics alone in locked libraries with their hearts stopped as if by an icy fist squeezing them dry. Men turned inside-out. Glowing green alien matter in wounds. Sea-widows drowned miles from water. Eyes or whole heads missing.

He couldn't think of the people who would become these bodies.

They were a necessary stage. Material he needed to work with.

Irene looked in on him.

"Looks like a chiller?"

She was commenting on the weather. But she spoke a deeper truth, asked a more pertinent question.

"Ayup."

He got up out of his chair, a process that became more difficult every single time. He saw Irene thinking about helping him, and knew that eventually she'd give in and step forward, reaching for his arm. He kept his grunt to himself, felt the ache wriggle up and down his back.

A bad one.

His intention was to stroll casually out onto the platform, but he creaked as he walked, every step as clumsy as Doc Stone's "child". Irene did open the door for him, the courtesy he should be showing her. He nodded a thanks.

The cold outside was good for the pain, froze it away.

The 7:32 was coming. He felt the vibration in his gums, rattling his partial plates, before he even heard the train.

Before he saw the sleek, dull metal tube of the commuter train, he held in his head the picture of a real locomotive. Pistons and a funnel, clouds of steam, a shrill whistle. When those clanking things were phased out, the bullet-headed electrical creatures that replaced them seemed like things off the cover of *Amazing Science Fiction*. Streamlined, beautiful *Flash Gordon* props. When did they become just a part of the furniture?

The train came in and stopped.

He looked for a door opening. Not all the town's visitors needed to open doors, but most did. He supposed it was fair, that even the unnatural needed to grip a handle and turn.

A door did open.

Another person might have thought no one got off, but Stockton saw clearer.

A man-shaped bubble, shot through with black filaments, moving slowly. The prints of bare feet among the wet leaves left on the platform. A chattering of unseen teeth.

He congratulated himself on having worked it out ahead of time.

This was the only one left. The Man.

"You," he called, "I've been waiting."

The bubble froze, turned sideways, disappeared into stillness.

There was a coughing and racking. Somehow with a British accent.

Stockton stepped towards the noise. He saw small movements in the air. Up close, the Man was discernible by dozens of tiny telltales. Feet naturally picked up dirt and so outlines that looked like grubby ankle-socks stamped up and down against the cold. Ten black crescents – dirt under fingernails. A shell-like spiral of clotted blood lining an infected invisible ear. A wrinkled, mottled sleeve of grey, dead skin. Irregular black discs that floated – breaks in bones set but not healed, suggesting a body bent and crooked by age and abuse. A squeezed tube of digested food, palely transparent in the twisted bulb of the stomach, blackening in the wrap of the lower bowel to form what looked like a nasty obstruction. And the dark tendrils winding around bone and through the meat, making unhealthy balloons of the weakly-pulsing lung-sacs.

He'd seen enough friends pass to recognise the symptoms. The crab. He knew the Man was a heavy smoker, liked to take the smoke in and fill out the shape of his gullet and lungs as a party piece. Now he was paying for it.

"Aren't you in bad shape, though," he declared.

The cough became a cackle. A cracked cackle. Never forget that the Man was mad. Even before disappearing, he'd been odd. Now, uniquely apart from mankind, he'd be completely crazy.

Before – on the *Late, Late Show* – when a man like this died, he faded into view. He could only be invisible when alive; in death, he appeared. Obviously, from what Stockton could see, he was a quarter-dead already.

"Welcome, stranger," he said. "Welcome to the Elephants' Graveyard."

This was where the monsters came to die. It was in the natural supernatural order of things that there be a place like this. And a man like Stockton.

"You're the last of them, as far as I can tell."

"Once, I – or someone like me – called himself Invisible Man the First," said a voice from nowhere. No, not from nowhere.

Stockton saw a faint funnel in the air, smelled bad breath, could even make out a brown tooth. The voice came through pain. It was cultured and croaky at the same time, speaking with the clipped, artificial tones he associated with knighted theatrical actors slumming as Nazi war criminals in very poor films. The Brits you heard on TV these days – Prime Ministers and pop stars – didn't sound like this any more, if any real folks ever had.

The Man wouldn't take much killing.

No struggle to shove a stake in its heart, or a dozen men tossed about like straw dummies as they tried to wrestle it down, no bell-book-and-candle recitals, no calling-out-the-national-guard.

He could just reach out and break it, then watch it turn into an old, naked, dead man.

The Man *wanted* him to do it.

That was what he had come to understand. These things came to town to make a last stand, to do their *schtick* one final time for an appreciative audience and then fade away completely. Or, in this case, shade in completely.

The clutch came, at his throat, surprisingly fierce, cold and dry as black ice.

That rotten tooth came closer. The sick breath stench was stronger.

Stockton cursed himself for thinking too much, drifting off. He had made the mistake too many folks made. He had momentarily been taken with the wonder of the creature before him; had felt not only an empathy with the Man's plight, a kinship with its all-too-familiar pains, but even a fondness for its uncomplicated madness, a *nostalgia* for the world it had terrorised and which was as long-gone as steam-trains and old-time radio serials.

For a moment, he had forgotten what it was to be a *monster*.

A thumb was under his ear, pressing on the rope of vein, long-nailed fingers were in his neck, ragged edges cutting the skin.

"You all right, Mr Stockton?"

Irene was looking at him. From twenty feet away.

He was being held upright by the grip on his throat. His arms and legs dangled. He couldn't speak, but he tried to gurgle.

"If you let her get suspicious," whispered words directly in his ear, "I will kill her."

He raised a hand and waved, tried to construct a reassuring smile.

Irene shrugged and went inside again.

His arm dropped. It hurt a great deal.

"Very sensible," said the voice, more conversational now, more upper-hand.

Stockton looked down, trying to swivel his eyeballs to the grip. He saw a seam in the air, an old scar.

The Man changed hands, letting him go with his right and taking up the grip almost as severely with his left. Bloody fingerprints floated in the air, and rubbed together.

"I'm most fearfully sorry, old son," said the voice, tittering on the edge of hilarity. "One of my great practical problems is trimming my nails. I imagine they're horny talons."

Stockton tried to get hold of the arm that must stretch out beyond the grip. His fingers scrabbled on greasy, cold skin.

"That tickles."

He was punched in the stomach. A solid drive, dimpling his padded hunter's jacket. The pain roiled in his belly, shook his bowels.

He did not intend to have an "accident".

"Elephants' Graveyard?" mused the monster. "I like that."

"You're all here," Stockton snarled, with difficulty. "All dead and gone. Dust and bone."

"You miss the point, chief."

The voice seemed genuinely friendly, amused, superior.

"Now, let us go for a little walk."

He was jerked along the platform, taking more puppet-steps. His left ankle turned and he yelped, then dragged his foot.

"Easy now, old-timer. Don't go on and on and on."

"Where are we going?"

"Why, to your house, of course. I could do with some breakfast, and you're having a trying day."

An old suit of clothes sat in his favourite armchair, casually comfortable, trouser-legs crossed, empty space between the cuff and a dangling slipper that pointed up or down as an unseen foot stretched.

Though they were indoors, the Man had decided to wear a hat, a hunter's cap with flap-downs over the ears and the back of the head. Stockton found it impossible not to look at the hole where the face should be and focus on the ragged fleece lining of the back-flap. The offer of a pair of sunglasses had been rejected with a tart "indoors and in autumn, I don't think so."

Stockton couldn't help noticing the Man seemed healthier, as if exerting his power over someone else assuaged his own hurts. He was bundled up and wrapped away now, but it seemed the black filaments he had noticed earlier were far less apparent.

His guest was disgusted that Stockton didn't have any cigarettes. He'd given up, on doctors' orders, years ago. The doctor who'd ordered him was dead. Emphysema, so he'd known what he was talking about.

"This is a very decent cup of tea," said the voice.

The cup tipped in the air. Liquid slithered around the shape of a tongue and mouth, then squirted down past the collar of Stockton's old wedding-and-funeral shirt.

"Far better than one would expect to find in heathen Yankeeland."

Stockton's throat still hurt. He had examined the scratches in the mirror, and saw rimmed white pressure-spots that would last for days.

"So you think we're the last?" asked the Man.

"You're the last."

"Invisible Man the Last?" Shoulders lifted in a shrug. "Perhaps. Though that's been said before, too many times. And I deliberately used the first person plural. We. You're a part of this too. You're as much a coelacanth as I am."

"Coelacanth?"

"Living fossil. Prehistoric fish. Thought extinct for millennia, until one showed up in some African peasant fisherman's net back in the '20s."

"I've heard of that story."

"Good. It's the duty of a lively mind to take an interest in sports and freaks, don't you think. You might aver that it was your specialist subject."

Stockton nodded.

"How many of us have you killed, Chief Stockton?"

The question was a surprise, a slap.

"Come on, don't be modest. I'll admit to all my murders. Little men and big, women and children. Dogs. I've happily killed dogs. It used to be that not a day went past that I didn't murder something. Now, as time creeps on, why . . . it's been months, maybe years. And the last time was a farce. Took forever to throttle and stifle some twig-like spinster I'd have done for in a trice on my best day. We're both professionals. We have licenses. I have my . . . condition," a handless sleeve up before an absence of face suggesting a gesture, "and you had a badge and gun. I imagine you've still got your old trusty service special around. You Yanks and your blessed firearms. Makes everything too easy. You're not a proper killer unless you get up close, feel the flesh part, the warmth dissipate, the heart stop. It's a good thing you can't see my face, because I know it's arranged into an expression you would find even more horrifying than my words. And you know why my words horrify you? Of course you do, Chief. It's because you *understand*."

Stockton remembered a scatter of dust on a red-lined cloak, a spike stuck into its folds; the pie-sized scarlet holes in hairy black hide made by a scattergun packed with shot mixed in with ground-up sterling silver dollars; various steaming piles of loathsome putrescence. Monsters dying. That he had seen a deal of.

"For you this isn't a graveyard, it's Death Row. And you pull the switch."

"You're all monsters."

"And monsters can't live? We kill people. No argument here, old thing. It's just that . . . well, chief, how can I put this without seeming ungracious about your hospitality, but perhaps you shouldn't enjoy *destroying* us quite so much. Your kind always hates and fears the extraordinary."

"Uh-uh," Stockton said, bristling, "you don't get me like that, Mr Clever Man. I didn't start this. We – regular folks – we didn't set out to hunt you all down and see you dead just because you were different. Nothing wrong with being different. We took objection to the murders. And the other things, the worse crimes."

A sleeve hung in the air, invisible finger tapping invisible chin.

"Of course you did."

They were argued into a corner.

"I put rat-poison in your tea," Stockton said.

"I know. I drank it."

White lines were winding up around inside his head, outlining a skull. Red wires crept over it. A face was forming.

"Soon you'll be face-to-face with the Visible Man."

And old face, of course. Weather-beaten. Eyes mushroomed in sockets, watery blue, lids forming around them.

"Then it'll be over," muscle-flaps in the shape of lips formed the words. "You'll have killed the last but one coelacanth, and it'll be down to you. My guess is you won't see out the winter. Spring will come and you'll be gone. Without us, what's the point of you?"

"That doesn't bother me. I've lived my life justified."

"I suppose you have. I say, this poison is rather painful. Stomach feels as if it's been through a mangle. You could have just shot me, you know."

"Then we wouldn't be having this . . . little chat."

He tried to mimic the Man's clipped tones.

The Man laughed. "What do you think you sound like?"

Skin was forming – pale from years out of the sun, withered over bone, white beard thick on the cheeks but scraggy under the chin. Of course, he couldn't have done much of a job of shaving.

"It'll start again, chief. It always does. It's what makes monsters monstrous, in a way. We can be killed, but we come back. When I'm fully opaque, some other idealist or madman will start to disappear. Knowledge is out in the world and can't be taken back. This town isn't just a graveyard, it's a spawning ground. Sure, we come here to die, but we also come to be reborn. And many of us are *from* here. Just like you."

The voice stilled. There was a dead old man in Stockton's favourite armchair.

For a while, the air was clear and the pain was gone. There were no monsters in the world, in this town.

Then, a black little bulb under a field somewhere nearby began to sprout.

Stockton saw it in his mind, and knew he was seeing a truth. It was part of his legacy, his gift. He also recognised that somewhere this morning he had suffered another stroke. He couldn't feel his left arm and a cord in his neck was spasming beyond his control.

Damn monsters.

He needed to do something about the body. This was a particularly inconvenient one. Some dead things resolved to bone and ash or were such obvious inexplicable departures from the norm that cops and coroners quietly absolved their destroyers from legal blame. This one lost its defining feature in death and looked uncomfortably like a poor old vagrant poisoned by a mad old cop. There were precedents, and he hoped his name still had enough pull – but it didn't matter. The way justice ground on these days, this wouldn't come to trial before spring and his visitor had been right in estimating that Stockton wasn't liable to be around when the leaves greened.

He picked up the phone, ready to dial – no, the rotary phone was long gone, to punch out – the familiar number. He would talk to the new Chief. No, he realised, he had to talk to someone else first. That black bulb had spider-limbs now, reaching above ground.

If the pests came back, so must the pest-controllers.

He stabbed buttons.

This would take some convincing talk, but there was evidence enough. A duty could be passed on, as it had been passed on to him.

At the end of the line, the phone rang once.

"Highway Patrol," responded a voice.

"Get me Stockton," he said.

"Is this police business? I can take your call. Stockton's out on the road, and won't be back 'til later."

"It's police business," he said. "And family business. Get her to call her father's uncle. There are things she needs to know."